THE TRAYMORE ROOMS

THE TRAYMORE ROOMS

A NOVEL IN FIVE PARTS

Quebec, America and Rome

NORM SIBUM

BIBLIOASIS
WINDSOR, ONTARIO

FIRST EDITION

Library and Archives Canada Cataloguing in Publication

Sibum, Norm, 1947-
The Traymore rooms / Norm Sibum.

Issued also in an electronic format.
ISBN 978-1-927428-22-1

I. Title.

PS8587.I228T73 2012 C813'.54 C2012-907648-1

Edited by Dan Wells
Typeset by Chris Andrechek
Cover Design by Kate Hargreaves

The author wishes to acknowledge Michael Carbert, Marko Sijan, Don McGrath, Dan Wells and Marius Kociejowski for services rendered as copy-editors. Also, he would like to thank Richard Labrosse for his translation of *Ballade pour mes vieux jours*, by Luc Plamondon and André Gagnon, found on page 692.

Canada Council for the Arts | Conseil des Arts du Canada | Ontario Arts Council | Conseil des arts de l'Ontario

Canadian Heritage | Patrimoine canadien

Biblioasis acknowledges the ongoing financial support of the Government of Canada through the Canada Council for the Arts, Canadian Heritage, the Canada Book Fund; and the Government of Ontario through the Ontario Arts Council.

PRINTED AND BOUND IN CANADA

FSC www.fsc.org MIX Paper from responsible sources FSC® C107923

Contents

Part Five: Moonface Returns

In Memory of Peter MacFarlane,
b. 1927, d. 2010 at 902 years of age

Part One:

The Traymore Rooms

Book I—Against Chronology

To Begin

Now Edward Sanders, aka Fast Eddy, hatless in winter, beetle-browed and barrel-chested, shows up in the Blue Danube, the left side of his face inflamed. He is not happy; deep-set eyes accuse. Silent, he joins us at our table. A round of greetings. He raises his hand to check our effusions. He will make the most of this moment, encased in layers of sweatshirts, nylon coat, baggy denims, his pale blue eyes registering what had been cataclysmic. Those eyes are absolutes, so complete is his revulsion for all accidents of time and space, he claiming a sparrow flew into his mug.

Well, how? He was turning a corner at the back of his duplex just as a bird endeavoured to do the same, its flight path minimizing the possibilities of attack from predators. Chicago School of Physics: two solid objects cannot, at one and the same time, inhabit the same space, unless one is to speak of hand-to-hand combat or acts of passion.

Eggy, old and decrepit, snorts, octogenarian bravado and envy asserting: 'She must've squeezed too hard.' Yes, there it is, what explains Fast Eddy's wounded pride. But Fast Eddy's love of our waitress Moonface is pure, as the girl is a noble creature. Eggy's hand begins its journey to his glass. Eventually, the glass secured, wine is consumed. Says Eggy, 'Just trying to cheer you up. Effing hell.' The old man would sow the wild oats he had failed to sow in past years long since dissolved in the wake his passage has left on the broad sea of life, the Ebenezer—his willie, his Priapus—now inert. One day, perhaps, Fast Eddy will declare to Moonface his love of her, and she will grant him the justice of his argument. He might have to see a doctor, his left ear shiny red, grown enormous.

It did not augur much then, the scene described above. It came about early in my Traymorean existence. Congratulations are in order, I think. Not only have I managed to take root in the Traymore Rooms, I have survived its inhabitants: Eggy, Moonface, Dubois and Eleanor R, Mrs Petrova our live-in landlady and others. In the end, they did not see fit to turf me into the street. They had threatened to do so now and then.

What has been more spectacular than spectacular failure, than the truths that did not quite endure, than the lies that all too often succeeded? I would put such questions to myself in the Blue Danube while filling up notebooks with my infernal chatter. I would observe the snow falling, how it settled on fur hats and tuques and caps; how a wind drove it against scarfed shoulders. I observed what, beyond the cold café window, had all the attributes of a dream: the afternoon commute, its sounds muffled. Though it has since changed, its dimensions, its floor-plan altered, the Blue Danube when I first knew it was not much more than a hole-in-the-wall. A few tables. A pair of coolers for keeping pastries semi-fresh and bottles of water and juices on the cool side of lukewarm. A tapestry I despised. The TV at ceiling level was usually switched off, the screen staring down at us a pallid eye. A small galley I never examined. A restroom off to its side. Potted plants came and went like literary experiments. Stacks of newspapers and magazines situated on a broad window sill. A hookah, so Dubois once said, commanded that window, its only reason to exist being to perplex passersby. Until a Slav took over management, the place had been a home away from home for Iranians. They consumed cow brains and sheeps' balls, so Eggy insisted, and Dubois did not gainsay him. The owner went to visit family in Tehran and was never seen in these parts again.

I believe, and you might agree: time is anything but linear, except perhaps when it comes to train schedules and the like. And yet, one might easily enough succumb to a memory or two while on the overnighter from Vienna to Venice. There you are, looking out the window under a dawn sky, brooding on the Italian landscape. And if you are not that child in your thoughts holding a sprig of meadow-clover to your nostrils; if you are not that wretch engaged in yet another miserable love affair, why then, you must be one of those Caesar fellows from a page of Tacitus. Here we go again, and though I am, so far as I know, in no train barreling along through two thousand years of time, I am back in the Blue Danube on the occasion of Fast Eddy's adventure with a bird. There are three bottles of wine on the table, two of which are empty, one half full. I, Randall Q. Calhoun, in addition to Fast Eddy, Dubois and Eggy, am a regular here, the café but a short stumble of a return to the Traymore Rooms.

Aphrodite's Little Helpers

At his table a leather-jacketed Slav is Lord Hades surveying his dreary underworld. His eyes evince mild contempt for us who have no idea as to how anything works, be it molecules attracting molecules, be it pay-offs in a dark lane. Moonface brings him his beer, she wearing a dark chemise under a coarse white shirt. Her countenance anxious, she had an attack earlier in the day, a fit. More physics, like those that confounded Fast Eddy in the body of a sparrow: she rubs her forehead where it banged against the loveseat in her Traymore digs. Well, sparrows in mythology carry the souls of the dead away. They are also Aphrodite's little helpers, emblematic of both lustful and spiritual unions. There is Lesbia's pet sparrow in the poem Catullus wrote, and it is known that small birds like sparrows and thrushes and such represented to the ancient Romans certain male body parts. But we are getting rather far afield here—

And the snow out there keeps coming down, passersby bent to the wind. Dubois gives me a look. He is right: there is no hope for me. Eggy, raising an admonitory finger, points out: 'The rain in Spain stays mainly in the plain. There's poetry for you.' Moonface, pressing her hips against the edge of our table, offers me comprehending sympathy. She knows what an orphan poetry is. What colour are her eyes, today? Two pools of rainwater set in weathered marble.

Fast Eddy still frowns, still suffers. I do not have the heart to rag him as Eggy had. Instead, I ask, 'So how did the bird fare?' 'Hoo hoo,' Eggy chimes. Fast Eddy glares. Then to Dubois I say, 'The first crossbow was most likely a Chinese invention.' He is incredulous: 'Are you serious?' Moonface rolls her eyes up and to the side, a characteristic gesture, she a chameleon. She is appealing. She is sullen and feckless. It perplexes her that she, waitress and Latin scholar, has the power to charm a special category of men—half-baked intellectuals who distrust intellectuals, her jeans skin-tight, her soft boots streaked with salt. Eggy's squint gaze is all over her and she surely knows it, now proud, now self-conscious, Eggy such a horror at times.

And when I suggest that I knew Buffalo Bill's great-granddaughter, Eggy interjects: 'Why, did she squeeze too hard, too?' 'Don't know,' I answer, 'but she was intense.'

And then Dubois who, in his youth, hung around with Chrétien, asks, 'What has this got to do with anything?' The man knows his politics; but regarding life on the American plains, he is in over his head: all that nasty and brutish stuff of conquering space one Indian and one buffalo at a time. Moonface pretends she has no idea of the import of 'squeezing too hard.' 'The rain in Spain,' says Eggy, this West Virginia-born homunculus who seems to have been everywhere, he no sparrow such as accosted Fast Eddy, but a sparrow of a man.

Thought-World

How often in the Blue Danube I would pitch headlong into a thought-world perhaps peculiar to me, history as ineffable an item as consciousness explained by a specialist. What about Josephus the Jew, his Roman monicker Titus Flavius Josephus? History qua history does matter to this writing, as you will see. But say that at a time of weak political control in the American West, a man like Buffalo Bill Cody could pretty well do as he wished, polite society be damned. Could hunt and happily go on benders. Meditate on mass and energy. Could scalp Sioux braves and make theatre of it while his biographer inflates the Cody reputation with exaggerated accounts of derring-do, titillating the fantasies of the well-heeled of the east. Enough. Dubois, his blue eyes glittering, abstracted himself, hears my inaudible sigh. 'There you go again,' he says, 'you're somewhere else.' No, nowhere else but here. And if I were to say I am a poet, it is easy enough to say. Say it once, it gets easier to say, and the rest of one's transgressions will follow in their own sweet time without hindrance or hitch, the way greased, as it were, by the first calumny. And the ice has no sparkle and the snow is already tinkled on by dogs. As previously pointed out, but a few steps separate the Blue Danube from the Traymore Rooms where my brine-caked body from another life came to rest. To Mrs Petrova I pay rent, she eighty-some, eyesight and hearing sound. Born and raised in what had been *Tsar* Peter's town, such heart-ache traces remain of her youthful beauty. How often I have waved to her in her street-level shop. How often I have pushed through a door, separate entrance. Here are the mailboxes and a radiator that gives off Saharan heat in a tiny foyer. Another door of dimpled and tinted glass, sheen of rose petal, *fleurs-de-lis;* and I climb the stairs to the carpeted hall that runs between the Traymorean apartments, three on each side. The wainscoting on the walls is probably bronze under the lavender-coloured paint, and it dates the building, this according to Dubois. How often I have unlocked the door of my digs and pretended I belong.

Moonface

How did Emma MacReady come to be Moonface? It is not even now clear to me, but Eggy is, no question, suspect in the matter. Moonface. She made a show of worrying for her men: Eggy, Dubois, her latest boyfriend of the hour, and yes, sometimes even me. And then, she could not give a toss for the lot of us. Of Fast Eddy who, so soon after I arrived on the scene, was to die of a diabetes-induced episode, Moonface said, 'I wish he'd seen a doctor when he had the chance.' I might have answered, 'Could be I love you. The odds are, I don't. As Brando said in *Last Tango in Paris*, men will worship at the altar of their John Hancocks. When people start talking life-affirmation, run for the hills. Now, what's this about Fast Eddy?'

She was right, of course, about our friend, but I can understand why he decided to give the doctors a miss. His world would become their world, no place in it for dalliance with Moonface. Once I thought her eyes were black; then I saw they were a golden brown. Russet has come to mind, russet against late autumn green. Virgilian.

And almost Virgilian in his own right, another regular—Blind Musician—would occupy a corner of the Blue Danube and get on his high horse about cigarette smoke. He was always recently returned from one of those tours by which Yukoners or North Saskatchewanites receive their cultural upgrade. Brahms and Delius. I would have the pleasure of women with parasols, men in pin-stripes doffing straw boaters as I looked upon Blind Musician who had not that pleasure; who did not like me; who did not like people, period. Well, would that a bear of the territories had got him. The Slav would continue to survey his Dis, his massive brow meditative, though five will get you ten he really was a thug involved in the drug trade. Once a poem of mine was accepted by a cheesy journal. Unusual. Portending what? I said as much to Moonface, her voice a rising note as she responded, 'Cool.' Infuriating. Her brows had gotten extra dark, the mascara on her lashes clumsily applied. In my span of years I had passed from the company of sophisticated women, and how can I put it kindly, to the allure of a girl who was far from having accomplished accord with her body. Now she was fatal; now she was as ordinary as a flash of sparrow feathers in alarmed flight.

On Being Unique

It is a question that has been plaguing me of late: are there ordinary readers? Are we not all of us in our waking lives unique, as most spiritual systems tell us; as bank ads tell us; as your army recruiting officer might have told you? Your book club, no less? Hear yourself described as unique and know you are being targeted by market forces. I ask because the question following has been put to me (and perhaps it was Dubois, that rotter, who put it to me): '*What ordinary reader would trouble himself with this writing of yours? You can't even decide where your story begins.*' It is true: I cannot decide. I am not even certain where I begin. The day I first drew breath outside my mother's womb? That day that probability dozed off, and I scored a touchdown? The moment I lost, as it is vulgarly said, my cherry? Some fatal hour when the government began to complicate my life? How about when I defied my father and thereafter was stuck with the fact I am not entirely devoid of backbone? One might say I was not a shell of a man when I moved into the Traymore, but I was getting there, me and my manuscripts of musings. I refer to them as *Calhoun's Follies* because, in all likelihood, they confuse a great deal more than they clarify. Who is this Calhoun? Is this me—so flighty in mind? So, at bottom, insincere? No, I am not insincere. I am nothing if not painfully sincere, even when I am most glib and flippant. The age wants a stand-up guy. There is not going to be any stand-up guy. The age wants its lies and adores its perversions. Perhaps, you have your own ideas as to what the age wants. This is as it should be. Ah, electric cars. Guilt-free sex. A Perfect President. All the pleasures without the pain. God without religion.

For a while there, distant wars, profligacy, and Eggy's old age were to be my literary themes. Love, too, if you choose to believe that love conquers all. Now, I cannot say. If I remain unable to find traction by way of a beginning to the tale I have to tell, how can I presume to speak of themes? Even so, I expect showers of rose petals, roars of acclamation to greet my prowess, come the moment when I will eventually extract order from chaos. I expect horses, chariots, even elephants, barbarians bent under the weight of heavy chains, the vulgar masses jeering at them, to honour my triumph. I expect lounging temple whores and grinning gods to accord me a thumb's up. I expect celebrities to drolly remark on what will have been my freakish rise to celebrity status. Are we so removed from the splendour of processions?

So then, patience. You will get to know, in time, so far as any of us can ever know anyone, Traymoreans, as well as Fast Eddy. You will learn how I came to discover the true colour of Moonface's eyes. You will hear of the pseudo-Traymoreans, the Lamonts and Osgoode; of future residents such as Marjerie Prentiss, she and her Cleopatra bangs and knobbly toes and militant free will. There are non-Traymoreans to consider. The names come fast and furious. How I deferred to Gareth Howard's moral authority even as I joshed him, the quality of my pessimism dubious to him. Vera Klopstock, amiable predator, married, is an old part of my life. How I had nothing to say, really, to Minnie Dreier. How I always have plenty to say to Bly, he who has the cloven hooves of the public intellectual. How I would, now and then, post letters to a dead man. How there was Echo, and how she faded. You will come across bells and whistles such as my notebooks of musings spawned, eccentric turns of mind that conform to no rational purpose, none that will rid the world of what ails it or retrieve the natural order from extinction. What, in any case, is the natural order? Moonface may or may not throw light on the matter. I will invoke the spirit of Sally McCabe, cheerleader of my high school days who, in her spirit-guise, was, on occasion, a structuralist. 'Structure? Chronology? Subject matter? Didn't you learn anything?' She will dock me points for my latter-day Neo-Platonism, one all too often hung-over. She will tickle my chin as I make mention of the screed of Eunapius of Sardis against chronology, yes, as if Socrates were only wise in the dry season. And were I to say 'Iraq and quagmire', she would answer, 'You expect me to explain why?'

Evening, and in the upper-storey hall of the Traymore Rooms where a window looks out on brick edifices, leafless maples and back lanes, I will watch the new snow coat stale deposits of the same banked against fences, each drift now a new-minted sculpture, a white dune. My name is Calhoun, Randall Q. But have we not done this, already?

Errant Memory

So many years ago, after having left the U.S., I departed British Columbia for this eastern province, for this island city in which I have skipped like a stone from one lodging to another. I flitted from affair to affair, disillusioning women as well as myself. I live among the generalities that inhabit my mind like a junkman's oddments; I lie about in my digs, listening to symphonies. And memory, dragging its lame foot, is hauled along by that music. Just now, I recall making love to one woman in particular. We managed what we could in the broom closet of her art gallery, the mops helping to render some discretion to our fervour, like so many postillions securing privacy while newlyweds eyeballed the artwork, looking for that something which would complement their furniture. (Soon after, the gallery closed for lack of sales, and the woman absconded, owing her artists.) What does any of this mean? Good fun, yes, but perhaps we are not moral creatures? In the morning, Mrs Petrova will clear the snow away from her shop downstairs and the effort will not faze her in the slightest, a curl the colour of burnt cinder loose on her forehead. When did I write the words that follow? *Moonface, my immediate neighbour in the adjoining apartment, is not quite sleekly full value for her self-empowerment, but she is getting there.*

No, there is no use pretending that the image of Moonface, lying about in her pajamas, committing Traymoreans to her diary pages (the act of which distracts her from the classics she reads at university), did not add a certain frisson to my capacity for lust. There is no use pretending that Eggy will not start early on his wine intake. Eleanor R shall whip something up in her kitchen or go out in the world and scratch an itch. Dubois shall pound his keyboard, besotted with his mind, his neck craned, his glittering blue eyes spooning at the computer screen. He will calculate that things will change not necessarily for the better but to the benefit of some. It is what we knew as history. Will the future offer us plutocracy light? Economic populism? Theocratic state? The slow burn of decline and fall? Comedy jamborees? If you must know, I direct you to Dubois. I, too, took to heart the professed ideals of the Great Society. Well, almost, I a skeptic counselled in my mother's womb—she who had not the sweetness and light of, say, a giggling starlet, my skepticism ratified by my father's reptilian brilliance. Fat lot of good it has done me, going around appalled.

Calhoun's Military Service

Momentous decisions are sometimes spur of the moment. Life is random except when it is not. There was a war in Asia; I went north. I opted out of military service, not a moral agent as such; rather I was a blind particle looking to collide with its fate. I claimed to understand what I did not understand, the year 1968, chasms in the national fabric both widening and deepening. My parents, most nominal of Christians, rendered unto Caesar. Of that period in my life, a great deal is now mercifully hazy. I recall the pre-induction physical. Along with my fellow cannon fodder, I was poked, prodded and otherwise examined like so much beef. If, for some, this exercise christened their love of country, I only got cold feet. The historian Tacitus would have sympathized with the demands of the state. He would have had little good to say of me; and he would have concurred that the war was pointless. Much in life is pointless for all that there are the campaigns of the hour: military incursions, new fruit drinks, corporate raiding, self-promotional stunts. Political progressives would arrange my thoughts to suit their pleasures, the reactionaries, likewise. Not much remains of any middle ground, and what remains is a sinkhole for makeshift consciences. Cynic, I please myself.

In Vancouver, B.C., a city double-parked by the sea, I married for complicated reasons, citizenship one of them. I could not hold down a job; I was all thumbs at the game of snooker. We divorced in short order, she and I; and I went off to Europe and further complicated myself. She threw herself out a window, and I must not think it had anything to do with me.

It is the old story of one's demons. They might be but garden variety demons, but even so, mine in perpetual Mardi Gras mode, I was, and I remain, a walking festival of them. I certainly do have pedigree of a modest sort, to wit, that I, the father of no one so far as I know, the son of Edna née Avesbury, socialite of minor magnitude, and Harry P for Prince Calhoun, chemical engineer and something of a Genghis Khan cum Scrooge when it comes to rapine and bank balances, am the spawn of an understanding. It does not deny the possibility of love, God, redemption and other intangibles; just that such concerns are better left to other people. The less said about my parents, the better, I in my 6th decade. If we are not moral creatures, I, for one, have endeavoured not to hurt anyone. A spectre in my mind that I name Boffo the Clown holds his belly and guffaws. Of course, it was not always the case that I was so high-minded; and one always hurts some unsuspecting soul simply by drawing breath. Generally, sex was the weapon; and when one had been on the receiving end, it sometimes afforded one a glimmer of the consequences. To be sure, I have indulged my share of delusions, among them the notion that this is the best of all possible worlds; that evil is a treatable condition; that America is blessed, her democracy a state of grace. Bent backs and the pieties of whores built the country. I would rather believe that than believe social justice had anything to do with it. The lone prair*ee* demanded improvisational skills. So when I stand on a street corner and smoke a cigarette, my middle finger in full index position, what you will see is not the athlete I was, however brief that career, but an aging boulevardier in American tweed, a kind of patchwork Main Street of an aesthetic sunset. I have had peculiar friends.

Jack Swain

Jack Swain was one of these peculiar friends. His mother, an Albertan, rolled cigarettes with one hand, even on horseback and in a wind. The father, Idaho born, knocked around with a toolbox. So that it was in Palo Alto where Jack, in his senior year, quarterbacked the high school football team. He resolved to write poetry, finishing up university in Vancouver, B.C. He went on to teach, to drink liberally and wench like a fool; he published once and never again. Too other-worldly for his Marxist-Leninist colleagues, for Billy Bly who described the Jack Swain verses as limpid and of no use to the working man, Jack came to spend his last years in Sicily, as far away from this continent as he could manage, for no other reason than that he could not stomach an actor become Commander-in-chief, first among equals. If Bly was the cool professional, Jack's sense of injustice was heartfelt. Even so, I thought the Sicilian idyll extreme. But to the memory of the man dead now these twenty years, I say, 'Jack, I'm afraid the Fat Lady still sings. Can you hear her, you know, the one who drove you around the bend?'

Jack was partial to plump women, yes; but that one, that porker, as she bellowed from sea to shining sea under spacious skies of onerous greatness, was more than a lover boy and a self-deprecating bard could bear. To put it vulgarly, and he did put it vulgarly, ram a fist up an intimate part of her anatomy and she would never notice, keeper of the American flame, the

Eternal Comeback. When America invaded Iraq, do you not suppose she invaded herself?

And you, Gareth Howard, deceased, would you prefer I forget these initials stabs at an accounting of some sort? Your mother and father, both Canucks, were reinforced by seven generations of colonial circumspection. For all that, it was in the U.S. where we first met and promptly got drunk on some vile muscatel, having just lost each our ripe cherries. You were a prospective journalist and a polymath. You were soon to pass through your first gateway to hell—there in Asia.

These lugubrious musings on the nature of time—Yes but, it snows as if it has never snowed before. It may never snow again. The white stuff comes sideways out of the wind. Plastered to awning and tree branch and parked car, to a jumbo-sized Christmas wreath affixed still to a lamp pole, it muffles tires and human tread. Gar, I have been to Rome and back in the past weeks but you could care less. 'Oh?' you would say like a man who had been there many times, 'how was the old girl?'

Smoking Towers

I did not know, once I had transferred myself to the Traymore Rooms and gotten to know its residents some, that I would take to writing them letters, slipping the missives under their respective doors. I had always written voluminous mail to old friends and longtime enemies; but I suppose Gar, Vera, Bly and Minnie—to name a few friends and enemies—were too used to me and my wiles for me to pull any wool over their eyes, as when I might claim I had, at last, seen the light. They certainly did not believe, for instance, that I was any genius. Just prior to taking up Traymorean life, I sat there in the basement suite I was about to vacate, my belongings packed, waiting for Reginald and his van. I was tired and down at heart and confused, a more than middle-aged man of no accomplishments, chary of principles, bedeviled by the smoking towers of an America I had only known by way of TV screens for the better part of my adult life.

I am caustic in regards to the notion that America is always able to reinvent herself. 'Out of what?' I ask. Hopes and dreams, as ever, for which someone will pay. I console myself Montreal is an old city, older than most cities on this continent. I trust nothing new.

Introductions All Around

It was Robert Dubois, impossibly handsome and rather vain, who introduced me to Traymorean society. On the following afternoon after my arrival, he knocked on my door, told me to get my coat, and he would treat me to a glass of wine at a nearby café. He would brook no refusal. Lucille Lamont, sticking her head through her door, made note of this invitation, and I could not be sure, but it seemed to me she scowled. The look in my new friend's eyes instructed me to pay her no mind, those glittering blue eyes companionable. 'We're all pretty friendly here,' Dubois said, 'and we're friendly there, too, in the Blue Danube.' He gave me a hand to shake, a somewhat worn attaché case in his other. On his head was slopped an outlandish tuque, creamy white with red stripes. He had the air of a man who had enjoyed modest success in life and was comfortable with his lot. I detest smugness. 'Well,' said Dubois, 'what are we waiting for?' I shrugged my assent to the man's proposal. I grabbed a coat and let myself be led down the Traymore stairs and out the door and to the corner where the Blue Danube was, a small café beneath some seedy-looking apartments where Moonface was pleased to serve us. Arthur Eglinton, wizened old runt of man whom Traymoreans affectionately called Eggy, had been awaiting our company with some impatience. Dubois having said that he had brought the new guy in for interrogation, Eggy hoo-hooed in my direction and said, 'How do you do?' And then he asked, 'And what do you do?' 'Nothing,' I answered. 'Well, that's something,' Eggy replied. 'Come on, now,' said Dubois, 'you must do something.' 'The nothing I do,' I responded, 'is to write verse. Oh, I read a little but mostly I sit around and brood.' 'I'm a reader, too,' Eggy volunteered, 'but brooding—that's too much heavy-lifting for me. Verse, you say? Problematic.' He reached to pinch Moonface's bum and missed. I thought perhaps something had moved in her eyes at my mention of the fact that I wrote, but I could have been mistaken.

Perhaps the wine went straightaway to my head; before long I blurted out a compressed life history, how I played football in high school—a depressing experience; how I left the States for Canada, knocked about the various provinces and Europe, as well; knocked about this island city; and in conclusion, could not make sense of myself. 'Welcome to the club,' Eggy laughed, not unkindly. 'It is what life's for—to come to know there's no sense to be made. The rain in Spain and all that.' 'Yes, it's all pointless,' Moonface pitched in with exaggerated solemnity, the timbre of her voice a little thin but musical. The look on Dubois's face said that, on the contrary, life has a point. 'I beg to differ,' he said. 'Beg all you want,' said Eggy, 'but it won't do you much good. Moonface, I can see the bottom of this glass.' She rolled her eyes upward and to the side as if in exasperation, and I could see she was touchingly oblivious to her charms. She replenished Eggy's glass. Dubois advised us, 'Eleanor should show up soon. She's one of your neighbours, too, Randall.' 'Hell of a woman,' said Eggy, 'but a trifle argumentative for my taste. Of course, the Lamont woman takes the cake in that department.' 'You just want women reduced to the level of slaves,' said Moonface. 'But of course,' said Eggy, 'the more the merrier. Hoo hoo.'

Eleanor's entrance broke up this exchange. 'Ah, the new Traymorean,' said Eleanor R, she sizing me up as she occupied a chair, setting three grocery bags on the floor, supper, so she explained. Dubois grunted. Evidently, Dubois and Eleanor were an item. She was not bad looking, on the plump side with frosted curls, her eyes intelligent. I read in them that, though she was no bully (as was Lucille Lamont, most likely), she was used to getting her own way. Here was a woman who might have spun Jack Swain around. 'Well,' she said to Moonface with a startling sharpness of tone, 'do I get a glass or do I have to fill out an application form for one?' An eclipse of sorts darkened the waitress's pale visage, her pleasant existence called into question.

A Prettier Truth

Perhaps, at bottom, everything is sex; but if so it is an ugly truth for an ugly world. I prefer a prettier truth, one infinitely riskier to my well-being: that there is something noble circulating in the Moonface brain.

She often began her day with Eggy, taking coffee with him in his rooms. What could they possibly talk about? There was certainly nothing noble in his disintegrating sack of a brain. Despite all his reading, he was interested, really, in nothing but wine and Moonface's bosom, of which he would get the full measure before he died. Moonface, he said, had promised him this. She did not mind he would try and grope her. I doubted that she did not mind. 'However,' so she let me know, 'I'm too quick for him. He treats me to dinner once a week. He considers you a rival, an interloper on his privileges. He wishes the best for me and I really do believe he means it.'

I would slip notes under her door. They amounted to no more than idle chatter. *Dear Moonface, trees aflame. Tulips in their tulip rows. Is the face of spring a young woman glad-footing around some maypole? Is it an old man with salty tears? Listening to* Gianni Schicchi *just now. The wise dude prepares for the fact he's never prepared. Wings it. Shall we meet? You tell me. Under your door.—RQC*

I would tell her about my Vancouver life, how I barely got by. How I married and how my father deemed the woman unsuitable. He cut my subsidies. Difficulties. The inevitable divorce. Her suicide that I must not think had anything to do with me. Reinstatement in father's books. The rain, the mist, the cavernous beer parlours. Loggers, miners, prospectors some of whom quoted Percy Bysshe Shelley for the price of a beer. "The Poet wandering on, through Arabic and Persia, and the wild Carmanian waste". The bird cacklings of Chinese matriarchs. The tribes down from their islands, each Indian locked away in his or her inner being. The half-savage daughters of the well-to-do. *It might surprise you how we carried on: moonlit back roads up the mountainous coast. Bottomless whiskey flask.* I would tell her Montreal is a cosmopolitan burg of cosmopolitan stalwarts, Francophobes sniffing, Anglophobes hauling English trash off to some landfill. I would tell her that Virgil, whose poetry was the object of her Latin studies, had been on a suicide mission. He meant to please Caesar but would stay true to his dark vision of what was shaping up. Some sickness got him, yes, but he died of the book.

Mostly though, I would, by way of a note, just invite her out. She almost always wore black denims and red sneakers, her hair done up in a ponytail, her shoulders hunched. I lacked the courage to steal a kiss. Once in a while she would give me a look. It said: 'I know what you're thinking. I won't think anything bad of you but I won't think anything good either. Poor man.' She had me over a barrel of some sort.

'Guess Who?'

Eleanor liked to talk sex and politics. Mid-morning, and I would put aside my notebooks in good, healthy, writerly disgust, and gravitate up a carpeted hall in the salacious light of early spring to her digs, the good woman greeting me, pompadoured. Often, she wore summer frocks. She, on the plump side, was supple and devastating. It would seem she enjoyed my company for all that I wondered what it had to do with me in the particular; just that I was male and could carry a conversation. Was Dubois so vain he was incapable of jealousy? Did he harbour secret torments, her body welcoming every sailor? What sort of arrangement had they fashioned from a messy froth of desire and trust? She would finger the spit valve of her trombone as I held forth. She would blow through it now and then as if to caution I was on shaky ground when it came to my reminiscences of Sally McCabe, who in high school allowed me to steal a kiss for which I had paid a heavy price. 'Goddess?' Eleanor queried. 'Goddess,' I affirmed, 'prime mover and shaker in the operations of the American mind such as manifest in every election cycle.' 'Oh, we're half Americans, anyway,' Eleanor said, half-relenting, 'Bob and I. Spent half our lives in Florida.' Bread was baking in the oven. The kitchen was all too often a disaster, Eleanor grimacing, 'It'll take me all day to clean up the aftermath.' It was very odd then, how she rose once and stood behind my chair, clapped her warm hands to my eyes and said, 'Guess who?' Her perfume overwhelming my thoughts, I went along with her caper, in any case, and then she backed off; and it was as if she sprang away, like a wrestler breaking a clinch and looking for a new hold. 'What you call goddesses,' said Eleanor, 'are made of clay. Teases and sluts. I was one of those, I don't mind telling you.' I pretended to be shocked. 'But if Bob,' she continued, 'were to start getting extracurricular, I'd break his kneecaps.' 'I bet you would,' I said out of respect.

I wrote Eleanor notes, too, and slipped them under her door. *I'll be there or I'll be square. By the way, I do want to hear out this notion of yours that Lucille L is a murderess. Really? How so?—RQC*

And then there was the night Moonface and I got back late from an evening out. It seemed Eggy had had a stroke and there was a commotion of Traymoreans and paramedics in the hall. The look on Eleanor's face wondered if Moonface and I were lovers. The look on mine suggested otherwise, and what is more, I was keeping a faith so obscure it was not worth explicating the matter, no, not to anyone; not even to a good woman who would serve me coffee and biscuits five days out of seven and go where I went in my conversational spacewalks. I was flattered, of course, that she made a pass at me. I was relieved, too, that Dubois would never know. I was taking my celibacy seriously, though a woman like Eleanor who played the trombone and baked cherry cobbler was not to be lightly denied. Every town in America has its Sally McCabe. That she was ageless, wise, cruel, free of doubt and self-reproach. I would say to Eleanor, 'This creature wandered to this continent on a Phoenician barge. I've told you already how, in the Utah desert, she took up with Coop and his pale red crew cut hair. They'd ride around in his pale blue Chrysler car. They'd listen to "Cathy's Clown". To "Teen Angel". "North to Alaska". "Sixteen Tons". "The Monster Mash" Me, I gummed up the works. Wrote poems to her. This made everyone nervous. And the more I was mocked the more I wrote, and it pleased her. I caught a football for her I wasn't supposed to catch. I was only following my own nature. Everyone around me, true to their natures, made me pay for my presumptions. Perhaps Sally McCabe caused Mr Jakes, our history teacher, to blow out his brains, who knows, proving the power of myth over the historically-minded mind, the petty materialist? Would I have lived another year if my father hadn't been transferred out of that hell-hole of a state? Now, as for your idea that we form a salon and have weekly get-togethers either here in your kitchen or in the Blue Danube, I'll think on it. I'm not at the moment keen.' And Eleanor grinned, saying, 'Mr Calhoun, you're one of a kind. Maybe with you I'm out of my league.' Oh no, I would protest. If anything, it was the other way around.

Bats

And I slipped notes for Dubois under his door, the fact of which bemused him. 'Randall,' he said to me, one spring afternoon in the Blue Danube, 'What are you trying to tell me?' Another voice: 'Yes, what's with all these notes, lately? And why haven't I been getting any?' That voice accusing me—was Eggy in his 8th decade, sensing treachery everywhere. 'Why nothing, Bob,' I answered Dubois, 'it's just that I know you think me extreme in my views. I applaud that you retain your faith in the innate good sense of the American people. It's a faith I lack.' 'As much as I hate to say it, I'm inclined to agree with you,' said Eggy, raising his glass to me, a collegial but wary gesture. A table of Slavs on the other side of the café regarded us with some derision. 'Bob,' I continued, alluding to previous business between us, his invitation to have me come and drink with him, 'your request is under consideration. My Internal Review Board is certainly taking it seriously. Whiskey? Enlightened discourse? Tempting. It's just that I've become such an autodidact of late I don't believe I can play the scholar and speak dispassionately on Caesar's lost legions, let alone current events. Then, too, knowing you, you'll wish to expatiate on gravity and anti-gravity, on Jesuits, on Mayan numbers while I struggle with the sum of my parts and the whole seems altogether short-changed. Is this a fair assessment of your druthers? And you, Eggy, how is it you're so besotted with *My Fair Lady* when you are, as you put it, the scion of a switchman and a roadhouse Jezebel? Why not *Richard III*? Whence the high Tory? Or is it just that we're out of earshot here of the Reveres and the Thomas Paines and Tinpan Alley?' 'You,' said Eggy, 'are going to take some getting used to. You do have a peculiar way of talking. Well, are you boffing Moonface? Because if you're boffing Moonface, I might have something to say on the matter.' 'Eggy, Eggy,' I said, 'I wouldn't dream of it.' 'I'll bet,' said Dubois, much entertained.

Bob, I enjoyed the other evening immensely, the warm evening, the bats flitting between the maples, the whiskey. Especially the latter. Oh yes, and the talk, you attempting to convert me to materialism and me letting you know I'm 99.9% there, just that I reserve the last one-tenth of it all as a means of keeping the house honest, though the house always wins. Does this sum up my spiritual position? And when Eleanor joined us and let out one great bleat of her trombone and then apologized to the world at large, I thought to myself life's worth living and it's good, on occasion, to kid around. I'll endeavour to reciprocate. But entre nous, *I'm not all that keen on her plot to organize a salon.—RQC*

For the Record

Twice in the course of a year, Eleanor will have come across corpses: Marcel Lamont, and soon, Edward Sanders aka Fast Eddy. Whom she will find in pantyhose with a grimace on his face. Here is the Keats he was reading: "La Belle Dame Sans Merci". *'Oh, what can ail thee, knight-at-arms, alone and palely loitering?'*

§

Book II—Follies Ho!

Calhoun's Follies I

—I have settled down somewhat in the Traymore Rooms. I write a little every day, if diffidently. I do not expect I will add to the sum of human knowledge. I do not expect I will entertain that much. It is always a wilderness for others, pleasing oneself. But were I to write up this place, were I to present a stage set to the world at large of unassuming rebels and cultists, who among my characters could best plead our case? Eggy with his death-is-just-over-the-horizon-for-me eyes? Moonface keeping a schoolgirl's diary?

Was up at five to catch the fabled worm. Grabbed empty air, the thought of my mortality just then a depressing thought. I laid down on the couch, switched on the TV, heard out a televangelist. 'Believe you me,' he chortled, 'when Christ comes, you will know it.' He was wearing a blue suit with a pink tie and silver clasp, an American flag pin affixed to his lapel. I pictured swarms of angels darkening the sun in advance of judgment. I switched off the TV. Sometime later, and I was, perhaps, in a sort of yogic trance as I brewed coffee and smelled toast and the homemade marmalade of Eleanor R that she foisted on me. Or perhaps I managed to hypnotize myself, turning the pages of my notebook, each page of it a sail otherwise becalmed, but each a testament to offenses against some tut-tutting Poseidon of a critic. In other words, in my endeavour to make sense of things, I had gotten to the bottom of exactly nothing.

The name Lucille Lamont was scrawled on one of those pages. Question marks followed. Was she, on that page, seeking intellectual justification for the murder of her husband? 'Evolutionary opportunism,' I imagined she said of a force she thought she could enlist to her advantage. I chose not to respond; she might have bested me in a quarrel. How does one rebut evolutionary drift? All the machete work I would have to do, hacking through the lost byways of God and free will and any number of related considerations. Was not up for it. Nor did I care to reassemble the fallen down pieces of the old patriarchal hegemony, if for no other reason than that one cannot turn back the clock. Still, it had been a power with which one could argue, however unsuccessfully; it is all that one can ask of power—that it listen. Well, it usually does not unless its own interests are involved. Lucille Lamont, no feminista, certainly no ballerina, no drawing card for some independent production company, no cutting edge of a turning tide, was just another broker of the everyday and the humdrum, petty cruelties her currency (as they are for you and me), the new pieties and platitudes of the hour hers to massage as she saw fit. I went for a walk.

Oh, but it was a glorious day, indeed. The early weeks of Traymorean existence had made spring seem a promise. Then summer and terrasses and flirtations. Now autumn. Now and then glimpses of Moonface passing beneath the yellow leaves of maple boughs, of a girl steeped in ancient verses. Yes, even as she was fatally of her time, as stretched and consequently frayed as a rag pulled at by the contending forces of a blank politeness and a rage she barely suspected her body harboured. Processions might prance and reverence gods; oracles might sing and pronounce, but she in her black denims and red sneakers was hunched at the shoulders and non-committal, the world of ancient verses less an injunction against our stale hypocrisies and more a theme park. More depressing than any thought of my mortality was to know I could do nothing for her, could shine no light on various confusions of intellect, the old benedictions and accidents of lust discredited. And even if this were not it at all, I was simply too long in the tooth for this young woman. It had been one thing to depart the Old World for the New; now it was a weary, fed-up new world; and every day dawning was already some bleached skull of an animated cartoon's desert floor. So it seemed. Glorious day, indeed.

To be sure, Lucille Lamont, as we all are, was guilty in her thoughts and at one with her urges. But could she be charged with a deed born of a plan? A method, not immediately apparent to her, was always right in front of her nose. Did she hate her husband so much? Was it the way he chewed his food? His smell? His snoring? Perhaps it is too easy, throwing the word hate around. Why not pity? Pity is an emotion that attracts its own dark arts. My exposure to her was limited to chance meetings in the Traymore hall. To the hello's, the how are you's. To, well, things are not bad but I have seen better. A tinge of whine in an otherwise all-knowing tone of voice—

We were trying to have it too many ways. Always in America the trumpets and cavalry of the triumph and the escape clause. A coffee machine in the window of a specialty store stopped me in my tracks. It was a beautiful machine shining with a bronze burnish. I would buy it just to have it for its own sake; that I might actually use it was another matter. Here was my materialism and my spiritual side. I stood there, admiring spigots and valves. What had Pompeii that could compare to this? But could Caesar have been a mystic by virtue of the fact Rome had no machines (siege engines excepted) and slaves did the work? A smartly-dressed woman was now beside me, inspecting the object. 'It's quite the thing,' I ventured to say. The look she shot me suggested I had just invaded her space.

Returned from my walk, and no more the wiser for it, I sit here performing the same old lustral rites, marking boundaries with words; I kid myself I am breaking ground. A bowl of orange slices, banana. Yellow foolscap, gray pen; the rolling tobacco, the amaretto. How precious, itemizing objects on a desk, itself a tawdry piece of furniture not Regency. A contemporary symphony, the music of which is not easy listening, produces an image in my mind of a heavy crock. Tipped on end, it allows so many yellow demons to stream out that had been pent up. It is as if they skitter now through some citrus grove such as I saw once in Sicily, the almond trees in blossom; the sea sparkling all the way to Africa, the island once as lusted after as was California. Geo-politics 101 is Fate. Eggy, whom I saw earlier in the hall, went on about Moonface, and how he expected to get the measure of her bosom.

—My first impression of Lucille Lamont was not favourable, she bored, clever, disputatious. Her idea of flirtation was Stalinist. I could not imagine her in flattering dress, her attire aggressively drab and shapeless; and yet, clearly and unaccountably so, she wished to be thought of as fetching. Yes, and given her boasting as to what a high roller she once had been, a winner and not a loser, why then had she married Marcel, good sport but self-destructive by the looks of it? That these thoughts enter my head at all give me pause, more reason to despair of myself for giving those thoughts the time of day. Is there more to add to them without resorting to damnable ologies, those articles of faith which claim to know why people gravitate to people who can do them no good?

Dubois, Eggy and I would discuss the war, afternoons in the Blue Danube. Well, sometimes we did, so as to fill in lulls in the conversation that, on occasion, arose, Eggy losing his train of thought. 'Hoo hoo,' he might say, 'I've mislaid my wits.' Moonface listened in now and then. She would only look puzzled as we pronounced on this and that, our grasp of current events coloured by our view of previous debacles that had transpired before she was born. If the war in Iraq was a staple of Traymorean discourse, I did not wish to know Lucille's point of view. I assumed it was a liberal point of view, but I could have been wrong. One evening, I heard through the walls of the Traymore, a Lamont shouting match in progress. There was mention of Graham Greene the famous novelist. A pair of drunken voices, one hissing, slurring heavily (Lucille); one in full-throated contempt of the lack of true sensibility anywhere (Marcel). I am sorry to report that, perhaps, Lucille had some justification for describing the writer as a muddleheaded mystic. Marcel argued otherwise, though I could not make out his every word. Just that Mr Greene had divined the human soul. And that was that. Then silence. Then, you gin-soaked Catholic stooge. Then, up yours. Then, worse, as Lucille was likened to an intimate part of her anatomy, and something made of glass was smashed.

There is no causal connection between the war and the death of Marcel Lamont; between the war and a belief by the police that Marcel's death was the result of 'misadventure'; between the war and the fact Sinatra might now sing: 'It's witchcraft, crazy witchcraft'. There is no causal connection between the war and the belief ordinary people have that this world is the best of all possible worlds, and they may well be right, just that they are not. History the tale of unfolding progress, surely evil comes along for the ride, moral outrage the luxury, spinnaker, the cherry on the cream. If Lucille had not set a trap for Marcel, gin the bait, she did not seem all that eager to dispel our suspicions.

—And so, in March, I moved to the Traymore. April had hardly come around, and Marcel Lamont was dead. Moonface and I converse. Often I drop in on Eleanor R. Sex is no mystery for her; it is physio. Eggy is quite the character, Dubois another egotist of conventional depths. Which is to say he assumes we live in the best of all possible worlds as there is no other.

None. Of course, one may imagine worlds. One may deduce their possible existences by way of mathematical formulations. '*Bonjour, monsieur, ça va bien*? Shall we talk red-shift stars? Iraq is nothing. No, really, it's nothing.'

And so, on a moving day, I had the intention to do something serious with my life. Ah, creative non-compliance. I knew instantly, as soon as I saw her in the hall with her copy of Virgil's *Eclogues*, that I was going to allow Moonface to distract me from my grand purposes. Just the sight of that book told me I was a fraud in any case. And was Lucille, in her own way, playing a similar game of non-compliance to the prevailing orders, Marcel her proof of sincerity, and she had the courage to expend him?

Evil is sometimes cause and always a consequence. The yellow wasps of September dart about in the deep peace of a late summer afternoon. Sparrows and squirrels lark about as if a life and death struggle were just that—a lark. So many middle-aged women in the streets seem so tired. If men can always plead their maleness, what can women plead? Is not Lucille Lamont entitled to her excuses? But she never looked tired, and I do not imagine she does now. Heavy of body, Lucille Lamont is as empty of soul as a hot air balloon.

But suppose Marcel had been trying to dry out, as it were, and get a grip on his life, get out from under? He had, in fact, checked into a clinic before I showed up at the Traymore as a raw recruit. Suppose Lucille, at first all for it, realized she could have none of it? Who could she then despise if, in fact, she did despise an innocent or a Marcel who, at times, was brutal to her; but who gave one and all the benefit of his doubt; who liked his sailboat, his booze and hearty laughter? Life is random except when it is not.

I have been much put out by Marcel's death; it is not because the man meant anything to me. It is just that his demise swamps me with a glut of Lucille Lamont thoughts. Have not written anything worth a damn. (*To Charlottetown: infinitive bespeaking a Canadian jig.*) Lack of knowledge. Lassitude. As Bly would say: amateur.

—It is quiet in the Blue Danube. Moonface sits, turned sideways on her chair, one leg slung over the other, her torso square with the book she reads. Her left hand is flush to the table, her right hand resting on top of it, bony elbows suspended in space. I cannot claim for her any elegance of body but the length of her thigh is terribly elegant, suggesting power and grace and promise beyond the scope of words. It almost seems that her lips move as she reads the Latin of Publius Vergilius Maro, as she employs skills I have long since lost, I now unable to coax latinities into accordance with English sense. Yes, she is having at the *Eclogues*, some lines of which render Scylla and powerful whirlpools and frightened mariners, her lips parted, she fully focused. She is no innocent, but she has much to learn. My eyes lock on a tapestry tacked to the wall, one depicting a snowy alpine scene. It speaks of no perils; there is in it none of life's chanciness. Demented landlocked item. As if it would sell more bratwurst and schnitzel to the Slavs who meet here, to whom I am indifferent. I cannot tell myself why this should be. They seem too comfortable with their uprooted lives, and smug. In walks Eggy, or rather he totters through the door with his cane. 'Wine,' he says to Moonface, 'toot dey sweet.' I rate a nod as he says, 'Oh, you here?'

Eggy is in a reminiscing mood. He starts up, saying, 'A few years back, I and My Fair Lady, why, we took a long drive. I footed all our expenses. I didn't expect to get to first base with her, but we did manage to raise Kamarouska, a village, you know, on the St Lawrence. *In Kamarouska a kiss and a thought for Algonquins*. Thereafter, it was New Brunswick, lobster tail and clergy in a village by the sea near the state of Maine. My Fair Lady thought herself a bluestocking of certain Scots forerunners, and Montcalm threw the battle, as I always say. Hoo hoo.' So much for Eggy's reminiscence. I look at Moonface and she looks at me, her look impish. Eggy promptly falls asleep, his chin having raised his chest. Would Virgil have understood the plight of the Micmacs? My best guess is in the affirmative. I leave Moonface to the old man. It is as if I leave them to some remote island of harsh winters, just that—between an old man and a young woman—there is no hope of regenerating the tribe.

—There are tides, human migrations, the consequent spawn. Evil? It is a game of charades for the blind, the attempt to posit it ontologically. If there is no such thing as evil, there are no moral creatures, only those migratory sweeps, a tumbling through space. We now ape beyond the earth's atmosphere what we have been doing for millennia on the ground, tumbling. And perhaps the chimpanzee that first picked up a stick and used it, in a string of causation raised the first Edenic crime. How much blame accrues to Lucille Lamont? Inevitably, conflicts arise. Whose corn, fish, copper? Of what efficacy the strange gods? The women are of use. Such remarkable craft, those birchbark canoes. Soon enough, however, it is the victor's turn to cry foul, immigration a hot button issue, nation-states collapsing, every capital a Troy. If there is no such thing as evil, there are hopes and dreams which, if immaterial, are certainly tangible and measurable, so much so history crushes them. One wishes to improve one's lot; unwittingly or, indeed, with calculation, one triggers a chain reaction of events. *In Kamarooska a kiss and a thought for Algonquins.* 10,000 orphan daughters of the French king, and the die is cast in the attempt to colonize Quebec. Fire dances from the eyes of Heraclitus as he whittles down a thousand tribal wars to a single word: conflict. If we are not moral creatures, we are lethal, and some describe the fallout as evil. Yet another glorious autumn day. And I scribble on paper, lose myself in history; and I am shrunk to a pin's head for a brief span of time. Angels jitterbug on my miniaturized mass. But soon enough I spring back to my full and rightful volume, will go off to the post office presently with a bundle, one slated for a literary redoubt.

It would seem I require a censor, a Grand Inquisitor with invasive counter-tenor voice, one who will save me from myself. Everyone else—they are throwing off their shackles, their doubts, their oppressors. I am scrambling wildly for my inhibitions. All the world's treachery and not worth the paper it is written on.

—Out for another walk, I pass among loathsome creatures far from being in control of their food supply. Shining head males who, due to the unnatural warmth, wear shorts and tank tops, the girls glassy-eyed and chitterish. Are we not all refugees from collapsed stars, the shock of separation so great we have forgotten everything we once knew; but that, as we make our way along the avenues, as if in a pop tune, each sparrow and blade of grass, each blond brick, the cigarette smoke pluming in the humid air, bequeath us the illusion we are omniscient, and we know all the why's and how's and wherefore's; except that the girl or the boy at one's side, well, maybe they will or maybe they will not gratify our wants? We are all of us traversing the edge of the world in our packs and sub-groupings in want of *X*, surfeited with *Y*; but that the mysterious powers of *Z* will come for our salvation, whether *Z* is within or without us, helping those who help themselves. An old woman in an old coat, getting about like a peg-legged sailor, gripping shopping bags, lets some boy on a bike know he should keep his distance. Her forays into the garden are becoming more arduous, more beset with dangers. She does not trust the best minds of her day; I, for one, cannot blame her. She arouses my curiosity but I am too cowardly to ask her, 'Do you feel life has gotten better since the day you were born? More amenities? Better medicines? Improved methods of conveying oneself through space? Or do you feel things are worse: more complications, more rules, more gadgets you can't possibly use let alone keep track of? On what are your opinions based? Good or bad health? Cheery or sullen temperament? Experience shrewdly appraised? Does it matter? Did your first kiss move mountains? How about the last?'

Rome tells you this: evil is not the end of this world, just of some. Ah, the small sadisms. But evil? Mr Calhoun, you know nothing of it though you have lived with it all your life.

In Eleanor's kitchen you talk Sally McCabe and tumbleweed and whiskey, the desert moon, the gloomy faculty of a high school for whom you had no respect, sad educators propping the sky, secret fantasists of the sort a woman named Rand encouraged to do their worst. Eleanor listens as she always does, her attentive face left in position, thoughts elsewhere. On recipes; on electoral reform; on Dubois.

Has she capacity in her thoughts for this: we are not moral creatures, kindness to strangers and muffins our 'let's party' redemptions? RQC: 'Do you know what Dubois said to me just a few minutes ago?' Eleanor R: 'No, what did Bob say to you?' RQC: 'He said I was going to drive everyone around the bend, obsessing about the White House lawn.' Eleanor R: 'He has a point, you know. It isn't the centre of the universe which, as we know, dear boy, hasn't one.'

How can the woman stand being this sane all the time?

—Moonface's two front incisors are slanted inwards like a double-door gate one opens from within. It is back to Plato and Montaigne and Darwin and Tolstoy and Shakespeare and Homer and Horace—to the canon, in other words. Except that you do not go back. The sum total of it all suggests you ought not to bother. Instead, a woman from your past occupies your thoughts. She gauges her wants and desires. Should she or should she not? Oh what the hell. And she grabs your neck and pulls you to herself; as if to say, no, you are definitely not the one, but there is no one else around, so pucker up. Up the stairs then to her boudoir. The shadows of a maple just outside the window fall across the bed. It is neither love nor sport, what transpires. It is marking time until the heavens part and trumpets announce the angels who, in turn, announce something significant is at hand, darkening the sun. And there you are, not where you are supposed to be but where you happen to be. Before you know it, you are saying once more we are not moral creatures. Once more the void nods off. In the meantime, you make tender love, until she wearies of it and springs her metaphysics on you. She is greedy and likes to play the slut. You have no objections. Her knees are nice to look at.

You go home. You write, apprentice of the word and of love. Such silly, pretentious stuff you write. Should you give the woman a call? And risk another three months of running in place? You are tempted.

So that is how it was once upon a time and not much has changed. Now I wind up in the kitchen of Eleanor R, the sanest woman around, this after I had popped into the Blue Danube, having spotted Eggy inside. There was grizzle on his chin. I teased him. 'Eggy, you old hoser,' I say, 'you look like you've been in bed for three days with whiskey and sweetheart.' Eggy beamed. Can a man as old as he beam like that? Moonface gave me a look and I left. Eleanor's rooms are so cluttered with knickknacks, sentimental debris that, even if I had the means of saying something, I could not possibly catalogue an item of it. And it seems a kind of failure. She is bored with me just now and so, it is a quick mug of tea. A bleat of her trombone sends me out the door. 'Next time, fella.' As if she had anything to say for evolutionary drift. I will go back to the Blue Danube under a grey sky; I will smell Halloween as I go. I will be a hobgoblin of outrage, shadow governments putting the kibosh on my love of country of a country I once knew, one inseparable from its attachment to violence, slavery and greed.

But in the street, debonair Dubois assails me. Like reformed drunks, these non-believers. He thinks me a fool but obviously, the fact of me entertains him. 'Are we closer yet,' he asks, 'to a non-materialist basis for the universe?' 'As a matter of fact, nowhere near.' 'A pity. I was so looking forward to your thinking on it.' 'Silence,' I say, 'the profoundest silence imaginable. As who was there to hear the Big Bang?' 'Well, that's something. Let's meet, later.'

And in the Blue Danube, Moonface. Cream is drying on her cheeks. Slavs swoop down on cabbage rolls like carrion birds.

—Moonface informs me that she in her diary refers to Randall Q Calhoun as Simply Q. Who is this entity? It is clear that she and Eggy have been talking about me. This is novel, I as scuttlebutt. I must confess I am momentarily titillated. Simply Q? He's somewhere about my person, God knows, slung around my ears, hanging off my nose or other appendage.

Her bosom, high with wide cleavage, is a lonely bosom. Moonface might make the best of mothers, the most misunderstood of mistresses. Perpetual virgin? Now and then a look on her face suggests that, no, she is not too proud to pleasure herself. Cynicism followed by trying harder—a great danger to her soul. Furthermore state that evil stalks the land, and see if even an iota of the heroic sparks in the dying embers of your soul. A Moonface sideways glance accuses you. It is as if her eyes know before her brain can tell them so that you will betray her simply because you are you.

—The man Marcel Lamont had been and Iraq in its dismemberment—it is what preoccupies me now. That I sit in the Blue Danube early in October on a humid afternoon. I met Marcel shortly before he died. He was coming out his door in the Traymore, and he was sober. 'So you're the new man,' he cheerfully ventured, but as if I were the replacement for some other tragic figure who was no longer in the Traymorean picture. I could see easily enough that when he was out front of his demons, he was agreeable, lively, curious. Powerful physique. Fond of handball. Otherwise, between us, not much transpired, Marcel's wife Lucille a strong deterrent to me for extending any social courtesies. She certainly rubbed me the wrong way. Early on she told me she thought most women insipid; that in life there are no guarantees except those one begs, borrows or steals. I had no idea what she was talking about. Foolishly, I suppose, I jumped into the hole she had so considerately dug for me. 'What,' I answered her there in the hall of the Traymore, 'what if you'd been up on a platform in Paris, 1790s or thereabouts, the blade of the guillotine poised above your neck, your privileged self at risk, your blue blood about to gush away? Wouldn't you plead entitlement then?' She shrugged. 'And,' I continued, because I was unaccountably irritated, 'what if some cruise missile, programmed to target a somebody in Baghdad, wipes out, say, thirty innocent nobodies, instead? Wouldn't you, a nobody, think you'd been roughly handled? Wouldn't you be a little put out? Is Mr 007 a god or Tinkerbelle?' She thought me a lunatic. I thought her perverse.

If it was a plan, it was certainly a sketchy one. Lucille Lamont was having none of those precisely-established minuets, so prominent in whodunits, by which alibis are built and police are misdirected. She brought a case of gin into the apartment. She took off for Ontario. It would take a few days, but presumably Marcel would poison himself in short order and enjoy doing it. But why? And to what end? Dubois scoffed. 'Murder? Not likely,' he said. 'What motive? What does she get from it? The software he'd been developing? A leaky sailboat? Marcel was no Rockefeller, no whiz kid. He was a wife-beater. Yes, well, maybe she did provoke him, but still, I mean, come on.' Eggy had no opinion one way or the other. 'Man proposes; woman disposes,' he said. Dubois scoffed some more, saying, 'There you go again with that poetry stuff.' The police had closed the case: death by misadventure. In the notes she kept on the Traymore menagerie, Moonface merely observed that Eggy had no opinion, that she herself had none; that life was pointless and had no meaning; that when she was a little girl she used to weep for Christ on His cross, but that had ended when her breasts began to develop.

—Eleanor R had discovered the body, the body, that is, of Marcel Lamont, about nine in the morning in his apartment. She was stepping out for smokes. She knew Marcel was on a toot, Lucille in Ontario. For no particular reason she could think of, she rather liked the man, and did not like to think he was doing all that drinking and not eating. But would not Lucille have gotten in some groceries before she left? Maybe. But would Marcel take nourishment other than that of gin? That was the question. So she went and knocked on his door.

And the door was unlocked, and this was not unusual. She stepped in and saw right away the old telephone had been upended, the receiver off its hook and buzzing. Then, caught by the sun streaming through the living room window, curtains undrawn, she saw a dark trail of blood; and she followed it to the bedroom where, nude at the foot of the bed, lay Marcel. In recounting this to Dubois, at first she said the body was blue; then she said the legs were orange. No matter; he was dead. The conviction immediately formed in her that Lucille was at the bottom of it. She had always had a hunch about that woman; it was not a flattering hunch. The place was uncharacteristically tidy, so much so the place itself was what was out of place, the empties stashed in the kitchen sink except for one or two looking like fish out of water on the couch. Lucille was a poor housekeeper, Marcel comfortably slobbish. Why, if he was that far gone in his drunken state, would he scruple to pile the empties in the sink? This was not like the man she thought she knew and rather liked. Dubois, scoffing as always, said, 'She was going away. She tidied up before she went away. Lots of people do. They don't like coming back to a mess.' 'Tidy?' Eleanor R nearly barked, 'tidy? An army of janitors had been in there. The kitchen floor nearly blinded me.' Dubois responded, 'I say she just cleaned up, banal as that might sound to you. And maybe she told Marcel to keep it that way—on pain of death.' Dubois laughed, touching the shoulder of the woman who was the apple of his eye, this woman in the service of whom he had placed his vanity and powers of deduction. Eggy really did have no opinion in the matter, saying only that if Lucille Lamont had once been a bit of a sport, a highroller, man-friendly, well, bloody hell, what was the harm in that? I myself placed little credence in Eleanor's suspicion. Even so, I could not get out of my mind that configuration between Marcel and Iraq, between the grandiose crime and the petty theft of a life. Would Euripides, defender of women, have looked with compassion on Lucille Lamont? The speculation was briefly rife over a bottle of wine at the Blue Danube one evening not so long ago. Yet again, we went through the possibilities. Was her motive the life insurance? Money-making patent? Property we did not know about? 'Perversity,' said Eleanor R. And I wondered if she was not borrowing the word from me, seeing as I make great use of it, and had been doing so in our kitchen chats. 'Sheer perversity.' 'Oil,' joked Bob Dubois, and then blushed, a certain glint in the eyes of the apple of his eye. 'Christ, I was only joking.'

Yes, what would a writer of genre fiction make of all this? Not much, I supposed, as I went to bed that night quite sloshed.

Calhoun's Follies II

—To hork. By virtue of the fact that a Viking, one day, squeezed a nostril shut and horked out the other and baptized a Newfie rock in the name of wanderlust? Some say a Viking squad traversed as far as Oklahoma where, no doubt, a friendly game of football was got up between Norsemen and Shawnee.

—Moonface. We could tumble into her bed and discuss Ezra Pound. 'He was only half right about Browning,' I would say, 'and that's where so much went wrong.' But she is as likely to paint her toenails right then and there as recite from *Pisan Cantos*.

—So America was not schooled in the Homeric. She slipped into her coming of age with puritanical spite, unwarranted optimism the medium. Space taunted her. All that space of prairie and mountain coaxed her forward in lethal spurts. It went hard on the Indians and the buffalo. And she, in the meantime, presented herself to the world with strangely theatrical social graces. Ah, Buffalo Bill Cody, yankee Bembo cracking a whip.

—Well, when the weather's nice and the Blue Danube's owner, pitching peanuts at a squirrel, puts out a few tables and chairs, Eggy and I take up positions, Eggy with his eyes on the girls. He is not unmindful of the grave import of grave political words; words like 'imperial overreach' or 'burgeoning civil strife', but he prefers to them the gravity of young women, especially those for whom a proper construction of the world is a serious matter. 'Dubois,' he said on one such afternoon, a wasp buzzing about his beer, 'had a time of it trying to convince me of the virtues of Black Dog Girl. You know of whom I speak?' But no, I did not. 'Oh, but you must. Well, I at first couldn't see what the fuss was about. And then she goes by, she with the dog, and I peer a little harder, and my goodness, Dubois was right. Unsung hips. Oh bloody hell.' 'Yes, but what of the Patriot Act? Will you make light of that?' And no, he will neither make light nor heavy going of the business, Eggy's mind on other business, to wit, Moonface's sacrosanct bosom and the fact that, it being his 81st, she is volunteering to fête him. '81st,' I say, 'I thought you just had your 80th. How many birthdays can you have in a year?' 'Why, as many as I want. I think she has the opera in mind. *Tannhäuser* I believe. It's not *My Fair Lady* I'll have you know, but it'll do. She gets points. Hoo hoo. Tra la.'

So we sit there, Eggy and I. He has his fancy glass of fancy beer; I have the cheap stuff in wine. The wasps sew tapestries in the air. All that is missing seems to be lederhosen and dulcimers. As if he were reading my thoughts, Eggy says, 'Innsbruck. Was there once.' And then—nothing. Thought closed, case closed. He might have met royalty in the town. Might have had a fling. I will never know. His mind, mostly alert, on occasion will falter. Pull up for a rest stop. He is a tiny man, as tiny as a sparrow; that is, if you can picture a sparrow getting about with a cane and a loopy grin. It seems to me the lovely physiques of lovely girls are what keep his mental operations in order; that they are a kind of alphabet for Eggy, those girls, a way of putting the world together. They are a way of keeping his hand in, now that he has weeded out, for us, at any rate, what bad memories he has had to preserve: Korea, wives, and the fact that Tricky Dick went from slick lawyer to presidential Othello, Desdemona the Constitution, Kissinger his Iago. And then, all of a sudden, the flow of his words seizes up; curtains draw down his eyes. As busy as the street might be with cars, trucks, buses and passersby and capricious taxis, it will get very silent. It will get as silent and as cool as a sepulchre deep in the labyrinths of a Roman basilica, no matter that the sun is quite warm in the trees and the breeze is a southerly. And just when I am thinking I should call for an ambulance, up he pops from whatever deeps into which he had descended, and he chirps, 'Oh, there's Prunella across the street.' Well, who is Prunella? And she, as it turns out, used to clean Eggy's rooms for a wage and sometimes consent to be his dinner companion for a Friday night when she was at loose ends. 'Oh but she's rather bi, you know, and she went chasing after some KitKat wench who, in turn, went chasing after some stewardess, suckered into some hell on earth in Cleveland.' And then we are in for a round of Balfour and Lawrence, as in T.E., and the Plains of Abraham and the Long Parliament. These things interest Eggy but not as much as does Black Dog Girl. 'Let's have another glass,' he suggests. 'Fuck my cardiologist. Oh my, I shouldn't say that. She's 35 and not bad looking. Hoo hoo. Tra la.'

—Moonface, shortly after I moved into the Traymore, slipped me a note. It observed I was leonine, the nose snubbed, hair in a state of arrested white. That I was a new section in her notes on the menagerie. The flattery is well received; even if, last night, as she brought me wine, I spoke these words to her, she thinking of pursuing her studies out of town: 'Ottawa? It may be a classics town. But it's a prig's town. It's a smug person's town. It's a making sin safe for the professional classes sort of town. I hope you reconsider.' She rolled her eyes.

—Now that you think of it, it was always in the air, as much so as Sputnik and Paul Anka, as white buck shoes and a missile crisis, as cheese spread and Budweiser: the spirit of Ayn Rand. Perhaps as some Aristolelian extension of matter into essence, she was the spectre attending the ceremony, one that tied the knot between Marcel and Lucille; one that whispered property rights into their ears. A magus-temptress. (Rhinestone glasses, scuffed highheels.) She might have said, 'The world's at your feet. You've only to take it. What persons in their right minds wouldn't? This is the Land of Use-it or Lose-it. So we're a little tawdry. So our eyes get too big for our stomachs. Look how far you've come already since your chance meeting at the supper club, happiness the rhumba that followed upon the tiramisu. To tell you the truth, I'm unsure as to whether I approve of this business that seems to require the state's imprimatur. Be that as it may, the ball's in your court, Marcel. Forehand smash. Deft backhand. Ace the serve. Pssst. Forget that Lucille, your May bride of a thundery afternoon, has seen better days. Morality is reinvention. Take her to Florida. Time-share unit. Fuck her in the arse. Meditate on the waves. Be the innovator you are. Hone the entrepreneruial skills. The computer's a grand machine. How right you are to hop on this bandwagon. Leave Nietzsche to me. I have a firing squad firing 24/7 at the likes of every Kant, mushy brain of every liberal.'

—It was wine in the afternoon. It was Eggy on a tear. As if 80 plus years of life had finally taught him how not to spoil things by cavilling; by unseemly selfishness and overweening pride. 'Oh bloody hell.' He was wise to himself as we sat there, courtesy of the Blue Danube, our libations on the table, Eggy a sparrow of a man. 'Moonface is going to fête me,' he said, 'but how and with what resources, I can't say. The opera, maybe.' With a very slight but nonetheless measurable trace of irritation in my voice, I said, 'I know. You advised me already that she has plans.' 'Oh, did I?' he shot back, yes, with a sparrow's worth of dudgeon.

But somewhere in this sparrow of a man was a page of Tacitus, the senate a cowardly aggregate of time-markers, their words a parody of words, their truths but senatorial heads affianced to body and fortune. The proles in the streets were restive, the lovers cynical who had dalliance in the deer parks. It was a contemplative moment, Eggy reaching for his golden glass of beer, his hand in delicate relations with the space it travelled through. He said, 'The rain in Spain. Hoo hoo.' His words seemed, for all that they were non sequiturs, a petty rant, a disavowal of the news cycle, a remarkable comment on the times. So that even I, as the American legislative branches played their games, as they pretended to what was good for the country; as they sent mixed signals in all directions, presumably for the benefit of the electorate and the Executive both; so that as the shadows lengthened, as commuters rumbled by in their high-gloss chariots; as the addicts smoked;

as lonely housewives engaged in all their obscure theatrics; as girl students roamed in packs and boys pounded basketballs; as birds sounded off in the golden trees and a mutt sniffed a hedge; even I who, more often than not, abide by decorum, said, 'Well, Eggy, one wonders if, before you die, your eyes ever will feast on Moonface's bosom in all its glory?'

'Oh but they shall,' said Eggy triumphant, 'they bloody well will.' Damnable lie, of course, but it was the sentiment that mattered. You had to give the man credit; how it was he had gotten free of his squalid origins to play the Grand Man without, in the process excessively violating justice. And yet, given that the bosom of Moonface was a kind of Holy Grail, how many good knights were hanging from trees, carrion birds pecking at their eyes, just so Eggy could redeem his spirit and bring life back to some blighted harvest? What if she embodied a stupendous hoax, one tantamount to a betrayal of the deepest magnitude; that she was already lost in her quest, her Latin studies of no earthly or heavenly use? Then Eggy said, 'We knew we were in trouble with Nixon. Montcalm threw the battle. Oh bloody effing hell.' He took a long, throat-rippling swig of his beer. The sky seemed to tinkle along all its faultlines.

—Much of what men think about women, women think about men. But I have yet to meet a woman who reasons like old Eggy. I could see he was excited about something, this sparrow of a man. He waved me over to his table as I approached the Blue Danube on a golden day. What could there be in the world that was 'off' or out of kilter or repulsive or morally suspect? But how convoluted that sounds! Must we always be drawing a line in the sand at which point body and mind separate? 'For God's sake, sit down,' said Eggy, his cane propped against the table, two glasses of red wine before him. He was drinking both.

I took a chair and, his brow suddenly troubled, his eyes went blank. Just then he looked the image of a stone portrait, one of those Roman busts one encounters in the basements of European museums. He came to, eventually, saying, 'Don't get cheeky with me. Oh bloody hell.' He must have been addressing general principles as I had not said anything—yet. 'Beautiful day,' I finally offered. 'True,' he said, 'true.' I went inside the café and came back with a glass of wine for myself. His tiny hands were those of a pontiff, folded together there on the table. They were penitent, greedy, magisterial. In the meantime, his eyes had gotten dull again. Ferocious anger, fathomless melancholy on his brow. Was there some Caracalla in this sparrow of a man? He said, brightening on the turn of a dime, 'I've got it. I've got what I meant to say. Deficit position. Hoo hoo.' 'What,' I asked, 'are you talking about? The Federal Reserve? Tantric sex?' 'Don't get severe with me,' he said. 'I rather think I meant the latter,' he said, 'and don't look now but there goes Black Dog Girl. My, she's splendid.' I did not stick around and get drunk with Eggy. The day was too burnished with some bronze sheen for that. I left him to his own devices of which he has more than meets the eye.

—Pay me millions to fake it, and I could not do it, not even as cheap genre; I could not fake some tale of the inner sanctum. And yet, deep in my bones, I know. Randall Q Calhoun knows, for power is wielded all around us. But one may as well watch the sun sparkle on the sea for clues as to what moves on its floor. What tin men we are who believe we choose and are not chosen. No word from Gar. None from Vera. But drinking whiskey on a ferryboat, waving at beachcombers on their Ithacas off the British Columbia coast, copping a feel as the seawind whipped through our hair—now that was something: those warm-hearted kisses that delighted the soul, the lips cool in the winter air. It is not to say we cannot see things for what they are. It is not to say we cannot distinguish right and wrong. It is not to say we perpetually deny ourselves states of grace out of spite. And it is not to say we cannot rectify a bad situation; but that, for the most part, we are blind, our blindness the broad thoroughfare into the real. So Calhoun opines. Cheap genre, indeed.

—There always has been and always will be a Lucille Lamont. She has in these times, how do I say it, good camouflage. That she irritates people just enough and no more. So that they see her as a nuisance, a person to avoid whenever possible. Besides, this husband of hers she allegedly did in, what was he but a nobody, a drunk, a probable wife-abuser? Eggy pleases himself. 'Lucille?', Eggy has said, 'I never minded her. Marcel was a trial. Unstable character. I know what Eleanor thinks, and Eleanor is otherwise of sound mind and all the rest of it and good company now and then, but when women get on about other women, well, you know, feathers fly. Hoo hoo.' Eggy is already a monument, one that occupies a public square and sees it all; whose answer to it all is strategic silence. It seems very wise.

With Moonface one never knows; one day she is glamorous, her lashes longer and darker (it does something for her high cheekbones), and she shines from a place within; and the next day, she is a colourless wallflower, prematurely defeated, without appeal. She complains of her fits; she lives in dread of them. And men are a pain and she has nothing to offer them but her fecklessness. What has any of this to do with fascism? It has much to do with Randall Q Calhoun, how he (how I) expends hours and hours and hours fingering the various loose ends of the life and the lives at hand, wondering if they interrelate, if at all; wondering how much is to be owed chance and what to design, and how much of that design is for good and how much for evil. Enough. What, will I organize in the streets?

—Slavs motion to Moonface to turn down the music here in the Blue Danube. One slams an empty beer glass on the table. No doubt, the ologies have something to say about this. How many lifetimes required for the unlearning of theatrical gestures one has enacted against repressive regimes or collapsing states? I give Moonface a look; she looks away. 'Do you know what you're up against? Do you know what creeps across the land, seriously unpleasant? You already tell me in a hundred different ways how I've failed you, and I'm neither your father nor your husband, much less your lover, and you're right, and still you don't know. Indeed, you can't cry on a pillow constructed of Latin vowels. The living don't help much.' Of course, I do not mouth these words; a look is sufficient. Black eyes and a sour expression push back.

There is narrative and there is narrative; you wheel the horse inside the walls of Troy and bad things will happen and continue to happen until, eventually, one arrives at some futuristic point of time in the slums of Rio. I will steer clear of Eleanor's kitchen at least for today. Whiskey, sex, large cars? The eyes of Sally McCabe blink, she under the weight of the boy who is on her and taking his satisfaction. Her delectable nose sniffs the wind, she giving it and not the boy her full attention. As if, by way of this wind, the dead were talking to her; were perhaps warning her, and if not the dead, then some other eternity. I have to stop seeing such things in my mind. Sometimes boredom brings it on: that baby blue Chrysler car parked on a rise overlooking a sea of sand and sage and mesquite. Crew-cut Coop leans against the front of his car. He smokes a cigarette; a pal boffs his Sally on the backseat. What Conestogas ferrying the pieties over the endless expanses? General Motors had been there before it was there. What will it get me at the drycleaner's, at the bank? What will it get me with Eggy should I, against my better judgment, interrupt his isolate trance; with Moonface should I sashay into the Blue Danube and barter for a cup of coffee, bravado and not coin the trade of the realm; and she, full-frontal assault, attack me with Virgil and her lonely bosom, her black eyes looking for their betrayer? (I had slipped my arm around her waist the other night, and, at first, she was fine with it.) I had crossed over a line—somewhere on the open Atlantic and yet, for all that, I was getting signs: debris in the water and birds in the air. Soon enough, I would raise some shore the inhabitants of which would paddle out and greet me where I had dropped anchor. But I stand there in the middle of a sidewalk stopped dead in my tracks. It is as if I am Socrates meditating on one leg, passersby in awe. I would like to take it back—that arm. God only knows what the Calhoun arm has set in motion.

—'Satanic forces,' I say. 'Colossal stupidity,' she says. We argue, she and I, in an amiable fashion, bread baking in the oven. Eleanor R wears one of those body-length aprons the logo of which reads 'Boss'. Eleanor R has frosted curls. And she has, just now, the demeanor of one expecting to be informed of what she already knows. Actually, we are horrid little creatures, she and I, the way we sit in our comfort at her kitchen table, she playing with the spit valve of her trombone, I pouring us out some amaretto, a sweet substance for which she has a weakness. We are attempting to come to grips with collective madness. It seems we are getting nowhere.

'Yes,' I say, 'for the sake of fancy, let's imagine that, here or south of here, the upper percentile of the populace, fabulously empowered, fabulously rich, behind their closed gates, worship some Belial or another and don't give a straw for the rest of us; whether we're consumed by pestilence or storm; whether by penury or helicopter gunships. Furthermore, let's picture the grotty rest of us in our tenuous relationship with a notion of the commonweal; how we're depraved, worshiping our celebratory demons, our two-faced angels such as turn the cranks of blue-haired old biddies and pasty-faced pulpiteers, of witless housewives and their honey-voiced but even more witless spouses, the kind who oversee franchise outlets and collect alms for their various sects, all the while their runtish broods are consigning themselves to the love of Jesus or are jacking off in the garage or both. Et cetera. For the sake of fancy, for sheer torpor of intellect, out of boredom with all the ologies such as would calibrate the distance between our soulless souls and some couch potato god, all the while insisting there is no such thing as God, let's imagine satanic forces. It would explain much if it were true.' 'It's as plain as the nose on your face, Mr Calhoun,' Eleanor R says, 'colossal stupidity. I don't know why you have to get exercised with the devil.' 'Because,' I say, 'and I admit I haven't much of a case, the standard definitions, the usual run of the mill diagnoses seem only to give the malaise permission to have its way. They're a part of it.' 'In other words,' says Eleanor R, 'you don't trust the best minds of your day.' 'Absolutely not,' I say.

SET PIECES

In Eggy's Domain

At loose ends one evening, I knocked on Eggy's door. I heard him slide in his slippers over the pinewood floor. It would take him a while to reach me. Soon enough, however, I was admitted into the Eggy lair.

'To what do I owe the pleasure?' I was asked as he, with the aid of his cane, shuffled and slid over to his old armchair before which was a carpet, on the other side of which was an another old armchair, a rack of shelves against the wall stuffed with books of varying thicknesses. I had not known what to expect. There was a scholarly side to Eggy the boulevardier, this I had known, but somehow seeing evidence for a creature more thoughtful than he might let on threw me a little. After all, here he entertained Moonface and endeavoured to pinch her bum.

'You do the honours,' he said. 'Wine and glasses in the kitchen.'

And so I did the honours, the wine on a counter alongside a box of crackers and an unopened tin of sardines. It was the kitchen of a man who dined out a lot on sausages and fried onions.

I did not know why, but I felt perhaps I had imposed on him. Suppose he had been sitting there given over to his memories, the world of his inner life superceding all other possibilities? On every available surface it seemed there were photographs of women, previous wives, most likely, and young smiling faces—progeny, I supposed, and there was a snapshot of a uniformed man who could only have been Eggy in his Korea days. As for the books on the shelves, I was not surprised to see Herodotus or Gibbons and other more contemporary historians, but I was surprised to spot the flashier book spines of spy novels and whodunits and instant biographies of political personalities. The room struck me as a compromise between the demands of those living still, and the silent submissions of my host to the bequests of the dead. I put it to the man: 'Suppose all hell breaks loose and you look around. Who's there in the trenches with you? With whom can you work? Who, by the very fact that they exist, can only make things worse? Who's all sweetness and light and can never be otherwise, no matter what corruptions they ingest?'

'Beats me.'

Eggy smirked.

Her Eyes Weren't Really Black

I said to Moonface: 'There are those who believe in Nemesis. Which is to say that the immoderate use of power and little regard for the consequences invite downfall. Still, there are those who find this explanation too much a party to myth, as if Nemesis were an old wive's tale. There are the more scientifically-based examinations of cause and effect. We'd be talking geography, food supply, population growth, climate fluctuations, the ability or inability to adjust to circumstance that is always tied to a system of governance, be it democratic, oligarchic, plutocratic, or outright jackboots and midnight knocks on the door. So that there are those who say morality has nothing to do with good or bad use of power, if we take morality to mean a regard for justice and distribution of wealth; that there is only power and the question as to whether, once power is attained, it can be held against all comers. It's a natural condition—to want power. It's so much more unnatural to refuse it. We couldn't be paleolithic wanderers, forever, in some wind-blasted Eden. Yet many do refuse it. Et cetera and so forth.'

Granted, it was a windy but pensive speech I gave, there in the Blue Danube after closing; there in the raw light of three candles set on the table. Moonface had loosed her hair and it spilled around her shoulders. The lover boy in me had flailed about; the pedagogue took over, that demon in me I was always pushing back. I hated holding forth. Wine had unhinged my tongue; I was enjoying holding forth.

'And what about poets?' Moonface asked, hands clasped to her cheeks, elbows on the table.

'Well, what about poets? Hopeless dreamers. But sometimes they're students of power and the powerful. They keep an eye on events, as well they should. Sometimes they know who got where and how and why and to what end. Poets, too, want power. Words are their consolation prize. Sometimes these consolations are nothing more than self-induced fantasies. Since poets are little valued in these parts, they're not much of a threat to the powers that be. Who in their right minds would place much value on semiotic gobbledygook, let alone take fright from it?'

It was then I noticed, in the raw light of three candles working its miracle with the wine, building grace and well-being and benign intoxication, three flames weaving a romance, that the Moonface eyes were not really black; they were a deep and richly glowing brown tending to gold. They were, at any rate, a startling colour. I worried for us both on account of them.

'Tell me,' she said, 'of Ovid.'

It was as if she were asking for a fairy tale or the legend of some hero.

'Well, what's to know? He was a jet-setter. He fell foul of Caesar's program of family values. He was a middle class soul of some wit and some flair for the pursuit of the pleasures. Perhaps Caesar thought him a buffoon.'

Her dimple flashed. She was beginning to have altogether too much fun at my expense. She asked: 'Do you believe in Nemesis?'

'But of course. And we're in for it.'

§

Book III—The Good Ship Lollipop

The Beginning of a Proper Narrative

I knocked on her door and she answered, Moonface in her jammies, socks on each narrow foot. Botticelli might have painted those feet and their martyrdom. She nodded me in. Perhaps her willingness to admit me had to do with the evening before when Clare Howard finally tracked me down, finding me in the Blue Danube. Clare was both majestic and drawn, bringing news of her husband's sudden death. The look on her face said I was to blame, but then she regained hold of better thoughts. Even so, Clare did not want my company, though I gallantly offered it. I told her that Gar, her husband, my oldest friend, had loved her very much. I was told, in turn, the particulars of the funeral. *Should the jackal eulogize the lion?* She left me at table with Dubois and Eggy, the two of them politely silent. She was out the café door, her lovely face unreadable. And then, as Eggy, irrepressible, said something about Jackie Kennedy, I glared at the homunculus. *Effing hell, I was just suggesting...* Dubois told the old bugger to shut up. Moonface had been a witness to it all, and now I was following her into her untidy bedroom. On her bed, on the off-white duvet, was something of a tableau. What looked suspiciously like an old primer was a hardcover edition of Catullus's verses. Dead worlds lived: the poet's Rome, and the decade (the 40's?) in which the edition had been printed. Perhaps Bogart had read out some of the smuttier verses to Bacall. In addition to the book were loose sheets of binder-paper scattered about on which were scrawled Moonface's notes. And there was what I took be the dear girl's diary. She sat now on her bed, Indian-style, her back flush with the pillows propped against the wall. She indicated I should deposit myself beside her. I heard myself asking: 'Are you sure?'

'Why not?' she answered, a little too brightly, gathering up the papers and books, making room.

'I'm going to flunk,' she said, 'if I don't get serious.'

Erotic burblings.

She was somewhat lanky in her physique.

'Well then,' I said, 'maybe I should leave you to it.'

'Oh no,' she said, 'you can stay a while, but just a while. I have to go to class.'

Perhaps there was time enough to steal a kiss.

'It's so sad,' she said, 'about your friend. No, really.'

'Yes, well—'

Clare Howard had been a figure of judgment in the café; as something more, at any rate, than a dead man's wife. Abandoning Dubois and Eggy to their bickering, I went back to my digs and began a letter to Vera Klopstock. I described for Vera a little of Traymorean life and how I had settled into certain routines. I asked after Karl's health. And how was life in Costa Rica? I pictured a seaside bungalow. Bananas. Fishing spears. Nets. I wrote that I had foolishly declared my love of Moonface to her and she responded: *wha-hah-hah!* The girl-woman was irked. Eggy was sniffing that Moonface was getting serviced by someone outside our circle. *Never offer a woman love when she wants sex. Conversely, hoo hoo, never offer sex when what's wanted is love. Effing hell.* Wise, old, Zeus-like Eggy. I figured Vera was gadding about the island in a grass skirt. I then informed her of Gar's death, wondering as I did so, if the news would take her aback; I wondered, as well, if there had been something between them once, as Vera had, on one occasion, complained about Gar's prickly nature. Her tone betrayed an intimacy. It was, however, well-known: Gar did not suffer fools. I wondered, too, if the early Christians were the prigs some assumed them to be. Eleanor, so I continued writing, had received a letter from Lucille Lamont. The Lamont woman would fly to Australia to visit relations. Well then, good. She should stay as long as she liked. No one would care if she never came back. It was not yet a full-banked fire, this ardor I had for Moonface, but Vera was to understand (not that she would mind, she in her own career was cheerfully amorous) that I would not lay a hand on the girl in question. It would be rather like kicking and scuffing away what thin soil there was of love on the rock on which humankind squatted.

And so, it was a bit disconcerting now, Moonface sliding down her pillows to adopt a prone position on her back, her knees drawn up, her hands resting on her belly. What was this? She turned her head slightly so that she could read my face, and she said: 'Did I tell you? My father's United Church. I lost my virginity when I was 13. The boy wound up in prison, but not because of me. There's this poem, Catullus's, where a boy's buggering a girl and then Catullus buggers him. When I first read it I blushed. You can kiss me if you want, but you don't have to. I have to get my teeth straightened. Anyway, so now you know, I'm not a virgin. Sometimes I find it so boring, the poetry, that is. Sometimes I feel like it's a language that only I and no one else gets, and it's my secret.'

I was terribly aware of the proximity of her body and its allure. But I was also seeing Gareth Howard in his future grave; and it was as if he had been penalized for his cold, Apollonian seeing-into-things. The cornlands of Ontario were, I suppose, restive, what with Lucille Lamont among them somewhere, she as inevitable as bad weather and taxes. Would Moonface change her mind and salvage an awkward moment by offering me coffee? Sally McCabe flickered briefly in my mentions, she enjoining me *to take the girl, for God's sake.* As it was beginning to verge on comedy, the situation, the dear girl artless and perhaps very confused about what she thought she wanted, I reached across my body to squeeze her shoulder in some collegial way. Involuntarily, I sighed. I had not the courage of my convictions, clearly. I got from Moonface's dark eyes what I took to be amused scorn. Perhaps she thought to confuse me when she said: 'The Good Ship Lollipop doesn't sail every day.'

Calhoun's Follies III

—The liberal believes he has conquered fear; the conservative knows it is so much hoo-haw.

—If Britain was the template of the modern, what with its factories and merchant classes, if America is the latest wrinkle in this perversity, then I have been useless since at least feudal times, the shortest route to absurdity one's refusal to sell out. If worship of the collective is a recipe for homicide on a mass scale; if worship of the individual is frivolity, but a way to have one's pockets more thoroughly flattered by every corporate thief in the land; if the death of the gods spelled the death of poets (was not Nietzsche but the first op-ed machine?); if there is even an iota of reality to the words above, then the world is in such a temper that I might, mistakenly or not, consider the authors of Genesis and all those who would be Flaubert to have been one and the same clown at which kids at the circuses laugh, all the cities of the plains sheer braggadocio.

—Minnie Dreier was my last chance at respectability, if, by respectability, we mean the honoured passions. I wanted the romance of it all. She wanted to be the Great Woman. She lacked the talent though her body had charms and her mind had scorn to spare. She might read the great historians and keep up with the news and cultivate a progressive bias in regards to politics, but if she thought me a loser, the other men in her life were bland and decidedly uninteresting. They were just dishonest enough to cut her the slack by which she deceived herself. I suppose I had played the same game. Jade cigarette holder, indeed.

—Moonface insists we only meet on neutral territory. It is to say she agrees we could become an item, but Platonically so. She is a great friend of Eggy, has no problems entering his lair, which she does nearly every day. She suffers his innuendos with good cheer, as if Eggy can be nothing but incorrigible. He will also expatiate, however fleetingly, on Picot-Sykes (or is it Sykes-Picot), on Kipling; on the end of the era of the Common Man. He will disremember the names of former wives, and Moonface will remind him, 'There was Cynthia.' 'Oh, screw Cynthia, mother of my children.' I believe Eggy has a true regard for Moonface's welfare, would like to see her get somewhere in the world; but he has no liking of pushy women and he has nothing but contempt for men who think themselves avatars of a new humanity. He has said, 'People fly up a horse's arse and think they're on the fast track to solving everything. Bloody hell.' His politics are old-fashioned: loosen up the purse strings; let people, like water, seek their level.

—Robert Dubois is the sort of handsome and vain man I cannot abide and yet, there is no percentage in actively disliking him. He likes his conversation; any topic will suffice. He listens, his eyes telling you, however, that you are on sufferance. On very rare occasions, something in them bespeaks melancholy and failure in life. This something flickers and then, poof, it is gone. And he is slapping your back or he is trying to tell you that, no matter what you say, the sun rises in the east, and there is an end to it.

But if you wish to continue to believe that it rises in the west, well then, fine, but please do notify him of the fact should it actually occur. He does not speak of his relations with Eleanor.

—Marcel Lamont kept a sailboat on a lake not far from town. The ologies tell me I have no grounds for thinking his wife evil, that I am only projecting a fantasy on her feral countenance. Eleanor R is much less complicated than I in this matter; she believes murder was carried out in the Traymore right under our noses.

—If truly there is poetry in me, I must owe it to the intervention of a god, one who never heard of the Enlightenment, one who was never wrong-footed by a rational mind. It remains a mystery, how mother suffered father in her bed.

Calhoun's Follies IV

—Well yes, we are all of us, in fact, showing up a little more grey around the edges, a little more grizzled and cranky. Damned inconvenient, what with the war on its multiple fronts, thorough-going sleaze and nepotism, religious hysteria, party-favour humanism, sham art. And we have no reason to despair, to mope across our spiritual squares from A to Z in our spiritual tutus? So pardon me my complexes as I, unschooled, un-tenured, unofficial, soldier on with McCabe deep in my soul, she that laughing harlot, the Authentic Existence's own prom queen who, at the head of every seaside procession, slathered with roses and reeking of incense, presents every man his choice: either accept the possibility that there are virtue and harmony in this life or, cynic that you are, believe it all a fraud, but do not waffle about in between, congressman with a gold toilet and celebratory shit.

So I go knocking on a Traymorean's door; I am granted an audience. King Eggy, dwarfed by his armchair, says, 'For God's sake, sit. Don't lurk. I've been noodling in my mind. Have you been noodling in yours?' 'Eggy,' I say, 'and it's impertinent of me to ask, but what I want to know is this: were you cruel to your wives?' Eggy, stand-up fellow that he is, a sparrow of a man, answers, 'No, I wasn't cruel. Who, me? It's the wives who got nasty and ill-tempered. I can't blame them. They expected a certain splendour because I, silly me, was foolish enough to promise them it. I had sex on the brain. They had other things on the brain. I made money but didn't worship money. The fact I may have a soul is entirely conjectural. But if I have one I got it in Korea, seeing as we shelled to smithereens a few villages here and there and dispatched the souls therein to their gods. A man can only go one of two ways after seeing something like that. Either he gets to be so much drifting about or, praying to obscure deities, he is the walking wounded. It is not to say I have a conscience or some other bauble of the mind. What I have can't be put in words. It comes with tears, if you're not too embarrassed to hear it. Oh dear me, not the tears that self-infatuated idiots generate but the kind of tears that a cold wind raises in one's eyes and can't be helped. You can choose to build a philosophy out of it, maybe even a religion. Or you can shut your mouth and cut your losses. I chose the latter. Hoo hoo.' I mock-bowed to the man's superior wisdom. He mock-suffered me, and I backed out the door.

So I go knocking on the door of Bob Dubois. He is banging something out on his computer. He is so steeped in virtue he has forgotten the word exists. He is so vain he has forgotten himself. He does not even apologize for the disarray his digs are in. 'Bob,' I say to him, 'I'm on a fact-finding mission. What I want to know is this: why do you continue to believe in the innate good sense of the American people?' His eyes get a little glassy. His jaws get a little slack. He has not been expecting the question, so it seems to me. 'I'll tell you what,' he says, after a moment's reflection, 'I think I know where your question is coming from, you being such a cynic and all. But I'll assume you're serious. The sort of man I am, the life I've led, the schooling and training received, all that what-not, has led me to believe all problems are solvable. And when they're not, it is only due to the fact we lack sufficient data, not inadequacy of mind. You don't agree with me on this? Let's say there is justification for your point of view. Let's say, alright, there are problems that are insoluble that will always be insoluble because that's just the way it is. I say, alright, but the odds are, even as we knock our heads against a concrete wall, that we'll muddle through, anyway. We always have and we always will. Hence, my faith in the innate good sense of any people. It has nothing to do with good sense, perhaps, but the odds have favoured us, and barring some cataclysm, an asteroid hitting us, say, they always will. Life trumps death. You ought to take up materialism, old man. Less arduous. Now I've got this letter to finish. I've decided I'm for impeaching the

President.' He laughs, the rotter. My eyes get glassy; my jaws slacken. For a financier enamoured of logic, he is awfully baroque. He is his own variety of madness.

To Eleanor's. I knock; she barks, 'What now?' I push through. Some acrid odour in the air. And in her kitchen I see that the good woman is incensed. 'I've been up since 5 this morning, baking. I burnt the cookies. Why? Because I got engrossed, watching *Advise and Consent* on TV. Most unlike me. And you? I don't like the look in your eyes.' 'Yes,' I say, 'I'm on a mission.' 'Christ, a mission?' she says, 'whatever for? You're no missionary. You're anything but. You're a man who pleases himself.' 'Could be,' I say. 'Well, it's true,' she rebuts, 'and most men I know have always pleased themselves. Anyway, let's get this over with. I can see I won't be able to put you off.' (Even so, she allows me a generous glimpse of her thigh, her robe parting as she leans against her kitchen counter.) 'Look,' I say, drawing out a chair for myself, 'all I want to know is this: what convinces you that Lucille did in Marcel?' 'Because he's dead, you ninny,' she says, a trifle short-tempered, 'because she's such a condescending, I-can-do-anything-and-get-away-with-it kind of witch that she did it for the hell of it. She didn't hate the man. There's no deep-seated bundle of twisted wires in her soul; and, in any case, she hasn't got a soul. If she didn't hate the man, certainly, she didn't love him enough to despise him, if you get my drift. Is she evil? There you got me. There I can't say. I prefer to think of the woman as a two-legged blob that simply absorbs and ejects impediments. Charge her with a crime, prove her guilt, put her in the electric chair or shoot her up with some cocktail, and you will have simply extinguished some protoplasmic endeavour organized along capitalistic lines.' She lights a cigarette and dares me to gainsay her. 'My,' I say, 'that's a dark view you have of crime and punishment and all things Lamont. You take my breath away. I had no idea.' 'Well, now you know,' she answers, 'I'm all for humanity and doing the right thing. Everyone deserves a second shot after screwing up. But for every rule an exception. I can't prove I'm right about that woman and you can't prove me wrong; just know that I'm right. Now, as you no doubt have discerned, I'm in a lousy mood and I wish you out of here.' Her voice saying one thing, her eyes another, I go. And it leaves Moonface. It leaves Moonface for me to interview. But life is pointless to her, and meaningless. She is rubbing our noses in it, she is, having sex with some cretin outside our circle. Yes, I am a little jealous but not as jealous as one might think.

She has got to get her toe wet, sometime. Take the plunge. A few laughs. A few tears. *A bowl of milk each year, Priapus, and these cakes are all you need expect…*

—I lie down on my couch in a semi-dark room, drink in my hand, music in the ghetto blaster. I close my eyes; images abound. Seaside temples. Lemon groves. Human cruelties. The ologists say that hunting in packs was our boulevard to a civilized state. So much for our noble natures. No, you crouch in your cave and you hope for the best. You get the crop in or you fail. You eat or starve like any other animal. The music says, 'No, no, no, you're barking up the wrong tree. Love exists.' 'Of course, you're right,' the cynic responds, 'but surely, even you'll agree that love is happenstance', love the thing that apparently suspends the operations of cause and effect and the grinding wheel of time. Music hisses, crashes with cymbals, percolates with flutes, and trumpets displeasure with my cynicism. 'What evolutionary drift?' it says, 'for every note contained within me has meaning and purpose, to wit, architecture.' 'Right you are,' I answer, in no position to argue, and besides, there is a knock on the door.

Why, it is Moonface. Moonface in tears. Cheeks streaked with mascara. No, it is not Moonface; rather it is Eggy who is of the moment, because she is saying the man's slumped over in his chair. Her eyes, once black to me, brown for all the world to see, are stricken; and they are saying, 'Calhoun, I love you like a father but Eggy, well, he's Zeus.' What, that sparrow of a man? Her voice is saying, 'I think he's had a stroke.' In any case, we rush over, Moonface and I. 'Look,' I say, 'he's just having one of his episodes.' 'I couldn't rouse him,' she insists. We are in Eggy's room now. If he was slumped over, now he is rigid, firmly flush with the back of his chair, his eyes wide and a little awed. His eyes comprehend they have got company. He speaks up, 'I think I fell asleep.' 'I think you're going to the hospital,' I say. 'Bloody hell I am,' he weakly thunders, 'the cardiologist will just get on my case about drinking. I'll have to mollify her. Then I'll have to go against her when I'm back on my own again. You see how it is. Damn nuisance.' Phonecall is made; ambulance arrives; medics troop up the stairs. Dubois sticks his head out his door. Eleanor, still ill-tempered, pads over, barefoot. 'Good Christ, Eggy,' she says. Moonface fusses, gives Eleanor a look, as Eggy is strapped to the stretcher. Dubois says he will drop by the hospital, later. Eggy says, 'Hoo hoo.'

Back in my room, the reverie broken, I now have no idea what I think about anything. It would seem Moonface, evolutionary drift or no, was born to love, the soil for it a tad thin.

—And, a few mornings later, fog hanging in the yellow trees, there in the Blue Danube, a tiny café that caters primarily to disaffected Slavs, Moonface turns up the radio, and the tune is "Funky Town", and she jives a little, her eyes half-closed in their boredom, and it annoys me. So much for romance however one-sided, and I feel patriarchal and judgmental and there is no joy in Mudville. I say nothing. The café is otherwise empty of clientele. It is as if a sign on the door reads PLAGUE, QUARANTINE IN EFFECT; and carts rumble by, adding to a pile of burning corpses in the street, birds looking on from high perches. And it is as if, besides Moonface's handcream and the coffee staling, getting downright poisonous, the smell of a cathedral's cold crypt—other-worldly, relentless nether region at the heart of everything—thumbs up my nostrils and stuns my brain. 'Eggy that devil,' says Moonface near to sighing. It is a coincidental choice of epithet on her part, as, last night in this place, Eggy against a backdrop of roisterous Slavs, had said of the President, 'He's an apostle of evil.'

'Pretty strong words, don't you think?' I replied. 'Well,' said Eggy, 'I suppose Nixon was worse. Hoo hoo.' He gripped his glass of wine and a coherent history of America fell apart in my mind. After Rome and Byzantium, I just have not the room, so many wagons ho wagon trains tumbling off the edge of a precipice in my mentations, mixing it up with buffalo and dinosaur bones. Moonface was on shift then, too, busy with the Slavs who were passing around one of those new gadgets that combine the functions of phone and computer and camera, or so I understand it; and I figured sourly enough that this technology, too, will go the way of wagon trains and musketry even as Moonface at their table was girlishly saying, 'Cool.' One of the men, as if peering around a corner, gave her bum a good going over with his eyes. Eggy sat there, saying, 'But I'm too old and I don't much care now, and you younger fellows are going to have get up to something, should you want truth, beauty and justice.' Moonface, overhearing, passing by us with an armful of used plates, girlishly snorted, 'Fat chance of that.' 'You behave,' Eggy laughed, 'you rotten girl.' 'How is it,' I asked myself, 'we can be both dying of too much history and not enough of it?'

—It was a small and sombre group at Gareth Howard's funeral. Clare avoided my unspoken entreaties. Old marble plinths tipped every which way. Yellow trees. The invasive caw of a crow. A minister parcelled out his words, and Gar, in a contemplative mood, might have found them poetic. Or, feeling combative, he would have parried with a grumbled 'up yours'. He rather disliked the homiletic: to all things a season. I skulked about the edges of the gathering. I made no attempt to verbally claim the dead person of Gareth Howard. I refrained from muscling in on the living memory of him, a memory which, in any case, looked to have a short shelf-life. I did not say, 'Yes, he was a great guy.' Colleagues in the news business lamented the passing of a conscience. It was what their eyes said, at any rate. I thought of the frustrated writer of short stories and novels. A smartly dressed woman with whom Clare was, shall we say, tensely diplomatic, folded her arms across her chest all the while she clenched her purse tightly, her knuckles white. Her face was otherwise appealing and open. From what world capital had she flown? Clare was, and always had been, a knockout. She may have had her affairs during her husband's many absences, but she was, all the same, ferociously loyal to some underlying principle of their relationship. Erotic warmth briefly pulsed through me before it flickered and died away. Ministerial words trailed away in a wind beginning to gust; the words gambolled down a gentle slope toward the river, funereal words that suddenly got playful. To everything a time under heaven. And, under heaven the *isolate*. And there it was, the word, the almost bardic word that conditions friendship, collegiality, lust and love. I noted a raptor in the sky and pictured the fur and bone, the bit of tissue of a mouse. Sex, so I was thinking, and unaccountably so, is a cold thing; a bucking about on a bed. Sometimes, yes, it is warm, and sometimes it is even hotter when lovers come together with their secrets and without walls. I was not dressed for the occasion, so it began to seem to me. I should have been decked in tights and bells and a jester's cap. The President was beginning to be seen as mad in some quarters, he and his vice-president and coterie; and I recalled that Gareth Howard had interviewed his share of the demented. The tinny, unforgivably rude hectoring of a cell phone. Curses. Mumbled apology. Finally, the interment. Dirt clods slapped down on the casket. A smartly-dressed woman threw in a rose. The redness of that rose was obscene in view of Clare; and she stiffened a little for all she was most likely past the point of whatever tears she had already shed. *In Kamarooska a kiss and a thought for Algonquins.* What is it about funerals in the New World that clutch at the land, whose claims are greater than those of rapine and slaughter and conquest and settlement? Die and it is yours. I did not attend the wake. No, I went instead to the Cloister, the old wateringhole Gar and I used to frequent. Defiantly, I gunned off its new clientele, the members of which had not the slightest understanding of integrity; a word those smug tipplers were trashing with gusto. But I raised a glass all the same and drank down my Sea Breeze. Then back to the Traymore. I slid a CD into my ghetto-blaster, heard in this new symphony grief amidst the dissonance of cymbals and drums. The real thing. I saw Clare majestic in her stockings. Another spell of erotic warmth. It was like taking a cup of hot milk for sleeplessness; but that I gag on milk. Now, at the window, that one which looks out on a back lane straddling lots and yards, I commune with sparrows and a squirrel. It is to say I mourn the various assemblages of the Gar face and the Gar voice, none of which, so long as I yet live, will ever again cohere.

—Last night, Dubois comes over, worry on his face. He ought to marry Eleanor but cannot bring himself to. Meanwhile, we may have a new lodger. Can he make the grade? I deeply regret I let Moonface know of the extent of my affection for her. I may as well have taken a length of two by four and whacked her with it, the way her head has turned vis-à-vis me; how she whah-hah-hahs me and wards off the Evil Eye. Alright then, Moonface, love? I'll forget it. You will see how scrupulously I will abide by your terms.

§

Book IV—A Proper Narrative

Salon

Sometimes when the maples are green with leaf, the wind gentle and not bringing too much heat; and the sky is clear or its cumulus dissolves in the evening air, and the day's last sparrows go to roost; and the girls are meditative in both body and mind, the boys not too puerile, people of all ages out for a stroll; then well-being is palpable, owing to something other than one's net worth in any mercenary sense. And sometimes Moonface, her shoulders hunched, walks the crucible of the street, returning from a night spent with some young man or other. I note how lonely her aspect is, how unmet. How useless I am to her in her search for meaning.

Four glasses of wine, and Eggy was lit: 'Moonface is my first reserve. I've asked a girl at the bank to marry me.'

Moonface tossed her head.

Eggy: 'Well, will you want to improve? Who can marry a woman who doesn't want to better herself? The rain in Spain—'

Eleanor R suppressed a giggle; now she had heard it all, Dubois grinning.

I leaned back in my chair. At the moment, Andrew Jackson, President the seventh of the United States of America, or some such entity, interested me more than Eggy on his fool's errand. (That AJ had happily set about annihilating those pesky Red Stick insurgents there where the Tallapoosa bends sharply.) Still, Eggy seemed to know he was indulging himself and yet, he did not much care. We were gathered in Eleanor's kitchen on the occasion of her first salon.

She, not the most fastidious of women (though she enjoyed mastery of her kitchen, it sometimes mastered her), had vacuumed and swept and wiped and dusted. A grumbling Dubois helped. Sweet Haven lovebirds they were not, if only because they maintained separate apartments. Eleanor, fingering the spit valve of her trombone, said: 'Well, Eggy, I suppose congratulations are in order.'

'Hear hear,' said Dubois.

Eggy beamed, Moonface disgusted. Eleanor put the spit valve which she was always fingering—as if it were a mood rock—aside. She reached for a fancy cracker with its slice of cheese. She shovelled it into her mouth. She reached next for a pickle and crunched it in half between solid molars. She was pleased with herself, the kitchen warm, homey and roomy. It was perhaps the finest room of all the Traymore rooms, excepting those, perhaps, of Mrs Petrova's ground-floor suite.

She assured Dubois she would not bring up the Lamonts as a conversational gambit, Dubois having drawn a line in the sand. Even now he did not believe anything untoward had happened in respect to Marcel's demise. *Too much gin, that's all.* The man paid for it with his life. Eggy would have no opinion, Moonface's jury quiescent. It would seem Eleanor and I alone were thinking otherwise; certain dark arts had been employed to repatriate Marcel Lamont to the realm of the dead. Eggy, sparrow of a man, was saying: 'Oh, I don't believe the girl will marry me for my looks. Nor will she necessarily marry me for my money. I haven't that much.'

'Then for what?' Moonface, on the edge of some irritation, interjected.

'Why, for my charm and considerable intellect.'

Moonface could not have been in a good mood or she would have laughed down Eggy's love of self. The rest of us were, so to speak, rolling in the aisles.

'Anyone for coffee?' Eleanor inquired, rising from her chair with a majestic lift to her shoulders, tra-la-lah-ing to the stove to put the kettle on, she sporting a flattering blouse and new pompadours. Perhaps later, Dubois would get lucky.

I had written about Moonface. Worse, I committed the mistake of informing her I had done as much. She was suspicious.

'I suppose you describe me as immature.'

'A point of view,' I countered, somewhat testily, 'to be arrived at through the arcana of physics, suggests we all had a hand to play in the death of Marcel Lamont. We're each of us fickle and inconstant creatures, mouthing our pieties one moment and silently stewing in darkness the next.

Or like so many Andrew Jacksons drunk on frontier liberties, we breed horses between campaigns. In any case, I dolled you up as a sex object of lethal dimensions. Those tiny ears of yours. Chew on that.'

And she seemed to be chewing it as I spoke the words, her eyes rolling up and sideways. We had been talking over and around the conversationalists in the room, Eleanor registering the fact, storing away this intelligence in her commodious mind. No doubt, the good woman thought us lovers, Moonface and I, and we were not. We were, however, competitive partners in a game whose rules and whose object were most unclear. But had not Constantine the emperor translated Virgil's fourth eclogue into Greek hexameters, and peace would come to the trembling cosmos? *iam redit et uirgo, redeunt Saturnia regna.* Latin words that speak to new beginnings. If it is nature, and nature only that works the great sea-changes in the life of humankind, Moonface was just a girl, and probably no great shakes in bed, at that. At least, she was not hanging around Mexico City, privy to the Second Coming of Diego and Frida, parasitically living off the reputations of those two artists. No, she was steeping herself in the malignant light of Virgil's moon, he who, so as to defend Rome's reasoned rule of the known world, would snatch from Homer's defeated and dead their lawful property: to wit, the poetry they had earned.

Later, in my own digs, supine on my couch, I reviewed the salon. I had not, in truth, enjoyed it as much as I would have liked. For all that, I was conscious of the fact that, over the months, I had served as a catalyst to Traymoreans for a certain kind of conversation. A claque of sorts, if one comprised of stubborn individualists, we would turn this way and that in our quarrels like a single flock of birds. Dubois, shifting from a position of indifference in regards to the war, now fired off letters to the editor castigating the President for his callow utterances and feckless helmsmanship. Even Eggy could be heard to say from time to time, as if it explained something, 'Apostles of evil. Well, it's true.' Moonface had no opinion. Eleanor's last political loves were Kennedy and Pierre Elliot Trudeau, and Kennedy was long since departed, his brains splattered still against the interior of the presidential limousine, and that was the end of it. Even so, politics as such, or so I figured, had little to do with our seeming comity. More so it had to do with each our standing-apart from the effluvium of war and profit-taking, from every theatrical display of moral gamesmanship. A wary outlook seemed to brand our foreheads with an identifying mark, one that said: 'I'm here for you if you wish. I don't expect to win. I don't suppose you expect to win. Please don't expect me to even try. I like my pleasures.'

If the materialism to which Dubois subscribed as a philosophy of life was entirely conventional, he, at least, recognized the power of certain intangibles to riddle life with mysteries. He tsked-tsked mention of God, but poetry was something, at any rate. Eleanor, more the logician than any of us, amateur trombonist, consummate in her kitchen and comfortable in her bed, nonetheless enjoyed her spells of solitude and respected her intuitions. She knew she could not prove Lucille Lamont a murderess, but no matter, she just knew. Moonface? Erotic fancies, no doubt, compromised my view of her; and yet, from what I could see, she was as likely to settle down, marry, have children as do anything only a mystic might comprehend. Eggy was, perhaps, the jewel of the Traymore crown; translucent, acerbic, kind, selfish, thoughtful, as silly as a goose; in short, he was all human possibility enjoying a last burst of brilliance. Dying star. Or rather, he was just effing decrepit but that he had lived a little.

The Lamonts never fit in. Marcel was welcomed, was considered 'sympatico', but he had kept his distance, Lucille always tugging on his strings. It was clear she could not entertain herself unless she was in the driver's seat and scheming this and scheming that. She was not well-liked, if at all. Mrs Petrova was necessary. She was a woman admired throughout the neighbourhood for her vitality and fearlessness and the tight ship she ran without hectoring her lodgers in the process. I lay on my couch, dyspeptic chrysalis. Virgil was a thief in the night. Old Hickory, or Andrew Jackson, split open the backs of his slaves with God's grand purposes. A new symphony shattered the universe with lyrical and dissonant passages. The music seemed to skirt the perimeters of full-blown madness, Bacchic frenzies, Dionysus hooting in a mountain wood; and I with my superstitious awe of grotto and grove, was an urban creature. I could not comprehend the American mind.

A knock at the door, and it was Moonface somewhat distraught.

'I love you, too,' she said, heatedly.

It was as if she resented saying as much; as if the saying it was costing her more energy than she wished to expend.

'But,' she advised, 'I won't sleep with you.'

'Of course not,' I replied, astonished.

Blutocracy

The bedroom a pleasant crypt. I half-awake. Bird chatter a conduit to consciousness. Sparrows, starlings, crows. I could see, as I looked out a window that Mrs Petrova had strung up a new squirrel-proof feeder. A bluejay, a nuthatch and a lone reddish finch were attempting to raid it. Life seemed rich and hopeful, the morning after Eleanor's salon.

Who was I kidding? Darker thoughts now, to do with the American mind that I could not comprehend, the national cruelties, even so, familiar; the Sally McCabes who were all beautiful and pragmatic in their seemingly necessary sadisms; the empty-minded brutalities of young men who peopled cheap horror flicks, who were sometimes parodied and mostly extolled. It was the funfair waterslide descent into barbarism on a collective scale. As Eggy might have put it, it was a blutocracy. I had an all too brief moment of seeming clarity: Moonface as Psyche. But mythology was suspect, Bly saying, 'Calhoun, forget the gods. Global capitalism is our handiwork.' Of course, and it was going to finish us off even before we would see its victory cross in the sky. Was not Mr 007 its Hercules, its John the Baptist, corporate foot-soldier who wenched and dispatched rivals and flirted with Armageddon? It was too early for the Blue Danube. I would go elsewhere to eat.

And a bus of lonely faces conveyed me downtown. It was a polyglot assembly of passengers. French, English, Spanish, Czech. Haitian and Jamaican lilts. Chinese. I read those faces for the miseries all had in common. I did not want to know. 'Time is a continuum,' my old friend Gareth Howard once said to me, 'in which past and future are indistinguishable.' He had wanted to carry a point by way of ironic effect. An old black woman praised Jesus. Next to her, a Lavinia all punked up, shot me waves of her drug-induced paranoia. My skin crawled. A Virgilian combat scene flashed through my mind. Spearing him through his thigh, Aeneas pinned Turnus to the ground and heard out his pleas. Then the victor capitulated to his rage, and a moral creature not quite moral expired. Huck Finn rafted down the Tigris. I was only just getting started, my mind its usual chaos. The city was steel and glass as well as the brick and granite of an earlier history. The bus clattered over potholes. The heavy hand of the church was much in evidence, as were strip clubs and universities, Ste Catherine's a fine street, in my view, worthy of the attentions of a Villon or a Baudelaire drifted in from Rivière-du-Loup.

Steerburgers. Cavernous joint. A squadron of waitresses fanned out to cover each their sections. Commandos. I sat at the counter, luxuriating now in the sense of belonging to a wider world in which the Traymore Rooms and its vicinity were ancillary. Were I to carry a business card, it ought to read: 'Randall Q Calhoun, Adjunctivist'. An overly familiar hand gripped my shoulder and I did not like it as it belonged to Arsdell who was All-Academe.

Who was a foggy-headed humanist, one of those men who were forever scheming up new ways to waste a student's time in the hopes of keeping a student interested. He stood there vacuously smiling, his overcoat forever chic, his only humanity his suppressed apology for his existence.

'Randall,' he cooed, the fellowship implied utterly bogus.

'Arsdell,' I said, barely suppressing my lack of regard.

A 40-ish blonde and attractive and very business-like waitress gave him, a married man, the eye as she wiggled by.

'I'm on my way to a meeting. We're going to rally against the war.'

'You don't say,' I said, perhaps too off-handedly.

'Wouldn't you be primed for that—to stop that insane war?'

'Of course, anything,' I shrugged.

Anything but line up in the trenches with an arch-enemy who was so much a part of all that had gone wrong it was impossible to elucidate the reasons why.

'Good luck,' I said.

And even he, as thick-headed as he was, could understand he had just been dismissed. He was betrayed, singularly alone. The legions of evil were numberless.

'Thanks,' he said softly, withdrawing his loathsome and martyred hand, 'we'll probably need it.'

He took his hurt eyes to the blonde with whom he spoke a few words and then he was out the door. Perhaps I should have been drawn, quartered and hung from a lamppost right then and there. I used to have faith in the Arsdells; that they were a bulwark against the barbarisms. Oh, they were the sort of men who, in the dead of night, always open the gates of the citadel from within to the marauding armies of the hour. I had my breakfast, my little hopeful excursion into the wide world otherwise spoiled. I went up to the cashier and paid my bill, and as I did so, gave an entirely innocent waitress an accusing look. Fool around with that man and she would be sorry.

I walked the drag. It bustled with people. Sex boutiques. Bookstores. A business college. A Protestant church. Restaurants devoted to themes Mexican or Thai or Japanese. I pretended it had nothing to do with a take-no-prisoners economic system. Like so, I figured, Chaucer once pretended his pilgrims had nothing to do with the feudal order; they were creatures who were simply doing and not being done by. My oldest friend was dead in his grave. He had been a man of ordinary good looks and restless eyes. His voice carried his character: a warring front between civility and impatience with stupidity. If he eschewed the dramatic when on camera in the field, he was caustic in his reportage. I could not picture, at that moment, the polished stone that marked his final assignment, so to speak. Just the surrounding grounds, the maples and birches at the edges, the slope down to the river. A crow very black against the orange and yellow leaves. A gloomy thought this: would Gar have joined forces with Arsdell in the quest for world peace? Is loyalty an absolute? American movies were full of ingenious escape clauses from these sorts of binds. I returned to the Traymore. The trouble with the wider world was that it could get very claustrophobic.

I breathed easier on a familiar street. Mrs Petrova in her shop, eyepiece screwed on, held a wristwatch between her hands. She was scrutinizing its innards. 'There it is,' I said to myself, 'bulwark against barbarism: time and those who defend it.' Of course, the opposing argument was always waiting in the wings, the one that blamed time for all human woes. Mrs Petrova gave me a thoughtful look as I passed by the window to the Traymore entrance, and she grunted.

I was about to unlock my door when Eleanor opened hers and crooked her finger at me. What now? I was in the mood for a drink and music and solitude. I had, after all, eluded the clutches of academe in the person of Arsdell, and I wished to celebrate. I followed the woman through her living room—all knickknack and macramé and potted plants—to the kitchen. Bread baked in the oven. She and Dubois were probably on again. Her waddle was flirtatious, high-spirited.

'Sit,' she said, and I sat, and she continued: 'Several things. One, that cop woman was around again, that bony blonde with the Nazi eyes. She was asking after Lucille. Think she's bucking for detective? So I gave her the address that was on the envelope of the letter I got from the witch. Two, Moonface has just learned she isn't really preggers. Seems the father would've been a Nigerian exchange student. The classic angry young man. They'd been to the doctor's. Three, Bob wants to take me to Disneyworld. Should I accept? I think I should. A little trip will do us good. Four, but then, you know: Eggy has asked some bank girl to marry him.'

Eleanor lit a cigarette. I wanted nothing else but music, a drink and a lie down. Gareth Howard was floating away from me on his river of death. Clare Howard stood revealed for the believer she always had been, and no one should ever have doubted her, not for an instant. That she was strong and lovely and good, and a terror when crossed. Moonface was a dull part of my mind, she and her troubles. She could not be but relieved that she was not actually preggers. In any case, it was yet another thing she had kept from me. I said: 'Russia will sell out somebody, but which somebody? That's the question. Putin has the look of a cynic who likes the feel of his plush poker chips. The President has the air of a man who has always depended on the kindness of strangers, his chips the cheap kind you can buy in drugstores. What has this to do with Lucille and a cop and Moonface? Did the girl at the bank agree to marry Eggy? No? No matter. He's living securely in Camelot, and everything is fine with him. Never mind that his soul is hideously black with the sins of a long life. I'm in a mood, I fear, and I'm going to take myself off. But I'm pleased you got me up to speed in regards to recent developments as no one tells me anything, and what I'm told is largely suspect.'

A commotion in the middle of the night roused me: paramedics, Eleanor, Eggy on his familiar stretcher. How does the woman always know to call for an ambulance? I would hear about it in the morning.

Moonface Was Forever Messing with Boys

Eggy bore up under a series of tiny strokes. Now and then I would know Moonface had had a fit, her visage as white as that of a Kabuki performer, mornings in the hall of the Traymore, her eyes other-worldly. Eleanor R was thinking scallops, lately, Coquilles St Jacques. She just had, she said, a yen for it. Scallops and butter and mushrooms and chopped onion and Miracle Whip. Mmmmm. The sight of her, in her pompadours and her apron, whisking something in a saucepan—was it, in a venal age, permitted? I should have considered myself a fortunate man (and for the most part I did), surrounded as I was by agreeable male company, by not unattractive women, comfortably anchored in my digs, pursuing my obscure ends. Now I was conducting an interview with myself, sitting in the Blue Danube, Moonface working. We had put to rest that business of her pregnancy; and she was, for once, in good spirits. In truth, I was feeling guilty. The news (as related to me by Eleanor) of her false alarm, of her having possibly been with child, struck me with no more force than if I had learned she had developed zits.

'What will you do with the Nigerian?' I asked.

'What do you mean—do with him? His name is James. He's my friend.'

'Ah, your friend,' I said.

'Indeed,' she shot back, her tone indicating that that was to be the end of it. Reginald, the man who moved me with his van so long ago last March, was jocular in a withering sort of way: 'Love the tupperware, refrain from philosophy. Some men speak truth to power; you, you speak to a void. You's crazy, mon.'

We were beginning to wonder, Eleanor and I, if Eggy had a new sweetheart in a hospital ward, was engineering his over-nighters with a view toward the possibility of a tryst. In any case, he would be out again soon. Whether or not any bank girl had agreed to marry him, Eggy was not saying, and I had thought it intrusive to ask. But it seemed only the other day that his lower lip was quivering a little as if disappointed, Eggy in the Blue Danube reading a book on the French-Indian wars, two glasses of red wine set before him, the maples outside in their coats of many colours.

Moonface, then leafing through a book, was seeing life through a bit of grim verse by the poet Propertius, some voice speaking out of a burial site to a survivor of the fracas at Perugia two thousand years ago. I had been there once upon a modern time myself, and all I could remember of the place, besides one excellent meal I had chanced across, were the local communistas unfurling their red banner in the main piazza.

'Well,' Eggy was saying, apropos of nothing, and lately, his sentences would spring up like water from nowhere: 'I've been to Quebec City. I've seen the Plains of Abraham. Is hers the face that launched—?'

Moonface came over, hands on hips in a gunslinger's pose. She said, speaking of Eggy to me: 'Is this man bothering you?'

I thought her eyes were getting more beautiful, if possible, and her not so ample breasts more alluring. In the realm of the erotic, once you commit to the charms of your beloved, that is it, you are finished. Still, I was too old for these Stendhalian romps. Clearly, Eggy—who had twenty some years on me—was not. And perhaps he was a better friend than I to the young woman, he saying to her: 'You know you're rotten, don't you. I'm going to have to have you on my lap and spank you.'

'Ooooh,' said Moonface in mock alarm.

It seemed we could live like this forever, playful, flirtatious, downright naughty, the past rendered pure by the poetry of tombs. This is why Plato distrusted poets; they did not lie, necessarily. They were seductive, distracting the mind from the present or that which men like Plato could never keep their hands off, inasmuch as they must always manipulate it and improve it to some dubious specification. It is bad enough, trying to keep one's balance in respect to their invidious claims as to what reality is; and here I was tights, bells and jester's cap, living off the fumes of a lust that was rising in Moonface and taking possession of every atom that constituted her unassuming self. I could see us having sex like wild dogs, she yipping and snarling with alarm and arousal and pleasure. Perhaps the scholar in her mind was attempting to make sense of that Propertian poem of a soldier's death. Perhaps a girl was lamenting the waste. I needed a loner's drink.

Calhoun Waylaid

The war, the war, the war. I was in for it now I had let thought of it rear its hideous head. Now it was abstract and remote; now it was as immediate as a throbbing knee, the ache of which one just managed to ignore. Who had not been knocked for a loop by dint of that Manhattan day a few Septembers ago, the towers collapsing like two accordions stood on end? In light of that horror, the war was an even more shameful business feeding on all the clichés, a vain stab at collective self-respect. *Tiberius? Oh he's off chasing the tribes around in Germania. He'll be back soon enough to darken the Roman sun with his sour countenance, to give the astrologers a hard time of it.* With words like these, I might distract myself. Or I would take a powerful whiff of Mrs Petrova's Sunday cooking through my nostrils, her pot roasts and cabbages the aromas of which vied with those emanating from Eleanor's kitchen. If the sun was beginning to weaken, I would tell myself it would become strong again in March when the snow—part purity, part dog piss and debris—would start melting away and reveal the dead leaves and stringy grass of the city parks. I would tease Moonface a little just to see her smile. She did not have a remarkable smile, not one that could light up an entire world with joy and insouciance, but even so, fair to middling smile that it was, it was a grace note of sorts, and necessary.

In my letterbox was a letter from Clare. I thrilled to the fact of it; then a warning sounded. Why was she writing me? She disapproved of Randall Q Calhoun. I had kept Gar out late at nights; I had hampered his development, what with my pessimistic and cynical attitudes. Even the drug runner on the street saw more of a future in his line of work than I in mine; he had more reason to smile. If she was good, beautiful and true, I was weak and callow and corrupted. Throw in a few more qualities, and the picture of me was completed. In any case, the missive consisted of all of three lines, not including the salutations; to wit, that it was silly of me not to have a phone; that she was driving out to Gar's old country shack with a view to selling the property; and, did I want to come along? There she was in my eye: tall and willowy, her chestnut hair long. Now I really needed a solitary drink.

Instead, I knuckled on Eleanor's door. Soon enough, I was in her kitchen, babbling away.

'Why shouldn't she write you?' Eleanor asked.

'Because she doesn't like me.'

'How do you know? Did she ever say as much?'

'She wouldn't. She doesn't go in for theatrics.'

'Maybe she fancies you. Stranger things have transpired in the course of human affairs.'

'Probably she just wants help clearing out the cabin of Gar's effects. Perhaps I owe her this, some squaring of a moral debt.'

And so, on the appointed day, Clare at the wheel of a battered import, I found myself being transported to the country, the shack just under two hours from the city, and set in rolling hills, east and west of which was land as flat as a billiard table. We were mostly silent; I had not a clue what to say. She was, as ever, dressed elegantly but simply. Leather jacket. Thick scarf. Skirt. Warm leggings and ankle-high boots. Knitted gloves. Then she said, her voice rich and to the point: 'You may as well know, Gar was going mad at the end.'

Dionysus had trucked with madness, but had a cold Apollonian trucked with it as well?

At any rate, Clare's words were most unexpected. When had we last had words? How is it that time plays these tricks by which, when face to face with someone, it seems that moments and not years have intervened between meetings?

'I knew he was hot and bothered, but mad as in clinically insane?'

'Politics,' she said, explaining everything, and she continued, I her pick-me-up confidante: 'He was convinced lunacy had taken over the world.'

'It has.'

She took her eye off the highway and gave me a look. A smattering of interest. A flicker of hatred. The radio was tuned to a classical station. If the music was, indeed, CPE Bach's, it was at odds with the RV park we were proceeding by now, the disposable architecture of the sales office.

'Look,' I said, 'what do I know? I can't speak for Gar. I, as it were, read the mists in the air. Gar saw things up front, down and dirty, knew and talked with men such as I can only imagine. Since when have I had a chat with any mayor let alone a congressional stooge? Who was I to gainsay a world traveller? I triangulate my views of the current situation from the musty pages of long dead books and that makes me, what, an egghead, a fool, and decidedly irrelevant. Are you saying you were jealous of Gar's obsessions?'

Another flicker of hatred. Tender, somewhat melancholy, a keyboard sonata only hardened Clare, she ignoring me her passenger, gripping the steering wheel more tightly. Semi-trucks barrelled by, shaking us with their turbulent wakes. She was cocooned by her sulk. I was made ludicrous by way of erotic fancies at a most inappropriate point of time. She laughed and switched off the radio, giving me a sideways look that suggested she had read my mind. She patted my knee; and it was as if I were a dog who knew the command to sit but had not yet learned the sense of the word heel. We were going up into the hills. White birches leaned in all directions. Scraggly spruce.

She had kept everyone, including me, away from Gar throughout the course of his dying. Perhaps she thought she was making up for this, driving me out to the shack, pretending that once I had mattered to Gar's life. What disturbed me just then was not what Clare was up to, if anything; it was the thought of Gar drawing his last breath in anger. I was confident he and Clare had reconciled, but only a fool, I supposed, would hate a country's politics in his last hours.

What can I say? Soon enough, I was to receive a shock. We had arrived, having left the highway for a series of secondary roads and then a road best described as tertiary, the car kicking up shards of crumbly stones. We drove up a hill, cows at pasture on either side of the road. Strange heapings of rock in the fields. Gaunt but stately maples. Now here she was struggling with the padlock of Gar's old cabin, I smarting from her silence. At last, she got the better of the lock, and she pushed open a creaking door. Must and mildew. Old paperbacks, ancient newspapers. A rumpled copy of Steinbeck's *Cannery Row*. Kerosene. Stacks of firewood and a kindling box. An old iron kettle on a cook stove. It was a mouse I heard inside a wall. Clare was no country girl, but rather than register disapproval of the shack in its neglected state, her eyes widened and seemed curious. She poked at dust thick on an old, cracked wood table; she inspected her mittened finger. Perhaps she saw all she needed to see. She grabbed me and put a kiss on my mouth.

Hours later, and I was back in my digs; and, as if wondering were possible, I wondered what it had all meant. So much for the beautiful and the good and the true. She had laughed after that kiss, and it seemed to me she said, 'Yes, just what I thought,' this as I was trying to get my hands under her sweater and up to her breasts, as if, contact made, I would know everything I ever needed to know. She guided them with her mittened hands. And then, in a silence as deep as the silence which greeted the creation of the universe, she put mine away from her; and she held me, or rather, she let me hold her; and she shivered a little in our embrace; and then she dabbed at something in her eye, pulled off me and said: 'I'm not going to apologize. It seems I've been doing this all my life. *Voila!* Marriage with Gar. It would be better if I just burned this place down.'

And then, an after-thought, perhaps, and whether it was clear-mindedness on her part or more confusion, she added: 'Don't think I didn't love Gar. I suppose you're a nice enough man in your own way. Silly of you not to have a phone. I'm going away for a while. Somewhere utterly unreal. Disneyworld? Fiji? Well, we once rented in Umbria, Gar and I, for a couple of months. I rather liked it. Near Orvieto. Have you been there? Maybe I'll look you up when I get back.'

The beautiful, the good and the true had departed her eyes. She was tired and angry. It was as if men like me had snatched the beautiful, the good and the true from empty air and foisted them on her, just because, well, someone had to have those eyes. She had been much younger than Gar when they married. She would be a handsome woman even in her old age. In a silence as deep as the creation of the universe, one was never going to know for sure how resentful she had been of men and their expectations. I was relieved our lovemaking had not gone further. I fervently wished it had.

As for myself, I was now branded an incurable loner; oh, not in any dignified sense of the word but as a law unto myself; a law that had come bearing no gifts. Clare's kiss had done the trick; she had been a solar wind that came my way and passed. My failure to draw us both one step closer to some emotional disaster gave me cause to wonder just how feckless I was, unfit for such chance as society brings. And this in what was effectively a commune, what with Moonface always traipsing over to Eggy's, Eleanor and Dubois banging away on Eleanor's four-poster. Mrs Petrova went to church, and maybe she played bingo, and so had a life beyond her shop and her renters. So that it was yet another shock when in moved a new lodger.

Breached

Traymoreans exchanged intelligence at the Blue Danube.

'He seems alright,' said Eggy. 'Don't know what the fuss is about.'

'Shining head,' I said.

'What's his name?' Moonface asked, 'does anyone know?'

'The name hasn't appeared on his letterbox yet,' said Dubois.

'I think he told me,' I said, 'but I was so flustered it went in one ear and out the other. It was something like Osgoode. He was carrying an open satchel. I distinctly saw a Bible and other religious paraphernalia.'

'You bet,' said Eleanor, 'and I know I heard a prayer meeting raising the rafters in his room. There's been a lot of traffic up our stairs all of a sudden. Women.'

'Maybe he's on to something,' suggested Eggy.

'He's a door-slammer,' said Dubois.

'A shining head,' I repeated.

So Osgoode, first name unknown, a shining head, had—in his late twenties or thereabouts—rented the old Lamont apartment, the one we Traymoreans thought Mrs Petrova was saving for her son. Except for Eggy, none of us had ever laid eyes on this mythical son. Perhaps Osgoode was that son in the spiritual sense; in which case I might have to modify my view of Mrs Petrova. We would get over it, I figured; we would soon enough accept the intruder, this enemy within our gates. I myself was a tolerant fellow, but what with the war and the corrosive political atmosphere; what with the zanies with their fingers in every pie; executive pies, Pentagon pies, Department of Justice pies; what with Nazis calling peaceniks Nazis and peaceniks calling Nazis fascists; what with terrorists skulking in the shadows of every lawn's pink flamingoes (and was it all horseplay or was the rhetoric a prelude to much worse behaviour); and so forth and so on, and my good graces were fewer; and I was more frequently drawing lines in the sand; and soon, as if I ever had much ground on which to stand, I would have no ground left at all to support my pins. Clare had kissed me, that much was certain, every molecule of me hissing I would never see her again. It had been a strange interlude. 'Copy that, Houston.' I could neither see nor hear Gareth Howard, my oldest friend, dead in his grave. I would have to wake him.

We Traymoreans had commandeered the Blue Danube for an hour; it being our purpose to discuss the new lodger. We alighted on the café's chairs like a single flock of birds. Eleanor called the meeting to order, she with her frosted curls. Dubois was handsome and vain, Eggy's shirt littered with bits of food. Moonface was luminous in her black denims and white blouse, one that she usually buttoned to her neck, but that now provided a glimpse of her bosom's swell. She had been getting her toes wet, no doubt about it, in affairs of the heart; James, her Nigerian friend, was the man of the hour, and yet she kept him from us. There was pain coming for her. I would be a cad were I to point this out.

'Well,' said Eleanor, touching the wrist of her beau, vain and handsome Dubois, 'are we going to Florida or not?'

'Are we? Do I have anything to say about it?'

'But of course,' said Eleanor, draining her glass of wine and wondering if there was more.

'One thing's money in the bank,' she said, 'it won't be the same—the old Traymore.'

'Stuff and nonsense,' said Eggy. 'Montcalm threw the battle. Hoo hoo.'

In actual fact, sightings of the Osgoode creature were rare. We heard him well enough, as well as his gang of True Believers trooping up and down the Traymore stairs. We heard him slamming his door. He was not interested in us. And then a letter from Vera told me all I needed to know: Clare was with her there in Costa Rica. I had visions of a thatched hut, one wired with the latest technological wizardry, including some gigantic plasma TV, Karl watching the World Series via satellite. For sure, I would never see Clare again, now that she was in Vera's clutches; now that I was effectively cut out of the loop. I could see them—Vera and Clare, each woman tall and willowy—carrying on like two kissing cousins, like two peas in a pod; Karl playing the bemused and mild-mannered and ever reliable patriarch. Normally prompt in responding to correspondence, I would sit on this one, this chatty treachery on Vera's part. I whipped up my inner turmoil to a fine froth. I knocked on Eleanor's door.

'Well,' she said, 'you may as well come in. But I'm betwixt things, if you know what I mean.'

I did not know what she meant.

'Bob, that louse, he's reneging on his offer to take me to Florida. He's saying he's lost his appetite for Disneyworld. He's heard somewhere that the people who work there work for next to nothing. Since when has he developed a conscience? Between what am I betwixt? Relationships are absurd. I need love. Hell, I'll settle for sex. True, I get sex. But he's got marriage without the commitments, one of which is that a promise made ought to be kept. I'm thinking a kiss-off is in the offing. What's on your mind?'

'Plenty. But first, whence all this venom you have for Bob? I thought you had things pretty much the way you wanted.'

'I was wrong.'

'Why this sudden craving for the mercenary and vulgar?'

'Don't know. But all the world goes to Disneyworld. Sometimes I'd like to be in with the world, if you know what I mean.'

'No, I don't know what you mean. And bear in mind, the world always exacts a price.'

'Sometimes you don't know you're alive until you pay the price.'

'Pay for what,' I said, exasperated, 'a spectacle? A little fame? Cuddles?'

'You're so damn Christian.'

'I'm as pagan as a grotto and a grove.'

So yes, the good woman was annoyed. With apologies, I took my leave.

And I knocked on Eggy's door. It being windy and raw outdoors, Eggy decided to stay in and read a book and drink himself senseless. It seemed sensible.

'Women,' I said to Eggy, he in his overstuffed chair. I was opposite him in another chair. It was as if we were opposing rooks on a chessboard.

'Women,' said Eggy. 'Oh really? The particulars, please.'

I gave him those particulars. Eggy then responded: 'I can't speak for those women. I never met them, but it seems to me your Clare is still hanging on to her husband. She smells him on, what's her name, oh, Vera then, and she smelled him on you. It's called grief. Don't interfere.'

'My God, you really make the most of a nutshell.'

'It's what I get paid the big bucks for,' smirked Eggy, 'the really big bucks.'

I took my leave of a sparrow of a man.

I had my forebodings: nothing good could come of Osgoode. I was addicted to symmetries, and the undoing of them made for chaos in my view. The unravelling of the Soviet Union slingshotted the West to some apogee, and then the tailspin. Or say that if a new breed of inner circle scoundrel had hijacked the Constitution, well then, one could expect other hijackings at street-level. The hearts and minds of the neighbourhood. As I myself was so tired of pointing out, I was not a political animal. Even so, I had long since noted a change of pressure in the air, the formation of fronts and storms and serious unpleasantness. My nose was out front of learned parts of my mind; parts that were cautioning against foretelling the future or reading false lessons from the past. Granted, polite society was a criminal world. Granted, the Underworld was the World of the Light of Day. One lived so as to obtain and exercise leverage: a committee vote or the barrel of a gun in some alley. One lived so as to secure yet another ordinance favouring the lifestyle of the rich at the expense of the poor man's bad habits. Some quarrel over a seat in the bus was a life and death matter. Would the waiter return one's cold scrambled eggs to the kitchen for a heating up? Or would he advise one to soldier on? Everyone was getting thin-skinned and petty and hankering for release in ever more bizarre entertainments. And the thing is, everyone knew it and would prefer to know nothing else. Like so, I figured, Germans had accommodated Hitler so as to accommodate themselves. I was certifiable, investing Moonface with powers she did not have. To Eggy who had given her it, her nickname was a joke; to me it was a sign. Life does not read as historical romance. You are born; you putz about; you die.

Social Beast

What was he going to do, winter coming on, his pins not as steady as once they were? In his rooms, I asked him, and Eggy responded: 'Oh, I suppose I'll hibernate. Live off the fat of my body, you know. Hoo hoo.'

Then it seemed he would now succumb to one of his spells, his head sagging. But he came around. And he reached for the wine on the lamp table beside him. Instinctive fingers secured the stem of the glass; and then, dreamy ballet, he swept it toward his mouth, sipped, and swept it back again to its place of rest.

'You're fishing, you know,' he said. He continued: 'Well, it were better not to have been born. I go to bed. Will I wake up? Will I touch a woman again? There are idiots I'd happily hang. Drink and Moonface keep me going. Drink and Moonface are not luxuries. Now and then a page of Herodotus gets me over some hump, if it does not put me to sleep. Most storms pass, as did the wives and my labours in the marketplace. What stays with you, what turns the soul hot and cold, aside from the business of having been born; well, what it was for me, is Korea. The things I saw there. Stupidity and intransigence don't even begin to tell the tale. Did you ever hear of No Gun Ri? No, I suppose not. Did you know I was in the Signal Corps? Ah, tropospheric-scatter. Hell, there were spies in my unit back in Aberdeen. It put McCarthy on the warpath. We drowned Pyongyang in napalm. Do I sound like I'm on a soapbox? My apologies. Moonface, get your sweet behind over here, your child-bearing hips. Think she heard me? Whoop-de-do.'

No, she could not have; she was at the Blue Danube, marking time while she looked forward to post-graduate life. She was seeking her niche or else she was terribly distracted.

'You know, she'll fall to you,' Eggy said, 'when I'm gone.'

'I don't know about that. She has a mind of her own.'

'She's lost,' Eggy insisted, 'and when she looks around, she sees there isn't much help.'

It had been a while since I heard Eggy this serious. *In Kamarouska a kiss and a thought for Algonquins.*

I was never going to know exactly what it was that chilled his soul when he had been a young sparrow in Korea; but it was as if something were trying to reassemble in his eyes so that I could view it; oh, not as a movie to watch at one's leisure but as a manifestation of pure horror that takes one unawares. Then Eggy's eyes closed. Gone for lunch. His chin drooped. My audience was over. For a moment there, as he was delivering me the fruits of his wisdom, Raphael might have painted him as he did some cardinal, or was it a pope? Then again, a cartoonist might have sketched the Eggy frame. Pomp and circumstance and the veiled fist of power were always somehow never far from the absurd; but when what is absurd is suffused with thorough-going cynicism, then what is merely absurd seems a thing to pine for, as in falling through time with tights, bells and jester's cap. Evolutionary drift.

Eleanor R, big spender, took me to the Blue Danube for dinner.

'Oh,' said Moonface, working extra hours, 'I shall have the pleasure of serving you.'

'Just put food on the table and a bottle of wine and don't be cute about it,' said Eleanor with some fire.

Moonface gave me a 'what's with her' look and set about her task.

I said to Eleanor, 'Why do you always give her a hard time?'

'She's a dreamer and she leads men on.'

'That's news to me. She's almost asexual by my estimation.'

'She's always got that maybe I'll let you kiss me, maybe I won't simpering in her eyes. It's supposed to drive men crazy. If I were a man, and happily I'm not, I'd find it boring and counter-productive. From the sounds of it, at least that McCabe gal of your high-school days didn't mess about. Wham, bam, thank you, gents. Now let's get on with the party.'

I thought the good woman was gravely mistaken but I was not about to swim against the tide.

'She's trying her best,' I said, 'in a not very helpful world.'

'Oh piffle. I wonder what God thought men would be useful for. Adam may've had a rib to spare but Eve copped the brains in case you're looking for yours.'

We ate in silence, now that Moonface had brought us the cabbage rolls and sauerkraut and Hungarian wine. To change the subject, and because I was still curious; and even though I sensed the justice of her suspicions vis-à-vis Lucille Lamont, I had never had enough of Eleanor's reasons. Perhaps it should have been as obvious to me as it was, apparently, to her. Even so. Even so.

'Have you heard from Lucille since her last letter?'

Eleanor was wolfing her food down. She gulped from a glass of wine. Then, absurdly dainty, she dabbed at her mouth with a serviette.

'No, haven't heard from the witch. I expect the cornlands of Ontario have withered and will never sprout corn again. Grass turns black where she walks. Men keel over dead at the sight of her. Who wouldn't, the way those frightful tits of hers clank together under her greasy sweatshirts? You know, some time ago, you got me thinking about redemption. I don't believe I've done anything so bad in my life that I have to think about the eternity of my soul. But, mind you, if I must, then it seems I'm to be stuck with the nasty business of prosecuting her in my soul until hell freezes over. This is a hypothetical, you understand, and it may seem petty of me, but how was that woman ever anything but guilty as sin, innocent though she might be (and I give her one chance out of ten that she is) of Marcel's death? I liked him. It's as simple as that. He may've been as guilty as sin, too, and she have her reasons. You have your notions and intellectual preoccupations, your writing and your musings, your woman-wary soul, but you're not so complicated as all that. Eggy is Eggy, which is to say life has refined him to a single pure speck of something or other, and the wind is going to blow away whatever it is soon enough. And Bob, well, Bob is pretty straight-forward, likes his mind, his body, his dinner, his nooky; but Marcel, his eyes were a battleground between joy and sheer terror the legions of which were in hand-to-hand battle and dying in one another's arms; as if, and you tell me, you're the expert in these matters, as if he were seeing angels all the time and it wasn't so wonderful.'

'Close enough for folk music.'

Eleanor gave me a look.

She said with some heat, 'Look, Calhoun, get this: Lucille Lamont is how I make amends between me and myself. She's my truth before God, seeing as I see the truth of that woman. Do you think He minds I must stick His nose in it? You bet He minds. She's low-lying evil, but evil all the same. Do you think I like this hang 'em high mentality? It's not my job to judge her. But if and when she ever looks in my eyes, she has to know I know. It sits in my gut like a greasy meal. By the way, who's in the kitchen? This is raunchy stuff we're eating.'

I had not noticed, so rapt I was in the operations of the Eleanor mind.

Moonface (and was she joking around?) had brought us over a candle and lit it, and Eleanor's frosted curls seemed to glow for a moment, a kind of divine apparatus.

'Thank you, dear,' said Eleanor. 'Now could you bring us coffee? And if there's something sticky and sweet and alcoholic to drink in this house, we'll have that, too.'

I was so caught up with Eleanor and her musings that I had been oblivious to the fact the Blue Danube had filled with Slavs; that Moonface had her hands full and that, dreamy-minded or not, she was competent and efficient in her work. Some swarthy and mustachio'd character was playfully giving her the gears, and Moonface was smiling, her eyes rolled to the ceiling, she holding menus to her bosom. She was Iphigenia operating on blind trust.

We fell silent again, Eleanor and I. It was one of those prickly silences in which judge, jury and the accused think the worst of one another. My dinner companion, the evening's benefactress, was getting glassy-eyed. I was restive now and wanting to go, staring out the window at human detritus in the street. Moonface served the coffee and liqueur. Then as if she were in a world of her own and we did not exist, she upped the radio's decibels. A harsh and unpleasant female voice sang of wham bam sex. Never had fire and desire been such an unlikely pairing by way of rhyme. I was weary of the emphatic. Somewhere in a nation-state a president was noodling in his brain, his base disintegrating, the one of Bibles and values and pristine principle; his generals sullen; his cabinet and advisers all scrambling about, pushing each their agendas. Spin doctors spun their cotton candies; and, would the man widen the war? It was not an unreasonable question to ask, though many in the pundit class tittered as, categorically, they asserted: 'Ain't gonna happen. That's money in the bank.'

'A penny for your thoughts,' asked Eleanor, as if trying to rope me back into her world, she preoccupied with some showdown between good and evil of a quite different order.

Truth to tell, I disliked the expression 'a penny' and so forth; it was intimacy on the cheap. Besides, who could think, what with the racket emanating from the radio?

'Oh hell, law' I answered, 'the *raison d'être* of law has undergone a sea change.'

'Oh, do you think?' Eleanor said in a twitting tone of voice, stealing from the current put-down phrase of the hour.

'Protect the rich, screw the poor, that sort of thing? Old news. What else you got?'

'I worry about Moonface. Sometimes I think she hasn't got the sensibility God gave a baboon.'

'She's young. What do you expect? You've had years to acquire your, what do you call it, sensibility; your druthers, your prejudices.'

'There's something more to sensibility than what can be learned.'

'Well then, either she's got it or she doesn't.'

Eleanor was dying for a cigarette. Any moment now, she would rifle her purse for one and light it in the candle's flame. She would waddle outside, puffing defiantly. And yet, a moment gone by, and still, she sat there, less an oracle than a cheap shot artist whose only aim in life was to pillory everything that moved.

'Thanks for the dinner,' I said.

'Don't mention it.'

'Ever hear of No Gun Ri?'

'Can't say that I have.'

Peering into a small pouch of coins, Eleanor added: 'Shall we leave a gratuity?'

'I'll get it,' I said, Moonface in the kitchen with the cook, kidding around. She was worth the fifteen percent, I supposed. I would dock five on account of the music. I helped Eleanor with her coat.

And she lit up on the short trek back to the Traymore, the air calm, cold, clear. She slipped her arm through mine, saying: 'You're not such a bad fellow, you know. What are you saving it for?'

Secular humanist? Was I that? Must I declare my particulars in a census? If I could teach Moonface anything, it would be this: do not let the bastards pin you down; but should it come to that, make them a pay a price. I had already been with her, if not strictly in the biblical sense. We had not had intercourse, but we had been intimate, so much so it constituted a minor betrayal on Moonface's part to her current consort. It was an hour spent in a harmless snuggle, each of us remaining clothed. Millions of baby boomers might have approved; or, *à la* Bly, a heavyweight, snickered. She had a knack for nesting, to go by her decorative and tasteful touch. There was a Veronese print on her bedroom wall, that one of Venus coddling (and twitting) Mars, little cherubs gambolling about. It was timeless, idyllic, and it masked a thousand horrors. There was a new epithet going the rounds: zero-sum gamers. It was meant to characterize the mentality of the President and his vice-regent. So that it would seem that Venus, squeezing her nipple, and Mars in his languor (and still armour-clad), nostalgically comprised the notion of a balance of power. Were we not hurtling backwards in time—to the wars of the Titans and other semi-coherent gods, and nature was not so much the battlefield as one of the combatants? A question perhaps too speciously asked. And then I would go out, and on the street, I would learn that the world is front and centre and immediate; which is to say the sun happened to be bright and the day cold, and in the Blue Danube, Moonface somewhat abstracted, Slavs were talking colonoscopies.

Dying in Brindisi

Calabria. The abandoned cantina on the beach had been a portal to another world. It was as sun- bleached as an enormous animal skull monitoring time in an arid wasteland. What dream had died in that spot? What humble aspiration? I photographed the ruin even if packing a camera around had been a nuisance. Then I dozed for a while on that beach, sand fleas or some other insect pestering me. Even so, I dreamed. Greek, Carthaginian, Moorish incursions. I supposed Virgil's return from what were for him classical lands was also an incursion of a kind, his great poem not quite ripe. Eggy said that east of Vienna people have a view of life different from ours. A commonplace remark, one that Eggy refused to substantiate. He had gotten around; I should take him at his word. A leader was wanted in America, unifier, backdoor messiah. Some impute to Ronald Reagan, President the 40th, this distinction. Who knows which America danced in his crinkly eyes to his barnyard fiddle or languid baton, those folks in Latin America needing prepping?

Caesar was in the east when Virgil went to Greece; in Megara he came down with fever. He had been putting Caesar off, who wanted reports on the progress of the great poem extolling the empire, as if the empire were a moral thing. Virgil would revise as he travelled. Spitting blood, he was, no doubt, tubercular. It is said he had carved grottos with no other tool but that of his intense gaze. I had read Mr Broch's famous treatment of Virgil's death. I did not believe the author understood in the slightest what makes a poet a poet. Even so, I pictured Caesar rushing to the poet's bedside—in Athens, say; then escorting him by ship to Brindisi, neither man truly the friend of the other. For each man was locked into each their function and role, Virgil's view of his lot strictly ironic, Caesar not quite able to indulge such latitude vis-à-vis himself. Had Caesar really loved Virgil he might have acceded to the poet's wish that the poem—ambitious, epical—be put away and forgotten if not destroyed. Rome would be Rome with or without it. But perhaps Caesar was a competent judge of literary worth. Eggy, it all too often seemed, was no competent judge of anything, given his prodigious wine intake, his pins sabotaged. Still, he would say the nonsense had gone on long enough. The apostles of evil, hoo hoo, had run out of gas, a first term black senator from Illinois the imminent man of an imminent hour. Moonface might as easily paint her toenails as divide her thoughts between Virgil and her suitors and her political druthers. Was homeland an American word?

As I predicted, Traymoreans were taking little notice now of Osgoode, the new lodger; though, in point of fact, he was noticeable, in and out at all hours, his door-slamming not yet part and parcel of mere background noise. Even so, and mysteriously, the constant trooping up and down the stairs of women had ceased, as had their voices lilting with hello's and good night's. Had he fallen out of favour with them? Had they no more use for him? Was he now in a state of apostasy? Was he, after all, no more than a seller of insurance? He was courteous, well-spoken. He was somewhat interested in the arts, so he had mentioned to Moonface whom I briefly feared might be tempted to take up with the man.

'No,' she told me with an imperious air, 'he's not my type.'

Eleanor, whose parents had been devout but not zealous, searched him out for a belief system, if any; and to her amazement she could find nothing out. Oh, he informed her, alright. He was a Yank. He hailed from a small town in the state of Washington; had enrolled in a small college in the Seattle area; had, by chance, drifted into the computer game; had come east to work for a software firm. (Firm, he called it, as if talking steel or railroads or pharmaceuticals.) Then Montreal. He did not think he was any more or any less religious than anyone else. He supposed there was some 'design' or structure to the universe. As for the women, their presence in his apartment was work-related. 'It's an out and out lie,' so Eleanor let me know, and I had to agree. He was a shining head and a holy roller, no question, but why the low profile? That it made him subversive and more chic than he deserved to be. He was evidence for the fact that not only did I not comprehend the American mind, I had failed to understand how the world had changed even when such change occurred right under my nose. My brain had been perhaps arrested in its forward progress when a president, a presidential contender, and a spiritual leader of the civil rights movement had been, one after the other so long ago now, in another country, assassinated. Except for that bit about the women, Eleanor pretty well bought his story, but I wondered if I was not as suspicious of Osgoode as she was of Lucille Lamont, and for the same reasons. There was in Osgoode's eyes, for those who wished to note it, ambition. There was a clearly defined purpose, the world in his sights. There was something revolutionary about the man, and it cautioned me, saying, 'I know you were revolutionary once. It was pathetic, how you failed. But Jesus loves you, anyway.' Whom would he find expendable on his way to grasping the brass ring? I did not fear for myself or other Traymoreans; we were out of the loop. Dubois, semi-retired, still kept his hand in various business ventures, but it had more to do with maintaining a social nexus than with making a buck. It was not difficult to imagine, as Osgoode held his hand over his heart and pledged allegiance, that bodies would fall. My father had been a knife fighter, country and corporation so much office politics; but the shining head was a different animal. For him it was more than power and financial gain all wrapped up in the flag, though it was just that; only that the flag had come to symbolize something other than a rough and ready republic labouring somewhat under the burden of its innocence.

I took the rent to Mrs Petrova. I asked her there in her shop, 'Want some money?'

She shrugged and answered, 'Sure.'

It was the most American of words, that word 'sure'. There were ancient imps in her eyes. And when she was done with time and time done with her, we Traymoreans might be out on the street, depending on what that mythical creature, her son, might have to say about it. She was far from frail in her eighty or so years. One moment she might be attending church in fancy red shoes and a rakish hat, and the next, she might be on her hands and knees digging in the earth for grubs. Versatile woman. A terror to thieves. It might require centuries for us to learn again that poetry and music are divine gifts, not commodities. The thought had nothing to do with the watches and the bracelets and the rings in Mrs Petrova's glass compartments; had nothing to do with the ancient calendars and their winter scenes; with the crazies who came off the street and talked gibberish to the woman on account of the fact she was a legend and favoured by the gods. The thought had everything to do with all these items. The rent paid, receipt received, the woman having written Natasha Petrova on it with a careful flourish—in the bottom right-hand corner, I went out the tinkling door to the Blue Danube.

Dubois and Eggy were already there. Moonface at school, a young man, new recruit, waitered in her stead. He was Albanian, as it turned out, and he seemed angst-ridden from head to toe but was otherwise a good sort, Eggy and Dubois breaking him in. I sat with my friends, endured their insults. I soon learned that in 1961, Eggy had a wife, and with her, had crossed the continent by car and raised California. I had visions of Desi Arnaz and Lucille Ball and comradely sex. Then Eggy said: 'And once I went by train through the tunnel at Kickinghorse Pass.'

And Dubois said, 'What has this to do with California?'

And Eggy shot us one of his standard looks, the one that said we had yet to live sufficiently to appreciate his wealth of experience. I wanted to be serious, but my friends were in a larking mood and would not have it. 'What's pestilence, famine and endless war?' asked the mocking eyes of Dubois. Perhaps it was true that he fired off letters to the editors only because it was hilarious fun.

The Albanian brought over another bottle of wine at Eggy's behest. Mikki seemed permanently stuck in a no man's land between a collapsed state and a discotheque. One perhaps associates exile with men and women of sentience, forgetting that exile also numbers among its supplicants the mute and the shell-shocked and the not so clever. I had no wish, really, to get drunk; but there it was, I was going to get drunk and count Eggy and Dubois as my closest soul mates. Gareth Howard was in his grave, and I could not see him or hear him or sniff him or otherwise sense his presence. His words had counted for something, if only momentarily; he a journalistic insect that mates with a deadline and immediately thereafter dies. Jack Swain materialized briefly before my eyes and was gone again, he the only dead man to whom I would post a letter. I did not recall what I might write. 'Dear Jack,' I suppose I would begin, 'It's untrue, the notion that there's no justice in this world. It's just that the justice you get is rarely the justice you truly need. But you know as much.'

Every cell in my body clamoured for something to happen. A president might own up to his crimes or pigs fly. One could get to like a purgatory, one's redemption nowhere in evidence. I looked at Eggy and for the first time thought him smug. I looked at Dubois, and damn it all, but he was deeply envious of his old friend's seeming air of immortality. Something had changed; and as Dubois explained what was wrong with the Democrats and their new lease on life (given the results of the last mid-term), I noticed he was now exuding saliva in a fine spray. I pulled back a little from his proximity. I noticed also that his facial skin was minutely scored: wispy scratchings on a coloured block of glass.

'There she is,' Eggy near shouted, 'Black Dog Girl.'

'Where?' said Dubois, leaning closer to the window.

'There. She's just now going by the bus stop.'

'But the dog, where's the dog?'

'She doesn't need a dog to be Black Dog Girl,' retorted Eggy with words that explained everything.

I looked and nothing much registered, save that the girl had a contemplative face. I rose from my chair, nowhere near drunk, made my excuses, and bolted. In the hall of the Traymore, I ran into Osgoode who was stepping out. For a single unguarded moment, he—with a glint in his eye—exposed his superiority. Here was the young Octavian, romantic, lethal, and, as always, underestimated. No doubt there was in his satchel an early draft of his infamous proscription list. His suit was just this side of a hideous green. I mumbled hello, and squelched the impulse to advise him that it was colder outside than he might think. I ducked into my rooms, knowing that whatever mood I had fallen prey to now, no Traymorean could help me. Even so, someone knocked on the door. It was Moonface. She looked fetching, her pale complexion set off with a shiny scarf. She said: 'I just dropped by the Blue Danube and the boys said you looked peculiar. I thought I'd check. Are you alright?'

'Of course, I'm alright. Do you want to come in?'

She thought it over.

'Can't stay long. I'm meeting James. I wasn't going to tell you because it's none of your business, but it's over between us. I'm too arty and not political enough. He's drunk on anger, though God knows he has his reasons. We make love and it's like two strangers having arguments with themselves inside their heads, and the other person may as well be on the opposite side of the planet. I don't understand it, Q, I really don't.'

Was she going to cry?

She had called me Q. I was only Q when she was in trouble. But what could I say? As for the pain of love, she had not seen anything yet. It was the one thing I could say, but in the saying of it, my tone would slide into the avuncular—a word which produced in my mind the rather comic spectacle of a worm bunching up and straightening out as it inched its way from A to B, predators everywhere. There was whiskey in my cupboard.

'How about a drink?'

'No, that would really set James off, me smelling of booze. I think I'll just go. You seem alright.'

'Come by, later, when it's over. Maybe there's something to see at the movies.'

'Sure,' she said, a little abstractedly.

It was hard to see in her just then the woman who read Virgil in Latin, something I would never accomplish; Latin had mystified me in high school. Besides, the Virgil I knew was a modernist Virgil, hostage to our platitudes and critiques of the past. Either he was at the core of our poetic tradition or he was a shill for Caesar, or both, and Dante's Jay Silverheels, to boot. Oh, he was an avuncular man, one rendered pensive by the evils of empire. The Virgil I had formed in my mind was a great heart with a mind to match, and in the end I supposed he had eluded both his time and mine; he had settled for pleasing himself.

Another knock now, and it was Eleanor. As she stood at my door she fingered the spit valve of her trombone. It was then a curious thought struck me concerning the good woman: she was somehow not as all together as she seemed, the trombone a sham, the valve in her hand a cult trinket, a clutching at straws.

'Greetings to you, kind sir,' she began, 'I have tea and muffins at the ready in my place. Care to partake?'

No, I did not wish to partake but I was not at the moment of any use to myself. So I followed her down the hall and through her door and living room into the inner sanctum, her kitchen. She said: 'I guess Bob and Eggy are out getting drunk?'

'That they are.'

'And you're not?'

'I gave it a go, but I couldn't really afford it—in the spiritual sense, if you know what I mean.'

'I know what you mean.'

'So what's this all about?'

'I want the pleasure of your company. I want to hear again about Sally McCabe and your old high school, scene of your trials.'

'I should think you've heard enough.'

'Because your motherland's in a nosedive, and maybe, in your tales of McCabe there's a clue as to why.'

'I doubt it.'

Eleanor looked short-changed by my response.

'A Sleepy Hollow of wheezy Wurlitzers, sexual ghouls, the over-bright eyes of vampires? Pyscho beach parties? Isn't all this reason enough? Wounded Knee. No Gun Ri, as Eggy says. Will the cure, proving worse than the disease, reduce us all to gibbering idiots or automatons or sieg-heiling fanatics?'

'But you spoke of her as a goddess and so forth and so on. I remember distinctly you saying so, and I thought it hogwash, here's a precious boy and all that, but now, I don't know.'

'Nor do I.'

'And then I wonder if life's nothing but a series of random acts like you say. Or do patterns form, and with patterns, predictable consequences, and with consequences, a tale of our own shortsightedness and egotism. I mean we do love ourselves so, don't we? We love the effing stuffing out of ourselves. Hey, my little pinkie is worth a thousand times more than your little pinkie. Does anyone come to mind? How about Lucille Lamont, the effing witch?'

'Have you heard from her again?'

'No,' Eleanor near barked, 'and if she'd sent me another I'm-fine-wish-you-were-here-letter I would've thrown it out with the garbage, unread.'

With an utter absence of ceremony, she slopped some hot water in our cups and dropped a muffin in my lap.

'Eat, drink,' she commanded.

No wonder Dubois was in the Blue Danube, drinking himself insensible.

'Well,' I said, 'better to love oneself than not. Self-loathing. So zero-sum.'

'Too many people who love themselves are taking us to ruin.'

'Shall we count the ways?'

She gave me a nasty look.

'The President is clearly self-enamoured,' she said.

'Well, when you've got God in your corner, it's hard not to be a little smug.'

'You can say that again.'

The tone of her voice, rather than a ringing endorsement of my thought, was more like the realization of the limits of her intelligence.

'I don't understand you,' she said. 'I just don't.'

'Get in line,' I drolled, 'behind me.'

We sat there quiet in her kitchen. It was a place in which Eleanor and I had so often conversed; and yet, how little I knew its particulars. Pots and pans on the gas stove. A fridge with those little magnets which pinned notes and lists and snapshots to the fridge door. A heap of unwashed dishes in the sink, the counters at either side of it sheer chaos, what with dishes and tins and boxes and scattered cutlery, bags and food bits and cookbooks. A young shoot of a plant on the sill just over the sink, the leaves touchingly optimistic. The window looked out on the same view as the window in the hall. Eleanor, too, would see Mrs Petrova raking her leaves. I decided to take matters in my own hands.

'Look,' I said, 'when I go on about McCabe, I'm just blowing wind up my arse.'

'How delicately you put it, Mr Calhoun.'

'Who was she?' I continued. 'She was just a girl who once let me stammer in her presence, on ceremony.'

'And you weren't supposed to win that football game. You spoiled a perfect losing season.'

'Yes, I certainly did spoil it, and the Furies have been chasing me ever since.'

'You're definitely off your nut.'

'Oh but I am.'

It was only then I noticed she had something else in mind, she exuding heat like a furnace; her breasts young, her smile a little foolish. Let a nation-state tear itself apart limb by limb; my hands could happily get lost exploring this woman who was all of a piece, our selfishness absolute. Then the moment went down like a plane shot from the sky. There were questions in her eyes and no answers in mine.

Doing Moonface

I wanted un-Traymorean diversion now, autumnal evenings beginning to hang in the trees. Lovers in the parks, as intense as peacocks in misalliance, were feeling the chill now, after dark. So Propertius might have viewed it, up to no good, wearing sun shades and a leather jacket, headed for some cult venue called The Sarajevo Club, verses breaking in his mind like news from a distant front. I would go downtown and pretend myself abroad. It had always been my fancy that, in my twilight years, I would live in Venice like one of those Victorian aesthetes in revolt against London fog and other rigours, against all complacencies. But I could barely afford dinner and a movie ticket, let alone a musty palazzo and a regimen of expensive coffees in the famous piazzas. I had failed at rapine and pillage, the rules of the game rigged, in any case. Was there anything anymore like honest thievery? I could not wait around for the Traymorean Moonface to reappear (we had planned to see a flick) and so I stuffed money in my pocket, grabbed a coat, went and boarded a bus of silent brooders.

I finished off the cannelloni, washed it down with wine that tasted of cobwebs. I enjoyed the spectacle of people on the street, all bundled up, cares in abeyance. Frosted breath. Enthusiasm for life. I had great affection for the scene. Somewhere Moonface was being ignoble and her James noble, or so the script should read; but that, of course, it would not. How did we become clichés? In walked Minnie Dreier with a new prospect.

Cogs and wheels and gears and springs that were Randall Q Calhoun disengaged, part from part. The mechanism crashed and scattered in pieces. I felt myself absurd. I read the telltale signs of what was uppermost on Minnie's mind; it was neither love nor even a date. She was one of those women for whom sex is a preoccupation, only that, when the chance arose, she got skittish and would argue terms. I hoped she had not spotted me. She had streaked her hair and had it cut close. It did not flatter her. She had aged since last I saw her, but still she had her attractions—the dark eyes and full mouth, the lower lip of which was somewhat pronounced; it had a rather maddening and enticing way of pulling away from her strong teeth when she got drunk enough to forget her fears.

If she had seen me, she did not let on, guiding her beau to the rear of the restaurant. He, and he was hard to read as to which of the honoured professions he claimed for himself, then walked back to the cashier and put in an order. By now, Minnie must have noticed me. Soon enough, as if the back of my head had eyes, I could determine that Minnie, my old passion, was working overly hard for scant returns. She was chattering on; he was all scorched earth. Perhaps he had character, a fact which might complicate things for her. In any case, I slid back my chair, rose, and went to pay my bill. I spoke two words of Italian to the cashier who was wearing a red apron. '*Stai bene*?' I said, and he smiled obligingly, humouring me. This time, I caught Minnie's eyes and she distinctly blushed as if caught out in a naughty act. I offered up a mock-wave. By the time I hit the street I had worked up a righteous and seething boil. Of course, I had no right to it. Minnie was a world I long since put behind me; or rather it was the other way around. It did not even feel all that good, the anger in me, and the movie I had planned to see with Moonface—*The Hustler* –(and yes, I had seen it many times) did not entirely satisfy on this viewing. Newman's performance seemed lazy, his smile saying, 'Oh come on, I'll ace this, just feed me the line'. Piper Laurie however was as doomed as ever as the drunken and lame-footed Sara who saw it all; saw what makes clowns of men. Jackie Gleason as Minnesota Fats, pool shark, wearily wise, was a massive Buddha. Though the Buddha had stated otherwise, the squinted eyes of Minnesota Fats said that pain is real enough.

All night the wind blew hard and further denuded the trees. I walked the last few remaining blocks to the Traymore, disembarking from a bus of more silent brooders. Apart from the ruckus of the wind, it seemed unnaturally quiet in the neighbourhood. It was Halloween, after all, and there must have been house parties; there must have been carousing in the bars. I passed by the Traymore, and in the wind and dark, it looked forbidding, something out of a horror flick; and I said to myself that on the other side of the door, I had a life of some sort. In the Blue Danube, incredibly enough, Eggy and Dubois were still at it, a pair of mewing kittens, silly, endearing, mildly destructive. The Slavs were at it, too, among their number a striking woman in furs, her face hard-bitten but somehow aristocratic, demeanor and attire suggesting money. I estimated her age to be near mine, and I wondered if she was not able to read my mind, disapprovingly, of course. She levelled haughty glares in my direction. The new Albanian waiter seemed quite at home, humanity in its cups a familiar enough spectacle. Dubois was on about something. He and Eggy hardly noticed my showing up, Dubois saying: 'Kennedy welcomed power. He had no compunctions about it.'

Dubois spoke like a man who actually knew something.

'He didn't always have to use it, but he had it should he need to make a point.'

'Yes,' said Eggy, 'like the Seventh Fleet.'

'The current President is something else again. Here he's got at his fingertips all the tools of an expanded Executive, but I don't think he's interested in power as such. He just likes playing the role. The real power is you know who.'

'The Veep,' said Eggy, supplying identity and role and scope for criminality.

'The rain in Spain,' he sing-songed, 'was always in Espawnya.'

'So yes,' Dubois said, 'I'd say there was, I'd say there's a lot of difference between now and those dear old days of Camelot.'

'And I suppose you'll still tell me Trudeau was his own man,' said Eggy.

'I'll still tell you that. Even in French the word maverick applies.'

Moonface blew in, as it were, on the wind.

'Happy All Saint's Day,' she said.

Her cheeks were charmingly flushed, and the way her face was set off by the scarf, it imparted to her eyes a look of gusto, a Marilyn Monroe look, the one that knows the game is rigged but that it is still worth playing. Even so, I could see she had had a bad evening of it. More censure emanated from the woman in furs who really must have been a minx once upon a time. There was an epic in her face. She sized up Moonface and found her fluff, no match for the grind of history and the abysmal predilections of men insofar as they concerned sex. Well, we would see about that. I would give Moonface a backbone, if that was what was wanted; and Eggy would help and Dubois. Eggy, checking his wristwatch, challenged her: 'All Saint's Day? You're somewhat early.'

Moonface ignored him.

'So how did it go?' I asked.

Her eyes suggested it was a matter best left for another time.

'How did what go?' Eggy demanded to know, unwilling to miss out on any fun.

'Yes,' said Dubois, 'what's the big mystery?'

Moonface brightening, her neck still wrapped in the scarf, said that it was no one's business, and if we were the gentlemen we claimed to be, one of us would treat her to a glass of wine, even if wine went hard on her stomach.

'Oh sure,' said Eggy maliciously, 'we'll get you drunk. Hoo hoo.'

I searched her face for pain and trouble. Quite the chameleon that face was, now lovely, now plain, now intelligent, now vacuous; and she was just another woman setting out on life's treadmill; and there was no reason to believe she would amount to anything, however dignified the treadmill was with notions of self-empowerment and equality of opportunity and all the rest of the platitudes by which the pursuit of power is disguised. Yet another glare from the woman in furs suggested I was close to the truth in this, but that she could state it better; and I was aching, strangely enough, to know her story; and it was not going to happen. I had visions of White Russians or Polish countessas or some such, but she was not decrepit enough for the lot, and the aristocratic cast to her face was, more than likely, an accident of birth. Still, she was clearly the personage to reckon with at the table at which she presided. I said: 'Well, boys, I've already had a long evening of it. I think I'll retire.'

'You wimp,' said Eggy, and a pair of Dubois eyes, glitteringly blue, said that no one abandons the field until it is time to abandon the field, so, sit down; we were not yet finished. But I carried my point, and Moonface, who did not really want any wine, followed me out.

'They'll be chin-wagging this,' said Moonface, 'forever', and I said: 'I know, I know.'

I took her arm.

Once we were in my apartment, and she had a cup of warm water in her hands (it was all she had wanted to drink as it soothed her stomach), she did not want to talk about it. Yes, bad evening, but she had expected as much. She was only surprised that James, her ex-beau, her prince of a guy, played the sex card and wheedled her with it; and it put her off. Then he got angry and slotted her in distinctly unflattering terms. I supposed nothing much had changed in the annals of revolution. I had spoken similarly myself in a far-off time when a grasp of history clanked oddly and dully with one's inability to perceive the odd truth. In any case, I said nothing, out of fear of unwanted collusion between myself and her antagonist; and because, well, there was nothing to say. I leaned back on the couch, Moonface at my side; and she set the cup of hot water down, shivered gently, and laid her head against my shoulder. She was lost and not minding it so much. She had experienced some pain but she knew she would get over it. She was a shallow girl who operated according to predictable laws. She was a young woman who stumbled onto a world that she recognized as out of the ordinary; that was rich and impenetrable, perhaps impossible to get to the bottom of; that she was a pilgrim; that she was not entirely the author of her own life, and that it was not necessarily a bad thing; that she was not alone in this, at least, not all the time; and lastly, that her mind and body would astonish, one day, some prospective lover, that is, if she played her cards right and did not throw pearls at the feet of the undeserving.

'From the sounds of it,' I said, 'James will sort himself out in due course. Meanwhile, there are Virgil and Beethoven, and there's new music, too, popping up on the horizon, however shaky that horizon is. And maybe you've got poems to write.'

She opened her eyes.

'Oh Randall, give it a break.'

I was being avuncular.

As I said, the wind blew hard all night, and it woke me at four, a terrifying hour. I sweet-talked myself into thinking that everything was fine, life unfolding as it should. And I left my bed to relieve my bladder, and there in the living room, on the couch, was Moonface, looking cadaverous. Perhaps it was the darkness, I do not know, and it was as if she had died, grimacing. Perhaps it was a bad dream. In any case, the sight of her shook me, unpleasantly so. Why was she not in her own bed? How had I come to forget she was in my digs? What sort of lunacy had gotten hold of the both of us? The wind howling like it was, all the world seemed deranged. Were it a movie, this scene she and I were playing out, I would draw her coat to her chin and maybe blow her a kiss, and humanity at large would say, 'There, you see. We're not such a bad lot.' I would have to sweet-talk myself harder than I had, and I piddled and then I padded, barefoot, back to my bed; and tossed and turned a while. In the morning, she was gone.

I went out my door and stepped into the hall, the Traymore somnolent. Not even a mouse and all the rest of it. Oh but there was Osgoode in his this-side-of-hideous attire, and now here he was, slamming his door and inserting his key into the lock with a flourish and turning it. He put the key in his pocket like a man about to set off on imperial business, his satchel his lethality. He saw me and said in his superior fashion, 'Morning', and he clambered down the stairs. I clambered after, and out on the street, he went one way and I went the other. I was happy to see the back of him. I supposed there is always someone in this world who may intend one no ill will but who always rubs one the wrong way.

I wandered into a restaurant in the adjacent district. Posh neighbourhood known for its airs and pretentious boutiques. I ate hungrily and without a thought for table grace. My thoughts were peopled, as it were, with people quite other than those seated around me; with Clare, for instance, and Moonface. With Gar whom I could not actually hear or see. With Jack Swain, an honest enough man who, instead of pretending to poetry, began pretending to radical objections to the prevailing world order. I saw myself in Rome, and this seeing myself there was a frequent occurrence. Now I was in the Forum, negotiating the ruins. Now I was on the Corso clogged with teenyboppers brandishing shiny shopping bags. Now I was in a deserted Piazza Navona very late at night, the fountains drowning the noise in my mind. Now I was up in one of the gardens, the Pincio, I guess, and Nero was cloaked and disguised and up to no good, but that it was fun. Back in the restaurant, spawn with rubbery legs and a too-bright face approached me and his sleek mother called him back. 'Evan', she said collegially with her brisk voice and well-accommodated existence. Who, these days, was named Evan but one who was doomed to a life of lawyering and cynicism and failed marriages? So this was the sort of place I was in and I had best get out of it, and I did; though in the process of my escape, I endured the humiliation of the fact that my shoe was untied, and the laces slapped against the floor as I perambulated out the door. The food sat uneasy on my stomach, and there was a presence in me who was not quite familiar, a pagan assassin or a very wary early Christian.

'Ah,' I said to myself, 'I'll hit the library.'

I would read up on the Korean War. It was going to be a hike but I could manage it. And as I walked I recalled London scenes I knew. Perhaps the cenotaph of a small park put me in mind of them. Sometimes Canada seemed most Canadian to me when linked to England and the last great war, Quebec the counterweight, one of church and sin and Oscar Peterson, and hockey, of course. In any case, London—how I had once stayed with Gar when he was posted there, back before the days when the money men left the news alone, and poetry, too; how we were to meet up in a pub near Covent Garden, how it was all red cushion and dark wood; how he had brought a degenerate old writer of plays along to introduce me to; how this old geezer had said, apropos of nothing: 'I'm perfectly willing to die. It's getting to be a loathsome old world.'

And still, I could neither hear nor see Gar, but clearly he had laughed. Clare remained in the New World, was teaching young nippers how to make a mess of things with crayons. At the library, I gave the Korean War a pass, opted, instead, for the fiction section. Since when had I bothered myself with fiction? Perhaps I was in the mood for writers like Dickens or Tolstoy. Perhaps I needed to know of a time when the road to reality was a broad boulevard, albeit one crowded with much traffic, the stuff of history; one graced with beautiful and misapprehended women. One in which hope had not entirely departed the world, no matter how bad things looked. But the library seemed to have no air and I could not breathe; and I checked my shoelaces; and I damn near ran out of the place. In a nearby park, trees in the last throes of shedding their leaves, I occupied a bench and smoked a cigarette.

'Randall Q Calhoun,' I heard.

Someone, relishing the syllables, had called my name. It was Dubois. He was out and about with his worn and honest-looking attaché case.

'Dubois.'

'The very one,' he said, a bit too heartily, and he occupied the bench as well. He had given up smoking; his cheeks were ruddy from the cold, delicate with their hairline cracks.

'So,' I said, 'you and Eggy were certainly at it, last night.'

'Yes. The old fart amazes me, the way he puts the wine away. He was in fine, fine form. He knows a lot more than he lets on.'

'Of course he does, and he's not really all that shy about it.'

'And you, what are you up to?'

'I think I just had a panic attack. Don't ask why. In any case, I'm alright now.'

'Panic attack?' said Dubois, as if the thought of it were as strange a thing as the sight of sailing ships was once strange to Indians on the shores of the New World, 'what's there to be panicked about? Moonface maybe? Are you doing her?'

'We're only friends. I intend it stays that way.'

'If you say so,' said Dubois, disbelieving.

How the man had gotten through life without any apparent scars to show for it was beyond me.

'Did Eggy ever tell you anything about Korea?'

'Korea?'

'His time there. He was in the Signal Corps.'

'Not a thing,' Dubois answered, 'nothing.'

And it did not seem that Dubois would have been interested, in any case. I allowed myself the thought that none of these people in my life, these Traymoreans, were who I imagined them to be. I had settled my cases with the Gareth Howards and the Vera Klopstocks and the Minnies and so forth, these people from my old life (even if I could neither see nor hear Gar who was in his grave), but as for Traymoreans, perhaps they were not as noble and somehow out of the ordinary as I had given them credit for; that Eggy was just an old fool who had never grown up; that Moonface really had the soul of an accountant; that Eleanor was a frustrated hostess of a salon not worth the mention; that Dubois had coasted through life on the strength of his looks and chance business connections and was not particularly deep, and so was amiable enough. He might have guessed what I was thinking as there was intelligence and a warning in the look he shot me. I was not to underestimate him. We all have our reasons. And the like. I could do worse for friends, and besides, who was I to strut about in an overblown condition of creative non-compliance? The world perhaps was no longer about to give us much, but we had gotten just enough, in any case, to get along, camouflaged and relatively free to pursue what we thought worthwhile, even if only paths of least resistance. The look that set up shop in my eyes, said: 'Don't forget. The way things are, the world can turn on a dime.'

Then Dubois said, 'I don't know what you know. I don't know if I even want to know, and if you're doing Moonface, I don't object, and if you're not doing her, that's alright, too, and probably better. She's a strange one.'

'She's not strange. She's really rather normal. So she reads Latin and has ill-advised love affairs—she's living and trying to sort things out. What else is there?'

'Well, a few million dollars would go down nice right about now. I'd take Eleanor off to warmer climes.'

He shivered. The wind kicked up again and was raw.

BYOB

It snowed briefly, and the snow did not stick, the day cold and bright. It was not yet so cold that the wind scoured your eyes with your abrasive tears, your sorrows beside the point. For some months I had been writing. I had words for my fellow Traymoreans, for the state of the world, for myself. The tallest maple in the neighbourhood, devoid of foliage, seemed violated, though this symbolized no human malaise. I would have had words for it, but—trees? Obsessive. Senators and congressmen who had once given reason for hope had revealed themselves to be dissemblers. The President spoke inanities into cameras. Perhaps if he squinted his eyes tight enough like some range rider facing the wind, he could change the world to his liking. Still, many were predicting a turnaround in the new year, a reversal of the past seven, a closing of the book on the Sixties, at last. But could a collective simply snap its fingers and the past vanish never to reappear? What of cause and effect? What of the misadventure in Iraq? Virgil might have sung arms and the man, and yet nothing he wrote obviated the fact of how it was that Rome filled in the wild and barbarian spaces at the expense of the indigenous tribes, and then ran a protection racket. How bitter were the tears the last Etruscan wept? As for the Colonies, the fledgling U.S. of A., well, the likes of Andrew Jackson, arch-democrat, were a kind of paint remover and finish all in one. Creative destruction. Move those confederations of savages along. We were not moral creatures; we were but occupiers of the time and space we would always abandon. All else flattered us. Perhaps Moonface truly loved poetry. Perhaps she was a gentle soul. Perhaps her eyes hid vast stupidities the substance of which aped some moral order or another, one rigged in Philadelphia or in communion with a contemplated pond. Walden, anyone? Ah yes, a mood of quiet objection to the vanities being ever the ascendant mood. Perhaps, however courteous, she was a succubus, boys and old men her prey. In which case, Eleanor was less the hypocrite, if one at all, making no apologies for her appetites. To say the cynic knows not the value of a thing is preposterous. I, for one, I knew the value of Clare Howard's turn of ankle, of Eggy's hoo hoo, of Moonface's tiny ears, of snow electric on the black boughs of trees. I knew the value of wine, how it gives rise to the heroic mood.

I had not yet committed Osgoode to my pages. I did not think I would accord him the honour. Superstition on my part caused me to hang fire, or else fear of some black sort of serendipity; or that, by writing out the man's name, I would set in motion events that would quickly get out of hand. Alright, as Eleanor would have it, I was off my nut. A theory in physics stipulates that if one observes and measures one alters the reality of the thing observed and measured; one suspends or speeds up time and detracts from the stability of the universe. How was I affecting Traymoreans? Dubois seemed more able, as each day went by, to penetrate the fog of the daily unfolding of politics, and yet he never seemed to take sides. Once in a while Eggy, sparrow of a man in a drunken stupor, said, 'The apostles of evil'; but one could not take the words seriously; they were the spoken detritus of a decrepit mind. In spite of his apparent decrepitude, and for all his foolishness, I was more and more protective of the man, our Traymorean Palaemon, Virgilian arbiter of song. Moonface and I had entered a quiet period in respect to one another: there seemed little to say.

Perhaps I had been serious when, a while back, I intimated that if one were to look into my soul, one would see Sally McCabe. One would hear the bleating of trumpets and the beating of drums. The calling out of play-action signals. The thud of colliding bodies on a football field. The cheers, the screams, the grunts. A coach swearing a blue streak at one of his athletes, yelling, 'What in hell is that boy doing?' One would see Sally McCabe looking up at one from the back seat of a car, a boy on her labouring away at satisfying himself. I could taste the lipstick on her mouth. One day there was Rome on its self-destructive path, and the next day there was Rome the empire; and it was as if not a single Roman eye had blinked before, during and after the transition; it was as natural a thing as the precession of certain stars; one season following another. As a certain Secretary of Defense had famously said, and it was difficult to improve on the sentiment: 'Stuff happens.' Unipolar Dominance would lead to something else.

The bank girl, of course, demurred on the question of marriage; and Eggy with his customary gallantry did not press her on the point. How this affected Moonface's position as 'first reserve' was unknown. No, I do not think Eggy cared much one way or the other; but he was a little lonely; and he did like the ministrations of agreeable women, be they Moonface, his nurse, the woman who would come every so often to clean his apartment; his cardiologist, or Eleanor, she his conduit to the paramedics. I figured his soul was black with the smut of Eggy sins and yet he would slip away into death, his sins unchallenged. Not that he had been Pinochet, a brutalist. Not that he was Milosevic, ethnic cleanser. In fact, I am certain that Eggy, apart from the small sins all of us commit in day-to-day living, had not done anything egregiously terrible or wrong other than disappoint his wives and hold a business together; just that, given that he had acquired a considerable span of life to boast about, he must have seen much and he must have said little, waving his tiny hand at events as if bringing up the head of a motorcade in a shiny limousine. To be sure, I was being grossly unfair. How was it then, whether we were young or old or betwixt things, we were all of us Eggy to some degree?

'Unanswerable,' I said to myself, there in the Blue Danube, the man in question across from me at the table, his chin on his chest; and it was a rare public display of his melancholy. For the management was threatening to cancel its liquor license, and henceforth, it was to be BYOB, and, according to Eggy, it made no bloody sense.

'You people haven't got the brains God gave chickens,' that sparrow of a man thundered.

The square-jawed owner, his greying hair cut flat across his head, had taken refuge in the kitchen and seemed genuinely frightened. He had otherwise the look of a man who had expected by now to be rich, but that, any day now, life, liberty and the pursuit of happiness would reward him. Moonface, thoroughly enjoying the spectacle of Eggy victimized, whispered in my ear (and the whispering was delicious): 'It's not true. It's just a prank.'

She stood away from me and I looked up at her and there was mirth in her rich, brown eyes. Somehow it was madcap Virgilian.

'Goddamn it,' said Eggy, waking briefly, and you can be sure that Eggy did not often resort to violent language, 'Montcalm threw the battle. The apostles of evil. The rain in Spain was unnatural. Your wine is crud, in any case.'

And if I had to come across the man dead, I hoped I would find him in his overstuffed chair, book on his lap, and it would have been that he had only fallen asleep after a rich meal and good wine; after reading Gibbons or Symes or some such, and he had not yet read *War and Peace*, and he had always meant to.

'But it's thick,' he would protest, 'awfully thick for fiction.'

Melody

Dubois was in hospital (heart murmurs), Eleanor beside herself. But her man was all smiles; it was an adventure of sorts, the nurses and doctors such good and dedicated people. When I heard of it from Moonface (who got it from Eleanor and was now in the good woman's good books), I was incredulous. I could not remember since when I had met a genial doctor, one who was not crabbed with virtue and reforming zeal and pharmaceutical dollars. It was still the heyday of the ologists, priests buggering their way into irrelevance. Poets? What manner of creature were they?

In other words, I had soured on everything again, the days uniformly bleak, no hard freeze as of yet. Rain and wind. Now and then an hour of bright sun teased one. Even the sight of Mrs Petrova on her way to church like a woman who fully expected to vanquish a widower's heart and have God smile on her for it, could not alleviate my bottoming gloom. I knew of persons who, the temperatures icy enough, had drunk themselves into an unconscious state, and then laid out on the snow somewhere and froze to death. Was I one of those? Moonface would draw away from me slowly but surely; it would be nature taking a hand. She may or may not want a child. She was, in any case, bound somewhere for post-graduate life.

'Why not London at least?' I would say once in a while, if testily, 'I mean they still do the classics there.'

But her grades were not good enough, she would reply. All that screwing around, however tentatively, had kept her from her books. Me, I was tempted to go to Costa Rica, where I knew of the existence of two mature and sensible women, and of a man who did not mind footing the bills. Even so, making a religion out of my loneliness was, perhaps, my only realistic option, as it was for the irascible masters of old, but of what was I a master?

There was not much by way of conflict among Traymoreans. Nothing on the order of Achilles and Agamemnon; of Ahab and the whale. No Chekhovian reasons to rage. No Gatsby flying the flag of capitalism against the odds until the boat up and sank. I would not be writing *Hamlet*. To be sure, Eleanor and Dubois had their spats. Moonface and I indulged our tiffs. With Eggy there was always going to be a difference of emphasis; his eighty odd years had steeped him in various schools of proportion (save for the drinking); but for all that Eggy and I both wanted the same for Moonface; that she hit upon something worthwhile and not fritter her life away on the asinine and inane. We had little say in the matter. If it were not for the obscenity of the war; if the reinvention, south of here, of class warfare were not unfolding before our astonished eyes; if we were not sensing wrong-footedness on every foot irregardless of political bent, the words I was consigning to my notebook, of little conceivable interest to anyone, would lull one to sleep with gentle comedy, perhaps entertain the odd senile pensioner and a dancing cockatoo.

On PBS wars were raging. The Revolutionary War. The Civil War. The First World War. The Second World War. Korea. Vietnam. And this list was decidedly incomplete. Geo-Politics 101 was Fate and Destiny. And so was our collective goodness now blighted beyond recognition. Even so, I would amuse myself, contemplating Moonface's tiny ears. I had by now come across an article or two on No Gun Ri in the library's computer. I supposed Eggy had not been in on the action, having been in the Signal Corps. But he must have gotten wind of the massacre—all those civilians the Americans machine-gunned under a railway bridge. I exhorted myself to commitment, even if only to Moonface's nose, to Eggy's petulance. It was the time of year when fallen leaves smelled like a chardonnay. A French poet, Ponge, wrote words to this effect: 'In the end fall is a cold herb tea'. Was Mr Osgoode, moral or not, a Traymorean creature, his shoes always shined? It was the time of year when fallen leaves smelled like an old paperback of Tu Fu the itinerant diplomatist and versifier.

Eggy was chuffed. The Blue Danube was, indeed, still threatening to cancel its liquor license. Now a man as old as he had to cross the street to the wine store for a bottle of the stuff and then cross over again, having traversed the equivalent of a march through some Mongolian waste, just to sit at a table and sip a glass. Here was injustice. Dubois took a philosophic view. Out of hospital now, he seemed to be drinking more, spraying ever finer mists of saliva as he conjectured and philosophized, his cheeks ruddier, their hairline cracks more hairline; his eyes more alert to the women on the street. I did not think he would begin fooling around; I think he was just commencing to feel his age, which was reminding him of what he might have missed. Eleanor, in any case, would thrash him within an inch of his sorry existence should he stray. Dubois said of the new BYOB policy (he was in on the joke): 'Well, it's an inconvenience but cheaper in the long run.'

'Oh bloody hell,' retorted Eggy, lost in his great coat there in the Blue Danube, 'not really. If I buy a bottle I feel obliged to drink the bottle. If I go by the glass, at least I have the option of cutting myself off.'

Dubois laughed. Here was logic and reason and all the rest of it. But the new policy was, at the very least, yet another assault on civic space, if we mean by civic the opportunity to congregate and pursue one's pleasures and confabulate, and in general, BS, and not worry ourselves with by-laws and such; and to teach the girls that everything their mothers taught them was not necessarily true.

Mikki, the Albanian waiter, had not lasted. Or rather he was fired *in absentia*, he having absconded with some petty cash. A young woman was hired to fill his shift, and Melody and Moonface hit it off. Immediately Eggy asked Melody to marry him.

'Well,' he said, 'you can at least let me take you out once in a while.'

Melody, a redhead, was not shy about her charms. Her knee-high socks were a great attraction until, one evening, and perhaps it was a grease spot or something, and she slid on her high heels and nearly fell. The Slavs applauded her acrobatic recovery, and she had the job. It was slacks from now on and flat shoes. I could not imagine what she and Moonface found to talk about; it could not have been poetry, but perhaps it was all for the best. In any case, despite the added inducements for stepping out by way of wine, women and song, I was, in fact, staying in more, dealing myself hands of solitaire.

It was Eleanor who noticed. She knocked and I gave her entrée into my grotto. She said: 'You haven't been around to visit me.'

I told her I figured she had her hands full with Dubois, seeing as he had been to the hospital and was eating pills.

'Bob can eat pills on his own time. What are you doing here? Plotting a coup?'

'I'm playing cards as you can plainly see.'

'Is that what it is?' she said, unimpressed.

'Well, I'm noodling.'

'Well yes, you're always noodling. I didn't expect you to be doing otherwise. Why aren't you out with the boys? I hear there's a new waitress in Dodge. I hear she's a honey and the Blue Danube has been painted red.'

'Yes, it's something like that, and Melody, that's her name, she's vivacious enough but she's not, how shall I say it, my type.'

'I'll tell you what it is,' the good woman said, 'you're in love with Moonface.'

'For God's sake, Eleanor.'

'Am I wrong?'

'You are. If I'm in love with anyone, it concerns someone you know little about. That's the way it shall remain.'

'I see,' said Eleanor, suddenly much less seductive and rather matter of fact, 'Mr Calhoun has the hots for someone and we Traymoreans don't deserve to know who.'

'You see, it's hopeless with you people. And besides, if love it is, it's a love going nowhere kind of love. Too late and out of the question.'

The eyes of Eleanor R could not quite conceal the fact that she had by now guessed the identity of the mystery woman; she had almost broached the name.

'Well, I don't know,' she said, 'and I can see you're occupied and I'm in the way.'

'Tell you what, I'll come over later.'

'Sure, if you want,' she said, indifferent, and now on the go.

Eleanor took the amaretto from her cupboard and two wide-mouthed glasses with ceremonious stems. She kissed the bottom of each glass with a touch of her favourite substance. She set the glasses on the table, attempting to read me all the while; and she sat and lit a cigarette. I rolled one of my own; and as soon as it was hanging off my lip, she started in: 'I'll bet that Clare is the sort of woman who wouldn't give Traymoreans a second thought. I'll bet she's elegant and as sharp as a tack. I'll bet she's *au courant* with everything; with fashion wear and foreign affairs and the latest books. Yes? No? Much too wide of the mark?'

'For starters, Clare is no snob. But why her? What's this about Clare?'

'Because,' Eleanor said, a hint of triumph rising in her throat, 'she's the one you're smitten with.'

'Oh really?' I said, exasperated, 'really? And now I suppose I'll get on my charger and gallop to the ends of the earth to save her from infidels. She, and how can I put it, she's a one-man woman, and, Gareth deceased, there won't be another soul mate. And even if there appeared a successful contender, he'd only ever have a small part of her.'

'That's funny,' Eleanor said, her tone of voice dangerous, 'because the picture I have of her, and how I have it I won't tell you, is of a woman who isn't shy when it comes to extracurricular activity. Know what I mean?'

'You're uncanny,' I said, the game up with me, 'and the truth of the matter is unavailable. In deference to you I will allow that I've had my suspicions. Even so, she's a one-man woman.'

'As for that, I'll bet Gareth was quite the skirt-chaser, one in every port.'

My silence betrayed my oldest friend.

'Look,' Eleanor said, 'it's not for me to judge. Frankly, I don't care. It's you I worry about; and if Clare is necessary, well then, she's necessary.'

'I thank you for your concern. But silly you. Necessary for whom? Huge assumption. She's not most on my mind. Nor you, nor Moonface. Not Eggy. Not Dubois. Not any of the people I knew before I knew you. Not McCabe. Not Virgil or Tacitus or Harry S Truman, for that matter. Though here, I'm beginning to get warm. The republic, yes? We're hanging from the trees, twisting in the breezes.'

Eleanor looked a little stunned. A long drag on her cigarette ensued. Her spit valve had magically materialized, and she was rolling it between her thumb and forefinger. I added: 'And you're whistling Dixie through that thing.'

'Calhoun, good sir, this is Canada. Besides, it's nothing new, citizens hanging from trees. An honoured pastime.'

'Well, we're used to it. You on your part of the tree and I on mine—we wave at one another. We talk the talk of lust and Caesar and the price of tea and our snot-nosed love brats; and we pass the salt and freshen up the drinks and maybe make a little money in the marketplace.'

'I think you're blowing wind up your arse, Mr Calhoun. I surely do think that,' my hostess and good neighbour pronounced.

'Besides, like I say, this is Canada,' she added, 'you know, the frozen tundra, True North?'

'Yes, and my arse aside, what a wind,' I said, oblivious to the finer points of geography.

I rolled another cigarette. I drained the last of the amaretto from my glass. I had half-ways vindicated myself in the eyes of Eleanor; and I might have frightened her, who is to say? But I had no idea what I was talking about. Perhaps one may only discern the lineaments of some intangible presence, of an avenging ghoulish god, for instance, by throwing everything and anything at it so as to see what sticks; and listen for the little mewings of recognition. *No, no Moloch here. False alarm.* I had not intended to frighten Eleanor. She was, in any case, a big girl. I had frightened myself so often in recent times that the only spectre I had left with which to frighten myself was my mortality; that, and a few other items not worth the mention. There was the item of Virgil's ninth eclogue, that bucolic ('who'll cast green shadows on the spring?') hinting at the failure of poetry to amount to much in the real world; no happy endings for the shepherds; across the board disillusionment with the program in general.

Calhoun, Lover

It was a shocker—the latest news: Osgoode a sexual predator. I nearly exploded with a guffaw when I heard of it; it was no secret how much I disliked the man. The police had been around to interview Mrs Petrova who had referred them to Eleanor, she who was always in the thick of things. The details of Osgoode's personal history had struck the police as a little vague.

'Well,' Eleanor informed the two community-minded patrolmen, 'it's vague to us, too.'

As for his supposed connections to the Faith Light Church, and, good God, what sort of church was that, this, too, was a mystery; and there had been those women who would congregate in Osgoode's rooms, only that the visitations had ceased fairly early on. The police believed Osgoode was not as devout as he made himself out to be; he simply drifted from cult to cult and preyed on the unsuspecting. He had, apparently, crossed over a line when he shifted his attentions from a mother to her pubescent child. No charges had been laid as of yet, but he was currently being held for questioning. So much for my view of the man as a young Caesar in the making; he was but the filth-infested underbelly of the beast, not the head. A meeting of Traymoreans was convened at the Blue Danube.

'Another blow for Priapus,' said Eggy, relieved to have discovered that the Blue Danube had not, in fact, cancelled its liquor license.

'Our dear Traymore,' said Eleanor, 'is now truly a den of iniquity, what with Marcel and now this. Poor Mrs Petrova. She must think she's rented out to sleaze bags and perverts and worse.'

Eggy, petulant, continued, 'Well, if some woman lets herself believe the Lord God Himself is shagging her, she deserves what she gets.'

'I don't know,' said Dubois, 'the woman is one thing, the child another. Sets my skin crawling.'

I did not know what to say. I supposed I should have pitied Osgoode rather than sit there with my I-told-you-so smirk of satisfaction on my face. Then Eggy turned his indignation on me, saying: 'You, sir, have been awfully quiet. No doubt you have something to say on the matter.'

'Nothing,' I said, 'I've got nothing. I completely misread the man, if you must know.'

'So did I,' interjected Moonface.

'Yes, we all did,' added Eleanor, 'live and learn.'

It was beginning to dawn on us Traymoreans, we innocents in a corrupt and dangerous world, that we would have to face Osgoode in the hall.

'Carry on as normal,' said Dubois.

'More wine,' said Eggy, banging his glass on the table.

'Don't just stand there,' he said to Moonface who was lost in thought; who, in the light of a dreary day, was my muse; and if she had the soul of an accountant, no matter.

'Yes, as normal,' Eleanor said, 'and yes, maybe we should have more wine.'

Moonface went for another bottle.

'In my day,' said Eggy, and then stopped. 'Bloody hell,' he said.

'In your day,' said Dubois, 'and when was that? When they burned witches at the stake?'

'Well yes, in my day, in the town where I grew up, we just sort of worked these things out amongst ourselves. Of course we didn't have police so much as we had a sheriff. He'd just nip things in the bud. When Sniggers got drunk, the sheriff put him in the slammer to sleep it off so he wouldn't go around bothering the women. Hell, my sainted mother was a slut, and she'd go around and bother the men, the sheriff included.'

'Sounds positively idyllic,' drolled Eleanor.

'I guess,' said Dubois, 'there's a line, and the thing is, where is it?'

'Please,' I said, 'don't play the ologist.'

Moonface brought the bottle and, wordlessly, she poured. I could see she was apprehensive. At length she spoke: 'He's going to know we know and it'll be creepy.'

A woman passed by the window of the Blue Danube, her bag stuffed with rolls of bright Christmas ribbon. I numbed myself with the thought that it was already that time of year. I recalled how Jack Swain, back in a seemingly simpler time, used to convene his friends in his apartment on Christmas Day, hand each a towel, measure out generous portions of mulled wine in mugs, and turn the TV on to *A Christmas Carol* and instruct us to drink and weep. An afternoon of Dickens and Che Guevara. Yes, back when we could still pretend we believed in America. I said, playing the reason card: 'Obviously the man did something that was not good, but it doesn't necessarily mean he'll be locked away. You know, they'll just feed him drugs.'

'Come on,' snapped Eleanor, 'you don't really believe that.'

'You're right,' I answered, 'I don't. He's a shining head. But Bob's right: we carry on as usual. It's not a medieval village we're living in. The ologists built this world, so let them play cat and mouse with their lab rat. No doubt they'll pounce on him when it suits them.'

Eleanor went out to smoke a cigarette. Eggy fumed, his fingers pinching the stem of his wine glass. If the world was utterly strange to me, imagine what it was for Eggy, this sparrow of a man, one who had come to maturity in a simpler time when the innards of a car were comprehensible and for all that his sainted mother had been a slut. He would have had a lot of fun cracking jokes at Freud's expense. To do so now would only date him in some hopeless way. Or there was this old saw: you get the president you deserve. Or if one out of every five men and women on the street were ologists of one kind or another, then what did that say for the rest of us? It was one thing to say we have our demons; it was another that we were phenoms, every man jack, woman and child, the world in its entirety a laboratory. What next? That I would come across Osgoode in the hall standing over Moonface, she on her knees praying; he going on about his Christian duty to get rich and she service his sacred hard-on? A morbid thought, to be sure. I disliked myself for thinking it. If there was such a quality as innocence in the world, it was, as the poets had always said, a lovely thing but oh so accessible. I was more certain than ever we were not moral creatures, not even we Traymoreans. Yes, we could make ourselves disappear, according to a certain theory of physics, simply by the way we were poking around in our minds so as to satisfy a so-called thirst for knowledge; ah, the thing observed and measured. There was no metric system for perversity. Eleanor threw her cigarette on the sidewalk, re-entered the Blue Danube and looked out of sorts.

'Come on, Bob,' she said to Dubois, 'I've had enough of this.'

What had she enough of? Panic was settling in me. There was a new edge to her voice, admixture of dread, rage and sheer indifference. It was as if she had wearied of seeing the world through my eyes, but that were I to see it through her eyes, the spectacle would bore me. Here was the nub of culture wars, the good Traymorean days at an end, a blip of unreality all along.

'So soon?' said Eggy, 'we were only getting started. Bloody hell.'

In Kamarouska a kiss and a thought for Algonquins.

'Anyway, what's with everyone?' Eggy asked.

The party was indeed breaking up. I said I would look after Eggy. Eleanor and Dubois departed. Soon after, Melody arrived to take over from Moonface. A few Slavs drifted in.

'Just leave me here,' said Eggy, 'I'll be alright.'

Moonface and I stole away.

We walked a little and shivered a little; we stared up at leafless maples in a park, trunks, branches, twigs more and more visible in the evening light of approaching winter. I turned down the collar of Moonface's coat and kissed her on the cheek. She did not protest.

'How about pizza?' she said.

I fiddled now with the rolling of a cigarette, my fingers cold.

'Sure,' I said, 'pizza.'

And as it turned out, we had not much to say. We sat in a place called Pepe's, listened to grinding and energetic music; and what was it for, to enable our digestive tracts? It was a smothering smell, the smell of baking pizza dough. We watched a young crowd; we ate and drank. Finally, Moonface asked: 'Do you worry about Eggy? He's getting so old. He drinks so much. One of his eyes is beginning to droop. He's shakier and shakier on his feet. I've gotten so fond of him even if he's such a bother at times, and he's always groping me, and, well, you know.'

'Look, I worry, too. But he is what he is. He's much too old to change. He's simply saving us the trouble of a wake. He's having it now while he can enjoy it and he's the star attraction. It could be so much worse. He's the last of those who, with a little luck and a little help, got somewhere, read a few books, had a few thoughts, and certainly had more to say about life than knuckle draggers and ranting evangelists.'

'You make him sound so ordinary.'

'He is ordinary, as much so as are we, shepherds about to lose the farm. Osgoode's ordinary, too, but who wants that sort of ordinary? Or maybe I'm wrong, and Eggy is not as ordinary as all that. And maybe we aren't either, given the crowd in here.'

'I know. I'm sorry.'

'What's to apologize for? You can't escape it. Always louts or arty pretenders or money men—what happened to people just being people?'

'You're a snob. These people are just people.'

'Of course I'm a snob,' I said, 'Self-defence. In any case, you'll get married and have kids. Or maybe you'll write poems. Or maybe you'll teach the classics to those who couldn't care less. Or all of the above.'

'Maybe,' said Moonface, her cheeks bright from the heat of the restaurant and the effects of the wine.

For singers heavy is the shade.

We might have become lovers, she and I, were I much younger and not so soured on things.

Calhoun Jealous

After closing time in the Blue Danube, to the light of a candle, Moonface read a letter. She had extricated it from an envelope opened earlier in the day. I may as well not have been there. Her lashes nearly brushed her cheeks as she read. Her lips were parted, I was sorry to note. She held the missive between both hands, elbows tucked in at the sides. It seemed she hardly breathed even as she lived only for the words some lover boy had spirited in her direction. Clearly, these were words that spoke directly to her of intimacies and declarations. Had I not written words that were spoken directly to her? I had failed, I supposed, to effect this transformation of her face. I looked for somewhere to be in the candle-lit wine. Had Dante punished Francesca because she loved not him but Paolo? How awfully tiny—those ears of Moonface, her hair bound in a ponytail. Someone banged on the glass door wanting admission. I waved off a trio of drunken Slavs who looked to get nasty. They lurched across the street to the doughnut shop, one of them grousing at the night sky. He flipped a motorist the finger. I drank some wine. By the time its burn hit my stomach, I had done the entire circuit of jealousy; been to every part of her body and come away at a loss. I attempted banter, saying: 'That's some letter you're reading.'

She looked at me with loving eyes but the fact of my presence did not register. She helped herself to my wine.

I distracted myself with Eggy's mention of No Gun Ri. I assumed that whatever happened there had been awful. I looked around the small café and was lost in a vast expanse of space that bore down on a single point of flame, Moonface pure concentration in its light. I tried another ploy: I was a poet in the receipt of a gift. And the gift was Moonface so thoroughly rapt by a sequence of words. She looked my way again with those love-conquered eyes. It was getting comic now—this situation, I some Cyrano without a chance. She had come to the end of the words and would now need to decompress.

'I'm sorry. You said something?'

'It was nothing.'

She folded the letter along its creases. She reinserted it in the envelope. She held it a while in her hands which rested now on her lap, her eyes closed. Then she rose.

'Finish up,' she said, sliding the wine glass back to me.

Calhoun the Gladiator

The lone prair*ee* demanded improvisational skills. I was Virgil charged with reading Caesar's face. How read what flickers in the shallows of human eyes? How many cockatoos were screeching in the halls of the Pentagon? Ask me to write an essay on the intricacies of the game of football, and I would make my excuses, pointing out that I was dreamy when a child, uncoachable. Had been a prodigy of sorts. Even so, I-formations, slant-six Dodges—it was all a nonsensical jumble to me. Civilization is always turning a corner. The coach is always saying: 'Douche-bags. Well, don't be afraid to wash your willies when in the showers.'

How does one say farcical in Farsi?

It has taken me all my life to atone for catching a ball and playing the hero. It would take me all day and most likely a good bit of wine to pay my debt to literature, the apology I owed it. Would Moonface have on her game face, one of these days, or Eggy's ticker go bust? Would the President give an order and all hell break loose?

The Supreme Folly

We crossed the hall to Eggy's rooms, Moonface and I. A matter of a few steps, the crossing over seemed almost biblical, all physical and human laws up for grabs as time and space succeeded time and space. But he was to be caught up to speed with things Calhoun and Moonface; how we had wine in the Blue Danube after the movie we went to see; how we argued Rampling's state of mind in *The Night Porter*. Had she in fact exercised free will, electing to strike up again with her old concentration camp tormentor? Or had she been so messed over by him, as it were, that she was ever his Eliza Doolittle? Was there a more delicate way of stating cases? For all that, Moonface, so far as I could determine, had no idea what she had just seen. She paraphrased Virgil to me: 'The banks of the Mincius. Reeds. Bees. Oaks.'

Eggy was jealous of our intake of wine; he had passed the evening disgustingly sober. Come morning, I accorded it an honour that Moonface knocked on my door before knocking on his, she having passed a guilty night on account of divided loyalties. To have spent the evening with me meant standing up one of her boyfriends. There was a new development on the street: someone had moved into the rooms above the café. He was blind and was, apparently, a member of the city orchestra, packing a violin. After the evening's concert, he decided to sample the food in the Blue Danube. He was a miserable hose bag, bearded and grey; and he sat there a few tables over, complaining about the smell of cigarette smoke on everybody. He had the face of one who had flown up a horse's arse and had encountered the Golden Age. Irritated, I had, at length, invited him to eat elsewhere—in an ology ward, a padded cell. I was getting up steam when Moonface shushed me.

'Why?' I asked her.

'If everything's pointless, why not let him have his innings?'

'He'd beat his wife if he had one. I don't care how well he saws away.'

I put it all down to evolutionary drift, how we had been hanging around the Blue Danube, Moonface and I, with a few Slavs and a blind musician who was an avatar. *Was ich mir den wünschen sollte, eine gute oder schlechte Zeit?* Or had the musician performed that evening a little something more seemly from Mendelssohn?

'Well,' said Eggy, 'now that we've established you two spent the night at the movies and then got drunk, to what else do I owe the pleasure? My intelligence? My matinee looks?'

He patted his lap but Moonface was having none of his lap. He said to her: 'If you're going to deny me your charms, missie, away with you two. I sit here remembering the cold, red hands of My Fair Lady and the night we spent by the St Lawrence. That's all that's left to me.'

Moonface was about to plant a parting kiss on Eggy's brow when in breezed Eleanor singing: 'It's my party and I'll come if I want—'

She was in a loose robe, wearing her mules. She was in a mood, her curls freshly frosted. She held in her left hand a cigarette, her right hand gesturing at the side of her temple that either she, or someone she had yet to name, was beyond the pale.

'Dubois. Need I say more?'

'What now?' I asked.

'I asked him to move in with me and he won't. He said everything was fine, why change things? I want a real relationship. "What's a real relationship?" you might well ask. You know, I don't know. Maybe that's why I'm upset. He comes over in time for his favourite public affairs TV show. We watch BBC news and then it's to bed, unless he goes off to his bed. In the morning, he's gone, and I have no idea where he gets to. What if he's got a little something stashed away in another part of town? Do you think I care? You can bet your bottom dollar I care.'

'Stuff and nonsense,' Eggy interrupted her, 'seems to me you come and go as you please. There are no *real* relationships. There are only relationships.'

What, was Eggy getting ological in his old age?

'Some relationships are better than others,' said Eleanor.

'To be sure. There was an old fart of Ischia whose conduct grew friskier and friskier.'

'Oh fart yourself,' said Eleanor, dangerously annoyed. Then, on the turn of a dime, her countenance softening, she said: 'I suppose I'm greedy. It's always been my problem. Bob has never mistreated me.'

'He's a prince among men,' Eggy chimed.

Moonface had no opinion.

'Well,' I said, 'I'm sure Bob loves you. You're made for one another, both of you as vain as Siamese cats.'

'Vain?' said Eleanor, 'as in vanity? Sure, my guy's handsome. Wouldn't have it any other way.' And then, indicating me: 'And you don't know what you're missing.'

Moonface blushed as Eleanor patted her hips and shimmied off. Eggy called out: 'You can sit on my lap anytime. Problem is, you'd squash me.'

Eleanor, apparently, did not hear this spate of bonhomie.

Later—and it should not have surprised me but it did somehow—the gang was all there: Eggy, Dubois and Eleanor R at table in the Blue Danube. Slavs defended their turf. Blind Musician was in a corner, grey, grizzled and unsympathetic. One could only hope that the Slavs would, perhaps, eventually prove too much for him. Moonface circulated about, bringing food and drink to the various parties. Gaetan Szabo sat next to a blonde, she wriggly, smart, and clearly enjoying herself. They were both outfitted in leather, he craggy-headed, half-Hungarian, maker of erotic verses; inordinately proud of the fact he employed the noun cunny as an action verb. He was as astonished as I at this chance meeting. The blonde wondered if I was important.

'So, Calhoun.'

A shock of white hair tinged with rust was making a last stand on Szabo's pate. The smile on his lips had long since succeeded in gutting sincerity while preserving its carcass.

'It's been a while. This is Lise. Lise, that there is Calhoun, a man of some talent and a serious fool. Me, I've been busy. Writing books. Lots of books. I've been otherwise entertaining myself. She blows me within an inch of my life and then reads *The New Yorker.* Do you think I can cure her of liberal bias? I'm all for bombing Iran, you know. May as well get that straight at the outset. Like I said, you're a somewhat talented man with an instinct or two but you fail to get the big picture.'

'That's what I always tell him,' crowed Eggy.

'It's what we tell him,' other Traymoreans echoed.

Blind Musician was startled out of his lonely peevishness; Slavs went silent a moment and then decided we were all of us children. Had Szabo taken on the apocalypse as his mistress since I had last seen him? An argument was in the offing and it was going to be futile. Dubois did not know that it was going to be futile; and I did not try to prevent him from joining battle. He addressed the stranger: 'Are you serious?'

'Of course, I'm serious except when I'm not. Which is to say I pursue certain frivolities, though I'm serious when I pursue women.'

Dubois was unimpressed, his eyes glittering. Perhaps just now he was beginning to realize that his interlocutor was not the kind of man to cave to superior logic.

'But bomb Iran?' Dubois asked.

'Either that or appease.'

'Appease?' Dubois repeated. 'Appease?' he said once more, as if appease were a word he could not get his thoughts around.

'The rain in Spain,' said Eggy, 'and they're off.'

Once in a while Eggy was quite capable of serious intellectual engagement; evidently, he figured this was not to be one of those times.

Wariness grabbed hold of Eleanor's eyes. Moonface stayed out of it. She had no opinions about anything. Szabo said: 'It's going to happen.'

He may as well have said that Caesar would cross the Rubicon.

Dubois asked, 'And how do you know?'

Szabo answered, 'I have sources.'

Eleanor was no stranger to 'sources; she had had a few in her time. Accordingly, her wariness increased. I wondered what Gareth Howard, my oldest friend, would have made of Szabo's assertion. He had had a few sources, as well, oh yes, in his time. I was quite prepared to ridicule this notion of sources; I bit my tongue. Szabo had written some interesting verse; it could not have been an accident. Then again …

'And what do you do?' Eleanor asked of the man, as if she had not already guessed.

And the man, in answer, put up quite an unnecessary show of false modesty. It was his way of saying Eleanor was a nobody, dismissible.

'Are you or aren't you a poet?' Eleanor asked again.

She may as well have asked whether Szabo was a monkey.

Sadly, I concluded the man was hanging from a tree, too, as we all were; but it was quite another tree from which Szabo was suspended, as he was reputed to be very rich. Obviously, his mistress, this Lise with the Cheshire grin and blinking eyes, had no idea that Szabo pitied us. Had Dostoyevsky written us a mad scene? Would I lunge for Moonface's bum? Eggy's silence was due to the fact he had fallen asleep. One of the Slavs, a regular, as he passed by to go out for a smoke, tenderly patted Eggy's shoulder as if caressing a shrine. That little gesture was a breath of fresh air. I was going to break up into little pieces inside and each of those pieces was going to guffaw. *Surgamus: solet esse grauis cantantibus umbra.* Blind Musician, my arse. Indeed, heavy is the shade.

One Last Kick at the Can

'What turns men into clowns?' I asked Eleanor R.

She wasted no time in letting me know: 'Sex, power, over-estimation of prowess. Ask me another.'

She was about to slide a baking tin into her oven. Oatmeal muffins of carrot slivers and raisins.

'Bob's new favourite,' she said in a tone of voice that ought to explain everything and set the restless mind at rest. So I ventured another query: 'Why is there such a plethora of clowns, these days? They give me a bad name. Who could be so envious of my lot they'd speak power to truth and deny that western civilization wasn't cracking up?'

'You lost me there,' Eleanor said, 'but I suspect you allude to your friend, that one with the exotic name.'

'Friend? Don't know about that. I suppose we've been standing pat in some sort of collegial formation but I'm sure he thinks me an idiot. It's perhaps my salvation.'

Eleanor in her pompadours and a light dress began cleaning up her kitchen. She was got up for spring and here it was winter. Flour and raisins went back in the cupboard; carrots back in the fridge; bowls and cups and mixing spoon in the sink. Now she swept at the floor with a few brisk flourishes of a broom, a frosted curl spilling across her forehead. The kitchen's warmth was a bit oppressive.

'I'll leave the dishes for later,' she let me know, and she plopped down on a chair and reached for a cigarette.

She would eventually answer all my questions, the wherewithal for it not so much in what she had to think or say, but in her eyes. It was the look that said that while I was a man she was a woman; and there it was, all either of us needed to know; she exempt from certain torturous processes of logic that would have me tied in knots.

'You know,' she said, 'the way he went on about his flavour of the month and how love orders his existence, well, one could smile if it all didn't smack of Health and Education and Holy Water.'

'There is that. There is that.'

'Now if Bob were to start fooling around, I'd thrash him senseless. But what would sign his death warrant would be some smarmy hypocrisy on his part. If you're going to be bad, well then, be bad. If you're going to play the patriarch, play it to the hilt; but don't use women to help you pretend to what you can't possibly be on your own cognizance.'

'Amen,' I said, somewhat glibly, 'but he's rich enough to afford his own set of rules.'

Eleanor gave me a look.

Even so, I could have kissed her; and not because she had brought me any clarity of mind; she had not. What turns a poet into a thug? The only grandiloquence I could claim was that I fought battles in an arena much sterner and lethal than that of mere politics and penthouse lust. Its ruins were more ruined, its dead more dead, its moonlight more stark. But why had not Eleanor brought out the amaretto and we really get down to cases?

I left Eleanor R to her muffins and trombone, to the management of her bed partner and "Stardust". I knocked on Eggy's door; he bade me come in. And he, a sprite of a man in his vast armchair, took one look at me and said: 'Hell's bells, Calhoun, I've got no answers.'

He sounded rather querulous.

Even so, he continued, 'You're a lover, not a warrior, and even at that, I daresay you're not much of a champ in the sack. Hoo hoo. Sorry, old man, but life's short, especially for me, and well, I've watched you trot about these parts playing the poet. I'm not much impressed. Can you say, "Sing, muse, of arms and the man"—all that rot? Can you even manage, "Beautiful soup so rich and green, waiting in a hot tureen"? No, I thought not. Have you plunged your hot shaft in the Moonface estuary? No, you haven't the nerve. Effing scruples. You male German feminista. Men like you drive me to drink. Causes me to question God's grand purpose. When you don't propose, women can't dispose. Now be gone with you. I'm going to stay indoors and drink myself insensible. Send Moonface over should you see her. I at least know what to do with her though my wacky willie is out to lunch.'

I left Eggy to his own devices, which were considerable, for all that his mind was a shrivelled bean and his body decrepit. There were bodies hanging in trees. We were not moral creatures, loneliness the engine that powered our urges and our betrayal of them.

Sally McCabe

Sally McCabe, long absent from my thoughts, began putting in appearances again. I would be in one of my funks, lying on the couch, listening to music.

'Hello, Randall, long time no see. Nice little set-up you've got here. Good people. Good talk. And that Moonface—she's such a sweetie. Why haven't you dinged her yet? What are you saving it for? You're not so old as all that.'

Or she would say: 'Who, me? Don't blame me for the country's parlous state. I did what I could. Think Mars would've been anything other than a brute if Venus hadn't worked her charms? You know the story. Think I liked the boys drooling on my tits? I thought you all perfectly ridiculous with your football. The coach was a nasty piece of work but I scared him right off. So you're a poet now. How things turn out. Are you going to write me something? Aren't I worth a line or two? The blood used to drain from your face when you saw me, you so precious and cute.'

Or she would really turn on the charm, saying: 'Randall, why do you mourn? Can't you hear the wind in the tumbleweeds? Can't you hear the moon swoon with her lust for kisses? Hear Gene Pitney on the radio of the Chrysler car? Falsetto voices? Wet knickers? Why can't you? Nothing's changed. It's all there still, you, me, Coop, Thompson and the sheep-fuckers. Even now Mr Jakes the history teacher is blowing out his sweet brains. All for us. So that history won't bother us. Isn't he nice?'

Fantasia on Greensleeves died away in the ghetto-blaster.

Afternoon Kiss

All animals dream, even mice. I said as much to Eleanor in her kitchen, but she ignored this declaration of fact.

'Here's something about Bob I'll bet you don't know,' she said, seductive, proudly so.

'I'm sure there's much about him I don't know.'

'He wrote his thesis on Camus. The money world came later,' she stated.

Did seals snuggle beach balls and starlets giggle? Camus and beaches and girls and killing Nazis in a spirit of good, clean fun—it was Dubois 'to a T'. Then Eleanor had other ideas: 'I want to get out of here. Bob and I, we could move to the country, be man and wife, put in a garden, keep deer meat in a freezer, cozy up on cold nights. I grew up out there. In a town so small it was barely a village.'

'What will you do for conversation? How cut a figure? Difficult to see you in high heels, what with corn stubble and wind-hardened snow.'

'We'll have each other. We can always find new friends. You can come and visit, and Eggy, and what the hell, I'll even put up with Moonface.'

I shrugged. I was through and through an urban dweller, though I had spent time, in the long, distant past, with Gareth Howard, my oldest friend, in his Townshipper's shack; weekends devoted to drink; to kicking around political and literary footballs.

'Then again I don't think I could get Bob to go for it. I've lived in this city for most of my adult life. I'll likely die in it. The Traymore is sanctuary, Mrs Petrova our guardian angel. Eggy assures me she has a son and he's met him and he's not a bad sort. He wouldn't just toss us out on the street after she dies or can't keep up with things anymore.'

'Good to hear.'

And it was good to hear that Dubois was perhaps so much more the renaissance man than I could ever be. Even so, I rose from my chair and draped an arm around Eleanor; I bent and kissed her on the cheek. Two shadows commingled with astonishing force. She turned her face to me; her eyes swept mine, her mouth asking for its due. I responded with what I hoped was an admirer's due, but one that said she was in her skin and I in mine; that we were but fellow travellers on a road, our fates separate. Sometimes it is verity: the body, not the mind, decides, for better or worse. And she recovered, telling me to get lost; a palpable hint of contempt in her voice. You cannot promise a woman something and then point out that, in actual fact, no such promise ever existed.

So yes, I was less than a satisfying whole on so many fronts. If woman completes man, I was an abandoned building site. I took away from a few semesters of post-secondary futility an incipient distrust of ologists. God was the sum of all we did not know, or so Jack Swain used to declare. Reason had its limits, religion no apology for the blunting of critical faculties. Both reason and religion were delinquent mortgages in respect to the house of the soul; and yet, things had come to such a pass that a poet could not claim poetry as a defense of that house.

'No soul, no redemption,' I would say to myself as I drolly regarded my visage in the bathroom mirror and wondered if it was worth the bother to shave.

Lollapaloozas

Canadians, phantasmagoricals, blinded by their relatively benign history, subscribed to the notion that humankind was perfectible. If the good were known, no one would do bad. It touted a shining collectivity that had not been tested by such thorough-going evils as had beset and were besetting other collectivities. Ethnic cleansings. Genocides. The sorry histories of achieving GNP. We were in the Blue Danube—Dubois, Eggy, and I—going on about foreign affairs in a feckless fashion when a voice from another table piped up. It said: 'Pakistan was already such a mess that the Yanks couldn't have made things any worse over there.'

It may have been an accurate observation, but it was, as a statement, untenable, and I thought it was designed to get the White House off the hook for its blunders. The voice belonged to one Edward Sanders who was short in stature, barrel-chested and beetle-browed. He looked serious. He had just done two big things in his life: he had retired early and had just purchased half of the duplex immediately behind the Traymore. We invited him over to our table, and then, to take some of the sting out of his insufferable gravitas, he said: 'Some of my friends, those I have left, in deference to my phlegmatic nature, call me Fast Eddy.'

Other details of his personal history followed. He was diabetic. He was old-school conservative, leaning toward the British wing of that particular view of observable facts. He had no love of either Ottawa or Washington. He had acquired, he said, a modest but adequate enough nest egg, this from his involvement with a software company. That, and the money he received from selling his father's house on the other side of town. He had come of age in love with late-night radio stations. Rhythm and blues. Bob Dylan. Dylan, after all, was a conservative, and if the Republicans, the party of Lincoln, had been wiser, they would not have let the Democrats outflank them on civil rights and social justice. And so forth and so on. Fast Eddy was a man after Eggy's own heart. Dubois was charmed. Moonface had no opinion.

Another newcomer on the scene was a skyscraper of a poet. If ever a poet deserved to be called by the name of Longfellow, this man was it. *Too Tall Poet.* As it was, he went by the rather nondescript appellation of Joe Smithers. Smithers came to us in much the same way as had Fast Eddy. Only this time, I had been the Blue Danube's only customer when in he loped, involuntarily ducking his head as he came through the door. He ordered a coffee from Melody and profusely thanked her. She gave me a look and then left Smithers to his own devices. I was at that moment scribbling something in my notebook. His giggles had far to travel from diaphragm via long neck to a mouth of irregularly spaced teeth.

'Are you an author?'

Well, I waved the man over. He was an instructor at a small college on the outskirts of the city. He had no love of his students. He paid next to no attention to politics. He had just moved into the area and would, in a few years, get out of the pedagogical game. He was embittered. The only view that women had of men was that men were always undergoing a mid-life crisis. This caused men to write books that women found specious. But when women wrote books pertaining to their mid-life debacles it was a literary miracle. I assured Smithers I was writing neither poem nor novel nor any other recognized futility. I was only scribbling. Scribbling was a form of therapy. My mid-life crisis had stemmed from the cradle and would, no doubt, accompany me to the grave. Smithers did not seem satisfied with my response.

Life could turn on a dime but decline and fall was agonizingly slow; so much so, that man, woman and child might live life according to principles of pleasure and not be inconvenienced by a debased constitution and a devalued currency and the gutting of the military. Such was Rome. I knew little of the Ottoman Empire in its disrepair but could it have been much different than the city of Baltimore in its decay? If the world was drifting backwards in time; if Russia was returning, via the ghost of the Soviet Union, to its byzantine beginnings; if China was reverting to its old imperial self; if India was going I did not know where, to what was America falling back on? Cotton Mather? The Philadelphia Congress? The charge up

San Juan Hill? Hearst in his castle? Who was it who claimed to have seen *Citizen Kane* a hundred times? Was he a nutter or was he prescient? Would Eggy ever see the Moonface bosom? Now there, there was a question, and perhaps, as far as moments go of transient and bittersweet epiphany, it was the most compelling question that the mind in crisis could devise.

'Oh,' Eggy said when I came to see him of an afternoon and run the gist of some of those aforementioned thoughts by him, 'I don't know. I suppose Moonface has got to go to Ottawa to advance her education. It's not as if Latin is dead in Montreal. She'll be hazing the boys soon enough. The Latinity of Stiffus Prickus and all that.'

Once more I had my heart in my hands as I left him there, more diminutive than ever in his overstuffed chair.

Fast Eddy's Guard

Politicians were speaking of moral tests. Silly buggers, did they not realize we were not moral creatures? In any case, Fast Eddy was now an intimate to Traymoreans, how he viewed us hard to read. Either we were all besotted drunks without substance or moral utility, or we were a lifeline of sorts, an antidote to his new dilemma: that in his retirement he did not know what to do with himself. He eschewed drink. It was his diabetes, so he said. Smithers would come around infrequently, and when he did show, it was to seek me out. I had become a project of sorts to him, a cynic to rehabilitate. The truth is, he was worse off than I in that department, only he could not see it; he could not believe he was the bitterest gall I had ever seen packed in a 6 foot 6 inch frame. Besides, he was shy.

It was not money that made the world go round; it was filthy money, that and the courtly ceremonies of ego. Iraq was the nuptials, the briefest of honeymoons, the wedded turmoil, the cruelties of divorce. Some believed it the whirligig of decline and fall. Some believed it the capstone of decades of maladministration and paths of least resistance, quick fixes rewarding an ever exclusive élite, the pyramid's uppermost tip, at the expense of the widening base. I was not a political thinker, just a man cursed with the gift of worry. I was a cautious sort, closet-conservative continually amazed by human audacity. I would tire of my petty consciousness and seek refuge in music. Even music, glorious music sometimes staled; and I could not hear in it the voice of God, just men and women lurching from measure to measure. Or I would hear the acid tongue of Tacitus, a man who was perhaps blind to himself but absolutely wide-eyed when it came to the hypocrisies of Caesars and senate and the Roman peace. I would walk over to the Blue Danube, a penitent, a clown in sackcloth looking for absolution. Eggy and Dubois might distract me, working their comedic routines against a backdrop of decline and fall. A table of Slavs might show what humanity looked like when stripped clean of illusions. Exit illusions; enter materialisms of a rather basic sort: a man entranced by his musical cell phone, a hairy-lipped old battleaxe appraising bootleg lingerie as the *summum bonum* of civilized life. I figured Moonface was hitting her books, so I left her alone. And just when one was beginning to get smug in the belief one had seen everything, well ... back from the Blue Danube, no absolution anywhere, and I am climbing the Traymore stairs. You would think they would have heard me, Moonface and a strange young man in a kind of clinch. Moonface's back was to the wall just to the side of her door, his hand on her crotch making claims, she not entirely displeased. The look I got from her hailed from a distant planet of superior beings. The young man, suppressing a scowl, attempted to grin. I shrugged and entered my apartment.

Melody brought beer to a table of quarrelsome Slavs. Noble scavengers. The nobility of animals lay in their lack of hypocrisy and pretence; otherwise, I refused to ennoble nature just so sedentary liberals as well as those somewhat more active could know feel-good moments. Eggy said: 'Ah, Mr Calhoun.'

'Evening, gents.'

Had I entered a saloon, desperadoes twirling the ends of their moustaches? How could it have been otherwise, Dubois saying: 'We've been discussing escapades of a sexual nature.'

'Such as when,' said Eggy, 'such as when, one night in Philadelphia, I met up with this tart and she ... oh ... oh bloody hell. It was the missile crisis. She thought we were all going to die. Hoo hoo.'

But if Dubois expected a recollection more X-rated, he was disappointed.

Melody, in the meantime, had approached the table. I indicated I wanted wine. As Dubois gave Eggy the gears for being a goof, she stood at my side, hand on my shoulder, the pressure her fingertips applied suggestive. It was certainly proprietary. I shifted in my chair, evincing my unease with this state of affairs.

Dubois saw what was happening and was amused. Eggy had not as yet succeeded in getting a date with Melody, and he reminded her of this. And she, not one to overplay a losing hand, at last got the hint I was attempting to kinetically transmit her way; and she went and got me wine. But I glimpsed her face just before she turned around to act on her appointed task; it was coarse, confident, optimistic, that face. She was a woman who, in her own mind, could do no wrong.

It was going to be tragic, I figured: Melody, though she was no beauty, still had charms that turned the heads of men. She would settle for some lout, live in a trailer with a pack of brats. The privileged at the top of the pyramid would feel vindicated in their snobbery. Liberals would at last accept the fact she had not a shred in her of transcendent talent. Should she elude the marriage from hell, she was perfect managerial material at a rather petty threshold of the capitalist way of 'getting it done'. I certainly did not wish to sleep with her; and, come to think of it, I had more than likely misread her gesture. It had perhaps more to do with a management seminar than with an invitation to sex. So that when Fast Eddy, barrel-chested and beetle-browed, with a look in his eyes that suggested good will to all good men, put in an appearance, I was in a pernicious frame of mind. We were crowded at our small table, so he sat at one immediately adjacent and leaned forward. Melody, without inquiring, brought him his usual soft drink.

'Gentlemen,' he said, 'I see you're well in your cups. I tremble for my sanity.'

'The rain in Spain,' said Eggy in comradely response.

'I know just the thing for you,' I said to Fast Eddy, 'I think I have what you need.'

'Oh?'

Fast Eddy's guard was going up.

It had become apparent to us that the man was lonely; that he was thinking he was long past the point where women might find him attractive. He had confessed to having had the odd affair or two in his adult life. They had not amounted to much. Now that he was retired he could no longer distract himself with work and other expedients; he was painfully cognizant of the fact he was an unhappy bachelor. I motioned Melody over. I said: 'Here he is, the man of your dreams. Footloose, fancy free. Financially solvent.'

There was no accounting for it, that she actually took the trouble to size Fast Eddy up, now that she saw him in a new light. Dubois gave me a look of warning, that I should not push it; but he was otherwise amused. Melody tactfully smiled, playing along with a harmless prank. Fast Eddy sniffed, his gravitas kicking in. He was not an aggressive creature. He did not like the aggression of others. He had assumed we were all free of those sorts of games by which people bully one another. His beetling brows knitted together. A flicker of hatred. Then, the only honourable way out, he accepted he had been briefly the butt of a joke. I was not yet drunk, and instantly I was ashamed. Fast Eddy said, looking straight at Melody: 'I'm afraid you'd find me somewhat out of practice.'

By the time I got back to my digs, I was decidedly drunk. My little stunt—ill-conceived urge to humiliate Fast Eddy—was tantamount to full-blown moral disintegration on my part. I switched on the TV. BBC was at pains to explain the world. I switched the TV off. I slid Schubert into the ghetto-blaster. *The Trout Quintet*. Fish rippled in a purling brook. It only served to reinforce my sense that the world, as an entity, was out of step with itself and I with it. I waited for someone to knock on my door, Moonface, even Eleanor. No one knocked. No one arrived to restore me to my humanity; to elicit my sympathies; to pick my brains about Nixon or Domitian; to mark time; to snuggle and laugh. In another life, women sometimes looked me up, and in the darkness of whatever room I happened to inhabit, they would caress me as I caressed them; and it was all profound and silent and beautiful, or so it seemed in retrospect; moonlight in the window, music in the speakers, fingers erotically charged. McCabe drifted into view, her smile cruel and unfathomably wise.

'Your questions have no answers, and even if they had, you don't want to know,' her laughing eyes seemed to say.

I thought I heard Mrs Petrova in her yard, raking leaves, and at a very late hour. If so, she was a peasant warding off evil when all else had failed, her talismans being her wristwatches and timepieces, her bins of jewellery and other ornaments. In her world, the debate regarding the matter of habeas corpus was not of the greatest importance; evil had much bigger fish to fry.

A Whole Lot of Concept

Moonface did not bother to knock; she walked right in, saying: 'I hear from Eggy you really tied one on. He said you were funny, trying to match-make Fast Eddy with Melody.'

'I was cruel to him,' I said, stating a fact.

'Were you?'

Her eyes were dubious. She spoke of the young man with whom I had seen her in the hall.

'I've taken up with my old boyfriend again. Well, I guess you saw that for yourself. Rick was before your time, before you moved in. Before James. He's a songwriter, plays the guitar.'

'Peachy.'

'He's good. He's interested in poetry. He wants to meet you.'

'Can't imagine why.'

Suddenly, I was the stern, unbending patriarch: 'What about school? Your studies? Virgil? The serious life? I suppose this guy thinks he'll be at the top of the charts any day now.'

'He's not like that. He's serious but laid back. He likes hearing about Virgil.'

'Virgil?'

Moonface would see me later when I was in a better mood.

'Laid back,' I said as she went out the door, 'a whole lot of concept signifying nothing.'

A Poet Matters

Eleanor, washing dishes, did not know if dreams could reflect on waking life. Then she wiped her hands dry with the apron she wore. The look in her eyes suggested she knew I had quarrelled with Moonface. She crossed to the table in her pompadours and reached for a cigarette.

'Settle down, Randall. Rick's a nice fellow. He was hurt when Moonface dropped him. I'm surprised he'd have her back. But then I'm not surprised. I have my problems with the girl but, at bottom, she's decent and means well. I guess I was a little jealous. Jealous of her youth, you know. And you, sir, you're jealous, too, and you're not man enough to admit it. You've always had the hots for her. Not that you should act on it and not that she, heaven forbid, should be silly enough to let it happen. I know, I know, I said once that nature has broad shoulders and a winking eye, and what harm could come of it? Have you slept with her? I hope not. Anyway, everything else aside, the timing's wrong. As gently and considerately as you might treat her, you're just too much the pessimist now for her mental health. You're even too much for me, and God knows, I take a pretty dim view of what's happening around us. Be that as it may, decline and fall is for the chosen few. The rest of us peons—there's nothing for us but to get on with it; with our living and our dying and our bumbling along. Ain't no one gonna to do a whole lot for us. Excuse my French. So yes, woman that I am, I changed my mind. And if nature intended Moonface to come to grief with a rogue, better it's a young rogue, one laid back, to boot. He'll sing her a pretty song and she'll love it. You seem to think you've no chance with Clare, and seeing as you're intelligent and wise to yourself (for all that you're a dummy), probably you're right. So get over it. I think you've got things to do. Weren't you going to write a book? Bob bet me you didn't have it in you. I took up his wager. You going to prove me wrong?'

At Eggy's, I brought up the matter of Rick. Eggy said: 'Well, a girl's got to get it from somewhere. Us old geezers can't do her any good.'

And when I next saw Moonface, and it was that afternoon in the Blue Danube, she was being jocular with a pair of Slavs; she viewed me, instead, with suspicion.

I was alone in the Blue Danube with Moonface and contemptuous Slavs. I reflected on this and that. Thought had not altered reality; it had not even served as prelude to idea, to the form and substance of such an item. With an idea one tilted at the world and the world tilted back; and the dance was comedic, farcical or tragic or all of the above. *I was dancing with my darling…* The pedagogue in me was on a tear, the afternoon bright, of eternal autumnal promise. Moonface played around with a derby hat, one left behind unaccountably; and she was doing a fair imitation of Dietrich, vexingly sexual. The eyes of the Slav men glittered.

In walked Joe Smithers, a real pedagogue stooping at the door as he strode through. It seemed Smithers had won a prize. He entered a poetry contest on the theme of thanksgiving; he submitted what he regarded as a spoof; and surprise surprise (so Smithers blushingly put it), the poem seemed to have struck a chord (or else the jury was witless), so pervasive the pessimism in the air. Perhaps this small acknowledgement of the fact bespoke good news, a shifting tide to come.

'Sure,' I said, 'stranger things have happened.'

I congratulated Smithers. I was a little jealous. No use pretending I was not. As always, the innocence of the unconscious man produces the timely poem, the one of the hour; and whatever I was about, innocence had not much to do with it.

'Oh,' said Moonface, 'cool.'

The Slavs took Smithers's measure and silently tittered.

I explained to her jocularly enough that the man in our presence was a war criminal, having won a prize; but that I would stand him a glass of wine, anyway. Perhaps she heard the edge in my voice; she did not make a fuss over Smithers as she might have done. Eggy, however, when he showed up, shuffling forward with his cane, settled like a decrepit bird in his chair and said that the occasion called for libations.

'A real poet in our midst,' he crowed, giving me a look from his drooping eye. He knew precisely what he was doing.

Smithers, uncomfortable, his small head engulfed by a large peaked cap, sipped his wine and looked glassy-eyed with the glory he had accrued.

'Politics,' he said between clenched teeth, speaking to Eggy, 'is something I don't concern myself about.'

'What effrontery!' some comic voice spoke within me, Stan waving his tie at Laurel.

'Nor do I,' said Eggy, 'but good God, man, it will concern itself with you.'

'Not if I can help it.'

Had the glory already gone to his head?

The Fast Eddy Effect

The effect of Fast Eddy on Traymoreans was to wean them from flights of fancy and bring them down to earth. Now we were talking leaky basements or the latest in reality TV. Defibrillators. The nuts and bolts of getting by. Fast Eddy certainly did not seem to have a metaphysical turn of mind. Eleanor thought Fast Eddy a nice man.

She finally met him one evening in the Blue Danube. Although it had not been necessary, Dubois had reserved us a table, instructing the cook to prepare us something, and Moonface would set it on the table. Fast Eddy said little, even when Eleanor asked him questions pertaining to his background, to his career and even to his love life. Fast Eddy demurred on all counts, and I thought he blushed. I was now a fish out of water, flopping about in my exertions to render Lucretius comprehensible, his paean to Venus and his garden of pleasures which may or may not have had room for a discussion of leaky basements. I may as well have been talking to a mildly alarmed stone statue of the Buddha in a lunar dry land. Moonface gave me a look of infinite sympathy but was otherwise no help; and besides, she was busy, setting the various courses down, topping up water glasses, bringing on the wine. Eggy had had new respect for her powers ever since that false report concerning the Blue Danube's liquor license. At the end of the festivities, Moonface brought the bill and we each kicked in our share; though, truth to tell, I was overly generous. It was my attempt to salvage my position as *l'éminence grise* of the group, the power behind the imaginary Traymore throne. It was only leading to the triumph of Bly, as I could hear him in my windy cranium snickering at an amateur. Eggy had fallen asleep. In a corner, beneath the silly tapestry of a winter scene, a woman in furs was holding court, royalty in exile. Two children, a boy and girl, sat at her table; and they were grave and dignified. Other Slavs at other tables had been carrying on, loyal retainers awaiting the hour of action. The Presidential character meant nothing to them. Tragedy unfolding anywhere meant even less. It served to put things in perspective.

Dubois the Realist

Downtown, a panhandler let me know it was a crazy old world. I forked over a fiver in a fit of foolishness. Wearing mittens that exposed her fingers, she was blind in a blind world; her other senses were not enhanced. I thought I saw Arsdell in a fashionable coat, academe's glamour boy, smoking a cigarette with guilty pleasure as he looked through the window of a bookstore of vain bestsellers. Here was glamour on which he had missed out. I was about to extend him the hand of friendship when Boffo the clown in me bleated: 'For God's sake, Calhoun, how about a little self-respect?'

Jack Swain had always said the worst sin a poet could commit was to write his verses in return for the love of the public: 'Lie and they'll love you. Tell the truth and you're a putz, one who can't be trusted to manage his affairs.'

This statement naturally invited a question as to what truth was.

I stepped into a small park adjacent an old stone church, and the sparrows and the starlings were competing glee clubs.

I rolled a cigarette, lit it, and smoked. Closed my eyes. Sally McCabe appeared, lovely chestnut curls set off by a green sweater, her face open and frank. She said: 'Nice set-up you have here. Tradition. Grass and birds. The noon hour tolling of a steeple bell. The next thing I'll hear you'll be rowing for Harvard or writing a book extolling the life of reason. You're tumbleweed, Calhoun, like it or not. You're the cruelties of Apache and cowhand, all the lawlessness.'

'Be gone,' I said to an image of Sally McCabe.

Then Dubois in the flesh joined me on the bench.

'We're always meeting like this,' he said. 'I might even begin to believe in fate if this keeps up.'

He set his honest attaché case on the earth. His eyes told me he wanted a cigarette but he had given up the habit.

'Who were you talking to?' he asked. 'Your lips were moving.'

I let it pass.

'You know, you've been touchy, lately. It's none of my business, but just in case, is it anything I can help you with? Eleanor thinks you're in love with Moonface. I tell her no, I don't think so. Calhoun's no lover. She speaks of some other woman, too. Well, come on. What gives? And none of that political crap, how we're all going down the tubes.'

'I was writing a poem in my head and you came along.'

'Oh that. There's a comet currently exploding in the night sky. There's subject matter for you.'

I gave vain and handsome Dubois a look, and he looked around like a man in search of better prospects.

'Well,' he said, rising, 'I'll see you, I guess.'

'See you.'

He smiled and shook his head. He was of such vanity that had he a plan for torpedoing Republican election chances, he would never once doubt that dirty tricks were anything less than a gentleman's honour; and he would go home and boff Eleanor, all's well that ends well. I felt a little like Noah minus the ark with which to ride out a storm.

An Epiphany

It was not that I was now unrecognizable to myself but that I was getting mystical; and no matter how it may have looked, I was a rational creature.

Had Melody doctored the wine? The light of day was departing the street, the passersby blind fish in a random current. The President could not know, of course, of my existence; and yet, he was an intimate of mine, as much so as McCabe; as Moonface sometimes was, she with all of the remoteness and the incomprehensible eyes of a muse figure, standard issue. Two of the city's finest on patrol now walked by, the one saying to the other: 'She either died by pills or …'

I did not hear the sentence completed. Some amateur astronomer had declared that between oneself and any event occurring anywhere in the universe there were zero degrees of separation.

But it was no good, I decided, explaining the Presidential thought-process by way of history's impersonal forces; or by way of a single cataclysm as had come to pass in New York. The man really was what he had been all along, the analog of all spoiled and immature and adolescent Caesars who played at empire; he was the spoiled, privileged scion of a dynastic enterprise. He was the boy a girl affectionately pushes into a lake. He was the triumph of hope over experience. He may have meant well until the glow of the wine of power faded and the shortcomings of character wreaked their havoc. All he had to do was draw breath and he further blighted a non-existent Camelot. He was every one of us living off the fumes of a remembered glory that had never been real; and like us he pretended to empathy and was cruel. He was a cult object. He was a male Lucille Lamont beautiful in his own mind. Oh I was playing the ologist and liking it; that somewhere in the man he was so uncertain and so terrified it brought him to discover certitude. He had mistaken stubborn passivity for will, all his kitchen staff forever dealing with the fallout that was the consequence of his wrong footedness. And perhaps it should have been obvious to me that, by way of the wine, I had leaped headlong into a cavern's sacred pool (and it was the profoundest of silences, the water delicious on my skin, its reflections on the rock walls enchanting). The wine said: 'It takes an upheaval of the proportions of a nuclear detonation to lose one's love of country. The shock wave has been slow in arriving, but it has come. Of course, every one of those dry lands on which Americans have designs has their own demons; it is what opens their gates to the enemy. Even in Montreal, no imperial city, just a backwater of French and Scots and Irish and Jews, not to mention Haitians, Brazilians, Iranians, Moroccans, Tunisians, one sees them on the streets—old men who had the glory of girls and hockey or football and maybe a war; who gibber at themselves; who've been squeezed from the dream. They cadge what drinks they can and piss alphabets on the snow. Moonface going by them, high-breasted, might as well come from another planet. Melody stands before you, gesturing at your glass. Do you want another? Do you have the stomach for it? Is that a snicker flickering in her proprietary eyes?'

Slavs came and went. They sensed perhaps I was in a state, and they kept clear. Eggy did not show. Moonface was, in all likelihood, carrying on with Rick. Perhaps he was performing on his guitar for her, playing an anthem of hope. Dubois and Eleanor were, no doubt, discussing politics in Eleanor's kitchen. Perhaps Dubois would stay the night. Sex as lamentation. A woman in furs entered the café. Her eyes, her somewhat tired demeanor, suggested they had seen the likes of me before; that there was no right side of history; that it either worked in your favour or did not; that life was so unaccountable that sometimes your worst enemy could be your best friend; but that mostly your worst enemy would do you in when it suited him, conditions ripe. You should not take it personally; and, of course, when you are dead it is no longer personal. She shrugged, I an ineffectual beast.

Calhoun Transfigured

When I woke the next morning, I found a note that had been slipped under my door. It read: '*Cher* Randall, we don't think you're crazy. Love, Dubois and Eleanor.'

Of course I was not crazy; I was demented. Moonface knocked. She was having coffee with Eggy—did I want to come over? She was a happy wench just now. She had her Rick, her Eggy, her Q-touchstone. Post-graduate life was in the offing.

'Give me a few minutes,' I said to her.

She went back to the Eggy domain, smiling.

Soon I was standing at the window at the end of the Traymore hall, as if to see what sort of day it might become. Sparrows were at Mrs Petrova's feeder, scattering seed. Pigeons pecked at what fell to the ground. A raw wind seemed to be burning what leaf-tatters remained on the trees. I walked through Eggy's door and he said: 'What ho, Calhoun? What calamities are about to befall us?'

'Three bags full of Pakistan and Iran and Iraq and Somalia, plus a banking system out of whack and corrupt courts and creeping fascism. Otherwise, nothing new. Will we have a female Caesar? Shall a black man beat the odds and be head of state if no one guns him down? Stay tuned.'

But Eggy was going to go to his grave, his faith in the sweepings of the pendulum intact. The fact that it might fly off its pin need not concern him. Moonface might have babies. She might cop a Governor-General's award, she who put a cup of coffee in my hands and said: 'Congratulate me. I've applied to Carleton.'

But there were no classics studies at Carleton, so far as I knew. In any case, she was going to Ottawa. Just to be going somewhere. Should I laugh, cry or feel immense relief that she had found herself a window of opportunity to fly through on her magic broom?

'I congratulate thee,' I said.

Eggy said, 'And well you should.' He reached for her bum and missed. 'Oh well. Hoo hoo.'

Moonface said, 'Rick and I celebrated, last night. We drank a six-pack and I don't even like beer.'

'She doesn't even like beer,' Eggy echoed.

He was going to miss the girl, deeply so; and he was struggling, this sparrow of man, against the diminishing ground on which he stood.

'It might snow, today,' Moonface said, apropos of nothing.

Eleanor entered. She was wearing some kimono-like thing and was pompadoured. She said: 'A party. How come no one invited me?'

'You're invited,' said Eggy, 'set your arse down. Moonface, another cup.'

Dubois, it seemed, was off to some meeting of concerned citizenry.

I would splurge on a taxi to Gareth Howard's grave, Moonface asking to come along. Such a loyal and committed friend, devoting me time from her busy life. I was barely conscious of the streets through which we passed. Erotic burblings. Even so, Gar had been my oldest friend; and if I could neither see nor hear him, I must come his way like a serious knight of the grail: no hanky-panky in the backseat of a cab. Moonface was, in any case, lost to her own thoughts. And we arrived and I picked out his stone on a slope above the river; and there were his name and his dates and the carved rose courtesy of Clare, she who was somewhere in the world if not in Costa Rica. I said: 'I think he's disappointed in me.'

'Why is that?' Moonface asked.

'My fatalism. What's more, he suspects I've always been in love with his wife but that I won't plead my case. It's my fear of rejection. It's my pessimist's view that it wouldn't work out. A drunken evening, a toss in the hay. A morning after of wry commentary on the frailty of humankind.'

'You've been in love with his wife?'

'Secret of mine. Though I did manage to let the cat out of the bag with Eleanor.'

'I'm not sure I like graveyards. It's cold.'

She was not, at that moment, comptroller of the universe. The cheeks of her pale countenance were bright with the wind. I would like to have kissed her. I thought I could hear Clare's laughter, rich and chesty and not malicious.

'Well,' I said, 'stupid of me to dismiss the taxi driver. I thought we'd be here a while, discussing maybe my old memories and your post-graduate life. I'm not sure about the buses, and it'll be a long hike back.'

She wanted to go. We turned our backs on Gar and walked down the slope to the river. A promenade followed it to the city.

'You speak,' said Moonface, 'of your friend as if he could hear you. Strange, wouldn't you say?'

'Could be. Thing is, I can't hear him. My excuses for my failures in life roar; his sarcasm goes mum on me. It's as if he stole my memory of his voice for no reason but that of spite. I never touched his wife while he was alive. I agreed, in general, with his politics. I liked what he wrote. I missed his company when he was off somewhere, reporting on this or that calamity. He had a chip on his shoulder that puzzled him. By all rights it shouldn't have been there, just that it was, and sometimes he lashed out at people, at me, at Clare, all the while he sipped cocktails with human monsters. Patterns are true up to a point. Reason has its limits. We're not moral creatures. You've heard all this from me before. The world makes us crazy, and when it runs out of games to play with us, we make it crazy. And off we go again, to the races. Sometimes I love you. Sometimes I'm indifferent. Just know that when I love you I want the best for you. Maybe you'll get lucky. Well, I got off subject—'

'I don't know what to say. It's such a backhanded compliment. You touched his wife?'

We walked in silence for a while. Like Eggy, I would miss Moonface, too, when she left.

Calhoun in Paradise

Later, much later, I saw that, in fact, there was postal matter in my mailbox. Among the bills and solicitations from various literary venues wanting money, there was a missive from Vera. Back in my digs I read that she, Karl and Clare had it in mind to spend the holidays in Venice but would start out in Rome. Vera even had the wit to spell out the itinerary and supply me with the names of the hotels they had booked, 3-star splendours. In Rome the Hotel Abruzzi. In Venice the Hotel Albergo Best Western San Marco. It was in no sense an invitation for me to 'come on over' and rendezvous. I supposed I was meant to feel a little jealous. I would have to cash in a few family chips, the blood money, so as to finance my last fling at kicking the can, oh, just to get a glimpse of Clare and the pines of a Roman sunset. Perhaps I fell asleep.

It was McCabe who spoke: *'You're in error, Calhoun. Only eggheads pine for those pines. You can't go backwards. Your only way out is the desert over which I preside. Tumbleweed and moonlight. Whiskey. Teen angels. Uncomplicated petting in the back of a Chrysler car. In other words, nostalgia, sir, for one's youth. If it's time travel you want, it's the safest there is. What do you desire ghastly old Rome for? Besides, you're so right: Clare's a one-man woman. She'll leave you with a shiv in your gut in some unlit backstreet.'*

And then it was the turn of other interviewers to have their shot. Szabo. Arsdell, academe's glamour boy. Would I address his class on a theme of creative non-compliance? Fast Eddy said: *'Life keeps throwing you life-preservers. You keep drowning.'*

Said Joe Smithers: *'Your opinion of yourself is rather exaggerated. I, on the other hand, am bona fide. Read 'em and weep.'*

In due course, I had words with Vera and Karl, each asking after my well-being. Clare was aloof. Dubois said: *'We'll take back the White House. Tomorrow, the world.'*

Eleanor said, *'But we're Canadians.'*

Eggy gave a speech: *'The name is Eglinton. I'm the senior Traymorean. They call me Eggy. I was always the runt of a litter of one. Then, when I gained my majority, I was the runt of the entire human litter. Still, I prevailed. Calhoun supposes too much. It's the rising and setting of the sun, that's all. Oh, sometimes it's personal when it's going good for us. It's personal, when from what's good in life, we're cut off. Can't find a drop of wine anywhere. Can't find a girl who'll tolerate one. It's when you have the vote but you're an arse if you think it counts. Oh, I suppose I don't make much sense. Just an old man seeing things through to a conclusion. There most likely isn't a conclusion. Breath will flame out in the windpipe, that's all. Whatever it is you're trying to comprehend, give it up. You're neither good nor bad. You're neither acted upon nor self-actuated. You're a fact of no essential character among billions of other flimflam artists. The artist-artist, especially, is a dufus, thinking he's the reason for something. Well, perhaps we have souls. Perhaps we're but machines of kinetic scope. I'll certainly shut up. Now what was I saying? Oh, bloody hell. I'm too old for this. Get some young whippersnapper on the case. Moonface wants a good hosing. Let's not mince words. Hoo hoo.'*

Moonface, not a stitch of clothing on her, kneeled over me. She alone was wordless. If I was to supply words, none were forthcoming, as her mere presence said it all. Silence, her eyes shut and rich with her inner mysteries. And then the world came rushing back in to sully us.

One after the other, presences appeared and disappeared and came around again so as to instruct me; so that I should not be mistaken on any matter whatsoever. I had not fought hard enough to hold on to Minnie Dreier, or so some bony finger was putting it to me. Gareth Howard, my oldest friend, was dead in his grave. I would embark from the container port on a container ship. Two days on the St Lawrence. *In Kamarooska a kiss and a thought for Algonquins.* Yes, some of that. And then, past Newfoundland, open ocean. Curried chicken and jigsaw puzzles. The channel. Thamesport.

Calhoun on the Head of a Pin

Dubois and Eggy were drinking wine in the Blue Danube. I smoked a cigarette on the street. A beetle-like bug scuttling along the sidewalk caught my eye. It had begun to grow dark, and it was going to get too cold for a bug to explore the cracks and chasms and culverts of its terrain. It put me in mind of Baghdad, this creature, and I could not tell you why. So many people had already been snuffed there like so many insects. Sectarian cleansings. Death-dealing militias. Divide and rule, Americans in on the game with special intelligence units such as trained death squads in Honduras during a time of mayhem. The moon would rise. People would die. Some passerby would inadvertently squash the bug underfoot. It was all so matter of fact, and I was not standing there, cigarette in hand, indulging outrage; I was getting drunk. I did not know who or what I was; I was a man occupying space in a time of evolutionary drift. I rejoined my friends, Melody attending to them.

Dubois asked, 'Have you noticed an odd thing? More women than ever wearing hats, these days? Gives me a bad feeling. A portent of something.'

'Stuff and nonsense,' said Eggy, 'and anyway, Montcalm threw the battle.'

I knew he had plans to see an opera, and I asked him about it.

'Hoo hoo. *Tannhäuser*. My cane might sprout and I forgive all my wives. But in the spring. Moonface will wear a slinky dress. Will I live long enough to see it?'

'Yes,' said Dubois, 'and I'm going, too. To chaperone.'

'Tra la la,' said Eggy, 'and not only that, she's going to try it on for me in my room.'

'I suppose,' said Dubois, 'I'll have to be there for that, as well.'

It really did seem like the three of us would sit there in reasonable humour, thoroughly inane; and when forever came around, we would still be there. We would still be there doing what? Reconstituting Big Bang theories? Remembering the dead? Fast Eddy walked through the door. He said: 'Gentlemen, greetings.'

Melody brought him his soft drink with the air of a woman selling real estate. He, too, it seemed, was going to the opera in the spring.

'I don't even like opera,' he said. 'I'm just going to cut a figure.'

Moonface was making it possible for three men to squire her and cut figures. Fast Eddy said to me: 'You should write a poem about it.'

I wondered if, perhaps, I should. I saw Virgil in my thoughts; and he, with wind-sculpted eyes, was drifting through the American southwest in search of shepherds, the Great Experiment showing early signs of going off the rails; and he would lose himself in the cantinas of a melancholy land. I rolled a cigarette and excused myself.

It had become colder, the bug I saw earlier nowhere to be seen. Moonface appeared. Immediately the fact of her divided my loyalties, such as they were; allegiance, for example, to Clare who was, no doubt, in Italy; to a book I would never write, if only because, as Bly would put it, I was such an effing amateur and not enough the cool man of reason and mastery. To kiss Moonface herself (just a peck on the cheek)—even this was, perhaps, an allegiance owed that I would fail to honour. She said: 'I thought I'd find you here.'

'What's up?' I asked, oh so carelessly.

She had that way of looking at you while not looking at you at all; it was as if, in the corner of her vision, she had spotted an angel and was being distracted.

'I'm not up to anything but I see the gang's here.'

And what she saw through the window was the sight of Melody bringing another bottle of wine to the table, Traymoreans plus Fast Eddy about to consume it. Yes, Fast Eddy had decided, his diabetes aside, to become bibulous. We no longer talked the Latin poets, Moonface and I. She was content with Rick, her old and now current beau. And how long would that last? Someone once said that every sentence a writer writes should carry a perception. I perceived nothing, try as I might. Now I was looking at a face that was sometimes lovely and sometimes not. We were not moral creatures. To the questions 'Were we ever and would we ever be', I had no answers. Opinion is not knowledge, for all that Eleanor had knowledge even in her effing little finger. I could love Moonface best if I did not submit her to my notions of love; and yes, such notions amounted to not much more than pride in my thought-processes. If I did not attempt to defend myself from whatever the charge she was bringing against me, about which she was unconscious, could it then be said I was committed to the fray? Perhaps I would love her best if I did not attempt to love her at all. It was ludicrous, she and I standing in the street, in search of a reason to be standing there. I nodded at the gang in the café. She declined to join us. Dubois, Eggy and Fast Eddy, having spotted her, waved at her to leave me to my own devices and join them. It would be so much more fun for her. But no, she was just out for a breath of fresh air, but that it was a little cold. She hunched her shoulders to which her hair had fallen; and she was hatless. People walked by. People were hanging in trees.

'Well,' I said, 'I'm going in.'

§

Book V—Returning Prodigal

As Noted

—Emma MacReady (Moonface) Jottings

Q took off for England this morning. Going by ship. Rough seas possible. Do we care? Bon voyage party for the man last night at the Blue Danube. Eleanor's tits practically hanging out of her dress.

Mom once said I'd look like Garbo, but I'm too clumsy and asymmetrically angular. Thanks, mom, for that. Randall phoned from London to say he'd arrived and was alright, though the ground was pitching about beneath him.

Eggy pines for Randall. 'Bloody hell, what's he doing' Quid non speremus amantes? What may we lovers not expect?

Rick and I fought some more. Sex, again. This is what I hate, this is what I really hate about Randall. He gets this other look on his face, the one that says he knows nothing, never did, and I want to scream he's lying. Liar, liar. Pants on fire.

Wonder of wonders, Randall's back. Surprised by all the snow. Then he told me about Clare and the Klopstocks. My God. He said he wasn't going to get cut up over his old friends.

Randall's Rome letters arrived.

Letters from Rome

Randall Q Calhoun to Moonface

Dear Moonface, I'm just back from a morning visit to the Baths of Diocletian. In the museum there a figurine of Anna Perennis, one dug up recently from where it was buried for centuries, put me in a tizzy. She's a very old deity whose festival fell on the Ides of March. She had a grove at the first milestone up the via Flaminia and she was popular with the plebs, and for her sake, and for luck, 'lad lay with lass' at the turn of the year. The sight of her many-breasted caused the back of my neck to tingle. She is the object of many stories and she was the cause of many off-colour jokes, a cult partner to Mars. Ovid had it she was Dido's sister who wound up in Rome, just as Virgil had it. Sometimes Anna Perennis was equated with the moon. She was also an old woman who, during a pleb revolt, fed cakes to starving rebels. Is there a tough, old biddie in you to give succour to the rabble? Altogether, it was a profitable morning. I saw also Tacitus's funerary inscription. Do you care?

It has rained much and it has even tried to snow. I'm perversely happy, broke and tired. I grieve of course for Clare, Vera and Karl. Oh my goodness, I didn't tell you. They're dead. Cable car mishap in the mountains. I'll fill you in on my return.

I got drunk the other day. *Bar Tempio* territory. Two bars over is a McDonald's. I try not to be snooty but it is evident that the more packaged sort of tourist frequents the obscenity. A thunderstorm broke in the course of my reveries. Brooding old Rome got madcap, everyone scurrying for cover, an army of touts appearing everywhere, hawking umbrellas. I pictured you and Eggy and Mrs Petrova's sparrows for some reason or another. I was stood up by a woman I've met here. Why do I always fall for women who write verse? Are you one of those?

Did I say I was happy? I'm near mad. Virgil signals me to get a grip. He's a way out of the coming cataclysm, only he can't be bothered with ninnies, especially one like me who has 'Q' for a middle name. How affected is that in these times? You see, I really have quite gone around the bend. And yet, what's sanity but knowing one is incurable? Knowing one is incurable means one trusts the operations of cause and effect to do their worst, Rome dancing in all the corners of one's eyes.

Now why is Virgil a way out as I see it, given that the man is nothing but a hostage of our platitudes? He's nothing but a prisoner of the Augustan agenda to dominate the known world. He's nothing but a calendar pin-up for those Christians who made of him an honourary Christian. He's a straw man for academe, a convenient target for all sorts of exercises in self-congratulations. You really do have to come here, some day. Surely, you could find something for Rick to do. He could play his guitar on the Spanish Steps.

I had so much I was going to write you. Here when a hand touches you, it's a hand, not the idea of one. When an ape imitates human behaviour he is more human than his human handler. Here I could fondle you within an inch of your life. Divine prurience. In America, it would be just more fodder for the ologists, all of whom drag around Ahab's harpoon like it's so much training for a blood sport. There's still life in this corrupt old heart at the core of our civilization, backwater now, and thank Christ that it is. Even Leopardi, in his day, complained of its provincialism. My regards to Eleanor, Bob and Eggy. They will have their work cut out for them, re-educating me on my return.—RQC

Dear Moonface, In continuance: that I went up to the Palatine in a light rain, the morning chilly. There was a crowd. I looked for a tiny goddess I'd stumbled across on a previous visit, years ago, and could not find her. Perhaps she'd gone to ground, deeply so. In any case, I hung around for a couple of hours if only to get my money's worth, the price of admission having doubled since that last visit. Then I waited for a vision of a hunched up man wearing a hooded cape; but no such vision materialized. Would I have looked kindly on a wizened Augustus leaning Eggywards at the shades, the curtain lowering on the play? Or would I have asserted my values and given out with a Bronx cheer, notwithstanding the fact that not one of those has been heard in many a year? Then in a bar, somewhere off the Piazza Venezia, two Vietnamese wenches serving, I the only customer (the music too loud), I warmed up with whiskey. Perched on my barstool like a winter-blasted sparrow, I prosecuted Virgil.

I imagined you were there also in defense of the poet. I speechified, saying he'd been no more than Caesar's shill. Your turn to speak, you countered, saying that in the *Eclogues*, especially, he'd given the little man a voice, albeit a grand one, a Theocritan tune he had perfected; that, if anything, it was too good a voice for stinky and sex-besotted goat herders. I thought you spoke well, but even so, I went on to say that, of course, our own epoch had not achieved much more than a carping critique of past glories, *Bitch, Bitch, Bitch & Whine* the sign on a law office's door. Be that as it may, it should not blind us to the fact that the man in the dock had an army of slaves under his thumb, enough with which to complement two football teams, at least; that in consequence he was not quite up to our standards, as we cherish our illusion that we have outgrown all that. Once more you countered, noting that irony is neither prosecution nor defense; and that, unless slaves had composed his verses and Virgil falsely got the credit, the way things were in the ancient world were not his doing anymore than wiping out Indian tribes was ours. At which point, you disappeared from my thoughts. The barmaids struck me as warm and friendly. How had they come to be in this city and under whose thumb were they? Guitars screeched and scrounged for oblivion; some rockandroller shrieked.—RQC

Dear Moonface, I sit in a tiny park, smell Marlboro smoke, the air damp and ineffable. The park, in turn, sits on top of some portion of Nero's architectural fantasia, his Golden House. I can eyeball the Coliseum and view the approach to the via San Giovanni di Laterno. If the devil's in the details, there are details in Rome beyond number. Did I say I was happy? In truth, I'm a little homesick, missing you and Eggy and the other Traymoreans. I am, after all, a boffo Yank, but one who drags a rather deep foot around. What gives me dread is coming home and getting angry again. I've had a vacation from anger. My old friends dying like that in some freak accident—they've turned my thoughts in other directions for the time being. Rome offers up the 'big picture'. It's all very neat and tidy, and just at this moment I don't trust the intelligence of my emotions. Virgil, in the end, is but another dead poet. A man smokes a cigarette and reads a newspaper. A mother pushes a baby tram. Some druggies are huddled together, conspiratorial. *Carabinieri* stroll by, unconcerned. Christ, in the end, is but another martyr. The clouds thin somewhat, and the sun struggles to shine down on an arena of bloodlust. I have not reached any terminus where curiosity peters out, but perhaps my energy flags. I have failed in my quest to prove by logic that time is a continuum; my senses take it on faith, my senses so many stray cats and whimpering dogs. They tell me I'm alone and you're alone and some peacocks in a gilded cage are likewise. The lover boy in me loves; the pedagogue cringes; the amateur scorns. Lucille Lamont is an unpleasant woman, but in some way she's right: she's so much more the true face of the world than are my mild objections to her triumph. Perhaps it's snowing now on the Traymore, the sparrows carbuncular in the leafless lilac tree, squirrels skittering along the top of the picket fence. Perhaps Eggy is three sheets to a very cold wind. I can smell Eleanor's marmalade thickening in a pot. Perhaps Dubois utters imprecations at the President. And this speculation brings us full circle. I look upon ruins and cogitate on the ruin he's brought us, some violets in the corner of my eye.—RQC

Calhoun's Follies V

—A hero's welcome among Traymoreans? I was quickly disabused. 'So how was Rome?' Eggy hoo hooed. 'Meet any signorinas there?' Did the look in Eleanor's eyes suggest I was now contaminated, having been exposed to exotic influences? Or had she, a homebody, reason to feel inadequate in my presence, I bringing back a whiff of the wider world to her kitchen? In any case, the sights and sounds and smells of a foreign place in my mind pretty much dissipated as soon as I hit New World air. Only in the privacy of my digs, in my solitude, would I be able to reconstruct those ephemeralities. Dubois, for once, had no opinion. He was a practical man. 'The pope,' he said, 'did you tell the pope the world's moved on?' Mrs Petrova had grunted when I brought her my back rent. Moonface had not even received my packet of letters. I should have posted them at the Vatican, their postal service more efficient than the regular venue. No, the news was all Eggy there in Eleanor's kitchen, Traymoreans sitting around. Eggy did not need now to see Moonface's bosom. That she would accompany him to the opera was enough. He supposed that on account of his advanced age, he ought to grow up, Moonface long since tired of the joke. It had been a good joke while it lasted. It had seen a worn-out old man through the rough patch that was his life's imminent end. 'Apostles. Those damn apostles,' said Eggy, and, as ever, one did not know exactly to what he referred—to a juggernaut made of *übermenschen* or to Mark, Matthew, Luke and John. Eleanor sat there unusually quiet, her feet shod in red pompadours, the fact of which was loud enough. There was a sadness in her eyes I was unaccustomed to seeing. It unnerved me. Had she been pining for Marcel Lamont all this time? While in Rome I had examined my loyalties and elected for my friends. I saw now I had only placed myself on the wrong side of a one-way street, expecting the traffic to come in my direction. In other words, I would have to go against traffic to get to the bottom of Eleanor's unease, if it were possible, as well as obtain what I thought I needed. Dubois, a man of some reserve, seemed acutely remote. Had he a new woman in his life? Had he reason to fear for his health? Immortal Eggy could kick the bucket at any moment; that much had not changed. Immortality did not vouchsafe wisdom, the usual two glasses of wine set before him. Moonface was, well, Moonface; now alluring, now a woman (excepting the eyes) of unremarkable charms. I began to wonder if I had not imagined everything that transpired between us, right down to the theatrics of Platonic flirtation. To Eggy I said that I had indeed met a woman in Rome, but that she had stood me up. To Dubois I said that some aspects of Platonic theory survive among certain physicists; that, so far as I could make out, the idea of the universe precedes the laws that govern it. I had read it in a magazine on the flight over. Silver-haired, blue-eyed Dubois looked at the floor, as if to avoid calling me demented. To Moonface I said nothing. To her I might have said, 'Seems the queen mum has out-queened Victoria. Doesn't high-spirited American speech have a way of one-upping other people's fun? Putin sure has a burn on, the west still thinking Russians are savages.' I assumed we would meet up later, she and I, and compare notes. As my letters had yet to arrive, she could not know the full import of my news—the death of the Klopstocks and Clare—except what I had stated matter-of-factly, almost in passing in the Blue Danube. 'Women are my religion,' said Eggy, waking from an evanescent snooze. This comment brought Eleanor to life, and she said, 'Have a care, you old fart, I'm a jealous and wrathful god.' Dubois looked at the ceiling. Eleanor lit a cigarette and adjusted her robe which had come away from her thigh. I searched Moonface's eyes. Was I being left out of some loop? In which case it was nothing new. No one tells me anything. There had been a big snowfall, the city still getting out from under. Every sparrow from miles around vied for a perch at Mrs Petrova's feeder. All that snow—it was strange to see after the ancient stones of the via Antica which had seemed to throb beneath one's aching feet, resentful. Here the act of perambulation lacked all that romance, America, however muddled, still capable of inventing itself. The notion that things could get better or get worse was less the whim of a dreamer, a whim fed by the passing of centuries; it was more a matter of the moment; and today or tomorrow or a year from now, and who knew? Now Fast Eddy let himself in. Since when had he been accorded this privilege? He had a gift-wrapped package in his hands which he promptly thrust at Moonface. 'I looked all over town for it,' he said, anxious and smitten, Moonface at a loss for words. This much had transpired while I was away: she had a new suitor. 'Look,' I said, 'something's up. You've all been acting a little strange. I can always go away, again.' Fast Eddy gave me a look. It was as if he only then noticed my presence in the room. Moony eyes for a dear girl replaced the rather sharp look he had bestowed on me. Moonface unwrapped the package. In another time Eleanor might have said, 'What have we here? Someone's in love.' 'Well, Randall,' Dubois said, the sloppy grin on his face suspect, 'we took a vote while you were gone. And when we were sure you were well and truly gone, we decided we'd have you evicted. Ask me why. Well, suppose you write that book you're always threatening to write? Who's going to read it? Eggheads? Who'd buy it? What bookstore stocks it? Do you think we're going to buy it? Life's short. Don't embarrass us. Sex and carnage, the dumber the better.' I was astounded. Eleanor butted her cigarette. Now she snickered, rising and tra-la-lahing to the stove to put the kettle on. She had now heard it all, I the measure of all that had put one on her and was caught out. Eggy hoo hooed. Wine, fruitcake and a history of Cuba had gotten him through the holidays. 'So how was the trip?' Fast Eddy asked me, some sliver of accusation in his voice. There it was: I had only been on a little trip, a jaunt of sorts. I had indulged a brief detour from Traymorean life. 'Apparently, I went away,' I said, 'but it seems one can't come home again.' This remark struck Fast Eddy as specious. 'Stuff and nonsense,' Eggy said. Moonface had no opinion. The spit valve to Eleanor's trombone appeared and Eleanor was playing with the thing. Would she put it to her mouth and wheeze *Stardust* into the aperture? 'Chocolates,' Moonface said, 'oh, my favourite kind. The really dark kind. How did you know?' Fast Eddy was near weepy, standing in this treacherous world like a guard on sentry duty, his beetling brows knit together. Mission accomplished. Then Moonface leaned my way, and in my startled ear (and her whispering was delicious) she whispered, 'It's the new joke, this bit about evicting you. Eggy's idea, the little devil. He thinks you need shaking up. We're only kidding. But no way I'm taking you to bed.'

Chittering

We have chittered in the rough-bladed grasses, Moonface and I. Had such high hopes of breaking through our natures to something truly civilized. As if naming the world forestalls its evils. It does not, really. As if taking pictures of snow leopards in the wild is a charm against evil. It is not. The saying so proves I am no romantic as Dubois has charged. But I am rambling, filling space. Leave some blank for all the troubled absences and the deities that preside over them. This will prove I am, if nothing else, damn near pagan.

A Bit of Academe

> The Common word for these figures was *oscilla*, and the fact of their swinging in the wind suggested a verb *oscillare*, which survives in our tongue with the same meaning.
>
> But here we must leave a question which is still unsolved. All we can say is that the old idea of substitutes for human sacrifice must be finally given up, and the *oscilla*, whether or not they were substitutes for human swingers, were probably charms intended to ward off evil influences from the crops.
>
> from "The Religious Experience of the Roman People"—
> The Gifford Lectures for 1909-10, Edinburgh University

§

Part Two

Echo's Gone

Book I—Phrygian Mode

Ghosts

Even as snow fell in thick, slanting gobs, it would soon be spring. Blind Musician knew it. One could almost bear him now, he the neighbourhood's sourest entity. At any moment, he might exchange his grotty coat for an Hawaiian shirt, even if he sat quite motionless, braying in the Blue Danube that cigarette smokers were anti-progressive. It was in America and perhaps the world over, the anniversary of the murder of a civil rights hero. Blind Musician observed with a voice that always caused my skin to crawl, that was a grating horn the burr from which no wretch, no matter how secure his refuge, was safe: 'A fine and noble man, that Dr King. Didn't smoke, so far as I know.'

To add insult to my injury, Blind Musician probably played a half-decent violin. Eggy ignored the remark. Eggy in his decrepit old age, sparrow of a man, chirped at me: 'This time next week, Calhoun, we'll be sitting outside and Black Dog Girl will walk by with her splendid hips, and all will be right with the world. Hoo hoo.'

'No, we won't,' said vain and handsome Dubois. He explained why: 'Because she's left the area. Didn't you know? Took the dog with her.'

Would Eggy cry?

Lately, he was writing me amorous escapades, Vincent and Veronica the two hosers of his imaginings. I was to append them to my jottings, Eggy waiving his claim to authorship. But that, and wait for this, I would find the Eggy words too hot to handle.

'Oh yes,' he crowed, 'too hot for your chaste little thoughts.'

Veronica then, concerning Vincent: *'He not only plugged my every orifice, he not only drove me to the point of exhaustion, he devoured me, nights on end.'*

What, here in phantasmagorical Canada? The words certainly had a familiar enough ring, but I had not the heart to accuse the old bugger of the tacky crime of plagiarism.

His words to do with Moonface, however, were strictly on the level. The young woman was a waitress at the Blue Danube (now under new management and soon enough to be rechristened as Le Grec; she a reader of Virgil in Latin and a lodger in the Traymore Rooms).

'We will see her in the end,' Eggy thundered, his tiny hand raised in the air as if about to unleash a lightning bolt, 'doing the chicken shuffle on our noble boulevard, headed west.'

A guffawing Dubois nearly died of his laughter.

Out of spite, I was thinking I would light up. This would certainly incur the disapproval of our blind prophet, blind fiddler not one of us had been able to abide for more than a minute or two, each subdivision of which was an eternity. Blind Musician? He was one who had flown up a horse's arse and bumped into the Golden Age. I must have muttered something uncomplimentary in respect to that avatar of high culture.

So that Dubois guffawed some more who used to smoke and longed to smoke again. He had become somewhat adept at reading my unspoken thoughts. This meant, somewhat disconcertingly, that he had been paying attention. The hairline cracks of his cheeks were, if anything, more spidery; it was difficult to say why. Had he had a dream which presented him with the back-stage activities of his soul, his mortality a matter of sliding facades and hoists and winches and cans of paint? Moreover, Dubois was bragging he would now fly to Rome and see what the fuss was all about, putting my powers of observation to the test by his sight-seeing there. Well, he was blowing smoke. A man reaches his middle 60s, he begins to tease himself with travails he would not, otherwise, contemplate undergoing. Dubois, semi-retired man of the business world, was suddenly expert in matters of Caesar, pope, architect and painter, not to mention filthy-minded poets. Why could he not take me at my word, that Rome was not our childhood so much as it was our fate?

Moonface served us, after a fashion. Mostly, she brought wine. We were her men, Eggy, Dubois and I, her little contingent of male stalwarts. We may not have been the stuff of her dreams but we were hers, for all that. Her old love of Virgil's poetry, her student days apparently behind her, was put on hold. She read Herodotus now, that amiable father of history; and she had not had a fit in a while, knock wood. A new boyfriend was in the picture. All we knew of him was that he was in media, headed for a sinecure. Too many boyfriends and not enough confidence in her intellect were besetting Moonface. It had been one of my labours to settle her down on this score and to instill in her some patience for the rigours of classical study. I myself had not the patience God gave a hummingbird. Eggy, I suppose, was her true mentor; he was always trying to clap his tiny hands to her body and then tell her she ought to take up the Hundred Years War.

There was at our table a presence unavailable to the normal operations of the eye: Edward Sanders aka Fast Eddy. The beetle-browed, barrel-chested spectre picked at his food, staring at it with some trepidation. It was hard for him to swallow, let alone chew. He had gotten hairier in his afterlife, the hairs on the back of his neck backlit by what light there was in the window. Fast Eddy assured me he was fine, pay him no mind. Now and then he just gave up on the chore of eating, the knuckles of his right hand flush to the table, the fork held loosely between thumb and forefinger, his shoulders stooped; and he would gaze at Moonface with touching entreaty. But just as it was not going to be in life, so it was not going to be in his low wattage Elysium; that Moonface would return his love in any meaningful sense. She was wearing a coarse white shirt and black denims. Her eyes were an indifferent black just now, registering her indifferent mood. In actual fact her eyes were brown, a rich, golden brown which sometimes charmed. I was as conscious of her body as ever. My lust for her even so was an intermittent force, my regard for her stable; she had my backing for anything she chose to do in life. But whether or not she pursued post-graduate studies in Ottawa, I would always wonder in what way I had failed her.

Dubois rose to leave, vain, handsome, tolerant. Even so, Blind Musician was getting on his nerves, as well; to Blind Musician Blue Danubians were philistines. Dubois gave me a look which suggested he had had enough. He reached for his venerable attaché case where it rested on the floor. He said, regarding its contents: 'I've got something to show you but not now.'

'What is it?' I asked.

'If you must know, a critique of your writing efforts. It's been fun, putting it together.'

Eggy struggling to his feet, pulling himself up by way of his cane, saved me the burden of a withering response. He said: 'I'll shuffle down to the bank, I guess. Got a little number there to see. Oh but I see it's still snowing effing hard. Bloody hell.'

Eggy collapsed back in his chair.

'So, see you around,' Dubois said.

'Well,' asked Eggy, 'are you going or not? Silly twit.'

Dubois was going. He slid his arms inside the sleeves of his coat and laughing, said: 'What a life,' he said, 'what a crew.'

He departed. He had read Sartre once upon a time; I pitied him for it.

The snow was everywhere banked in heaps, black, filthy deposits of the stuff. It was the shabbiest time of year for this, my faded Jezebel of a town. Still, if one looked out the window at the end of the upper floor of the Traymore Rooms, one could see that the lilac tree was beginning to bud, birds and squirrels more frenetic. Mrs Petrova in her eighth decade, landlady to Traymoreans, was even so vital and energetic. She still had on her hands a vacant apartment, and it was being held, we were led to believe, for her mythical son. Eggy always insisted there was such a son; he had clapped eyes on him once. I wondered if the spirit of Fast Eddy would not gravitate there, and that he would become, at last, a full-fledged member of our little tribe. It was going to be a terrible thing, so I figured, were I to hear emanating from that apartment the flushing of a toilet in the middle of the night. A restless spoon stirring tea. Yes, and cigar smoke? Fast Eddy, when alive, had smoked cigars in his loneliness. I witnessed, the other day, Mrs Petrova transporting an armload of folded bedding to the apartment in question. She gave me a look. It was a look of innocence accompanied by a Russian shrug.

Emma MacReady

Verses? I had not written any in a while; either I was done with them or they were done with me. Perhaps it was due to the fact that Virgil, as an object of study, vacated the Moonface eyes, and so poetry vacated Calhoun. I have lived some 60 years of a life; I am not entirely pleased with how things have panned out. A man dives for cephalopods so as, one imagines, to advance scientific inquiry as well as get his kicks. Unadventurous to a fault, I confine myself to music, and, failing that, movies. So I took Moonface to a seldom-viewed film: Kurosawa's *The Idiot*. It was almost like old times, how, in the odeon that had seen better days, I was as conscious of her body as I was of the famous director's craft; how she played with her ponytail, sighing and restless, the film long and slow of pace. It was a great work of art despite its imperfections. I insisted on it, and she said: 'Well, maybe.'

'Your objections?' I asked.

'Oh, I don't know.'

Afterwards, we drank wine in the Blue Danube aka Le Grec. Echo was the new young waitress of the moment. Impossibly bright, frighteningly enthusiastic, she improved on Wendy who had the face of DeGaulle and lasted a week; who was middle-aged, ill-tempered and lazy; who knew everything about everyone just by looking at them. Eggy? What a disgusting old fart. Dubois was not much better though she flirted with him on the off-chance he might favour her with a response. She viewed me with neutral eyes; and now and then I would impart to her the courtesy of a greeting when our paths crossed on the street. Then she looked prematurely old, always rum in mood. Defeated. There were so many Wendys out there. Echo, however… Well, if one could describe a girl as cute as a button and not insult her loveliness in the process, she was that. Her voice was a pleasant and mischievous warble: 'Here, let me light that candle for you.'

Moonface gave her colleague a collegial glance. She waited for the girl to go away before she startled me, saying: 'We should've done it at least once, you know, had what you guys call a tumble in the sack.'

Perhaps I blushed.

Her eyes growing blacker in the candlelight, she inspected the end of her ponytail, her mouth slightly parted, her two incisors slanted inward like two halves of a gate. The pedagogue in me got the upper hand: 'You can sleep with any number of people and not gain one jot of experience from the exercise.'

What had my remark to do with anything?

We were Echo's only customers, the café once more under new management. Two Greeks owned it now; they took turns working the galley. They were affable enough, their English language skills suspect. They just assumed we were always joking with them; they kept smiling and laughing back. We took care to look astonished when it was admitted that the cheesecake now on the menu was homemade; that Cassandra, wife to one of the partners, was responsible for this fact. Gradually the clientele changed; Slavs, one by one, drifted away. There were more Greeks hanging about, as well as locals from the neighbourhood who had been leery of the place when it was under other management. And, come May, and if one were an ancient Roman . . . but enough of beating on pots and invoking deities. Moonface said: 'I never told you much about my father, did I? Don't you want to know about my father?'

'Not really.'

'United Church. The boys, you know, they thought that because he was a minister, it meant I had to be a slut. Don't know where they got that idea.'

She rolled her eyes up and to the side—

'What about your mother?' I thought to ask.

'What about her? She's crazy. Reads philosophy. Thinks I'm almost a Garbo look-alike. It's her way of telling me I never quite cut the mustard—'

'That bad.'

'Yes. But I blame my father most for me being what I am,' she said, airily.

'Which is?'

'Can't stop being nice to everyone. Because he can never think ill of any idiot, and nothing gets done, and everything's allowed. If he'd been one of those hardboiled detectives, nobody's fool, it would've been so much more cool.'

'A lot of people use certainty as an excuse to be mean.'

'Avuncular, Randall, avuncular.'

Her voice was a little thin, and yet musical in her contempt.

Phrygian Mode

Echo was a miracle, a delight to have around. Her air of 'places to go, things to do'—from where had it come? Her eyes were round and tawny, like the eyes of certain cats when they are alarmed or intently curious. Her stature was short, her body compact, bosom full. She once asked me in the Blue Danube aka Le Grec what I happened to be reading just then. I explained I was reading over something I had written with a view toward making it better. She then said I ought to let her have a go at it; that she was the best reader I was ever likely to have. Was it true? In comparison to Echo Moonface now seemed world-weary and jaded and much overrated. Was she beginning to get her first taste of how it is life so very often disappoints and just keeps on disappointing? Moonface was now in her digs and I in mine.

I had poured myself more wine. I would hear out the *Tallis Fantasia* –a piece composed in 1910, Phrygian mode—as I flopped on the couch. It was a mode about which I knew nothing, just that the violins and violas taken all together had the full bore resonance of a great pipe organ. *Against the Lord with false accord.* Something like emotion stirred in me; then emotion and music died away.

Eggy had said that when he was gone, he with his death-is-just-over-the-horizon-for-me eyes, Moonface would fall to me. She was his great friend and he was hers, but he viewed her as lost and confused. In light of what Moonface had just confessed, that business about her father being somewhat of a flake, and that consequently she might be an apple fallen not so far from that tree, I could perhaps understand a little more clearly how she was suffering. I attributed it to her love affairs, all of which turned out mildly disastrous. Fast Eddy was now in the room, his eyes squinted behind cigar smoke. He with his insufferable gravitas advised: 'You should make sure Moonface goes back to school.'

'Should I?'

'In Ottawa, even.'

'Classical studies?'

'Accounting.'

Fast Eddy disappeared like a spirit who had a mission elsewhere.

Moonface, so I thought to myself, needed a little of what Echo had. There was a brief blast of music, her CD player. Led Zeppelin as a retort to my existence. Then accusing silence.

I could go knock on her door. I could go all of a few steps up a carpeted hall and recommend myself for an hour's worth of solace. It had transpired before, our lovemaking not lovemaking as such, just proximity and exchanges of thought. Even Platonic relationships must bear up now and then under the pall of disillusionment. I could go but I did not wish it. I could go just to hear her protest: 'But you don't like my ears. You wrote about not liking my ears.'

I would tell her she was exaggerating. And more than likely, she would be committing to her diary acerbic asides about Calhoun and other Traymoreans. It was her leisure activity. I could go hell-bent for leather, and Dubois in his digs, hearing my intentions loud and clear, would grin. Or Eleanor, in hers, might smack her lips and figure I had finally caved. Eggy, Zeus-like, his death-gaze immortal, would remain above it all. The rain in

Spain and all that. Kennedy had done for sex what Eisenhower did for the game of golf—all that stuff and nonsense. Mrs Petrova might hear the old floorboards creak and she frown, she who ran a tight ship. Later, I would rise with the birds, as would most Traymoreans save for Eggy who rose around nine, Moonface lying in her pajamas, playing with the ends of her hair. Then she, too, would get up, don a robe and cross over to Eggy's. And he would reach for her bum and she would evade his clutches; they would carry on like a house on fire, saying vile things about vile people.

Attack on Iran

It was a day in April, light-years into a dark Presidency. For all that a palliative and enabling media was suggesting otherwise, the darkness was much remarked upon. Melancholy had gotten the best of me. I was flat on my back on the couch. This time the music into which I would crawl and curl up was comprised of a piano, an accordion and an oud. But it was as if the musicians, both worldly and cenobitic, were making music from within the sanctuary of a flame; not that the music was fiery, it was not; it was remotely jazzy and somewhat cool in tone. But it had put me in mind of heat and summer skies, of southern winds just passing by, moody maples shimmering each leaf of which was an episode of my life. Indeed, it was madness that I lay there in that state of mind.

And here was Sally McCabe, one auditor, among others, of my mentations; and she meant to goad me into authorship.

'Why yes,' said Sally McCabe, politician's daughter, pom-pom girl, beauty queen, fellow student of a high school I once miserably attended, and for years an hallucination peculiar to me, 'I exist. Randall Q Calhoun has his theme.'

I went out of the Traymore, and there was Wendy on the street looking over the time-pieces in the window of Mrs Petrova's shop. From the looks of it, life had just insulted this Wendy yet again. I nodded; she scowled. A few more steps and I raised the Blue Danube.

How long would the place stay the Blue Danube in name? The present owners who hailed from the north of Greece had other mythologies and geographies to honour, other dead grandeurs. Eggy was there, as I expected he would be. He had survived another winter, winter one of his besetting fears; snow and ice restricted his movements, his pins shaky. He ached for the warmer weather when he might sit out on the terrasse and eye the passing girls. No more Black Dog Girl? No matter. There would be others just as fascinating to behold, just as pleasing to regard, just as essential to his construction of the alphabet of the world.

Dubois was there, too, but not Moonface, Echo waiting on tables in her stead. A hairy old Greek with thick-lensed glasses and ugly khaki slacks was nosing about everything. Perhaps changes were coming. Already, a large, unframed photograph of the Acropolis replaced the obscenity of a tapestry, one of a snowy, alpine scene; one fit for Tyroleans, perhaps, but not the Slavs who used to congregate in the café. Ah, those steepled cypresses.

And I was surprised to hear that even Dubois believed it possible, air attack on Iran, the Vice-President pulling the strings for this in the background. Eggy said: 'I keep saying it, Calhoun, and if you've been paying attention, you'd know the U.S. of A. went from adolescence to senility without passing through maturity.'

Yes, Eggy had said so many times, he so old now and having been in Quebec so long that he had forgotten he, too, was a Yank, a West Virginian, at that. Now he was on about the nosy Greek.

'What do you suppose he's doing?'

'I'll bet,' said Dubois, having recourse to a bottomless well of expertise, 'that he's in the restaurant supply business, and he's looking for a way to make some money out of Gregory. Upgrade, upgrade.'

Gregory and Elias were the two partners who made up the present management team.

'Oh the rain in Spain,' said Eggy, 'it falls mainly on the plain.'

His chin raised his chest.

I had yet to speak a word. I certainly had opinions to offer on the current political situation. But here was Echo come to take my order and my eyes filled with her, her face so open and frank and honest, her fine hair swept away from her brow and tied in a ponytail. I had wanted to put a question to her, and finally, I did so: 'Echo,' I said, 'really? How did you come by that name?'

'My grandparents,' she promptly warbled, 'they're Greek and they wanted to spite my other grandparents who are, guess what, Italian.'

This explained everything. Her smile let me know that it should. I said I would have some wine though it was early yet. Off she went with a bound in her step.

'I'm impressed,' said Dubois, 'I really am.'

'With her?'

'No, with Hitler, you cretin.'

'How long is that look of hers going to last?'

'I know what you mean, but let's say forever. Though, of course, we know better.'

We looked at Eggy, Dubois and I, at the half-asleep half-man, half-angel who seemed to have lasted forever with all his accumulated sins, his soul, beyond question, black with them.

'Has the old sod asked her out yet?'

Dubois laughed, saying: 'He's intimidated. Can you believe it? That slip of a girl has got him knocked back on his heels.'

'Poor Moonface,' I said.

'What about Moonface?' Eggy thundered, that sparrow of a man awake again.

Gypsy

Eleanor was despondent. She knew things between her and Dubois were fine but that, somehow, they were not. She wanted marriage; he was good with the status quo—her dinner table, the postprandial bed. I was taken aback by the woman who answered my knock at her door, she of the frosted, the gilded curls. What was with the gypsy skirt which, as she spun around on her high-heeled slippers, was crimson and full-bodied and the very spirit of death-defying gaiety? Confronted by sharp fluctuations in mood, and I run for the hills. She tra-la-lahed: 'Mr Calhoun, to what do I owe this pleasure?'

'I'm not sure. Have you joined a folk club?'

'Funny, Randall, momentously funny.'

I followed her into her kitchen, one that was perhaps the finest of all the Traymore rooms; that skirt of hers twitching and switching and twitting me. The commodious kitchen was conducive to talk and the baking of edible delights, to political forums and all around philosophizing. It was a refuge from mean spirits and idiot minds. Even so, I knew she wished to launch into a tirade concerning Bob Dubois but was holding back out of deference to my tender sensibilities. She was a woman who usually got what she wanted without too much blood being let in the process. Yet she expected her men to have backbone; she was often perplexed by demonstrations of male diffidence, especially mine. She said: 'So I hear there's still another new waitress in Dodge.'

'That would be Echo.'

'What's she like?'

'That pixie, she's unstoppable. A terror. A warbler. A winner of hearts. It's not clear yet whether she can win minds.'

'A warbler,' said Eleanor, 'you don't say.'

It was as if she had an idea of what I meant.

'Yes, she's got me believing again that anything's possible. I haven't felt this way since the days of my youth, that is, before I caught that fatal football back in high school and incited all the furies of the universe to hound my steps ever since.'

'I'll bet Moonface is feeling something like a pinch.'

'The possibility has crossed my mind. And Eggy's, too, I might add. Bob? I think he's vastly entertained.'

'That sounds like my man.'

I rolled us a couple of cigarettes. I wondered if she would break into the amaretto, a substance for which she had a weakness. She made no move to the cupboard. She sat on her chair, her thighs spread wide apart under that voluminous skirt, her thoughts elsewhere. Once in a while sparks had flown between us, but it had never amounted to anything. It had always been my belief that she harboured a secret crush on Marcel Lamont, a one-time Traymorean no longer in the world. Eleanor convinced me that Lucille Lamont murdered her husband by way of leaving him with a case of gin, right in front of our noses, in the Traymore. It is to say she went away to Ontario for a family visit, and Marcel not only drank himself silly, he drank himself dead. Lucille Lamont would never be caught out in her soft-core crime; Eleanor and I, we could only hope that, one day, some god, some agency of fate, some glaring flaw in the Lucille Lamont character, something, at any rate, would get the best of her in a spectacular and emotionally satisfying way, satisfying us. But what with the ghost of Fast Eddy flitting about Traymorean haunts, why not then, the supplicating ghost of Marcel? Was his death not a classic instance of a man having been prematurely cheated of his just desserts, the very thing that terrified those most superstitious of people—the ancient Romans? Who had no love of vengeance-exacting spooks? Perhaps Marcel believed he had deserved his lot; and death was final.

'Moonface,' Eleanor ventured, 'is not going to like this other chickadee stealing her glory.'

'Maybe, maybe not. She seems adrift. She's frightened of something.'

'Tell me another. She has always been scared, scared of her own shadow, scared of men.'

'I don't know, she's never been particularly frightened of me. And she's never been afraid to be left alone with Eggy.'

'You're not the intimidating type. Eggy's decrepit.'

'That's not what I want to hear.'

'You're a softie, Calhoun. The classic liberal mind that's had too much high life.'

'Eleanor, my goodness, you're threatening analysis at my expense.'

'I've got a brain. It's served me well.'

'Of course it has.'

A not unfamiliar silence took over the room, Eleanor on her side of things, I on mine. There was nothing baking in the oven, so I only just noticed. Dishes had been washed and put away. Counters were bare and clean. A clear vase of store bought freesias on the table. True spring could only be just around the corner. I only just noticed them, as well. Eleanor rose and then, slowly circumnavigating the table, she came to a stop behind me. She rested her hands on my shoulders. I cannot say she sighed so much as she sang some brief but undetectable dirge. She had operatic tendencies. I was worried she might attempt to kiss me. She grazed the back of my neck with a mischievous finger. Then, stepping away, she went and pressed her midriff against the edge of the sink, all her weight on one foot, the other foot lifted from the floor. She was now and then inimitable. I had the overbearing sense that there was so much flying around in her mind by way of thought and worry (not to mention her penchant for flirtation) that it would prove futile to say, 'A penny, my dear, for your thoughts?' Besides, it was an expression I detested. I could only say: 'Eleanor, you seem awfully restless.'

'I am, Calhoun, very much so.'

Herodotus

Love of father for son is as fraught with blindness as any other love. I have long suspected the futility of thought, for all I have been rational enough to eschew the mysticism of loons. The less said about my father and his reptilian brilliance, the better. I was in no danger of receiving his blind affections. Sometimes the father, perceiving all too clearly the flawed character of the son, simply cannot stomach the view and turns away from it. Perhaps Marcus Aurelius, Roman Caesar, believed that responsibility would activate the better parts of Commodus's nature, Commodus his son and Caesar to be. There was nothing to activate but the appetites. A great deal of pollen swirls about in the air.

Fallujah. The Americans, thinking it payback, having at the place with all their ordnance. The mad going mad. Imperial pique. The mind stretched so very thin between two polarities of absolute illogic. It was what happened to bodies that fell into black holes, subjected to unimaginable forces. I would have loved to know whether Tacitus ever giggled in the face of beastliness.

Moonface moped. Perhaps Eggy was right about her and she was lost. Despite the odds, Gregory, the new proprietor of the Blue Danube, was making optimistic noises in the galley. It was as if he would cook and people eat and pay him for it, and his labours and his expectations have rhyme and reason in dark days getting no lighter. He took the world on faith, his boyish grin impervious to the mutability of fortune that was, in any case, nothing he could not address. New toys, new for this café, at least, were popping up almost every day. Touch screen computer for tabulating orders and bills. A flat-screen TV replaced the old set, where it was attached high on a wall. In time for the hockey play-offs, and I supposed, the Euro Cup. Various other electronic gadgets whose functions escaped me. A new menu, its cover cobalt-blue, its gold lettering Greek script. More images on the walls: white coastal villages. Sparkling seas. Pomegranate sunsets. Such-like. A rise in the price of a cup of coffee. I wished Gregory the best. I wondered, could I excite myself enough to make a play for Moonface? The cynic in me was beginning to wallow in cynicism.

The previous year or so had been a time of transfigurement for one Randall Q Calhoun. A grand enough word for that little something that had shifted in the Calhoun soul, that perhaps amounted to nothing more than a wave-tossed pebble, than particles of sand streaming down the sides of a depression in a lunar dry protectorate. Fast Eddy was now at my table, stub of a cigar in his mouth, unlit. He nodded at Moonface, saying to me: 'Have you told her yet?'

'Told her what?'

'To resume her studies.'

'Her trail's gone cold on Virgil.'

'I would prefer she do accounting or take up some useful science. I know Eggy wants her to dedicate her life to the study and the writing of history. A reasonable enough Plan B.'

'Even as we speak, she's reading Herodotus, playing with her ponytail.'

'A pretty picture.'

'But maybe she needs to drift a little. Often the young are in too much of a hurry.'

'There's drifting and there's drifting.'

Fast Eddy, in his new travels, had picked up some wisdom. He vanished, presumably to go and get more.

So I said to her, to that chameleon of a young woman now attractive, now nothing remarkable: 'Are you funked? Or are you actually captivated by what you're reading?'

No,' she answered brightly, 'I'm really really reading. It says here on page 410: *Bear thou unbearable woes with the all-bearing heart of a lion.*'

'Fancy that, you've become oracular. Pythian priestess.'

'Pythian priestess? Avuncular, I'd say.'

'Yes, but one high on a gas-rich artesian stream.'

'What a life you have, Randall. You read, you write, you lay about. Not too many people take you seriously, so that not too many people obstruct you in your endeavours. You quaff your wine. You make your comments. You flip off the world.'

'I was, after all, the class clown.'

Perhaps Moonface, too, was acquiring wisdom, and if not wisdom, a capacity for accurate observation.

'I don't believe it.'

'I didn't either, not for the longest time. I was such a serious, such a sombre boy. My betters knew best, and it was my sacred duty to honour their view of things. But sometimes wisecracks did escape my mouth and it shocked everybody, including me.'

'You were a rebel, like everyone else in your generation.'

'Perhaps so, but I stopped after a while. What was the point? Those who were wrong wouldn't own up to their errors. Those who were right just got more heated and sanctimonious. It was like a nightmare Thanksgiving dinner, everyone in the family at everyone's throats. I hate scenes. I haven't the stomach for taking prisoners. I've even less for taking none. In light of this, I suppose I'm not entitled to an opinion about anything much.'

'I don't know. It doesn't seem to have stopped you. Especially when you go on about poets.'

The dear girl was getting cheeky. Erotic burblings.

A Letter to Jack Swain

Dear Jack, These words I write you will, of course, not bring you back, you in your Hades reading smut, drinking swill, fending off your nagging muse. What had she ever done for you that you should present her with lines of verse? Otherwise, what news? Do you track the obscenities of my realm? I don't suppose you do. But then, now you've attained a sort of omniscience among shades of reasonably civilized behaviour, how would you pronounce *spanokopita*? Do you chuck a football around, say, with the likes of an Ajax or a Red Baron? Is the circle you inhabit multicultural? Well, and though it's been asked numberless times by persons more gifted with comedic gab than I, is there sex in the afterlife? *The rules of morality, therefore, are not conclusions of our reason.* I dreamed I went to bed with Moonface. As Eleanor R, one of my fellow Traymoreans, would have it, I caved. Moonface was neither pleased nor displeased. It was neither chore nor pleasure, though, of pleasure there was a certain quiet partaking. It was an occurrence that had to occur. Details? You want details? As I said, she was neither pleased nor irked. When she was not in some secret part of her mind communing with God knows who, she teased and minxed, pretending it was quite the event, this pairing of Moonface and Calhoun, her bed sheets the darkest of blues, her body pale. More than this, you'll never know. It would violate discretion and it would be rude. And I'd be lying through my teeth, what I did to her; what she did to me. We are lonely and frightened creatures who, on occasion, chance on moments of unpremeditated grace. In my waking hours, somewhat liquored up, I have amused myself, penning a trial draft of my Last Will and Testament. *To Moonface my Tacitus, Eggy too old to care. Liquor goes to Dubois, CDs to Eleanor. He'll drain the whiskey down to the last bitter flame and she'll just adore the Shostakovich. To Minnie Dreier my ancient mash notes, and she may do with them as she wishes. Five will get you ten she'll make, she'll build, she'll cause to happen a cold holocaust of them in her fireplace. I, Randall Q Calhoun (Q to Moonface when she's in trouble), weak in flesh, weaker elsewhere, remark that I, the last man to rate the mind over and above the pleasures, kissed a girl in the light of dawn, and the shiver of it ran down my spine, and a note too low for my ear to detect went back up it and out to the stars. But in conclusion, this: there's never any help even if, on time, we love by appointment and routinely love. To succeed in a world gone berserk, to fail in a kinder one—yes, it's the devil itself to come by a choice.* End of reverie. Now up springs Sally McCabe, as beautiful as ever, as mischievous. She says, 'Fine little moment you got going there, Calhoun. Who, by the way, is this Jack Swain? Anyone I might find of interest? And Moonface? You know what I call that, what you're doing with her? Taking advantage of a dim bulb.' Jack, did you ever comprehend the American mind? Just now, I'm looking at pictures in a book. Poussin's *Dance of Nymphs*, for instance. That Priapic deity at the center could be Eggy. *Adorn Priapus; adorn Hymen.* This I understand even with my eyes closed, one hand tied behind my back. Baroque grandeur. Dinah Washington I understand, too. 4 in the morning, and what's this, I'm pouring my heart out to a dead man. The other day, Jack, I'm sitting in the Blue Danube. In lopes Joe Smithers, that skyscraper of a poet. He's beside himself; seems he'd been invited to an evening of French and English poetry, he the tallest reader on the dance card. Would I come? Why would I go? I've got Moonface and Eggy when I want a literary evening. Even Dubois once wrote a treatise on Camus. But I went. It was a warmish supper hour when I got downtown, 10 Celsius or thereabouts. After a long winter, people could be forgiven for thinking themselves in Miami. The boulevardier in me sought the upper hand and achieved it, close on his heels Boffo the Clown. All those girls smirking in a thaw, and what, would I sweep one of them off her feet? There was the-going-home-from-work crowd, the-coming-down-to-party crowd. Young perps of either sex looked for mischief. The young homeless had already checked in from the prairies with mongrel pets and blankets, hardcore sex logos plastered everywhere on that stretch of Ste Catherine's. Limo drivers, communication devices clipped to their ears, received their marching orders. The driver of a cream-white hummer could only be looking for one thing in this video erotica part of town. It's where the bookshop was in which Smithers was slated to perform. I'll cut to the chase. Midway through his spiel, and I noticed a woman of interesting profile. Black page-boy cut to her hair which was silvered, so it seemed, with white filigrees of hair. Black pea coat, skirt and boots. But it was the way she sat, leaning forward slightly, really listening, perhaps a little disappointed—it was this aspect of her that caught my attention. Poor Smithers, he angry with all those women who consider that men have nothing to say worth hearing. Well, his vignettes in regards to our faded Jezebel of a town have some charm, but no, there was nothing much at stake in what he read, at least, not on this night. Was the woman a little embarrassed for him? Could she not discern his competent craft? A few days later, I'm in the Blue Danube again. I enter; Moonface gives me a look. Well, what? She rolls her eyes to the side in that way she has, and I follow where her eyes are leading me, and what do you know, there's that same woman. Seated at her table, she's deep in thought, and writing. Eggy, that sparrow of a man, death on poets, he's appraising her with not a little pity. Dubois is absent or he would have been arching his brows. I'd gone to the Café Cherrier after the reading in the hope I would meet the mystery woman there, but she didn't show. I knocked back the wine while Smithers went on about Yeats and Klein and Miron to a group of disciples who humoured him. In any case, here she is. Light red sweater, dark slacks, red socks, black loafers. A scarf of some subtle pattern is draped around her neck. But I notice just now, what I had not seen before, a mass of raised, pinkish flesh on her left cheek. What's this all about? Moonface seems bemused, Eggy bored. —RQC

A Bit of Academe

> So the *Lemuria* did still correspond to an anxiety which was felt deep down in the consciousness of most Romans, however much they might disown the Elysian Fields or the tortures of Tartarus. Nothing shows this so clearly as the violent outburst of the elder Pliny (*Natural History* VIII, 190) who attacks 'the stupidity of those who renew life in death; where will creatures ever find rest if souls in heaven, if shades in hell, still have feeling?' Pliny's question could be answered: 'by celebrating the *Lemuria*.'
>
> *The Romans And Their Gods In The Age Of Augustus*
> R.M. Ogilvie

§

Book II—Piano, Accordion and Oud

As Noted

—Emma MacReady (Moonface) Jottings

Can't toss the boys out of bed fast enough. Watching them pull on their grotty briefs, how unnerving. Hearing them in my bathroom, how off-putting. I suppose dad loves me. My man-of-the-cloth father figure, my breakaway, stud-in-his-ear, paterfamilias, he calls me up, talks silliness at me his beloved child. Am I okay? How's work? Do I have enough money? When will I go back to school? Am I practicing safe sex? Did he? Randall has taken up with a female who has taken up with him. If she was looking for sex, she might've done better. His mind, his vaunted intellect? His mind's a mess. He'd be the first to admit it. At least here he doesn't sell you false goods. Knows what he knows, and what he doesn't know, well, he gives you a look, the one that says, 'You're on your own.' I wonder what Lindsey Price (she's the siren, she's the sparkling half of the au pair*) is going to do when she realizes Calhoun will never scale the summit of literary derring-do. What lion sits in a café, fiddles with a notebook, looks out a window like a lost puppy muttering 'Iran' under his breath as if to effect a charm against the end of days?*

She's a regular now, that spoon-eyed scarlet. 'Randall tells me you read Virgil.' What's Oh Alexis, have you no time for my tunes to her? Alright, she has a terrific figure. Has this scar on her face. Eleanor can't stand her. I can't stand her. Eggy is Eggy, Dubois titillated. What's Randall thinking? Nymphae risere.

Calhoun beatific is not a pretty sight. They hold hands. They play at knees-ies. She's got her Raleigh. He's got his regina. His—well, the word that would rhyme commences with v. Doesn't he realize how truly nasty I can be, once you rub off Upper Canada and the fact my French is ex-cell-ent?

Didn't Randall and I used to sing in the park to the tune of some Irish ditty when we were drunk enough, 'No more ologists no more…'

Anti-Follies I

—It is a bright morning, sparkle in the air, I in my grotto, fully garlanded. It is to say I am not an object of worship; rather I am a supplicant of some as yet unspecified deity, that sparkle a harbinger of promise. And yet, it is only a season handing off to another, the end of snow for a while, a morning fit for the robins of childhood. A book of Gombrich rides the low-slung table that sits before my couch, item of furniture bordello-green. Essays on art. Ghiberti's doors, for instance. A visitor might assume I have been reading it. Moonface might wander in and say, 'Oh, Italian paintings. I like Italian paintings.' Fast Eddy the spectre has been and gone already, cigar stub in his mouth, his visage somewhat peaceful, as if he rather likes being a ghost. Italian paintings mean nothing to him. Or Eleanor might sashay over in her pompadours, note the fact of the book, examine it briefly and put it down, the book holding no clue whatsoever to the mysteries of her existence. Dubois might suddenly announce his expertise in chiaroscuro. In this faded Jezebel of a city, population roughly two million, perhaps all of a hundred cognoscenti know of Ghiberti's doors. It is conceivably an astounding number, but whether it reflects the high-end or the abysmal bottom of collective knowledge I cannot say. The question is, does it matter? Should the operator of a grocery truck have the knowledge? The cashier at the poor man's super mart where I buy my bread? Where the men are brave and the women good-looking and the vegetables are indifferent? The doors of paradise. Made of bronze. It would seem the artist had been ambitious, won the prize, his paradise his bragging rights to those doors, back in 1401. I go out my door, cup in hand. I stand at the window at the end of the carpeted hall. On earth saturated with snow beneath Mrs Petrova's bird feeder sparrows contest territory and mates. It is that time of year, birds collecting nest material—tissue, grass and twig. This much I have witnessed as if an alien. Harsh chittering displaces human news. Human news? What, on a bright April morning, is the most salient characteristic of a spate of human news? The universe is slowing down; catastrophe unfolds in slow-motion. Score one for hyperbole. Had the universe slowed down for the darkest days of the last Great War? Or did it hum along smoothly in its infinite expansion, human events of no especial concern to this moving toward a space not yet created, moral judgment absolutely irrelevant, people dying in their millions nothing compared to the imploding of a star? I have this great feeling that something is about to happen. Mrs Petrova's yard will get raucous with sparrowlets insane with hunger, all other dins driven out of the Calhoun mind; especially that din that concerns a certain nation-state, its internal gyroscope out of true. The last thing one ought to trust is one's great feeling.

A Roman grunt could expect 16 years in the field and plenty of scope for mutiny, there in the cold boggy forests of Germania. But what of that in Diyala Province? I go to the mart and buy prosciutto. Moonface and I shall tear at it with our teeth. It shall be our sexuality. If Moonface will have none of it, then Eleanor. She will eat anything, save for chocolate-flavoured grasshoppers and such-like. Eroticism burbles in my bones, a morning of sparkling air. It cannot possibly last, this state of affairs. I shall open my mailbox and detect in a cubicle galactic portions of absence. I tear at bread and a prosciutto slice alone, back in my digs.

—Yet another enduring obscenity, those coins struck in commemoration of the dead of September 11th. One imagines, going by the TV ad and its obnoxious voice, that the metal was extracted from the rubble; was gleaned from the entrapped molecules of those dead. Americans enjoy the grotesqueries they have become. It certainly cannot be claimed that the houses of Congress have been anything glorious of late. From Tiberius on, the Roman senate drifted, was not quite what it had been even if, over the decades, its makeup altered, reflecting the changing demographics of the Roman scene, gentleman farmers from beyond the Alps in on the fix. Last night, in the Blue Danube, Eggy sang, after a fashion, "Three Blind Mice". His voice rose to a falsetto as he expelled from his ancient throat the words *see how they run*. Dubois said, 'Horrors!' To me he said, 'We can't let this happen, again.' Echo came over to investigate. 'A sing-fest?' she asked hopefully, her eyes round like a cat's. 'A sing-fest. Hoo hoo,' said Eggy, who had the wit to cease and desist. Moonface was out on the town with a new beau. Was he in communications, too? I imagined love-making with Echo. It would be brutal and sweet, brutal because there was nothing of the dreamy or languid about her, not in such a small but compact body. Sweet because she had a lovely nature. Yet she was already lost to the enduring obscenities, one of the ologies her chosen field of study. She would learn, presumably, to standardize grief, that it has various discernible if not quite measurable stages. As far as it goes with me, science concerns itself with what can be weighed and measured, or in some reasonable manner, observed. The pseudo-sciences take the rest, and what they overlook is, well, poetry. The harder the poet sings of blossoms and blooms and the love of the young for one another, young and in one another's arms, the higher the heap of shadow-dark bones that haunt all our ceremonies. Famine, war, pestilence. (How many glasses of wine had I had? What was bringing this on?) It was an idiot who surmised that poetry is our anthropological destiny; in a certain sense he was more right than he could possibly suppose. That afternoon, a trace of heat in the air, the air however still too chilly for the Blue Danube terrasse, a skyscraper of a poet, Joe Smithers, announced how, inside a week, his father died and his long-time girlfriend went insane. Goodness. But he had only been stating facts, spitting them through his teeth, as it were. He had not been looking for sympathy, his head bowed to the weight of some yoke. More likely than not, he actually had a poet's soul, if one stretched a little thin between two pontoons that were his feet and the stratospheric elevation of his pedagogical head. I had no right, for all that, to estimate the breadth and depth of that soul, and there you have it, a poet's scruples. To be ignored only in times of emergency, as when a pestilential Executive is on the prowl. Moonface had been on shift and overheard what Smithers had to say. She moaned slightly in her musical way and otherwise said nothing. She retreated to the galley and Gregory the cook with deliberate steps. She seemed distracted. Erotic urges occur at the oddest moments, her nape exposed, her hair upswept. I had Joe Smithers on my hands, he in a dark and panicked mood, as might have been expected. I made conventional noises; he thanked me for them. What would Echo eventually learn to say of this current phase of his grief? Was there an organization, a union, for example, that grief counsellors might join and pay dues to in return for lobbying privileges? Moonface had no clue, Echo less, but she might go farther in life on the strength of her boundless energy. Dubois had informed us, to judge by junk mail that popped up on his computer screen, that he was to go and do something obscene with some starlet of fabulous notoriety. 'Now,' said Dubois, 'why would I want to do that?' He sounded on the up and up. Soon we would be attending barbecues and coming away from them with lumps of leftover cake and sacks of peonies, with news of new colonial postings for cousins and in-laws. We

Traymoreans, save for Moonface who was a student and Mrs Petrova who sold time-pieces from her shop, were more or less retired from the fray.

—There is no plot-line to the twists and turns of one's existence, but there is impetus; there is something like fate which one's momentum attracts. And yet, there are joys to life in Quebec that have not been hopelessly polluted by the joys of 'lifestyle'. The first sustained snowfall sifting through the trees that makes of everything a hush is one of those joys. The first warm robin day. The deep afternoons of late September, the maples and their vestments. Even so, some old hag on the street seems to have been off her meds of late. If I do not go to church she will not only call the cops, she will fly up my arse with her ratty sneakers and tumble-down socks. Echo, a Blue Danube waitress, is not the brightest penny, not by a long shot, but she is the sort of girl who will conquer your heart, any heart in the blink of an eye. The ologies do not deserve her.

—The primaries: Roman circus. Americans pretend to outrage at the liberties the contenders take with their credulity. Some object to the gender of a woman running for presidential office, as if gender were but some abstract notion of a living and breathing body. I am not a political animal, but it is as if I have been left with no choice but to watch ritual acts of copulation. Boogie days and nights. Jack Swain sat it out in Palermo where, perhaps, he had a better seat, lobbing long-distance peanuts at the interchangeable shadows of a senate. Sicilians thought him a character, they otherwise nonplussed with most human antics. My interlude with Lindsey Price began, as I have already described, in a French language bookshop. She was aware, she later told me, of a pair of eyes burning into the good side of her face. Joe Smithers had been holding forth with his verses, and he surprised me. I had expected cloying allusions to his dying father; he had recourse, instead, to his affection for his faded Jezebel of a city. It was his stab at continuity.

—Lindsey Price had, she told me, packed a suitcase and closed up her cottage. She got in the car and drove. She supposed she would head into the city on a dreary day. It had been a long winter.

—Down out of the hills and into the cornlands. Abraham would not have believed these cornlands. He would have prayed to his Sky-Father, saying, 'Lord, there's nowhere here to hide the shadow I cast. All the snow. All the ice.' You cross a grotty old arching bridge, then a long causeway—the river wide and grand. Potted concrete, decrepit system of thruways and on-ramps and off-ramps and trestling bridges. Tattery Jezebel of an island city. Walter, to whom Lindsey Price was once married, used to say she drove too fast. Walter, Walter, good egg, dead of an Arab's bullet. She stopped somewhere and rang up Hilda, her old mentor. 'Sure, you come stay with me, my precious.' Hilda Riesendorf taught Lindsey the world's old god-systems back in her student days. This was before Lindsey met Walter, who took her on a whirl around the world's modernity.

—Here is how I imagine it. Hilda is 90, effervescent, stooped. Weighs less than the scent with which she sprinkles herself. A Haitian woman cooks and cleans for her. There are eight rooms and a hall the length of a cruise ship in Hilda's apartment, the building of which she owns, passed to her from her long-deceased husband. It is not far from the Traymore Rooms. She has no children to whom she might bequeath property. She talks to her African masks that hang on her walls, dubbing them Al and Putzie and Dizzy and such, little terrors they are who will accompany her on the next leg of her journey. Were she to leave them behind they would be sure to misbehave. A woman like this could certainly be significant in anyone's life. Lindsey Price has her own mask that she calls Spot. It was the central ritual item of our ceremony.

—Her first city gambit: to bathe and luxuriate. It is a lovely body in an old cast-iron tub. Women are narcissists, so Lindsey Price told me. I pretended to astonishment. 'Intelligent men,' she said, 'understand this. Women who don't are fools. Walter used to mock-bow at the foot of the bed before plunging into me and splashing about with great vigour, that is, until he tired of me. Even then, he adored me, like a sad old bear getting arthritic. But I do hate the word adore. It's a word the high and mighty use when they wish to appear affable.' Yes, she talked like this. After her bath, she rang up a few people and got their news. She made appointments for lunch. Hilda snored gently on her wide couch, a woman about to meet her gods, shawl tucked to her chin. The Haitian woman flapped about in slippers, a terrible anger in her eyes. Lindsey did not want to know. Music tinkled. Haydn.

—I would have thought that, for Traymorean society, she would have been a natural. It was not the case. I came across her in a French language bookshop where we exchanged no words. I came across her again—in the Blue Danube. She had burned the manuscript on which she was working; she had started over again from scratch. Some tiny old man kept looking at her as if he knew her; and of course, Eggy, the man in question, did not. He was looking for an excuse to make her acquaintance when I appeared on the scene. Lindsey said, 'You were white-haired. Snub-nosed. Leonine. Startled. Kind eyes. But a terrible lecher, so I surmised. A bit old, to be sure, but not yet doddering. Nothing might happen in the sack but we might talk. I hadn't talked, really talked, with anyone in ages. Walter would always put up with my silences, that is, when he was around. Then you saw Spot on my left cheek. Deep in your mind you were aghast. Don't deny it. Well, we didn't talk, at first. I had to make the first move. Slowly, I got the lay of your land. You were great friends, clearly, you and the old man and the waitress. Oh well, the war. It obsessed you though you claimed it didn't. It is what we talked about in the beginning. I told you I was married once to a man named Walter. He worked for the State Department. Now and then he would mutter "48" when he thought no one was in earshot. You looked quizzical. "Palestine," I said, "Deir Yassin." "Oh, that," you answered. I loved Walter. An Arab's bullet got the best of him. "Oh dear," you said, wondering how much it had to do with your life. Your eyes were all over my body. You could not make heads or tails of Spot. Some day I would tell you how Spot came to be. For the moment, impulsively, I told you I would have made a good prostitute. "But why?" you asked. I explained to you it was not the sex so much but the company. And when you pointed out I could have the company without the sex, I begged to differ. I failed to convince you. It was not a thing, I guess, that I could explain. Some women will say I have a poor self-image. Yes, and tell me another. What's more to the point is the hostility I incur from your women. I carry on with you in the café, and the smiles all around are sheets of ice. Moonface sniffs. Eleanor is oh so aloof. Only Echo maintains any sort of neutrality, presumably because she's fairly new on the scene, and has yet to really take the measure of Traymorean males. She, perhaps, doesn't know yet what to measure. Yes, a witticism. Walter never had an embassy of his own to run; he was what they call in the trade a go-fer, fixer, expediter. No, I really don't know the precise word that described his business, but that the Arab hadn't meant to kill him.

Stray fire. Wrong time, wrong place. Sex was a way by which I could return Walter to some creature to whom I could relate. His tastes in most things were conventional. He hadn't the time to explore literature as much as he would have liked. I did him the service of reading certain books he thought he should be reading. I would present him with a critique; he trusted my views. He had been privy to certain rumours which, if proven correct, would indicate the world would get to be one unholy seething cauldron of a toxic brew. This was a long time ago. The rumours seem to have been on point. I am not a fatalist as I suspect you are, Mr Calhoun. We should not be surprised, I think, by certain coincidences, for example, that your good friend Gareth Howard had crossed paths once upon a time with my husband. I myself had no opinion of Mr Howard, an opinion, in any case, that had to rely on a single meeting in a Rome bar. It is where the paths crossed. The Americans were up to some funny business regarding terrorist suspects. Walter was an American who, nonetheless, sometimes regarded his fellow citizens as aliens. Then he was posted to Ottawa. We bought ourselves a vacation cottage in the Eastern Townships. Shortly thereafter, the bullet did its work. I have done with mourning. I suppose my love for Walter was more respectful than deeply and insanely passionate. I don't know if I will ever feel that way toward any man, as much as I like men. It doesn't seem to have been in the cards, but then, you never know. It isn't likely to transpire with you, I can see that now, but your company is agreeable, and even a little instructive. It is easy to turn your head. I wouldn't have thought you would let yourself get foolish over any woman. I don't know what you can possibly see in Moonface. It's the name, I fancy, the name and the fact of Virgil; that and the twinned facts of imperial Rome and contemporary America. Say as much to you and you get defensive. Then we got as far as your bed. You keep a rather Spartan apartment. It does not meet my comfort level. In any case, there we were in a post-coital state, and you were rolling us each a cigarette. You had already poured drinks. We could hear music in Moonface's rooms. It was loud on her side of the wall, and it seemed hostile. You thought it high time I tell you the story of the scar on my cheek. What I liked about you was the way you sucked in your breath at the first sight of my body. I also liked that you left it to me to bring up certain matters in my own sweet by-and-by; you're not pushy. In this instance, however, you were insisting. And so I told you. It was a violent tale. It said I was fifteen at the time, petting with a boy on my parents' couch, a fire sparking in the fireplace. It said my father was away, he a high-level civil servant. It said my mother came home and caught us, she who had been at a meeting, to do with church finances. She was a very strict, very proper, repressed woman. Something, I suppose, gave, and she exploded. To keep it short, she branded my face, as it were, with a half-blackened log she grabbed from the fireplace. We will never know why. Jealousy? It seems too pat. There must have been a thousand causes such as came together in a single moment. This episode was only the beginning of the insanity that encroached on her mind. I don't know if my father truly loved his wife and if love was returned, but it broke his heart, what happened; he had loved me. My beauty, however marred, has been, even so, triumphant. Perhaps every man I take to bed is a way to punish my mother. I suppose what you call the ologists would say as much. I say it's what I would have done, in any case. Men are not saints; I could have done without some of the company I have received. I understand your woman-wary soul. I am pleased you are the confidante of the Eleanor woman and that you worry for Moonface. You were silent after I spoke my piece. Clearly, you were trying to picture it all in your mind. Before I met Walter, I was already taking men to bed. I would accuse them of feeling sorry for me. It would seem I had to punish them, too. Walter cured me of that. He said, "There are a thousand reasons why we go to bed with one another. Do you think you understand the implications of each and every one of them? I certainly don't. Can we not just enjoy the fact that we do go and have a romp, and sometimes it's marvellous?" The boy. Then I related to you what happened to the boy on that God-awful night. As beside myself as I was with my pain and rage and my mother's fury, I did see in his eyes a look of terror from which he would never recover. I never saw him again. I have heard through the grapevine he's married, has children, lives quietly somewhere. He should not have held himself responsible for what happened; I rather think he has done so. You poured us each another drink. I was worried just then you would tell me you had fallen in love with me. You didn't; you sighed. It was the sort of sigh that indicates the universe is a mystery for good or ill. You said, "Life is random except when it isn't." You placed a warm hand on my thigh and squeezed. You got out of bed and went to the bathroom. I heard you in the bathroom, relieving yourself. It was a sad sound you made, a lonely piss on a lonely night. Then I knew you couldn't possibly love me nor I you, at least not in any deeply insane way. I might understand how your mind worked but it didn't necessarily follow that I *knew* you, or that there was any guarantee that I could know you and vice versa. I have sometimes seen how Moonface looks at you. I don't know what she has by way of imaginative powers; I suspect she flatters herself in this regard, but she's protective of one Randall Q Calhoun. It's all that's important, that we are able to feel safe now and then. I may have struck a false note when you returned from the bathroom. I said, "Anyway, that was the story of Spot." You looked horrified. We exchanged a collegial kiss in the morning; we agreed to meet up, later. I returned to Hilda's. There I prepared a light breakfast. I set her tray on the ottoman at the side of her couch. All the while I had described for her the events of the previous night. She said nothing. Then, reaching for a slice of toast, her look somewhat impish, she said, 'Really, my dear, you ought to check your *Golden Bough*. What we are about, what we have always been about, is to effect good outcomes. Science is only the latest wrinkle, though science is very powerful. Listen to your gentleman friend. He has no clue to what you are but even his silent testimony is worth something. You were not meant to be alone. He is not your answer. But you are to face your dilemma honourably; you are to find yourself someone suitable, before it's too late." She chewed, and then her eyes closed. A sensation of infinite weariness nearly bowled me over. I had been on my knees, pouring her a cup of tea. Hilda had been my true mother; she could not last much longer. I was cognizant of my true age; I was not anymore, as it's vulgarly put, a spring chicken. I had been thinking like a college co-ed. I was just about to cry. Hilda spoke again: "My precious, I won't have the tears. Effecting good outcomes sometimes brings disaster. In fact, it all too often does. But unless you can tell me there's another way, I can see no other way. Now hand me my cup of tea and go about your business. I'll be fine."'

The above are words Lindsey Price spoke to me. They were my pink slip, as it were, delivered to me in the Blue Danube and in other places. I cannot say I had fallen for her, given that what goes on in the mind has a separate reality from what transpires between a man and a woman face to face. She certainly seemed brave; she may also have been an incurable egotist and near insanity; I may have come to regret her. Hopping into bed with persons does not always add to one's experience; in this case, I would say it had. Moonface, I think, is relieved to see the back of her. Eleanor certainly is. Echo stood back and observed, furiously taking mental notes, as if recognizing she is not the brightest penny but that she is not afraid to work hard at addressing any shortfall. Eggy, in the end, thought the woman strange, Dubois bemused. He asked, 'Well, did you sleep with her?' I shrugged, and he took my shrug for a yes. Then he said in a lecturing tone, 'I hope you enjoyed it. Where we are in life, it's not something one can take for granted any longer.' It was his turn to come off avuncular. Eggy had the sense not to press for details; he would have been keen for them were I in the mood to spill. She had gathered her writing materials and slipped them in a large handbag. She had put on her pea coat, watching my face all the while. She walked to the door of the Blue Danube, then for a moment turned around. The raised mass of flesh on her left cheek was what it was—briefly hideous. She went out the door, waved through the window, and was gone.

Anti-Follies II

—I had been to Rome at the turn of the year. As I may have said already, I may as well not have gone; what I might recall of its sights, sounds and smells had dissipated in a North American air that does not forgive an Old World coddled by museums. Over the course of our brief set-to, Lindsey Price let me know she, too, had been to Rome; what is more, she had even met my old friend Gareth Howard in a Roman bar. I asked her which bar. She answered she could not remember but that it must have been in Trastevere where the meeting occurred. There were plenty of Americans about, and, come to think of it, she could remember some number of them arguing the merits of a war in its early phases, the outdoor patio trellised. Faux-ornamental grapes. She had had a powerful wine. Her husband Walter and Gar shouted at one another over the din. To Lindsey Price, Gar seemed a little dour. I might as well say now of our affair that it, too, may as well not have been; the savour of it as strangely out of sight out of mind as a scent that disappears in the shifting of a wind. Perhaps it will also return to me at a time when I least expect it. Just now a woman of quite ample charms, a stunner, pounds across the Blue Danube floor in her high heels, headed for the washroom; Eggy steadies himself, placing his tiny hands at the edge of the table. 'Did you see that? Hoo hoo.' Moonface, on shift, is not all displeased with the man's unabashed chauvinism. She is getting, so I surmise, worldlier. Perhaps in their aggregate her various liaisons are beginning to make a difference, Champagne Sheridan the latest. It all depends, of course, on the quality, not the quantity of such couplings. Finished with the washroom, the stunner in question reoccupies her table at the window, makes Eggy's day with a friendly glance. It happens, sometimes. He may take the memory of it into eternity. Moonface brings her a tall glass of beer, and she has a lusty swig, her hair long, thick and lustrous. Will wonders never cease?

—Echo will gain experience in the Blue Danube, then move on to a grander venue where, no doubt, she will earn better tips. We will not get to know what otherwise makes her tick, though we will endlessly speculate, and in the process, mark ourselves as the old fools we are, Eggy, Dubois and I. And perhaps Moonface will allow Fast Eddy to unlace her red sneakers and massage her feet, perhaps not, Fast Eddy, in any case, an hallucination. The radical right has mirrored the antics of the old left in the previous century so as to get and exercise power. 'Well, of course,' says Eggy, three sheets to the wind, and feeling fine, 'they were lefties once and would know.' Gregory the cook fiddles with the new high-resolution TV. He thinks the sports channel will attract customers. He is going to get his deadbeats. Dubois explains sub prime mortgages, economics now his specialty; and when I suggest that profit-taking is a bit like pulling a rabbit out of a hat, he says I am getting the hang of it, at last.

It is evening in the Blue Danube. Blind Musician, older and shaggier, is uncharacteristically silent, his thick lenses reflecting light and futility. 'I saw a robin, this morning,' I say, 'strutting in Fast Eddy's backyard.' 'But of course,' says Eggy, 'it's spring. Get up, get up out of your bed. Cheer up, cheer up the sun is red.' 'Oh boy,' observes Dubois, 'we're firing on all cylinders tonight.' 'And how,' Eggy continues, 'did Fast Eddy get to be on Moonface's A-list of paramours? That's what I want to know.' 'Because he truly admired her,' I suggest. 'He dreamed of massaging her feet,' Dubois adds. 'Doom,' I say, 'the definition of doom is precise logic scuttling back and forth between two absolute points of illogic. Doom is what madness brings us.' 'Not again,' says Dubois, 'thank you for bringing that up.' 'What, is he on about that again?' The voice belongs to Eggy, its pitch rising and querulous. 'More wine, *messieurs*?' asks Moonface, rolling her eyes up and to the side. She stands there, sexual and prematurely schoolmarmish. Her eyes are on a distant object, a menacing star, a future devoid of humans. She is considering how that might sit with the Hostess with the Mostest side of her. Or so I believe, very tipsy.

—I am on my couch, and it does not take long: Sally McCabe: 'Calhoun, you dog, who would've thought it? A hot little number comes along and decides to take you seriously. Sex becomes politics becomes metaphysics becomes proper burial rites, gratitude all around. Well, you haven't amounted to much as an author, but it would seem you have a new fan, even so. I'm a little envious. But, kisses. Got to run.' Then Fast Eddy, he with his jaw-clamped cigar: 'Randall, you're shirking your duty. I told you, you must have a serious talk with Moonface. She's lost and getting more lost. Alright, so you'll insist it's none of your business, her future, but who else is there but you? Who else could read her the riot act? Eggy, maybe, but he can't string more than three thoughts together, being too old. You're a not unintelligent man. You've been around, seen what becomes of dreams and drifting over time. You don't have to play the heavy. It's not fascistic to interfere, to insert the odd word of caution now and then. Can the world afford another lost soul? You mistake me. I don't wish to see Moonface get to be just another efficient economic unit. I want to see her fulfilled. Got that?' And though I am, for all practical purposes inert and dead to the world, in my thought I dismiss Fast Eddy, he a ghost, with a wave of my hand. Fulfill. It is a large verb, a very large one, indeed, fraught with much risk and misdirection. There is something to be said for the operations of chance. Life is random except when it is not. There is also something to be said for sticking with something or someone, come what may. Still, the Presidential stick-to-itness has given serious purpose a bad name; it has gotten a great many people killed. How redeem this balance sheet? Tomorrow it will be warm enough for the Blue Danube terrasse. To sit and admire the passing women. But why cannot I just lie here and sleep?

—It is touching how Dubois trusts the system. It is even more touching, his loyalty to Eleanor. There are hints, now and then in our general conversation, of an unhappy marriage in his past. Hints and nothing more. Even Eggy knows nothing. 'You know Bob,' Eggy will say, 'good for a tipple and teasing the girls. Knows his politics. Wrote a paper on Camus way back when. But here I am stringing more than two thoughts together. Hang the bastards. That's what I say.' Well, what does it mean, to trust the system? One may not trust its politics, but one expects to receive one's pension, the warming up of the earth be damned. I go back over the business to do with Lindsey Price. I had treated with her honourably. I had had the wit to recognize she was at a crossroads, the best and worst of times to take a lover to bed. We had gone far beyond the everyday concerns of Traymorean society, so much so it had frightened me. I had licked behind her ear and stated we are not moral creatures. She then made a nest of the bed and shivered herself into sleep. In the morning I drew her a bath. Every wall of the Traymore Rooms was listening. She was splendid, immersed in her baptismal fountain, her knees drawn up. I could have wished, however, that she had forgotten she was one of those supreme egotists, cause of all effect. Could she not have acknowledged that things might have transpired differently, only they did not? Too late for this little vexation on my part. I had otherwise squelched my sometimes overwhelming sense of futility that is human endeavour. She may or may not have noticed. We were on trial; we had on trial the parlous state of the world. Such is a purely private affair. Men performed music from within a sacred flame; the oud rang the changes on man, woman and God. We should have sold tickets, she and I, our little tryst a rip-snorting affair. That afternoon, as we sat around with Eggy in the Blue Danube and played a game of what was the best meal you ever had, Eggy answered, 'Oh, that's easy. British Rail. Kippers and scotch.' For the first time in my hearing, Lindsey Price guffawed. That moment alone may have justified everything that transpired between us. As far as supreme egotists go, Eggy is a battle-scarred, wily veteran of the campaign.

—Eggy is beside himself; he cannot make his rounds fast enough, the sweethearts he has to see. From bank to physio to the Blue Danube and stops in between. He has got a string of them, women with whom he must liaise, his strokes apparently in abeyance, wine intake holding steady. It is the weather, of course, the shorter skirts, easier smiles. For now. Come the dog days, and they will come, summer at its muggiest will slow a tiny sparrow of a man down. More than once Dubois has said to me, 'You should write a book on him. Why not? But make it light.' 'What,' I have replied more than once, 'you think his life has been all humouresque?' 'Make it light,' Dubois always repeats. I will never be able to satisfy these Traymoreans, these culture critics who do not mind the fact of the Prousts and the Tolstoys, just keep such-like out of their hair. 'Upon my word,' says Eggy in the Blue Danube, he regaling us—Dubois, Eleanor and I—with his latest close shave, 'I've got lucky stars.' Well, what's the story here? Seems a car had lost its brakes and nearly pinned him to a tree as he was crossing the intersection to the bank corner. 'Too bad,' says Dubois, his blue eyes glittering with bonhomie, 'that it didn't.' Moonface, hearing him, tsk-tsks. Eleanor shifts in her chair, rearranging her legs. 'Eggy,' she says, 'you've got more lives than a herd of cats, I swear.' 'Hoo hoo,' the man responds, 'it seems so.' For the first time Gregory the cook appears deflated; the hockey playoffs underway, the expense of the TV and the cable feed, and he has yet to enjoy a full house in his establishment. He has trusted the system: build it and they will come. The Blue Danube, if nothing else, is a laboratory for testing the efficacy of the various clichés, some of which, no doubt, will fall away when the ocean currents change. What Oedipus will pick what daisies from what roadside ditch? What Electra will honour what grave? What sparrow strop its beak on what twig? The lilacs are budding. A pestilential Executive is getting away with being pestilential. 'You're at it again,' observes Dubois, 'stop it.' 'Let him be,' says Eleanor of one Randall Q Calhoun, 'he's noodling.' 'Oodles of noodles,' hoo hoos Eggy. 'You like the looks of that?' Eleanor asks, she a little chuffed, seeing as Dubois's eyes have wandered to a stunner in the street. Dubois rolls his eyes, a grin semi-frozen to his wine-ruddy mug. All this time, and save for the occasional tsk-tsking, Moonface has been sitting quietly at another table, inspecting her red nails. She has the look of someone awaiting an interview. We are on very thin ice, she and I. We have not between us even the excuse of sexual passion with which to enrich an argument of man, woman and God. She has slipped through my fingers and I through hers. What disasters, emotional and otherwise, have we managed to avoid?

—Mrs Petrova's shop window, in what it reveals of time-pieces and curios of sentimental and atrocious taste, of gewgaws and cheap gems sparkling and gleaming in soft April light, is a time-warp. She has exchanged the snow shovel for a broom, the immediate area scrupulously swept, a winter's worth of accumulated debris disappeared. Say the word happiness to her and she will grunt. Happiness? But of course. What, otherwise, is the point? Nature gave her a strong and optimistic disposition; she has a powerful shrug for those moments when life does not at all go well. I calculate she has been a widow for some twenty years. I am one of Mrs Petrova's colourful lodgers. Another is Eleanor. I sense dangerous moods in the woman. Something between her and Dubois has gone awry. She is an intensely sexual creature; she has ungratified nesting urges. Dubois responds to the sex and is indifferent to the nest. It is significant that she has put away her trombone on which she would wheeze out "Stardust"; it was a crucial part of her mild eccentricity, as are her showy skirts and pompadours and frosted curls. Is she threatening to grow up, she who considers most men mere boys, if men at their sexual peaks? Push come to shove, Dubois will confess that the only movies he cares for are westerns and thrillers. Here perhaps is the great clue to his inner being: that reality is systemic, therefore amenable to improvement. Fast Eddy is not going to be one of the quiet dead.

—Gregory the cook got his wish, Echo run off her feet. Families had commandeered Blue Danube tables, game six of the first round of the playoffs, the Habs in the hunt for the cup. Echo in profile, so I was startled to realize, is classical. I have seen her many times in a Greek or Egyptian or Etruscan past, she the modern child of Greek and Italian confluence. Full frontal, and she is all moxie, some table clamouring for an extra fork, and she responds cheerfully enough, warbling, 'I'm on it.' Dubois would instruct her in the art of extracting wine corks. 'It's all in how you use your instrument,' he said, his wink perhaps unintended. 'The deeper the screw goes, the more leverage.' Sexual entendres got the upper hand, Eleanor stone-faced, Eggy in 7th heaven, Echo's cheeks in full blush. Eggy has lived for Moonface and wine; now Echo provides lift for his wings, he more a spiritual essence than a physical manifestation of old age, he the wisp of a wine-dazed grin. This grin only deepened the more that Echo hovered at our table, she a brazen hummingbird. Eggy's grin was an ancient shadow lengthening outward from the marble pillar of a god, especially so when I remarked, 'When her mind catches up with her body she will devastate.' Yes, she expends three times as much energy as she needs to do her work, but even so, she is everyone's darling, Eleanor cold and aloof and inwardly hot. For all that, Eleanor is too classy to just sit there and pick apart Echo's faults as she has done with Moonface.

—All one saw and heard in childhood was true and real, though the attempts of adults to reproduce the child and the events are only so many lies. The trees did talk, as did the waves of the sea and the clouds in the sky. Witches slept in closets and under beds, their power to turn one's blood ice-cold indisputable. Dogs were always one step ahead of one's thoughts and intentions, and were wise and not a little sad, given the ways of the world. Harm a shiny red and spotted bug, and one would die in some gruesome manner. Louise was beautiful beyond compare, hers the pigtails that one yanked in class, and one would marry her, and the irony is, in one way or another, one did. And so forth and so on. And the truth is, there is much

I cannot remember. There were, for instance, now and then outbreaks of my mother's blind fury, and one knew one had been touched forever by them, there at the dumbstruck roots of one's heart. There was my father's reptilian brilliance which repelled the moon and turned its face. But I have chosen to speak of my parents as seldom as possible, just that I did not pop up from under a rock. One was not aware that, as a child, one loved life. I love life now in the way that old and decrepit Eggy loves women, through wistfulness and the memory of how the women once fit in his arms.

SET-PIECES
In the Country

We rented a car, Eggy, Dubois and I, and into the country we went, Dubois at the wheel. It was a bright, April morning warming up. The snow seemed to have largely disappeared from the countryside; we would see more of it in the hills, above the cornlands. Eggy's chin raised his chest. I had the backseat to myself.

'You're going to like this place,' Dubois said. 'I know it well.'

In other words, we were headed for a lake an hour and a half out of the city. There, at lakeside, stood a five-star hotel, the bar our Mecca. We left the highway for the country roads. Eggy woke now, his flat nostrils quivering at the memory of various watering holes he had once frequented out here in a long career of frequenting.

'Me and a certain bluestocking,' Eggy said, 'laid up in a B&B somewhere hereabouts. Until a certain husband and a certain wife got wind of it. Thus ended the tryst. There was hell to pay.'

'Was it worth it?' asked Dubois.

'Well, depends on how you look at it, I suppose. I thought it was worth it. Bluestocking wasn't so sure, I believe. Ungrateful wench.'

'One of those,' observed Dubois, swerving to avoid a ditch in the road. The earth the colour of straw, hawks circling lazily in the air.

Eventually, we arrived. A narrow gravel lane, pricey automobiles parked to the side in a not as yet full shade.

'Seems a busy place,' I said, not looking forward to the company of swells.

It was a chore prying Eggy out of the car, but I got him out.

'The bar?' he asked.

'Just follow your nose,' said Dubois. And then to me: 'See, he's got his afterburners switched on.'

Eggy was caning his way, stutter-stepping, not wasting any time in his approach. Two men in baseball caps and wearing sunshades and speaking French were raking dead leaves from an embankment. I had not known what to expect, but at first glance the hotel was colonial heritage, painted white. Shamblesome. A comfortable old shoe in which to drink away one's last years should one have the bank account and the inclination. Now in the holding bar where the uptight staff had decided to stash us, Dubois sipped from a medicinal-looking dry martini. He wished it had been served in a beaker rather than in the fluted vessel he had. Eggy was working on his Jamieson's. I had asked for a *maison rouge*, and not knowing the vintage, guessed it was Californian and very good. Dubois was treating us. He pointed at the wine.

'96 bucks a bottle,' he said, having seen the drinks menu. In some circles the price was but the market value of nothing more than potable plonk.

Through a doorframe painted olive-green that separated the holding bar from the dining salon, a conference group of a sort now passed, heads bowed, feet shuffling. A junior management seminar? Dubois saw my look, and said, he who had once been a player in the business world: 'It's a good thing to do. You take people like them to a place like this, they get a taste of class, and they never forget it.'

Really? But I did not have the heart to give him the gears over his educational methods. My back had gotten up for reasons due to another cause. For one of those vultures of the merchant class, casually and sleekly dressed, designer shades, pristine white ball cap, had stuck his nose in our little realm and leered in a patronizing fashion, his wife cold and critical.

'Small fry,' I said, 'but with serious amounts of spending money.'

Dubois grinned. He knew what bravado made the world go round.

Two ducks exploded from the surface of the lake still thinly iced over. Eggy then said the ice was flowing northward. Dubois wondered what was in the whiskey that he would make a comment like that. We had not much else to say to one another. But we were content.

In Her Bad Books

Eleanor was too seasoned a woman to speak ill of Lindsey Price; even so, her eyes said it all, she saying: 'Well, I imagine the earth moved.'

I ignored the cattiness inherent in the remark.

'What can I tell you,' I said, 'it was just one of those things.'

'That's what they all say.'

'It had no legs,' I said, referring to the affair.

'Seems to me I could see plenty of fins and flippers.'

'Eleanor, really.'

'You smirked. I didn't like it.'

We were in her kitchen. She had bread baking in the oven. An old black and white TV sat on a counter, the sound off. The scheduled offering was a soap of some sort. A blonde who looked like she had had too much physical exercise was speaking words at a hunk, looking thoughtful.

'I apologize,' I said, 'for the smirk.'

Eleanor puffed loudly on a cigarette. I was enjoying her bout of jealousy.

'For God's sake, Randall, she was a predator. How could you fall for that, seeing as you've spent a lifetime avoiding predators?'

'What makes you so sure I have?'

'These women who care for nothing but themselves—'

I cut her off: 'I wouldn't go so far as to say that, but yes, she was rather self-involved. Aren't we all?'

'Sally McCabe wouldn't look on her kindly.'

'Sally McCabe would have thought the more the merrier.'

'You're not the type, Calhoun. You're not a hoser. You're just, what, one of those liberal losers history has passed by.'

'That's harsh, Eleanor.'

'Well, I say it.'

'Say on.'

'Dubois isn't going to marry me.'

'No, he isn't likely to.'

'But I guess it doesn't matter.'

'Maybe yes, maybe no, I can't say.'

'You mean you won't say.'

'Not my business.'

A soft April light blossomed in the window. It lit up Eleanor's frosted curls. She butted her cigarette, rose and went to inspect the bread in the oven. It was now almost too warm in the room. She shut the oven door and sat down again.

'Roll me another cig,' she commanded.

We might have talked about torture memos or the pending oil contracts in a lunar dry land once called Shinar. We might have discussed the election campaign that looked to have no end. We might have gone on about the three senators in the running who, despite being three, were a twosome Punch and Judy show. Of course, I was an elitist in the privacy of my being, one well-camouflaged. For a while I had thought Traymorean society was breaking apart; it was always unclear what we actually had in common besides a residence. There were the staples of sex and politics. Moonface had a new Sheridan Champagne whose mother, evidently, was flying into town to nip the affair in the bud. This was something we might have talked about with some relish. Or Fast Eddy who had died wearing pantyhose, a book of Keats in his hand. Eleanor had no room in her commodious head just now for Tacitus. I handed Eleanor her cigarette. Traymorean society was, in fact, more or less intact. Her eyes had softened and they looked a little spoony to me, and I was alarmed. I saw myself unlacing Moonface's red sneakers. The blonde in the soap was not in a good frame of mind; she had just slapped the hunk across the face. What, as if to stimulate self-awareness in him? Senate reform? Peace in our times?

Yet Another Blow for Priapus

Dubois, Eggy and I her only customers, Moonface was radiant; it seemed the mother of her new Champagne Sheridan was enchanted with her. Suddenly here was Fast Eddy to say: 'Yes, but the boy has neither looks nor talent nor great riches nor ambition, so that the fact that the mother approves of her son's sweetheart is neither here nor there.'

Fast Eddy had spoken, and now he was gone.

I had unkind words for a certain senator from Arizona. Dubois, gentleman that he is, decided to defend this presidential contender: 'Well, he's big on free trade. Can't be all bad.'

I said, 'He was shafted in the year 2000 by the same people he's all kissy-kissy with now. You call that honour?'

'I call it politics,' said Dubois with a Gallic shrug.

'Hoo hoo,' said Eggy.

How few words it takes to sum things up.

There but for the grace of the treasury go our grotty selves.

Even so, I was surprised when a serious look got hold of Dubois, he saying: 'Now don't say I never told you anything. But there was quite the scene the other night when we were all here watching the hockey game. You left, I think, at the end of the first period. So you missed it. But anyway. Seems Cassandra's partner was pawing Echo in the kitchen. Finally, she had enough of it, and she phoned her boyfriend who soon after that showed up, ready to take the guy's head off. The upshot is that the police came around. Echo is going to press charges.'

'Hoo hoo,' said Eggy.

'Moonface, too—she's rattled by this,' Dubois added.

'What will become of the place?' I asked.

Dubois shrugged and Eggy squinted.

I said, 'I don't think Echo is the type to play games. So if she says something happened, it must have.'

'Another blow for Priapus,' said Eggy. 'And we'd been having so much fun,' he continued, 'bloody hell. Why can't you boys and girls get it sorted out?'

'Us boys and girls? What did you ever get sorted out?' asked Dubois.

'Why,' said Eggy, 'I was always a gentleman.'

'I'll bet,' said Dubois.

It was hard to imagine Echo in distress, she all good cheer and gusto and determination to master the arts of waitressing. It was a very bad business, what Gregory's partner had brought about. Echo might very well leave, and even Moonface might. She moaned slightly in that musical way she had. She agreed, standing there at my side, that it was a bad business, enough to sully what had been a couple of good days for her.

'People are always spoiling things,' Eggy observed.

Gentleman Jim

Gentleman Jim had discovered our company and of what a generous nature it was. He was a drinker with a cane. White Bermuda shorts and pristine white socks were his garb. Rain fell of an evening in gloomy torrents. The thing is, we had not seen the man in a couple of days.

'But what's his story?' I asked Dubois for lack of anything better to ask, my questions welded, as it were, to the doomed superstructure of the American ship of state.

Doom consisted of a shortfall in honour and the lies told so often they were now truth. It was the triumph of hope over experience. It was the sentiment that problem drinkers like Gentleman Jim should be locked away as he, most likely, would always lack the money to buy his way out of trouble, unlike the men who caused most of the trouble. Dubois answered me: 'Insurance. Says he was a backroom boy. I guess that means he didn't knock on doors.'

'I think,' said Eggy, 'that he has much to forget, the way he puts it away.'

'So where is he?' I said, indifferent to the man's whereabouts, in any case.

'I don't know everything,' said Dubois, shocked at himself.

'He got pretty disgusting, the other night,' Eggy offered.

'We left him at the bus stop howling at the street,' said Dubois.

I had visions of a drunk being rolled for what sanity he still possessed. There had always been in the eyes of the man a look of untamed apprehension. It made him authentic, however weak. He had seen the face of God and wished he had not. He lived in a care facility for the semi-infirm. The wine was, strictly speaking, what put him there; it was also his way out now and then.

An Evening for Vulgarities

Eggy, flattering himself, fancied he had been a security breach at some point in his life. The fact that a government official had left a top secret document on the seat of a London commuter train had brought this on. A passenger, finding it, handed it to the newshounds at BBC. Meanwhile, in Canada, an ex-biker's moll was in the news for having slept with a cabinet minister.

'What,' I said to Eggy, 'you managed to get into Hoover's bad books?'

'Why just his,' Eggy countered, 'why not Special Branch as well? The rain in Spain. Hoo hoo.'

'What do you think my life's been about,' he thundered, 'Holy Mass?'

'I suppose,' I said, apropos of not much, 'that if one were to have sexual relations with a tree, and if one is high enough up on the political food chain, even the tree in question will have to be vetted.'

It had been a while since I had manifested a thought as vulgar as this.

'Go on,' pshawed Eggy, impressed with this turn of my mind.

We were at the Blue Danube, he, I and Dubois.

'Now if Arizona Senator gets a black man, preferably a general, to be his running mate, he just might win the election,' observed Eggy.

Dubois did not think so, as the only black man he could think of who was a general had been badly burned by the machinations of the current administration. Furthermore, Dubois did not believe Illinois Senator stood for anything that he could see, so that Arizona Senator was quite likely to win, anyway, no matter who he picked for his running mate.

'He had better not run on foreign policy,' said Dubois of Illinois Senator.

'So how many women have you taken to bed?' I put it to Eggy, tiny sparrow of a man.

'Six,' he answered, without blinking a tough, old eye.

'Only six,' I said, 'and you such a rake? 901 years old at that?'

'You asked. I answered. Why should I lie?'

We would get deep into the wine, our voices rising through the branches of the lush tree shading the terrasse, up and out to the stars above.

'I want to smack that girl's arse,' thundered Eggy, speaking of Moonface.

But Moonface was not available, busy with customers inside the café.

'Howsomever,' said Eggy, eyeing me with a drooping eye, 'how many women have you slept with?'

'I lost count,' I drolled.

Both Eggy and Dubois threw up their arms in disgust with my vanity.

If anybody was in anyone's bad books, it was Dubois. He had chanced across Moonface the other day, a hot and steamy one, and she was wearing something flimsy revealing of her bosom, and he made some sort of gesture, taking hold of his shirt with the thumb and forefinger of both hands and pulling on it. She did not countenance well the implication of said gesture; she told Dubois he could go and eff off right then and there. Yes, well, the dear girl. Truly obscene were the fantasies of world domination on the part of Republican Party apparatchiks who had brought so much grief to so many. Miss Meow passed by, miaowing in the evening dark. The Whistler was not far behind her, striding along with his usual exaggerated motions. It was a disconcerting spectacle as he, being Jewish, was very nearly goose-stepping. Absent so far were Too Tall Poet and Blind Musician. Still, it was quite the neighbourhood, one chock-a-block with characters.

The Quality of Eleanor's Tears

'I don't know,' I said, 'we're mostly sexual creatures, don't you think?'

I had just echoed some ologist, much to my horror.

'Really?' said Dubois the materialist, we at table with Eleanor in her kitchen.

'Well then, what are we? Chemical soups? Electrical discharges? Nothing else?'

'Pretty much,' was Dubois's lazy answer.

Eleanor sucked on a cigarette I had rolled her.

'Living,' I said, 'we live to what end?'

Dubois and I noticed Eleanor's tears at the same time.

'It's mostly the bloody footprints I remember,' she said. 'And how hard I tried not to look at his eyes.'

'But getting back to what you were saying—', said Dubois at me.

'I'm not finished,' Eleanor interrupted with some heat. 'There he was, you know, Marcel Lamont. There he was on the bloody floor, dead. There wasn't any sign of a soul in or around or about that body. Maybe it had already flown the coop. Still, and don't give me the gears for saying it, and it was the ickiest, spookiest feeling, but I had the feeling he somehow knew I was looking at him, ashamed I'd found him the way he was. I mean the dead speak, you know. Somehow they do. Don't ask me how I know, because I don't.'

She sipped from her glass of amaretto. Dubois and I had recourse to wine. Neither of us was going to insist on chemical soups and electrical discharges.

'It's just ego that makes us think we're the point of it all,' said Dubois.

'Don't trifle with me,' said Eleanor to her Bob.

It was time to go. I kissed the dryer of Eleanor's cheeks. She nearly extracted my heart from its cavity, the way her look entreated me. Dubois just sat there, somewhat astonished and too drunk by far.

§

Book III—In Continuation, a Proper Narrative

An Odyssey of Hands

There was Eggy's drinking hand on its journeys to the glass, its pilgrimages to Moonface's derrière. Excursions fraught with peril and no guarantees. Another birthday was imminent for his death-is-just-over-the-horizon-for-me eyes, and he was immortal. The hand of Eleanor R was soon to embark on some foray or another, this theatrical hand, devil-may-care hand, at home in bed, competent in the kitchen, imperious in both the Traymorean and the wider world hand. If the prose of some slutty novel was more suited to it than the pentameters of Homer, perhaps I could redress this state of affairs. And what to do with the hand of Elias, how it darkened Echo's smile and compromised her spirit and robbed Cassandra, his wife, of her honour? That is, if Elias was, in fact, guilty of molestation and more. Lop off the offending item? My own hands had had their voyages, some of which I would not care to repeat; some of which had introduced me to delights; some of which had been as humdrum (and yet compelling in their own unremarked ways) as a walk to the poor man's super mart, dangers all around, treacheries, jealous gods. It is said of North African women that they overwhelm one on account of their wild and beautiful energy. I had of course no way of testing the assertion though, in the neighbourhood, the sight of a tall, green-eyed Moroccan mother who wore short skirts and ankle bracelets, who was ferociously devoted to her children, whose husband was a chump, whose smile was grudgingly tolerant of all we lesser mortals (including Eggy), would always stop me in my tracks. The political hand. The warring hand. The loving hand. The rapacious hand. The indifferent hand, the one oblivious-to-the-air-through-which-it-travels hand. To the storms that knock it about, to the marvels, dangerous or not, that ought to bring that hand up smartly and cause it to sing praises of the living and of the glorious dead. The reasonable hand. The industrious hand. The economic unit of a hand attached, by way of nerve endings, to the cold madness of a calculating brain. The romantic hand. The futility. There was always that—the futility and the next day's hangover, an affliction to which Eggy seemed immune. I began to suspect that for a brain a crystal bowl sufficed for Eggy, its surfaces wine-splashed, its glintings and sparklings a record of all that Eggy knew, had experienced, had done, a Zeus-like comprehension of the Zeus pigpen, our universe. Moonface was now painting her nails. She bedded boys who, so I believed, presented her with diversions but otherwise bored her, her golden brown eyes the light of summer trees, her nostrils alert for some exotic scent such as might reveal her life's meaning. Perhaps it might travel her way all the way from Venice or Cairo or Kabul. Perhaps it would cover no greater distance than that which separated her Traymore digs from a library's stacks. Echo the new waitress had astonished me. She knew she had; and she enjoyed the fact of it.

Eleanor claimed she was going to visit her brother. It had been ages since she had seen him. I do not know why I did not believe her. Something in her sexual eyes shone with a plan. She did not say that, well, things had gone amiss between herself and Dubois. She did not berate the man or otherwise verbally cuff him around. No, she just needed a break. To this end she bought a bus ticket. She would brave the six-hour tedium of a passage down the 401 to Toronto. She supposed she could smoke at rest stops, if there were to be rest stops. Nothing was civilized anymore. She had been close to her brother, whose wife had left him. Oh, and he was now drinking heavily. Besides, what did Dubois need her for, he who was self-sufficient? That, I supposed, was a cuff of sorts. In respect to Dubois, I begged to differ, saying: 'Bob's proud, but he'd fall apart without you.'

'Fall apart, my arse.'

It was to be a significant exchange of views between us, so much so that, there in her kitchen, though it was still morning, she had brought out the amaretto and poured. I rolled cigarettes. I handed her one and sat back, swirling the amber in my glass. She was wearing one of her gaudy dresses. She ran a hand through her frosted curls. This was a highly theatrical gesture on her part, even for a woman prone to such gestures. Something was on her mind. I ventured to guess that that something had nothing to do with her brother, let alone Dubois. I knew enough to keep what I was thinking to myself. Usually, we resorted to politics, she and I, when we had nothing else to say. We were awaiting developments such as pertained to Echo and the charges she might bring against Gregory's business partner in the Blue Danube. Eleanor was less than impressed with either party. She had said: 'Cockteasers and stupid men—just leads to alpha silliness and stainless steel bras and pointless laws.'

Bringing the subject of Echo up again, I said: 'I don't think Echo is a tease. She's just enthusiastic.'

Eleanor gave me a look.

'How enthusiastic?'

'She's friendly. Elias is, well, I don't know, sullen, weird, unhappy all around. Maybe he was drunk. Should Echo have been expected to discern the state of his psyche and forgive him it?'

'You believe her then?'

'I do.'

Eleanor seemed a little disappointed that I did. I shifted themes.

'How long are you going for?'

'Don't know.'

'What's up with you?'

'Couldn't tell you. I know you don't want to hear me speak ill of Bob. It's not as if he's doing anything wrong. He isn't. I have an itch, to put it simply. Don't know how to scratch it. You apparently aren't interested in scratching it.'

She took a drag on her cigarette and knocked back a swig of amaretto. She leveled her eyes on me.

'You know, you're getting to be a bore. I would never have thought that of you, Calhoun. You may not have been good for much, but at least you were good for some booze and smoke and a bit of chat.'

'If I gave into you there wouldn't be anything left of me.'

'You can take that to the bank.'

'How does Bob survive you?'

'You'd be surprised at what a little demure thing I can be. It's part of my dirty tricks campaign. It's what every woman has in her arsenal.'

'I don't believe it.'

'You'd better believe it.'

'I imagine you two rolling around like apes on a Congo mountainside, no-holds-barred.'

'If the image entertains you—'

'Any chance of a refill?'

Eleanor wondered if I was worth it.

Evidently I was, and she poured. She had to reach across the table in order to pour. A generous glimpse of her bosom. I am sure I was meant to have it. Her air of triumph would outlast the glaciers. Sometimes she was insufferably full of herself.

'And what's to become of Fast Eddy's house?' I asked, changing the topic yet again.

'Don't know. The yard's going to seed.'

'He never did much with it, anyway.'

'He was a strange fellow, I'll give him that,' Eleanor sighed. 'God, that it should've been me to come across his body, and he wearing pantyhose. How awfully strange.'

'Yes, that was some touch. I'm sure he never intended anyone to find him in such a state.'

'Are you sure?'

'He was a very private man.'

'Private men, you know, have wild inner lives.'

'I'm a private sort, and I don't consider the inner me to be all that wild.'

'No, you're just a bore through and through. At least, you've been that way ever since you got back from Rome. Like Rome was too good for us for you to cut us in on the spoils.'

'What's to say about it? Besides, I wrote Moonface the odd letter or two, dwelling on things Roman. Ask her for them. She'd let you read them.'

'Don't want to read them. I want you to tell me.'

'There's nothing to say. I hung out, drank wine, brooded. It's pretty much what I do here. The scenery was different, that's all.'

'Yes, but that wasn't what you were there for. You were there to get in Clare's pants, if I remember right.'

'If there's one thing you're subtle about, it's sex.'

She gave me a look.

'Clare liked her men to be direct but she didn't like thugs. There's a difference,' I explained.

'You don't say. Well, I like men to be direct. And five will get you ten the odd thug isn't to be sneezed at.'

'Don't look at me. I'm not much for the rough stuff.'

'Not looking at you. As Eggy says, "Bloody hell."'

There were layers upon layers of hurt and anger in Eleanor's tone. How much of it was real? How much imagined, a dollop now and then of self-pity? Theatrical woman are quick to avail themselves of self-pity. I liked theatrical women, always had, but the pity part could be bothersome. Lindsey Price was rather unique; she was so much the egotist she had no need of woe is me. As for Clare Howard, dead wife to my oldest friend in his grave, she had been neither the theatrical nor the self-pitying sort, but she was able to go from hot to cold and back again on a dime. She had been a magnificent woman, and since her fatal accident I had relived the single kiss we exchanged, over and over again in my mind. Life the Great Tease.

I feared for Eleanor, and it only followed I would have to fear for Dubois, too. It would prove a bad business if my hunch was borne out, Dubois betrayed. Echo was betrayed. Wrong place, wrong time. The dirt done her was in the fact she was open to life and a cretin took advantage of her smile and the favours it bestowed. There was so little grace in the world, however rough and ready that grace, that years might pass before one would ever encounter it again.

The book I was writing was not going anywhere. Words succeeded words succeeded words at which the likes of Dubois only laughed. Perhaps it would serve him right should Eleanor pull a fast one and he get wind of it to his own disadvantage. Dubois's worst fault as a materialist was that words were as much subject to consumerist appraisal as a toaster or a pepper grinder or the child-whores of Bangkok. And this was a man who had idolized Camus. Where had the romance gone? Had the hairline cracks of his cheeks spread to his brain? Perhaps I was not as impressed with his Jesuitically-formed mind as I should have been. In fact I was in the act of scribbling when there was a knock on my door. It was Moonface, all smiles.

'I don't know,' she said when I let her in, 'I'm just in a good mood.'

'For once.'

'For once.'

'And to what is owed the pleasure?'

'My boyfriend's mother likes me.'

'Hallelujah. Huzzah. But we know that.'

'But that's not it.'

'Then what?'

'I've decided you're right, you know, when you said I don't have to contribute anything to my classics studies other than my love, and that some day, I can pass the love on.'

'A red letter day in this, my faded Jezebel of a town.'

'You're such a cynic, Randall. But you keep trying, I guess.'

'Trying? Trying what?'

'To be good.'

'Would that I could do some good.'

'You are. You do. You inspire me.'

'Spare me the encomium. Look at this. These words. Here's real betrayal. Literature will never forgive me.'

'Well, maybe you've got a point there.'

That was Moonface for you. Just when you thought her feckless and dull, she could slip one in you and twist it a little. She was seated now beside me on the couch. She leaned back, tucked a red-sneakered foot under her denimed leg. I had forgotten my manners. Would she like a drink?

'A shot of something?' I asked.

'No, that would be pushing it.'

'So does this mean you're going back to school?'

'Could be. I'll have to take my bachelor's all over again. Awful grades.'

'At least you'd know what you're about.'

'Oh Randall.'

She hated it when I got avuncular. But was she going to kiss me? Something had just flashed in her rich, golden-brown eyes. Her child-bearing hips were alluring. When all is said and done, there are stages in their lives when women are infinitely more sexual than civic-minded.

'I think Eleanor's going away,' I said.

'I heard it, too.'

'But don't ask me. I don't know what's up. How's Echo, by the way?'

'Haven't talked to her. She sure was mad. I thought her boyfriend was going to shoot Elias.'

'Are you staying on?'

'I think so. It's been hard enough going to work lately, and now all this.'

'Yes, I can imagine. Sometimes I'm afraid that Traymorean conviviality has only made things worse for you and Echo.'

'Well, it's not your fault or Bob's. Eggy sometimes gets so loud, he embarrasses me. But he's so old and he's going to die soon.'

She was only stating a probability but I did not like her just then for stating it.

'Eggy is not going to change,' I said.

'He's stubborn, alright. Is it true Fast Eddy was wearing women's clothes when he had his heart attack?'

'Partially true. He was reading Keats.'

'Oh. Right. I forgot.'

Now Moonface was getting feckless, as if she had reached the limits of her attention span. Then she rebounded somewhat, saying: 'I did like him. He was sweet. Not like you guys.'

'Point taken.'

'I should think so.'

There was an edge to her voice. She was, indeed, like the moon, changeable. Now innocuous, now menacing. She had slipped through my fingers and I through hers, and yet, here we were, getting on with Traymorean life.

'Well, I think I'm going to have a drink,' I said.

'I think I'm going to go,' she said.

Hours later, and the knock was Eleanor's. I hoped I was dreaming it, that she was drunk and wearing something very thin. Dubois could poke his head out his door at any moment. Her words were slurred.

'Kith me, kith me, you fool. You know you've always wanted to.'

Elias puttered about in the galley; the look on his face—half grin, half grimace—suggested he knew no girl named Echo. Moreover, if he had known of such a creature, he certainly would not have groped her. Eggy was silent and content to be so. I worried for Cassandra, Elias's wife. She came in now and then with a cake she would have baked at home to sell in the café. We did not see much of her but even so I liked seeing her: she was shy, undoubtedly intelligent and determined. When she felt sure of her ground, her smile ravished. The last thing she could possibly want was a train wreck of a marriage, there being two daughters in the mix as well as a business to run. I supposed there must be qualities to Elias she could respect but he was such a closed man I could not discern them. I could see he was homesick, sometimes, his being here a favour he granted lacklustre Canadians of no apparent traditions but hockey and bagpipes. I said to myself, 'There's rage in this individual that could very well get the better of him. Also, he looks as if, at any moment, he will burst into tears.' I was playing the ologist, a shameful pleasure. Eggy asked: 'Did you say something?'

We sat by the window in the bosom of the sun, Eggy's demeanor near angelic. Whether or not he was aware of the tensions circulating in the café, he was certainly far removed from them. I waited for the halo to form above his inverted pyramid of a head. Of course, Eggy's soul was black with the sins of a long life and multiple wives, but his loopy grin just now was beatific. Verily, the cliché was true: the grip of the old on life is as fierce as the grip of the newly born. Love Eggy or despise him for his antics, one had to admire his commitment; he was going to see things through. With any luck, he might even see a few bastards hang. He would say that one does not die as such; one simply runs out of breath. There is only life; there are only what may live and what must die by way of the dictates of natural selection. Husband and wife love one another deeply, yes, but they will pass on to progeny what shall kill the children, unless other operations of chance get them first. Despite Cassandra's prominent sharp nose, her face was attractive. Perhaps it was the large, dark eyes and the smile. She was busty, her hair long and almost purple in its tint.

'Sure,' I said, smiling back, when she asked if I wanted more *ko-fee*.

To me she extended an almost exaggerated respect. Eggy she humoured.

Now Cassandra and Elias had a verbal exchange in Greek. The words seemed tinged with pain and regret, though yes, I could have been imagining it.

'How much longer,' Eggy asked, 'do you think this place will keep its name?'

'It'll be the Blue Danube forever, at least to us Traymoreans.'

'Hoo hoo,' Eggy said.

From the night before, there were revellers on the street, ugly because swollen with excess, the Habs having won their seventh game first-rounder, moving on to the second. I prayed these revellers would stay clear of the Blue Danube, and they did, crossing the street against traffic to the doughnut shop, pumping their fists. Was there evolutionary advantage in obnoxiousness? Cassandra, too, seemed relieved. Elias might as well have been on Mars. I could feel a spell coming on. As if its messenger, here was Fast Eddy now, he saying: 'So, you've spoken to Moonface. Good. You're not such a fly-by-nighter, after all. I always wondered if you really cared.'

I waved my hand in dismissal and he was gone. Can a ghost pitch woo at a girl, especially one named Moonface?

I made a count of nation-states in deep and dire trouble; I abandoned this barren exercise. How often can you say 'He shoots, he scores' in a phantasmagorical land? In any case, Canadians were no less expert in rank perversions and psycho-dramas than any other collective. Cassandra tugged at her wine-dark hair, seated now, worried and abstracted. Elias, blinking his eyes, looked every inch a murderous warlord. The collective, in the deepest recesses of its cave-black psyche, was crying for a bloodbath. Politicians pandered to this request. A Pan would have been spooked; would have led his revellers to higher ground, away from the teeming valleys of burned-out Apollonians and New York senators. I looked at Cassandra who looked at me; we had no idea what was afoot in one another's mind but, gazes met, we understood perfectly. Such understanding cannot be borne for long.

'Wine, Cassandra, wine.'

The woman ravished my thirst with a smile.

Le Grec

The heat, not unwelcome, was unnatural to the time of year, leaves not yet on the trees. Even what snow remained on the ground looked parched. The Blue Danube, save in the hearts of Traymoreans, was no more. It had been swept from the field by the rather prosaic soubriquet Le Grec. I suppose this satisfied the enforcers of the French sign laws. I could easily enough picture 'The Greek' as a gangster, as a larking Zorba. The philosopher Diogenes shuffling about the streets in his barrel, paying the price for the liberty of his mind. But pizza cook? Yes, the old Blue Danube, now Le Grec, was offering pizzas to an unsuspecting public. I had nothing against pizza but it was a travesty of sorts, in light of the schnitzels and debreciners and sauerkraut the place used to serve up. And Eggy and I and Dubois made our compact; from here on in, we would always say we would meet up at the Blue Danube at some specified time of day or night, to hell with Greekness à la the Gallic rendition of it. Now, given these changes, Eggy was terrified that management (and Gregory carried on with the air of a man who had ideas) would drop the liquor license and institute a BYOB policy. Snow and ice, extreme heat, boozelessness—these were Eggy's degrees of difficulty, his wars. Moonface and I had gone through our wars of which lust, jealousy, and uneasy affection were part and parcel. Then she slipped through my fingers and I through hers. Even so, there remained between us something of a bond. We were mutual witnesses now to other combatants and other wars such as was life swirling about Traymorean existence. Echo had made a serious impact on the hearts and minds of Traymorean males. On Elias, too, perhaps. How would Gregory, he more or less the captain of the good ship Le Grec, handle the lapse in discipline that had occurred? Echo had not been seen for a few days; there was no news of her. Eleanor was away. I suspected she was pursuing trouble, Toronto not a bad burg for that sort of thing. If in our faded Jezebel of a town the arts of self-gratification were *de rigueur,* there they were so many life skills one honed to perfection; or one was sent back to Battle Harbour or Saskatoon, disgraced. Eleanor, I was sure, needed no lessons.

What had the most of Gareth Howard's mind in his last lucid moments? I always assumed that Clare, letting sanity back into the house, had spared Gar my oldest friend the ignominy of dying a bitter and dejected reader of polls, the republic to the south having veered wildly from its course, its appointed destiny as the world's last best hope. The country did not require a president; it wanted an exorcist. Moonface, noting my mood, kept clear of me in the Blue Danube. Gregory was nattering into a cell phone as he attended to chores in the galley. Liverpool and Chelsea duked it out on the televised soccer pitch, the great brand names of the world encircling the field within the arena. Gregory, too, was a complicated being, wiry and athletic, frustrated footballer, perhaps, with sensitive eyes. I believed that, at bottom, he lacked confidence and was even more passive than I. He would simply overlook Elias's transgression, who was his business partner, after all. An old woman entered the café, took one look at the TV screen and sniffed. It reeked of maleness, what her senses reported, and as Moonface rose to see what she might want, the woman turned around abruptly and shuffled off. Moonface seated herself again and tugged at her ponytail. She had been using Herodotus lately as an oracle; she opened the book to page 362 and read: "Thus far the history is delivered without variation … ' The blouse she wore, though it revealed nothing, was suggestive. The sight of her modest bosom unbound was what Eggy had lived for until he gave it up. It was to be a pleasure reserved for Moonface's Champagne Sheridans and no other, Eggy's tough old eyes usurped by kinder, but perhaps, less dedicated ones. It was not believable that Eggy lived now for virtue; no, it was the wine and the prospect he might see a few bastards hang. Sally McCabe appeared in my thoughts just long enough to say: 'I keep telling you, Calhoun, you belong with us, me and Coop and the other hosers riding around in the desert in the Chrysler car. You're not a huckster. You're not much of an Apache, either, but whiskey and boffing one another senseless are better than a poke in the eye with a literary stick.'

The wind picked up in advance of a storm. It might get thundery for the first time in the year. Having left the Blue Danube and Moonface, I did not walk far; I went only as far as the little park, giving Mrs Petrova in her shop a nod as I passed by. I was sniffling and snuffling, leaves beginning to unfurl like so many millions of tiny sails. Echo spotted me on a bench and walked my way. She was, as ever, up-tempo, indefatigable. She spoke: 'Do you mind?'

Of course, I did not. I looked into her pale blue eyes. They were round eyes the colour of a hazy, summery sky. Her bronze curls were spectacular. Whatever she might have had to say to me was lost now in a silence that established itself between us from the get-go, as it were, as if silence were the better thing. Manfully, I struggled not to break the mood, though she looked at me invitingly. It is to say it would have been alright to talk. She took it upon herself to speak: 'Look, I don't want to impose.'

'Not at all.'

'Well, I didn't actually think I was,' she almost giggled, shrugging her shoulders upward, her lovely arrogance in direct opposition to an outburst in her of humble pie. Perhaps here was a clue to what made her tick: she simply ignored contradictions. Two sparrows copulated in a nearby maple, the male flitting on and off and flitting on again until the female seemed to have had enough. I was terrified my nose had gotten runny. I said as much: 'I think I'm getting allergic to things in my old age.'

'To me?' she laughed.

'To flora.'

She gave me a look. She was a tiny thing of serious power as yet unrealized. She could hardly be conscious of what the gods had given her.

'I heard about it,' I said.

'Oh that,' she answered promptly, her tone dulling.

'Well, it's none of my business, but I wish you the best.'

'Thanks,' she said, a little confused, and she added: 'I'm taking a few days off until I decide what to do. I really need the job. But I don't have enough experience to work elsewhere. It's kind of, you know, a dilemma.'

'You're between a rock and a hard place.'

'Rock and a hard place. You bet.'

All sorts of madness were fluttering about in me. Some awkwardness flaring up between us, it was time to relieve the pressure.

'Look,' I said, 'I have some things to do.'

'Oh, for sure.'

'I guess I'll see you when I see you. If you decide to move on, let me just say the Blue Danube won't be the same without you. You'll be missed.'

Echo blushed and inspected the grass. Somehow, it should have been the other way around; that she should have walked away from me, eternally triumphant, humming a song as she did so. I figured if she really had something she wished to say to me, if it was genuinely important, other occasions would arise.

'Oh for God's sake, Calhoun,' so I berated myself, 'you've done it again. Been a perfect idiot. She had something to ask and you frightened her off.'

I awaited the affectionate mirth of Sally McCabe; it did not come.

I had dozed off, the TV on. Moonface simply walked through the door. She shook me gently as the audience in the Ed Sullivan Theatre tittered at Letterman the talk show host and comic. At first, she plopped herself down on the couch and I made room for her, drawing up my knees. It was intimacy that dared but who was daring whom? She took the initiative, kneeling now on the floor at my side. Though I was still sleepy, I knew that, despite what had transpired between us, it was new territory she was establishing. Perhaps she thought she was improving my morale. Perhaps she was atoning for recent decades of gender wars. Perhaps it was just so much nothing, but I would put a stop to it. It looked as though she might lay her head on my chest and go to sleep. I breathed; she breathed, the fact of our breathing like this maintenance for the universe. I smelled her hair.

'Oh, I have news,' she said, brightly. 'Well, not really,' she half moaned.

'Which is it then?'

I wanted a cigarette.

'Echo. I talked with her. Or she talked with me. Anyway, she doesn't know what to do. She said she'd seen you earlier. You were awfully nice. She wanted to talk to you but she was intimidated.'

'She could've talked to me. I would've listened.'

'I told her you were a pushover and wouldn't hurt a fly.'

'Don't be so sure.'

Were we not all things at all times? I said: 'I don't know what Echo should do. I don't think Elias is as bad a man as all that. But he has a streak of something in him I don't like. The world owes him, I guess. Poor Cassandra. What she must put up with.'

'I know.'

Did Moonface really know? Still on her knees, she rolled her eyes up and to the side in that way she had, staring at something that was not there. It was her sexuality, her fear, her gentle nature. It would make for her a hard life to come. It struck me then, as if I were to have been the first man on the moon, that I had come within an ace of beholding what Eggy had once lived for. Fast Eddy was in the room, looking thoughtful. It was possible then I had dreamed this interlude, having fallen asleep to the drone of the TV. But no, Moonface was there, her eyes shining down on me.

'A drink?' I asked.

I still wanted a cigarette. The Moonface visage fascinated me; I supposed I could read in it past, present and future.

This time, she accepted a drink. Whiskeys, smokes, and long talk on various matters. We were two old friends who had much to discuss but just let our words take us where they would. Had anyone heard from Eleanor? No. But then I had not seen Dubois of late. Moonface was almost charming in her denunciation of the President. It pleased me to see she was not saying as much so as to curry my favour. She did have, after all, some idea of what was going on in the world. Out of the blue I said: 'You need a much younger man than I.'

'Oh Randall, don't do that. It's patronizing.'

'You should be mothering a dynasty of poets.'

'Maybe I'll want to write poetry, myself.'

'Why not?'

'You could take me to Rome.'

'There's a thought,' I said, much too carelessly.

'I like the boys but they haven't any brains. Rick had a brain but he was always jealous.'

'What about your latest?'

'Him?'

I yawned. I hoped she would not take that yawn of mine amiss.

'Well,' she said, 'I'll have much to say about Q in my diary.'

My ears burned a little with the news she would exercise her muse in behalf of her diary, I her subject matter. She rose and I rose. Space separated us where we stood. She got up on her sneakered toes to kiss me. There was mischief in this kiss. I was meant to have learned a lesson of some sort. It was evident, however, that good humour would attend our parting. At least there was that.

An Untouched Meal

I could hear Moonface rousting about in her rooms, the Traymore walls thin. Soon she would nest in her bed, pen and diary book at the ready. *Calhoun uncooperative. Echo's in a pickle.* In my mentations Virgil the poet had gotten himself to some exotic clime; he was shambling from one Mayan ruin to the next in tropical undergrowth. What were the Mayan rites of burial? Were bird livers read before battle? Bodies had been stacking up in precipitous fashion over the last century of the first deep blush of the ologies, so many sacks of bones making for a causeway to the stars. I retired to my bed, window cracked open. After the frigid winter air, the cold night air of spring seemed a bonus, a boon, the only excuse one needed to delight in living.

A party would rise from the ashes, win all the marbles and never quite recover from victory. Here was the history of American politics. Some thinkers contended this explained Nixon and Reagan and the current occupant of the White House who was ruinous. The road out of Rome in a time of knife-fighters was a lonely one for Cicero, who watched his republic die of an overdose of irony. Elias, business partner to Gregory of Le Grec, had an air of sheepish stupidity about him. He looked as if he were continually amazed at his capacity for errors of judgment. I figured the café to be too small an enterprise to support both Gregory and Elias and his family. Were there other sources of income? Cassandra, I was told, was a schoolteacher once. It is said only impersonal forces shape history. Tell me another. I knew in my bones Eleanor was up to no good in Toronto, and that, on her return, there would be storm-rumblings in Traymorean skies as had already withstood the Lamonts and Osgoode the pedophile.

Again, Echo seemed to have just disappeared. Eggy did not think it significant, he saying of an afternoon in the Blue Danube, Dubois seated with us: 'These days, girls come and go as they please. In my day, well, it wasn't that there weren't any goings-on, just that maybe one girl out of a hundred had the time and the wherewithal for it.'

'In your day,' said Dubois, 'when was that? When they burned witches at the stake?'

Casting aspersions on Eggy's great age was getting to be a stale conversational gambit. Eggy's countenance soured. I said I was sure my mother had been a virgin when she married. She had expected happiness, to which sex was decidedly an obstacle. Dubois then said his mother had been a merry old girl, his father a patient workhorse.

'You mean stud,' said Eggy, somewhat meanly. His mother had been the town slut.

Dubois threw up his hands. Cassandra was waitressing, an unseeable weight on her shoulders, anxiety in her face.

'Oh Cassandra,' said Eggy, attempting mischief, 'we're dry here.'

Like an automaton she went for the wine rack. There was absolutely nothing one could say to her as she brought over a bottle and uncorked it and remembered to smile.

Moonface showed up for dinner at my place in a short skirt and red sneakers. She was ungainly now, hardly the sophisticate who had tried to put one over on me of a recent evening. I put a CD in the ghetto blaster: piano, accordion and oud. In the arts of humiliation, so I was thinking just then, we were amateurs. The Brits, for example, had those arts down pat, to go by their recent literature, whereas we were crude in comparison, pretending to an innocence that had never been, was not, and could never be, not even in some American way of life. We occupied the couch, the fixings of the meal I had cobbled together on the low-slung table before us. Moonface non-sequiturred: 'I don't think Virgil's shepherds were all that merry.'

Was she just trying to make conversation?

'Clearly not,' I said, adopting a pedagogical tone.

'I do like you, you know,' she said, somewhat primly.

I was flabbergasted. Had she something more compelling than 'like' in mind? Piano and accordion rippled; the oud struck deep notes. I wished to smoke, my plate hardly touched, my wine glass a cliché, one half-empty or half-full of drifting and indifferent sorrow.

'Well, I don't like you in that way, necessarily,' Moonface added, pulling now at the ends of tresses nestled on her shoulder.

'How then do you like me, might I ask?'

'Like a father. Like an older brother. Like a friend. Like that. But Eggy's Zeus,' she said, ending her peroration on a note of levity, her eyes rolling up and to the side.

'Zeus,' she repeated, somewhat distantly.

The girl, the woman, the girl-woman was a chameleon.

'He's certainly a right old numero uno,' I said of Eggy, tiny sparrow of a man.

The piano tinkled; the oud stood off at a respectful distance, awaiting its turn. The pianist was a romantic who had turned away from the world to indulge his soul, the oud a worldly figure of pessimism. That left the even more worldly accordionist to worry about how to make ends meet. I do not know why I had Brits on the brain who sometimes were as cruel to one another, so it seemed to me, as Islamists stoning adulterers in their stadiums. Perhaps it was the presence in my digs of Moonface, who had something of an island nation in her blood, her fecklessness her way of avoiding what it might cause her to do in the name of passion. Now the oud rippled like a lion in the chase. Moonface perched on her end of the couch, a sneakered foot tucked under one leg, her thighs very much a force. We were going to tease one another to death. I thought we might as well get it over with but it was not there; that is to say, were I to fall through space she would only shrink away and pull at the ends of her hair. I went to the kitchen for my tobacco and cigarette papers. Moonface, too, thought she might have a smoke. She followed me, at odds and ends. It was a dull kiss that ensued. It should never have happened as per an old unspoken agreement between us, she the mischief-maker, of late, not me.

Holes in the Fabric of Time and Space

In Le Grec (Blue Danube to Traymoreans), Eggy, lifting his chin from his food-specked shirt, put it to us: 'Where's that girl gotten to, I'd like to know?'

Eggy's tough old eyes, his loopy grin—I wondered if he truly cared as to where Echo might be. He reached for his glass, and in the wine were all his consolations. Dubois, in imitation of a movie screen cowboy, laughed: 'My gut tells me she ain't coming back.'

'Afraid so,' I said.

'Bloody effing hell.'

Eggy set his glass back on the table with infinite care.

There was a chill in the breeze; it was not yet terrasse weather. Even so, other people were availing themselves of it, extending the territory Moonface or Cassandra or indeed, Echo, should she return, would have to cover. Women with dogs at their heels and cell phones clapped to their ears. Shining heads of over-loud voices. Youth with their eyes on other venues, other destinations all cachet, the Blue Danube aka Le Grec but a way station on the silk and spice road to paradise. Eggy's chin dropped again. He was out for the count.

'Heard from Eleanor?' I asked Dubois.

'No,' he answered, his tone that of man who did not expect to hear from anyone let alone the good woman in question. Things between us had always been collegial, though Dubois's materialism was anathema to the on-again off-again mystic in me. Once he asked what I really believed, expecting to be highly entertained by my response. I answered: 'It's not something that just spells itself out in words at the drop of a hat. Do I believe there's a god? I don't. Is there a soul? Who can say? You're enjoying this too much.'

Dubois observed that my response was interesting for someone who was otherwise delusional.

Blind Musician, he who had flown up a horse's arse and found the Golden Age, seemed to have aged in a dramatic fashion, his beard whiter and longer and perhaps pricklier to the touch. It must be harrowing, bringing culture to remote outposts, soothing the savage breasts of bush pilots and glue sniffers and seal hunters and the odd oil man poking around.

With that voice of his that could cut one to the bone, he intoned we were all of us in the Blue Danube corrupt and unfit for the beauties of art. We were the half-breeds of the life of the mind. I half-believed him. Dubois was saying about Baie Shawinigan: 'You know, it did pretty good for a tiny little town, total population 433 max, and it produced three NHL hockey players and one prime minister, who himself played hockey, team captain in his youth.'

Dubois had grown up in Shawinigan proper. Blind Musician sniffed.

We were going to get drunk, Eggy, Dubois and I, and monitor the hockey game as we did so, no matter what Blind Musician thought of us. Moonface now chatted with the man, taking it upon herself to demonstrate for our benefit that he was perfectly civilized and in complete possession of his marbles, probabilities I found improbable, Moonface's eyes rolling up and to the side. Now Elias and Cassandra entered the café, husband and wife team bringing in sacks of supplies and Cassandra's home-baked cakes. I examined her face and noted the absence of anxiety in her eyes. Eggy and Dubois had noted it, as well, and the three of us exchanged significant looks. Elias seemed to have a new lease on married life. I said, apropos of nothing in particular: 'The voice of doom will have a BBC accent.'

Eggy started going on about a man's reach, how it should exceed his grasp or what's it for? Blind Musician must not have known his Browning as he went silent, confused perhaps, as to his whereabouts. That here, here in a faded Jezebel of a town, was the real outpost, true heart of darkness stuff. Even so, Washington was calumniating Syria and North Korea on the strength of partial truths, causing Israel to purr. A motorcade, no doubt that day, pulled up to some conference site, each limousine loaded with state secrets and lies and policy tweaks. The senate would debrief a true professional, a tall and dour Tiberius back from his labours in the forests of Germania, the tribes, for the moment, cowed and pacified by way of bribes, life's real terror Rome's high society. We were scuttling along, Eggy, Dubois and I, like creatures of the sea in a rising tide, merrily bubbling with our inanities, knocking back the wine. Eggy piped up, his voice precisely tailored for the part: 'Good evening. This is BBC Home Service. Now the news. We're scuppered.'

'What?' asked Dubois.

The Habs could not control the puck, pressing too hard.

A new creature came on the scene. He was wearing a light windbreaker, slacks and sneakers. He looked around as if to see whether the Blue Danube aka Le Grec were his kind of place. He caught Moonface's eye. Perhaps she had already guessed what this man was about. He approached her and said something and she pointed at the galley where a Greek and a Greek wife and the cook were stowing away the supplies. I heard Echo's warble in my mentations: 'Oh, will there be a sing-fest?'

Fast Eddy was now immanent, a look of concern on his spectral visage.

A Greek and a stranger went outside. The Greek lit a cigarette while the stranger, hand in pocket, seemed to be asking questions and the Greek (Elias) looked a little defensive and worried, examining the sidewalk. Anxiety returned to Cassandra's dignified countenance. Fast Eddy seemed awfully sad. The Habs finally scored one. Even Blind Musician cheered up.

'Yay,' Moonface moaned.

Had she turned at random to page 176 of Herodotus she might have read: *but such as think so err very widely from the truth.*

When I was next conscious it was first light. A hullabaloo of birds. It was too depressingly early for waking life. A disjointed dream claimed me, a fragment of which was Fast Eddy, he addressing Randall Q Calhoun: 'About your writing. Better a rough diamond than a polished turd.'

'Good God, Sanders,' I said, 'what do you know about writing?'

'More than you think. Since I died I have been much about. It hasn't been all that pleasant. Imagine a ghost having to shoot up insulin.'

The dream world dissipated. Then it was Moonface in my eyes, and she was real. She stood over me as I lay on the couch, blanket drawn up to my chin. I must have fetched it in the middle of the night. Bursting with definitive knowledge, she said: 'That guy was a cop.'

'That guy?'

'Yes, that guy. He was a cop.'

'Don't know what you're on about.'

'Come on, Randall. I'm not making this up.'

'Is there any coffee?'

'Just made some. I'll bring you a cup.'

So she went and brought me a cup. She was wearing a gossamer thing of a robe over her pajamas, her feet shod in soft slippers. *Two pale yellow gazelles are nibbling at the young shoots of a pomegranate or apple tree.* The Habs had won the night before, rather lucky to do so in overtime, so I managed to recall. I awaited words of explanation from Moonface.

'Anyway, that guy,' she said, seated now by my feet, my knees drawn up. I held a scalding hot cup of coffee in both hands, blowing across it.

"He was a cop and he was asking about Echo.'

'So she pressed charges after all?"

'No.'

'Well then, what?'

'No one has seen her in a while. The boyfriend called Echo's parents who called the police. The cop, the detective, I guess, came around.'

'He thinks Elias has something to do with this?'

'I don't know. No one knows what to think.'

'Eggy and Bob—do they know of this?'

'They were pretty drunk. So were you. But you had left before Cassandra told me what was up. I guess I mentioned it to Eggy and Bob. I don't think it registered. It certainly has with me.'

'I need a bath,' I said.

'I'll leave you to it then.'

One of these days I would understand the Moonface visage, what it conveyed to me of the meaning of life, if anything.

'I'm worried, Randall.'

I shrugged.

'How can I keep working in that place?'

I shrugged again. Where would we find a new Blue Danube? Without Moonface, what would be the point? *Arabesque, a form that repeatedly denies or negates closure…*

'I don't suppose we should jump to any conclusions. I really need that bath. Unless you want to frolic with me—'

'Going. Maybe I'd better check on Eggy. He could hardly walk when we closed up.'

'I know. I heard it all, he and Bob clambering up those stairs as if those stairs were the bloody Matterhorn. You know what I worry about? Eggy not being able to climb them even when sober.'

Was Moonface going to cry?

A Closing Window

It surprised Dubois to think that he knew so little of the local constabulary. How many gradations of rank were there among detectives, for instance?

We were in the Blue Danube, he and I, Eggy at another watering hole nearby his weekly physio. Serge the cook was in the galley. He had the look of a gangster from Marseilles, his hair close-cropped military fashion. He had a peculiar posture and gait. Martial arts? He was fluent in French and English and Greek. He seemed, in fact, too intelligent for his menial position. For all that, I was hazarding a guess he was there by choice, not force of circumstance. Perhaps he was a philosopher. Dubois said: 'It'll go like this, I think. The local police will hook up with the *Sûreté*, and other provincial police. Somewhere along the line, the RCMP might get involved, I don't know. To tell you the truth, I don't know how it would work. Maybe we ought to read more thrillers. She stays vanished long enough, and we'll be hearing about Interpol.'

Dubois was cutting into a slice of pizza. I figured that were Eggy here, he would have piped up, saying: 'And MI6.'

He would have hoo hooed. Why not the FBI? The CIA? So then, still no word of Echo.

I had been scouring my art books for a portrait of her. On a hunch, I started with del Sarto, but though the overall look of his madonnas was a close match to the sensual force of Echo's countenance, the eyes were always wrong, Echo's peepers more round than almond-shaped. It was much the same with Botticelli. It was as if I were a detective, myself. I even took to sitting in the tiny park just down the street where the girl had recently assailed me with her presence. As if she might have left a clue there as to her current whereabouts. Nothing. No Echo, no gusto born of life force. Sparrows and dogs and squirrels. It might be that this business had turned into an obsession with me. No one of us had known her long; we could not be expected to mourn her absence in any profound way, but there was no question she had caused us to notice her simply by her whirlwind hold of the sun. Eggy had never seen anything like it, and he had seen much.

Ah, but in a book of Gombrich, a young woman (*Head of St Apollonia*: Perugino altarpiece), was very approximate to Echo's look. That air of sauce and challenge. In another volume, the central female nude in Piombo's *The Death of Adonis* was quite suggestive of her profile.

Dubois, having treated with matters of police procedure, his hunger sated, leaned back. He began an account of the human record, starting with the origins of language, that the first sentence ever uttered must have been: 'I want this' as opposed to 'I love you'.

'Well, what do you think?' asked Dubois. 'Do I rate the palm?'

Well, were we moral creatures? Two observations were undeniable, at least: America once made a covenant with knowledge and the moral courage knowledge ought to vouchsafe; but that America had often broken faith; and in the past eight years had not only broken faith but had smashed the covenant beyond recognition. For all that, and despite the fact they seemed to be the source of more op-eds than any other source, I knew too many so-called secular humanists to be much reassured. They were Arsdells 'to a T': callow time-servers, egoists. I rolled a cigarette that I would smoke outside, the evening's revelries ramping up around me, parking spaces claimed, the traffic in and out of the liquor outlet a steady stream, hooded young males, girls in the briefest of skirts and stiletto heels. Pensioners walking mutts. Business as usual. Humanism's highlight reel.

'I suppose we should put it to Eggy. He must've been there. He's old enough to have witnessed the birth of language.'

Dubois availed himself of mirth. It had been a satisfying exchange of views.

Prodigal Girl

I saw at a glance, coming out the Traymore door, that she had spent a great deal of money. The black, flat-capped cab driver, having already popped the trunk, was unloading her suitcases as well as the shiny tote bags, and setting them on the pavement. I offered to help Eleanor with her booty up the Traymore stairs.

'That's mighty white of you, Calhoun,' she said, oblivious to the driver, her voice edgy, her smile defensive.

She was dressed better than when she had left, or so I figured, not having seen her leave. If the attire was conventional, it was nonetheless tasteful, suitable for an ambitious woman of politics or business, her new high heels tony. Her hair was freshly frosted. She paid off the driver with a theatrical gesture, presenting him with a sheaf of twenties and suggesting he keep the change. He needed no encouragement. I grabbed the suitcases plus a bag, and she managed the rest, and together we clambered up the Traymore stairs which did not exactly bespeak Corporate American life. As she unlocked her door, she said in a somewhat curious manner: 'Come see me in my kitchen.'

Ah, Eleanor in full thrall to Aphrodite, the jealous Aphrodite, the pay-back Aphrodite, no goddess bitchier than she save for Hera, Zeus's other. But of what had Eleanor to be jealous? Dubois, so far as I knew, behaved well in her absence, whereas she, I would have wagered, had not. I said I would give her a chance to settle in after so long a bus ride; I would come by in an hour. It dawned on me then that she must have taken the connector flight from Toronto; it would explain the freshness of her outfit and the twenties, airport fare. It would not explain, however, what she was up to, what mischief she was contemplating, which rug was about to be yanked from under whose unsuspecting feet. I hoped Dubois had a healthy centre of gravity for he was going to need it, he who was always going on about physics; or how, in a universe some 13 billions of years of age, a short history of the Democratic Party was not even worth the blink of God's eye. Of course, there was no God, religion a cheap stunt. No, we inhabited a planet that was but a corpuscle in the bloodstream of some vastly larger entity than our galactic purview. This last supposition, product of Dubois's thinking, was unworthy of a rational mind. I went about some business to which I had to attend, but in an hour or so I was back, my heart pounding. She could only have intended, of course, that we would smoke, imbibe and chat.

Her look was a searching one as she admitted me, her eyes momentarily soft and seductive. I smelled the amaretto on her breath. I hoped Dubois was across town, pursuing one of his vague projects. She slinked away from me and then stopped in the middle of her living room. She had slipped on something else, semi-formal evening wear. She spun around, light of foot in her new shoes. I made the proper noises.

'Well done,' I said.

'You bet your bottom dollar,' she said, unexpressed expletives breaking the spell.

I followed her into the kitchen, admiring the performance of her walk.

I rolled two cigarettes. Something was amiss. The new edition of Eleanor did not seem to suit the previous edition's kitchen. Even so she topped up her glass and poured me a measure of the liquid amber. Somewhat fussily, she seated herself, a crazy grin beginning to form on her mouth. Was she starting to get glassy-eyed?

'Here it is,' she said. 'You're not going to know. Tit-for-tat. Your tat mightily irked me. You know, back when you were carrying on with that woman, what's her name.'

'Lindsey,' I said.

'Whatever.'

'I don't understand,' I said, mounting a weak counter-offensive against as yet unknown threats.

'He doesn't understand, he says. Well, how's this then? You want to know? Sure, I threw myself at all sorts of men. Got lucky a couple of times. You might ask what I was doing. I might answer I was fit to be tied. I want Bob to marry me. You know he won't. Meanwhile, and my, how inconvenient, I still have an itch. Do you care to scratch it?'

She leaned forward. She leaned back.

'No, I thought not.'

She was dangerous, I surmised just then, perhaps the most dangerous woman I had ever known. It had less to do with sex and more to do with territory. She had always let me know she was infinitely more dangerous than Lindsey Price, to whom I had falsely accorded that particular distinction, and I had always pooh-poohed the claim. I was missing my cenobitic existence.

'You know you want it,' she said, like some co-ed trying out newly discovered leverage for size.

'Look,' she said, 'I believe in sustainable resources. I wouldn't leave you a heap of bones. And you're worried about Bob. Honour between friends. You see how Bob thwarts me at every turn?'

'You're a handsome woman, Eleanor R, but I thought it was understood: we are not fated. I nearly wrecked a home once. I'll not do it again.'

I more than halfway lied, seeing as Gar my oldest friend was already in his grave when Clare and I had come together in his country shack however briefly, even if for an eternity.

'You always say we aren't moral creatures. So then, what's your scruple, if I say scruples don't apply to me?'

I lit my cigarette and handed her the thin stick I had rolled for her. I lit it as well, taking my time in the formulation of an answer. She held my hand with the lighter between her two hands. The pedagogue was rising up in me; he would strike too many trumpery notes. I shoved him back down as I spoke: 'We aren't moral creatures. I haven't changed my mind about that. You would, in fact, leave me a heap of bones. I'm not the lover boy that once I was. Too much disillusion and drink.'

A husky voice said: 'I'll be gentle.'

'Eleanor.'

'Well, you seemed to have gotten it on with what's her name smartly enough. Your smirk was so loud it broke the sound barrier.'

'What, you think it was sex?'

'What were you doing, pushing daisies?'

How explain to her what I could not explain to myself, but that that woman, that what's-her-name had passed through my life just at a time when she was, for whatever reason, entitled to a piece of me and I had it to give, no explanations necessary?

'We were, how does the parlance go, hanging out.'

Eleanor shrugged and wilted. It was not a pretty sight or one in which I took pleasure.

'Bloody effing hell,' she said, her theatricalities chased from the stage.

The upshot was, I gave her a kiss, a longish one, one I hoped would leave us both with our dignity intact. I enjoyed the kiss. I suspect she did, too. Resurrecting some good humour, she then pushed me off, saying she could not have dalliance with just any Johnny-come-lately, what sort of woman did I think she was?

But if I thought everything was going to be fine from here on in, in the Traymore, I was mistaken. Eleanor and Dubois were having rows. Shades of the Lamonts. No, strike that, those last words an all too convenient comparison. Eleanor and Dubois did not throw furniture. Eleanor, out of exasperation, may have wished to kill Dubois but she loved him, so I will always submit. Dubois, in his feckless, can't-pin-a-man-down fashion, loved Eleanor. Theirs was not a love the poets might have sung and have caused to be put up in lights; but it was love, a love, and if nothing else, an avowal of mutual need. Booze got drunk; voices rose; the atmosphere was stormy, but Eleanor was not Lucille and Dubois was not Marcel expatriatable to the realm of death. What then was the problem? Love between Eleanor and Dubois did not require a reason, only that Eleanor had got it in her head that she wanted one. I said as much to Moonface, who had come over for hamburgers, bringing Louisiana hot sauce. It was perhaps Virgilian, her gesture, and if it was a Moonface touch, it revealed an aspect of her I had not yet suspected. It was such a worldly note for the unworldly Moonface of my thoughts. It, of course, reminded me that Virgil's shepherds were not mere literary fancies. The Caesars were up to no good; the world was crashing down around our ears, but we would season our meat with a concoction made of peppers, vinegar and salt such as would have really stung the wounds of Christ. Moonface said: 'You're sure it's love?'

'I think so.'

Well, I preferred to think so.

'What a romantic you are, Randall.'

I took offense.

'No, I'm a cynic, high echelon. But cynics, at least those such as me, have an undeserved press. We don't question the existence of the basic constituents of the universe; we don't question the existence of the universe itself. Carbon we can weigh and measure; love is so much more intangible, but there nonetheless. Moral behaviour is the shell game, is misdirection, a turkey shoot. Moral behaviour can mean many different things to many different regimes. One might die for the sake of honour. One might die for love. But moral behaviour? I'm hardly a romantic.'

Calhoun had spoken. Moonface consumed her burger with enthusiasm.

I did not indicate to her that, on any given day, I did not object to Eleanor's flirtatiousness; it had been a great pleasure. But that, lately, it was something other than play; it was hurt and anger and God knows what. I supposed the prospect of old age disturbed women as greatly as it did men, but Eleanor was far from having arrived at that pass. She leaned toward the pulchritudinous, but it was a lovely pulchritude worthy of a Rembrandt. I further supposed that one cannot always find a reason for seemingly unreasonable behaviour. It was as if something had flown up her nose and was pounding her brain. Dubois might relent and marry her but I could see he might be protecting what had made their liaison work in the first place, its below the radar operations. I could see it might be nothing other than selfishness on his part, a form of leverage, an imposition on the Eleanor R soul. What an impenetrable thicket of suppositions plague the human mind.

'No,' said Moonface, 'you're a romantic. Even I know that.'

She ran the back of her hand against her mouth, her rich brown-gold eyes large with appetite. She always came out of nowhere—the lusty Moonface. The lust in her always receded like dying thunder, and the feckless Moonface then came to the fore. By now I could almost time it.

'What shall we do now?' she asked with mischief.

'What have you in mind?'

Women are perverse. If there had been no Lindsey Price, I doubted that Eleanor and Moonface would have found me as much of interest of late. Had they taken note of a satisfied customer?

We would take in a movie, a new release. It was something that we, at any rate, could do with ourselves. We did not know of any other way, it seemed, to be with one another's bodies. But as we stepped into the carpeted hall of the Traymore, Eleanor stuck her head out her door. She said: 'Stepping out to play, you kids?'

Well, she had always assumed Moonface and I were lovers. I would have thought it obvious that we were not. To her credit, she did not usually violate justice in her machinations. She abjured woman as victim and she was quick to call out any woman for bullying, as she had done with Lucille Lamont. But Eleanor was jealous now, and it was not attractive.

Downtown, somewhat disorientated by the throngs of people and the clamouring traffic (I had forgotten about the hockey game), we made our way as best we could along Ste Catherine to the Cineplex. Moonface had my arm, walking at my side like a lover. If the venue was garish and off-putting, it was a pleasure palace for those who wished their pleasures undiluted with the subtleties. Look into the eyes of the movie-goers and there was erotic flux to be seen and even high spirits. Yes, there were always the loners marking time. There were always the dull-eyed. In other words, what was there to criticize? The feature itself impressed us. We left the place in a sober and chastened frame of mind, and we were out of place on a street of revelment, painfully so. I hailed us a taxi. In the backseat, Moonface's knee grazed mine. Finally she said: 'You've done it again.'

'What have I done?'

'We go to a movie—I get depressed.'

'But you said you liked the movie.'

'I did like it.'

'So what depresses you?'

'I don't know—that people can be people like that.'

'You mean so violent, so petty and lost.'

'Yes, like that.'

The cab driver coughed. That cough seemed to subsume everything, even the air Moonface and I were breathing. It was a statement, that cough, but whether in accord or discord with our dialogue, I could not say.

A cell phone tinkled with inane melody; the driver answered it and was now in his own little world to which we were but adjuncts, Moonface and I, paying customers, souls to be freighted between points of a compass.

Later, I almost caved.

Page 272 of Herodotus

We had retired to our apartments. But shortly after, I listening to piano, accordion and oud, Moonface reemerged, Herodotus in hand. With some heat she read aloud from page 272 of the book: 'Such then were the governments, and such the amounts of tribute at which they were assessed respectively.'

'Your point?'

But she had no point; for once the oracular powers of the text seemed to have failed her. She joined me on the couch, uninvited. Chameleon that she was, cynic that I was, it was more parody than passion, what followed. It was only fantasy, that I undid the buttons of a coarse shirt and slid hands under the cups of her shiny bra, her small breasts indignant. Even so, she looked stricken, holding Herodotus against her chest. Even as, in my mentations, I would study her countenance, the eyes the window of the soul, she was deeply unsure of herself. We were, so I noted with some irritation, still teasing one another to death. No human urge is more tough and resilient and obdurate than the sexual urge. None connects as devastatingly to the most fragile parts of the psyche. But I did not want a million pieces of Moonface to reassemble. I did not want regrets, her eyes now shut, expression sheepish. She was helpless and perhaps a little humiliated. It was going to be awkward, conversation in the coming days. In the old days, I would have already taken my pleasure and hoped she had taken hers, and we would be sharing drinks and smokes and talk by now. Godard the filmmaker was oh so full of it, for instance. In the end, I said, and perhaps it was beside the point that I said it: 'What you want is a man your age.'

'Oh Randall. Randall the avuncular.'

She was irked. But the fact she was irked was each our release point, a way out of an impasse. Even so, her mouth drawn tight, complexion flushed, she was just then no liberal-minded daughter of a community-inspired idiot. She said: 'Now I don't know why I came over.'

'You know why.'

'Anyway, you're not much help.'

'No, I guess I'm not.'

'It's because you're old enough to be my father.'

'Something like that.'

'Or maybe you can't, you know, perform.'

'And if I could, what then, you nasty, little minx?'

Was Moonface snickering?

'There are remedies,' she said.

'There are always remedies.'

'It's easy, pleasing men. Why are you so difficult?'

I was scattered about in a million pieces.

She rose, Herodotus still clasped to her chest. The look she gave me was one that suggested she had much to think over. She would get back to me, as it were. At any rate, we could each consider ourselves as having been assessed.

I could hear Moonface in her digs, preparing for bed. Plumbing rumbled and knocked. I could see her, knees drawn up in that bed of hers, her diary book rested against her hips, pen at the ready. *Q in one of his theological snits again. Didn't fuck me. Well, plenty of boys have, and I've seen no great light, as a result. With Q it's all dark, but I can see everything distinctly, flowers and trees and birds and the like. Means what, exactly?*

The piano, accordion and oud had played themselves out. It was just me and silence and whatever Traymorean sound blundered through Traymorean walls. Fast Eddy wandered in. He whose curse had always been his insufferable gravitas was all Churchillian cheer, he chomping on his cigar, pale blue eyes suggesting we would fight them here and fight them there, in the villages, on the beaches. And so forth. Great fun.

'Moonface,' Fast Eddy said, 'does not appear to want to go the distance with you. And you, who would've thought it, but you have scruples.'

A ghost could not have been more pleased that was once deeply smitten with a girl named Moonface. Then Sally McCabe: 'You're slipping, dear boy. You're letting down the side. But then you always flattered yourself you were some sort of swashbuckler. Let me tell you, you were humoured. It's what women do. Still, you were always sweet. Well, not always, but most of the time.'

'I wouldn't be so sure,' I addressed some ethereality, my tone black.

Speak a truth, and in an instant, a truth will invite its untruth; and I was a weak and shallow creature of fevered delusions of spiritual grandeur. How was spiritual groping-about in a rank and dark and horror-infested cave any different from Elias having groped Echo in the light of capitalist day? How any less primitive? I might flatter myself that I was *X*, *Y* and *Z*, but I would never flatter myself that I was any avatar of enlightened reason; of any moral claptrap that had addled the human mind and permitted it to slaughter and rape and oppress in the name of values religious or secular. Was Echo even alive? Perhaps what I needed was Rome and the shambling and haphazard sexuality of her narrow streets, a lethal moonlight in the pines. I felt at home there, half in ancient history, half in the waking moment. Where there was not such a grotesque distinction to be drawn between the glories of the body and the glories of the spirit, though of grotesqueries Rome had plenty. Traymorean society was not going to accept the fact that, almost overnight, one Randall Q Calhoun, could suddenly mouth the word spirituality without gagging, whatever he meant by the word. They would not trust it who knew me for my wine intake; who could see I was not dead to the charms of women, whatever my so-called scruples. Perhaps on this score I was only tormenting myself like some anchorite in his filthy hole, living on locusts. Perhaps it was as banal and contemptible and as unprofitable as this. Lust had, and would always have, pride of place in the human heart, out of which grew love as Plato once avowed, and I had always thought him right in this, if in little else. Only that, what, something in our era, in our kick at the can, was out of kilter, and more lust was not leading to more love. Politics would not solve it and law could not legislate the emptiness. The voice of redress was as wild as Esau baying in the hills for justice and for love of wild song. Eggy just might possibly understand. I would go see him in the morning.

Eggy's Little Speech

Eggy said: 'Haven't you been paying attention? I claim no high purpose in life. Wine's my purpose. Will lovely Moonface allow me to pinch her bum? We must wait and see. A pity about Echo. I spin my prayer wheels such as they are. The rain in Spain and all that. Do you do table hockey? I was shuffling by the Sally Ann the other day, and there it was on display.

The table and the hockey. Hoo hoo. I was in the Signal Corps, you know. Korea was my crucible. That and my wives. Bloody effing hell, Calhoun, if you can't take the breeze in your sails, get out of the wind. There's no soul to find. Exactly when did yours go missing? I close my eyes, and there it is: the scarecrow I saw once in a field when I was a boy. I think something clicked in my mind just then. Click click click. I mean, look at the thing, the way it's exposed to the elements and mocking birds. Almost a pun, that. But that was me. That's you. Wind and straw. The rain in Spain. Always.'

A rich man from Toronto called on Eleanor. She was unwise enough to entertain him. Later we were to learn he called her 'Ellie', that he was no millionaire's millionaire, but give him time, he was just getting started. Dubois (oh, bad luck!) unwittingly knocked on Eleanor's door, was told to go away, she was busy. It was unmistakable—the appearance of entitlement. A smart pant leg, the one leg crossed over the other, ran parallel with the couch. Not only that, here was Eleanor in high evening mode and it was only mid-morning. An emergency session of Traymoreans was convened at the Blue Danube at the stroke of noon.

Gregory at opening time assumed that all was fine for Traymoreans. But things were not fine; there was none of Dubois's usual horseplay as he ordered wine from Cassandra. Eggy, however, was amused; and he would have his usual sausage and onions and customary libation.

'Well, did you get his name?' Eggy asked Dubois.

'How could I?'

Dubois was not a man who generally lacked for answers. If he was not Irish, he had the luck of the Irish, so to speak. He was smug, and because smug, pleasant. And because pleasant, he was every man and woman's *bonhomie*. Say Russia to him, and you would get analysis of Russia's newfangled oligarchic practices. Say the U.S. of A, and you would receive the lowdown on the dollar's plummeting value. You would think you had just been treated to a charming tale. The last thing he expected was that Eleanor would take not just another man into her bed, but a future husband.

'What now?' asked Eggy, as if there were anything to be done.

'Don't know,' said Dubois, a riot of his cheek's hairline cracks threatening to pull his face apart.

'I'd smack her bottom,' said Eggy with some conviction.

The wine came, and Eggy's food, by way of Cassandra, nothing but a waitress's boredom in her eyes. How could this be, her husband a groper, a suspect in a missing person case? But through boredom one might stave off unwanted thoughts. The sight of alarm on Dubois's visage was most unfamiliar. Even the man's immense vanity could not prevent the dawning upon him that, somehow, he might have driven Eleanor to a transgression.

'She was always on about getting married. I've been married.'

'Oh you could've married her,' Eggy surmised. 'But I daresay the sex would've fizzled, thereafter. Standard procedure.'

'Actually,' Dubois confessed, 'it hasn't been that great, of late.'

'Marriage counsellor?' Eggy chirped. 'Not that I much believe in them.'

'But we're not even married.'

'Well then, somebody,' Eggy huffed.

How futile was it, exactly, swimming collegially with cephalopods, seeking cancer cures, looking for lost love that flew the coop? Cynic that I am, even so, I said: 'Bob, wait it out.'

'Why, you know something?' Dubois put it to me, a little suspicious.

'Well, we have our chats, you know.'

'I'll bet,' he said, somewhat heatedly.

'Randall's right,' said Eggy. 'Wait it out. She'll be back to you.'

Elias entered the café. The look on Cassandra's face was the resignation born of giving a cheating husband the benefit of the doubt. There was no end of pain. A man gives his all elsewhere; a woman gets her all elsewhere. So it seemed. The sky was beginning to betray us with rain, though the earth hereabouts needed it.

'Well,' said I to a stricken friend, 'do you love her? Because if you don't, it's only games.'

Eleanor and Dubois—the most proud and vain of lovers—deserved one another, but I, strange role for me to play, was fighting for community.

'Games, you say,' said Dubois, suddenly remembering that, in this, he was an old hand; but that, even though he was a man of business, he was honourable.

'Who's been playing games around here?' he asked.

'Now now,' said Eggy, presenting a calming influence.

The man's probably a fly-by-nighter,' I suggested.

'Hoo hoo,' said Eggy who had been that often enough.

A Rite in May

It was pouring outside, rain drumming on the new-leafed trees. Except for Moonface, on shift, and Serge the cook, I was alone in the Blue Danube, the radio broadcasting ugly music. All the siss-sissings, coo-cooings, phony intimacies such as were the mercies of the marketplace. Serge, a philosopher escaped from a mismanaged nation-state, approved of this music, however. He heard principles of self-determination and the testament of energies. My ears told me otherwise. Paint-by-numbers decadence. Meanwhile, Dubois was up against it, things having gone from bad to irretrievable. A rich man from Toronto, a certain Gambetti, was going to hire a catering hall in the east end among the industrial parks and strip malls, and he would invite friends and relatives to a feast, and he would, in public, propose marriage to Eleanor, as if marriage, in this instance, would transcend life's claptrap. Traymoreans were included on the guest list, and Dubois, too, if he wished. But did Eleanor know what she was about? The lilac behind Mrs Petrova's suite was in blossom, so I noted earlier as I sneezed. Life was like this. A Presidential pronouncement incurred one's outrage; good friends were in disarray, the peace of Traymorean society disturbed, and then, one caught cold or developed allergies, to boot. I supposed I would have to trot out some old suit I had not worn in years and dance along with a rite in May, all in honour of the wrong gods. I stepped outside to smoke. Raindrops popped like so many polyps on the street.

Agent Provocateur

A favourite downtown eatery, smoked meat joint, had closed after years of doing business. I took Moonface elsewhere. To a restaurant that cooked a decent and peppery burger. We had been roaming the shops. Underground, at some venue or another, she had even sampled perfume. She held her wrist to my nose; I got a whiff of *Agent Provocateur.* Supposedly I had just been presented with saffron and coriander by way of scents. I shrugged. Moonface shrugged. State secrets were safe for now. In the restaurant, we sat at a long counter with high swivel chairs. We drank weak coffee, waiting for our burgers. I liked the place; it was often busy but relaxed, the waitresses generally middle-aged, no-nonsense types who switched from French to English and back again in a flash. A bus man's holiday for Moonface, her hair loose about her shoulders now that she had let the hood slide off her head, rain outside and wind. The burgers arrived; she bit into hers, her mind distracted by considerations other than those of the taste of food. She said: 'I've been thinking about Echo.'

'Yes?'

'Well, I've been thinking that you think about her.'

What sort of statement was this?

'Not always,' I said, telling a partial truth.

'I think she's just another excuse for you to play at being noble.'

My only reservation about the place was that, here, I might run into Arsdell. Arsdell was one of academe's finest. He had most of my contempt. I looked around. Thankfully, there was no Arsdell organizing some campaign against famine, pestilence and war. He ought to be treating with student illiteracy, which was rife.

'Echo,' I said, 'is the life force personified.'

'And me?'

'You're such a chameleon I often don't know what you are.'

'Some compliment.'

'We are what we are.'

'I don't believe in love. Do you?'

'Having our troubles with Champagne Sheridan are we, or with his mother or both?'

'That's not an answer to my question.'

'Love,' I said, beating back the rising pedagogue in me, 'is real. It's not a hoax. It's to be found in and around the wreckages of human hearts. It has nothing to do with compatibility between lovers. Getting on with one another—it's the luck of the draw. Maybe the Lamonts loved each other once, but that didn't stop Lucille from offing Marcel. Dubois loves Eleanor, who loves him; they just might survive one another if Eleanor ever settles down.'

'Why are you telling me this?'

'You said you don't believe in love. Of course, you believe in love. Just that, well, beware. That is, don't deny its existence or it'll bite you on your arse. Love of man. Love of woman. Love of poetry. Love of life. These loves are real. Not even Dubois can darken what's sacred with his materialism.'

Moonface looked impressed. Our waitress (*Monsieur, Madame, more coffee?)* replenished our cups. She had seen it a million times: silver-haired lecher, young woman getting snowed.

No, I was not noble. But I was effing spiritual.

Moonface, I figured, had squandered her affections on too many rat-like boys. I was on my couch, listening to music. From within their sacred flame, piano, accordion and oud seethed like distant thunder. Earlier, I had spoken nonsense to Moonface about love, but it had to be said, even if only to arrest her eyes rolling up and to the side. Let her disagree if she wished, but let her quarrel with a reality, not a phantasm. Did she not see the ghost of Fast Eddy flitting about who was insane with love of her? Sally McCabe appeared now, saying: 'Yes, Calhoun, you really are slipping. There's only the romance of the body and the consecrating whiskey. This love you have of mind for mind—it darkens the night's desert floor. Don't you know? You were there.'

She sounded almost wistful. Could I now be her only remaining friend?

In Eleanor's apartment there was a fight in progress. I had been mistaken; love is no sack bulging with the gifts of truth and lie. It was its own truth, its own lie. One accepted the burden or one did not. There was no miracle of logic that Dubois could pull off and return Eleanor to her senses. A door slammed. Another door was kicked open. Such was the petulance of Dubois.

Echo would not have one child; she would have ten. She would not write one poem; she would write a thousand. She would not bake just one chocolate layer cake; she would feed a legion, and the lowliest grunt would lick the spoon. Moonface might not know what was at stake; Echo did not need to be told. Piano and oud matched her footfalls with a jig. So far as I knew the police had not been back around to the café. Perhaps they interviewed Elias at his home, perhaps at the station. Perhaps interviews had been discontinued. Cassandra's smile could still ravish, but it ravished less frequently. She had the look of a woman who had dodged a bullet. Elias had the look of a man who had survived the front but might not next time. It was as if their destiny were holding, if that destiny was that they should run a café and raise daughters. Echo was, in any case, gone. What did I know of any Echo? She was a slip of a girl with whom I had barely spoken. I might be wildly wrong about her character; I doubted I was wrong.

Once I thought Moonface was born for love, thinking it in one of my more expansive states of mind. I stood corrected; Moonface had been born for the mutability of it. Echo was born to love life in no uncertain terms. For all that, I supposed Eggy had by now forgotten her. How swiftly things change, and with what indiscriminate sweep.

Four in the morning, and I was awake with the rag ends of a dream in my thoughts. In it, there had been many people, elegantly attired, sitting at the long tables of a catering hall. Eggy was Master of Ceremonies. He invited revellers to the microphone to sing or joke or just talk. Dubois and Moonface worked the bar. Dubois, of course, was miserable. This was understandable. The conspicuous absentee? Eleanor, for whom the charade had been wrought. Gambetti's degree of difficulty consisted of this, that he must convince jaded old matriarchs and bemused patriarchs and their children and their children's children that Eleanor was worthy of his love. Booze and cake. Accordions. At this point I awoke. It was not a nightmare as such; it was a question asked in the form of a dream. Where was Eleanor? Where was Echo, for that matter? Why was everything ever so slightly out of synch? I went to the bathroom and piddled. The trouble with being awake at four in the morning was that all answers to all questions were bleak in their view of life.

On the morning that followed, I went to the neighbourhood library. I would reacquaint myself with a few items: orgones, L-fields, morphogenesis, *qi*, *pneuma*, and the like. I was perhaps sinking to new lows. Echo's energy could have been explained by rational means. Really? In any case, it was not her energy so much as its quality, the way it seemed to have left a sparkle on everything she touched. The library could have used her at the desk so as to cheer things up a little. I bolted. And in a park, one frequented by mothers and their preschoolers, I sat and smoked, the wind chilly. There are times when the life we live lacks rhyme and reason, science a side-show, poetry The Bearded Lady and her glassy eyes. Birds hopped. Squirrels plumed. The sky spun cloud. Toddlers, already socialized, had already been warned off me. I must have been there before I was there, a Delian problem, the doubling of a cube on a bench. A familiar voice called my name. It may have projected itself from a leaf or a twig, pebble, bit of debris, blade of grass.

'Calhoun,' spoke Sally McCabe. 'I see you're upset. Echo disappears. Eleanor acts up. Death and evil are triumphant in the republic, every day their pageantry. Did we not teach you well? Because you're one of us: leering grins, limbs attached. The wind blows forever in our hearts. You see, we're blameless.'

I pushed back: 'Loveliest of women, you sullied your character. You, even you bought into the notion that, even if we're great no longer, we remain adorable. I present you with Fallujah. You counter with Las Vegas and honeymooners and true love and the teen angel choruses of tunes. You can't admit to your own disbelief. You seek me out in desperation. Because you are an unquiet spirit and because I'm the last person still standing who bothers to reflect upon what you were. Even so, I can't help you; you can't help me. I would dearly love to have it back, that moment we once had, that kiss we exchanged at the victory dance after the football game. For you I may have been just a shy, awkward boy, hero of the hour. For me the kiss was already redolent with the cinder and ash of prophecy, though of course at the time, I couldn't have known it. One more of these conversations and I may go mad. The prophecy has long since staled. It has all the freshness of the daisies Oedipus in his blind condition once picked, long before there were Caesars, long before there were Joint Chiefs of Staff, long before there was an operator like Freud.'

I ran out of bluster and words. Sally McCabe spoiled her face with hurt.

I did not know if this was the last I would see of her, but if she came for me again, armed to the teeth, I might try a more conciliatory posture.

Noble Romance

I knocked on Eleanor's door and was greeted by a fuming woman. She said: 'You.'

I followed her into her kitchen. She was dressed in a T-shirt and denims. Red pompadours. Smoke curled from a cigarette in an ashtray as if in mimetic sympathy for the frosted curls of her hair. She was near snarling, she saying: 'Did Bob send you? Isn't he man enough to argue his own case? I suppose you want to talk me out it. I'm going to marry that guy Gambetti, and that's all there is to it.'

I was regretting my little visit.

'I do what I want,' she continued. 'You do what you want. I sleep with whoever I want. And if you don't want to sleep with me, well, that's all on you. And you don't know what you're missing.'

I had a pretty good idea. I studied the coffee mug she was handling, that smudge of lipstick on the rim, the spoon at its side with its smear of cream, a bit of stain on the table cloth. Eleanor was not fussy about order and tidiness, but even she, she would not place a wet spoon on pristine linen. Other than this, I was no more enlightened than when I had walked in and taken my usual chair.

'So when's the big day?' I asked.

'Big day for what?'

'Your marriage.'

'Hell's bells, Calhoun, that's still a ways off. Next Saturday, we do the catering hall. I don't suppose you'll come.'

'I don't know. Maybe.'

'Roll me one of your thingies,' she said, her voice softening.

But how did Gambetti treat her in bed? How much money did he truly have? These were not questions a gentleman asks a lady, but then since when had Eleanor and I ever rested on ceremony? For a certainty, Dubois wished to know. Echo was gone and I was disgusted with much that had nothing to do with Eleanor slip-sliding her way to grave error, one that might prove more fatal to her than the Unitary Executive. Still, she was not the sort of woman one could gainsay, that is, once she had up a head of steam and knew her own mind by her own lights, however delusionary the knowing was. Cynic that I was, callous creature, I idly contemplated taking her to bed. Now would be the time to do it. What she really wanted was sympathy for her muddlement. She wished for Dubois to play a hand. Outside, city workers tore up the sidewalk; a massive drill bit pounded the pavement, the Traymore Rooms shaking as if earthquake-struck. Spanish gold had been found off the coast of Namibia. Iraqi gold, melted down, was now used to make the spurs on American boots. Eleanor pursed her lips around the end of one of my hand-rolled cigarettes and inhaled. She eyed me.

'What's on your mind, Calhoun?'

What, she did not know?

'Well, this would be a hell of a time for it,' she observed. 'You could knock me over with a feather,' she added.

Obviously, she was of a sudden amused. Then, she took matters in her own hands: 'Tempted, but I don't think so.'

'No, no,' I said. 'I was only thinking how little blessed our lives are with beauty and noble romance.'

'Come off it.'

She might spring for marriage, but as for beauty and all the rest, *fuhgeddaboudit*. I hoped she had had a good time in Toronto.

Gregory and Elias were sinking too much into their little project Le Grec. Large potted ferns had appeared. Purple glass teardrops, suspended from the ceiling, demarcated the tiny bar area, and they could not have been cheap. All the staff was there: Gregory, Elias, Cassandra, Moonface and Serge. A new girl, tall and very slim, was hanging about, waiting to be trained. She seemed much too shy and slow of wit in spite of her loud, metallic red hair. (Melody, another redhead, had moved on to greener pastures, downtown.) Eggy, at the sight of it, would be most pleased. He had yet to show. Dubois had yet to show, the hockey game soon to be on TV.

'How's it going?' Gregory asked, as I took a seat, he King Arthur in his Camelot.

I could not read Cassandra's mood for what it might indicate of her husband's guilt.

'Fine,' I said in answer, and with one word was noncommittal.

I suppose Gregory was counting on it being a busy night, the Habs down two games to one and needing to win, lest the entirety of this faded Jezebel of a town riot. Elias studied something that looked suspiciously like a blueprint. Moonface came over to speak. She had but a single word to offer me: 'Expansion.'

Ah, the dreamers.

I could see how they might knock out a wall and extend the seating area into the adjoining rental space. But would not they have to enlarge the galley already cramped with the new pizza oven so as to prepare more food for a larger clientele? But why should I consume my noggin with these considerations? Moonface was fetching: short black skirt, black tights. I looked for Virgil in her eyes. The President had admitted as much that his administration tortured. I had had yet another chance with Eleanor and had yet again, passed on it. Her eyes told me I was diffident, spineless, and oh so transparent; but that, good golly, Miss Molly, she was flattered I would bed her just to keep her from straying off the reservation. She would marry a fellow named Gambetti, so it seemed, and he would spirit her away on a magic carpet of marriage and wealth. No more feckless Traymorean society. Yes, look out, all you somebodies. What, would she take up writing short stories and organizing charity drives? Dubois would drink himself to death, no doubt, and Eggy die just a little lonelier. Who would call the paramedics for him in the advent of one of his strokes? Moonface continued to stand at my table, at a loss for anything to say. Her eyes rolled up and to the side. She tugged at her ponytail. Well, what? What was her thought that evidently I was meant to divine? That love was the answer, and failing that, the Roman peace? Here was Eggy hoving into view, shuffling with purpose, brandishing his cane. Here was Dubois behind him, carrying his honest and worn attaché case. Sometimes I wondered if his vaunted business career had been a myth. And here they were at the table, my best soul mates of the hour, Eggy hoo hooing at Moonface for a libation, Dubois saying forget that, bring a bottle. Quebecker that he was, he was looking forward to the game. Eleanor was some other agenda.

'Praises be, new blood,' said Eggy, catching sight of the tall and slim and redheaded girl.

From the inner pocket of his grungy linen jacket he pulled out a small notebook and checked his social calendar.

'Ah,' he said. 'I seem to have next Friday free.'

'She won't know what hit her,' said Dubois.

So then it was a not good time to pick a fight with those two over politics, the one too sanguine, the other a man of business who still trusted the system. To Dubois I said: 'It's no joke, the politicization of the Justice Department and its strong-arm tactics.'

Eggy I cautioned, saying: 'Don't tell me there's an article of interest in the *Gazette* because it's not possible that it would run an article of interest.'

Eggy opened his mouth to speak, Dubois preparing to laugh: 'The rain in Spain, you know. What's a man's reach for?'

'Speaking of which,' said Dubois, 'it's a pretty strange game of hockey the Habs have been playing. *Pas de deux* along the boards.'

'Look, Calhoun,' Dubois continued, winking at Eggy, a tiny sparrow of a man, 'when the Yanks come up here to bring us democracy, I'll be the first to insurge. You don't believe me?'

'Insurge, insurge,' Eggy hoo hooed. 'My cane shall sprout lethal blossoms of love. Moonface, oh Moonface, why are you not here with your child-bearing hips and pouring my wine? It's a disgrace. Bloody effing hell.'

And the young woman in question, whispering something into the ears of Very Tall Slim Girl, stuck out an editorial tongue. Cassandra stood behind the bar like a woman in possession of grave secrets. For Gregory, things were going according to plan. Elias had about him an air of eleventh hour resolve. Serge was a protagonist in some paramilitary raid, a parachutist firing from the hip as he floated out of the sky. And so it was. So it was that I was told how to behave, as it was, after all, Hockey Night in Canada. The instruction rankled.

Evolutionary Drift

Back in the Sixties, poets, mystics, philosophers, ologists, cons, pushers, pimps and politicos called for an opening of the mind, and, in the end, wound up as ungenerous and dogmatic as the old closed shops against which they agitated. Even I had said, *But of course. Liberty. Free and untrammelled.* And you might think that, as a consequence, intuitional capabilities enhanced, I could spell out what made Eleanor Eleanor, once I accounted for sex and security and all the rest of it. Even so, it was sheer perversity—to attempt to go Dubois one better in his powers of analysis. Well, marriage with Gambetti was Eleanor's evolutionary drift. Random molecules having brief relations in random sequence. Or it was that Eleanor was used to getting her way, knowing of no other mode of behaviour. Or because Dubois did not resist her so much as withstand, and withstanding, infuriated the good woman. No one may ever know what booted it for her. The vast majority of us will take our secrets to the grave, even those that remain sealed to our own comprehension. Still, an Event of Proposal, a prenuptial bash, the hiring of a catering hall was cancelled; Eleanor got cold feet. A hangdog Italian came around a couple of times to plead his case. In this, Eleanor received her full measure of satisfaction from a crestfallen ego that had been cut to the quick. Then she sent the man packing. Marriage? What marriage? Who said anything about marriage? Dubois allowed himself a guffaw or two in the Blue Danube, Eggy going on about the old days of the Shah, and then Dickens and Zola. The look in Dubois's eyes said three things; one, that he could care less about Iran's difficulties; two,

Zola Schmola; and three, as far as he and Eleanor were concerned, mind you, it had been a close call. And pressed to account for the fact that the Habs were eliminated from the playoffs, he shrugged.

'They need someone on the wing,' he said. 'Bigger, faster, stronger.'

'Yes but,' so Eggy would point out, 'that Dreyfuss Affair was a nasty piece of business.'

'Well?' said Dubois, looking at me. 'You will, of course, have an observation.'

'I have none,' I said. 'Three bags full of none.'

Cassandra applied Windex and cloth to a window, her long purple hair swaying from side to side as she wiped the glass. It was her blind faith, this housekeeping. If, in the film version of *The Golden Bowl,* the billionaire Adam Verver believed he could break his wife's infatuation with Amerigo and gain her affections for himself and set her on the straight and narrow, and invest her with true purpose, it was because he had all that money. Cassandra had no such recourse. Blind faith was the poor man's leverage, and it might win you a battle but never the war.

'What,' I asked, 'possessed you? And why did you break it off?'

Eleanor laughed, the good woman did. Her body rippled. She ran her hand through her frosted curls. Then, sipping amaretto, she licked her lips and answered: 'What possessed me? God only knows what possessed me. Why did I break it off? The man had ugly toes. Can't stand a man with ugly toes. Do you have ugly toes? But the other thing of it was, I'd always be seeing in my mind's eye the sight of Bob with my successor. I'm territorial, I guess.'

About my toes, I could not say. No woman had ever critiqued my toes. Perhaps there had not been the time, so much else about me that might incur their displeasure. My grotty mind. My leonine sloth.

And everything I had ever spoken to Moonface of love, spoken in some bright flush of infatuation and avuncular concern, I now retracted, love being but an electro-chemical sleight of hand born of a primal soup back when the sun was hotter and the earth less stable. And then we toed and heeled our way out of grassy Africa even unto Vladivostok. And whatever words we managed to construct so as to keep afloat a fantasy of the thing barely flattered us. The gods wondered why they bothered; they should have left well enough alone with squirrels and sparrows and stick-waving chimps.

Or I could choose to see Eleanor as a clown, were Boffo ever a woman, and know that no real harm was done; just that an Italian experienced some diminution of *amour propre.* I had resolved at age 35, as I became more deeply aware of the true height and depth and breadth of impudence humankind has been pleased to describe as literature, not to let bitterness ever get the best of me in view of my failure. My progress in this business had been spotty, given my weak and callow nature, but even so, it struck me just then, as I watched Eleanor handle a cigarette and regard me with narrowed eyes, that should I wish to indulge I had excuses with which to do so. How much more bitter I might have been, a loner, an expatriate of sorts, a man whom no political ethos represented, as bad faith was everything; a man who was not honoured by a wife; a man who had not done his duty by way of children, that is, had not given the gene pool the benefit of his doubt; who was no patriot; who was a so-so poet. Who had been average in bed. (The law of averages, not honesty, spoke this news.) Eleanor, of course, would have none of it just now, she the chuckles-inducing catastrophe of the moment who had had a brief pratfall with an *uomo gentile* and was on the mend. She switched to politics and said: 'It seems the senator from Illinois will prevail.'

'Yes, I think he has the nomination sewn up. It remains to be seen whether he'll be allowed to live.'

'You don't think—'

'I do think. But who can say?'

'The wheels are falling off everything. They nearly fell off me.'

This, at a relatively early hour, was to be her one concession to the demands of the life of the mind. I bit my tongue lest it cut loose with some news presenter sharpening his enunciation skills: the BBC accent of doom. We sat there quiet, there in her commodious kitchen. I had erotic notions. I saw us, she and I, as the last woman and last man left standing in the world. I could see her wrinkling her nose at the sight of my ugly toes. I wondered if she were pleased or displeased at how things had panned out. Or did she even know?

There had always been Blind Musician and the like who would appear at the Blue Danube aka Le Grec for a day or two and then disappear for weeks. It was the same with Joe Smithers the too-tall poet. Gentleman Jim was a more regular presence, but he would sit so quietly and so unobtrusively tipple his bottle's worth of wine that Traymoreans hardly noticed him. There was the old woman who directed traffic in the streets, be it vehicular or pedestrian, and she made it clear to the citizens at large that all were at fault, but that men were most at fault, and they were good for nothing. One evening, new blood poked a head in the Blue Danube door. The man wore glasses and looked scholarly.

'Is this place licensed?' he asked.

No one answered, and he addressed his own query, saying: 'Good, because I have a thirst.'

He parked himself at our table with brazen flair. Eggy blinked. Dubois prepared to guffaw. I examined the creature. Well, as it turned out, he was a photographer. Antiquities were his specialty. For this purpose he travelled a lot in North Africa. His name was Hiram Wiedemayer.

'Nice place, this,' he said, blinking foolishly at a photograph of the Acropolis.

'Ah, the Acropolis,' he said.

Eggy waved his arms. This brought Moonface over. Eggy said: 'I think we require another bottle.'

'I'll pay,' said the newcomer with enthusiasm.

'Promising,' said Dubois.

'But I have to eat, too,' said this Hiram character. 'What have you got to eat?'

Hiram settled on pizza. And then we shook hands all around.

And then we argued everything, how we were still fighting the first Great War; how Germany had been the centre of gravity for western civilization; how, as that was no longer true, there was no more western civilization, just an arrangement between nation-states of expedience, their old imperialist bag of tricks still in play but more discreetly so; that the Arabs needed Israel more than Israel needed Arabs; that America was in freefall. Dubois thought Hiram awfully glib in his historical analysis. Eggy had been listening with care. Then he said: 'I haven't spoken on this matter much, but after I mustered out way back in the Fifties, Korea, you know, I toured North Africa; I visited the clubs, the whorehouses, the KitKat places—'

'And what has this to do with anything?' interjected Dubois. 'I think you're making this up. You haven't lived long enough to have been to all the places you say you've been, and God knows you've been hanging around for 900 years.'

'Why, everything, you silly twit. That Hiram here just possibly might know what he's talking about. Hell, you only read Camus. You didn't live it.'

And so forth and so on. I began a disquisition on bad faith. I was getting very drunk. I said: 'What's Iran doing that's any different from what the Americans are doing, the Israelis, the Russians, the Chinese, the Europeans, the Indians? Get my drift?'

'And what has Baghdad got to do with Berlin?' asked Dubois, getting Jesuitical, his blue eyes glittering, he leaning forward for the kill.

'Ah, Berlin,' said Hiram. 'If Europe is ever to be Europe again, and not just some deal tricked up in Brussels, Berlin will have to take the lead. It's got the right energy.'

'Hoo hoo,' said Eggy. 'Bloody Krauts.'

'I agree with Hiram,' I offered. 'We're still fighting that Christly war.'

'All those empires gone,' said Hiram. 'And all these bits and pieces of them still around that are wondering who's boss.'

Then Hiram praised the pizza he had just demolished. Then he asked why Moonface was called Moonface.

'She just bloody is,' said Eggy.

'And why are you Eggy?'

'Short for Eglinton. And I'll have you know those Moroccan damsels were the best.'

'You've got a point there,' said Hiram. 'I took the picture of a Moroccan prostitute once. I still do, over and over in my mind. And you, what do you do?'

Dubois answered: 'I'm semi-retired from the world of business.'

'We need good business,' Hiram replied. 'Boy, do we ever need good business, not this corporate stuff that leaves no one with any reason to live but buy, buy, buy.'

Ethical Dubois nodded; perhaps he was impressed.

'I'm reading about Louis XIV,' said Eggy. 'Well, how else understand Montcalm and Wolfe and why Montcalm threw the battle? The rain in Spain and all that.'

Now Hiram Wiedemayer wished to photograph the Eggy countenance, that inverted pyramid of a face, its angular severity somehow softened by an inner sweetness of character the old bugger had stumbled upon in old age. I was always poking at that sweetness to see how real it was; I was not unlike the doubting Thomas who prodded the Christ wound. The droopy Eggy eyes. Now Hiram Wiedemayer wished to photograph Dubois. Perhaps he had it in mind to unleash some trick of light on the hairline cracks of the man's ruddy cheeks that did, at times, seem caked with cosmetic powder, the fact of which put me in mind of a double-lived ponce: the Scarlet Pimpernel. Perhaps Hiram Wiedemayer was very drunk. Me he did not wish to photograph. At least, I received no offer. Perhaps there was no way to adequately document my inner reserve, my rich pessimism. Moonface he inspected with the eye of an artist and then discounted as portrait material, yes, with the eye of a man who, knowing his pleasure, knew he had had better. A senator from New York had gutted the soft fruit of the Democratic Party in her bid to represent it as its presidential contender. Could smashed fruit acquire the plum of the White House? Unquiet spirits, bad faith everywhere. Götterdämmerung in pantsuits. A ghostly Nero laughed, seeing in this part of the world something he recognized. He whacked away on his lyre, tried on for size pop-apocalyptic tunes. The ghost of Fast Eddy looked especially worried, regarding his glass of wine as some corrupting agent, and he needed his wits about him. Perhaps he saw Hiram Wiedemayer as a rival. Gentleman Jim seated nearby us in a freshly laundered shirt and dark Bermuda shorts, his legs woefully pale, wished to salve and soothe and otherwise calm the world down, but he had been fresh out of kisses and caresses for years. And before Hiram Wiedemayer took his leave of us, we his new-found community and potential audience, he and I stood out on the street and smoked. He said he hoped he had not come across as one of those neo-liberal apologists for the high-handed way Israel treated with Palestine. I answered, oh no, and besides, who among us would remember a thing in the morning? Hiram had enjoyed himself. Likewise, I assured him. Then he took off with rapid strides, a man who was late for other engagements. One look through the window of the Blue Danube at my friends, and I could see that Hiram was already forgotten, Dubois and Eggy most likely arguing the merits of something or another, Gentleman Jim staring at the bitter dregs of his libation. Moonface was busy preparing the café for closing hour. I went straight to my digs. There I watched the weather channel with a dull, uncomprehending, inebriated gaze. To whom at this hour could the weather-presenter, ludicrously sexy, pitch her weather-wares? She had the look of a woman who frequently availed herself of office sex. Then there was something about clouds forming in the likenesses of corporate logos. Maybe there was more to this woman than met the eye. In any case, it was decidedly too much to bear.

Poor Mrs Stone

An unholy racket woke me in the morning. Chainsaw, woodchipper. Men had come to delimb maples out back. I worried for the sparrows and the squirrels. Later, I heard Moonface crossing the hall to Eggy's. I envied Eggy his morning audience. It was somewhat of a mystery to me what they found to talk about day after day, although I was sure Moonface's future had always been on Eggy's mind. I heard Dubois lock his door and head down the Traymore stairs. He kept his business dealings to himself. Not even Eleanor knew what he got up to; sometimes she suspected there was another woman. However, at this juncture in time, she had not much ground on which to stand. I would eventually come to some semblance of consciousness. I would amuse myself with my jottings while the saw shrieked through hard maple wood and did violence to the integrity of the trees. Around eleven I would pay Eleanor a visit. I dealt myself a hand of solitaire, and after a while Moonface appeared at my door, on her way to keep an appointment somewhere. She said: 'Herodotus, page 518: *Behold, I change to another mind.*'

'But of course,' I answered playfully, 'you're a changeable one.'

'Well, I'm off.'

'And where are you off to?'

'To visit a girlfriend of mine whose father is a poet.'

'Poor girl.'

'Ta-ta, then.'

'Tra la.'

Red-sneakered Moonface went down the Traymore stairs with a boundless faith in the life force.

'It's astounding,' I said to myself, 'the countless ways we have of slipping through one another's fingers.'

I went, that afternoon, to the grave of Gareth Howard, my oldest friend. It required roughly an hour's worth of public transport, getting there. And there it was on its hillside overlooking the river—Gar's headstone, this marker with its carved rose, name and dates. It seemed to me a grievous shame that his wife Clare was not buried beside him. They had loved one another, after all. She, I supposed, came to rest in a respectable family plot, her family respectable and prominent. In Kingston where she was born? I had nothing to say to Gar who, in any case, could not hear me. It was not on account of the fact that he was dead, but that he was, as I had always claimed, punishing me by way of denying me memory of his voice. Crows. Robins. Birch, spruce, maple. Ceremonial wreaths sprinkled here and there. *Hello, Gar, how the hell are you?* A stiffening wind, cumulus in the sky, made for fast-changing shadow on the ground of the dead, on a spectacle of finality. I shut my eyes. I could barely behold a memory of Clare. A sweater that flattered her bosom. Her pensive smile. A timbre of voice that suggested seriousness of purpose and great intelligence. All the hard thinking that Gar occasioned in me, that Clare occasioned, as well, to what did it amount in this a vain struggle on my part to preserve continuity, life's transience the law of every land? Gar had been a serious man, committed to the exposure of lies and abuse of power and all the rest of it, Clare proud of his endeavour. And I had been, what, their clown, comic relief? Even when Clare, that day in Gar's old shack, Gar passed on to his reward, had allowed a kiss to transpire between us, and just a little more than that, I had been but comic relief. Virgil the poet immortalized his obscure shepherds with their grotty little lusts and cares. A counter spin to the grinding Wheel of Time, sparks flying. All I had accomplished was a pile of jottings. Perhaps I could boast of a moment of ecstasy—her mouth on mine. We are all of us thieves in the end, and some, like Clare, steal better than others. Virgil, I surmised, looked long and hard at death, so much so he became his shepherds, words become flesh. Too many people, extravagant types, who shout they love life, always aroused my suspicions; that they had not looked at anything, especially not death in its absolute grandeur, and were only spouting some party line so as not to be cut from the herd. And if the festivities required the deaths of millions, even so, to spoil the party could cost you your life. I loved life. I began to follow the promenade along the river. I would walk a ways and catch a bus somewhere. Gulls and crows. It seemed to me I could hear Clare encouraging me to write at least one decent poem. I minded her schoolmarmish tone. I would rather she had wished a follow-up kiss, and failing that, a drink such as might lead to one.

Eggy was having too much fun to die. The Blue Danube. Wine. Genteel talk. Served hand and foot by the likes of Moonface. Even the new waitress Anna, tall, redheaded, looked like she might get into the spirit of things. As for Traymorean society in general, its pursuit of frivolity was not likely to amuse oligarchs whose fascist notions of virtue had only masked an appetite for depravity. Our social and political betters were, of course, amused by the fact that they were not us.

In any case, we were seated in the Blue Danube of an evening, Eggy, Dubois and I. It was an evening like any other, we situated in a deep trough of sea as calm as the water of a bath, but between two gigantic and rolling swells. Eggy had indeed said he was having too much fun to kick the bucket yet. Dubois responded that he may as well die, and we would all jump up and down on his grave, and we would have one hell of a party. Eggy sniffed that if we were not too cheap, we might contribute a bottle of scotch to said grave, yes, for that long journey he was about to take. Dubois supposed it could be arranged. Moonface looked a little alarmed. Gregory the cook asked how it was going for us. For him, we were just business. There was hockey on TV, the Habs long gone. Echo was gone. How many articles could one read on American foreign policy and remain human? What, in God's name, was 'dual containment'? Literate slaves ran the show that was Claudius's rule, this after the madness that was Caligula; but those slaves were, at least, competent and smarter than your average bear. Elias was on the street examining a dent in his car. He squatted by the fender in question, and he was pondering, what, life's great questions? He did not have the air of a man who might have done some horrible thing to a girl like Echo. But then, what would such an air look like? The ghost of Fast Eddy was now at table, complaining that the delimbed maple which once shaded his backyard was a ghost of its former self. Moonface was thinking again of a post-graduate career. I regretted encouraging her; I had a dim view of academe. Who was she really? It was alleged that Laurier, an early Canadian prime minister, had got five bucks a head for every Russian immigrant who was prairie-bound. Would that the black nurse of enormous heft had drowned Eggy when she had the chance, scrubbing him in his bath, Eggy a tiny sparrow of a man. And Eggy sniffed that, at least, he would not have the bother of attending at our funerals, that is, with any luck. I took my leave of my soul mates, repaired to my digs. There was a movie on TV: *The Roman Spring of Mrs Stone*. I wallowed in nostalgia for the ancient corruptions as they were portrayed, ancient loneliness by which some of the privileged of the world do fall. Poor Mrs Stone. She tried to grab love with her passion and with her expendable dollars, and she grabbed a chimera. Still, she had been, in the end, more honest than her cynical gigolo. Later, on the Letterman show, there was that insufferable blonde celebrity, her tits and her tanned legs and her family's money her excuse for exciting our attention.

'Echo's gone,' I said to my four walls.

Rot Your Socks

Said Eggy: 'According to Bob, you're getting worse.'

'Worse than what?' I answered, playing it straight.

'Why, moody. It won't do, you know: constant doom. And what, by the way, what's that on your head?'

'Baseball cap.'

I had found it, that morning, among some forgotten effects of mine, its bill furled just so.

Hey batter batter. No batter batter.

Though the wind cut a little in its chill, we were seated outdoors at a Blue Danube table. Eggy raised his glass to me.

'Whatever. Rot your socks.'

'Rot yours,' I said.

We fell silent, Eggy and I. It was Eggy who caved first, breaking the silence: 'I told you I was in Innsbruck, didn't I?'

'A hundred times.'

'You needn't get snippy.'

'Must have been some wench.'

'She was no wench. She was, well, I suppose she was a wench, at that.'

An angelic grin did grotesque things to Eggy's face.

'I'm sure of it. Rot your socks.'

A two o'clock sun in an indifferent sky seemed shoddy somehow, the birds just birds. Tulips. Dandelions. Tiny ants in their eternities. The fragile purple blooms of some ground cover. So much for Eggy's 81st. Perhaps Eleanor was baking a birthday item. Perhaps Moonface would present it with its candle and we sing *Happy Birthday, Zeus.* Zeus the rotter. Amiable rotter who had had killer instinct enough when joining battle with those

Titans, moody, implacable earth spirits opposed to the airy lightness of the sky. So it must have been. Passersby were jacketed. The more intrepid wore only shirts. It was a national pastime, defying climate. A dachshund rebelled against its leash, was yanked to order by a white-haired, stoop-shouldered biddy punch-drunk with the banalities. Now here was the too-tall poet, Joe Smithers.

'Ah,' Eggy called out, hailing him, 'a real poet. Not like some I know.'

Too Tall Poet was confused. Some believed poets were a vanishing breed, and one did not insult the remnants. I begged to differ.

'Can't stay,' the too-tall poet advised. 'My laundry.'

'It can wait,' surmised Eggy.

But it could not wait. And Joe Smithers had recently buried his father and watched his girlfriend go starkers. It seemed he would cast a cold eye and move on. Real poet, indeed.

'Oh well,' observed Eggy, 'passing one's birthday with a depressive like you—it isn't so bad.'

'Rot your socks.'

'Up yours.'

And so, come that evening, we celebrated Eggy's 81st. Dubois, teasing, was sure it was more like Eggy's 901st.

'1107,' said Eggy. 'That was the year a pope took on the Empire.'

We none of us had any idea what he was on about. For sure, Gentleman Jim did not know; he was still coming to grips with the Truman Doctrine, but that Eggy should not expect anything grander than vermouth, seeing as Eggy had agreed to pay him a visit on the morrow. Fast Eddy the ghost offered to find me a literary agent. I was surprised at how much he was getting around. But since when had Fast Eddy developed a sense of humour, he with his insufferable gravitas? Moonface, as it turned out, did not present our table with cake. Eleanor, who would have cooked one up, opted to enter Eggy's digs earlier, instead. She kissed his horrid little pate. She pleaded to a sore throat and would not show that evening. It seemed to me that relations between her and Dubois had been strained since that time that Dubois cast aspersions on her bust. So that a stir was caused when it was revealed that, on the next Monday, Dubois and Moonface were to date. It was, as Dubois explained, not an assignation so much as a long-standing pledge to wine and dine at a fancy old town restaurant; that it had been in the cards for months and had always been put off. I was jealous. Outside, the trees were getting their boulevard airs. Perhaps it was the effect of the twilight in the new foliage, each leaf pert and aroused, tingling with life force. Women with immense buttocks, some wearing shades in the dimming light, were walking dogs. Some, resting on bus stop benches, were nuzzling dog noses. Everything was so dear. The world was threatening to do us all well-being, yes, as opposed to rape, rapine and pillage, and holding the White House hostage. Eggy said: 'I even got a phone call. That woman, you know.'

'Here we go,' said Dubois. 'What woman? Which of the hundreds with whom you have relations?'

'I beg your pardon. Nothing to extremes. But if you must know, it was International Sales Manager.'

'Ah, the clothing woman,' said a comprehending Dubois.

'Well, I don't suppose she's in lanjeray.'

'Lingerie,' Dubois corrected.

'Oh well then, lawnjeray. Bloody effing hell. Anyway, it wasn't Henry V the English guy; it was Henri V the French guy who said Paris was worth a mass.'

Gentleman Jim looked hopelessly confused. His face was red with wine as was the face of Dubois, the hairline cracks of his cheeks more fine than usual.

'We've been getting our Henry's mixed up,' thundered Eggy, a tiny sparrow of a man.

This, of course, explained everything. Eggy continued: 'But I won't be taking any pills. 36-hour boner, indeed. Bloody hell.'

Clearly, Eggy and Dubois had just referred to an earlier conversation known only to them—

'And you lost your virginity where?' asked Dubois.

'Why, it was Beirut,' Eggy answered, not blinking an eye; and then, quoting Marlowe: 'Was this the face that launched a thousand ships?'

Gentleman Jim looked even more confused. Did a thousand ships have something to do with sex? With what sort of men was he hobnobbing? Eggy expressed his disappointment with Moonface, addressing Dubois: 'You two going to paint the town red. And she'd promised to take me to the Ritz-Carlton, that ungrateful wench, after all I've done for her.'

'A little out of her pocketbook range, don't you think?'

'Yes. Yes, I suppose I shouldn't hold her to it. So why don't you take me to the Ritz-Carlton?'

'Because,' explained Dubois, 'we're having a good enough time here.'

'Gentlemen,' said Gentleman Jim rising, his voice a little severe, 'I wish you a good evening. Remember, three o'clock sharp.'

He was buttonholing Eggy with this injunction.

'I'll be there or I'll be square,' vowed Eggy.

And then, the man having departed, Eggy whined: 'What am I getting myself into? Why do I want to go to that death house of his? I guess just to see what it is I wish to avoid. Well, I'll kill myself before it comes to that for me.'

'We'll help you,' laughed Dubois.

But Eggy had been serious. Eggy looked weepy.

We covered a great range of topics. We even touched upon Agincourt, the battle of, this battle that involved the longbow, so Eggy had pointed out. Even Moonface allowed herself a moment of bawdiness, doing a little dance with her hips as she stood in place, just seeing how things were going at the table. We were her men, Eggy, Dubois and I, and perhaps Moonface did see herself as a warrior princess, a queen of some rogue confederation of tribes. She expected to begin her pursuit of a Masters in the fall. She leaned down to kiss Eggy's sour old cheek with her thin but royal lips. I am sure the old man at 901 years of longevity caught a glimpse of the royal bosom. Happy Birthday, Eggy. Then Gregory the cook came over to perform his *how's it going, guys, with you guys*? Elias had been the only one moping in the Blue Danube. Cassandra kept herself to the galley throughout the evening, preparing some food item for the next day's menu. I was not able, as a consequence, to glean any intelligence from her eyes. I took my leave. I had not played much of a part in the festivities though I consumed my share of the wine and contributed the odd observation. For instance, I conjectured that the New York senator was finished in her run for the nomination, and now was the time for serious political hanky-panky such as I was convinced was in the offing. Eggy shushed me. Later, in my digs, I heard Dubois hauling Eggy up the Traymore stairs. Eggy was in a good mood, quoting Marlowe again. *Was this the face that launched a thousand ships, and burnt the topless towers of Ilium? Sweet Helen, make me immortal with a kiss.*

'That's enough for tonight,' said Dubois, obviously tired.

'Oh rot your socks,' thundered a tiny man.

What's Bred in the Bone

Two notes were slipped under my door either earlier that morning or in the course of the night, Dubois and Eggy the culprits. Dubois, describing himself as a Senior Business Consultant, wrote: *Chassez le naturel et il revient au galop.* He then provided the English equivalent: *What's bred in the bone comes out in the flesh.* The meaning of Eggy's note was obscure, its origins even more obscure, as Eggy, for the life of himself, could not remember the proverb's author. Eggy, with his bird-like scrawl had written: *Better is the poet who is acquainted with erudites as he shall be able to avoid putting his finger in his eye. The New York Times*? No, the quote smacked of the hoary old age of an ancient culture. Hebrew? Arab? Persian? I woke with these words, not mine, in my thoughts: *Those vast, venerable walls were not meant to keep out cows, but men-at-arms…* One might have assumed that Dubois and Eggy would have passed out on the night previous, returning from the Blue Danube to their digs in the Traymore; instead, they went and got literary. At some point in recent days, the Secretary of Defense (the Kansan who replaced the infamous Rumsfeld) quoted Churchill at the end of a speech he had given, saying: 'The price of greatness is responsibility.'

So then, the Americans, according to an American, would remain a beacon.

And well, it would seem that this man, when he first came to Washington, summer of 1966, at the height of the American build-up in Vietnam, could look forward to the following intractable items, while he went to work for the monumental ego of Lyndon Baines Johnson, to wit,

—violent domestic turmoil; two major assassinations at home; a major war in the Middle East; the seizure of an America Navy ship by North Korea; the Soviet invasion of Czechoslovakia; the resignation of a president in disgrace;

—and then, by the end of the 1970s, these items, to wit,

—a collapse in Vietnam, and the death of millions across Southeast Asia; high inflation, high interest rates; two energy crises; the Soviet invasion of Afghanistan; revolution in Iran, the capture of American hostages there; tens of thousands of Cuban soldiers in Angola and Ethiopia.

Had I been paying attention throughout those years? Why, it had been a tempest.

And then, the Eighties,

—and the fall of the Berlin Wall was in the works; victory in the Cold War; reunification of Germany in Nato; the dissolution of the Soviet Union; the liberation of millions of Iron Curtainites and other entities around the world.

And in what ways were American cruelties different from those of the Canadian and British modes of persuasion? Eggy, Dubois and I might argue it, as if comparing cheeses. Eggy seemed to have fallen head over heels in love with a black nurse, much to Dubois's bemusement. We could none of us recall when Algeria got independence, but that DeGaulle, in Eggy's words, was a piece of work. A spectre named Fast Eddy threatened to defect to another neighbourhood, he in and out of insulin shock. Born and raised as an American, I was expected to succeed. It went without saying, the steady drip drip drip of failure everything that I was.

And I was, once more in a book of Gombrich, looking at Piombo's *The Death of Adonis* for hints of Echo, when Moonface came over to tell me that, she too, got a note from Dubois. She said: 'Bob's giving me the option of cancelling the date. I never actually thought it would come to anything.'

'Oh you should go,' I said breezily. 'Bob's a noble host. You'll eat well.'

'Randall.'

'You'll have to dress up.'

'I was thinking my opera dress and red sneakers.'

'I suppose in some circles that would pass muster.'

'You don't think he has ideas—'

'I honestly wouldn't know,' I answered, lying.

Away went Moonface like the brave young woman she was, even if, at times, she feared her own shadow. I could see it now, as I took note in a book of Gombrich of Cellini's gold saltcellar: Ceres about to recline, legs slightly parted, her left hand on the left breast of her otherwise modest bosom. And then, Neptune or Poseidon opposite her, his trident poised. Yes, that would be just about enough foolishness as anyone, god or mortal, could handle for a day.

'Make it up with Bob,' I said.

'Mind your own beeswax. Roll me a cig.'

Eleanor, of course, knew she was wrong. Her damnable pride was obstructing the flow of her affections for Dubois. And here was yet another one of those mysteries how, for all the man's vanity, and it was considerable, it had never hardened into pride. So it seemed. He was simply waiting her out. And when she was ready, ready, that is, to be herself again, beauty marks, warts and all, they would resume relations. One could argue forever who owed whom what and, in the arguing, forget to live.

'You think I did wrong,' she said.

'Yes, no, I don't know.'

I hated to equivocate, but there it was. I continued: 'You had an itch. You scratched it. It scratched back. But now you see where your loyalties lie. It's possible one can cheat in sexual matters and not betray a trust. It's possible, but only just. On this score most of us delude ourselves. What's trust? What are its characteristics? Informing ourselves of its physical properties, as it were, we create a chimera—'

'Calhoun, stuff it.'

I was being avuncular. I handed her a cigarette.

We were in the privacy of her kitchen, the finest room, perhaps, of all the Traymore rooms. The table hosted coffee mugs, ashtray, sugar, cream. A single tulip in a vase. She had pinched it somewhere. She lit her cigarette. She regarded me with narrowed eyes. I had never been clear about the colour of her eyes. Mottled green, blue, grey. I was a bit tired, not inclined just then to precise observation.

'Well, if you must know, I miss his company. And now, what to do about Hillary?'

She referred to a certain New York senator who, in her ambitions, was likely to be denied triumphal re-entry into the White House; who had been First Lady once upon a hallowed time of apparent boom and plenty.

'Again, I don't know,' I said. 'Is she to be lauded and extolled or buried up to her neck in hot coals in one of Dante's hells for the politically reprehensible? What's more important? The integrity of her lust or the health of the party she represents?'

No answer. Evidently, Eleanor R had her own questions and her own answers. Or she had Dubois on her mind or rising food prices. Earlier, at the hall window, I watched Mrs Petrova in her yard. Sunday finery that she wore did not stop her from puttering about. Here was neither woman as slave nor woman as Caesar, but woman as comptroller of her universe. After a long winter, others in the neighbourhood were slowly returning to their yards to rake and sift and seed and prepare for the barbecue season.

All the little sparrows were feathered coquettes. Someone was playing a mouth organ somewhere. State a truth and you invite its opposite. Which is to say that the stuff of life was like the flashing, silvery fish of the sea; too mutable, too restless a business to pin down. And yet somewhere in all this evanescence, were the heavy imponderables that never change.

Marvellous America

There was a time not long ago when America might, with some derision, ask of Europe, 'What have you done, say, since the 1600s?' The point is, of course, that the Old World was a museum. But apart from all her space and natural wonders, what was so marvellous in America? Baseball. Dance halls. Late night radio waves of a certain era. '47 Chevy's. Low-slung Buicks. Even so, America's unceasing triumphalism has long since dulled the memory of what I once loved. Romans used to twit Greeks for their pursuit of the life of the mind; that it was a vainglory; that it was a mark of unsuitability for managing the affairs of the world. And yet, look at Rome as she is now, a city so obnoxious in ways peculiar to herself, so haunted, and in places so breathtakingly beautiful, that one almost begins to believe that time, a great deal of time, does, indeed, heal all presumptions. What American city in future will claim such distinction?

Yes, Eggy was depressed. It was the first I had ever seen of it. He had his mood swings like the rest of us, but this was something else. A shadow on the inverted triangle of his face said that death was not to be borne, no, not with a pair of death-is-just-over-the-horizon-for-me eyes. For all that, he was a tough old bird; he would get over it and hoo hoo us to distraction. He had given Gentleman Jim a reason to live: Gentleman Jim now had drinking companions. Eggy had honoured the man with a visit, and ceremonial portions of vermouth were, no doubt, meted out. I saw in Gentleman Jim's wrecked, booze-soddened self a meticulous soul, a natural inclination to speak softly and dress neatly, to maintain a decent standard in all matters of comportment. His table, when he sat alone, was a study in order. One imagined one would not find so much as a smudge on the bottle of wine from which he replenished his glass, no iota of food crumb either on the table or adhered to his shirt or littering the floor at his feet. Some might view his drinking as self-destructive; if so, his attire was spotless, used serviettes pristine. It seemed he often went into a trance even as he would sit within arm's length of a Traymorean conclave, and he was in another dimension, one unavailable to any other human agency. Only Moonface seemed able to slip in and out of his reveries without disturbing their structural integrity. He possessed the unmistakable aura of a seventh-generation Canadian; I had come across a few of this type. Difficult wretches. Gareth Howard, my oldest friend now in his grave, belonged to this exclusive club by right of birth, and had, with his wandering ways, rebelled against its strictures, one of which was to talk the talk of excellence but not tarnish a legacy of mediocrity. The ghost of Fast Eddy came and went like rays of sunshine that appear and then vanish according to the whims of wind and cloud.

Meanwhile, Eleanor nursed a funk of her own, Dubois away in Ottawa. He was probably having the time of his life; Eleanor was sure of it. Dubois was always having the time of his life, it being the sort of man he was. Eleanor was always going to get her curls freshly frosted. It would seem the recent Dubois-Moonface outing had also rankled the good woman. Details had not been forthcoming, lost as they were to Dubois's vast sense of discretion. No Traymorean even had a hint as to what had been on the menu of some old town eatery. A happier Eleanor would not have given it a second thought that Dubois would walk Moonface through a 5-star meal, or that Moonface could have been a threat to Eleanor; Moonface but a girl afraid of her own shadow, not to mention men. When I pointed out to Eleanor the number of Champagne Sheridans she had on a string, Eleanor only sputtered with some dismissal of the fact; that they were mere boys, and the boffing, such as it was, could not be mistaken for major league boffing. One does not casually gainsay a woman as seasoned as Eleanor. It was conceivable, however, that Dubois was looking for payback; if so, what a blow to Eleanor's pride should he suddenly develop a passion for babes of an amateur hour. One could almost admire the subtle workings of the Dubois mentality, and yet I, for one, believed that relations between he and Moonface were entirely innocent. Moonface was simply collecting another mentor.

Dubois back among us, Eggy immensely relieved (he had missed his boon companion), we sat around the Blue Danube. Traymorean chaffers had harried Cassandra, and she perhaps wondered why she had ever gone in for restaurant life. As used as she was to men drinking wine, the sight of lily-white Anglos and one Francophone so deep in commaderie and so flush with *bon mots* must have unnerved her. Of immediate concern was the fact of Eggy's recollection of a black bath-nurse, her immensity as opposed to his Lilliputian private parts. What had been the politics of this? Eggy had replied: 'It was I do my own, thank you very much.'

Gentleman Jim dryly observed that it was standard procedure.

Eggy was fairly advanced in his wine intake. *Effing this, effing that.* Gentleman Jim had the look of John the Apostle at a convivial Last Supper, quiet but attentive, applauding the better exchanges of wit. The Saviour figure, I supposed, was supplied by Dubois, who had been after all educated by Jesuits, though he was strictly a materialist, entirely secular in his view of the mysteries. He was now telling tall tales of perilous flying, how once he flew in a DC-3, all engines leaking oil, all available landing strips fogged in; how, the pilot's hand forced, the pilot had glided the plane down on a wing and a prayer there in Newfoundland. Then there was the white-knuckle service between the Victoria and Vancouver harbours, the taking off and landing in serious chop, the near collisions with the Lion's Gate Bridge and with men in boats foolish enough to be out fishing after dark. And so forth and so on. Eggy described flying into Innsbruck, mountain peaks leaving no margin for error. Dubois shrugged. Fast Eddy reminded me that Moonface's birthday was imminent. She would like a book for a gift. He had accepted the fact that she was not likely to take up accounting as a way of life. This left Eggy's Plan B: the study of history. Tipsy myself, I could see plying her with *The Annals* or the *Twelve Caesars.* We would see just how serious the young woman was. I was astonished to learn she was approaching 25 years of age. Or was it 26 now? She seemed so much younger, so unformed. Eggy was chuffed now, charging the younger generations for having short-changed his, as if his generation had been all duffers and retards and hopeless in the sack. Dubois continued playful, saying *Ver-sigh* in reference to the infamous treaty that failed, in a sense, to close the window on one war, leaving the door open for another. I was tempted to go and fetch Eleanor, to have her resume her rightful place among us; to remind us that our intellectual capacities were a matter of some doubt; that they were overstated. If the world knew the truth about us, it would resume its channel-surfing without the slightest trace of a bad conscience. One other person was back among us. Blind Musician. He had been to Seoul. There Canadians had performed Delius and Hovannis. As if any Traymorean cared. Whatever happened to Joe Green, Eggy wanted to know, having recourse to a stale jest on the name of Giuseppe Verdi. Blind Musician had only just learned of the blind eye the State Department had cast in respect to the corruption and graft that was the government in Baghdad.

'I mean,' he brayed with his foghorn of a tempest, 'what if that money was supplying the extremists and costing the coalition lives?'

'Coalition?' I asked of an invasive baritone.

The knock was Eleanor's, she dressed for trouble: the bosom-accentuating blouse, tight denims, pompadours. And she was going to get her way, even should Dubois pop his head out his door and I give him a look, one that said would he please come get his woman, he had punished her long enough. The good woman shoved me with one hand; the other hand clutched amaretto. She kicked shut the door behind us. And now she was grabbing at my fly, and now, thankfully, it had jammed. I led her to the couch, the sight of which elicited her giggles.

'How many women have you biffed on this thing?' so she put it to me, incredulous.

'Clearly, one too few,' I was about to retort, and thought better of it.

Seated together now on the offending item of furniture, she made half-hearted attempts to fondle my person; she would rather shut her eyes and drift. Now she was nestled, as it were, in the crook of my arm. I had retrieved the amaretto and placed it out of harm's way. Now, with unbelievable timing, here was Dubois. Ah, Dubois to the rescue. He sized the situation up, making rapid calculations like the man of business he had once been. He ignored me utterly. He shook her gently. She squeezed open an imp's eye.

'Well, look what the cat's drug in.'

Eleanor had spoken. And with some bother, Dubois got Eleanor to her feet, and with some bother, he removed her from my presence, she smiling all the while.

And I returned to my jottings. Where had I been? Yes, marvellous America with all its trillions to spend. And yes, I thought it time to write Billy Bly a letter I would never post. Correspondence between us once flowed thick and fast; it was now down to the barest trickle, some once-every-six-month note of threats and insults.

Dear Bly, it's been a while. How much more glammy and glitzy have you gotten? The fault is ours and no one else's, what's gone amiss in love, literature, politics. I hope you are busy preparing your plea for your forgiveness.—RQC

Soul-Seeking

I went for an early walk in a heavy pollen season. Here were workers in their clusters queued at bus stops, so many stragglers in the lee of a mountain storm. Fanatical old women walked fanatical dogs. Birds took possession of territory. Tulips were so many castle turrets in their beds. The world was in moral drift, and I was not a moral man, far from it. I had no quarrel with the pursuit of pleasure, silence and lies the decadence. I entered an old diner, one of the last of its kind, and discovered that Wendy was there, serving customers. She looked tired, as defeated as ever, an automaton. Still, she recognized me as I took a seat at the counter, and she said: 'I hear there was trouble at the Greek's.'

It was no use pretending I had no knowledge of it.

'Yes, it would appear there was.'

She grunted and turned away. Had she news of Echo? Could she see through to my soul? She brought me coffee with a distinct air of dismissal. She peered about the restaurant as if in search of the limits of a property. Echo was a force that rebuffed despair. The glory of the morning was worn away by the commuter rush at its most intense. The door that had been opened to admit the breeze was admitting traffic noise and profanities. Sparrows scrambled along the sidewalk, birds in a bird dimension of ceaseless hunger. I saw myself in the haggard Wendy eyes and was not encouraged, she bored and looking for a live wire, looking for her favourite brand of trouble. Lone workers, one each to a booth, read newspapers. When I got back to the Traymore and to my digs, Moonface crossed the hall from Eggy's. She was in a fine mood.

'So?' she said, possessing the couch.

'So?'

'I don't know,' she said brightly, rolling her eyes up and to the side, her focus on some fancy or another.

'If you don't know, I don't know,' I said, just a little peeved.

But it seemed she was on the verge of applying to a school in Kingston, there to further complete her studies. I should have made supportive, enthusiastic, high-fiving noises. I blew her a kiss which had the effect of gainsaying her fine and sweet mood. She recovered, saying: 'Tell me about Ovid, please.'

Moonface the student smiled cattily, and so honoured the pedagogue rising in me.

'I already have. More than once.'

'Well, again.'

Moonface the minx. But Eggy did not believe Moonface was the sort of woman who would ever truly enjoy sex. I disagreed, but with a caveat: that sex was less important to her than, perhaps, the dreams it gave her of a pampering glory. What would Ovid have made of the dear girl, if anything? I said: 'Well then, despite his reputation as an agent of frivolity, he was an unassuming man who understood what was at stake and knew his limits. He certainly knew what Virgil was about, as did, for instance, Horace—'

'Oh Randall,' she cut me off.

I was being avuncular, as always. She was looking for a father, I for my soul.

'I trust the aforementioned poets dead these two thousand years more than I trust the current crop.'

It was not what she wished to hear. No matter. Even so, she was polite enough to ask: 'Why do you trust them more?'

'Though they got more things wrong, they lied less.'

'I don't get it.'

'You will.'

I accosted Eggy, tiny sparrow of a man, in the Blue Danube. I berated him with my desire that Moonface should become a true force for poetry one way or another.

'To thine own eyes be true,' said Eggy, tippling from his glass.

'To thine own self be true,' I corrected.

But Eggy did not wish to hear of it. Even so, he put it to me: 'Has she a mind? Has it been established that she has a mind? We know she has child-bearing hips. Hoo hoo.'

'Yes,' I said, annoyed with the man's flippant tone. 'Best we back off teasing her so much. But I would hate to see her get with some lout and get with brats.'

'Point taken.'

'Evolutionary drift.'

'What?'

'Never mind.'

There had been a sculpture recently retrieved from the bottom of the Rhône. It featured Julius Caesar's mug. There was a sudden flash of white wing in the Blue Danube window, a gull's. Anna was waitressing, the tall redhead as quiet as a ghost. But Eggy was only interested in the street's new talent, as he called it, the procession of girls passing by singly, paired or in packs. West Virginia, his state of origin, had just voted overwhelmingly, in its primary, for the New York senator. The race card had been a decided factor. Dubois entered the café.

'Greetings,' he said, occupying a chair, setting his worn and honest attaché case on the floor beside him.

'What's new?'

'You,' said Eggy. 'And what I want to know is, with what victuals did you ply Moonface when you took her out?'

'Victuals? Ply?' asked Dubois, a bit of laughter stuck in his throat.

'Why yes. The nitty-gritty, please.'

Dubois gave me a look. I searched his face for hints of how it was with Eleanor. Nothing. Now Anna approached the table, she so shy and unobtrusive that I did a double-take, finding her of a sudden materialized at the table, as it were, immanent. She took away the instructions of Dubois who said to me: 'I have to say I'm getting worried. In fact, I've been worried for some time over this. That Illinois senator. You know, he might not survive the campaign. It might throw the country into some darkness—'

'It's already been thrown,' I interjected.

'The rain in Spain,' Eggy said. He continued: 'Anyway, Bob, you're avoiding my question. With what did you ply Moonface? Oh come on, you must've plied her.'

'I resent,' answered Dubois, 'the implication that I plied her.'

Now the laughter in his throat was unstuck.

'So you didn't ply her.'

'It was very civilized, what transpired between us, and it's none of your business, I think I can say.'

'Well, I guess you can say it.'

Eggy tippled some more. Dubois slathered his soup, the soup Anna had just brought him, with a ton of pepper. Anna, a scrawny beanpole of a sylph, was not otherwise going to allow three Traymorean fuss-budgets to intimidate her.

'Well,' Eggy said to me, 'I can't seem to ply Moonface.'

'Maybe because you would ply?' I said, somewhat prissily.

'Oh you're always so superior,' Eggy thundered.

Dubois delicately managed his spoon, Francophone in an English business world. One had to hand it to him: he was often better spoken than his Anglo counterparts. The old hag came in for her glass of wine, and Anna sighed, the old hag gesticulating wildly at entities only she could see. Serge the cook, usually stone-faced, rolled his eyes. He had the look of a man so organized he could squeeze 36 hours of work out of every 24 hour day of earnest endeavour. When the invaders from the south came for us, I would hide behind him, throwing Eggy and Dubois to the dogs.

Eggy asleep on the Blue Danube terrasse. Were time comprised of so many mischievous cherubs, I could easily enough see them draping Eggy's ears with flowers as he slept, stuffing his pockets with sea shells or pebbles (anything that might startle his hand upon waking), and cherubs titter. More signs of aging marked him. His skin seemed shinier at the temples. The shadow was darker where he shaved his chin. He had never been known to be in want of a shave. A splendid Roman he might have made, his life predicated on his desire to transcend his hayseed origins. A stint at Caesarship, too, might have fallen to him naturally enough, his character bearing some resemblance to that of Claudius, the lame one who thought himself somewhat of a catch, even so, and was twitted by his wives. Eggy was the loneliest man I had ever come across who yet had such a strong instinct for the social. And then my thoughts would turn to Echo. I would not have believed her possible had I not seen her with my own eyes. Her qualities were all the more precious the longer her whereabouts remained unknown. It was just one of those things, this fact of Echo. Her being was not going to stem a tide or change a thing; no one who encountered her would live more fully and to better purpose, but that she was a force for life. As was Eggy with all his sins.

What with the thickening cloud, the humidity ratcheted up, the deepening darkness of the airy spaces between the maple boughs, and it would seem the sky was kissing all arboreal crowns, gods meeting gods. For yes, the language of science fails the man, the woman, the child, for that matter, lost in contemplation of it all; who do not write it off as so much carbon; who hear the mother calling for the child; who see the boys smoking cigarettes on the sly there in the lane, TVs lighting up the windows of brick dwellings, lilacs brooding in the dark. The cat's nocturnal prowl. And yet, all it meant was that rain was coming.

Eleanor, she of the frosted curls, a bawdy wench, cancelled the picnic. A leaf-glistening rain was falling. We had thought, she and I, to eat cheese and discreetly knock back some amaretto in the nearby park, the one shaped like the bow of a ship. We would pretend we were voyagers seated deck side, amiably exchanging intelligence, sparrows and pigeons our companions, and the odd river gull. The fate of the world was at stake. A lone, mad squirrel would put us in mind of some untidy element in the body politic, how that body politic was frustrated; how something had to be pulled from a hat, and soon. Instead, we sat at Eleanor's kitchen table. I rolled us cigarettes. She said: 'It's not that he took her out that burns me; it's that he took the trouble to buy a rose and present her with it.'

'I don't know,' I said, licking the adhesive strip of a cigarette paper. 'I should've thought to do it myself.'

Eleanor gave me a look. I was vaguely jealous of Dubois's gallantry.

'Bob thinks she has other needs,' I offered.

'It's a waste of a perfectly good flower. She hasn't got the wit to be flattered, let alone romanced. And then they wind up at the Queen E for nightcaps. Posh drinks. 20 bucks a pop. And what could they find to talk about for an hour and a half, I ask you? Her menstrual cycle? Identity crisis?'

'Israel-Palestine. The demise of the middle class.'

'Just give me that cigarette, damn you, anyway, and watch your lip.'

We were, Eleanor and I, referring to the fact that Dubois, a true citizen of this my faded Jezebel of a town, had squired Moonface to a fancy spot, then took her for drinks afterwards. Eleanor was just now getting her objections out of her system. I had decided that a certain f-word did apply, indeed, to a political situation south of the border. Eleanor had decided that the intentions of her Bob concerning Moonface could not have been entirely honourable. I would have disputed this, but what would have been the point, Eleanor seething? She was dying to know details of which

I knew nothing. My own view was this: that Dubois, without prompting from any source (myself and Eggy, for instance), saw Moonface as a lost soul. Here she was at age 25 or 26, tentative, feckless. There was something dark in her that wanted airing out. Dubois was a pragmatic sort for all his vanity; one goes and gets a rose. One rings up for a reservation. One sits out on a fine evening among vines and candles and chows down on shellfish or lamb, and one works one's way through a bottle of the appropriate vintage and makes appropriate noises at critical junctures of the conversation. Perhaps I would write a comedy of manners, one fraught with futile but expensive gestures, such as when a man, honourably or not, would take a woman on her wing and she feel like a somebody. Eleanor quite capable herself of noble and theatric flourishes, was no romantic. She had taken me to atmospheric restaurants where we might as well have been truckers in a hamburger joint. It was difficult but not impossible, I supposed, to see an Eleanor demure with her Gallic swain, he explaining the culinary facts of life to some liveried waiter clicking his heels; and then, having got the misunderstanding sorted out, attending to the fair lady's train of thought. The night before, I was with Eggy and Dubois in the Blue Danube. I had hopes that Dubois would reveal all the doings of his evening with Moonface. No chance. We fell to quarreling as, outside, citizens promenaded with dogs in the twilight. A young woman was staggering drunk, and it looked that she might heave. We argued alien life forms and the origins of life on this planet. I beat Eggy about the shoulders with my baseball cap who, for that moment, at least, was stating that aliens had messed with the DNA of primates, hence, humans. Moonface on shift looked tired and drawn, her lips more thin and unattractive, mouth more small. Had it to do with Dubois or with some Champagne Sheridan she had on a string? Had she had another of her fits? I submitted we were more than likely all there was of conscious life in the universe; that I could not see how some corner of it could have had that much of a head start on us, all things being equal. Eggy submitted otherwise, as did Dubois the materialist. Then we had a set-to about the fire-bombing of Dresden: whether it had been a city of military value. Eggy believed the Russians had wanted it done, and the Brits and the Yanks, taking paths of least resistance, accommodated Stalin. Gentleman Jim did not know the particulars; I confessed my ignorance of the history of the Great War. Gentleman Jim sat there indifferent. I was getting snaky and would have to mind my tongue. Dubois was saying now that, in any case, it is the winner who writes the history. I begged to differ, citing Tacitus and his peace made a desert. He had been on the winning side, true, but winning had cost the Romans a great deal, perhaps too much, and forever. Dubois, on a roll, submitted that all our knowledge is a hazy affair. How can we say we know what was what, circa 4,000 B.C.? I answered that we had a general idea; we were beginning then to get organized. Food surpluses. Priesthoods. Politics. Read the books. Had I just suggested that Dubois and Eggy did not read? It was pointed out to me that books did not guarantee truth, and of course, they were right, these soul mates of mine who would commit to nothing but wenches and wine. Since when had I become a professor? And so they sat there, those two, like a couple of Shakespearian rustics. The Queen Elizabeth Hotel served up a martini, so Dubois claimed, that was the real thing, not the kool-aid one got elsewhere.

'Eleanor,' I said, 'I don't know what to tell you. We could get post-Freudian. We could just accept the fact that Dubois and Moonface had an evening of it, no harm done.'

In No Mood for Consoling Noises

As if Eleanor were not enough for one morning, I went and knocked on Moonface's door. She answered, she in her pajamas, still. She stood there tugging at her tresses. The look in her eyes rolling up and to the side said I should go away. Thin lips pouted. The cynic in me noted she was deep in the throes of martyrdom. I shrugged and turned on my heel. And back in my grotto, one rife with unquiet spirits—the Sally McCabes, the Jack Swains and the like—I listened a while to piano, accordion and oud. I took up again an old history of Tiberius, a Caesar in whom Moonface claimed to have interest. But when I would press her as to why she found him interesting, she could not answer; I figured her guilty of making false claims. Later in the afternoon and well into the evening, I sat with Traymoreans at the Blue Danube. At first, it was only Dubois and I attempting to inaugurate the terrasse season at an outside table. He handed me a newspaper article to read, to do with the too-high price of commodities, buyer beware. Dubois confessed he was getting more worried vis-à-vis the *situation*—the coming general election, the possibility of an air attack on Iran. As he expressed his concerns, a stunner passed by. Leather jacket. High-heeled sandals. Plush shades. Clearly, she was a woman who enjoyed the fact of her body and did not care who knew it. She gave us what I thought was more than a casual glance, but I might have been mistaken. The way she walked suggested we ought to know what we were missing. She had under her arm a large portfolio of some sort such as an architect might pack from office to office. She was one more creature to chalk up for the annals of the boulevard in a time of late empire, trees by way of their foliage chorusing the sun and the birds and the sappy sexuality of men who did not, even so, stand a chance with any stunner. Dubois finished his peroration on dirty tricks. If the Republican Party was electoral toast, it would seem that extraordinary measures were required should certain operators behind the scenes wish to retain their hold on power. The President had made, even by his own standards, an unusually offensive speech that day. He likened a certain senator from Illinois to a Nazi appeaser. He forgot, perhaps, that his own grandfather had business ties with German bankers of Nazi sympathies; that this man had also participated in an attempted coup against FDR. Worse, the President delivered this speech in the Knesset, and all that remained to the imagination was to determine to what extent Likudists had engineered the applause. We moved inside, Dubois and I, and were joined, in fairly short order, by Eggy and Gentleman Jim, each arriving from different directions. Eggy was coming directly from his weekly visit to a bar in the adjoining district. Gentleman Jim was escaping his surroundings at the institution where he had his bed. Moonface was now on shift, her mood improved. Gregory was in the galley. Cassandra wiped dust from ferns, seemingly content with her lot. Wine flowed. Our dinners arrived. Moonface was perhaps pleased to see her men enjoying themselves. She was attending to us with panache. The ghost of Fast Eddy picked at his slab of fish. He was now muttering unflattering asides in respect to an Illinois senator. What, was there prejudice after death? Night fell. Now there was a Métis girl at our table whose parents had been born in France, their parents hailing from Winnipeg. It seemed an exotic history. She was studying to be a pharmacist and was a friend to Moonface, whom she described as a girl who did not think things through. Eggy was besotted. When the Métis girl confessed to having a boyfriend, Eggy was dashed. He said that, oh well, the rain in Spain, hoo hoo. He said he supposed she would find him too old and used up. And I said that, yes, the fact that he was 901 years of age, if a day, did not mitigate that well in his favour. 'Bollocks to you,' said Eggy to me. The girl blinked. Was she among savages, she who had been to Paris three times but found Parisians closed of mind and supercilious? I began beating Eggy about his shoulders with my baseball cap now that he was drunk enough to suggest that Muslims were taking over his home state of West Virginia, causing trouble. It looked to be a bad wine we were drinking, a crescent moon in the sky, girls in their packs giggling at the corner, preparing to cross the street against the traffic. Dubois was merry and immune to all calamities, Eggy chuffed. Gentleman Jim, like me, had voices in his head. Fast Eddy glowed with his stolen march against the probabilities. Moonface minxed and flashed her red nails like a dancer, chameleon that she was. I was uneasy. Dubois once reminded me that the word chameleon more properly applied to a lizard that had the use of protective colouration, that it had nothing to do with a girl of changeable personality. Of course he was right, he a Francophone who maintained proprietary relations with the English language. Even so, I was uneasy. What was happening in the café I likened to the desperate shenanigans of a Berlin nightspot circa the Thirties, even if we were but pikers when it came to decadence. My uneasiness was but a sign of my boorishness; that I had not fully aligned myself with my tablemates and was holding out on them. Moonface, bringing water, rolling her eyes up and to the side, released me, saying: 'Tiberius.'

Traymoreans wondered what was now afoot.

I laughed and answered, 'Snaky old goat.'

It was a magic incantation, one that permitted me to take my leave.

That night, in unsettled sleep, I dreamed of Echo. Even as I dreamed, I laughed. It was too obvious, too transparent a dream. The girl had quite ordinary ambitions. She would get her ology degree and perhaps marry and have babies and keep peace in her family between its Greek and Italian factions. That she would command a rebel force in the outback of Indiana was positively ludicrous. She pointed her fingers at her eyes and then, reversing those fingers, she pointed at me. *I see you.* I now realized that when she responded to every word Eggy uttered with 'amazing', she had been having him on all along. At some point in the morning that followed, Eleanor shanghaied me in the hall. She finagled me into her digs. It turned out that I learned something about her I had not known, to wit, the nature of her bedroom décor. Cherry veneer. It was the bedroom of a woman serious about nesting. And the bed, well, the bed was not the four-poster I had always imagined. It was a sleigh bed, classic Quebec, Eleanor explained. But could she explain what was I doing in this room? She kicked off her pompadours and then I knew. She backed me to the sleigh's edge. And we rolled around a bit until, finally, I returned to my senses. She had the grace not to be miffed. That she simply sighed and said that well, if that was how I felt about it… It was how I felt about it, Traymorean life complicated enough, her kisses rather searching and bemused. I passed on an offer of the hair of the dog, she having noted my hangover. She supposed I had been carrying on with the 'boys'; she supposed right, so I let her know.

'Don't be that way, Calhoun.'

'I know, you had an itch to scratch.'

She gave me a look.

'It's Bob,' she said, 'it's always Bob.'

'Do you love the man,' I said, exasperated. 'Are you going to make it up with him? If you don't, I think you'll be sorry.'

'I am, already, seeing as I can't get any cooperation from you.'

§

Book IV—Sex on the Beach

Anti-Follies III

—Eggy is still having too much fun to die. He once was in the south of France, having fun in his 5th decade arguing American decline with a movie star. What, had Eggy been prescient? Sex on the Beach is a drink. It is a drink which Moonface drinks when her Champagne Sheridans take her out. Combine vodka and peach schnapps, plus the juices of the cranberry, the orange, the pineapple. Serve with lots of ice in a highball glass. It is not to be deemed a classic drink, and so champagne is what Rumsfeld offered the first man who would solve the complex algorithms of Iraq. Rumour has it that in Baghdad there is a crematorium. *It's war, so suck it up or move on.* We are not moral creatures. Should Dubois get to Rome, let him begin at the forum with the Basilica of Maxentius erected on an earlier site where pepper and spice were sold. Let him contemplate what must have been a grand structure of groined and coffered vaulting. Then let him of an evening drink *limoncello* under a trellis of vines at a bar on the Janiculum. Let him hear from Nero himself the value of trusting the system, of the innate good sense of the people. Let Dubois return to this his faded Jezebel of a town, his thought hemorrhaging, his socks blown off. I am in the Blue Danube, and I am wearing socks. Anna the tall, the very slim, redheaded waitress is on for the afternoon. Talks hospitals with an old biddy. The Blue Danube aka Le Grec now serves moussaka that Cassandra prepares in her home kitchen. It is, I am sorry to say, heavy and tasteless. One hears on the radio some musical group whose music resembles nothing so much as a snapping of wet towels. For whose buttocks are they intended? I would refer Anna to the Villa of the Mysteries, Pompeii, her mute incomprehension her very solemn business.

—It is said the novelist requires a world; the poet makes do with a patch of grass. I pace the limits of my universe. From the Traymore Rooms to the poor man's super mart a gauntlet of attitudes. One flatters it with the epithet of 'cultural mix'. Augustus Caesar stood at the head of a rough and ready world-state. To be sure, there were peoples not included, the Parthians, for instance, the dangerous Germanic tribes. I am a creature of the boulevard, but one alienated by those in high office pseudo-civilized enough to make a hash of it all, their lawns always pristine.

—Is Eleanor to be faulted for wanting happiness? She has Dubois, but not as she would like him. Is not this what always breaks the bank at Monte Carlo—he or she has what he or she wants but not as he or she would like it? One cannot get from a person what a person has not to give. Dubois is the proud conveyor of looks and vanity. He is more or less civil; he is more or less interested. Has a certain *joie de vivre,* even that which cultural stereotyping insists he must have. The fact that he is a materialist of a most conventional sort is not necessarily off-putting. Even I, Calhoun, Randall Q, find I can live with it. Is it so much of a cliché to suggest that Dubois breathes best when his affections are freely given and Eleanor freely takes them? Well, I can only speculate, approaching my second summer among Traymoreans. I have not known Dubois or Eggy or even Eleanor, for that matter, in their darkest hours such as most people undergo alone. I myself cried out, last night, in a nightmare. Then I knew myself to be utterly ridiculous. Moonface is still just a girl. It is a privileged culture that allows this state of affairs. Even so, last night in the Blue Danube, she gave me a look of such impishness and it touched me to the bone; I could never wish to see that look replaced by one of banal maturity. Dubois was going on about sovereign money and private capital. I have to say his words went in one ear and out the other. Eggy wished to see a few bastards hang. Gentleman Jim protested that, on the contrary, he was not obliged to observe a curfew; he could come and go as he saw fit. 'But Christ,' said Eggy, 'you have to bribe the night nurse when you go out.' I said all of life is curfew. No one gave much credence to this observation. I noted that Cassandra's hands were plump and child-like. I wondered with what force they might strike her Elias. Who seemed to be emerging from under the cloud of suspicion that had dogged him of late. No one spoke of Echo, not even a whisper. The ghost of Fast Eddy bragged of the chocolates he had given Moonface as a gift, how he had put her figure in jeopardy. Blind Musician, his locks newly shorn, his eyes immense behind his thick lenses, showed up and was stunned; he had nothing about which to complain. He had a new blind man's stick to play with. Even Eleanor showed up, and it had been a while. To be sure, there was awkwardness in the situation, but I thought Dubois handled it fairly well, asking her highness what her pleasure might be, which gave Eggy his opening, and he said, 'Drink to me with thine eyes.'

—Shameless liar that he was, FDR, scion of privilege, gave Americans hope and true reason to have pride, so much wiped out in the downturn of the Thirties. Current Occupant of the American nation's sitting parlour, deluded fool, just makes everyone feel shabby. Redemption will not cost you a thing, just your soul and your house and your country. Late night comedians are fine as they go, but the chuckles are mostly showbiz. I sit here in the Blue Danube at the crack of noon, blind man in a cave. Cassandra lets rip with a joke and it so knocks me over that I fail to respond. Poor woman. She tries. Since when has Elias laughed at her levity? I will eat cream of potato soup. I will watch wind blow rain along the street. I will see passersby seemingly in control of their lives. A few of them might know it is a crock. We will, in any case, participate in a collective delusion, doing laundry, haunting a café, punching numbers at a bank machine, taking pets to the animal clinic. I envy Moonface her confusion and even her ambivalent sex life; at least her body is a kind of theatre, however absurd, of possibilities. I envy Eggy the fact he is having too much fun to die. What is Cassandra's hand doing on my shoulder? What is a puffy, child-like hand looking for? Do I look like a priest? A lover? Some woebegone who requires a mother? Surely, it is an accident. Her husband, Elias, who already views me not so much as a rival but as a man who might cause him trouble, would not look kindly on this. When one has lies to maintain one is alert to presences that bear disclosure. Her hand withdrawn, Cassandra retreats to the galley where Serge with his paramilitary haircut is, no doubt, plotting revenge against all the nincompoops who have trifled with the serious business of living. These tiny, tiny betrayals. Sometimes I believe I hear the creakings and the saggings in some unseen-to-the-eye rigging, the sound of a craft that is barely making headway, that is complaining, and no one listens.

—Mrs Petrova's tulip tree produced but a single blossom; however, it was huge. And while it grew, while it went about its business, attaining full, meaty volume only to fall apart and drop to the earth, I listened to the oud. Dhow boats hissed across the sea. Debussy played like a cenobite, but one in a salon of frocked women holding aloft their parasols. Some eyes were violet; some were green—like the colour of a liqueur. Sometimes sound travels well in the Traymore. Mrs Petrova on the telephone: 'Okay, okay. Nyet, no, nyet.' One heard in her voice impressionist paintings and black-scarfed women haggling at market. Then Dubois came over unannounced. 'Calhoun,' he said, opening his worn but honest attaché case, extracting from it a book, 'I see in this anthology one of your poems. Translated into French. I have to tell you it's not the equal of your English. What have you to say?' What could I say? Better to have been translated than to have lost? Now Eleanor, and right after her, Moonface. My, but here was a crowd gathered in my living room. Dubois offered up his chair to Eleanor and parked on the floor. Moonface joined me on the couch. 'It's peculiar music you listen to,' said Dubois. 'Are you sure it's legal?' He went on to say we should not expect a new world order anytime soon. Eleanor clucked her agreement, inspecting a pompadoured foot. Moonface wished to know if I thought Tiberius had truly been a perverted old goat. Eleanor's eyes narrowed with some interest. 'Well,' I said, 'there's fact and there's fiction. And then there's supposition—' 'Oh god,' Dubois interrupted. Eleanor massaged her ankle. 'Let the man speak,' she said. I continued: 'Here's the supposition. Where there's smoke, there's fire.' Eleanor said, 'Roger that.' She caressed the vain and handsome wrist of Dubois where it now lay across her lap. Dubois did not withdraw it. I minded this spectacle. Moonface rolled her eyes up and to the side. A dimple formed in her cheek. She was not as afraid of Eleanor as once she had been. The music faded to the evident relief of all. Eggy, who rarely passed through my door, now shuffled in on his cane. He surveyed the scene, I and Moonface on the couch, Eleanor squatted on a chair, Dubois on the floor like some college kid gathering up the thought-crumbs of a mentor. 'Bloody effing hell,' observed Eggy. 'Bloody effing hell, is that all you have to say, you old fart?' This was Eleanor. 'You have something better?' thundered Eggy in return, tiny sparrow of a man. Nor was he afraid of Eleanor. My eyes filled with the good woman's ankle. Moonface stared into space as if averting her countenance from shenanigans such as haunt the earth. 'Alley alley in for free,' I said, clapping my hands. It was my way of enjoining the people to depart. 'He thinks he's a poet,' said Dubois to Eggy. 'I know,' said Eggy, 'sorry case.' Eleanor clucked once more. Moonface moaned in that slight musical way she has of moaning, her sense of justice violated. 'I'm for the Danube,' Eggy let us know. 'I've got thirst.' He lowered his cap over his tough old eyes, turned around and tottered away.

Anti-Follies IV

—Eggy, fellow Traymorean, tiny sparrow of a man, decrepit at age 81, is waiting to see a few bastards hang. He lost interest in art in the year I was born. It was the year of the Truman Doctrine and the Marshall Plan. It was the year India and Pakistan gained independence. The Dead Sea Scrolls turned up at Qumran. Jackie Robinson joined the Brooklyn Dodgers. Toronto beat Montreal for the Stanley Cup. Meet the Press debuted on NBC. *Dr Faustus* was published. It is a gloomy sky. The darkest of grey clouds will unload their rain. I stand on the street corner, smoking a fag. My jottings are in the café. Moonface the waitress may steal a look at them to see if I have impugned her tiny ears. Eleanor does not think Moonface good for anything but marriage and the burbs. 'What do men see in this silly maid?' Eleanor has wondered, Moonface living proof that men are saps. Eleanor, you see, has no sentimental notions regarding either child-rearing or a woman's empowerment. If history is irony and self paradox, Eleanor is most selfless when most herself, stealing kisses when and where she can. Otherwise, she plans her nest in which she intends to install Dubois, her longest serving lover. It is almost endearing, her relentlessness of purpose. I continue smoking my fag. I note the cloud, the pale leaves beneath. Oh the Phoenicians, do they know what they unleashed, bringing an alphabet to Greeks? I raise my arms; I spin around. My signature gesture of disgust. Like so, William Blake in his dying hours, painted while naked out of doors. I spin until a swoon threatens to poleax me. If history is irony and the world a prison and the chatter of eggheads little improvement over the chatter of the masses—if this is it, and all there is, I would rather boff some girl against an ilex tree in Roman shade, tipping my hat at a procession of Priapus, no news hound anywhere in sight. Let idiots mew, 'Transcendence! Transcendence!' I return to the café. Moonface gives me a look. Eggy will go on about how history is bunk; it is written by winners. I offer Tacitus as refutation. He wrote for the winners. He did not necessarily coo with pleasure; he did not gloat even if he retained all the prejudices of his class. Eggy says,

'Alright then, have it your way.' Which is fine with me. His tough old eyes are tough for a reason. He supposes he must express his gratitude to the mothers of his children. He does not otherwise believe he must say he loved them.

—The only remedy for love, if remedy is wanted, is egoism. It suggests what love is not. Moonface reports that Eggy is beside himself. He has run into a girl he used to know and took out. She has returned to a bar down the street where once she served drinks. This may be the last we will see of the man. Farewell, blithe homunculus. But Moonface does not seem jealous, no, not at all, and she flashes her nails and she pulls at her hair. She has the look of a woman who has something on her mind, the contents of which I am not worthy. 'Soup and wine,' I say, 'and not necessarily in that order.' She rolls her eyes up and to the side. I glance at some jottings, mine own. I scowl. Serge the cook, he has the look of a man just back from a psy-ops interlude, mission successful. His air of utter competence infuriates me. Discipline, discipline. Cynic that I am, I search Moonface for a hint, any hint at all, that she knows what is at stake. She places the soup before me; no, she has no idea. Yesterday, perhaps yesterday, she might have found herself if only she had had a different father or read a more demanding literature among the moderns she does read. A wind kicks up. Maple leaves lash about in turbulence. In strides Dubois, a man on top of his game. Perhaps he has just been to the barbershop; perhaps he has just left Eleanor contented, having Henry Miller'd her. Immediately, he starts in: 'Pursuant to our previous conversation—' 'Which one was that?' I interject. 'Business,' he continues, 'plays by a set of rules or else it can't do business. However, I grant you this: free enterprise is a myth.' Moonface wonders if he will have wine. Dubois wonders why it has not yet materialized. Moonface flashes her nails once more that are oddly at variance with her otherwise benign manner. Must look up the latest scholarship on John the Apostle, I decide; it seems he was not the Beloved Disciple after all, the one who laid his head on the bosom of Christ. And Eggy, I explain, is down the street at some bar. Got a new honey. To which Moonface replies, 'Yes, he roams far afield.' Dubois laughs, the hairline cracks of his cheeks threatening to widen. But now we are a quorum as here is Eggy with his cane. Here is Eleanor in spiky shoes. Gentleman Jim has already taken a post, and like a Darwinist investigating an island, he examines Blue Danube space for terrors. Now talk to do with the price of oil. Well, it's a bit much, the price. Now fatwahs. Now computer viruses. Now politics. 'Alley alley in for free.' Ah, cloaks more cloakier, daggers more daggery. Hooded figures in a Roman shade. Pronounces Eleanor, 'I'm sick of politics. Sick of it all. Roll me a fag, won't you, dahling?' A burbling in her throat reminds one of the power of her personality. As for vain and handsome Dubois, he observes that while the dollar may be falling, and while that fact and the fact of speculation are spiking oil prices, the world still has to trade in those dollars. 'Not for long,' says Gentleman Jim, and his remark startles us; he hardly ever weighs in on matters of a socio-economic nature. He levels melancholy eyes on us all, those eyes his death rattle. On the street, an old woman walks a dachshund. Young louts walk their hounds. The hag occupies the bus stop bench. She utters no interdictions, but she is waving her hands about. Cassandra and Elias are in the galley, are a couple making a living. Serge is the Holy Ghost. It disturbs me, it panics me that, while Elias may be innocent of Echo's disappearance, he may not be and so, what does Cassandra know, if she knows anything? How unreal might her marriage be? And to what extent does the unreality mirror what goes on around us? Ahkmatova's cabaret poem. Must reread the thing.

Judicial at the Blue Danube

Cast:

Hanging Judge—*Eglinton aka Eggy*
Jury—*Blind Musician, the Whistler, Joe Smithers aka Too Tall Poet, Eleanor R, Mrs Petrova*
Defendant—*Randall Q Calhoun*
Prosecution Team—*Gentleman Jim, Allecto and the Furies*
Defense Team—*Robert Dubois, Emma MacReady aka Moonface*
Officer of the Court—*Edward Sanders aka Fast Eddy*
Disinterested Spectators—*Gregory the Cook, Elias, Cassandra, Anna the redheaded waitress, Serge, Hag, assorted irregulars*
Witnesses—*Billy Bly, Sally McCabe, Gareth and Clare Howard, Karl and Vera Klopstock, Minnie Dreier, Jack Swain, Lindsey Price*

Setting:

Le Grec aka the Blue Danube, a café. Eggy sits alone at a table. He wears an American battle helmet of the Korean War. A dish of strawberries is set before him. Chairs are arranged against a wall which seat jury members. A table each for the prosecution and defense. Gentleman Jim wears Bermuda shorts and is sockless. The Furies are dressed conventionally but smartly; one of them, Allecto perhaps, sports a tattoo of a snake somewhere on her person. Spectators are seated at various tables. Cooks and waitresses migrate between them and the kitchen or galley. Fast Eddy stands by the café entrance. As it is a small café, the place is crowded. Randall Q Calhoun has his chair in the middle of all this.

Scene I: Reading the Charges

Eggy, irritated: Well, I don't know what to say. Court's in session, I guess. O Mortals, blind in fate, who never know to bear high fortune, or endure the low. Well, I'll bet our prisoner in his dock doesn't recall that bit from Virgil, and he's an expert. On what shall man found the order of the world which he would govern? I'll bet his lawyer doesn't recognize those words as Pascal's? No matter. Bloody effing hell. Hoo hoo. Officer of the Court, I direct you to read out the charges. (*To Gregory the cook*): Gregory, these strawberries won't do. Miserably small.

Gregory, dubious: We're having fun, yes?

Fast Eddy, with insufferable gravitas: The charges against one Randall Q Calhoun, our defendant, are as follows. This could take a while. (*Clears his throat.*) I hardly know where to begin. Well, homicidal negligence, for starters. Ran over his kitten when he was a boy. Pretty heinous, if you ask me. Paterphobia. I think we're to understand by this he disrespected his father. He doesn't respect any authority we know of. This would make him an un-patriot. Bad literary taste. It's not so bad he retains affection for the works of Robert Browning and other authors about whom no one much cares, but that he should write his own claptrap, this is criminal. (*Hisses from among the spectators.*) Womanizer. Oh yes. I've seen it with my own eyes. He gets them all excited, then he abandons them. They weep in all the pizzerias. Lacks purpose, lacks ambition. He's a fantasist. He dabbles in religiosity. He mouths specious generalities about evolution. His wife of long ago threw herself out a window. Surely, he drove her to it. Drinks too much, has too many bad habits. Takes girls to art movies and expects them to like it. What, Fellini? Kurosawa, Bergman? No James Bond? Ummm, there's more, much more, but this ought to get us started. He's a walking catastrophe. The sooner we settle his hash, the better.

Dubois and Moonface in unison: Objection, your honour.

Eggy, dismissive: Shut your cakeholes. I'll have no faux procedurals in my court. These strawberries really are a travesty. He's guilty. We know he's guilty. What we're doing here is making it official. One for the books. The rain in Spain. Hoo hoo. Rise, defendant, and tell the court how you plead. (*Calhoun rises, looks around. Murmurings among the spectators. The Whistler whistles and stamps his feet. Calhoun waits until he calms down.*)

RQC: I am innocent of the charges you have been pleased to bring against me. You are of course a hanging judge and this is a show trial.

Eggy, thundery: Yes, I'm a hanging judge. What else would I be? It isn't worth my while, otherwise. Now get on with it. Or have you pleaded?

RQC: I am a reasonable man. I don't lord my opinions over others. I am entitled to the court's mercy. I ask for the truth. I've broken no law of the land so far as I know.

Eggy, incredulous: Law of the land? This isn't about the laws of the land. You're on trial because we're not sure you're one of us. You think you have a case? You haven't got a hope in hell, not with Dubois there and Moonface arguing it. Truth? Be careful what you wish for.

Dubois and Moonface in unison: Your honour. (*Dubois separately*): This is irregular. (*Moonface separately*): See if I ever come visit you again.

Eggy: Ungrateful wench.

RQC: Anyway, I thought this was to be a private affair among Traymoreans only. Ological experiment. Otherwise, I wouldn't have agreed to play the offending party.

Eggy, raising his forefinger: Jahcooz. Oh I accuse you, Randall Q Calhoun, of beating me about the shoulders with a baseball cap. Abusing an octogenarian, how shabby. I accuse you of boffing Moonface behind my back. What say you to these charges?

RQC: Slander. Nothing but slander. That I whacked you a couple of times is a demonstration of my affection. Moonface? She threw herself at me. Nothing happened. A few kisses. It was all quite ridiculous, really.

All the women in the café, in unison: Ridiculous?

RQC: I am accused, it seems, of being human.

Eggy: Don't flatter yourself.

All the women in the café, in unison: Don't flatter yourself.

Eggy: Order. Order in the court. Don't I get one of those pounding things, a whatdoyoucallthem?—

Fast Eddy: I believe you mean a gavel, your honour.

Eggy: Gavel. Thank you. My kingdom for a gavel. The rain in Spain. Hoo hoo. Order. Order in the court. (*Eggy pounds an imaginary gavel to comic effect. Fast Eddy steps forward, clears his throat. Silence. All except the Whistler who whistles and stamps his feet.)*

Eggy, to the Whistler: You ought to take that show on the road.

Whistler: Sticks and bones, you know. Watch what you say.

Eggy: Don't watch what you say me. I'm the judge. A hanging one, too.

Whistler, pretending to be mollified: Yes, your honour.

Eggy: Officer of the court, where were we? Ah yes, the list of charges. Surely, you haven't exhausted them. Take a look.

Fast Eddy: Yes, your honour, there's more, much more. But it could take all day.

Eggy: Get on with it.

Fast Eddy: Yes, your honour. Toot sweet, your honour. Ummm. Perverse. This item appears here with nine question marks attached.

Dubois: Objection.

Eggy: Well?

Dubois: I object to the use of the word perverse. It is open to interpretation.

Eggy: Point taken. We are, after all, a perverse society, and everyone's a poet. Sustained. (*From everyone assembled a murmuring of assent.*) Proceed.

Fast Eddy: The defendant refuses to believe in American Utopia. The defendant suspects the Truman Diaries of specious reasoning. The defendant worships some god unknown to the rest of humankind. The defendant lives in the past. The defendant is exceedingly judgmental of other persons. The defendant has failed love. (*General hissing.*)

Eggy: Alright, that's enough. Defendant, what say you? Are you innocent or guilty of these charges?

RQC: I am in somewhat of a quandary, your honour. Innocent, guilty—these are awfully limiting terms. We are all of us guilty of failing love to some extent. And what do we mean by love?

Eggy: Don't get pedagogical. Besides, we're not on trial here, you are.

RQC: The technologies of the Fifties released my mother from the drudgeries. She had too much time to sit around and drink and brood, to realize just what a monster her husband was. No, he didn't beat her. He was married to his work. Biological and chemical agents. Weaponry. It made him rich. He was cold, ruthless, dedicated. My mother died a lonely lush. She never stood a chance. Truman? He may have closed one door in the name of cessation of hostilities but you can't deny he opened up another which might lead, one day, to our extinction. God? There are no gods but shadows. I can't deny that those shadows are an inalienable part of my mind, whether I choose to recognize them or not. Love? But I have already addressed the issue. You may as well put a flower in the dock for withering. Oedipus acted in good faith and look where it got him. Selena Cross in *Peyton Place* acted in good faith and look what it drove her to do. Offed her stepfather because he raped her. Judgmental? I don't believe I must always apologize for my sensibility. As for living in the past, I don't live in it so much as I'm curious about it. I read books of history. I read ancient poems. I would like to know what remains of the ancients in our mentality. I suppose it's impossible to quantify.

Eggy: Well, that's straightforward enough. The human condition. I think Malraux had some words on the subject. He was an uneven writer, to be sure. But *Peyton Place*? Are you serious? You know the authoress used to go about in furs with nothing underneath. She drank herself to death. I don't know about you writers, not that you're much of a writer, Calhoun. I approve of history books. I'm a bit of an historian myself, amateur, of course. I am in need of wine. Court is adjourned for fifteen minutes.

Scene II: Plea and Arguments

Eggy, pounding an imaginary gavel: We're back. Settle down everyone. I don't believe we've yet had a plea entered. Will someone please enter one?

Moonface: Innocent, your honour.

Eggy, irritated: How many ways can you have it? The defendant has already acknowledged the possibility of his guilt. I think he's guilty. We all of us think he's guilty.

Dubois: Seeing as we have to start somewhere, we start by saying our man is innocent.

Eggy: Fair enough. Well, what do we do now? I suppose the prosecution should have its say.

Gentleman Jim: I should think so, your honour. May it please your honour, I shall leave it to Allecto, a member of my team, to present our case. She's really quite something.

Eggy, narrowing his eyes: No doubt. Not someone I would want to tangle with in a back alley.

Allecto: Your honour. We have been amused by the proceedings thus far. Ladies and gentlemen of the jury, the defendant has said it himself: he's on trial here for being merely a human being. How quaint of him. We Furies, we are daughters of Gaia, which is to say, of the earth. And we are daughters, too, of Night. It is to say we do most of our research after sundown. We are avengers of every transgression against the natural order. We were feminists even before the women of Athens went on strike, withholding sexual favours from their men because of their silly addiction to silly wars. You might think we have some points of sympathy with the defendant here, on account of his objection to the war in Iraq, but nothing could be further from the truth.

Eggy, interrupting: The court doesn't require your bona fides.

Allecto: In case you missed it, I am your worst nightmare.

Eggy, tittering: Don't think I don't know that. But try and keep to the matter at hand before this thing becomes even more of a farce than it already is.

Allecto, mock-bowing: Yes, your honour. Well then, here it is. Ladies and gentlemen of the jury, we will endeavour to show that the defendant is a man and is, *ipso facto*, guilty of maleness. And then we will show that—

Eggy, interrupting: What will you do? Offer up his balls as Exhibit A?

Allecto, continuing: That even in his maleness, he's not much of a male. He has contributed nothing to society, much less the gene pool. Times have changed and he refuses to acknowledge it so. He refuses, as well, to accede to the authority of the academically-trained. In fact he believes we are not innately moral creatures, that it's all a game, the rules made up by whoever talks the loudest for the longest. He is a cynic. We have not gone through the genocides of the not so distant past just to let cynics strut about. Furthermore, the reasons he gave for not boffing Moonface are disingenuous. He was more for being self-involved than he was for that bimbo's happiness—

Moonface, rising: I beg your pardon.

Allecto: Cool your heels, sister.

Eggy: I'm the judge here the last time I checked. No one but me gives out orders.

Allecto, smirking: My apologies, your honour. (*Turning to the jury*) We will show you what a little hypocrite it is. That's a line, you may remember, from *Dr Zhivago* the movie that we will turn on its head. I have nothing more to say, may it please your honour.

Eggy: It most certainly pleases me that you've nothing else to say. Bloody effing hell. Now for the defense. And, dear God, what next?

Dubois: I am a business man, not a lawyer. But somebody's got to do it, speak for the defendant. He's almost a classic in that he's a boulevardier, although I must say he doesn't look the part, he just behaves like it. And it's on this basis, ladies and gentlemen of the jury, that I defend him. Without him and his like, there would be no Blue Danube, no society. There would be even less discussion of the issues that confront us than there is.

Allecto: Objection. The defendant may be a drunkard, but Socrates he isn't.

Eggy: Overruled. I'm a drunkard, myself, and it doesn't keep me from speaking my mind now and then. Which reminds me. Counsel, are you going to wind this thing up? It's getting late. I'm thirsty again.

Dubois: But, your honour, I've hardly begun.

Eggy: It's neither here nor there, all this to do with the man's vocation. He's a self-obsessed sot with pretensions to literary grandeur. The third kind is the madness of those who are possessed by the muses, speaking of Socrates. Good poet, bad versifier—I think Montaigne allowed for the distinction. Of forests, and inchantments drear where more is meant than meets the ear. Enough. Only wine can cure this. Court is adjourned. Back in fifteen.

Scene III: Eggy's Ruling and His Finest Hour

Fast Eddy prods Eggy, who has fallen asleep, his chin nestled against his chest.

Fast Eddy to no one in particular: I think he's with the virgins in Paradise. Your honour, it's show time. Come on, wake up.

Eggy: What? What's that you say? What I hate is the girl who gives with a feeling she has to. Ovid. In case you're wondering.

Fast Eddy: Everyone's waiting.

Eggy: Waiting for what? Bloody effing hell.

Eggy raises his hand like a man wishing to get someone's attention. Cassandra scoots to his table, troubled.

Eggy: Wine, and don't stint. None of the watery vintage.

Cassandra: Wine? Water?

Eggy, thundery: Yes, you know, the blood of Jesus, woman.

Cassandra, comprehending: Oh.

Gregory, to no one in particular: How's it going, guys?

Eggy to Calhoun: I've got Moonface reading *Etruscan Places*, you know.

Calhoun: That ought to expand her horizons.

Eggy: Don't get cheeky. Now where was I? Oh, I guess I get to execute you. Hoo hoo.

Calhoun: So it would seem.

Witnesses rise en masse to indicate their pleasure, which it is they wish to see the defendant hang. Some jerk on an imaginary rope; some pass their forefingers along their throats; others assume the position of a firing squad.

Eleanor R, calling out: How much longer is this going to take? I've got better things to do than hang a man.

Eggy: Right you are.

Eggy, mock-gavelling the café into silence: I suppose the jury is just chomping at the bit to do its bit. Will one of you rise and pronounce the verdict?

Mrs Petrova kicks Blind Musician who elbows the Whistler who whistles at Too Tall Poet who looks at Eleanor.

Eleanor, snarly: Kick me and I'll snap you like a twig.

Too Tall Poet, rattled and rising: Your honour, we the jury find the defendant, Randall Q Calhoun, culpable and compromised. Of being a human being he is most certainly guilty. On all other counts he's up to his eyeballs in shame. As for his verse practice, God hasn't given us words to express the enormity of his crime. In this, too, he's blameworthy, guilty of fraud.

Eggy, hoo hooing: That's rich, one poet condemning another. Live and learn. It remains for me to sentence Mr Calhoun. Well, you know, it's been stuff and nonsense, what we've been about here. Farcical. Still, it's what goes on every minute of every 24-hour news cycle all around us. (*Murmurings of outrage. Eggy mock-gavels.)* Order. You know, the bottomless pit, the newshounds, the court of public opinion. That's what I meant to reference. And here's my ruling. Since one can't possibly be guilty of being a human being, hoo hoo (one doesn't ask to be born), and since, Mr Calhoun, you are guilty of something, God knows, and because there must be some point to this charade, and because I have a thirst and I feel a great sleep coming on, I sentence you, oh, what can I sentence you to, what's the severest penalty I can conjure up? Well then, sir, I sentence you to six months hard drinking subject to parole, that is, if you behave. I am not a wise man. I never claimed any such distinction. I am, if anything, so Moonface tells me and every other woman, a very silly man, but it seems to me, Randall, you ought to have more patience with humankind. Stop beating me about my person with your baseball cap. The court doesn't expect you to write paeans to the masses. Yes, spare us that. Everyone's alone; everyone's terrified. We just pretend we're not. We help one another pretend. So pretend, Calhoun. *Oh yes, I'm the Great Pretender, pretending that I'm doing well. My need is such, I pretend too much. I'm lonely, but no one can tell.* Come on, repeat after me. Oh well, suit yourself. Court's adjourned. Cassandra, where's that wine? Bloody hell.

§

Book V—Whirligigs

Anti-Follies V

—The whirligigs are falling, spinning through the air. 'Little helicopters,' Dubois said, as if stating one of life's well-established facts. We had been in the Blue Danube, Moonface working, Eggy absent. He was angry with everyone, Moonface, in particular. 'They're like a married couple,' Dubois explained, speaking of them paired. 'They push one another's buttons and it's fun and games until, one thoughtless slip, and someone crosses the line. I don't know who started it. I think he was giving her the gears. She got snippy. He took it badly.' Moonface overheard these words and came to the table, appropriately alarmed. Moonface: 'I was only half-serious.' 'Half-serious,' said Dubois, 'is serious enough.' 'I don't know what to do,' Moonface almost wailed. 'You could apologize,' Dubois suggested, 'irrespective of whether or not you were in the wrong. Of course, he could apologize, too, but he won't. But I think he's looking for a way out.' Dubois loved being the man who could make a difference. It was then we saw through the window Eggy tottering by on his cane, shoulders stooped, his head sunk between them, his progress determined, his anger having given way to sadness and martyrdom. 'Where's he been?' I asked. 'The bar down the street,' answered Dubois, 'he's boycotting this place.' Dubois laughed. He was the oldest of eleven siblings, familial politics water off a duck's back. 'Well, Eleanor thinks,' I said, 'that, at age 901, Eggy's no different than he was at age six. Mean, selfish, spoiled. Because he's kind of cute, he gets away with much.' 'Will the real Eggy,' laughed Dubois, 'please stand up?' Moonface frowned. Her frowns are something else as they suggest her world is fragile and easily upset. I had always thought she was born for love, a silly thing to avow, I admit, but she did have in her a capacity for diplomacy, or that which is not love, exactly, but is not something to be sneezed at. Then Dubois, figuring Eggy was in his rooms by now, called the old geezer. He produced a cell phone from his venerable and worn attaché case. The cell phone was news. He saw my look and said, 'I need it sometimes for business. And this is business.' The upshot? Eggy was not going to have anything to do with that ungrateful wench even if it had been her birthday recently, and so what if he had been mean to his wives? He had not asked them for favours; they should not have expected any from him. His kids were rotters. They were going to do well and survive because they were bloody hypocrites and, underneath it all, as mean as lawyers. The apple does not fall far from the tree. But what had this to do with Moonface? Why, nothing. Why should it have anything to do with Moonface? She was a strumpet who was getting a free pass because she had everyone thinking she had an intellect and was interested in intellectual matters. (This meant, by inference, that I was an effing fool for taking her seriously.) 'Yes, but,' said Dubois, 'her father's a minister, a theologian sort of, and for all he's a goof, he has scholarly tendencies. It's how she was raised.' Eggy shot back, 'He's shorter than his daughter by a full head.' 'I'll check on you, later,' said Dubois, and he rang off to Eggy's 'don't bother'. He said to me, Moonface standing there, 'He's really committed himself to this course of action.' 'Oh dear,' sighed Moonface, the guilt of a two-timing Eve written all over her visage. We had been by now treated to a glimpse of her father, who dropped by the Blue Danube one evening. The relationship between father and daughter was more like one between sister and older brother. The father, boyish, bore a vague resemblance to Robert F Kennedy, and he had a minister's air of accepting one and all. The Stanley Cup finals were at game number three. I began speaking to Dubois of linear time; he just waved his arms about and said, 'Back off.'

—Here is Eggy, stone-faced. His face is as stony as the marble-dark countenance of a long, dead imperator, the bust of which one might come across in a museum basement. He pokes by me on the terrasse with his cane; he would enter the café. So this is what it is to be Traymorean Zeus bringing fire and brimstone to Moonface, the party who has done him injury. But suddenly, the winter, the long winter we had had is a distant memory, as distant a memory as the Social Wars. It would seem that Eggy, inside now, has just spooked himself, thundering at Moonface, 'To hell with you.' Moonface the waitress awkwardly laughs. In any case, it sounds serious. I am shamelessly bemused. Shall I wait until all the pleasure has gone out of the balloon, oh, not my balloon, but that of Eggy in his dudgeon? Then shall I attempt some peacemaking? Cynic, I opt for the pleasure I am at the moment receiving: street life of stunners, of warm breezes and whirligigs. In respect to Eggy, will the boy of six pull down the man of 901 years to his grave at last? Moonface's excuse is to come out and see if I require anything. She rolls her eyes up and to the side. Eggy, of course, takes a dim view of this maneuvre, considers it treachery, betrayal and all the rest of it. One does not necessarily betray poetry by writing prose; one betrays poetry, in any case, by betraying something in one's soul. I ought to confront Eggy, saying, 'Come on, enough is enough.' *You scrawny old lecher, haven't you cocked up things enough?* I do so. I am thundered at: *Eff off.* Fine then. I shrug at Moonface. From her I get the commiseration meant for herself. Yes, a man can blow it as easily at 81 (or 901) as he did when he was in his prime, full of piss and vinegar, the consequences be damned, the wives but wives, variables in a grander scheme of things. Moonface, who had been wading through some investigation of the Roman mind, now switches on the TV to a movie. Squealing tires. Explosions. Serge, with apparently nothing to do in the galley, takes a seat in the dining area, arms folded across his chest. He seems almost to have a professional interest in the proceedings, as if once he had been intimate with such goings-on. Eggy's chin has raised his chest. Shadows play. The long hair of a woman streams in the wind. Truly, terrasse season is official. Two lovers at the corner kiss briefly and say nothing, each alone in their separate universes.

—A friend of a friend of Dubois invites him to a *vernissage.* He presses me into service. But could he not go on his own with Eleanor who, for an hour or so, would love to be squired? In any event, he treats us to a taxi, Eleanor, I am certain, overdressed. It will prove to be a dreary affair. How do I know? It is Dubois who wonders how I know, irked by my negativity. I plead a rich experience of 'art happenings'. The three of us squeezed together in the taxi's back seat, Eleanor presses a hand to each of our knees and says, 'Boys.' Downtown, the evening shadows are rich and long. Summer settles onto my unspoken sighs, the sky a benign blue, the trees lush. For a moment I believe I shall be introduced to Manet or Degas at some bistro on the banks of the Seine, to the last time that the seriosity of art and the pursuit of pleasure combined in civilized entities. We are deposited on Crescent St, the party crowds in full force at all the bars and cafés. Up a flight of stairs. We hear a gathering of people above us as we climb. We hove into view; we are checked out, dismissed. We circulate. Precious bits of bone on precious bits of linen set within precious frames. Ah, art. Swells from the professional classes. Even Eleanor has the sense to realize that what holds sway here over anything truly serious and truly joyous is pretension. Arsdell, one of academe's finest, wears a suit and tie such as one of Wyatt Earp's buddies might have worn to a shoot-out, but his art palaver is all thumbs. I extricate myself only to bounce off Gaetan Szabo who leers. He is smug with his various superiorities, ideological and otherwise, at the assemblage of connoisseurs. I bounce far. To Eleanor I say, 'One more glass of wine quickly quaffed and I'm out of here.' 'Likewise,' she says, a few shrinking violet males noting the regal grandeur of her bosom. There is a doctor in the house whom Dubois recognizes from his old days; they catch up on gossip. Eleanor signals her restlessness. How so? Eleanor, heavy-hipped, clumps about on her high heels among chinless sylphs and civic-minded biddies. Dubois recognizes mounting pique, disaster in the offing. Dubois steers us to neutral territory. At a bar now where we snagged a table on its terrasse. *Lumpen* packs of hosers of all genders throng by. Our conversation concerns itself with Eggy: what to do with him? Eleanor has few kind words to offer on the subject. Dubois believes the old bugger will come to his senses, eventually; he will realize what a pain he has been. 'Not possible,' says Eleanor, 'he could never believe he'd ever been a pain to anyone.' 'I have faith in him,' announces Dubois, merriment in his glittering blue eyes. I suggest that 901 years of *amour propre* is a lot of *amour propre* to of a sudden suspend. 'I'm with you on that,' says Eleanor. 'You wait and see,' affirms Dubois, 'he'll come around.' And then, like two men in love with the same woman who loves her men in turn, we form a human shape on the street and walk among the thrill-seekers. We are insulated from all debacles. Dubois hails a taxi. Back in our neighbourhood, at the Blue Danube, we see

Eggy sitting alone. He is forlorn. Moonface grimly brings plates of food to a table of revellers. Eleanor, however, has had enough. 'See you upstairs,' she says to Dubois, who informs her he will not be long, and he and I sit down with a tiny sparrow of a man. Dubois waves Moonface over. She approaches like a dumb creature vaguely aware that her end may be imminent. 'Wine,' says Dubois, and then adds, 'and by the way, I've had just about enough of this. The Chairman of the Board now issues a directive. It's this. You two shake hands.' Risky strategy. Eggy flinches. Moonface has her doubts. Then, like a nymph who has some blackmailer's edge on Zeus, she bends and implants on an hoary old cheek a kiss that the god does not deserve. Eggy is much too old and desiccated for tears, but it is a tear that very nearly puts an end to the Eggy countenance. He is cherubic. He is back in the fold, returned to the holy of holies which is his august peerage among Traymoreans. He had been frightened out of his wits. He had been subjected to the worst of punishments. He had been banished, turned out, exiled.

A Proper Narrative, Resumed
Of Values and Things

From now on Eleanor was going to play it by the book. No more dalliance outside the nest. I was both disappointed and relieved. Perhaps this in and of itself bespoke the weak and callow creature I was. But surely, she could toss the odd freshly baked biscuit my way, and in doing so, not compromise her standing with Dubois. In any case, it was not that Dubois had lowered the boom on her; that was not his style. It was entirely her own idea to truck now with fealty, abstinence, true devotion. I did not think it would last; she had not the patience, too vain a woman to remain unaware of her talent for trouble. It is to say she was perverse. I made the appropriate noises.

'So,' I said, with what were admittedly uninspired noises there in her kitchen, 'you're turning over a new leaf.'

'You're mocking me.'

I rolled us a couple of cigarettes. And I wondered if she would break out the amaretto. The stuff always put a purr on her tongue. It always made her randy.

I have always thought it a mistake in life to turn over more than one leaf at a time. Then again, the counter-argument, that of effecting a clean sweep of things, was a compelling one. But I supposed what worried me most was that Eleanor might lose herself in her makeover. It was not to suggest she should sleep around, far from it, but that sackcloth and ashes would only aggravate her intensely sexual nature as was an inseparable part of her intelligence, difficult to live with for any partner she might have on a string. I supposed that Dubois's own vanity was what preserved him from the agonies of jealousy; it was not a bad theory as theories go. For some reason or another he was able to take Eleanor's flirtatiousness in stride (for all that Gambetti had been another matter); it was just that this new Eleanor might cause him to break stride and put him off balance. What was more, Eleanor losing herself could possibly cost me a source of conversation. Occasionally, she was truly interested in what made man, woman and child and presidents tick, and it did not hurt that she, from time to time, enjoyed me holding forth. I did not mind being addressed with her best bourbon voice as 'sir' or 'Mr Calhoun'. I did not even mind her relishing a witticism at my expense. I would mind phony virtue. I supposed it was simple-minded of me to believe that love and affection had nothing to do with virtue; they were gifts to be freely given, without strings attached. Even this notion was suspect. Who could say why one person loved another? Who could say why some persons loved well and others badly? I believed Dubois would always be more comfortable with Eleanor, as she had always been bawdy, volatile and hopelessly vain. It was her sincerity. On the other hand, if there was anything genuine in Eleanor's desire to play the faithful concubine at the cost of her old habits, Dubois was going to have fancy shifting of his own to do, should he wish to hang in with her.

'Well,' she said, 'are you? Are you laughing at me?'

'To be honest, I prefer the old you.'

'And who was the old me?'

'The girl who smoked my cigarettes and plied me with drink.'

'I still smoke your cigarettes. As for drink, well, you know what that stuff does to me. Even you found it a bit much.'

'Yes, I did. But even so—'

'We should've done it at least once.'

'Good God, that's what Moonface said.'

'Did she now? I wouldn't have thought she had it in her.'

There it was again—the bourbon in her tone. Whether or not she had ever touched the swill was of no importance.

'Did you make up for the shortfall?' Eleanor asked.

'No.'

'And why was that?'

'Don't know, really. My age. Her inner confusions.'

'Yes, it would've been messy, no question. But how else is she going to learn?'

'The way I learned. The way any of us have learned. The way you learned.'

'And what way was that?'

'Lurching from one catastrophe to the next.'

'It was as bad as that?'

'No, but you know what I mean.'

'Do I? I enjoyed my conquests, Mr Calhoun. I didn't mind being conquered now and then. You seemed to have suffered unduly. Why?'

'Because I guess I'm the suffering type.'

'Come now, sir, you take to pleasure like a duck to water.'

'True, I like my pleasures.'

'You're a romantic, Mr Calhoun. That's your trouble. You're a romantic in a troubled world. And Hollywood has made such cheap currency out of your affliction.'

'Something like that.'

'I wish you well.

'Is this a brush-off?'

'No, sir, it's not.'

She blew me a kiss, the good woman did, from across the table. It was accompanied with a smirk. It was a statement of sorts, a new wrinkle in some Traymorean game, the rules of which I had yet to grasp.

Eggy got around: assignations, interviews. He was still having too much fun to die. I sat in the Blue Danube, looking out at the street, nothing much registering. Plain old, garden variety, down-to-earth self-preoccupation had me by the short hairs. There it was—the one inalienable right no *coup d'etat* could make disappear. Moonface, whom I had barely acknowledged, spoke at me: 'Earth to Calhoun. Earth to Calhoun.'

What was this miserable attempt at levity? Her voice was a slightly musical moan.

I saw in my mentations RFK's funeral train, mourners saluting the passage. Flags on hand-held poles, brandished horizontally, were pointed at the train. Perhaps an eagle capped one of those poles, a Roman battle standard. I entered Canada the day after the man was shot, wondering if the whole of the U.S. of A. was mad. Forty years later, and I was still wondering. Some were avowing they saw in the Illinois senator's White House run an echo of the martyred Kennedy. I had nothing intelligent to say about any of it; I did not wish to trigger presentiment. History, stated a famous writer recently, is full of surprises, most of them unpleasant. Moonface opened her Herodotus and recited: *I, O King, who has seen many mighty empires overthrown by weaker ones*— I raised my hand for her to cease and desist. Serge in the galley looked thoughtful.

'Anyway,' said Moonface, her voice musical, 'here comes trouble.'

Trouble was Eggy scuttling along with his cane, his head sunk between his shoulders. One could easily enough picture him as a scavenging bird among the battle dead.

I went to the door to help Eggy with his entrance.

'Wine,' he thundered.

'And you, sir,' I addressed Eggy, now that he was ensconced at table, 'what crimes have you been up to? For we are all guilty of something. Even of having been born.'

'What's with him?' Eggy inquired of Moonface, and then to me: 'And you, sir, are a damnable depressive. But you shall not dim my lights. I have just come from a rendezvous. Was at the Claremont with International Sales Manager. Drank Pernod. The lady had chardonnay. I'm the last man in this town to bother with Pernod. Keeping faith, you know.'

'Cool,' said Moonface.

'Yes,' said Eggy, 'cool.'

Sparrows copulated in a boulevard tree.

Moonface's chuckles were not a pretty sound.

Tristisimmus Hominum

It is difficult not to conclude that Tiberius Caesar hated the Julian clan into which he had unhappily married (at the cost of his early, happy marriage to Vipsania); into which he had been adopted. And whether, after Augustus Caesar's death, Tiberius already installed as princeps, he had grudgingly accepted full powers or had only been coy, remains a matter of speculation. For all that, the record is clear he used his powers with reluctance; the senate ought to deliberate and act on its own. The poor senate was thereby confused, Tiberius thinking it a body fit for slaves. Perhaps his *intima causa* had been all along his lost love Vipsania. While he brooded in Capri where he had secluded himself, Sejanus, Praetorian Prefect, schemed and plotted and murdered until, at length, Tiberius realized he, too, was the object of conspiracy, Sejanus wishing to be Caesar himself. Finally, Tiberius took back power into his own hands and had Sejanus executed and the senate purged. Quite the little bloodbath. Besides the books of Tacitus on Tiberius and his rule, I had read other books, modern and ancient, that purported to explain a difficult man. None of this was neither here nor there, I sitting at table with Eggy and Moonface, a slow afternoon at the Blue Danube. Miss Meow, new regular, was miaowing at a separate table. The only persons missing from a tableau were Blind Musician and the Whistler; between them and the miaowing woman, they could make theatre and tour. Serge kept to himself in the galley. Moonface soundlessly aped Miss Meow and broke it off after I gave her a look. We need not have encouraged the woman. Who was wearing a long and heavy coat, the air outside humid. Somewhere down the street, a drill bit chewed pavement. And when Moonface went and upped the radio's volume, and a female voice sulkily rendered some ballad of regret, even this did not deter the feline impersonator. But what sort of man was Tiberius, really? He had been one of Rome's great generals. He was the son of the world's most powerful woman. He was embittered. He may have been something of a versifier, and he was steeped in Greek rhetoric. He kept an astrologer on hand as a comic foil, so I surmised, to his own unhealthy morbidity. How would Tiberius Caesar have run the American empire? I put the question to Eggy whose chin was drifting toward his chest: 'What? You mean that old goat?'

'Yes,' said Moonface, 'he was cool.'

'From what standpoint?' countered Eggy, tacking back to wakefulness, suspicious.

'I don't know,' she admitted.

'Haven't I taught you better?' Eggy asked.

'Well,' I said, 'he wouldn't have gotten us into Iraq. Of that, I'm certain.'

'Well, I wouldn't know,' Eggy said.

Then all at once, the sun broke out in a ponderously clouded sky; Dubois showed up, as well as Gregory, who immediately cut the radio. He switched on the TV. Soccer match. It was all he had ever wanted in life: the glory of the soccer pitch. Dubois, even he, was now sporting a baseball cap. He removed it as he took a chair, revealing newly barbered hair going silver. To Eggy he said: 'I think you need dusting off.'

'Oh no, not that,' Eggy mock-cried.

With the advent of the sun, I figured it could get thundery later, Eggy chipping in with his own brand of thunder.

'So,' asked Dubois of us all, 'what's up?'

'Plenty,' said Eggy, and then explained: 'I just had a date with International Sales Manager.'

'Another date? I can't believe she still bothers with you,' Dubois laughed.

'What's that supposed to mean? That I'm too old? There's always penile enhancement.'

'Cool,' said Moonface.

'You're not supposed to hear that,' snapped Eggy, and he meant it.

'Tiberius,' cooed Moonface, in answer to Dubois's question.

'Doom,' I said.

'Nothing's changed,' said Dubois, a guffaw caught in his throat.

He had been drying out, the past few days. Eleanor was stuffing him with biscuits and Hungarian white bean soup. Moonface, even so, brought Dubois his wine.

'Rot your socks,' she said.

Echo, in the old story, loved Narcissus to no avail. And when Zeus lay among the nymphs and took his pleasures, Hera snooping around, Echo warned the god of his wife's approach. Hera got punitive. And now Echo was always the chatterer; it was impossible for her to shut up. And still she loved Narcissus, and still he did not respond, put off, perhaps, by her chatterbox mouth. And she in her grief pined away, reduced to nothing but the voice of a voice. Certainly, the Echo I briefly knew was irrepressible and talkative, she who had acted in good faith. Life is random except when it is not, dark energy the truant in the universe.

Café with Parrot

When Moonface played me or her world false, her voice got girlish. It was rebellion, I supposed, her balking at trodding the path to adult realities. That she pursue the niceties of empowerment; that she study and account for herself in this way; that she marry and bear children—it was none of it just then to her liking. That throat-high voice was an irritation to me, and yet, I could sympathize with its reasons. She was wearing her hair in a new style, wrapping it up at the back and keeping it in place with a clasp. This gave her a somewhat regal air, eternal adolescence notwithstanding. Either Anna the tall waitress or Cassandra had relieved her, and Moonface left Dubois and Eggy at the Blue Danube to carry on; she came and knocked on my door.

'Up for a visit?' she asked.

'Sure.'

There it was again, that most American of words—sure. She took up her usual position on my couch. I asked if she were hungry, and she was. I had nothing in the cupboard; so perhaps we could eat out. Well yes, she was amenable. She had been front and centre when she knocked on my door, the equal of any challenge; now she was withdrawn. Such a chameleon-like creature.

'Oh,' she said, 'I don't know what I'm doing.'

She had been quiet, of late, about her Champagne Sheridans. I inquired after one of them—Rick the guitar-playing mechanic. But no, he was not in the picture. In fact, he was in Alberta, looking for work. Moonface figured he would be happier there, among the Jezebelites of a faded Jezebel of a town. She noticed my book on Tiberius.

'Tiberius,' she giggled.

Some little bit of her died as she giggled.

'So,' I asked, 'when are you going to get serious?'

'Serious about what? What's there to be serious for?'

'Yourself,' I said, 'simply you, the fact of you.'

'You mean like take responsibility for my life.'

'You don't have to put it that way.'

'You're always saying I should do what I love. I love classical studies. But it seems so beside the point.'

'Beside the point of what?'

'Of life.'

She unclasped her hair now; it fell down around her shoulders. It should have caused my knees to go weak—this spectacle. It did not. There was a rather hard and pinched look to her mouth, signalling a shapeless, disorganized anger in her. It had been a while since her last fit. That she might undergo one of these fits at any time always frightened her.

'I know you care,' she said, 'and Eggy cares. Fast Eddy used to. Well, I guess he's dead. Even Rick cared when he wasn't just lusting after me. As if I was some bombshell. Which I'm not. Do you think I am?'

I disliked her then for putting such a cheap question to me. I made the appropriate noises. What I wished to say was: *Girl, you're a ditherer.*

'We don't quite compute, you and I,' I ventured to say, 'in this realm. But I can't make it any easier for you, and you don't make it any easier for me.'

'How so?'

She was astonished to hear it. I could lower the boom. But how does one lower the boom on a child? I suggested we go to dinner.

And we went to dinner, Moonface and I, traversing some remote escarpment of a frontier. Treacherous footing. Such blossoms as were left on the trees had begun to rot. A new hole-in-the-wall had opened up a few blocks away, and we decided on it, or rather I did, not content to drift. I directed Moonface inside. We were greeted by a man who wore a baseball cap; who was evidently cook, waiter, dishwasher, owner. He was in no hurry to attend to our needs. Even so, reading off a chalkboard menu, I ordered two specialties of the house (burgers), and, our conversation at a lull, I examined the photographs displayed on the wall next to us. They comprised a record of the historical city, our faded Jezebel of a town. Too Tall Poet territory.

'So, about Echo,' I put it to Moonface, 'any news?'

'No, none,' she answered, her voice a distant, slightly musical moan.

'I wonder what happened to her?'

'Let's not think about it.'

'Strange,' I said, 'that someone can just be there and then they're not.'

How lame was this observation?

'Yes, isn't it.'

I do not think she cared all that much for what had become of Echo, something on her mind. The hamburgers were indifferent, a garnish of radish slices ludicrous. Our proprietor was sleepy-eyed. He was like a man who had gotten fat and complacent and endlessly amiable, coaching a baseball team of children.

'Echo,' I said, 'has been much on my mind.'

'Really? Why?'

Moonface knew she was being ungenerous; I gathered from this that there really was something nagging at her. I prodded.

'Come on, what gives?'

'This is disgusting,' she said, putting her uneaten portion of burger down. 'I like sex. I know I like sex, but I'm not enjoying it.'

A bird screeched somewhere nearby. Perhaps the proprietor kept a parrot in the back.

'Well,' I said, 'who are you sleeping with? Could be he has something to do with it.'

'None of your business.'

She rolled her eyes up and to the side.

'And who's to say it's a he?' she said, mischievous.

'Well,' I drolled, 'I hope you haven't discovered bestiality.'

The dear girl blushed.

Still, I had not ever spent such a feckless spate of time with a feckless Moonface. A vicious crack of thunder underscored her perpetual ambivalence about seemingly everything. It imparted to her an air of erotic languor, a quality I sometimes found attractive. As if we could lie about forever, caressing to no particular end. The rain poured down. I had been itching to leave this hole-in-the-wall.

'I should hand you over to Eggy for a good thrashing. General principles.'

'I suppose you should.'

'Doom,' I said.

'Tiberius,' she giggled, and this time her giggling recovered for her the ground she had forfeited thus far to her more girlish self.

'Are we in trouble,' she asked, 'really in trouble? I mean, you know, politically?'

'Too much polarization. Too much hatred. Too much self. Too much weak-headed brotherhood. Too much of all the right things gone hideously wrong. Stop me when I begin to bore you—'

'You're not boring me.'

'It's gotten so vast in my head I can't put it into a few words.'

'I wish sometimes that you weren't old, not that you're at death's door.'

'How reassuring.'

'Even if you were just ten years younger. And maybe if I were just a little older. I know I'm immature. I know when you were 25 you were more grown up.'

'I wouldn't say that.'

'Oh God, yes, I'm still an adolescent. Woman-child.'

'You've had lots of boyfriends?'

'I don't know, how many is lots?'

'You tell me.'

'I'm not telling.'

'Suit yourself.'

The rain had stopped, and we could walk back to the Traymore. My treat, I paid the proprietor who knew we were not likely to come back. It did not seem to trouble him much.

I was not surprised to see them still at it, Dubois and Eggy in attendance at the Blue Danube; they were wine-lit. Earlier, Moonface had thanked me for dinner, such as it was, and she thought she might drop in on a girl friend. I said fine. I watched her go her way, her walk meditative and forlorn, her hands jammed in the pockets of her jacket. The neighbourhood resumed its more familiar aspect as I retraced my course. Ragtag storefronts. Well-being at a remove from the glitz and the glam of all the headquarters of the fashion world, at a far remove. After the thundershower, the air was more a concoction of exotic gases rather than an element one simply breathed. I supposed I was equal to the energy of my friends.

'Speak of the devil,' crowed Eggy, his tone evil.

'Himself,' said Dubois.

'Tonight's the night,' I said, taking a chair.

'For what?' countered a tiny sparrow of a man.

'That the Illinois senator makes history. I mean, it's really something when you think about it.'

'And the wicked witch is dead,' ventured Eggy, referring to the other contender, the senator from New York, hard-knuckled brawler, her backers frenzied, as grim as the bacchantes of Euripides. Then I saw hooded figures in a forum, daggers at the ready, marbled gods sucking in their breath.

'Hardly,' I said, 'she's playing a game on eleven dimensions. She won't go quietly, if at all.'

'Spooky times,' said Dubois.

Cassandra, on shift for the evening, brought me wine. Her smile ravished. Why? There was Elias in the galley, checking us all out. All of life, so it seemed, was fraught with treacheries beyond counting. A bonanza for ologists, especially those who loved to talk up the poets, beings who, what do you know, had not been such putzes as had always seemed the case.

'There's a bullet with his name on it somewhere,' Dubois added.

'Yes but,' said Eggy, flailing away in his inebriated condition, 'I knew a man who was in Palestine in '46. He said some Nazis escaped to Israel.'

'You wonder,' mused Dubois, not at all taken aback by Eggy's rabbit leap in the conversational drift.

I looked around. Blind Musician. The Whistler. The old hag and Miss Meow. Gregory had built it and they had come, even if Gentleman Jim was absent. Elias had the air of a man enduring warm-up comedians. Too Tall Poet passed by on the street, his eyes unnaturally bright, his head, even so, in gloomy cloud. Why did he not come in? Was humankind nothing more than an ordeal for him?

'So why am I the devil?' I inquired of my friends.

'You're an evil man,' thundered Eggy, 'because you beat my frail body with your chapeau.'

'Because you've gone radical,' said Dubois.

This was news to me.

'I'm nothing of the sort,' I said. 'I'm a cynic. A weak and callow creature. I ingest wine. I watch forces swirl around.'

'May the avenging hound of hell terrify your vile bones with hungry howl,' said Eggy.

Perhaps I recognized a quote from Propertius. In any case, predator capitalism was low in the water but was otherwise buoyant, like a treasure-laden pirate sloop.

Dubois, on general principles, said: 'You two are incurable.'

'Precisely,' said Eggy, 'that's the point.'

'Gentlemen,' I said, rising, 'I think I'll go.'

'What's this? You only just got here,' Dubois protested. 'Well, go. See if I care.'

'The rain in Spain. Always.'

Contretemps

There is a line in Shakespeare, one he put in the mouth of a mad, old king, something to this effect: that as long as one may say worse, the worst has not yet come. What my fellow bus passengers might have thought of the goings-on in America, if anything, I could not fathom. No doubt, they had plenty of their own preoccupations. Traymoreans, push come to shove, did not expect much from life by way of truth, beauty, justice. And even on a city bus, were I to suddenly shout, 'Praise Jesus', no one would pay me much mind; but were I to quietly announce I was looking for some unassuming path to a god who was more or less indifferent to the human lot, I could make quite a few people twitchy, if not downright antipathic. For a moment, I was tempted.

The great evil, of course, was the quest for perfection, hard on its heels the mindless pursuit of perfection's opposite. A duck would always be a duck; humankind, however? I wandered the streets. I even bumped into Hiram Wiedemayer at the Bay. He was in panic; his whole life had been a mistake but only in such a way as is true of all human lives. We promised to keep in touch. Then I felt a sudden twinge of affection—it was an overwhelming twinge, stark affection—for the woman I had married in my youth, she who, when leaving me, had left us both strangers. Words in a bookshop window asked: was there a pre-Clovis culture in the Americas? I wondered if Lindsey Price had ever completed her manuscript on goddesses. Had she a new lover? Male or female? I began walking back to the neighbourhood, the day muggier now. An hour later, and I was in the Blue Danube, knocking heads with Dubois. He was snippy, saying: 'I don't know what the man stands for. Elect him and we're saved? Is that it?'

Dubois spoke of the black senator from Illinois. Who had given a speech to some Jews that pleased them while antagonizing Arabs. I had no answer for Dubois, none that would withstand any test of logic, and I said: 'Your guess is as good as mine.'

Dubois, disdaining me, folded his arms across his chest. It was a gesture that made of his mind an unassailable fortress. Moonface and Serge spoke to one another in French, Dubois's eyes glittering at the sound of his mother tongue. The government of the hour seemed to be going against form. The Prime Minister had the look of a man with a glass jaw. Perhaps Eleanor knew what mattered, she less interested in the poetry of sex than in the wherewithal.

I left Dubois for the terrasse. He could join me, if he wished, so I let him know. Bevies of summer girls were going by; it seemed I could reach out and touch their joy, if joy it was; that it was very simply no longer winter. A tree getting lusher by the hour shook me. Metaphysics? The cold hand of mortality? All the clichés about lust and death being in one another's pockets were just then true, made all the more true by those girls and their predilection for black nail polish. As I sat there, Moonface checked to see if anything was amiss with me. I shrugged her off with a smile. In a nearby flower bed, such fat peonies. Could they be the product of thin Jezebel air? I may as well have been in Rome or Lisbon. Dubois came out to me, shaking his head. He had been slowly working through his thoughts over a tall glass of beer. For a man who trusted the system, collective enthusiasm for anything remotely resembling a political saviour would always arouse his suspicions. How could I blame him, given the history of the past hundred years? He said, taking up his position at the table with something like injured dignity: 'I can't see what your reasoning is, Randall.'

'What reasoning,' I answered, about to squelch a soliloquy on the rise in me, 'unless it's that one that says man in history puts his faith in illusions, but every once in a while an illusion trumps all else, even a prayer. I don't how much better I can explain myself.'

'You can't. And you haven't explained yourself. What's the next president going to do about the price of oil? Israel-Palestine? The war on terror? These are the things that matter, not eternity. Not Jesus Christ.'

'If you say so.'

'Well, I say so.'

Dubois laughed. But he was redder in his cheeks than he had been a while, not since he was chuffed with Eleanor for fooling around with Gambetti.

'But then,' he now said, 'if we want trouble, here comes real trouble.'
Eggy picking his way toward us with his cane…

Eggy said: 'Candy is dandy but liquor is quicker.'

Girls? The free market system?

'It would seem he got it,' Eggy said. 'But that woman is going to hound his every step. She's in it for the long haul. She's got plans that go far beyond his.'

Eggy was referring to a bitterly contested primary campaign between a woman and a black man.

Moonface appeared, happy to please.

'Well, wine, you know,' said Eggy. 'I didn't come here to sightsee. But wait a minute, what am I saying? I miss Black Dog Girl. Where has she got to?'

It had been explained many times to this tiny sparrow of man that Black Dog Girl had left the neighbourhood; the dog presumably went with her. Dubois said: 'Not this again.'

'Bloody effing hell. She had splendid hips.'

Moonface rolled her eyes up and to the side. She went back into the café like a woman with the fate of the world in her hands, shoulders set against turbulence.

'Well,' said Eggy, giving me a look, 'what doom awaits us?'

'He's saying that salvation is at hand,' Dubois laughed.

'I said nothing of the sort,' I replied somewhat grimly, 'and there's every indication that things will get worse, yet.'

'Oh, wonderful,' said Dubois, still laughing.

'I'm inclined to agree with Calhoun,' Eggy hoo hooed, 'partly because I've lived a great deal longer than you two and partly because I see no reason to trust our species and partly because all I give a damn about is girls. Cheesecake, wine and girls.'

'Oh, it's that now—cheesecake,' Dubois said.

'You bet, and with big strawberries. Think I'll have some now.'

Eggy called out for Moonface. He called out like a man whom death might suddenly silence and he have no more calling out to do, ever again.

Breviarium Imperii

It was awfully moist and awfully warm, the evening that was gathering to itself the end of times and the hours of revelry. Dubois, Eggy and I occupied a table outside the Blue Danube. Moonface, who sat with us for a while after her shift, was now off to rendezvous with one of her Champagne Sheridans, a 'rumply teddy bear'. Or, as Eggy would have it, have a look at her father and have at look at Current Beau, and one would know a lot about Moonface. Animated from the wine, and on account of his penchant for introducing historical trivia into our talk, Eggy now spoke a single word. He said: '*Breviarium.*'

Dubois guffawed. If nothing else, Eggy always entertained him with sudden rabbit twists in conversation and logic.

'Oh, I don't know,' Eggy said. 'It's just a word I came across, you know, around about five hundred years ago when I was taking a Latin class to pass the time, girls few and far between.'

'Well, what's brevyareeeyum?' Dubois wished to know.

'I can't remember. It just popped into my head.'

The pedagogue in me shot to the surface like a fish snapping at a bug.

'Allow me,' I said, 'it has to do with Augustus Caesar. Don't give me that look. Just happen to have read about it, recently. It refers to a record of the imperial accounts he gave his successor Tiberius shortly before he died. Seems a large part of the treasury was his private fortune. He had compelling reason to want good governance. History is irony, given the state of the treasury to the south of here—'

'Which is, in theory, public money,' interrupted Dubois.

Eggy looked delighted; he had sparked discourse.

But do not suppose for an instant I had any idea what I was on about. I missed just then the company of Gareth Howard. He would have addressed the concerns of Dubois in respect to the senator from Illinois, and he would have, in doing so, exposed Dubois as fundamentally un-serious. Jack Swain, on the other hand, would have had us dancing for joy right there, his old nemesis Reagan, once a president, at last discredited. Dubois would have balked. He would have pleaded a larger picture, a broader historical context, to which Swain would have icily remarked that his picture was so much larger, comprising, as it did, eternity. But now and then Dubois could surprise you, he troubled by the implications of this and that originating from on high and eroding further the premises of a constitutional republic. In the meantime I was in love with the fact of the Moonface nose, the bronze curls of Echo, even Eleanor's swaggering libido, and Tibullus's love muse who was named Delia. Erotical irruptions. They were like so many birds flitting about in a tree.

'Well,' asked Eggy, 'what does it all mean?'

'What does what mean?' Dubois laughed.

'I'm not asking you, I'm asking him—Herr Professor.'

'It means,' I replied calmly, 'that Tiberius, on his succession, had enemies. And he was on thin ice with the senate. So that the fact he was privy to Augustus Caesar's accounts made him, I guess you could say, official.'

'Oh,' said Eggy, 'like getting briefed by the CIA.'

'Something like that.'

I was restive, bored with my company. I caught the gaze of Gentleman Jim who had been sitting inside all this time. His eyes were focused on something remote. Also inside were Blind Musician and Miss Meow, each sniffing at the presence of the other, Blind Musician defiantly Anglo, Miss Meow a Francophone. These sorts of quarrels had never meant anything to me. We sat there, Dubois, Eggy and I, the wine in each of us softening hard edges. Or perhaps it was the humid air that softened. It always fascinated me how faces could change character in an instant, like the silvery flashings of fish; and here was Eggy angelic; and here was Dubois vain and handsome and almost courtly in manner, soul mates of the moment. Here was Cassandra very busty—her eyes large and soft, her smile impish—to clear our table of some plates.

'We're behaving, Madame, don't you see?' said Eggy.

'I know,' she answered.

Elias glowered.

Hiram Wiedemayer surprised us, showing up with his camera. He would not be refused. He took pictures of Eggy in his digs, Eggy royally homuncular in his arm chair. He took a picture of Moonface standing at Eggy's side, she looking for all the world like some Indian princess undaunted by a future of white colonizers. If only we were not parodies of what we seemed. Dubois, for all his vanity, was uncomfortable with the camera, as I was. So Hiram got our portraits later, in the Blue Danube. He explained he could not get Traymoreans out of his mind since that evening when he had by chance met us in the café. I suspected him then of Zionist sympathies but he was otherwise frankly liberal, dedicated to the arts, and the sanctity, as he put it, of the individual. It is to say he saw in us peculiar qualities; we were somehow noble for being what we were, a something he could not quite define. Nor could we. Let us just say that in Eggy he saw majesty, a creature occupying happily the niche for which he was born: Mr Common Man, but with book learning. I nearly giggled. It was a mystery, those two or so hours he spent with Eleanor in her digs. Dubois, who rarely suffered from bouts of jealousy, was frantic, the hairline cracks in his cheeks writhing like snakes. Later, Traymoreans in session at the Blue Danube, Eleanor slyly whispered in my ear that she had always wanted to know what it felt like to be a centrefold. Dubois shot me a dark and evil look. In any case, Hiram Wiedemayer stood us all drinks; he felt he had accomplished something tremendous. It was his business, he said, to record dying cultures and antiquities. We were not sure we liked being depicted as antiquated.

'Ah,' said Eggy, 'you should've seen Echo. Now there was a girl to photograph. Hoo hoo.'

'Who is this girl?' asked Hiram.

Eggy explained, over and above my shushing him, Elias and Cassandra within hearing distance.

'Oh, shush yourself,' snipped Eggy back, a tiny sparrow of a man. 'Effing hell, she just ran off with some young stud. Happens all the time.'

'Why,' asked Hiram, 'what else do you think happened to her?'

Even Eleanor saw good reason to nip this in the bud.

'She has that classical profile,' said Eggy, persisting.

'She used to work here,' I added, 'only she took off, and we don't know where she got to or why.'

Moonface bit her tongue.

'She was an honourary Traymorean,' I said.

'Was she honoured?' asked Hiram, cheekiness to his tone.

'No,' I said, 'we were honoured by her presence.'

There was in Hiram's mild eyes a suspicion we were holding something back.

'Later,' I told him, 'I'll explain, later.'

(But I did not, in fact, explain anything later, certainly not the who and the why and the how and the what of Echo. I flattered myself by thinking that Hiram had no need to know.)

He looked around. At Blind Musician and Miss Meow. At the hag. The Whistler was whistling and stomping all the while. Too Tall Poet had looked in the window, but then decided to pass on us. Gentleman Jim was just beginning to work his way through a bottle, he a dying god who understood to the last possible decimal point the cost of realms that die away. Hiram shook his head, somewhat awed.

'In my neighbourhood,' he explained, 'you just don't see this, this many characters in a single place.'

There it was then; we were characters. Truth to tell, Traymoreans had not been this excited about anything in quite a long time. We should have charged a fee.

Some men only derive meaning for their lives from history-altering times; I was getting mine from each humdrum hour that passed. From a certain lilt in Moonface's voice, for instance. From something glimpsed by chance on a TV screen. The page of a book randomly selected. The sight of sparrowlets shivering with hunger. The way Eleanor might hold her cigarette and sip from her favourite drink. Tiberius had lived in the inner circles for so long that, when his moment arrived, and he was sole princeps now, the whole of the known world at his feet, he might have regretted it had come to this. Let us not assume that every man welcomes power, even absolute power. Moreover, he had sacrificed the love of his life to his predecessor's grand designs of continuity of rule. As was usual for me, I lay on my couch, reviewing events. I switched on the TV, the BBC voice of doom just signing off. Here was the weather, the pornography of storm and ultraviolet and pollen count. Here were talk shows, each host jesting at the expense of politicians, especially Current President. Here was an inane movie, espionage the theme. Homburg. Umbrella. A starlet was a wit. Moonface and I had slipped through one another's fingers yet again. Fast Eddy flashed in and out of the living room, swift photon of light.

Echo Glimpsed

Moonface approached me where I sat outside the Blue Danube. Golden brown eyes shone, but with clouds. She waved off Cassandra who was inside. To me she said: 'I'm not staying.'

The pedagogue in me was rising. The voice with which it would speak was the voice of a hooded figure, one familiar with secrets and the exercises of power. I put it to Moonface: 'Before you go then, let me ask you, do you suppose New York Senator who is possibly grossly misunderstood, do you think she stayed in the race for the sake of women? Or was it simply power and leverage, she the party's most likely choice for the next election, should her rival lose this one? That it's conceivable she may even contribute in some subtle way to his losing it. Do you suppose Livia, Augustus Caesar's silent partner, wielded more clout than the senator will ever wield, even if she were to succeed in her ambitions? I should imagine that Livia, out of her devotion to power, understood its limitations, but then, I can be only supposing.'

'Randall, stop it.'

Moonface had just spoken rather sharply.

'I wanted to ask you something,' she explained, 'only it's kind of personal. Embarrassing even.'

'Ask away.'

Moonface looked long and hard at a point distant in space, then grimly said: 'Sheridan wants to tie me up.'

'Tie you up?'

'Sex, you know.'

She rolled her eyes up and to the side. Ah then, the body was still the last frontier for some. Moonface was a hooded figure in a park of ilexes.

'And?' I asked.

'Should I let him?'

There was just the barest hint of a musical moan at mention of 'him'.

'Why ask me?'

'I asked Eggy. He just laughed.'

'Well, he would.'

'I don't think I like the idea.'

'You aren't bound, of course, to like the idea.'

'Pun? But no, I don't like the prospect.'

'So there's your answer.'

''But I like him. Oh I do.'

'How much do you like him?'

'I guess not enough.'

'So it seems. Tell you what. Just giggle.'

Moonface giggled.

'Not now. Not with me. With him. And if he fails to see how absurd the situation strikes you, you can draw the necessary conclusions. He'll draw his own, if he's not mentally enfeebled.'

'I don't know.'

'What don't you know?'

'Anyway, I think she's more power hungry than she is an idealist.'

'Who is?'

'New York Senator. It's so obvious.'

'You might be right.'

'I have to run.'

'Run then. Run like the wind.'

'Avuncular, Randall, avuncular.'

Moonface headed down the street, shoulders stooped. She was Delia, Lesbia, Cynthia, if a little on the gauche side. She was that ancient in the early years of the 21st century.

§

Book VI—A Note on Progress

Anti-Follies VI

—At some point in the night, Dubois slid a note under my door. I quote: 'Some great philosopher (it may be Yogi Berra for all I know) said that bullshit baffles brains.' Dubois went on to intimate that if there has not been much by way of progress since progress emerged as a concept (late 1800s?), it is only that we have yet to give it much chance. We must keep striving. *L'homme révolté.* No situation is to be accepted as definitive.

—Eggy is having too much fun to die, going for year number 82; hopefully, he will see a few bastards hang. It is a better bet than that he will gaze on the bosom of Moonface.

—Eggy rattles around in his memories. I am startled to hear *Paris, 1919, Ho Chi Minh.* 'Well, you know,' says Eggy, 'it was the beginning of the end. Bloody Europeans—they should've taken the man seriously. Moonface will drop her drawers for anybody, fancying herself desirable. Well, she is. The Haitian is doing voodoo on me. Where's my bloody sausages?' It is Serge who brings them from the galley, and, as he sets the plate on the table, he grips the old man's shoulders with affection. 'Dubois,' says Eggy, 'has been a good friend. Moonface has been a good friend. Even you, Randall, have been a good friend. The rain in Spain. Always.'

Anti-Follies VII

—Eggy, near puny in his linen jacket, sips a tall glass of beer. He is in a mood, and the mood is bittersweet. It is to say he is now cantankerous, now an amorous old sod. It is to say he wants us out of Afghanistan and into Haiti where the judicious use of money might civilize the island. It is to say he is in love with a Haitian nurse who takes night classes. Eggy would attend class at her side and carry her books. Now Dubois figures he has heard everything. Well, I reckon Eggy is sincere; in the day's last hour of light, he is a romantic fool. Certainly, he knows it. His 81 years (his 901 of them, should one be measuring poetic time) have brought him to this pass, and the realization is just about more than his poor brain can handle. But there is triumph in his new-found suffering; he is in love. 'Her voodoo works,' he cries to the neighbourhood, not giving a tinker's cuss as to who knows it. 'Hell, I don't care,' he says, 'if she has this other stud on a string. Bloody effing codswallop, but I see more of her than he does. Ought to count for something. Don't you think?' Dubois bites his tongue. For even he, as vain as he is and impossibly handsome, knows enough not to rain on this parade. It is not that Eggy's tough old eyes are zealous, but that they are absolutely consumed with a dedicated love. We had been talking the economy. The sky had been briefly ominous. Dubois was certain none of us, and that would be Eggy and I, knew a pissant's worth of what was what in respect to the subject. The price of a barrel of oil was the price of a barrel of oil. I supposed this expression of market value was the product of an autonomous system, one impervious to the whims of human nature, let alone government regulations. Only Dubois knew the true innards, the cogs, gears, bells and whistles. Dubois had the knowledge, being a man of the business world, wherein the only integrity that mattered to other realms at large was to be found. A poet's integrity was but a puff of air. Furthermore, Dubois did not appreciate my cynicism concerning such matters as the Federal Reserve and the price of tea in China and Walmart supplicants. But had anyone seen Moonface's new come-hither earrings? 'Yes,' Eggy asked, 'do you think she's aiming to get laid? Hoo hoo.' Well, was it as incongruous as all that, the fact of her young womanhood, the fact of those earrings, the fact of the Champagne Sheridans at her beck and call? And Gregory has gone overboard. Sea blue shuttered windows now adorn Le Grec's (aka the Blue Danube) walls. Elias had made them. Expiation? Are those windows what occasioned his quarrels with the wife? God only knows how he must have fussed over them. Beetle-browed, barrel-chested Fast Eddy, a spectre, materializes. He takes the name of Champagne Sheridan and abbreviates it to Sherry. 'Sherry,' he says, 'hasn't the wit to realize what a hot little number he has.' Fast Eddy vanishes. The old hag goes by, exhorting the godless operators of motor vehicles to go to church. Even Eggy has kind words for her: 'There's a lost bride in that woman.' Dubois thinks not. She is purely a man-hater. As if by stealth, beautiful young women have begun occupying other tables on the terrasse. Has the Blue Danube become trendy, at last? I could swear that the eyes of Dubois are beginning to ache. It is on account of the poetry of the flashing ankle, the almost innocent laughter he hears in the soft air of the night. Yes, in this my faded Jezebel of a town. But who among us is innocent? Traymoreans? No way. It is clear Dubois would abandon the subject of politics for other possibilities, good golly, Miss Molly, at the drop of a hat. He might have devoted his ardor not to business but to endless rounds of cotillions. Indeed, Dubois in a pinch is all *Gone with the Wind*. A Mayan breeze brings Natchez riverboats. 'You know,' Eggy says, 'and well, I don't want to shake you fellows up, but the bomb can drop anytime now and I am ready to depart.' There manifests in Dubois's throat a throttled guffaw. Eggy's sincerity has upstaged materialist convictions for the present hour. The inverted pyramid that is Eggy's face is waggish, is cunning, is in full thrall to love of life. It is the beating of a sparrow's heart. Dubois sits there, arms folded across his chest. It indicates he is here and not here, front and centre but distant. The man is entitled to his regrets. It perhaps suggests the man is not wholly a smug operator. Eggy raises hand or bird claw or fleshly apparatus that boasts an opposable thumb, and he cries, 'Mam'selle.' Two tables of beautiful girls turn their exquisite heads. Tall Anna the waitress appears. '*Plus* beer,' says Eggy. Dubois's mouth gapes open, his mother tongue mutilated. 'And, don't go yet, don't be in such a goldurn hurry, why, bring Randall, this estimable gentleman to my right, bring him *mas* wine and put it on my chit.' I am honoured. Tall Anna, smiling, holds her head high like some Nefertiti.

§

Part Three

Consecrated Souls

Book I—What's a Good Woman?

Letter to Sally McCabe

Dear Sally, we exchanged mash notes and verses in Mrs Major's journalism class. Lipstick validated your slips of paper. It drove the old woman wild. She had no idea it was as bad with you as that (or perhaps she knew well enough): that you were sex, whiskey, the Chrysler car, the desert and the mutability of the moon. Good, as moral value, meant little to you. There was something of the ancients in you: what was good was excellence. Achilles would have gotten on just fine with Sitting Bull. We have all the ethics and pieties and moral concerns in the world; we think nothing of blowing away entire cities at the push of a button. Yours was an astonishing beauty that you neither denied nor advertised, you VIP's daughter. You would have gone to some tony college; might have landed a job in publishing; might have married an up and comer; perhaps had progeny and even divorced. Perhaps your notion of paradise has long since disappeared from any scene you may still recognize. I've been less than stellar, though unaccountably a stalwart. I suppose I must apologize to you, seeing as I cannot picture you ever as anything other than ageless, not eternal youth so much as just eternal. Perhaps you long ago grew weary of the burden. Your consorts and attendants? Those boys were my mortal enemies whom I fought to a draw. The one party could not quite vanquish the other. That endlessly grim siege. I thought I had what was moral on my side. Perhaps you were right: there is nothing to be done. Kiss and boff and drink, and otherwise mark time. There is, in a Roman catacomb, an early image of Adam and Eve and the tree and the serpent. It is what it is, but a depiction in which there is no hint of a moralizing agenda. A man and a woman may as well be waiting for a bus as standing around, knowing, for the first time, the weight of the world. Could be you martyred yourself to your old wildness, one carried too far into maturity. Some divinities were known to have done so, rather than live a lie.—RQC

A Bit of Academe

> "And Artemis they introduce... and say that she is a huntress, and carries a bow with quiver; and that she roams about over the mountains alone with dogs, to hunt the deer and the wild boar. How then shall a woman like this be a god, who is a huntress and roams about with dogs?"
>
> —from the Apology of Aristides, allegedly presented to Hadrian Caesar in Athens, 126 A.D.

One imagines Hadrian was somewhat bored with the Christian's play of mind, the literalness, the lack of poetry, especially as Hadrian had just been initiated in the Eleusinian mysteries, and probably had had the wits scared out of him unless, being emperor, he got a milder version of the rites.—RQC

§

Book II—In Continuation

Bridgehead

Marjerie Prentiss moved into the Traymore unheralded, her consorts performing the grunt work of moving up boxes and furniture from the van parked on the sidewalk below. Soon after, she began to assert herself, making friendly with Eleanor, who was welcoming. Prentiss must have calculated right from the outset that if she could charm the good woman, the rest of us would fall to her designs. Eleanor was both her greatest obstacle and our weakest link. Eleanor loved sitting around, talking sex in the particular and men in the abstract, and whatever the newcomer threw into the mix of politics, so much the better. I disliked Marjerie Prentiss at first sight. I was not unattracted. She aroused erotic burblings in me as seemed independent of my nerve endings. It was the oddest thing, how this woman radiated not so much sexuality as a flair for theatre (I had a weakness for theatrical women); and yet it was cold, this theatre, its sexuality but a sideshow to the main event. Her hair lacked lustre, her eyes watery and seemingly dead. To be fair, she could now and then muster a look of surprise that the world was, indeed, capable of defying her analysis of its parts, her freckled cheeks enhancing what the consequent astonishment lent to her face so that she seemed like she could be fun. How else explain her power then, and one felt oneself unable to take one's eyes off her? Eleanor described her body as gorgeous. I supposed it was. Eggy sang her praises.

'New blood,' he crowed after he had had his first look at her, he, Dubois and I on the once-named Blue Danube now Le Grec terrasse, taking stock of things.

And Dubois smiled that smile of his that indicated Prentiss was nothing he had not seen before. Perhaps she reminded him of his college days. Even so, while he allowed that, what's her name, oh, Ms Prentiss as Eggy would have it, was certainly attractive, but that there was something strange about her: he could not put his finger on it.

'Effing hell,' said Eggy in response.

Eggy was ever gallant when it came to new blood. Dubois then raised his arms in an attempt to ward off evil in the person of Eggy, the homunculus about to quote Marlowe, something about a pair of eyes launching the Seventh Fleet.

Yes, and before we knew it, the Prentiss woman was in Eleanor's kitchen day and night. She introduced her beau into a configuration of Traymorean souls, and not only her beau but her beau's rival and best friend, hard drinking fellow of roughly 50, his eyes unceasingly clapped—with some violence—to the Prentiss body. It now seemed impossible to have a private audience with Eleanor, as I was accustomed to having. So that Eleanor, not entirely unaware that she had been besieged, had recourse to an old Traymorean ploy, and she began slipping notes under my door. In this way I learned that a certain Ms Marjerie Prentiss worked for a technology firm, translating its documents from French to English and presumably back again. I learned that Ms Prentiss got on well enough with Dubois; they had plenty to talk about so far as it concerned the world of business in this, our faded Jezebel of a town. I learned that Ms Prentiss intended to marry Ralph her beau, but that Phillip—the rival—was better in the sack, though he would make an untenable husband. I learned that Ms Prentiss believed all Arabs should be fried; here was the solution to a vexing problem. I learned that when she was teenaged, her brother had passed her around from friend to friend for the purposes of cheap thrills. Perhaps this explained something. She was obsessively talkative, a fact which put me in mind once more of Echo the chatterbox who had won all our hearts. From the bits of intelligence that Eleanor leaked, as it were, I surmised that the prize Ms Prentiss sought was not so much fame, fortune or any other material boon, let alone any man's undying love, but an unassailable position in the rather fragile universe her watery eyes were forever constructing. Indeed, she moved through space and carried her lissome body somewhat rigidly, thereby announcing she was a precious bit of porcelain, have a care. As for Moonface, she had no opinion one way or another in regards to Marjerie Prentiss.

There we were, Eggy, Dubois and I, drinking and talking on the Blue Danube terrasse. I expatiated on the Lamia figure. It was the first Dubois had ever heard of it.

'Yes,' I said, 'a daughter of Poseidon, child-devourer. Had an affair with Zeus. What else?'

'Oh, I know,' Eggy perked up, and Zeus-like Eggy, raising a solemn finger, recited: 'Shall Lamia in our sight her sons devour, and give them back alive the self-same hour?'

Dubois shook his head.

'*Merde*,' he mooed, 'how do you do it?'

'Virtue,' lied Eggy, 'and because the rain in Spain falls mainly in the plain.'

And whatever I might have had to say about Lamia was now shunted aside (that such seductresses, despite their air of intelligence, were really rather thick in the head). Dubois rattled on about an ex-prime minister, one caught up in a scandal that just would not go away.

'Of course he told falsehoods,' Eggy the liar thundered, enough said.

Two Anglos at a nearby table, one wearing shorts and baseball cap, taken aback by Eggy's thundering, interrupted their conversation and gave us a closer look. Words like American army, private investors, stock market, oil bubble, ponzi schemes, Palestine, Israel, and shares, lots and lots of shares, had imparted point to their talk. They might have been local commies or garage millionaires, impossible to say. But so much for a mythological entity who could pluck out her own eyes and screw them back in again, a gift of Zeus.

'And here we thought,' I said, 'that Mrs Petrova was holding that apartment for her son.'

'What son?' Dubois asked, just to get a rise out of Eggy.

'She has a son,' said Eggy. 'I've seen him.'

'You were probably so plastered you didn't know what you were seeing,' observed Dubois.

'I tell you I saw him,' a tiny sparrow of a man insisted.

'She has a rather subterranean voice,' I said of Ms Prentiss, 'as if it emanates from an echo chamber somewhere in her.'

'I take it you're referring to the new lodger,' said Dubois.

'Whom else?'

'I don't know,' said Dubois, 'the way you two have been getting, lately, I never know what you're talking about, not really. Now I, on the other hand—'

'Bollocks,' said Eggy, 'you're no more coherent than the man in the White House at his worst.'

'You see, there you go again,' Dubois shot back with some heat. 'Everything comes back to this, to bashing the President, and it won't solve anything.'

'The bastard ought to be impeached,' Eggy said.

'Since when,' I asked of Dubois, 'have you become so forgiving?'

'Christ, I give up,' was Eggy's answer.

And Eggy looked so distraught that Dubois relented: 'Alright, he's one of those bastards who should be impeached. But really—'

'The rain in Spain,' said Eggy.

His inverted triangle of a face was a smirk.

'That Prentiss gal,' he said, 'she's a babe.'

In Eleanor's kitchen, I was about to unleash, between me and myself, a Jane Austen send-up on the gathering. But what can one say of casual people in casual dress who talked in casual sentences; who had deep pockets of invective? Eleanor, seated at the head of her table, shook a pompadoured foot. It signified she was interested. She was pleased that what she had here in the making was a new and improved salon over the salons of the previous summer; still, she was not unaware of the tensions in the room. Immediately to her left sat Marjerie; next to her Dubois. Eggy and I more or less shared the other end of the table, Eggy's chin having raised his chest. Standing and keeping their own counsel were Marjerie's love interests. Ralph nursed a beer, leaning against the counter. Phillip paced like a caged lion, and he was drinking rye, a cigarette in his workingman's hands. When he could he would interject a bottom dollar man's reality; he would admit that, as an economic unit, he had no clout, had not amounted to much, and would never amount to much, given the way the game was structured. One was not sure whether he was congratulating himself or whether he was simply stating a bitter truth, that the world and its market forces had passed him by, but that he supposed it could always use a handyman. Later, I was to learn that Phillip had come of good family in the Townships, had married badly, had recently and tempestuously divorced, and that he had a daughter whom he dearly loved. Meanwhile, if looks could devour he was devouring Marjerie with a violence of passion that was unsettling to the sentient among us. He was going to dig a ditch in the kitchen floor, his pacing back and forth that energetic. Ralph was clearly the quiet, competent sort, though he had none of Phillip's virile air, and he fully intended to keep his little band of stalwarts afloat by way of his contracting business and vouchsafe the Ralph-Marjerie household that was being contemplated. Marjerie, I was willing to wager, was in no hurry to play the great lady and wield dynastic clout in behalf of her as yet unborn progeny. And now, her voice a modulated boom, she suggested that Arizona senator, presidential contender, was the only sensible choice. That other one, Illinois senator, was smoke and mirrors. Dubois agreed: 'Policies? What policies?'

A look of triumph momentarily brightened Marjerie Prentiss's watery eyes.

To be fair, she might have had some justification for her view. Yes, what if Illinois senator was but a pop star, his skin colour of no account, really, so long as he sold a product; and the product he had to sell was a bonanza of all the ways a collective might flatter itself. It is to say that a technologized, affluent aggregate of whites had turned a corner, if not a page; had gotten ahead of the curve, and were not obviously racist or in any way reactionary, and were prepared to prove it. No matter that class warfare had hardly touched their insulated lives. In Eleanor's kitchen, there were seven corks bobbing on a roiling sea. Moonface might have made eight, but she was on shift at the Blue Danube.

'We are going to go Roman,' I said.

'What? Roman?'

The voice belonged to an incredulous Marjerie.

Well, we were not going to go Dutch or prettily to hell in a hand basket.

'Oh, he's always on about Roman stuff,' said Eleanor. 'And anyway, I like Illinois senator, I don't care what you say.'

She flicked cigarette ash into a dish, thrilled to be in the heat of battle.

Perhaps Marjerie had identified me as a force with which to reckon. Perhaps I was only stroking my ego. Even so, in the past hour or two, my, how time flies when you are having fun, the woman had subjected me to her unblinking gaze even as she was the object, the shining apple of the eyes of Ralph and Phillip. What a little circus it was. I noted her bare feet shod in sandals, her big toes prominent, tuberous, suggesting perversity. Not perversity of a sexual kind but stubbornness, rather, and with just enough intellect to get by.

'They want to bomb us all to hell,' she said, speaking of Arabs.

'Who wants to bomb us all to hell?' thundered Eggy, momentarily waking.

A tiny sparrow of a man slid back into oblivion. It did not seem that the question was worth answering. Dubois got a look on his face, one that would bring reason to the table, but then he lost heart. Eleanor sipped her amaretto. She looked good enough to eat. I had a terrible thought: five would get you ten she had Phillip, who would not cease his pacing, on the brain.

It was one of those hot nights when even the idea of sex was one idea too much, even though I had known women for whom heat unlocks their sensuality. Was Marjerie one of those? One of Eleanor's gilded curls was moist at her right temple. Phillip was like some stallion bucking in a barn.

Afterwards, prone on my couch, I waited for Moonface's knock. I was certain she would stop by for a report at her shift's end. Traymoreans had withstood interlopers before. Lucille Lamont, for instance, had murdered her husband right under our noses, leaving him a case of gin to drink while she buggered off to Ontario. She got away with the crime. Osgoode the pedophile was simply no more to be seen, once the police received complaints concerning his activities. So far as I could tell, what booted it for Marjerie Prentiss was the getting of leverage for no other reason than the sake of getting it. She would get the better of Dubois, I figured, he an entity, like her, who did not like to lose arguments. She had won over Eleanor and Eggy. She was accustomed to the sight of men tangled in their feet on her account. I was staring at a muted TV, Letterman the comic and talk show host regaling his audience with topical patter. 'We may as well amuse ourselves,' his facial expression seemed to suggest, 'as do anything else.'

'You're awake,' she said, brightly.

Moonface had let herself in, and she had unmuted the idiot box.

'They're talking about torture,' she observed with neutral tones, indicating Letterman and the woman with whom he was conversing, the mental health of the republic apparently on the line.

'So?' Moonface asked of me, wanting the goods.

I had nothing to say. I thought I might have had a great deal to say. I drew up my knees, providing Moonface with room on the couch. She loosed her hair, a gesture which announced the termination of her working day. I reached for my tobacco; I began rolling a couple of cigarettes. Eventually, I handed her a thin stick which she placed between her lips, unlit.

'Well,' I said, 'a good time was had by all. You had your basic Phillip fellow. I would say his testicles are in a vise. He's got it bad, 999 hells of jealousy and another thousand of unrequited desire. I can't say she leads him on, but I didn't see one signal from her that he should try his luck elsewhere. Ralph just stood there watching. Did he seem upset, concerned, perturbed, irked? Did he give the appearance of a man about to put his foot down? As in, look, we're going to get married and we're going to buy a house. Discipline, discipline. No more fooling around. No, not really. Maybe they're a threesome. Maybe they're recruiting Eleanor so as to make it all Even Steven. In which case, I should imagine Bob will have a thing or two to say about it as, liberal-minded though he is, he's not the type to share. Or else, truth to tell, I haven't a clue. And you?'

Letterman's guest, even as she chided Current President, did not seem at all the self-righteous type; and she looked like she might be fun on a rainy afternoon. But then I was on record as not liking fun. Moonface started in: 'Oh God, I had them all, tonight. Miss Meow. Blind Musician. The Whistler. The hag. Too Tall Poet took an hour and a half to drink a half pint. Miss Meow miaowed. The Whistler whistled and stomped. The hag was going to have us arrested for not going to church. Miss Meow miaowed harder. Blind Musician thought he might move. Too many philistines in the area. Cassandra and Elias spatted. Just for you, Randall, I came by, because Sheridan wanted me to stay the night at his place, and I'm not in the mood. You should be pleased. No, I haven't finished watching *Night of the Iguana*. I've only just met Ava Gardner. I don't know what I think about Marjerie Prentiss. I don't see what men see in her. She reminds me of Lindsey. But Lindsey was nicer.'

'I don't know,' I said, 'that Lindsey was nice, but I know what you mean.'

I avoided telling Moonface that certain women, Eleanor, for instance, could not see what men saw in her person, but that it proved that men were, for all practical purposes, in want of a clue.

'—We Americans don't do those things. We're not Nazis.'

The woman journalist and book author had just made a declaration of sorts, the audience applauding, Letterman blinking his eyes. Half of a smile was frozen to his face.

'Anyway,' I added, 'what's Marjerie to you?'

'You're not interested in her, are you?'

'Don't be daft.'

The dear girl, the unlit cigarette dangling mischievously from her lower lip, squeezed my foot and took herself off.

It was a dream, of course, one in which Moonface stood before me, her shoulders thrown back, a complicated creature. She was often in my dreams. And here she was a solitary entity, looking out of troubled eyes at things she saw as wrong but did not understand, her bravado her maidenly bust. And yet she was utterly selfish and not a little narcissistic, her smile revealing two incisors slanted inwards, two halves of a gate. How a woman could appear so lost, so afraid and yet quite capable of occupying space, the dream failed to tell me. She spoke, saying: 'I was thinking about what you said, remember, about love, about Virgil, about his shepherds, and I want to tell you you've been right all along, but the world tells me to tell you you're out to lunch. So sorry.'

She unclenched her hand, and there, crayoned on her palm was a pink valentine. It was inscribed with Latin words that I read as English: *The world is not workable.* Such a strange girl, this girl. Hapless seductress. Prophet with impromptu prophesy. The space between us took on a life of its own, seemed perplexed, indecisive.

What's Up with Calhoun?

The face that stared back at me from the bathroom mirror was not unattractive, not unfriendly, and not yet entirely run to jowls. Even so, that look of incipient shock affixed to my mug I could have done without; it nearly floored me. To what extent had it been molded by the knock-on effects of my own virtues and vices, and to what extent was it but a trophy to the prevailing geist? What was up with Randall Q Calhoun and the state of his erotic burblings and his cynicism and his sense that all was in drift and in thrall to a near universal imbecility? One saw it always, in the streets, on television: the self-congratulations of louts of either sex. So much celebration of so little. What was up with Calhoun that he could not say yes and he could not say no to playful Eleanor, to feckless Moonface? There was the old injunction that one does not foul one's nest with ill-considered notions of lust and love. I had skimmed through a book of the art of

Balthus for hints of Moonface. Much girl-ness, yes, girlish thighs, mocking eyes, the savagery of the life force, but no sign of a Virgilian strumpet of the Traymore Rooms. Perhaps she was a mutation of a kind; or she had been engineered; was a harbinger of a world in which nature herself would drown in doubt and self-recriminations of every sort. Perhaps drift was the wrong word with which I should depict the vertigo, the torque, the physics of coming unhinged; and yet I would come off prim if not self-righteous, accusing a collective of spiritual suicide. Mrs Petrova's backyard roses, mutely occupying space, induced, perhaps, a swooning sentimentality in her Russian soul. They were time incarnate, so far as they concerned me, because beautiful and transient. Life was easily enough stripped of God and poetry, yet no man or woman could entirely escape the suspicion that it all might actually mean something.

As I walked a noble boulevard connecting the Traymore to the poor man's super mart and points beyond; as I passed by boutiques and cafés and depanneurs and fly-by-night operations set in their brick edifices; as I was irritated by such pedestrians who, in their phantasmagorical stupors, had no grasp of yielding the right of way; as I took care to avoid dog feces dried in the heat, I mulled over the fact of Marjerie Prentiss and her consorts. She had introduced into my little world all the unwanted variables of premonition. I did not know how or when or even why, but she would shake Traymorean life to pieces. She was akin to some right-wing media host on a mission to undermine liberal sanctity, her brooding suitors running interference on the field of battle. By endlessly talking about Ralph and Phillip, especially there in Eleanor's kitchen, Eleanor perhaps getting a little tight-fisted with her supply of amaretto, Ms Prentiss would eventually succeed in convincing her immediate world that she was, indeed, its queen bee, repository of all right thinking. It was true that Europeans had no understanding of American realities, could not quite comprehend in just what way and for precisely what reasons the average American had no interest whatsoever in anything beyond their coasts, but were, nonetheless, the centre of the universe and the only populace that, by any criterion, mattered. Iraqis or Icelanders lived on sufferance. Such was Ms Prentiss; in other words she could see no effing reason why she should not be endlessly adored, her watery, dead eyes astounded by those who would withhold their genuflections. I went as far as the Polish delicatessen at the start of the next district over, and from a woman who might as well have expertly commented on the novels of George Eliot as slice ham, I got the ham of which I was fond. And a link of kabanos. And the woman's warm and frank smile.

I was making a ham sandwich when unfamiliar knuckles rapped against my door. It was Marjerie Prentiss.

'Hullo,' she said, blinking twice. 'Ralph and I are fighting.'

I had not heard any commotion. Did they yell at one another under water?

'May I cross the threshold?' Marjerie asked, with a proprietary air.

Put upon, I sighed that she might.

'And Phillip called and he wants to have it out with us, with me and Ralph, and I can't be there. Eleanor's not in, you see.'

She spoke as if from a treasure chest at the bottom of the sea. Now she was standing in the living room, at loose ends; I took my time extending her the courtesies. I munched on the sandwich and mock-bowed.

'I get the feeling you don't like me much,' she said, claiming the couch, a low coffee table between it and the chair on which I was seated.

She was wearing denims that flattered her hips, a sleeveless red blouse with shiny buttons. Flip-flops. She swept aside coarse tresses from her brow.

'I don't,' I replied, much too carelessly.

'Why?'

'Can't say why.'

'Because you won't say why or because you don't know?

Her inquiry was toneless.

'Or maybe,' she said, exploring, 'you don't like women.'

It was a stupid thing for her to say.

'You're twitting Phillip, from the looks of it.'

'Twitting?'

'Playing him.'

'Really?'

'You're keeping him around just to keep him around.'

'Yes, I am. What of it?'

'It's not nice.'

'What has nice to do with anything? He likes it. I like it. Ralph likes it.'

'Well then, maybe you ought to get back over there.'

'Not just yet.'

I saw that she would submit to any sex practice, she a long-distance runner who could run forever. Perhaps she read my mind, she lowering her lashes. Somehow, she contrived to appear both sleepy and insolent.

'Who says men aren't illogical,' she said.

'I'm a far from rational being,' I crowed.

She adopted no pose, really, made no gesture such as could be construed as seductive. But she emanated something, a something I could not pin down, and she did so with a powerful will, just by sitting there.

'Well,' she said, 'I say bomb them before they bomb us.'

One might think she was addressing the senate. I could hear Dubois jangling his keys, locking his door, clambering down the Traymore stairs. The phone twittered in Mrs Petrova's shop. Eggy was probably at his weekly physio from where he would engage a taxi to the Blue Danube and compromise a morning's worth of health. Marjerie Prentiss certainly did have inspiring hips.

'Why do you want to go and bomb people?'

'Well, I don't. I just think someone should.'

She had not the slightest interest in sleeping with me or that I should lobby her for her favours.

And she was the sort of woman who put other women, about whom one might have had doubts, in a better light. Whatever might transpire between myself and Traymorean ladies, be it sexual, be it otherwise, even so, was not likely to preclude friendship. It was not so with the woman on my couch; and she was recumbent now and this infuriated me, the intimacy she presumed unearned. I had eaten the sandwich but was unable to appreciate the ham's flavour, caught up in low grade hostilities. Here was beetle-browed, barrel-chested Fast Eddy, a spectre, and he was disgusted.

'She's not a nice woman,' said Fast Eddy, addressing me.

'Oh, I don't know,' I addressed him back in my mentions, 'what has nice to do with it, like she said?'

'She's not a nice woman,' Fast Eddy repeated, he with his insufferable gravitas.

'I take your point.'

'You'd better. She's eye candy. Looks delicious and goes down like gall.'

She had the unshapely feet of a bumpkin. And since when had Fast Eddy, for all practical purposes a virgin, gained worldly-wise wisdom? I would be surprised at how much he now got around. Someone was being buzzed in. Strange footsteps on the Traymore stairs. Marjerie sat up, ears perked like a dog recognizing its master. Perhaps it was Phillip come to settle her hash, as the saying went. The footsteps continued on, all the way to her apartment.

'You should go now,' I said to the woman, 'I don't want him coming here.'

I was just this side of livid.

'But I might be in danger of my life,' she said dully, knowing that she was as unconvincing as she was dull.

'I doubt it.'

Against All Flags

The Blue Danube terrasse. Moonface, flashing her nails, addressed me: 'Here you are, good sir.'

She brought wine. And it seemed to me she wished to make love to Randall Q Calhoun, not to the flesh of him so much, not to his ridiculous body, but to the idea of him. And thundering was on the way. Besides the humid volatility in the atmosphere, here was Eggy, tiny sparrow of man, moving right along with his divining staff, his octogenarian's cane. Moonface, aware now of his approach, gave out with a throaty giggle: 'Trouble.'

'Wine, you ungrateful wench,' he called out as he made the turn to pass under the overarching ferns to where I was seated. 'Wine, and I don't care who knows it,' he thundered.

More giggling on Moonface's part. What the dear girl required was a ruby for her navel as would complement the redness of her sneakers. The observation was Eggy's. The homunculus dropped into a chair.

And we were silent a while, as he caught his breath. Inside the café, Miss Meow miaowed the hearty patois of one who was forever talking to herself. The hag at the bus stop exhorted one and all to go church or she would call the cops. A wind was in the maple.

'I got cherried, hoo hoo,' Eggy said, able now to resume discourse.

'How so?' I asked, gamely enough.

'Why, you know, it was the cake I ate. There was a cherry in it. In it, you will note, not on top of it. The whole enchilada of a cherry. The real deal.'

Eggy was most pleased. But as Le Grec, save for its cheesecake, did not offer such temptation, I had no idea where Eggy might have availed himself of his godly and delectable dessert.

'So where was this?' I thought to ask.

'Why, up on Monkland,' Eggy let me know, referring to a better appointed but less noble boulevard.

It seemed a hot little number knew of him there, Eggy saying: 'And I walked all the way to and fro. Took a while.'

'Well,' I said, 'it would seem, sir, that cherries certainly have a way of finding you.'

And Eggy beamed like a man for whom truer words could not have been spoken; like a man on whom the gods have smiled; except that, wait a minute, he himself was Zeus-like, the vast entirety of the cosmos and all its mysteries his cherry ripe for the picking.

'The rain in Spain,' he hoo hooed.

His chin raised his chest. And yet something had to give, even at the risk of disturbing an old bugger's catnap. The electioneering. The economy. The distant wars. Prentiss. Gaza. It began to thunder.

And it looked to be a nasty little squall.

'Come on,' I said, shaking the old man's shoulder, 'let's go inside.'

Eggy was having none of it.

'No,' he thundered while thunder growled in the troubled pearl of a sky above.

He raised a finger in the air and declaimed: 'I am ready, sir, to depart from this life.'

Moonface showed her anxiety as she stood by the window. She blew some wisps of hair off her brow.

'Don't be silly,' I said.

'You don't be silly,' Eggy countered with the vehemence of a child. 'I'll be here when it's over, sitting just fine. So in you go. Bloody effing hell.'

He withdrew his finger, folding his hands on his lap. His mouth hung open a little, his eyelids drooping.

'Rot your socks then.'

'You rot your socks.'

I went inside, rolled my eyes at Moonface, who was rolling hers. One might say she knew a great deal about difficult men, having a father who was not as perverse as Eggy but equally a handful. Even so, as it transpired, not much happened. Eggy slept. He slept throughout the thunder and spitting rain, a tiny sparrow of a man intensely quiet beneath a beach umbrella. He might have been sculpted from stone. As Miss Meow miaowed, I fell into a mood. Perhaps it was the harsh wine on my palate inducing the recollection, how I once took shelter from a storm—there in the portico of the Pantheon in Rome. It rained so hard the blood and gore of ghosts danced on the stone where I stood, the place of which had been a pagan temple, a fish market, then a Christian church. Something in me was acting up as I sat by the window and kept an eye on Eggy; as I regarded Moonface with the eye of a connoisseur. What lies was she telling herself? Whether or not she deserved it, she was headed for a fall, she the brave chrysalis about to metamorphose into a creature with suspect wings. So it seemed. Perhaps it was all that any of us could expect to achieve, those suspect wings. There was no such thing as mastery of one's little craft of self. War had been declared on the poor of an hellish earth, whether the war be a matter of animus or but a consequence, nothing personal, of how things had panned out—since when? Since cheap billionaires had become as thick as locusts. I settled my bill with Moonface and she pretended to cheer, maintaining her girlish optimism over and against the pathologies that were the prenuptials to almost every human exchange. And though, in the course of a day completing itself, it was, as yet, afternoon, she said, a silly grin dimpling her cheeks: 'Good night, sweet prince.'

'I don't know why I bother,' I said.

She looked dashed. Then I thought to sneak by Eggy. But no, as I emerged into the still more humid air and was about to pass him by, he pounced: 'Calhoun, hear me out. It has come to me late in life, I admit. Oh, I've been circumspect. I might've played around just a little—it was mostly jabber—but I was circumspect. You don't go rocking the boat. My effing shame. But I can see how it is. Go against all flags. Hoo hoo. Oh, and by the way, when I'm eating cherry ice cream, I think of Moonface. Bad of me. Well, you know. Effing hell.'

He was having too much fun to die.

A Poem in the Window

All appearances to the contrary, Death was patient. True, Death snapped up young life in obscene measures. Death took thousands upon thousands of entities in one fell swoop. But Eggy, having too much fun to die, was proof of the patience. Or else Eggy was testament to the fact of Death's capacity for bemusement, Eggy—all gristle and spleen—endlessly endearing. Well, he was still besotted with some Haitian nurse of his acquaintance, she who would ring him up from time to time when she got, as Eggy put it, lonesome. Even so, he was not all the show. One evening, as I stood at the end of the Traymore hall, looking out the window at Mrs Petrova's birdfeeder, sparrows in the failing light getting one last peckful of seed, a woman appeared in a window across the way, a window that once was Fast Eddy's to look out, that is, before he died in pantyhose while reading Keats. She was naked from the waist up, at least. It was all I could see of her, the window's dimensions permitting no more comprehensive view. I could not make out her face; just that, so far as features went, it was rather plain, if regular. By now she was aware I was conscious of her or perhaps, I was *unconscious* of her and yet, she made no move to back away or recover her modesty. If anything, she was nonplussed. If her eyes bespoke her state of mind, it was a language I could not understand, be it a language of sorrow or joy, lust or loneliness, grim self-satisfaction or utter disgust with *X*, *Y* and *Z*; in short, I could not read her. Perhaps hers was a brazen language, one that dared me to make something of the fact that there she was starkers at the window. Perhaps she was as shy as a shore bird feeding in a flaming sunset. She was wide-shouldered, amply bosomed. One arm hung down at her side while, with the other, she had reached behind her neck as if, with her hand, she would alleviate some tension there. Her eyes were wide apart, her nose Roman. In any case, it would seem I was the first to find the situation uncomfortable, and stepping back, I retreated to my digs, wondering who or what the effing hell she was. Pianist? Archaeologist? Children's author? Perhaps Fast Eddy's old domicile had passed to her, though I was under the assumption that his brother and Vietnamese wife were going to commandeer the place. Did Fast Eddy have an amour we Traymoreans knew nothing about and she was grief-stricken, looking for what used to be? No, it could not be. Perhaps I had once again imagined something, in which case I was getting far gone, and it would seem that reality, such as it was, was insufficient gratification for my pleasure-seeking senses.

Cigarette in hand, Eleanor knocked. Yes, well, I heard the good woman shut her door; heard her pompadours grabbing at the hall's carpet all the while they slapped against her heels. She was going to catch me in a pique; I lacked the powers with which to telepathically warn her off. I admitted her, objections born of I know not what in her eyes.

'I need a sympathetic ear,' she explained, 'and no nonsense.'

'But nonsense is all I can offer just now,' I very nearly whined.

'I talk, you listen,' she insisted.

I indicated that, well, if such was the case, she should have the couch while I took a chair. And she reclined and was a pretty picture. And she balanced an ashtray on her belly, twirling the ash end of the cigarette in the ashtray's groove, deliberating on how to begin. I said: 'Well, to get the ball rolling here, let me say that life dines on itself. It devours itself; it consumes its various parts for no other reason than to obtain energy ostensibly for the purposes of procreation, and there is no other excuse, none of love of God or of Michelangelo's handiwork or of the tattoo on your inner thigh, glorious prospect that it is.'

'Not now, Randall. And just so you know, I have no tattoo on my inner thigh, and some day, maybe, I'll let you see for yourself. But not now.'

'So that we humans are nature's perpetual adolescents, the pursuit of fantasy our original sin such as distracts us from harvesting life so as to restock life.'

'Randall.'

'Well then, what brings you to my lair? Has Bob chuffed you? Are you sick at heart on account of, what, I don't know, all those enduring obscenities we cherish and behold, each requiring an Aristotle for the sorting out? Collateral damage, for instance, is what genus of our perversity?'

'Randall, Randall, Randall, whatever are we going to do with you?'

'Outsource me.'

'I'm tempted. Go bother the Chinese.'

'There was a naked woman in Fast Eddy's window.'

Eleanor shook her head of freshly gilded curls.

'There surely was. Here's how it was. She looked at me. I looked at her. Had we each recourse to a satellite link, perhaps we might've communicated. I might've said, "How do you vote? Ever so slightly left of centre? Don't you think the Prime Minister has a glass jaw? Oh, he's rather cute in your estimation. Does broccoli give you gas? Do you think people change over the course of time or just stand more revealed? Plato's Eternal Forms? Well, obviously, he couldn't have figured on and so, allowed for talking calculators, nose rings and the Edsel. How's the sex life? Do you find the male beside the point? Is blue your favourite colour? Burnt sienna? How rare do you like your steak? I'm not much for seafood but I do like salmon. Ah, lemon meringue—"'

'Marjerie Prentiss, Randall. Remember her?'

'That wench? But what need has the great white shark for ologists? Oh then, well, we hunt the shark to extinction, but then, along come the ologies to save his sorry arse or help him, at least, to deal with stress. More fantasy, of course. Tell me, Eleanor, what I mean when I say we are not moral creatures, and if we were once upon a time but not now, then when again?'

'I can see I'm not going to get any satisfaction here. The woman, well, she's beginning to get under my skin but in all the wrong ways. Know what I mean, jelly bean?'

'Sure.'

'And that's all you have to say?'

'Lamia. Bred and born. She's one of those. Devours without replenishing.'

'Here I am all upset, and you—'

'But you don't really know why you're upset, just that it's all in a name, and she's a neighbour of yours.'

'Why don't you suck my big toe, you clown? Here, kiss my foot,' Eleanor, close to laughter, continued, burbling, waving a foot in the air.

'Arizona senator is a self-loathing nutter who lost his honour somewhere along the way, the Beltway having chewed him up and spit him out, and he's going to cause us to yearn for the good old days of Current President, should he beat out Illinois senator for the brass ring.'

I spoke those words with grim relish, notwithstanding Eleanor's offer of something like sex.

Even so, she withdrew her foot from a list of things to kiss, and I learned she had become weary of the company of Marjerie Prentiss and her leering swains. It would seem they were buggering one another senseless. Then they would come and park in Eleanor's kitchen, grinning stupidly, disciples seeking a master's blessing.

'But I'm no master of anything,' Eleanor wailed. 'Sex is fun. It's a bumper car ride. I drive, you drive. Sometimes, sparks fly. What's there to brag about? I like to gossip as much as the next person, but there's a limit. Do I give a toss about the fate of the species? We're going to outsmart ourselves. That'll be our undoing. In the meantime, I'm going to find a man—'

'You have Bob.'

'You would say that.'

'I do say that.'

'Randall, Randall, you're beyond human help.'

'Precisely. Why else do you think I seek a religion the name of which I might speak without gagging?'

'I have no idea.'

And a few evenings later, and at roughly the same hour as before, the mystery woman stood at the window again, a black choker her only attire. It was not an easy equilibrium, the roles unfathomed, the roles unclear. Sinister was a word that came to mind, as did the word heaven and how to get there. Perhaps I could discern in her eyes a question, even if it was only a question she asked of herself: *who am I?* I supposed there were a thousand reasons out of which one and only one answer might stand the light of day. I supposed it was a great deal of space through which to fall should I wish to reach her. I did not think I wished to reach her. Words of Mandelstam the poet occurred to me: *What shall I do with this body they gave me, so much my own, so intimate with me?* One after the other, sparrows departed Mrs Petrova's feeder for their roosts. I looked for fireflies in the lilac, but none danced. The next time I saw her she was somehow less present, as if, all along, she had been but a shadow of limited and diminishing light. I never saw her again. The idea of making love to her crossed my mind, yes, and yet, how deep may the exhalations of a bird penetrate the waters of the sea? It is to say I could only presume as to what had brought the theatre about, but that it involved, somehow, my being's core. What was she trying to tell me, if anything? It had been drama, to be sure, compelling stuff, but so casual in its ceremony, so unremarked.

Early Christians

The afternoon was middling humid, maples beginning to redden and yellow, putting on their autumn vestments, shadows rich. For all that, it was still mid-summer such as drives starlets to lounge on beaches, away from the bother of their celebrity. And there was in the eyes of Phillip Dundarave the rather steely recognition that Marjerie Prentiss was, indeed, a conundrum; and yet she was not just any conundrum: she was a dear girl who could do nothing wrong. One could only hope, as the expression went, that he got it off well and truly with her, because she was going to marry Ralph the less exciting but more stable prospect. Phillip had joined me, unasked, there on the Blue Danube terrasse, my usual companions not around. Cassandra, wife to Elias, was filling in for Moonface. Cassandra. The large eyes. The ravishing smile such as could bring one gratitude for the fact she had been born. Then her melancholy. It would have done her a disservice to suggest the melancholy was due solely to her not having married Mr Right, though Elias, I am certain, must have often tried her patience. Phillip was already drunk, if coherent. Truth to tell, he was frightening me. Some gruffer than usual timbre to my voice defended my existential lot in this treachery of a universe over and against the possibility of violence. Phillip had it in him, the ability to simplify discourse with a swat of his hand. Even so, at bottom, he was somewhat honourable inasmuch as he took people at their word; was fundamentally honest for all he had an alcoholic's cunning. Ms Prentiss must have aroused in him exquisite pain.

'Oh, I know I can't marry her,' he was saying.

'Why not?' I asked, endeavouring to sound interested.

'No money.'

'Does she care about money?'

'Every woman does.'

'I don't know about that.'

'You weren't ever married.'

'I was. Once.'

His eyes were getting glassier, grin loopier. Not a good sign. Then it came out he had borrowed from Eleanor money with which to pay a traffic ticket. This meant he managed to arouse the good woman's maternal instincts such as they were; he was likely very much on her mind in the way men often were. Worse, and diabolically so, through Phillip, Marjerie Prentiss had a broad avenue to Eleanor. One could only thank one's stars that Prentiss was not running the show on Parliament Hill. Then again, perhaps she had a gift for such things. Hooded figures arose in my mentations like so many cemetery ghosts. Pagans? Early Christians? The Christ-figure meant less to them than their conviction that the corruptions and the cruelties of Roman life were so intractable they had little choice but to turn to other worlds, as it were, and from such ephemeralities derive the notion that life had a point. I could easily enough see Phillip crossing over to their side, consoling widows and orphans and the dispossessed, and being loved for it; his build athletic, his manner pleasing, that is, when he was not besotted with Marjerie and consequently rendered stupified. He was reticent about his daughter, and I liked him for this. It suggested that, whatever his state of mind, she was no pawn to employ in his convoluted love life, only that if he could contribute somehow to her college education he might acquit himself of the charge he had failed her. Old stories came to mind, ones in which the hero, under an evil spell, need only mouth the right formula, perform the right ritual, and he was released. In truth, the man's company was beginning to wear on me, and he must have sensed it, saying: 'Well, places to go. People to see.'

His eyes were not, just now, friendly.

'Alright then.'

'Good to talk with you.'

'Likewise.'

'Well then, see you.'

It was on the tip of my tongue to exhort the man to straighten himself out; that he was, at bottom, a good soul. That it was not about what Marjerie was doing to him; rather, it all had to do with what he was doing to himself. She was never going to change, but perhaps he might. I did not know everything there was to know about blinding lust but I knew enough; that a lover's embrace was a lovely thing, perhaps the loveliest thing of all except when it was about taking prisoners.

'All the best,' I said.

He gave me a look. He shrugged and left. And then here was another forlorn soul: beetle-browed, barrel-chested Fast Eddy the spectre.

'Haven't you settled down yet?' I asked him, not entirely pleased to see him.

'It's a nightmare.'

'Nightmare?'

'I retired too early. I didn't think it through. I'm in love with Moonface. I haven't got anything she could possibly want or even remotely consider using.'

'Yes, well, you're dead, you know. But in the meantime, can't you get yourself a hobby or something?'

'Don't get cheeky.'

And yes, what would Israel do to keep America in the game? What strings would America yank, and so many skeletons on key chains chatter? I have known women who, secretly religious, attended mass. They knew it was futile to explain their behaviour, lighting candles signifying weakness, a less than stellar intellect on their part. Having known powerlessness to the point of abject fear, as she was passed from leering boy to leering boy, I supposed that Marjerie Prentiss, from the outermost extremity of her pate to her protuberant toes, was now all foreign policy realism, the balancing of ends against a middle that cannot hold. She should have had all my sympathy and understanding; something in her watery, dead eyes was sucking that particular well dry. I further supposed that humankind could, on occasion, behave beautifully. Who was it said that mutual aid within and between the species is evolution's central, shining law? Kropotkin the anarchist? If so, another sort of central committee had overruled him, its various snouts even now poking about the carcass of Iraq. Phillip Dundarave had gone his merry way, a man who always meant to do his best even when supine in his stupors. Was there something of a Buddha's school of hard knocks in him, paths of failure that eventually bring one to one's senses? We would have to wait and see. Fast Eddy, too, had spirited himself off, restless spectre, a barely discernible grimace on his sombre mouth masking the marauding energies of regret. There was a certain kind of male the flesh of whom, just prior to a fit of tears, seemed to undergo a molecular change, become perilously brittle, and both body and personality might disintegrate into a million pieces. Fast Eddy was one of those. A tree scene in bas-relief (Hadrian's Tivoli), carved on a marble pillar, depicts a bird catching a bug with which to feed its chicks, coiled around a branch a serpent about to strike at the nest. No, it was not exactly Disneyland, but it could still speak volumes to reality TV. As I sat on the Blue Danube terrasse, scribbling in a notebook, touchingly but unerringly exposing my ignorance of what booted it (be it pain, be it death); as shadows lengthened; as a procession of girls and louts and widows with dogs and old men with angry beer bellies passed by; as the neighbourhood even in its shabbiness was sometimes as eerily compelling as one of Hadrian's gardens in its ruin; as I snipped, string by string, what connected my body to its youthful idealisms, its belief that humankind, for the most part, was a decent lot, and by way of a tautological leap of faith, so must be I; now Eggy came chugging along, master of his cane. He was breathless to let me know of *X*, *Y* and *Z*; how Illinois senator was in danger, and to what extent his pockets were owned. Bloody effing hell, why, hang the bastards. He settled in, started in: 'Seen Dubois?'

'Not lately.'

I met his death-is-just-over-the-horizon-for-me eyes. Even so, there was something like a twinkle in them.

'You know, why, you must know, he's all managerial class.'

'But of course. Upholds the standard. Otherwise, he couldn't live with himself,' I said, addressing the twinkling eyes of a homunculus.

'He'll never credit you with any knowledge.'

'To be sure he won't. It would go against his nature. It would violate nature in general.'

'But he means well.'

'I suppose he does.'

'That Marjerie whatshername, oh, I don't know, but she's quite the little number.'

'Inspiring hips. Otherwise, I can't say.'

'Is that all you think of her?"

'Pretty much.'

'Suit yourself.'

Eggy's eyes began to droop and take counsel with themselves. Then he rapped against the window with his cane, this to alert Cassandra of his presence and his need. At length, she brought the old bugger his wine, he hoo hooing his gratitude. Her smile faintly ravished us, which is to say she was otherwise preoccupied—with her family, her garden, the restaurant, her complicated spouse, the human lot, the state of the world, Current President, God in His heaven, or not-God and no-heaven. I was fond of this woman; I would like to have conversed with her on many subjects, and I knew it was not to be. Better perhaps that our eyes, and our eyes alone, exchange subject matter—certainties, secrets, justifiable doubts, compass readings.

'Fine woman, that one,' observed Eggy, deeply sincere.

Perhaps it had taken him some 82 years and change to chance upon a woman he could compliment with every iota of his being and not stint on the praise. I believed he had been mean and not at all gallant with his wives. I believed there was something angelic in him, unaccountably so, and it was, in his person, one of God's parting shots, or it was nature confused and perhaps experimental, as nature was forever circling back on herself, alley cat or splendid jaguar, nature insisting on her mysteries.

Muse and Sugar

Sometimes Sally McCabe came to me as Keats's muse, her aim to haul one up by the scruff of one's neck to show one the spiritual heights of poesy. Then she was pleased to let go, and one fell and got to know one's true vista: a dung-smeared floor. But perhaps to a poet's company, she preferred her little band of high school hooligans, her crew-cut Coop and his baby blue Chrysler car. She preferred the pop tunes of the day; the moon and chilled sagebrush of a desert that had welded together once and for all, in my memory, indescribable beauty and human pettiness, let alone the brutalities of sheep fuckers. Then years and years later, and I was in a taxicab in this, my faded Jezebel of a town, and the driver turned up the volume and I heard: *if I should take a notion to jump into the ocean, t'ain't nobody's bizness if I do.* It seemed the perfect philosophical riposte to just about anything; to Big Brother; to the Unitary Executive; to all the numbing conformities; to social Darwinisms many times refined as gave us our civic condition. Was Marjerie Prentiss a variation on a muse-theme, she knocking on my door, beggar's bowl in hand? She stood there, blinking.

'I was wondering if I could borrow some sugar,' she said, yes, with that modulated boom her voice was.

She bit her tongue so as to keep from laughing. Ah, an evil sense of humour. I might have slammed the door in her face but I played it straight. She got her sugar. She got other goods on her foray all reconnaissance. She might have picked on Eleanor, but perhaps her welcome there had worn thin. I was, of course, curious. If Prentiss had designs for me, what might they be and how would they come about? The pedagogue in me as well as Boffo the clown informed Randall Q Calhoun that he was what the girls call a tool. A fool.

Phillip Dundarave's escapade by way of muggers, one night, in a party part of town where the touristed streets turn ugly at a certain hour—and he had been punched about, beaten unconscious and robbed of the money Eleanor loaned him for his traffic ticket—caused her to cluck her tongue.

Not so long ago, she had come across the corpse of Marcel Lamont in his Traymore digs; it had been the same with Fast Eddy in his domicile abutting Mrs Petrova's yard. And now this. It put into the watery and dead eyes of Marjerie Prentiss something like pity for a fellow being. Well, he was her lover. And what lover did not know the game of patient and nurse? For Marjerie decided to tend to the man's wounds after the hospital was finished checking him out. Ralph had no objection to the arrangement; Eleanor had her kitchen back again. I might once more visit as used to be my wont; and I would roll her cigarettes and drink her amaretto, and we kick around Traymorean life as well as the politics of two nations. These were days of fairly constant weather: daytime heat, late afternoon showers or thunder showers, mild evenings and nights. They were nothing days, so to speak, the news all conjecture, so many trigger fingers poised but not green-lighted on so many fronts, not just those of war; and we might, we Jezebelites of a town, consider that it was but one more summer in a long succession of them; ones much too short, given the extremities of winter. Then again, though I did not pursue winter pastimes—skiing, snowshoeing and the like—I did not mind the snow, not really, and as it would drift down in the shine of city lights, I would wax poetic, the aroma of hardwood smoke intoxicating. Still, for now, summer evenings were lived on terrasses; on balconies among potted flowers, the toes of student girls clenched to balcony railings. In any case, Marjerie's attentions were consumed by Phillip's needs, and who is to say he did not revel in it nor she begrudge him tenderness? And though I was not privy to their conversations, I could easily enough picture a much chastened, soft-spoken carpenter lamenting his bad habits; he had gone to some barn of a KitKat place for the booze and strippers and pills. He would get, as it were, his act together and be a proper dad to a proper daughter. And I could imagine Marjerie nodding her head, looking awfully solemn, she in her new guise as an agent for redemption. Eleanor, too, went and bestowed her affections, the Traymore Rooms now a retreat for convalescing veterans of harrowing campaigns; and I heard it from the good woman that Phillip knew he had botched things; made a right hash of his existence; and he would make account. From all this, Dubois maintained some distance, his glittering blues eyes letting Eleanor know she had to do what a girl had to do, leave him out of it. And at the Blue Danube, when Eggy would inquire after Phillip, Dubois only shrugged and guessed he was alive and on the mend.

What had it been, really? Bruised ribs? No big deal. Meanwhile, Moonface was keeping late hours with her Champagne Sheridan; and soon they would fly to Vancouver and stay with his parents; and it would seem that they might marry or otherwise pursue a serious relationship. She seemed rather smug with the possibility. For all that, she was wary of Prentiss for no good reason that she could think of, and she put it to me: 'Why, Randall? Why shouldn't I know why I don't like her? If I let myself think about it too much, it drives me crazy.'

'Beats me,' I said.

I had stepped inside the café to use the facilities. I repeated my answer for good measure. Moonface rolled her eyes up and to the side in that way she had; and I thought of how I had been, for a spell, infatuated with her and was not so infatuated now. Something had changed in her changeable eyes; she was, after all, a chameleon-like creature of no fixed psychic address, but what had changed, exactly, was yet another thing I did not know. I shrugged, Moonface flashing her nails.

'Aren't we silly?' she suggested.

At the table on the terrasse, Dubois stared into space. He had the look of a man who thought he might have reason to express anger, but that it would require such energy as he lacked at the moment. Eggy's chin raised his chest. The old bugger supposed he might spend eternity with Moonface in some equanimity had he recourse to Edith Piaf albums.

'Can you,' he chortled earlier, 'imagine a Moonface orgasm?'

Dubois guffawed. I could not.

'Why not?' thundered Eggy with some heat.

The wine, perhaps, was settling on his brain. I suspected that Moonface among her peers, and this excluded Traymoreans as they did not haunt blues bars, might easily enough have described Marjerie as a slut; just that Moonface would not let the word escape her lips while in our company. She had an image to maintain with me, Dubois and Eggy: that of a virtue-minded, hard-studying, decently-behaved young woman. Even so, we were rotters and yet, the fact that we were such now and then amused the dear girl.

Eleanor had her own guerilla campaign to wage: her pompadours and wide, gypsy skirts. She read *The Economist*, which is to say there was more on her mind than fashion sense. Did I not watch Letterman on TV, justifying his show as a modern analog to Suetonius? For a while Eleanor had even subjected herself to my dog-eared copy of Tacitus, but she found him a little arch. There were once more, in the persons of Prentiss and her swains, interlopers in the building. Perhaps their boffings and jealousies and leveragings set them apart from celebratory sleaze such as one knew from the tabloids. But Eggy, as he and I encamped on the Blue Danube terrasse; as we braved the likelihood that it would rain, was still exercised with the challenge of imagining a Moonface orgasm. Heavy overcast. Tropical air. The green gloom of lush maple boughs. I saw hooded figures, each one a poet, whispering *Moonface* at the moon, the fate of the world dependent on her cries and moans. I did not believe Eggy would appreciate much these hooded figures of mine, and so I said nothing. Meanwhile Arizona senator, presidential contender, attempting to vilify his opponent, the Illinois senator, described him as so much glitz and glam, too much in thrall to the white bimbos such as grace the aforementioned tabloids. I made mention of it, to which Eggy replied: 'Why, hoo hoo, I'd like to be in the orbit of a black bimbo I know. Oh, sorry, I should say she's brown.'

Eggy gave himself over to a mock-show of looking around, yes, should there be monitors behind bushes, methodically recording his every unsavoury utterance. But here was Dubois. And he, so far as we knew, was no stoolie or creep or exotic growth in cahoots with thought police of any particular political bent, there being no centre worth the mention. Dubois, sockless and in shorts, looking somewhat muscle-bound in one of his patented worse for wear polo shirts, was up for our chatter. To Eggy he said, the hairline cracks of his cheeks prepared for laughter: 'And you, *monsieur*, how are you?'

It was the man's princely air that had won over Eleanor.

Eggy, unsuspecting, replied: 'Why, I'm fine, thank you.'

'Are you sure?'

'Effing hell, why wouldn't I be sure?'

'What day is it?'

'Tuesday.'

'Are you so certain?'

'Damn it all, Bob, it's Tuesday, and you very well know it, and furthermore, the lotto's set at 24 million and I'm going to play, and when I win, and if you're good to me, not likely, but if you're good to me, I'll set you and your woman up on Hispaniola, and you can play at pirates, which is all you're good for. Effing hell.'

'I give up,' said Dubois, gesticulating at a god he did not believe existed.

And then as Dubois took possession of a chair, as his buccaneer eyes reconnoitered the area for I know not what—American marines?—Eggy started in: '*With dextrous ease she flexed her knees, her grip on his cock keener, and with ecstatic sighs she sucked him dry, with the ease of a vacuum cleaner.*'

Eggy was pleased with himself. Dubois knew he had been chased from the field.

Pixies

Eleanor was preparing poutine in her kitchen for Phillip still on the mend. I was rolling her a cigarette as I read the newspaper, when in drifted Marjerie Prentiss with her showcase hips. Here she was, latter day Poppaea, Nero's second wife and a real piece of work.

'Hullo,' she said, blinking, annoyed, so I thought, by my presence.

'It's coming,' Eleanor chimed, 'it's coming.'

She referred, of course, to the poutine, Quebecoise concoction. Comfort food. Eleanor was happy in her element, making food. Gypsy-skirted. Pompadoured. Marjerie took a chair and slid in to the table. She was not best pleased.

'And how's the boy?' Eleanor asked of the man for whom she was developing a besetting fondness.

'Oh, he's shamming,' she answered, dully. 'He can get out of bed and start going about his business, any time,' she added.

Eleanor gave Marjerie Prentiss a look. And I noted that the watery, dead eyes of the woman had gone velvety. Disconcerting. Perhaps, so I lamely surmised, she had been steeped in political science studies while at university, and this was what ruined her for polite society. Poppaea had been more than a match for Nero's vaunted cruelty; it had been an equal opportunity marriage. For all that, it was alleged that Nero kicked her while she was preggers and this did her in.

'You two have probably got much to talk about,' I said, 'so I'll be trundling off.'

'Alright then, trundle away,' said Eleanor, cheerfully enough, raising no objections to my proposal.

Marjerie's eyes narrowed and accused. I was feeling somewhat queasy: the smell of the poutine, the time travel through history, the proximity of Prentiss, the demented logic of power in the grip of unbalanced persons.

For all that Moonface was insecure about her attractions, she understood that for some men, at least, she was alluring. All this, while Miss Meow, slagging her meal in a private tongue, was somehow unaffected by the heat despite the heavy coat on her. Blind Musician back, I supposed, from one of his tours, sat erect in his chair and held his blind man's stick perpendicular to the floor. His huge eyes blinking, his mind was intent on deciphering Miss Meow's inscrutable language, one sprinkled with *nuns* and *quoits,* all else incomprehensible, every Blue Danubian a philistine and unworthy of Schubert or Haydn and such. In perfect Angloese, the hag was in full-fledged mezzo-soprano mode that we go to church or she would call the cops on us frickin' sodomites. From which libretto had she gleaned such words?

'Eleanor and Phillip?' Moonface asked.

'Worse,' I said. 'Marjerie's a pimp, if the word can apply to one of your sex.'

Moonface shrugged. She had witnessed the Lamonts and Osgoode, and now here was Calhoun, and what a little busybody he was turning out to be.

'So?' Moonface put it to me.

Perhaps, because she was flying to Vancouver soon with her Champagne Sheridan, she, a chameleon, could believe she no longer had to care. I could have pointed out that Eleanor frisking with Gambetti had been one thing but this was another, this business with Phillip, as it had Marjerie Prentiss all over it, a woman of no good intent.

'Just get me some wine,' I said, piqued with Moonface.

'I'll get right on it,' she answered, too brightly.

Even so, I could see she was dismayed. The dear girl was clever enough to know I was not just imagining things; and though Eleanor had no high regard of her, Moonface had always respected the good woman, and would not wish to see her come to grief.

I went outside to the terrasse, the strangers there all laughing men, the source of their amusement a mystery. A wind blew up, the maples manic. In confused silence Moonface setting my glass on the table, regarded me at length. When I did not respond she turned away. Civic smiles passed by, buoyed, I imagined, by the inherent comity and fair play of Canadian life. The War of 1812 was a Canadian victory… And yet, so I was hearing it now, there had been a beheading onboard a bus near Edmonton. One of the strangers reported it, having ogled the electronic device in his hand for the news.

'Ooooh,' said a table of strangers in mock-alarm.

And then my throat caught the wine wrong; I spluttered and spewed and fouled my shirt. This got me a look from the strangers. Even so, I got out my notebook and jotted, to wit: *Her head was cut off and taken to Rome for Poppaea to see.* And the strangers appraised Moonface as she came out to attend to them. I cannot say that they were rude, but there was menace in their jocularity. She knew it, her jaw tight. It was a sight from which I averted my gaze. I supposed I could not begrudge Eleanor Phillip, but she would pay a price. Poutine, indeed. I pictured Dubois stiff-shouldered now as he made his rounds between the Traymore and the Blue Danube and his office, destiny unjust. He would pretend indifference.

There was, speaking of sport, another side to the story. This assertion was Eleanor's; and she, defending Prentiss from my prejudice, so to speak, agreed that the woman was a handful. A right royal pain in the arse. But that Phillip, in Eleanor's mind, was a fine fellow, confused, yes, and too much caught up in Marjerie's hypnotic glare, but even so. Even so. And here, Eleanor's thought trailed off as she reached for her half pint glass of beer. We were inside at the Blue Danube, ours a weak attempt to avoid any chance meeting with Marjerie and her entourage, yes, should they just happen by. Moonface treated with us as if we were visiting VIPs, fussing with our water glasses, inquiring as to how Eleanor's salad was. Eleanor thought the feta rather salty, not knowing what else to say, and she wished she could smoke a cigarette indoors. The look on the face of our waitress, the way her eyes rolled up and to the side, suggested that yes, it was a shame she could not. Eleanor waved her away, a regal eminence letting an usurper know of what thin stuff pretenders are made. And then, wonder of wonders, Eleanor took me on a rare excursion to her past, her Townships birth and girlhood; her coming to the city; her knocking about with men. How eventually she hooked up with a financier named Dufresne; and it was on-again off-again between them for, God knows, a lot of years; and it was, in fact, how she met Dubois, whose path in the world of business had intersected with Dufresne's. Life with Dufresne had not lacked for affection, but that he had never wished to be tied down by marriage; and she had assumed she had not wished to be, as well; and everything seemed fine, as things went; but that, in return for Dufresne's generosity, she was expected to help him entertain clients and the like; and help with certain other aspects of his dealings. Then he died, and to her amazement (she had honestly not expected it) she found he had left her a sizeable chunk of change and she thereafter drifted into the life of one Robert Dubois. Well, she had always liked this man; she liked that he was less interested in money than in the more creative side of business; that he thought himself forward-looking, so many problems looming on the horizon as would affect all of life. Why then the Traymore when, between the two of them, they could have afforded a grander lifestyle? Eleanor did not know, really. Just that the Traymore was quiet and clean enough. Just that she still had in her her Townships girlhood and its lessons in frugality, even if, now and then, she had bouts of extravagance and excessive emotional outlays. As for Bob, he had never gotten quite clear of his small-town boyhood, money a means and not an end. Besides, vain and handsome as he was, attractive in social situations, he was not, in actual fact, a show-off, and he liked his periods of solitude. The advantage of their rather modest appointment was the freedom it offered from money cares. So then, whatever happened to Bob's vision for a future, the problems he would solve? Gradual disillusionment. Yes but, disillusionment? With what, pray tell? And it was hard to say, so Eleanor's thinking went. It just happened in the way time happens. One can only tolerate so much. Mercenary greed. Spiritual greed. The politics of moral ascendancy. The departure of common sense from life. And I thought Eleanor might cry just then as, despite how well things had seemed to turn out for her, perhaps she might have done better: she had had passion, yes, and steady and reliable affection, and still, something was missing. If Dubois would only marry her, she could finally, one way or another, put the nagging to rest.

'Nonsense,' I said, 'we've got these pixies in our brains that contrive to keep us from our satisfactions. There isn't a man or woman alive who doesn't suffer from their schemes. What else is Marjerie? And what else is political life but those pixies that run amok on a collective scale?'

'I think it's a kind of failure on my part,' Eleanor said, with what struck me as unnatural quiet, 'not to know.'

She shook a pompadoured foot.

'Failure,' I said, 'sure, we've all got that, but then, what those pixies like to do is hound us with failure that isn't really ours to shoulder. And I think then what happens is that the ways in which we're truly blameworthy get lost in the shuffle. In other words—'

'In other words, yes, I know, in other words—'

Eleanor gave me a look. She was either 35 or 50-some, such were her looks. The pleasing near-plumpness, the curls, the intelligence, directness of manner.

'In other words,' Eleanor continued, 'we get distracted.'

'Something like that.'

I enjoyed being right; I was always leery of it.

'I have trouble seeing, sometimes, what you're good for, Randall.'

'Oh, so do I.'

'Closet author?'

'Ah, the shabbiness.'

'Dufresne would've put a man like you to work, and to good purpose.'

'I have a powerful capacity for loyalty,' I explained, a pedantic edge creeping into my voice, 'but I don't like taking orders.'

'Randall, Randall. You've always got an answer.'

Eleanor wanted a cigarette.

Blindsided

However it is that the laws of physics operate in dreams, one was certain that if Eleanor slept with Phillip nothing good would come of it. It would only bring her, as she worked her way through the treacheries of a maze, to some minotaur-like creature: Prentiss perhaps. I would have asked Moonface to the movies, but I knew she would not care for the bloody gore of a gladiatorial spectacle. I went alone to the old odeon. I would miss her body seated next to mine. I would miss the fact that no movie had yet been made of which she entirely approved. If I suspected that what she really liked were those old roadies Hope, Crosby and Lamour, I was gentleman enough not to challenge her on it. Still, to spot silver-headed Dubois seated four rows up from the front, a tub of popcorn on his lap, was something of a surprise.

'Trust you,' he observed, 'to go for something Roman.'

'It's a good if historically inaccurate flick,' I answered, the pedagogue in me rising to the bait.

'I'll bear it mind,' Dubois promised.

And the lights dimmed, and then the movie. And we were presented with souls who touchingly believed in an afterlife. From this belief, in the cases of a few, stemmed conscience and honour. That a few men and women were capable of conscience and honour seemed awfully exotic to me, a cynic.

Afterwards, we walked in silence to the Blue Danube for a late evening libation. Dubois was stiff and unforthcoming. And when we arrived, Cassandra on shift, even her ravishing smile was not sufficient to dispel Dubois's funk, Elias and Serge in the galley, a few regulars indoors, young revellers on the terrasse. Perhaps they put Dubois in mind of Moonface, he saying: 'I guess she's out getting serviced.'

He almost smiled. Cassandra brought wine.

'*Merci,*' Dubois said, extending to her his better manners.

I raised my glass to the woman. And Cassandra turned, her ample buttocks cantaloupes, and she went back inside among such regulars as Blind Musician and Gentleman Jim in his stupor. There he was, sockless, slightly astonished at the tricks life plays on one. Then Dubois guffawed, yes, for no reason at all, and especially as there was no Eggy about; and then he got serious.

'It's hit me recently: I'm going to die, some day.'

His eyes, glittering with intelligence, were making something like an appeal. Those words of his seemed to go against the grain of an arch-materialist's catechism that death was only to be expected.

'What,' I somewhat cheekily responded, 'and you haven't made your peace with your Maker?'

'That's below the belt, Calhoun.'

'I assume most of us think we'll be in our right minds at the moment of death, everything squared away, nothing left but a few regrets to inconvenience one's spirit. I figure it'll be so much emptier than that, that we'll see we've lived to no particular purpose but to extend the gene pool and the like—'

'Who's the cynical materialist here?'

'Why, it's yours truly.'

'Do you believe in God?'

I had no idea Dubois was even capable of troubling himself with the question.

'Irrelevant question. The question is: do I believe in anything?'

'Well?'

'Don't know.'

'Eleanor,' muttered Dubois, 'she's up to something.'

I reviewed the evening, a CD in the ghetto blaster. Corelli. For starters, and as Eggy would have it, just how deep were Moonface's affections for her Champagne Sheridan, the latest one? *Why, hoo hoo, if Bob and I plan another jaunt to Quebec City, and she agrees to it, agrees to come along, that is, it can't mean they're very deep, those affections. Oh, I guess she's a young woman looking for her way. Effing hell, she's but an adolescent. Ungrateful wench. After all I've done for her. Well, I fell over backarseward the other night. Hit my head. She called the medics. But I was alright. No harm done.* And then, Eleanor. She was priming herself, so I figured, for a suicide mission, one last kick at the can. The can was a fling with Phillip Dundarave, the carpenter. But had Dubois finally run out of his capacity to pretend not to care, his mortality reaching up for him like some monster in a bog? It went like this for a while, one question succeeding another. Where was Sally McCabe? Under which rat-like footballer was she ensconced while she sniffed the wind for the answer to life's mysteries? There could not be much about the male she did not know or otherwise suspect. And so forth and so on. And rendition. And torture. Dismembered economy. Fruitless wars. And here was Corelli on a Roman balcony, sawing away on his violin, an infinitely more sympathetic figure than Blind Musician, some poor lout in a cart on the street below being hauled off for hanging, this music the last he would hear of *la bella vita* without the jeering of his fellow louts dinning his ears. Fast Eddy appeared. Fast Eddy sat there in a chair, struggling with spectrely emotions.

'I hear,' he said, 'how you and Eggy like to picture Moonface on her back. It's most ungentlemanly, I must say.'

His insufferable gravitas. He had said his piece and now he was away. Great swathes of melancholy that a bow drew across lengths of gut. I had theories about melancholy, but not now, not here. Cruel life? No, life was good. Ask the billionaires.

I dreamed police dogs and admonitory headlines. I woke and heard Moonface run a shower. Was she pleased with her life? Troubled? I rose, dressed, and went to the window at the end of the Traymore hall. Here was Mrs Petrova in the cool of the morning with the old push lawn mower, she in a print dress that blazed with colour. I would head to a breakfast diner I knew. Eggs, sausages, toast. Food that tells one all systems are go; that life goes on, familiar pettiness the bedrock from which civilization's pillars derived rootedness and stability. A pity Le Grec only opened at noon. Would our kind ever have again a thing about poetry and shepherds? Someone had, in fact, beheaded a young man in the back of a Greyhound bus, there in the boonies of Manitoba. It confused people.

Bougainvillea and Stone

I recalled the countless Roman streets I walked in fascination, commercial, residential, historical streets. But that, sometimes, an air of menace would chill me. Hooded figures. Murderous hands. Consider that there was no automatic weapons fire in those ancient, imperial days, no bombs, no missile strikes. Save for the clamour of sacking armies or street riots, murder was a silent business. Coalesce all the cries on the part of all the victims into a single groan, and it would raise no more ruckus than a butterfly's wings. And here, in this my faded Jezebel of a town, I loved sitting out on the terrasse, watching the world go by. A cigarette. Glass of wine. The town's old history was so many images in my thoughts of snow-fed fires and uprisings. Sin and church. Here would come Miss Meow miaowing or Blind Musician blinking stupidly, hectoring philistines. The hag would whirl around and jab pedestrians with a forefinger. Just now, Eggy seated with me, had it in for Gregory. Gregory, part owner of Le Grec aka the Blue Danube, was in the galley along with Serge, a large order for chicken pita having been phoned in, and they were seeing to it. Moonface was a bit red-eyed, having had a late one of it the night before.

'Why?' I asked Eggy, 'what's Gregory done now?'

'He's Greek,' Eggy huffed. 'He has ideas beyond his station,' Eggy added.

'He seems to be making a go of it,' I suggested.

'He's a peasant who's trying to create a classy eatery. Isn't going to happen, not with this clientele. Why, we're it, we're the only class he's got.'

Cassandra was fussing with some potted flowers the names of which escaped me, but that they looked like tiger lilies.

'Now there's a nice woman,' observed Eggy.

'Yes, I like her myself,' I said.

'She's the classy part of the joint,' Eggy went on to say, 'and it's not Moonface. Ungrateful wench.'

I turned so as to ascertain whether or not the dear girl was in ear shot.

'Oh well,' Eggy hoo hooed, 'a girl's gotta do what a girl's gotta do.'

And then he was on about the Balfour Declaration and Jews, and what a right cock-up it had been in the ensuing years.

'Oh well,' a tiny sparrow of a man shrugged. 'In any case,' he said, 'I'm ready to depart.'

'What, and miss out on all the babes going by? I don't think so.'

'Seen one, seen them all.'

Eggy was being obstreperous.

'I'll tell you one thing I'd like to see,' he now piped up, his voice pure lasciviousness, his finger raised, 'is Moonface on her tummy, her arsehole winking at the sky.'

New heights of vulgarity on Eggy's part. I was taken aback.

And now, his finger still raised, his voice Zeus-like, thundering, humankind was but a cancer on the earth. All the collectives as have had their days had funked their chance, and he supposed no one people were any better or any worse than any other. This much philosophizing was tuckering him out; his chin began to raise his chest. I was rereading, perhaps for the *nth* time: *In Rome's earliest years as a city, its rulers were kings* (the words belonging to Tacitus) when I heard Moonface addressing me, she saying: 'I have a question for you.'

'Preemptive reply,' I said, 'if life has no meaning, what can it matter?'

'Cool,' she said.

Then Lucius Junius Brutus created the consulate and free Republican institutions in general. Dictatorships were assumed in emergencies.

'So what's new?' she asked.

'Rome,' I said, 'the coming Principate.'

She seemed to know what I was on about. She nodded, her mouth drawn tight. It had been weeks, if not months, since she had last had a fit, knock wood, or else she was keeping mum. Eggy stirred.

'Bloody effing hell,' he said.

'Why, I was just having a dream about you, Emma,' he added, addressing Moonface by her proper name. 'Oops, I'd better not say.'

'Why, was it dirty?'

'Not saying.'

He went back to dozing. The Moonface smile was triumphant, but of what the victory consisted, I had no idea. Eleanor, of course, thought the girl a twit. Dubois figured she was born for the civil service. Marjerie Prentiss was dressed to beat the heat—light blouse, skirt, flip-flops. Ralph and Phillip walked on either side of her as they came upon us. Moonface's smile went away.

Cumulus was building, the sky looking distinctly stormy. I did not think I had the spiritual wherewithal for the visitation about to transpire. A scraping of chairs along the pavement roused Eggy, and he lifted his head.

'Oh,' he said, 'Marjerie. How do you do?'

And then to Ralph and Phillip: 'Why, I don't think we've been properly introduced.'

Hands were shaken. Ralph, the steady one, explained that they were not staying; a garage sale beckoned. They had hopes of getting themselves a ceiling fan on the cheap. Eggy thought that they must have the time for a beer, surely. Marjerie's eyes, for all that they were watery eyes, drilled holes in my jaw, erotic burblings in me now. Inspiring hips. Moonface, who had retreated briefly at the sight of these people, reemerged and asked if they wanted anything. Ralph repeated himself. Momentary interest to do with the waitress flickered in Phillip's eyes that struck me as somewhat glassy; perhaps, he was stoned. He set them again on Marjerie. God only knew what the threesome had been up to. *Scrabble?* Verse recitation? Leisurely buggering? A white butterfly flitted by, heartbreakingly beautiful, seemingly lost. Moonface stood around, unsure of herself. Marjerie asked, her voice a modulated boom: 'Well, are we going or staying?'

'Why, stay,' said Eggy, 'you know, I've been meaning to ask you out.'

'Who, me?' said the unsuspecting woman, caught a little off her stride.

'Don't mind me,' said the old hoser, 'I always ask the girls. Keeps me young. I don't expect, you know, oh bloody hell—'

Ralph, leaning forward, endeavouring to look interested, was anxious to leave. It was then I took note of him seriously for the first time. Longish hair. The famous Julio-Claudian ears large and flap-like, almost independent of the head. His eyes were not unkind. Phillip was one of those men who hid their intelligence and did not mind, rustic sidekick to his intellectual betters. He could not, however, disguise the intense curiosity in his gaze. I would not have been averse to his presence at a Blue Danubian table, just that I now had the impression he would make one pay for it sooner or later. Moonface excused herself, the phone ringing inside. Marjerie broke the gathering tension, thunder rumbling above.

'If we're going to get that item—'

'Nice to meet you,' said Ralph to Eggy.

'Likewise,' said Phillip.

Marjerie folded her arms across her chest and began to walk away, her arms hairy, the men scrambling after her.

'What was all that about?' asked Eggy, his brow furrowed, his eyes disturbed.

I saw the threesome laughing themselves silly in the corner of my eye. Tight little group.

I helped Eggy through the door, then brought in the libations and my book. What, had something adhered to my being that Moonface found repulsive? She would not meet my eyes.

§

Book III—Iron Skies and Potted Flowers

As Noted

—Emma MacReady (Moonface) Jottings

No sleep. Boffing lots. I don't know, do I love my Champagne Sheridan?

Oddments

—Moonface tells me she is going to Ecuador. She worries that bugs will bite her between the toes. She really did mean to write a poem for me, but that 'the world turns one way and words another, and it's all a lie anyway'. Evie is her favourite person ever, though she does not see much of her. She is also going to Vancouver, Moonface is. False Creek condo. Where the Champagne Sheridan Srs will vet her for the position of wife to Champagne Sheridan Jr. BBQ's. Pompeii with kayaks and dragon boats. She will mainline guacamole. I told her the spookiest moment in American political history was when Kissinger knelt with Nixon to pray. But if Americans do not like phony two dollar bills, who are the biggest phonies around?

—I cannot claim to understand what makes a Quebecker Quebecoise, but I suspect Robert Dubois set himself to play the game of life by enlightened rules. 'Canada exported 2.265 million barrels of oil to the U.S. of A. in May of this spring,' a grinning Dubois has said, proving something or another. But that Phillip is as likely to drink himself silly and pass out as caress any and all of Eleanor's ample charms is all Dubois has going for his other suit as of this moment. He suspects Eleanor is up to something. I look out the window at the end of the Traymore hall. Iron sky. Bright red geraniums two yards over, Fast Eddy's yard a demolition site. Ecuador's highlands have few mammals. If I can picture Virgil seeking out Mayan priests, Moonface ought to be able to spot her Thyrsis in a fringed poncho.

—Eggy, adamant and impish, pipes, 'What we need here is badinage and nosh. Are you listening, Gregory? Gregory, where are the nuts to go with my beer?' And Gregory, uncomprehending, asks the old bugger, 'What you want?' His sad smile, in respect to Eggy, suggests the Greek equivalent of *insufferable old bastard.* 'Oh well, the rain in Spain,' Eggy hoo hoos. Outside, a white torrent of rain. A pair of teenaged lovers take refuge, hip to hip, in a telephone booth. Cassandra smiles a shy smile where she stands at the cash box, Eggy but something to which she has grown accustomed. Badinage and nosh—the alpha and omega of this faded Jezebel of a town where the days of prohibition brought the Yanks northward for the booze, an interlude of sorts in the roughly 8,000 years of human history on the site. Oh, and the conscription crisis. But Eggy raises a finger in the air, and he, back among us, says, 'If you haven't heard it before, I don't care. I'll say again: *caviar comes from a virgin sturgeon, virgin sturgeon very fine fish, virgin sturgeon needs no urgin', that's why caviar is my dish.'* Otherwise, Eggy is not best pleased, Browning poorly represented in a book of immortal poems. Where is sartorial del Sarto, for instance? 'Bloody effing hell. I won't tell who's kissing who down by the well.' Can hear it now—neo-Nazis busting through the door to beat the bejesus out of Eggy, he, Zeus-like, thundering away: 'Yes but, guys, *Ich hab Mein Herz in Heidelberg verloren.*' Eggy knows best how to conquer hearts and minds. He has a gift.

—Cassandra's brainstorm: she will provide the old bugger with a bell to ring should Eggy require service. No longer need he bellow; need he rap against the window with his cane, terrifying half the neighbourhood. Zeus-like Eggy getting godly by the hour. Children shall fashion wreathes of marigolds and affix them to the god. We sat around the terrasse, last evening; braved a couple of downpours. Dubois made mention of politics. I said something about critics I have read who stipulate that one ought not to treat with the moon anymore; it smacks of sentimentalist drivel. Clearly, these thinkers who would deny poetry its moon are sultans of swat and such mentatious rigour as would own civilization for the next thousand years. 'Yes,' said Dubois, 'Putin has won a round of poker.' 'The rain in Spain,' said

Eggy. I was baying at the moon. I was certain I had developed a snout. 'Yes,' I went on to say, 'we'll just pour mold over Eggy's frame and cast it in bronze and bolt the frickin result to the wall, put out candles and incense and tinklers with clappers, compose psalms and drinking songs, and women shall bring their troubles and men their worst nightmares, and this faded Jezebel of a town, this noble boulevard of ours, shall have its tutelary deity, at last, no matter what the doxology of *Ephesians,* no matter if the spirits of the ancient Hochelagans shall rally about, scratching their heads; no matter if the beat cop on his mountain bike shall write up tickets and disperse the crowd. Even so, sparrows shall convene in its august presence. Dogs shall cock their legs in respect. Gregory will kiss its pate for luck. And when the Americans invade, it shall inspire insurgents. And when such a one as Calhoun finally pens the Great Poem, it shall head up the honouring procession.'

So it went, last evening, smiles and guffaws luminescent with bloom, with ease of expression, all the world's ills treatable. Dubois threw up his hands in surrender, given my verbal onslaught. Eggy was having too much fun to die, his eyes brimming with tears of joy. I beat him about his person with my baseball cap. Fast Eddy sat there, grinning that it was like old times. Moonface, alas, was not in evidence, she at some concert with her Champagne Sheridan. 'I was at Baalbek, once,' said Eggy, 'and I bought a bell there. Still got the thing, I believe. Hoo hoo. It never occurred to me to actually use it, you know, for the purposes of securing my quota of wine.' 'It's not the animals that'll get her (Moonface) but the rebels,' observed Dubois. Eggy thundered, 'I've been to Quito. Fine place.' I returned to my digs; I promptly dozed on the couch. Woke to a rerun of Letterman. He had everything under control: mom, peach cobbler, sleazy corporate behaviour.

§

Book IV—'It Would've Rhymed But It Was a Dry Summer'

Cowgirl in Slippers

Hard to imagine, but Eggy and I had had a spat. And so, on the evening following the sorry episode, I brought a peace offering to him at the Blue Danube.

'Here,' I said, '*Immortal Poems*. A book of the things.'

Straightaway, like a duck to water, he went to the Wordsworth. And he was three sheets, already, to the wind, so that, he burbled rather than read aloud a few Wordsworthian offerings. I cannot now recall which lines the old man highlighted as if remembering to himself forgotten loves, just that the poet in question had loved the woods, and now Eggy the consummate boulevardier thought he loved them, too. He then peered over the top of the book; he was tearing up, so to speak. It was obvious he blamed himself for what had transpired, our exchange of insults.

'Let's not speak of it,' I said, 'and besides, I was as much at fault, if not more.'

'Yes but—'

'Enough.'

'Eff you.'

He had been to London once, but Tintern might have been a better place to bring a lady. Otherwise, we sat a while, not speaking. Twilight. A trifle humid. A touch cool. And Moonface, it seemed, had been in the washroom, changing her clothes. She was through waitressing for the day. And she was going to walk right by us without so much as a word. Eggy, however, raised a finger; he thundered: 'No, you don't. Not so fast.'

She sighed. And she turned around just shy of the archway made of ferns; she stood at our table and said: 'Drop it, Eggy.'

'I won't,' Eggy answered. 'Oh well, effing hell,' he added.

Something, I did not know what, had incurred Moonface's displeasure. Sleeveless tank top. Faded jeans. Red sneakers. Her jaw clenched, mouth drawn tight, a less than amused girl took her leave, though she had, in the meanwhile, given me a look that acquitted me of any wrong-doing.

'What was all that about?' I asked Eggy, she now out of earshot.

'Oh, it's Gregory, you know. Silly twit. He accused her of talking too much to her customers, namely me. I was going to have a word with him. She's more than just a serving-wench.'

It was a quiet night, business-wise, the café empty inside, save for Gregory and Cassandra and Serge. Elias had not been around of late for reasons unknown to me. Gregory, being an easy-going fellow on the surface, what had set him off that he would rag on Moonface? And then, of a sudden, it got busy: two Greeks whom I knew to be friends of Gregory took a table while a woman took another, one adjacent to ours. Immediately, the Greeks were voluble, and though I had no hope of understanding what was being said, I did recognize the word 'Santorini', and by its mention, knew the gist. It was in the news: yet another beheading in the world. A male had been seen walking the beach, holding the severed head of a female by its long hair. The one interlocutor, tall and white-haired, said to the other in English: 'Stupid Greek. Bad for the trade.'

He meant, of course, the tourist trade. Apparently, Eggy knew the woman who was conspicuously sitting alone.

'Why, Evie,' he addressed her, 'where have you been? Effing hell, in any case. I may as well tell you, I'm drunk.'

The woman grinned. This seemed promising. From where did Eggy know her? And it seemed I had my answer, Eggy explaining: 'But you just missed Moonface—'

'Moonface?'

'Alright. Emma, then. '

'Oh, I wanted to see her.'

Evie's voice was pleasant, that of a mysterious entity promising treasures: kisses, keys to the kingdom, sonnets polished to perfection. The long black dress she wore flattered her bosom. My eyes filled with her very pale ankles, her feet shod in shiny slippers. A frilly pink shawl sat on her shoulders. Much jewellery. A gold serpent coiled three times around her right forearm. I supposed she might have walked out of the pages of some gypsy romance, her hair dark, medium length. Her brow was prominent, eyes set wide apart. Hers was an interesting nose; it suggested, perhaps, strength of character and that she was not averse to pleasure. I chose to ignore the barest betrayal in her eyes of the fact she was lonely and seeking a solution.

'Oh,' said Eggy, 'I am bad. Evie, meet Randall the poet. No, you know, he really is one, but we try not to remind him of it or why, well, we'd never hear the end of it. You know, poets do go on.'

Evie extended her hand and I shook it—in some collegial fashion. Evidently, she was well-acquainted with Eggy's mode of discourse, its twistings, its rabbit leaps of logic. Yes, and she had the look of a woman who had been disappointed. She had been foolish, too, but even so, she continued to hope for the best. It was all I could immediately make of her presence. Still, she made one aware, as one regarded her, of one's past follies and unworthiness. It was too late, I calculated in regards to my chances; it was always too late. It was too late when Paul on Mars Hill chided the epicureans of Athens for the prevalence of so many idols about. What was gold, silver, and wood; what was constructed by human hand could not be God Known or Unknown, as God had no need of human enablement. Really? This flew in the face of certain streams in modern theological thinking, the pedagogue in me inconveniently rising, Boffo the clown not far behind. And Evie might have smiled; might have heard me out, too polite to show she could have cared less. She had, what, I could not put a finger on it, had *the courage of her vulnerability*, if nothing else. There they were, reasonable enough suppositions corresponding to what my eyes were telling me. Or else, the wine was affecting my judgment or she was quite the performer. Eggy was almost desperate, trying so hard to play the gallant, on his best behaviour, so much more now than three sheets to the wind. It indicated that Evie had power, sufficient power, at any rate, to render Eggy apologetic for being Eggy. Eleanor, who might also have dressed as outlandishly as the object of Eggy's deference, seemed coarse now in comparison. Arizona senator was nothing if not fatally jealous of Illinois senator and his charms. But here was Dubois now come upon us, and he wasted no time, going direct to Cassandra for wine. Then he would sit back, drink and watch sparks fly. Eggy, as he was territorial with my right ear, hoo hooed his cacophony into it, terrified we might ignore him, all our attention on Evie. With my left I learned that the woman was raised an Alberta girl among cowboys, rodeos, airplane pilots. Her grandmother had even looked like Kitty in *Gunsmoke,* owned a bar-restaurant with the unlikely name of The Golden Matador. In Red Deer? Evie had knocked about with bands and poets; had been to Paris; had a horror of conceptual art; spoke well of Kenneth Rexroth, but perhaps did not know a good book from a bad one, and yet, one cannot have everything. Dubois's blue eyes glittered; they were the most rapt I had seen in a while, though I could not say he had sex on the brain, only that his pleasure in the woman's company was genuine and abiding. The sky was mostly clear, a few approving stars up there. There could well have been rioting in the street in this, our faded Jezebel of a town, but we would not have noticed, well-established in our own little world of dialogue and not a little sympathy, that other world pleased to overlook us. Yes, Evie was perfectly at her ease, three bibulous gentlemen nothing strange or threatening. And yes, her grandfather had written a poem, once, and he had said of it, drolling, *'It would've rhymed but it was a dry summer'*. So much for the terror of beauty and angels in Red Deer. And later, back in my digs, I supine on the couch, more sloshed than I might have wished, I accorded her distinction, that she had the honour of being a true daughter of a country I did not understand or would ever understand, though I had lived within its boundaries for forty years. *That many already*? For she was not besotted with the usual *isms*, the kind that disguise what is, in the worst sense of the word, provincial. A false cosmopolitan outlook offends against truth. Even so, she had a weakness for this and that spiritual trend currently going the rounds. She had deemed it necessary to apologize for the fact her name was similar to some starlet's of a hit TV show. Well, I threw up my hands. It had been one of those evenings; no point in getting carried away. Clearly, she would enhance Traymorean society. Why she had not, thus far, it did not occur to me to ask. When I managed to rouse myself from the doze into which I had fallen, Letterman had long since waggishly cracked his jokes at a void; America still mom and apple pie and siren song cleavage; still a forensics laboratory; still a paradise for shills and corporate arselickers; incapable of doing wrong though Current President, with much dispatch and enterprise, had shot all the grim self-satisfactions to hell.

Echo Seen

In the morning, Dubois knocked on my door and was admitted. He had a grip on his attaché case, the item a well-worn, venerable, honest object.

A most business-like look took up his countenance; and indeed, he was on his way to his office, some point of interest that no Traymorean, not even Eleanor, had yet to clap eyes on.

'I just wanted to tell you,' Dubois said, 'I've seen Echo.'

He certainly had my attention.

'Well, I've seen her twice, actually. That's the good news. The bad news is something rather different. I mean the first time, she's walking her dog. I'm just coming out of the bagel shop. I ask her how she is. She doesn't really answer. But am I still wining and dining at Le Grec? Yes, I say. The look she gives tells me she doesn't think well of this. She then says her mother went there and made quite a scene, ranted at Gregory, I guess. Anyway, Echo has had her hair cut brutally short. And she doesn't have that pep she had, not by a long shot.'

'And the second time?'

'We didn't talk. She was just up the street from the café with her boyfriend. She did not look in a good way.'

So, Echo, then. At least, she was alive. So Dubois, bearer of news. I shut the door behind him. I might as well perform some chore, I figured, as sit down and have a cry over Echo. Those marvelous bronze curls—all shorn. The summer look? I took out the garbage. A thunderstorm at dawn had ushered in the day. Dubois ushered in another sort of day. Perhaps Echo, though she had not disappeared, though she lived, was in actual fact, fading away, yes, as it was in the old stories recounted by ancient poets.

Setting newspaper on a wet bench, I parked myself under weeping maple boughs, the sky grungy with cloud. It might thunder and it might pour at any moment, but that it would only drown not so much the grief in me but the low-grade despair with things in general, the sorrows on the cheap. Or a melancholy made of Echo, just a girl, she, but what a girl she had been. Sally McCabe appeared, green-sweatered, red-lipped. She was the pin-up genius of a night's desert air.

'You took your time,' I observed.

'Saw no reason to bother you,' she said.

'You're mistress now of some temple, burdened with temple chores.'

'Don't be silly,' she said. 'Those days are long gone.'

'You're right. It's finished. The ologists have it all.'

'She'll get over it,' McCabe suggested, 'whatever Echo has to get over.'

'I can't imagine what she's been thinking and feeling, lately.'

'Why should you imagine anything? None of your beeswax.'

'I fear she won't recover.'

'You have a low opinion of human wherewithal.'

'True, most people bend but some break. I wonder if Echo isn't one of those.'

'And what could you do about it, in any case? Cluck a brotherly, fatherly, unclesome tongue? Didn't I teach you better?'

'You taught me well, I must admit.'

'I surely did.'

'No kidding.'

'It's my birthday, as of three days ago. Two years running now, and you've missed it. You might light a candle for me, sing my praises if only under your breath in your next wine-induced stupor.'

'I will make amends.'

'That's it then. All I have to say. Yes, I do look rather like that starlet who played Caesar's daughter in the gladiator flick, same bearing, smile and insouciant air of privilege. Cautionary note, however: she didn't get her true love, not really. Got a whiff of his honour, though.'

'And you're saying what?'

'Never mind.'

'That's all there is ever—a whiff now and then?'

'Remember, you owe me a candle, a poem, too, if you can see your way clear.'

I waved my hand in dismissal; I was so poor in verses I could afford my cavalier, failure-masking attitude. I might have asked Sally McCabe what part of sex she liked most. The act itself? The aftermath, that one of lovely quiet, time a gently flowing river sun-dappled, paradisal, sheltering? I might have asked her only to hear her respond: 'Come on, Randall, get real.'

And who was Evie Longoria, come to think of it? Why was she not the belle of the ball, that Traymorean ball in which the long odds were always preferable to the short ones, though we all of us drifted on currents of expediency, having no other leverage?

Another severed foot washed up on a British Columbia beach. There was no one left to kill in Baghdad. The head of Orpheus once floated on the seven seas, but I could not recall the tale's mythological import, something about bringing to all the world's parts wisdom, medicine, mystery religions, wild singing, unassuaged grief. I regarded Moonface with a jaundiced eye, there inside the Blue Danube, rain falling now. She was no Eurydice but then, hang on, of course she was, in the way all women are, always waiting—

'How is my good sir?' she asked, her voice much too bright for my liking.

What sort of theatre was this? Champagne Sheridan would soon take her to Vancouver, and if it was theatre she wanted, she would get it there.

'I'm fine,' I answered, 'and you? How's Sheridan?'

'Taking Spanish classes.'

'What for?'

'We're going to Ecuador, too, you know.'

'Ambitious, are we?'

'It's his father. He studies music. And we're going to Chile. Maybe Argentina.'

'As folklorists, I imagine.'

Moonface gave me a look. And besides, though she now and then privileged me with her future plans, somehow she never actually told me anything.

'Aren't you pleased for me?' she asked, 'I'll have adventures.'

'I should think you will.'

It was churlish of me to picture it, she doing the chicken shuffle through some mountain jungle, burdened with a backpack, wondering perhaps if Virgil's poetry and a classroom had not been more her speed, after all. Her father, getting to be a lost soul, would be even more lost. Her mother, apparently, periodically went bonkers.

I rolled a cigarette, would stand in the rain and smoke it. I could hear it now, Eggy hoo hooing, hailing Moonface as Indiana Jane. To be fair, it had to be acknowledged that Ecuador might bequeath the dear girl what she needed: life without safety nets. Malaria and tainted food, undrinkable water, altitude sickness, rabies, drug trade, Chevron's messes. I took the cigarette outside, noticing for the first time another Cassandra touch (it had to have been her touch); that in one of the fern pots there was now a red parrot on a stick, attached to which were tiny wind chimes. Some passing rube, failing to respect the whimsicality of the gesture, would be sure to trash it, the neighbourhood another sort of jungle. Here was Dubois, making his way along our noble boulevard, head bent, shoulders stiffened against the rain. So soon? Had he not work to do at the office? He carried his honest attaché case as a badge of honour. He made the turn under the fern archway, and standing on the terrasse, he said: 'I didn't feel like working.'

He motioned we should go inside. Where, after he greeted Moonface and she him, and it was all very jocular as Dubois liked it, and he had his soup now, and his beer, he said: 'Eggy fell again. Maybe you don't know. It was after you left, last night. He got up to go. He got through the door and then, I guess his knees just buckled. He's pretty bruised. In the end, I hauled 140 pounds of dead weight up our stairs, he yelling all the while that it had been some senorita he'd had in Beirut. Senoritas in Beirut? I think he was raving.'

'I didn't hear a thing. I dozed off.'

'There wasn't a lot to hear but it was a lot to hear.'

'Oh, is Eggy alright?' Moonface asked, approaching the table.

Strictly Calvinist

Was it possible an honest man might not be honest enough, should his world be too narrow a confine? That the bubble in which he breathed preserved him from experience, for all that he was seemingly uncorrupted by a wider and deeper engagement with things? If so, perhaps Too Tall Poet was that man.

'Life sucks,' he said, and then giggled at his own vulgarity.

And yet, he delivered these words with the solemnity of Ahab knowing the whale was going to win out, even so, irrespective of Ahab's focus and commitment. Joe Smithers aka Too Tall Poet was steeped in the American classics.

Moonface had just gone back inside the Blue Danube, pleased to see that discourse was building between us, her stellar versifiers, her men of the arts and scholarship, of all that would dignify her burgeoning universe. And Eggy, poor bugger, was confined to quarters, too bruised to venture out.

'But Paul,' I said, 'you know, the man of the gospels, was certainly most judgmental.'

But who actually gave an effing hell? Eggy might, so long as I brought him back some beer from the depanneur. The pedagogue in me, rank amateur in view of the fact that Smithers was a professional pedagogue, was spreading his peacock fan of feathers and strutting. No, strike that; I was bored, reduced to listening to the sound of my voice.

'You mean you've actually read the book?'

Too Tall Poet meant the holy book.

'After a fashion. Not that I can quote you chapter and verse, but it puts pictures in my mind of worlds trying to sort themselves out, like this one we're in. Despite what Paul had to say about it, censuring the activity, what was the guy who made statuettes of the goddesses, idols, as it were, going to do for a living? Work in the tin mines—as a Christian?'

'Don't know to what you refer. I'd rather read Fitzgerald.'

Smithers, though the ancient towns of Corinth or Ephesus might not readily form points of interest in his mentations, was a literate denizen of the neighbourhood; on occasion he dropped by the Blue Danube aka Le Grec. The solitariness of the loner, so I figured, was not to be based on the length of time one went without human company but on the intensity of the self-incarceration. He would begin to cross the street from the doughnut franchise, the one Traymoreans called Drunkin' Donuts, as it was a hang out for a low-level criminal element; he would look this way and look that way for lurking vehicular traffic, and he would stride over, and now, he would have to duck beneath the archway of ferns, coming out on the terrasse, the look in his eyes one of a fugitive seeking temporary succour. Now and then he had words with Moonface; he was professionally disinterested in her body, and yet, one often saw him lost and agonized on our noble boulevard, some throwback to the days when one battled the temptations of the flesh. For him I had grudging respect; at minimum he did not run with any literary pack. And he was too sensible to ask if I were working on anything, though it might have been nice, had he inquired. Just now he had the look of a man indulging some delicious sin but knew he would have to pay for it. Some men, assured that God was grace, needed constant reassuring of the fact, were strictly Calvinist. Yes, and he did not pretend he was anything but a wretch, there being enough of the boffo-liberated running around, smiling into cameras, organizing cultural events. He did not know what to do with his legs, they were so long. One day, he would die, and there might be discovered among his papers stunning little bits of verse, demonstrating once and for all the extent to which life, as he had just quaintly put it, sucked. I preferred to think so rather than concede he lacked the courage of his pessimism. He had absorbed the death of his parents and the crack-up of his girl friend. In light of which he still had a few things going for him; that he did not speak like a computer print-out; that his social palaver was not just some reprise of a TV sit-com. Even so, now he was rising to leave. He was wearing a pinkish, candy-striped shirt, his slacks a thoroughly-repellant shade of green. Perhaps he just could not sit still too long; that his body might attract quantities of pain he might never sluff off.

'It's good to see you,' he said, looking at me out of the corner of his suddenly panicked eyes, 'but I have to go.'

Perhaps it had been good for him to see me. He was something the drift of a river had brought this way. And so, he went, tall-masted ship of self, all those classics in him of an American strain, though he was purely a citizen of this our faded Jezebel of a town, intimate with its drifting snows and steamed hot dogs and east end crime stories and copper roofs. And I was alone now of an evening; that is, there were no Traymoreans with me on the terrasse. Even so, it would seem Miss Meow had found herself a friend, and together they were braving the out of doors, miaowing away to their mutual content. It drove a passing terrier mutt crazy.

I brought Eggy his beer. He was miserable in the light of a lamp; he was dwarfed by the expanse of the chair in which he was ensconced, the TV switched to PBS and Hitler's Germany. He could see I did not wish to stay and keep him company, his tough old eyes deliberating as to whether they would put on a show of his irritation at the fact. They opted, instead, for his frailty.

'Yes but,' he said, 'it hurts to move. Could you bring me the opener before you eff off?'

I rummaged in his tiny kitchen for the device he had requested. I supposed it was still within his power to use it.

I had affection for the man even if he had been mean to his wives. He was not without courage; he had, once or twice in his life, seen himself for what he truly was, even if he had flinched at the result. It was more than a great many men achieve. We were not moral creatures, none of us, yet one might posit such questions of right and wrong as would challenge the assertion. Here was Hitler; here was Buchenwald. Here was the notion that nothing had changed, except in the matter of degree and means and the policies by which men and women of policy mask intent. The Pythian oracle was as efficacious as any ologist's post-holocaust memoir such as would ward off future outbreaks of evil. Eggy might raise a finger and object, yes, as the man still retained some smidgen of belief in human progress; it was, after all, how he was educated. All he lacked was a yacht with a well-provisioned liquor cabinet.

And Eleanor and Marjerie were up to no good, the one glassy-eyed, the other snakily drunk. They arrived at Eggy's door as I was about to bid the man good night, leaving him to his laments and chortlings and war documentary, Eleanor sing-songing: 'You can run but you can't hide.'

Marjerie, meanwhile, peered in at Eggy who, for all that he was dwarfed, was Zeus-like in his royal chair. Who was this creature, anyway, this troll, this homuncular grotesque? Marjerie's eyes were watery, dead, lethal. Eggy, peering back, was reduced to a single word.

'Oh,' he said.

He could not, for all the tea in China, recall her name.

'The rain in Spain,' he said.

Marjerie shrugged; she had now seen everything. Her toenails were painted the colour of turquoise, her flip-flops azurite. And I was marched off to Eleanor's kitchen, the finest room, perhaps, of all the Traymore rooms. Marjerie stalked behind us, lioness.

'Roll me a ciggie,' Eleanor commanded, 'and I'll give you some of this.'

She pointed at a bottle of amaretto; she pointed at the cupboard wherein I would find myself a glass.

'No,' said Eleanor, 'he rolls them better.'

Marjerie had grabbed the tobacco pouch and cigarette papers I placed on the table, and she was making a mess.

'I'm just rolling one for myself,' she said, a little peeved.

'Anyway,' Eleanor put it to the woman, 'where were we?' She answered herself: 'Oh yes. Monumental.'

'Indeed, prodigious,' said Marjerie, she with that dull booming voice.

It did not require much imagination on my part to suppose that the who and the what in their exchange had everything to do with Phillip. It would not matter how much liquor I managed to knock down, I would remain insanely sober.

'One is plugged,' said Marjerie, lazily suppressing something like incipient mirth.

'I'll bet,' Eleanor drolled.

A pompadoured foot took on a life of its own.

She, unleashed, was nothing new to me; it was her companion of an evening that gave me pause, her eyes studying, it would seem, Eleanor's every move. And for what? I wondered. She had made a hash of the rolling job, the cigarette too fat in the middle, too thin at the ends.

'And Ralphie boy,' Eleanor asked, 'ample enough?'

'Adequate.'

'Brand *X*?'

'No name brand.'

'The usual.'

'The very same.'

'Well, Randall, are you blushing, me boy? Ah, look at the lad. Hell's bells, it's only girl's night out. We're having ourselves a little fun.'

But the way Eleanor put the question to me, her tongue getting just a little thick, it was as if she were lost and looking for familiar ground.

'I'm shocked,' I said, falsely.

Then I stared into the Prentiss eyes. Was there anything in them that might bespeak warmth and a capacity for affection? Her silly grin proclaimed her adorableness to one and all. Cigarette smoke caused her to squint. Eleanor might come up to the very limits of cruelty in her behaviour, but even so, she was not cruel. Marjerie Prentiss, so it seemed, was like a cat that had long since lost interest as to whether the mouse she killed would return to life and run around again. I rose, feeling theatrical. I walked around the table; stood behind Eleanor. She reached up for my hands as I nuzzled my nose in her hair, whispering as I did so: 'Eleanor. Eleanor.'

I had bought my way out. I smirked at Marjerie. Territoriality was one thing, kinship another.

Yes, Paul had been clever on the Areopagus of Athens, long ago in a spiritually opulent time, the pagans he addressed too smug and self-satisfied. Even so, it had resolved nothing, though the church might claim otherwise, the Unknown God still unknown and unknowable, perhaps irrelevant, love a butterfly in loopy flight.

And I lit a candle for McCabe, there in the sanctuary of my digs. And as the flame bloomed up like a July lily; as Corelli bore down on his violin strings that bespoke a Rome whose pursuit of pleasure was not without the melancholic, that is to say, the body is everything but flesh is vanity, I offered my supplications, saying, 'And may all your boffings be jolly, and if not, I'll always be your friend.'

More Psy-Ops

Dubois was already at the Blue Danube when I got there at the crack of noon, needing something, Moonface perhaps, who looked fetching, bustling about inside the café. The man's newspaper was neatly, no, was folded ever so precisely in half, and one assumed he brought such exactitude to all his endeavours. He cleared his throat.

'I was downtown, last night, having drinks with an old friend. This friend of mine, well, I can't say how accurate his information is, but he told me there's a naval task force, an armada almost, enroute to the Persian Gulf. Americans, Brits, the French. Since I know this will get you exercised, and how you get exercised, I couldn't resist telling you.'

So then, he had been downtown, having fancy drinks. In the Ritz-Carleton or the Queen E, one might obtain a stellar martini. And while he was away, playing man about town, Eleanor and Marjerie had been at play, women beholden to no strictures of the patriarch. In any case, I had been privy to so many false alarms in the last year or so I did not know what to make of the news. And yes, it was quite evident that Dubois was waiting for my face to set its jaw against the face of war, his eyes peering over the top of his newspaper at me, his mouth set to guffaw. It was true, as of that moment, that Georgia and Russia were edging toward war, South Ossetia the bone of contention, Israeli military advisers in the mix, and, who knows, Americans, too. Where was Evie Longoria, cowgirl in slippers, a woman with whom I might idle away a missile crisis? Well, it was an idle question. Moonface stepped onto the terrasse and asked how I was, and in neutral tones I said I was fine, had she any coffee? She had.

'Well?' said Dubois, not to be deprived of his fun, ignoring Moonface, whose mouth was drawing tight.

'So, just coffee?' she interjected, those paltry three words reverberating through all the dimensions of a cosmic order.

I nodded. The sky, just then, began to brighten with sun. Through the open door, one could see on Gregory's flat-screen TV the Olympics in full sway.

'Who knows,' I said. 'It's chilling, if true.'

'Chilling, if true,' Dubois mimicked. 'I don't think it's true,' he added, 'and even my friend doubts the veracity of the report, saying his source is one of those hysterics of the blogosphere.'

'They are, in fact, considering more sanctions,' I said, 'seeing as the Iranians still haven't told the Americans what they want to hear. A naval blockade would, presumably, form a part of those sanctions.'

'That's an act of war,' said Dubois, and by his tone of voice, I could not tell if the man was simply having fun with me or if he, too, was not just a little worried.

I assumed that Dubois, living by his enlightened rules, still retained his faith in the system and in the good sense of people everywhere. And here was Gregory greeting us, hands on his hip: 'How's it going, guys?'

'Having fun?' I said.

'Sure. Fun,' he answered.

Gregory went back to firmer ground. What was it, sometimes, about the sun in the sky, that it was the source of all treachery? Moonface showed with my coffee, and blowing at the tresses sweeping down her face, she said: 'I was going to drop by this morning, but Eggy wouldn't let me go.'

'Aha,' Dubois guffawed, 'the old bugger finally got his hands on you.'

Moonface blushed, and it was a sight.

'No, he didn't get his hands on me,' she said, some stagecraft frog in her throat, 'but he tried. He was just lonely. Maybe you guys don't pay him enough attention.'

'Trust me, we do,' said Dubois. 'Well, maybe he'll wise up,' he added.

Eggy's foolishness was, of course, his wisdom. I had a naughty thought or two in respect to Moonface. Why did old men (such as I was getting to be) rage against the decrepitude of their bodies and torment themselves with the charms of young women? Why not simply dream on, accepting, all the while, that the dreamed-of embrace was but a hedge against one's irrelevance, a purloined bit of peevish passion as per Eggy, floundering in his armchair? So much for psy-ops, a looming world war. Moonface's rich golden brown eyes had just now trumped even Dubois's grand sense of mischief, as well as passing fire trucks, ten thousand athletes amassed in Beijing, and the sparrows at our feet.

Girls in Flip Flops

Brit sitcoms, especially those that traded on the idea that humankind was an endearing kind, as were the sheep it violated, were particularly abysmal. One watched the shows anyway, for the laughs, then caught the bestiality on CNN. The force of the sun, broken by maple boughs, was still strong on the terrasse. Moonface flashed her nails in such a sun, exchanging niceties with girl students come to avail themselves of sodas and salads and spinach-stuffed cakes. To the red parrot in the fern pot, Cassandra had added a green bird and a butterfly. I was even beginning to miss Elias, her husband, who had not been around. It was said he was in Toronto, tying up a few loose business ends. Even his perpetual grimace had been a kind of metaphysic; for all that I had turned from the transcendental, it reminded me I was transcendental at heart, obstreperous poet, wine-imbiber slowly and gently subsiding into drunkenness. *And they that be drunken are drunken in the night* (*Thessalonians* 5). The pseudo-Tibullus had written something to this effect: why master what depresses one unless one has a partner in love? The sparrow on the pavement had no answer. Even so, I had a new epithet for Moonface: long-bellied. A bank of storm-cloud on the horizon, and I was watching toes curl and uncurl of girlish feet shod in flip flops, sun shades pushed back over girlish brows, as it was in every sun city of the world. Giggles and shouts. Boys looked upon all this, pretending they were not bewildered. Body parts were washing up on British Columbia beaches. It was as if we had run out of room in which to bury the dead.

Gregory was in his galley, along with Serge, who once struck me as a paramilitary type, then a philosopher, then simply a surprisingly amiable citizen of the world. Cassandra puttered about, Moonface handling the customers. It was Moonface who gave me a look of warning, her throat flushed, lips thin with alarm. Marjerie Prentiss was the cause of this alarm, her sunshades owlish—that is to say, large, she in a black chemise, jeans. She, too, wore flip flops. Straightaway her opening was pure King's Gambit; and as she drew back a chair and occupied it, as she pushed back her sunshades, her hips splendid, she said: 'You still don't like me, do you?'

A thousand souls had just perished for the sake of her accusatory tone. She sat there, her shoulders hunched, her watery eyes relentless. My, but she expected an answer. She turned down my offer of a cigarette; she had brought her own, and there they were, the cigarette pack tucked in her waist. She waited until I had rolled one, and then she lit us both up. It was as if we were stealing a smoke in a high school lavatory. Moonface, I had just noticed, had not gone away. She was standing her ground, ready to defend a comrade to her last breath. Or she might hear what Marjerie's desire was, if she hung around long enough. A toneless voice delivered it.

'A beer, please.'

'Large or small?'

'Small.'

Perhaps Marjerie supposed it was not going to be a long interview; that I would soon come to my senses in respect to her likeability. And Moonface, so I was touched to see, had no defenses against the woman, and she retreated.

'What do I have to do,' Marjerie asked, 'to make you like me?'

Whence this need on her part for legitimization, and from me, of all people, my body ridiculous, mind a liberal cesspool?

'Shall I bad-mouth the President?' I heard myself being asked. 'You'd like that,' the voice added.

'He deserves it, alright,' I said, 'but I hear you think him a great man.'

'Oh? I don't recall saying any such thing.'

'No? I thought Eleanor told me you had told her as much.'

'So Eleanor talks to you?'

'Of course, she talks to me. We're friends.'

'He is a great man.'

She blinked. It was impossible to estimate the depth of her sincerity. I felt a curious absence of sex, of any attraction I might have had for the woman's charms. It was perhaps a dangerous development, that, in her company, I was not among peasants so much as I was making deals with cynical powerbrokers. She might have just gotten out of bed, all the same, her coarse hair tousled, her eyes a little sleepy. Still, they were as animated as I had ever seen them.

'It's kill or be killed,' she said, with a genuine effort at philosophy.

Once more she blinked, her voice as solemn as a crypt.

'Et cetera,' she said, for good measure.

It was possible I grudgingly admired her quasi-independent stance, one that seemed to disdain the usual platitudes. By now, her beer had arrived by way of the good offices of Moonface, who now looked adolescent and sexless, some girl labouring in a fast food outlet. In truth, I had no idea of what to make of Marjerie Prentiss. Given the right circumstances, I supposed she could render herself pleasant, agreeable, even adorable. Yes, I could see, even if they were not materially with us, I could see Ralph and Phillip frowning, upset, wondering why I could not see what they could see—a bosom buddy loyal to their obscure cause, loads of fun. Cumulus had broken free of the horizon; from between piles of them flat cloud was spilling across the sky—storm sheen. Summery girls seemingly as light as air, even in life's ponderous embrace of them, reminded me that, yes, it was summer, no time to match wits with diabolical entities, it being, anyway, a slow news period, two weeks into August.

'Well,' I said, 'you've got the ethos down.'

'I think so.'

It was a pitiable protest on my part; her expressionless look suggested as much. If Moonface might make a politician an honest wife, Marjerie Prentiss was that politician, a Livia, a Theodara, Salome as House Speaker. Ah, here were the late lamented erotic burblings. The woman yawned.

'Beer,' she explained dully, 'it puts me to sleep.' She yawned again. 'I can see,' she said, 'you're not going to like me.'

My silence in the matter was perhaps childish.

There was nothing at stake, in any case, no outcome of war or peace, no fate of a nation, no nothing; there were but two bodies, voices attached, and there was a wondering, one might suppose, if between the two bodies there was a fit. Her curiosity, if she had any, might have been mathematical: Do one and one add up to three? My curiosity came with the dust of centuries.

And she rose as I rose; she waited as I settled the bill, Moonface disturbed. And she followed me back to the Traymore, grimly patient. And then up the stairs and then into my digs and onto my bed. She transformed herself, made of herself one of God's milder creatures, curled at my side. She studied my eyes for what I was seeing in hers. All men were Adams, and all Adams were louts—it is what her eyes were intimating, her disgust lazy, even easygoing. There was no question of sex; it was not what she came for, though why exactly she was in my bed I was never going to know. In knowing, I would only horrify myself. We simply fell asleep. My last thought was that Moonface was most certainly aghast; she divined, for all that her mind was sometimes thick, what was up and what was coming.

We had played one another to a scoreless draw, or so I supposed it could be said of us both, Marjerie Prentiss and I in this our faded Jezebel of a town; and yes, it was her town, too. It seemed I snored. In any case, reality beckoned her; it is to say she had an assignment to complete for the company that employed her.

'This isn't going to happen again,' she said on her way out.

I was not about to dispute her. Churlish of me to think it, but perhaps it was what she had, all along, wanted: to be the first to raise an expectation and then shut it down. Moral creatures or not, we certainly did not lack for pettiness of spirit. But now I was seized with a bout of loneliness. Eggy? He was having too much fun to die, and yet, I found it depressing to visit him. Dubois? He would hit on something to critique me for. Eleanor? She would only make a great show of disinterest, feeling that she had been upstaged by Prentiss and Calhoun, a pair of trapeze artists. I returned to the Blue Danube, Moonface still on shift.

'So,' she said, furiously wiping the table I claimed. 'I don't like that woman,' she let me know.

And then the penny dropped: 'You mean you slept with her?'

'Well, she was on my bed.'

She stood there betrayed, a cloth in her hand, sandy tresses spilled over her brow. Long-bellied Moonface was certainly troubled.

'We didn't have sex.'

'You're the most perverse man I've ever known.'

She went to bring me wine. It was almost reassuring, I supposed, that she could read me so well. The storm that had been building all afternoon was taking its sweet time.

Chaos was rubbing my soul raw from the inside, Marjerie Prentiss the abrasive. What had transpired between us was perfectly innocent. We were none of us innocent. Her hunger for security was so intense she would turn the world upside down so as to obtain it. With one foot throttling the neck of God, her other was firmly planted on the agenda-producing soil of realism. Meanwhile, I bore up under Moonface's censure, she among her regulars. Finally she came to me, and I may as well have been a man on death row, unjustly accused, as she said: 'Well, if you say you didn't sleep with her—'

'I told you I didn't. But it was all very odd,' I added, 'and maybe I understand her now.'

'Really?' said Moonface, too brightly. 'Oh good,' she said, schoolmarmish.

She did, in fact, seem pleased that there had been progress on that particular front, Moonface willing to see the best in everyone. It seemed I was doomed to wonder for the rest of my life: was Moonface beautiful? The heavens, as they had threatened to, opened up and poured. I had been, with my drunken eye, gauging the darkness of dark cloud over and against the darkness of the wine and the abysmal depths of human shadow. Getting out of the rain, going inside, it seemed to me I, at last, comprehended Moonface, a dear girl, waitress, once a student of Virgil's Latin. She was, on account of her sensibility or lack of one, the last line of defense against the collapse of values we imagined we still had. She did not know she was a lonely outpost and expendable. Were I a gentleman of any note, I would have advised her she was in peril. Who is to say I had not already tried? If she had fantasies of saving the world, even as she flashed her nails in the jungles of Ecuador, she had best take stock of her true situation. In the grotto that was my mind, I saw hooded figures.

Indeterminate Genus

Flying things of indeterminate genus were devouring my wardrobe. When I woke from the dream and heard the first crows and their primordial but celebratory calls I figured that, perhaps, the dream augured something good. Rebirth. Old duds disposed of. I was, spiritually-speaking, already defrocked. The evening following upon the dream (I suppose the hairy flitting things were moths of a kind, and yet, lacking mouth parts, how could they eat my attire, so, welcome to Dreamland and its peculiar natural laws?...), I sat with Dubois and Eggy on the Blue Danube terrasse, Eggy back among us. And the recipient of a little, porcelain bell, one Cassandra had provided him, Eggy rang the thing and it brought Moonface out to us.

'You rang?' she drolled.

'We want to know,' said Eggy, a raised finger looking for mischief, 'what your old boyfriends think of Sheridan.'

'None of your business.'

'Oh,' said Eggy, and then: 'Well, do they know?'

'Know what?'

'Know about Sheridan. Bloody effing hell, woman, whom else?'

Moonface was irked, Eggy relentlessly naughty. Even so, he read her mind, and he lied: 'I'm a gentleman.'

Moonface rolled her eyes and went back inside. Meanwhile, I had lost my train of thought, listening to Moonface and Eggy chaff back and forth. Dubois was now preoccupied, and what preoccupied him was the sight of the old woman who, at this hour of the evening, was always out walking her dachshund. She wore a black rainslick in the event it might rain. It was threatening to rain. The world might be coming to an end, and still, so far as she could help it, she would not deny the dog his appointment with lamp post or postal box.

'I'd say,' said Eggy, 'that our dear Moonface is playing her Sheridan false.'

'I doubt it,' I said. 'I don't think she likes things that complicated.'

'I'm inclined to agree with you,' Dubois said.

'Carroll Baker once likened a pair of glossed lips to pink sausages,' I said, tacking in a new direction.

Dubois guffawed.

'You mean the sexpot?' said Eggy, with renewed enthusiasm.

'The very same. You might have, in your 901 years, you might have run across her somewhere, if not in Rome, then in Baalbek, say.'

'I wouldn't have minded being a dog between her legs.'

Dubois, guffawing, indicated his disbelief. Moonface appeared.

'Uh oh,' said Eggy.

One could not say he had been behaving. Moonface just stood there, flashing her nails.

Going up the Traymore stairs, much pleased with the evening thus far, I heard laughter in Eleanor's digs. No doubt she and Marjerie were in session, smoking cigarettes, knocking back the amaretto. If men could find women a source of endless fascination, I supposed the reverse was true, and if men were the butt of their mirth, well, anything for a laugh. I could hardly believe they were quoting one another casualty rates for the various armed conflicts now in progress around the globe. And who had been those hooded figures, anyway, so amiable with one another, so equal to what life could throw at them, of such wit as would rival Voltairean patter? Why, they were Eggy and Dubois cosmopolitan under a patio umbrella of the Blue Danube terrasse, two stalwarts laughing their way through a dark deluge with its poetry of rain and city lights, Eggy rhyming umbrella with fella, Eggy always looking for an edge. I ran a bath. I soaked in water oily with Syrian soap the smell of which I liked. I closed my eyes, Eggy and Dubois the last true blues of a silver age, let alone an age throwing up its feeble excuses at moons as pale as jellyfish.

'Benevolent victory,' I had heard Eggy whisper at a puff of wind, at maple boughs, at passing revellers, at Dubois, his cheeks red and patterned with their hairline cracks.

Benevolent victory—it was the old Virgilian apology for Roman might. But it was as if Eggy had just prayed. The next voice I heard belonged to Moonface; it was a near musical moan.

'Hello? You in?'

I supposed I was in.

'What, no Sheridan?' I called out.

'He gave me the night off.'

Here was tacit acknowledgment, so it seemed, that sex was the primary occupation of their relationship, all other gambits so many far-flung suns of a galaxy at some incredible remove from our time and space.

'Ah,' I said, not knowing how otherwise to respond. I said, 'There's whiskey in the cupboard.'

'No thanks.'

I pulled the bathtub's plug; it was a comic sound, the consequent gurgling. Towelled and dressed my ridiculous body.

'Sorry,' said Moonface, 'I'm not interrupting anything, am I?'

'What's to interrupt? *Auditis an me ludit amabalis insania?* Horace. Loose translation: Are you hearing me, muse, or does inspiration, the pleasuring madness of, twit me?'

I could almost hear the blush that would be spreading up the Moonface neck. She had taken up, by now, the couch. She would be half-recumbent, her hips a force, her long belly a goddess's.

'Eggy's a menace with that bell. I feel like a maid in the employ of a rich old lecher.'

'He's becoming divine,' I said.

She did not care, it seemed, to pursue that line of thought.

'So, Vancouver?' I said, in light of the fact she was headed there, soon.

I was clothed and in her eyes now.

'A week from tomorrow,' she answered.

'Anything special? I mean, is there anything in particular you plan to do there?'

'Not really.'

'There's not much I can tell you about the place. I'm told I wouldn't recognize it.'

'No need.'

'You seem a little, what, pensive.'

'Life,' she said.

'As in—'

'I was happy. Now I'm sort of happy. Why is it always like this?'

She rolled her eyes up and to the side. She tugged at the ends of her hair that fell straight to her shoulders. Erotic burblings. But I put them out of mind, seeing as she had come for counsel, not that I had anything that could possibly bring her ease of mind.

'What's wrong,' I said, 'with sort of happy? Think of the millions and millions of people who lack even that.'

'I hate that argument, Q. Millions and millions of people aren't living my life.'

'Well, are you? Are you living your life? My apologies. I'm just a moody drunk. I have nothing more intelligent to offer.'

'It's the love thing, I think.'

'Oh, the love thing.'

I bit my tongue before I found myself off to the races with a notion of Plato's theory of love.

'What's your favourite part of sex?' Moonface asked.

I was astonished at the question.

'Talk to me,' she said.

'The intimacy,' I answered, playing it straight, 'but even so, we're all alone, as in really alone. The more you understand that the more you'll appreciate what you have and don't have, and why sex can both put your head up among the stars and bring you crashing down to earth.'

'Avuncular, Randall, avuncular.'

'Just trying to be of use.'

'You smell nice.'

'It's the soap.'

'Maybe I'll write a poem.'

'Why don't you?'

'Because you'll read it and laugh.'

'*Douse me with water and let the ivory pipes—*'

'Oh God. Must go.'

'That was Propertius I was mangling—'

'Who cares?'

'No one, really.'

'I'm getting snippy.'

'Well, I'm going to pour myself a whiskey and objectify my mystical bent.'

She stifled a yawn. She rose and patted my shoulder, collegially. She proceeded to my door. She turned and said: 'What if—what if nothing means anything, anymore, what do you do then?'

The tentative tone of her inquiry suggested there was something stuck in the corner of her eye. Moonface the girl could see it was an item to dread; the woman could but stammer.

'There are standard operating procedures,' I said, 'but poetry and whiskey usually do it for me.'

'And if those don't work?'

'Then you're beyond help.'

'Avuncular, Randall.'

'Shoo. Go away.'

Fuzzy and Buzzy

The oneirocritical functions of my brain were playing me silly, so I surmised, as when I dreamed I must go and write about onions. I went to the library and read up on the subject, to wit, *allium cepa*—edible bulb. The green onion, the chive, the garlic, the leek, the scallion, the shallot. Did I not know my onions? Which is to say, of what had I any expertise? *I feel all fuzzy and buzzy, said Baby Doll, Vacarro's hand presumably on her knee.* The leek was sacred to Apollo, the onion to Isis. I had enough of myself and my fuzziwuzziness in the library. The smile of the clerk at her check-out counter had all the politically correct healing properties of this week's trendiest herb. In a *certain phantasmagorical land, what is not gelded in life is neutered in death and deified on postage stamps.* Such was the reflection I carried away with me from my pilgrimage to a temple of books, the maples still, sun glorious. And on a certain noble boulevard, I ran into Dubois.

He was returning from his office, whereabouts unknown, just that I was beginning to suspect it was in the next district over of pricey boutiques and overrated restaurants. His smile said: '*We have to stop meeting like this.*'

'Just back from the library,' I said. 'I was reading up on the noble onion.'

Dubois reached for a rejoinder, but there was none immediately forthcoming. Then his smile brightened: '*Ail des bois*,' punned Dubois at the expense of his name, 'I've eaten it myself.'

We stood useless in the street. We would meet later on our favourite terrasse.

As it was at hand, I went and sat in the little park, the one shaped like the prow of a ship or an arrowhead. Pigeons, sparrows, crows. A thoughtful squirrel. Since when had I ever encountered a thoughtful squirrel? The shadows were still crisp of a late morning. One might lull oneself to sleep with thoughts of well-being, flowers bright and lively against granite and shadowed brick. The cast and crew of *Baby Doll,* in the year 1956, did not believe they had filmed anything untoward, though of course the sex as presented was pure erotic burbling, pungent, oily, sulfuric. Israelites fondly recalled the onions they had eaten in Egypt. It was here in this park I had last seen Echo, who was now, by all accounts, dulled, after a fashion, drug regimens making for vacancies in her round eyes. Miss Meow walked by in a heavy coat; she was on the arm of her newfound but smaller companion, a woman who had the look of an entity who had never known a dark moment. I supposed it was possible. Were they to pass through shadow and disappear among the dappled maple leaves, proto-angels, well, why not?—more power to them.

I enjoyed all the sports when I was a boy. Football, baseball, basketball, tennis, to be sure. There were the games we invented from which stemmed epic contests, no quarter given. We observed, I have to say, a crazy, byzantine code of justice for whenever disputes arose, and it worked. And any girl who could handle a bat was, willy-nilly, on equal footing with any male would-be slugger. One way my father had of not completely alienating my affections was to keep me well-stocked with athletic gear, and in this, no matter the neighbourhood in which we happened to reside, my popularity was vouchsafed. When one had in one's possession the toniest catcher's mitt or first baseman's trapper for blocks around, the shiniest and sleekest bats, one could count on the unfailing company of friends. From this state of affairs, though it was a gradual process, one expedited by the travails of high school, to state it briefly, I passed from 'popular' to 'loner'. Somewhere along the way, poetry reared its ugly or lovely head, depending on one's point of view. One assumed the making of it was as natural to the order of things as polishing the family car or roping calves or joining a thespian club just to be near some girl. One was shocked to discover it was not. One went on to assume that the practice of poetry was the one last, honest endeavour left to humankind. One was further shocked to discover it was not. *Whither are you whirling me away, O Bacchus, to what sacred grove et cetera?* Enough. Now and then, residence in the Traymore Rooms brought me back to my old place of esteem among fellow beings. Drinking on the Blue Danube terrasse was a kind of play; one brought to it one's stock of conversation. Even so, though Eggy wished to see the bastards hang, to politics and metaphysics he preferred sex and his loopy memories of the same. How he ran afoul of the FBI. (Dubois was skeptical of this.) How he drank with Sophia Loren in Innsbruck. And then it was Ava Gardner or Lana Turner or that minx, what was her name, oh, Natalie Wood. One knew then that Eggy was making it all up. Even so, he was an unceasing fountain of verse committed to memory. I supposed ologists had an explanation for the miracle that, in old age, in regards to memory, one's centre of gravity shifts. I, for one, believed that Eggy, were the conditions right, would recite such liturgy as was mouthed by King Numa, priestly office part of his résumé, crops, animals and marriage rites the mandate. It was Eggy who divulged to me the fact that Dubois got a kick out of my person. It was easy enough, I figured, to amuse an arch-materialist with one's shabby superstitions. As for Eleanor, I had been replaced in my role as confidante by Marjerie Prentiss, and, on occasion by Phillip Dundarave. If she was a well-camouflaged deity, which herbs were sacred to her? Once again the question arose: just how much longer could Eleanor rely on such forbearance and patience as Dubois seemed to have in spades? Though they always maintained separate digs, there was much they had done together, including travel. And now? Dubois's vanity was not the sort of vanity that fatally compromised relationships, but perhaps the man was sufficiently vain he would go about the world in his years of seniority as he did when he was boffo on campus. Moonface was not the beauty that Caroll Baker had been, but every now and then one got the look; that is to say, some power emanating from some remote fastness of her being ventured out and sampled the air, and it could turn one's knees to jelly. No doubt, the celebratory cause of sex had been grossly cheapened—too much mindless celebrity, but even Moonface might muddle through, perhaps on the strength of Eggy's traversals in the matter. Why else had she visited the old bugger nearly every morning, walking across the hall from her place to his in her pajamas and robe, to gossip and wink conspiratorially? Due to Champagne Sheridan, these visitations were now curtailed. But perhaps she had found a trail that had not long since gone cold and so, seen her way clear to a modicum of love and contentment as ought to satisfy any citizen of a phantasmagorical land. Then again, that she was in my room so recently; that she believed she had yet again found the love thing not quite as advertised—it was not the best of signs.

Caligula's excuse was that he was mad, bonkering mad; besides, he was vulnerable to every assassin's knife. We had no such excuses, we in our suburban constellations so many self-empowering, self-enabling mall cashiers with a soft spot in our hearts for drive-in churches and the winks and nods of the Unitary Executive. And then, speaking of devils, here was Eggy, behind him Moonface. There was Dubois half a block away. And lo, there were, coming from the opposite direction, Eleanor and Marjerie on the arms of Phillip Dundarave, he a yesteryear Parisian dandy squiring his debs. Now was our noble boulevard a particle smasher. Eggy hove-to at the table I occupied and seated himself. Moonface continued on inside without a word of greeting.

'My bell,' thundered Eggy.

Cassandra brought it, and it tinkled, I supposed, with undue respect for the thunderer.

And Eggy thanked her. Dubois, however, at the sight of the threesome headed his way with every intention, apparently, of stopping by the café for drinks, stopped and consulted himself as to where he stood on the matter. It was a quick consultation; he was, after all, a gamer. He resumed his progress. As Moonface might, I rolled my eyes.

And, at the next table over, the jovial threesome parked themselves.

'Hail fellows, well-met and all that rot,' Eleanor called out, feeling no pain, silly smile backlit, as it were, by her freshly gilded curls.

'Hail yourself,' Eggy responded, not in the least intimidated.

Marjerie Prentiss said nothing, her eyes on Dubois, who now gained the terrasse, his eyes searching Eleanor, then Eggy and I. It was an embarrassment of riches: at which table should he park? It seemed to hit him then: he was going to be gamed, no matter which table he chose.

'Effing hell, sit down, you twit,' thundered Eggy, deciding for him.

'Hey, Bob,' said Eleanor, '*didja know those who do it more live longer*?'

There was pain in her voice, and derision too. Pain and derision manifested in her now and then, like monsoon rains. There was in the eyes of Bob Dubois a sudden hunger for peace and quiet.

Moonface stepped out to see what we wanted to drink. My eyes caught the promise of a breast sheathed in its cup. If she noticed, she did not let on. Otherwise, she was not in good humour. She collected our orders.

'Did you see that?' asked Eggy.

'See what?' said Dubois.

'Her eyes. They're all purple underneath.'

'No sleep,' I said.

'Maybe her Sheridan beat her about,' Eggy suggested.

'You sure have an imagination,' observed Dubois.

'I do not. Effing hell.'

Then to me, Eggy put this question: 'Do you think she's going to find herself?'

'Who knows,' I shrugged, 'it's not easy to tell about her. She's a chameleon.'

'You're always saying that,' said Eggy, 'but I tell you what, it's the rain in Spain. Bloody effing hell, no one pays me any mind.'

And I did not think Phillip meant anything by it when he, perversely Anglo, remarked that for every by-law the English dreamed up, the other official half of the polity dreamed up three. Dubois seethed. It was an assault on the fact he had elected to live his life by enlightened rules. Eleanor laughed. Eleanor shook a pompadoured foot, one in solidarity, perhaps, with the wrong faction. From such a one as Eggy, Dubois might accept insults, but Eggy was the limit. The sight of Eleanor's ankle erring on the side of a cheap shot might have vexed me as well, had I the pleasure of her intimacies as Dubois certainly had, and for once, I believed he loved her. His chin about to raise his chest, Eggy perked up his ears; even he could sense something was amiss with remarks that would have been, otherwise, so much barnyard noise. Marjerie studied Dubois, as did Phillip, realizing now, inadvertently or not, he had rung someone's bell. Moonface brought beer and wine, and no, she had no sense of who might prevail in the American general election; in Canada, however, Current PM would hold his position. Sometimes, it was like this: she spoke as if she had authority on the subject at hand. Eleanor, I believed, had no idea with what incendiary material she was playing. Marjerie sat there, a woman quietly supreme among rivals, snipping at yet another sinew of Phillip's self-respect. And by this or that gesture, she staged her charms to advantage, my sinews in no better shape than overused and brittle elastics. Dubois took a deep breath. His tone unusually pedantic, even for him, he began to patiently explain the weaknesses each of Harper and Dion, gladiatorial opponents in a possible snap election. Rotweiler versus unicorn. I said, more in hopes of forestalling hostilities than in advancing the cause of understanding: 'But with the one, all one hears are the shutting tight of sphincters. The man's what they call a control-freak. And what with his glass jaw, should anyone actually manage to deliver a hit, and no one's managed it yet, he'll shatter. Trudeau, Chrétien—they could shrug things off.'

Dubois's guffaw should have been more full-bodied; it came off as a squeal.

Eggy, raising his finger, thundered: 'Yes but—'

He lost his train of thought. The cumulus above was impressive.

'Yes but, well, Mulroney, you know, and, effing hell, have you ever seen Mila shop? I have.'

And Eggy was grim with self-satisfaction, he who had had drinks with Sophia Loren or somebody in Innsbruck, and had seen the wife of an ex-prime minister buy herself shoes. What sort of homeopathies would have had favour at Caligula's court?

Quiet Night

I left the Blue Danube, the wild west show of the terrasse, the Roman bacchanal, beer-tent aspect of it all; Dubois going on about Chrétien the knife fighter, Eggy the Balfour Declaration. I was drifting into virtue and self-righteousness—always dangerous, inwardly moping on account of the waning prospects for truth-telling in the U.S. of A., my alma mater, as it were; that the citizens there wanted change, but not so much change as would compromise their lines of credit. And I knew I was profligate, oh, not with money, perhaps, but with matters of the spirit; that I pursued the pleasures; that I was, even so, cenobitic; that I was half-infatuated, still, with Moonface, even as I could see she was lost, was awfully confused, *and inappropriate*; that I could see my failures in her eyes that now and then claimed me as their trophy. As for the future in a general sense, that one whose bones public intellectuals were already fighting over even as we spoke, it was as if I lacked the social skills for the forced marches out of bondage that were imminent. Eleanor, Marjerie and Phillip occupied an echo chamber of their own; relations had grown elaborate between them, this much was obvious, though I could not follow every turn of their talk. But it seemed Marjerie had had an abortion when she was not yet beyond her teens, and that Phillip, well, he had every intention of doing right by his daughter. Eleanor, I supposed, fulfilled the role of den mother, supplied cookies and lemonade for such intrepid scouts as made it home from each their rites of passage, merit badges in hand; and I was a little surprised and a trifle vexed when Eleanor appeared at my door, looking disconsolate. She was armed with amaretto; it was her peace offering though war was as yet undeclared, its objectives, in any case, ineffable. I should have done the good woman the courtesy of a show of compassion when she confessed that, yes, she had been behaving like a jerk. My silence in the matter caused shadows to gather in her eyes (and I could never get to the bottom of their true colour—gray, green, flecks of topaz?). She looked as summery as she had an hour ago, looked sumptuous in her blouse and denims; her allure, the guarantor of dreams now largely irrelevant, given what had shifted over the past years, less viable in the winner-take-all economies of desire. Eleanor commandeered the couch; I got us drinking glasses.

'Yes,' said Eleanor, 'I've been a shit. Well, aren't you going to say something?'

'Don't know what to say,' I replied.

'You're always saying something—'

'That doesn't mean I'm saying anything—'

If I was ridiculous and she sumptuous, we were both veering toward the absurd.

'Bob loves you,' I said.

'So what that he loves me, he won't marry me.'

'Well, I've run out of grand things to say for love,' I said, 'just that, in the end, in spite of everything, we do come to care for each other. I don't know how, I don't know why, but it happens. Cynic that I am, I have to say it seems to me this fact sometimes defies all odds.'

'You're not a cynic. You're a romantic, and a damn fool.'

'Alright, Bob doesn't love you, but he cares for you.'

'What do you mean, he doesn't love me?'

I wished to believe in Moonface's theatre of self-empowerment; that is to say, I wished to believe she was truly proud, and not just putting on a show for her various mentors. Boffo spoke, and he sounded more like some dreaded grief counsellor than a circus performer afflicted with a perpetual case of the giggles: 'Your desire for marriage is a chimera. You want a prize, not a husband. True, the one addresses some need in you, but the other would—'

'Calhoun, for God's sake, you've gotten boring. Either kiss me, say something that matters, or get off the proverbial pot.'

'Why would I want to kiss you?'

'Because you want to.'

'What makes you say that?'

'Because all men want to kiss me. Because I don't mind that all men want to kiss me, only I don't necessarily want to kiss all of them.'

'What would you say if I said, no, I don't want to kiss you, at least not now.'

'I'd say it again: you're a damn fool.'

'I'd say I don't want any trouble.'

'That's all men want from a woman: no trouble. That's what Bob wants from me: no trouble.'

'Perhaps.'

'Oh, perhaps to you, too.'

'You don't do me justice.'

'You're so, I don't know what, so prissy, sometimes. Effing Quaker.'

'Thanks for that.'

'Alright, Randall, I'll simmer down. Can't hurt for a girl to try. It was Marjerie's estimation, by the way, that you're prissy.'

'What does she know? She's a piranha in a goldfish bowl. Everyone's prissy to her. She thinks she's the antidote to political correctness, liberal puritanism.'

'You really don't like her.'

'No.'

'I suppose I love Bob. No, I do. He was a great travelling companion. We haven't travelled in a while.'

'He carried your luggage, did he?'

'There he is, the real Randall, sarcastic to the bone, even if he is a dreamer.'

'It's the true condition of the poet.'

'Poet schmoet.'

We were almost managing it, pure dialogue, one untrammelled with the machinations of thought.

'You can't change the world, you know,' so the good woman reminded me.

'I never expected to. I'm still holding out for a little justice, though.'

'Good luck.'

Ah, Eleanor. What man in his right mind could turn her down? Perhaps Dubois was not in his right mind, or else he was too greedy or too finicky in his terms. I lacked the energy with which to push back against her egoism, lack of energy my age-old excuse. Even so, I did not really mind it, her egoism, and, as such, it was much to be preferred to the hubris of civilians playing at generals or generals shining up their ribbons and stars. Our wretchedness consisted of, and here I was the cynic, if nothing else, of some capacity for truth-telling, of our existential isolations, of such bliss as never frees us from mortality. And when Lucretius, for example, was in his writings sanguine in the face of death, I did not believe him, though I might for a moment admire his Roman pluck. Eleanor, realizing the conversation had run its course, was rather reluctant to clear off the couch, hideous item of furniture, its colour bordello green, an item of furniture in which I took perverse pride. We had not even broken into the amaretto; I had not kissed her when I might have been welcome to; I had not insisted she go. She just knew. When the woman was right she was right, and she knew.

'It was a hoot,' she drolled.

She was more tired, I suspected, than she realized. I must have hallucinated: for a moment I was looking not at Eleanor's comfortable countenance but, rather at, Prentiss's grinning visage. The Prentiss entourage had been, perhaps, taking its toll on us both. Soon enough, I would hear Eggy and Dubois on Traymorean stairs. The bloody effing hells. The *Come on, man, lift your foot.* I might hear Moonface, too, if she were not spending the night with her Champagne Sheridan in righteous sin. I doubted that Mrs Petrova gave her tenants a moment's thought, she a woman of an entirely different order of obsessions in comparison to ours, her origins a great deal more troubled, ours getting to be troubled, here in Canada, in the prop wash of American realities.

'Well, I guess I'll take myself off.'

Well, I guess she would.

'Maybe I'll throw a party,' I said, right at the end.

'Why don't you do that?' said Eleanor, a hint of frustrated justice in her voice, 'I might even cook something, if you ask me nicely enough.'

The Love Book of Marjerie J Prentiss

Haitian women, dressed for church, waited for bus service. Secular moms with tots in tow hung out together at the health food store. Singularities drank coffee at outdoor tables catering to those in the loop. For all that, it was ragtag St Tropez up and down the street, though what one was to think of the bag lady, sorrowfully scrutinizing a pizza flyer on a park bench, one was not sure. I had abandoned my writing project. For in my jottings I would have itemized every commercial sign, the retail bent of every shop, took note of such humankind as graced the poor man's super mart where I had gone for bread. Too much bother, those jottings. But it was in the mart where I ran into Eleanor, who regarded me with something like a chill to her countenance. I was not, I suspected, in her best books. As we stood by a shelf of jams and marmalades, she let me know that, in general, I lacked the courage to deal with the real world, unlike Bob, for instance, who had wiles to match its wiles. I did not doubt it. Be that as it may, in view of my one very serious shortfall of character, to go with so many lesser ones, Eleanor, however, relaxed her critique, chortled and said: 'I've seen something you have to see to believe.'

Well, this was mysterious.

'I'm supposed to keep it to myself. But you know me, and besides, you could use a treat.'

Which would be, what, news that Current President had fallen off the wagon or that Palestine had gotten its state?

'But later,' she said.

She was buying aubergines.

'Later,' she repeated, 'at the terrasse. If Eggy's there, he may as well hear of it, too. It'll curl his toes.'

As for Dubois, he was gone to Boston for reasons of business. He had got it in his head to rent a car and drive the distance. All this had come about of a sudden, the details of which were initially unknown to Eleanor.

'No matter,' she said, disguising her disappointment, 'that's Bob. He's still got the get up and go. I like that in a man.'

So why was she so besotted with Dundarave, a layabout like myself, so far as I could tell, only that he tiptoed through the tulips without literary polish? We returned some way together until she detoured into the drug store, for toiletries, as she put it, and I went on alone. I would have liked to believe that the Jamaican speedster, the fellow who had just smashed the world record for the 100 metres, *who flew it*, had grown up poor and unscientifically. For he ran the last 10 metres like a child, one ecstatic, without regard for technique or regimen. Perhaps it was so. It was, in any case, a stunning performance, one for the ages, as it were, the event wanting its Pindar, strophe and antistrophe of heart and grit and God-gift, as well as mention of a tiny nation's GNP.

One of life's worst fears was not so much to die having accomplished nothing, but to have barked up a wrong tree with one's ambitions and labours. All those rigours, all those expectations, let alone the accidents of love and the hazards of sex—all beside the point. Of course, I was, as self-described, a cynic; as such I was anathema to the Civic Smile. Was I to posit that the gateway to Unipolar Dominance was Central Asia, the Middle East a side show, would it make of me a think-tanker in pancake makeup, Mr and Mrs Civic Smile parked in front of their TV, nodding gravely in agreement? And was it not just a little obscene, comparing the weekend receipts of one blockbuster flick compared to the gross take of another? Was it not just a trifle celebratory of spiritual suicide? (The cynic in me was thinking now that Illinois senator would not prevail; he was not enough of a grotesque as was his rival, for all that there was in him a bit of the schoolmarm or the prig.) When I got to Le Grec aka the Blue Danube, a faith group, along with squirming, noisome, obnoxious brats, had taken over the place. Moonface, usually so accommodating, was disgusted. Cassandra was panicked, Gregory and Serge in the galley officers of a submarine undergoing depth charges. Back from yet another tour of a culture-deprived geographical entity, Blind Musician was trapped with Miss Meow at a table, high water rising higher. The one personage despised the other. Perhaps the faith group regarded the whistling and stomping Whistler as a manifestation of the Holy

Spirit, but even he appeared somewhat nervous. I retreated to the terrasse, and with my eyes gunned off any overzealous child with proprietary designs. Mothers had already thrown in the towel. Poor Moonface. Here was a moment of truth for her diary, that nothing she would encounter in Ecuador could possibly imperil her as much as what was swirling about her knees. Mothers in flip flops and shorts. Fathers in baseball caps. Mood pills and God-providing. And she stepping out to see what I wished, was coming up for air.

'Stick around,' she said, her mouth drawn tight, 'I may need you.'

Beach volleyball was on the flat-screen TV. Build it and they would show.

Well, I was curious to see what Eleanor had in store for me by way of a treat; she seemed to be taking her sweet time. I ordered coffee from the dear girl, then had recourse to a book of verse. It was one I had had lying around and not yet investigated. I read: *Rein in your mares and weep, for a love and a campsite—*

A hot breeze seethed amidst the maples leaves. And Eleanor, when she, at last, showed, took one look at the doings in the café and shuddered.

'Oh my,' she said, 'feeding time at the zoo.'

Had it been any woman other than Prentiss, I might have applauded the intention. It seemed she, too, kept a notebook, but one in which she recorded her sexual dealings with men and rated their performances; one in which she listed their physical charms as well as their peculiarities. As in *So-and-So's left testicle hung lower than his right. Or that So-and-So was a good kisser, but his breath*... And so forth and so on. But to have entitled this dossier as The *Lovebook of Majerie J Prentiss* seemed overly grandiloquent.

'You're kidding,' I said to Eleanor.

'Oh no, it's for real. What's more, she has headings for you, Eggy, and Bob.'

'Surely, she doesn't intend to sleep with Eggy,' I said, incredulous.

'Of course not. Eggy is, so she said to me in that way she has of saying things, beyond the pale. She thinks you and Bob are prissies. Too stuck on yourselves. Need treatment.'

'What treatment?'

'She didn't say.'

And Eleanor did not know for what the initial *J* stood, the *J* that separated the sex enthusiast Marjerie from the empirically-minded Prentiss of a name.

I wondered what Prentiss would make of a certain Gerald of my Polson High days, the boy who was addicted to weight-lifting and something of an exhibitionist? He was hopeless at football, just that he would whip out his immense manhood whenever Sally McCabe was conveniently in view; and she, surely as much the empiricist as Prentiss, would smile and say, 'Impressive, Gerald. Very impressive. But your timing is a little suspect.' In any case, the surprise element Eleanor had promised me was now a stale prospect; and the fact that Eggy had now joined us was also ruinous to revelation and further wonderment. He looked to be establishing a moustache on his inverted triangle of a face, or else he no longer cared to bother with shaving. He was exercised with *them Russkies,* so he hoo hooed it, old Cold War warrior that he was; and who, after Georgia, was next? Poland? The Ukraine? There were bastards who ought to hang, yes, but they were not necessarily such luminaries as once lit up Russia's political class in by-gone times.

'Jill,' I said, 'or, God help us, Josephine.'

'Jasmine would be worse,' Eleanor reflected.

Eggy gave us both a look with his darkening countenance.

'Why, what's in a name?' he huffed, having no idea, even so, what we were on about.

Then Eleanor volunteered other news. Dubois had been detained at the border for a considerable time; had been subjected to unpleasant questions all because *Robert Dubois* showed up in the computer and was, at it were, red-flagged. He phoned Eleanor, afterwards, from somewhere in Vermont, put out enough to consider turning around and denying the U.S. of A. the boon of his cash and credit card and business savvy.

'He was not a happy camper,' said Eleanor.

'Imagine that,' crowed Eggy, 'Bob a terrorist.'

'He's mad enough to blow something up now,' Eleanor observed, and then added: 'Pig. Well, that's what Bob said, only in French.'

'*Cochon*,' said Eggy, who knew a few of the more picturesque words, his finger raised.

In the meantime, the faith group had dispersed; they had subjected Blue Danubian staff to terrorism of a kind, so much so, Gregory, Cassandra and Serge were exchanging words in Greek while Moonface doggedly cleared tables, in English, one assumed.

'But,' said Eleanor, reverting to our earlier topic of discussion, 'what woman would keep tabs like that?'

'Like I said, an empiricist,' I answered. 'And why not? Just that Prentiss is a mean spirit and has a false estimation of her own qualities.'

'And Montcalm threw the battle,' Eggy said, apropos of so very little.

'I don't know,' said Eleanor, 'love book? Sex book is more like it. All the men she's slept with. Their inclinations. Their perversions. I mean—'

'Yes but,' Eggy piped up, 'every Madame of every whore house in every world capital has their little notebook. Big bucks, you know.'

Eggy was most pleased with himself, this worldly-wise, tiny sparrow of a man.

'She swore me to silence,' said Eleanor.

'Oh she knew you'd talk,' Eggy observed, then went on to say: 'But I don't know the woman. Comely wench.'

I wondered aloud if the so-called love book was not trimmed in gold leaf and leather-bound, as would befit a genealogy of sorts, or state secrets. I wondered, too, how long I would remain a blank entry in it. My wondering was truncated, Eleanor snorting: 'You don't seem to think it's all a little bizarre? Don't you think it's bizarre? I do.'

'The rain in Spain,' observed Eggy.

'Maybe she's researching a novel,' I said.

This put Eleanor's pompadoured foot to increased agitation.

'Judith,' I said, 'Julia.'

'Jackie,' said Eleanor, gone absent-minded.

'Yes but,' said Eggy, 'here's one: Jezebel.'

The old bugger hoo hooed in this his faded Jezebel of a town, his finger raised in exclamatory mode. Eleanor and I, we gave him a look.

'Jan,' I offered, wearying of the game.

And Moonface came out to ascertain how it was with us, though Eggy had yet to tinkle his bell. The humidity was stinky, the maples looking a shade less splendid, looking rattier. Soon enough, however, one would awake to their autumn vestments, and one would be consumed once more with dread and awe, courtesy of the passage of time.

Innocent Cute

I was summoned to Eleanor's kitchen, that commodious room, finest, perhaps, of all the Traymore Rooms, barring Mrs Petrova's suite below. Marjerie Prentiss, knocking at my door, issued the writ, she looking sharp at a mid-morning hour, ready to do battle in a world all corporate mergers. Red, sleeveless blouse, collar raised, the two ends of which seemed to nestle her chin. Kim Novak look.

'Your presence is required,' she said, her voice a dull boom.

She did not bother to indicate where, exactly, my presence was required; it was assumed I knew. She was a *grand vizier* of the female sex, smug and lethal. She turned so as to retrace her steps, her body, sylph-like, presenting challenge. It was not, I figured, that she always had sex on the brain, just that there was no such thing as chance in her universe. And there was no contest she might engage of which she could possibly get the worst. Passing through Eleanor's comfortably cluttered living room, I feared for its occupant. There was a zone, so to speak, where the pursuit of the pleasures bespoke the virtues of intelligence and kindly regard; there was a borderland that delimited the zone on the other side of which was only vice without sensibility, human feeling at risk.

And it was a Rembrandtian scene, at first glance: Marjerie, Ralph, Eleanor at table. Phillip stood behind Eleanor, his arms loosely slung over the good woman's shoulders, the grin on his face brazen. And Marjerie's eyes told me that while she did not object to this two-person tableau, there would be a price to pay for it, eventually. I was incensed. The table offered amaretto, whiskey, beer, packs of cigarettes. A nondescript blues band played nondescript blues on the radio, the very music I could not bear.

'Randall,' said Eleanor, greeting me, her leer apologetic. 'Here's the thing. What we want to know is this—'

Her voice was dangerously thick.

'Yes,' said Marjerie, attempting levity, 'we want to know—'

'We want to know,' Eleanor continued, 'whether it's Tuh-blisi or Tee-blisi.'

'Teh-blisi,' said Marjerie, who considered herself something of an expert on geo-political realities.

'I have no idea,' I answered, cheerful and urbane in a pit of vipers.

'What in hell does it matter?' said Phillip, perfectly sensible.

'Because,' said Ralph, with the tone of a concerned citizen, 'we're talking the next world war.'

'Oh rot,' said Eleanor.

'Shove over some balm,' she commanded of no one in particular, and Marjerie, grabbing the amaretto by its vessel's neck, emptied some of its fiery sweetness into Eleanor's glass.

'You poor dear,' she said, 'you've gone dry.'

'Catastrophe,' Eleanor agreed.

She looked up at Phillip and puckered her lips.

'But that's enough now,' she added, ridding her shoulders of his arms. 'I am, after all, spoken for. I might be kind of loose, you know, but I'm no push-over.'

'Oh no,' Marjerie boomed, 'perish the thought.'

Phillip took a chair with the air of a man who would live to fight another day.

'Well,' said Eleanor, regarding me, 'what are you bloody good for?'

'He imagines he's a thinker or some such rot,' she said to Ms Prentiss, 'a poh-weet.'

'Indeed,' a voice boomed.

My damnation was forthcoming, and when it came, it went like this, the judgment Eleanor's.

'You know, I've had him in my clutches and he gets right sprightly, you know, real spright. But he's a reluctant hoser. *Ah hates a re-luck-tant hoser.* It means some jackass is looking down on you all the while you've got your hands in its pants.'

'My, my,' boomed that voice in its subterranean depths.

Ralph and Phillip did not envy me my status. I had business elsewhere.

§

Book V—*Scéance*

What Eggy Knows

—My first words to Eggy of an evening are '*capote anglaise*', and the old man replies, 'Oh, those bloody things.' The words are, in any case, obsolete, their Portuguese equivalent—shirt, perhaps, or blouse of Venus, I am only guessing—also unjustifiably extinct. Nevertheless, under a canopy of maple boughs, the Blue Danube terrasse is busy; the air is rich with silky voices, some of which hold forth on the games in Beijing, some on love and men and lawyering. Eggy, meanwhile, knows his Stuarts, his Williams and Annes, his South Sea scams, his Treaties of Utrecht, this homuncular Zeus of infinite consciousness. He, so I belatedly realize, has been keeping me young. And now that Gregory, Elias and Cassandra have had their write-up in a restaurant review, the terrasse has been attracting customers somewhat more worldly than your nunnish Miss Meow, though perhaps Blind Musician has trotted his Scots burr and violin all over the globe; though the Whistler may have been a warrior for the Israeli air force. Gentleman Jim, his presence sporadic of late, even so, would not look out of place in an impressionistic depiction of an exotic drunk, his pessimism riding the green-feathered wings of an exotic drink, his missions all kamikaze. Too Tall Poet does not easily cavort with the demimonde. Our local high-flyers are, in any case, leery of him, his stratospheric noggin as if top-hatted like Ahab, his hand occupied with an harpoon. For all that, Cassandra is run off her feet. Dubois, almost absurd in cargo pants, sockless in yachting sneakers, come now on the scene, catches her eye and she runs her hand through her purple hair and nods and will bring on a half pint, no words necessary. Just back from Boston, he has showered and is among us. He has not much to say, not even on the subject of his having been detained at the border and hassled beyond reason. He just indicates they are nuts down there, gone overboard with the patriot game. He is pleased to be back among his bilingual roots, where, though church and state were once joined at the hip, one was not so brainwashed in one's youth as are the Yanks forever talking about their generations in sermon and song. Once Blind Willie Johnson rumbled: *Trouble will soon be over, sorrow will have an end.*

—'Effing hell,' as Eggy might say, 'life is no journey; it's a hijacking.' Marjerie Prentiss? What is it with this pseudo-Traymorean? She has done nothing especially bad, though men dance on the strings she pulls. She is not unique in this, and so long as there are men who are up for it, there will be women to oblige. But no, she is no Ava Gardner shimmying with her beach boys on the beach, as Prentiss has not a shred of honour in her soul. She is not stupid, nor is she particularly brilliant; she observes the means, tenaciously so, dull in her ceaseless machinations. She has not the power to ruin a state, let alone a cottage industry, and yet, she is in her person a reflection of those women who do enjoy such power. There is no deeper devotion a man may experience than that which a strong-willed woman of incorruptible justice might elicit from him. Was New York senator such a woman, calling on Americans to give her the White House? Or was it too much to ask—that she be both ambitious and just and in the fray for the good of the country? Eleanor, of course, is a babe with the cunning of a ward boss. She approaches her mid-way point in life, lacking ambition. Her intransigence is, perhaps, her acknowledgment that she might have gone further in life and did not. The indifference with which Dubois regards her fooling around must be especially galling to her. I would happily hand her gavel and gown and let her preside over the inanities, but she would rather cook up poutine and playfully twit Dubois for being her almost perfect love mate. Some dismiss it as pillow talk; others call it love, the kind that seemingly aches forever in the heart. No one has heard from Moonface. We are given, we Traymoreans, to understand that, for the dear girl, Vancouver is a test of sorts.

—When Nero bade his retainers go and bugger with his blessing, he was moral. When the thirteenth apostle bade the opposite, to marry, for instance, as a last resort, he, too, fulfilled the requirements of moral logic.

Moral is maxim backed by the loudest, most sustained voices; if necessary, it is backed by might. Moral is *force majeures*. Moral is trivializing Jane Austen as having been very, very smart.

—Eggy, sporting a bib, peers speculatively at a plate of four miniature cheese pies. Dinnertime at Le Grec aka the Blue Danube. Serge, horsing around with the radio, lingers a moment on a station putting out an aria. Placido, so I reckon. There is soccer on the TV. In the hands of Dubois, fork and knife meet over the body of a steak. '65 years,' says Eggy, 'why, they're 65 years behind. You know, health insurance.' Eggy's America. Dubois, always in the vanguard, nods assent as he chisels himself a morsel of meat. I have gone overboard again, to his way of thinking. Americans are not that stupid, that craven. 'I'll believe they're serious,' I say, 'when they own up to Iraq. Otherwise, nothing will change.' '*Plus ca change, plus c'est la meme chose,'* says Eggy, finger raised. Dubois is somewhat restive at this foray into his mother tongue. The café is otherwise empty. Gregory, Elias, Serge—they huddle and watch European sport. Beautiful girls go by in the evening shadows. Here is the old woman and her dachshund. What, does the mutt smell some debacle in the offing? Cassandra, who has been tending to the plants on the terrasse, who stands alone there surrounded by a vast tract of darkening dune, alone, alone in the whole wide world, looks up at the twilight blue, sweeping it with her lovely, large eyes. She expels breath which she had swallowed and held in.

—As a teenager, I thought *Sexus* pretty much the work of a clown. America, it is said, had a genius for community. Tell the Sioux another.

Brava!

—Oligarchs: the necessary evil in every system. Augustus Caesar gave the world its greatest object lesson in the getting and the keeping and the maintaining of power. The American genius, so say its champions, is that power may pass peacefully from hand to hand, is, in effect, distributed and balanced. A partial picture of the reality. A picture explaining less and less. Devotees of transcendental politics will, eventually, have to play the game. Bare knuckles, 'mom' inscribed on one. My sense of futility deepens. Prentiss cannot bear the fact that Eleanor, despite her greed and insecurities, does not bring pathology to her practice of sex. *Brava!* Eggy snoozes inside the Blue Danube, Zeus-like. Roman Zeus was no true Zeus, too busy being august; that that other Zeus was ill-organized and partisan and inclined to dalliance. 'I'm so lonely,' croons a pathetic radio voice, that of an emotionally expressive male. I jot these words with hooded figures and the gardens of Lucullus in mind. In those palatial shadows sex was achieved and, perhaps, *libertas* died.

—So Dubois tells us he played baseball in his Shawinigan youth. And I should read Fregault for Quebec's history, should I wish to take it as seriously. Eggy, it appears, was never an athlete except, perhaps, in bed, and Manifest Destiny was, you know, the Philippines. Seems the last car he owned (he clocked 180,000 miles with it) was a brown Ford Comet, two-door, and in this chariot he went to see where Washington crossed the Delaware; he was pleased to have done so. Bloody effing hell. We occupy the Blue Danube like a trio of bibulous Hessians, we Traymoreans, hail fellow, well met, and all that. What sort of word is *scéance*? Why does it not appear in my Dictionnaire LAROUSSE? 'Well, it's what we're doing here,' says Dubois, 'being kind of minor, not quite a full-blown spectacle.' So far as I can see, he has no envy of American dynamism, and who knows, but that maybe China now rates the palm on that score, given the Olympics just concluded, rave performance; and neither can I see Eleanor in his eyes. Perhaps, what with the Prentiss woman and her beach boys hanging about in Eleanor's kitchen, Dubois cannot get a word in edgewise, let alone a foot through the door.

—The cynic is on the right side of history until, *mutatis mutandis*, he is on the wrong side, twitted, pitied, derided. Illinois senator, by acclamation, is the man of the hour.

Antonio

—Old Eggy would not have rice on his plate. 'Take that away,' he thundered. Antonio, the new waiter, an Albanian, shrugged. 'So, don't eat it,' I suggested. Dubois told the homuncular grotesque to behave. 'I don't want it. What a mess. Don't even want to look at it,' Eggy wailed, his voice rising against the ruckus in Le Grec aka the Blue Danube. Busy night. Even so,

Antonio beatifically smiled, bent down, cradled a Zeus-like pate with his arm and kissed the brow; it chuffed Eggy even further. 'What, are you queer on top of everything else?'

—Marjerie, Ralph and Phillip—perhaps they groom one another before initiating sex. Perhaps they burn votive candles to Venusian spirits such as hold sway over the various regions of male and female anatomy, ensuring optimal performance. Perhaps they are throwbacks each to the Sixties when a new comedy of manners arose from this or that college campus, authority snubbed, curriculum trashed, the Pentagon evil, and then the resorting to communal strictures. I do not mean to second-guess the results, let alone ridicule the presumptions, and there were many such presumptions; just that those shoes all Hansel, Hansel and Gretel outside Marjerie's door; shoes that say times are tough but we will get through this and live happily ever after, seem an affront to Traymorean sensibilities. Eggy is having too much fun to die. Moonface boffs the boys, no question, but hush hushly. *A sweet Tuxedo girl you see, Queen of swell society, fond of fun as fun can be, When it's on the strict Q.T.*

—I settle for an afternoon of Tacitus and baseball on TV. The Optimates. The neocons. The merits of first pitch fastball hitting. *'It's the most hitable pitch you're likely to get. If it's in your zone, drive it somewhere.'* As per Tacitus, hacks will commit any crime for advancement. Lawyers lawyer, preening and stropping. If Moonface is back in town, she has gone with her Champagne Sheridan straight to his place. It suggests they may as well be married. The Jays chase the Yankee hurler to the showers. Tiberius Caesar slips into seclusion at Capri. To pursue, one imagines, the existential side of rule; to appease the inner demons. Sejanus, his right arm, then lords it over Rome as the worst sort of cockatoo, playing all ends against the middle, whipping up bloodlust, keeping the Imperial Mind in the dark. A voice dully booms in the Traymore hall: 'Bring back some chips, too.' She may as well have said: 'Bring back So-and-So's head.' One of her corsairs is on a beer run. Evie Longoria has the grace of one who was at least loved, but that life has a way of, well, interjecting nasty little surprises.

—We were silly out on the terrasse, Dubois, Eggy and I talking of Moonface. Eggy: 'I'd just smack her bottom. Effing hell.' Dubois searched for the Grand Cause such as might explain the lesser effects of Moonface behaviour: 'Her epilepsy might explain her suppressed anxieties.' 'Her father,' said Eggy, 'it's her father. Deadbeat. United Church. And the mother's a loon. Why, she's apparently a qualified academic. What qualified academic goes and hides in Sudbury?' 'Is there a bar in this province,' I asked, 'where you have not imbibed?' 'I swear he can smell them from miles away,' remarked Dubois. It was Breughelian on the terrasse.

—Eggy lets it be known Evie Longoria will come clean his digs once a week. She could use the supplemental income. Still no sign of Moonface. Already, it is a scorcher of a day. At the poor man's super mart, it occurs to me to put it to myself, as I test the nectarines: *what may we lovers not expect?* Ralph and Phillip plan to scavenge Fast Eddy's old place for its oak. I have run into them, hearing out their plans. Erotic burblings as Marjerie emerges from an aisle of tinned goods. 'Hullo.' The dull booming voice. The sound system pipes *Hotel California.*

—It has been written, recorded, painted, in a hundred ways depicted; catalogued, downloaded as items *X*, *Y* and *Z*—every iota of perversion humankind has set loose on the world. And when one would meet with it, surround its parameters with words wise or unwise; when one would troll for it in one's own inner deeps; when one would simply ologize, 'This is it and this is how it works', one, in the end, knows even less. One may as well squeeze photons into a tube of toothpaste. Antonio, speaking of Eggy, says, 'That little man, he's *fonny*.'

—Eggy, his countenance pained (and when a man is Zeus-like and, still, he fears extinction, it is not a sight for the faint of heart), presents me with a riddler. If I had my life to live over again, would I go for it? He expects a straight-up answer. Well, an instant of time might last an eternity. Eight years of a malignant presidency may elapse in the blink of an eye. We are a few minutes shy of total sunset. It is 30 degrees Celsius. Wine. Eggy's plate of little cheese pies. A tall woman goes by in a pale yellow frock, her eyes glassy with the inferno. Dubois paces the sidewalk, smoking a cigarette. Otherwise, yes, his mood is upbeat: Americans are finally coming to their senses, and there it is, his faith in the innate good sense of the people justified. I am, predictably enough, not so sanguine. In any case, here is Eggy, his tough old eyes fixed on mine. 'Well?' he says. 'I asked you a question,' he reminds me. 'Indeed, you did,' I answer, not stalling, not rehearsing a reply so much as I am staring at some particularly abysmal sector of my mentations. He is such a tiny sparrow of man, this Eggy. His one eye is rage; the other features sorrow. Yes, it is rather like this: some rare alignment of celestial bodies, those eyes. 'No,' I say, 'why live it over again? Handed another life to live, one will muck it up anyway. I should think once around the park is enough for any insufferable ego. Progress? Tell me another.' Eggy shudders. That he shudders disconcerts me. I hope I have not been overly flippant. 'Yes but,' he raises his finger, 'yes, I'll say to you, I'll say that for someone like me, born on the wrong side of the tracks, you know, well, that I married the daughter of a bank manager, that's something, don't you think?' Well, it is the first I have heard of it, as whenever Eggy invokes his past, there are just 'wives' in the generic sense of wife, and spawn. I nod my assent. I have nothing, at any rate, to say. It is too hot for riddles. Antonio, the new waiter, asks if we want coffee. 'No, six virgins,' thunders Eggy, 'and a piece of heaven.' 'Six virgins? What is this?' asks a waiter, his accent thick with incredulity. 'Well, what do you think? Six virgins? Effing hell. Do I have to spell it out? Oh, just bring the coffee. Bloody Albanian.' Antonio bends down, kisses the Eggy pate. Eggy protests. The wine in me reaches up for the highest hanging fruit.

—And still no sign of Moonface. Perhaps she came in the dead of night for her change of underwear.

Letter to Emma MacReady (aka Moonface)

Dear Emma, Before I begin to fulminate and froth, let me say I hear the trip went well. Now it's on for Ecuador, no? If so, when? Of course, you don't tell me anything. You were missed.—RQC

Letter to Gentleman Jim (surname unknown)

Dear Jim, I think you've drawn a line in the sand, as it were, the bottle your improvised explosive device. Now the ologists, of course, will state you only commit violence against yourself, alcoholism a disease. What's more, you make yourself unattractive to the human family. You hide from your problems, unable to deal with the real world. And yes, the odds of the ologists being right in this are greatly in their favour; the odds are next to zero for our chances at a declaration of what's real. I contend, however faintly that I do, that the stupor—you staring out the window, you looking at God knows what (but presumably, it involves the shambles of your life)—is that line you've drawn, beyond which you do not comply. By means of drink, you deny the occupiers a smoothly-functioning capital: you burn it down. It is a cheap sort of romanticism with an ugly aftermath; it is cowardice of a kind. But you are entirely within your rights, so far as I see it, to deny those bastards whom Eggy believes ought to hang the wherewithal of your heart, mind, body and soul. Just thought you might like to know. The intent of all hypocrisy, so far as it concerns each and every collective, is to keep one in line and productive, or, at the very least, to enlist one's acquiescence in extending the shelf life of lies. Soon, you'll be so far gone you'll no longer find yourself able to follow any logic but that of your internal dissolutions. That you might comprehend my thought process will be pretty much moot. Mr and Mrs Civic Smile shall be glad to see the back of you. So shall Dubois who finds your communication skills somewhat wanting, your stupors sheer intransigence. It is otherwise conjectured that Moonface, remember her?—she's the one who was kind to you, and she's the one whom you've stiffed more than once, cheating on the bill—anyway, she's slated to return to work, this evening, after an hiatus of a couple of weeks. A Traymorean or two may rejoice. A Miss Meow might miaow in contralto and purr. A beetle-browed, barrel-chested spectre—perhaps you, too, have seen him—might show and genuflect at the object of his shabby and yet somehow noble infatuation. See you there.—RQC

§

Book VI—*De Incendio Urbis*

Squeezing Out Moonface

It began to chill as soon as the sun went down, Eggy, Dubois and I on the terrasse of *Le Grec* (aka the Blue Danube) even so. A few regulars, Miss Meow, the Whistler, Blind Musician among others, preferred to sit inside. A postcard Moonface mailed from Vancouver had only just arrived that morning in Eggy's box. It exhorted Eggy to hug Bob. And if Eggy was feeling up to it, he could slap Randall on the back as well. Nothing doing. Too much ardor required. Eggy, nursing thin tumblers of Jack Daniels, said: 'We are poor little lambs that have lost their way. Bah bah bah. Lord have mercy on such as we.'

'Baudelaire,' said Dubois, 'tried suicide, but he only scratched himself.'

Since when did Dubois know anything about Baudelaire? Even so, poets could not do anything right. We talked Moonface.

'You have intelligence for me,' I said to Eggy, 'what do you know?'

Eggy had recently taken the dear girl to a garden restaurant, then to a bar owned by some Irish with connections to Mafiosi. A nightcap at the Blue Danube was the *coup de grâce*, Eggy pinwheeling home on his pins afterwards.

'You see,' I said to Dubois, 'for days he brags he's going to get the skinny on Moonface for me, and now, he's got it, and he won't tell me a thing.'

'Fork over some dough,' Dubois suggested, a disinterested cowboy, a gangland enabler.

'I beg your pardon,' said Eggy, not a little miffed.

'Well? So what's the story?' I insisted.

'She's a heavy sleeper,' Eggy offered.

'Heavy sleeper? And you know this, how?' Dubois guffawed.

'Why, because Champagne Sheridan told me so. He met up with us at the bar. Seems Moonface is well known there. Says she goes out like a light. And there's a roommate. That is, if Moonface moves in with Sheridan, there'll be someone else to consider,' observed Eggy.

'Hansel, Hansel and Gretel?' I drolled, 'or Hansel, Gretel and Gretel?'

Eggy gave me a look.

'Yes but,' he said, getting it all out now, 'she said, and she said it voluntarily, I didn't force it from her, that not only was Echo groped, remember her, but that she herself, you know, Moonface, she had to fight off Elias. It's what happened to Tall Anna, too. And now that Gregory has hired Antonio, well, it's the writing on the wall for Moonface. The place is going to be all boys except, of course, for Cassandra.'

'We've seen it coming,' said all-seeing Dubois. He continued: 'If I'd been Echo's boyfriend, I would've handled it differently. I wouldn't have made a scene like he did in the restaurant. The cops see all that, they don't want to deal with it. The thing is, you have to make the cops take the allegations seriously. To do that, you have to play the game by the book.'

'I don't know about that,' chuffed Eggy.

I had no opinion, knowing now that, once more, I must revise my estimation of the man Elias, husband to Cassandra. I must also wonder about her. How much did she know or suspect, if anything, when it came to her man's predilections?

'Bloody peasants,' said Eggy, 'they come here and start treating their women like dirt. Bloody uncivilized, if you ask me.'

'And you're civilized?' Dubois countered.

'Well, I keep my hands to myself. They don't go where they're not wanted.'

'Like hell,' said Dubois. 'We know what goes on when Moonface visits you.'

'That's different,' Eggy protested, 'and anyway, she's my complementary function.'

'Complementary function?' said Dubois, having yet another occasion to laugh.

'Yes,' said Eggy, 'I could see out eternity looking at her. Forever, you know. Why, it has nothing to do with sex.'

'Do tell,' said Dubois.

'I worry about Cassandra,' I said.

'Howsomever,' said Eggy, 'I want to sleep with this young Haitian woman I've gotten to know.'

'But you're 902 years old,' I could not help but notice, 'she isn't going to want to sleep with an old bugger like you, not in a million years.'

'Yes, dream on,' said Dubois.

And Eggy looked more surprised than hurt. He had the look of a man utterly unaware of his age and other particulars. It had been a while since we sat out this long on the terrasse, past BBC news time, at any rate. Gregory had built it, and some regulars had showed, and then they were gone, save for we hardcore Traymoreans. Dubois looked natty in his knee-length coat and baseball hat. Eggy looked rather like Lenin, what with the hat he wore. I said as much.

'But I always get mistaken for Kissinger,' Eggy crowed, his finger raised, 'why, back in '87—'

'Which '87,' asked Dubois, '1787?'

'Don't get smart.'

'I think Cassandra wants to go home,' I observed.

Yes, and I wondered what she did for a treat, for kicking back, as it were. A shot of something from the liquor cabinet? A square of chocolate? The intermezzo from *Cavaliere Rusticana*? Snuggle with hubby who just might be a sex pirate? A lonely sob on the back porch?

Sleek Babes

Dubois, bored with me, turned the better part of his attentions to the meat on his Blue Danube plate. The occupants of the galley had finally acquired the knack of preparing it to his specifications. Dubois possessed, right down to his fingertips, the air of a man who was in no especial hurry to begin digging his bunker or run for the hills. Life was good.

'So,' he remarked just to be civil, 'it sounds like that Wiedemayer fellow got a phone call from Putin, and Wiedermayer's leaking the gist of the conversation.'

The cool Francophone brushing-off the politically overheated Anglo. I had spent the afternoon with Hiram Wiedemayer, photographer of antiquities, a traveller in ancient lands. We drank at a bar on the city's party street while talking doom with a capital D, the day bright and crisp, sleek babes going by, leggy in their heels, cell phone clapped to well-coutured ears. Hiram was entranced.

'How surreal is this,' he said, 'we're sitting here with our wine, all these gorgeous women, and western civilization is going down the tubes?'

My sentiments, too. And now suited men, men who had the look of men just gotten off airplanes; men who had *X*, *Y* and *Z* to hawk, expense accounts to honour; men with briefcases milled about and took stock of their surroundings and the girls. Hiram Wiedemayer, American transplant, capitalist to his core, nonetheless bemoaned the fact that America was passing up its best chance in years for national renewal. That he was Jewish and obsessed with Israel's fate only added to his pessimism. He was convinced that, in recent weeks, Putin had backed the U.S. of A. into a corner, forcing its hand on Iran. The Americans would bomb because it now had no other choice, and—

'Interesting,' said Dubois, cutting me off as I recounted what Hiram the realist had to say.

But the girls on the street had also exercised Hiram.

'Good god, those babes. Just look at them, would you? I'm going nuts here. I've got to separate myself from America. I've got to separate myself from Israel. Can't keep agonizing over the mistakes they keep making over and over. This is a good city we're living in. Good place to be.'

I was so agog with the import of Hiram's words, so inwardly miffed with Dubois's apparent indifference, that I barely noticed Moonface's cheery hello, one that proclaimed her contentment with her life for the moment. Even so, I thought it good that she could not and would not ever match for prowess those sleek babes of Crescent Street; she had neither the looks nor the resources nor the killer instincts of a predator. She might wish her men to think of her as pretty Emma, but it was only whimsy on her part, an interlude on the road to Ecuador; or indeed, as Dubois would have it, on the royal path to Ottawa and the civil service.

The Last Comic Standing

Marjerie Prentiss, so I was convinced, wished for Eleanor to continually second-guess herself. It was not enough that Eleanor suffer the occasional lapse of judgment; she must also sour the pursuit of pleasure by way of self-doubt, and then seek advice and pointers from Prentiss as to how best proceed. Moreover, men were not to be enjoyed so much as secured. What hit me about Marjerie's digs was that her place was unexpectedly Spartan, more so than mine. There was the entertainment console, to be sure. A queen-sized mattress on the living room floor. Black sheets, overstuffed pillows, rumpled blankets. Such a pallet would feature from time to time, so I figured, three loving bodies. A large philodendron and some other plant I took to be a clematis. There was a photograph pinned to a wall, one scissored out, I supposed, from a magazine, and one I suspected I was meant to see. Her pretext for having me over? She had wished my opinion on something or another. But at first, my disbelieving eyes did not quite register the import of the photograph; I stepped closer to it. And saw a male of indeterminate age but younger rather than older, naked save for the black hood that enwrapped his head and the red briefs he wore; he was bent over in an institutional-like corridor, hands clasped behind his knees. Eyes burned into the back of my head. I shrugged, disgust with the image and hatred of the eyes taking possession of my thoughts.

'And?' I said.

'Oh,' spoke that dully booming voice, 'it's just that you've never been here.'

Tank-top. Denims. Knobbly toes. The splendid hips. Brittle hair. A gaze that looked at one with intense curiosity, yes, from the bottom of the sea.

'Well, now I can say I've been here,' I said.

'You're not ever going to like me,' said Marjerie Prentiss, her smile terribly innocuous.

'I don't suppose so.'

'Eleanor says you're the nicest man.'

'I wouldn't bet on my being nice.'

'Oh, I'm not.'

'I don't think you're nice.'

'Not at all.'

'In fact, I think you're rather twisted.'

'Decidedly.'

There must have been something like a grandfather time-device in another room; the hour was bonged—three o'clock—and time sounded hollow. Was there not a Lorca poem in which an hour was famously struck? Of course, I was going to have this moment on my mind for a while, her little triumph. That, and the allure of her body, even so. And if the world was going to get any more twisted than it already was, she, she was its clown.

And Moonface, standing before us, flashed her nails that were not, in this instance, painted. I searched her visage for I know not what, in light of the fact that Eggy had spoken of her sweet mood of recent days. Was it sweet still? Had she broken into a soft-shoe just then, I would have not been much amazed. And fauns appear, and Silenus and satyrs gone mellow, a wine-heavy retinue; all of it as if depicted by Watteau or Titian in dreamy light; Moonface to be anointed Prom Queen, Roy Orbison plucking on a lyre. I shivered. I asked for a whiskey. Moonface rolled her eyes up and to the side, more a maid-in-waiting than a sceptre-equipped queen; and she spoke of how pleased Champagne Sheridan had been to have sat at table with us not so long ago so as to have words with Blue Danubian luminaries.

'Yes,' said Eggy, 'I thought he was rather delighted.'

'The rookie has promise,' Dubois guffawed.

'Now boys,' said Moonface.

We were, after all, her men. And to speak of Marjerie Prentiss just then would only have sabotaged the pleasantries. Even so, northern light and northern chill were ill-suited to the sweet agonies of desportment; for all that the forebears of Gregory the Greek might have worshiped at shrines of Eros; for all that Gregory's radio spewed assembly-line burblings of love and loss. Even so, here was Blind Musician as officious as ever with his blind man's cane, he for whom I suspected Brahms was just a pill to give the unwashed; and presto, the beast was elevated a notch. Here was Blind Musician come for lentil soup. His baritone filled vast subterranean acres with contumely; that we were all of us Philistines. Moonface went to him who had ventured inside. She had developed stratagems for dealing with the man, one of which was to broach the subject of Scriabin and hear, in turn, that the Russian had been an airhead. Blind Musician might sense but he would not see the dear girl rolling her eyes, let alone strike a somewhat saucy pose with her slimmed down hips.

Damnatio Memoriae

Rain fell heavily through the maples. Evening. It seemed I was rooted to the spot, there on the pavement, and were I to move just then I might disintegrate. The window of the Blue Danube framed Moonface, she arrested on her way to a table with plates of food, her attention turned to another table and the customer who had obviously called to her. In a flash, as it were, I saw her life unfold. She was set to love her Champagne Sheridan a while and he her, and this love might or might not deepen and come to define each their needs and wants. A successful foray into Ecuador might seal the bargain they had struck; it might just as easily inaugurate the beginning of the end. No matter, they were young, and the young wade into life, blind to its hazards, optimism a hormone. Moonface might turn her back on Virgil and his poetry (I suspected she already had); she might scale down her ambitions, if any; modify her passions in respect to those of her man; she might even get pregnant and carry the Champagne Sheridan child, but there was always the civil service. She was unfailingly courteous; it was the one thing that could be said for her, and perhaps she had her loopy parents to thank for it. She was just cheeky enough to think herself on the right side of history's judgment, however she defined it; it was a prerogative of the young, but she had no sense of the ironies. It was only political correctness on her part to suggest that winners tend to die of their success. Politics, then? America, certainly, was nothing but a series of headlines, and yet she would count herself liberal and believe what liberals were expected to believe, whatever that was. And if America was sagging at the knees, then sag away; it had nothing to do with what made Emma MacReady Moonface to Traymoreans. She might, in time, come to have an affair, one that was a reaching back for something she had yet to suspect she had lost. Was she all for true love? No, I was that absurd creature, even as every bone in my body told me that love was only love, and if true, it was never the whole truth. Moonface was in her working mode, hair tied in a ponytail. Coarse blouse, black denims. Her posture seemed exaggeratedly proper. Now she set plates before a bored looking middle-aged couple, she looking straight into the eyes each of a man and a woman having already made preemptive adjustments to anticipated disappointment, Moonface's smile rich with hope and *bon appetits,* and was there anything else? Suddenly, standing behind the cash box, was Cassandra, the look on her wide face that of a woman who had just been rudely startled into wakefulness. I knew that look. I had always known it as the Medea look, and whether turned inward or outward, it was lethal. Here was Elias now, and sheepish, he was blinking. Pedestrian traffic parted around me; rain pelted me, the ordinary commotions of an evening remote in my ears. I had no urge to enter the café; I lacked just then the courage with which to fend off Miss Meow's miaow. I could continue up the street; if I walked far enough, there were other eateries, including a little nook whose Japanese cuisine I once thought to sample. Eggy, I figured, was in his rooms, saving his money for another day. Perhaps Eleanor and Dubois had gone to a movie. Prentiss and her band of merry brothers were to be avoided. Even so, I could not seem to move my feet. Just then, Moonface caught sight of me. Her mouth opened as if to say that, in regards to my person, something had slipped her mind. She was, once again, so sorry.

The next morning, Evie Longoria, once an Alberta girl, Montrealer now, 50-ish cowgirl with a smattering of culture, took Eggy shopping. Eggy paid her for this service. He complained of it later at the Blue Danube; that the woman critiqued how he shopped. Also, he drank too much. Marriage, I supposed, was Zeus-like Eggy's self-imposed penalty for his vices. For instance, he thought himself married to Moonface (though not to Eleanor), Evie yet another prospect in a string of hectoring Heras.

'Come on,' I said, chaffing an ancient sparrow of a man, 'you love it. It's attention.'

The look Eggy gave me was that of a rat who knew he was cornered and would fight to the death. When Dubois, joining us, was brought up to speed, he guffawed. Mid-September, the day was humid, warm enough on the terrasse for our pleasant little lives. There was news of Gentleman Jim.

'Yes but,' Eggy said, 'Moonface said she saw him barefoot last night. And, you know, why, it was wet out here.'

'When was this?' I asked.

'Last night.'

'When last night?'

'She didn't say. But he didn't come in, Moonface pretty happy about that. Yes, he was standing right there, just staring at her through the rain.'

'Well, it couldn't have been me.'

'Of course, it wasn't you. Effing hell, what are you talking about?'

It was too complicated to explain, Dubois narrowing his eyes. Antonio brought medicinal beer and wine, Traymoreans so many Chairmen of the Board whose bad tempers he must placate.

They were a pair of potted plants joined at the hips—Eggy and Dubois. And when I was once again among them at the Blue Danube, Phillip

Dundarave was seeking commiseration in their company, he bent on drinking. He had become, so I figured, a bottom dweller in the pecking order of a three-way.

'She turfed him out,' Eggy said, explaining the suppliant to me.

She could only have been Prentiss. Her putative lover had rue slathered all over his powerful frame and sheepish mug, one pint down, a second one breached. Meanwhile Dubois was dangerously silent, and in this perhaps he revealed his true intelligence. Dubois liked to chatter and benignly dominate; no doubt, from Phillip, he was seeking hints as to Prentiss's intentions. The woman had, after all, wormed her way into Eleanor's affections; she might even attempt to turn Eleanor against his affections for her. Phillip, too, was also a possible rival, one who seemed to think highly of Eleanor's indisputable charms.

'Cunt,' said Phillip, simply.

'The rain in Spain,' Eggy hoo hooed.

And the evenings were getting shorter, Eggy sensible of the fact, his fun threatening to be curtailed by a spoiler called nature. Cassandra brought out lit candles, Phillip slouched in his chair, his inebriated state threatening to shift gears from mere ruing to outright hostility by way of slurred speech turned inward. He reiterated a word which bespoke Prentiss in terms of an anatomical particularity.

'My, my,' said Eggy and once again hoo hooed, pleased to hear it said, push come to shove, as the word had, at times in his life, summed up his feelings exactly.

Dubois was, however, uncomfortable with the epithet. It was a highly charged word, and one must pick one's spots, employing it judiciously.

'In point of fact,' said Dubois, 'what is the nature of your relationships?'

There was no doubting what Dubois wished to get at, Phillip sitting up now, glassy eyes alert.

'Oh,' he answered, an innocent pup, 'we just hang out. We aim to buy a house in the country and renovate it.'

'Yes?' said Dubois.

'Oh,' Phillip responded, 'do you mean me and Eleanor? Relax, man. Nothing's going to happen.'

The humidity of an evening threatened to swallow the flame of our candle. Eggy had the look of a man who had just witnessed marvels. Dubois sunk back into silence.

After Phillip took himself off, a lonely man without a secure port in which to lay his weary head, I helped Dubois get Eggy up the Traymore stairs. It had begun to rain again, in any case, the front end of a scaled-down Texas hurricane upon us.

'Come on, man, move,' Dubois commanded.

'I'm moving. Effing hell.'

The stairs negotiated, and free of our clutches, Eggy immediately tottered to his door, his head sunk between his bent shoulders. Dubois knocked on Eleanor's. I already had it in mind to go back out on the sly. Moonface just might be at that Irish bar down the street. Dear girl that she was, gentle if chameleon-like, she now and then irritated me. I always assumed I was blind, to some extent, to her shortfalls in character. I had to admit that, on her part, passivity as a ruse to control and manipulate was a less than attractive feature of her being. She had every right, of course, to marry her Champagne Sheridan. She had every right to cashier her Traymorean membership for a position in the upcoming Ecuador Expedition. She could decide that Virgil had, after all, bored her to tears; that art required no more sensibility than what was needed to push the buttons of a video-camera. I heard: 'Well, look what the cat dragged in.'

The voice was Eleanor's, she at her door. Heard Dubois being scooped up. Heard Eggy potter about with his cane. He was, no doubt, pouring himself a nightcap, settling into his armchair, the TV on; and he would soon commence to curse the fare.

'Effing hell. More fundraising. No news? Does anyone care? What if they dropped the effing bomb?'

Eggy thundered. I went out. Rain and wind. Even so, I had not far to go. Perhaps once or twice I had been to the bar in question; Eggy, so he said, used to go on a fairly regular basis, so much so a woman had photographed him there, and from the photo painted his portrait. This portrait now had pride of place in a downtown gallery. The homuncular little bastard. A bevy of cigarette smokers hanging about the entrance despite the rain and wind. I pushed through them, and inside, Celtic music was pitched at excruciating decibels. I saw at a glance that there was no Moonface. I squeezed between two young ladies standing at the bar. They were aspiring to the dramatic arts, by the sounds of it, their looks and appearance and patter utterly conventional, vaguely street edgy. As Moonface was not about, I may as well have been absent myself, a stranger unremarked by strangers, bored out of my skull, drinking too quickly a glass of wine that would not go down well. What did I think I would achieve?

'Moonface, sweetheart,' I might have said, 'inebriation is lovely, I grant you that, but mindlessness is not the point of the exercise.'

'Oh Randall,' I might have heard, 'you're so effing avuncular. What's real is not being real. Don't you get it? Being real hurts people.'

And her golden brown eyes, on occasion rich and inviting and seemingly paradisal, might have carried her talking-point, she puffing out her modest bosom, her hands on her hips, nails flashing. She might have been what was the going rate in the bar, her Champagne Sheridan a toy, Virgil the poet but a neurotic queer, no more than a press agent, spokesperson for empire, interpreter of the imperial whim. *Emma pretty. Emma pretty.* She was ready for the next wave to ride, one that just might silence, forever, all distinctions between truth and falsehood, she a dear girl and the nicest person in the world.

Aviator Glasses

Wind roars. Rain spits. Babies are getting born. Wall Street is set to panic. Hooded figures flit from pillar to post in pumps and wingtips and Rockports. My teenaged life was football practice, Holsts's 'The Planets'; gin, fried eggs and bacon; friends slated to die in 'Nam, Johnny Unitas; the odd poet or two as swacked as Li Po drunk on the moon (this before I knew Lucan was a crank and J Caesar was a supper club comedian). My late teenaged life had very little to do with courtly love; but I do, of a sudden, recall seducing a girl who sold encyclopedias door to door, or perhaps she seduced me, she who paid me the tribute of her lust, from A to Z. Such recollections lie buried at the bottom of an ocean of memory. Girls randier than the Lydia Pinkhams of the hippy communes did it for self-respect.

Cassandra admitted me early, Elias grunting. He had the look of a man who wished to make amends with some collective or other, but must first fire up the grill and put on the soup. Cassandra poured me a cup of coffee, serving it with a ravishing smile. She certainly was a sphinx. Perhaps her thoughts were really quite simple thoughts. *Does my husband love me? Should I let my daughters wear lipstick? How much do we owe the bank? If there is a God, why is He so fickle with Greeks?* I noticed her ears. There in the morning light of the Blue Danube, they struck me as miracles. Her hair swept over them, erotic burblings sweeping through me, one could see they were neither too large nor too small nor too thick; as ears go, they were perfection of a kind. A pleasing roundness of shape suggesting liveliness and mischief. I did not know why a man might become utterly fond of a woman with whom he could not expect anything remotely resembling intimacy, whose thoughts he would never divine; who was not, perhaps, as beautiful or as intelligent as other women of his acquaintance, but who was, nonetheless, in her own right, compelling. With her he might exchange an unspoken confidence—on a bus, for instance, the reasons for it forever unknowable, or to be left for another lifetime. I could not let her distract me; I had jottings to make, even if I had sworn off jottings; and yet she seemed to find my theatrical display of earnest endeavour amusing. She was not entirely indisposed to an egghead like me. More than likely, she had no desire to know the extent of the world's parlous state; she had a household and a restaurant, troubles enough, and the French lessons for which she had signed up were on hold—insufficient quorum, and she was homesick for the Mediterranean sun. I worried for her happiness.

At the stroke of noon, a dangerous trio entered the café. Dubois, Eggy, Evie Longoria, she wearing aviator glasses.

'Beers all around,' thundered Eggy, stutter-stepping with his cane, his afterburners still firing.

'Why, we're planning an excursion,' he continued, 'I always wanted to visit that pub in North Hatley again.'

Dubois guffawed. Three desperadoes commandeered my table, Evie apologizing for her lack of make-up.

'Hence, the glasses,' she explained, 'don't want to frighten anybody—'

'But you don't need them,' Dubois interjected.

And Evie Longoria blushed, and was appealing as she did so.

'Care to come?' Eggy asked me.

'Will there be room?' Dubois put it to us. 'We'll have to hire a bus,' he added, 'if Moonface comes and Eleanor, too.'

'Of course, there'll be room,' Eggy thundered once more, 'there's always room for knights of the table. I think we ought to become terrorists, seeing as no one is going to hang the bastards.'

Once more, Dubois guffawed and Evie blushed, the temples of her forehead, however, pale.

'I'll think about it,' I said.

'What's to think about?' Eggy said, severely.

And I supposed it was to be another birthday bash, Eggy's second or third, already, of the year. At the rate he was going, he was going to be as old as Adam was old when he died, three times over. Even so, Eggy was having too much fun to die. Now Antonio, come on shift, approached us, warily.

'Beer,' thundered Eggy, 'effing hell. Damn peasants. Have to repeat everything.'

But Evie was not having any beer, and I was having wine, and Antonio's feelings were not at all hurt. He slid his arm around Eggy's tiny shoulder and kissed the old pate.

'Oh, go on,' Eggy spluttered and blushed, if blushing were possible in a man of his age.

Evie, picking up on some earlier conversation thread, now said: 'Clark Gable. He's my hunk.'

'Really?' This was Dubois, incredulous.

'Of course,' said Evie, 'and he never got over his wife dying in that crash, who was she?'

'Carole Lombard?' I suggested.

'And he never claimed he could act,' Evie went on, 'he was just himself.'

Evie Longoria adored *The Misfits*; it was one of her most favourite movies.

'Oh,' said Eggy, 'I should think Errol Flynn's more the man.'

'Oh no,' Evie protested, 'not at all. Except that my mother used to tell me, because I think she had a thing for him, she'd say, "Never say in like Flynn to me."'

Dubois guffawed. He had a good working knowledge of Anglicisms.

'I ride an old paint and I lead an old Dan, goin' to Montana to throw the houilhan,' said Eggy.

'Feed 'em in the coulees and water in the draw … oh, I forget the rest,' softly sang Evie, swaying side to side.

Dubois guffawed. Eggy, raising his finger, completed the stanza: 'Their tails are all matted and their backs are all raw.'

'Good God,' I said, 'folkies.'

'Terrorists,' thundered Eggy, 'effing hell.'

Original Sin

There are moments which occur in life that, if successfully negotiated, vouchsafe a future free of doubt. And one's gentleman's agreement with God—He keeps to His neck of the woods and one will refrain from impugning His office—will most likely remain intact. And, perhaps more importantly, one will not second-guess the operations of love. Such a moment arrived for me in the summer between my 4th and 5th grades of elementary school. Missouri. And when my mother described thunder as God moving furniture, though I appreciated the poetic element in her image-making, I knew it for a falsehood. Even so, I did not snicker or in any way fail to respect the point of view. Which made it all the more hard on me when, on a certain Sunday afternoon, no black clouds anywhere in the sky, a church picnic in the offing, I expected to be among the faithful for the softball and the food. Mother had other ideas. She got it into her head that she would much rather spend the afternoon sunning herself at some lake; that we did not need a church in order to have fun; that, as a family unit, we ought to be self-sufficient in the matter of fun. Father sided with her, if only to keep the peace. It was, in fact, the oddest behaviour on his wife's part; she had no quarrel with the church; she had entirely conventional views on religion, politics, and the mechanisms of society; she was all for keeping up appearances. And yet here she was about to risk a future and interrogative visit from the local pastor, all for the sake of showcasing a scanty two-piece bit of beachwear at some mountain spa. Even my father, and in spite of the fact that his work provided him with scope to live in the shadows, beyond the banal reaches of religion, politics, society, not to mention questions of law, was shocked.

In any case, I felt myself betrayed. I did not take the betrayal well, and worse, I discovered in myself a capacity for willful and obnoxious argument, for the vanities and specious pleasures of argument, father rolling his eyes as he drove the car, mother's temper red-hot. This also was a development as new as the swimsuit would eventually prove to be. It could have been any moment at any point in my life in which my trust in the orderly procession of days and the satisfaction of my desires was to be challenged and essentially crushed; all the Big Questions rendered moot, as suddenly one lacked the leisure, could not count on the old saw that *all would be revealed in the fullness of time.* But it was not any moment; it was that particular moment at that particular juncture in my life when I was perhaps most vulnerable to a soul-jarring surprise. My mind was, assuredly, a pretty primitive enterprise, all ego, urge, and surly instinct; even so, it was then, just then, that the true lay of the land was revealed: life a caprice, there was no justice, middle-class comforts notwithstanding. It was an epiphany which, if kept before one's gaze 24/7, would drive one mad. So that, as I grew older, I was not always mindful of the lesson that had been served me such as would, at other moments, in other guises, catch me up short of rope and wherewithal. And I could almost believe, given all the evil and wrongdoing so apparent in the world, that no one was to blame for it; it was part of the very substance of life itself, Original Sin nothing more than the recognition of the tenuous nature of human relations. As for the banking crisis now unfolding on Wall Street, Zeus-like Eggy took the Olympian view: there was only Moonface. Yes, the old bugger knew he was a hopeless old fool in this regard, his self-directed laughter a kind of tight-lipped chuckle.

'Yes but,' Eggy said, 'I don't know that going to Ecuador is such a hot idea. It's not as if she'll be cycling through the Lowlands, beer and cheese available every 10 kilometres of the way. Her epilepsy, you know. I tell her, you know, to get clearance from the doctors. She won't listen. She thinks she knows everything. Well, I guess that's what being young is all about. The rain in Spain. Always.'

The evening turning nippy, he stubbornly bore up on the Blue Danube terrasse with his pint and his tough, old eyes. Darkness was settling on an old woman and her dachshund, those two loopy integers of an almost endearing farce. Clearly, she believed she and the mutt shared a wavelength. I had hoped Dubois would be around so that I might gainsay his faith in the system and score cheap debating points.

'Oh, he's probably skulking about somewhere,' said Eggy, 'you know him. One minute he's all agitprop for justice and fair play and the next he's financing a bridge or a shopping mall.'

If I had taken Moonface to Rome, sat her down on the terrasse of a Janiculum bar beneath a pergola of vines, talked poetry and history, plied her with a deadly white wine, rendered her boffable, I would not have ventured to compromise her virtue. Drawing on the example of Plotinus or some Average Joe early Christian, of Rome's infinite capacity to contradict her eternal reputation, I would have let Rome come to each of Moonface's six senses and carry out the buggering of her soul. Otherwise, I would happily destroy the polite constructs as have already ruined the Moonface mind.

Marjerie Prentiss was beyond the pale, and proud of it. She was in her person the sole repository of value as she saw it. And we, we rubes and marks of either gender, had not the wit to credit her with the fact. Nuke the Arabs. Rip up the safety nets. The market rules. And that a feminista without slaves is only whistling Dixie in a sterile academe, pissing on the possibilities. She forced me to give way on the Traymore stairs, no doting mother she, *diabolical regina caeli*, her retinue in tow, Hansel and Hansel brandishing amulets and snakes and golden penises. She was almost a revelation, and I could almost take her seriously and get behind her—in a political sense.

'Ah,' I said, 'esteemed crew.'

I was answered with blank stares. Obviously, they considered my remark less than civil. I was headed for the post office, the envelope addressed: Jack Swain, Palermo, *Poste Restante*. I was sending him, for his amusement, my impromptu review of the latest work of Fidelio Snorris the poet, one of dismaying longevity. Jack, though he was dead, though he was probably in Hades knocking back some vodka and sucking on a tangerine, could draw his own conclusions. And what do you know, and speaking of other devils, I ran into Moonface doing the chicken shuffle on her way to work.

'I'll see you at the café,' I said.

She smiled, much preoccupied. I simply kept going. And back at the Blue Danube, Dubois was holding forth: 'The value,' he said, 'of the asset is this, mark my words, it's the price paid for it.'

'Yes but,' said Eggy.

True love, too, was an exchange, but that what was exchanged was the rueful acknowledgement of one's absurdity. Eggy's sneeze was a Zeus-like furor.

'Yes but,' he repeated, attempting to block his nostrils with his forefinger.

A bright, late afternoon, the maples reddening, looking somewhat glazed. A bus now delivered Blind Musician to the bus stop, his disembarking theatrical. He was not packing a violin. Had he failed to honour his union dues? His blind man's stick was most definitely dispirited, so many Philistines about, five of his six senses reporting back on that score. I never much liked the man, but just then he had my sympathy. For he had the look of a man who would be the last man on earth to learn of his own absurdity. Dubois continued: 'And the strongest currency—well, are you listening?—look, I won't say it again, the strongest currency is that one which has the longest nose ahead in terms of stability, thus—'

Another Eggy sneeze. A terrible violence done to his frame.

'Effing hell,' said Eggy recovering, 'and why, well, you know, even if you don't credit me for it, I generally make sense, but you, why it's you who never listens.'

And what was my excuse? I had none. And what was up with Moonface? For by now, she had brought me wine and seemed out of countenance.

'But it was the grey parts of the TVs,' said Eggy, 'that assaulted my young adulthood. Even so, we still had a moral absolute or two.'

'No wonder,' said Dubois.

'No wonder what?' Eggy thundered.

'That you're so off base about things.'

'Well, I remember the missile crisis.'

'Yes, so?' Dubois smirked.

'I was scared.'

Eggy's tone was sheepish.

'Moonface,' I said, 'why the long face with her?'

'Oh, tarnation and bother,' Eggy began to explain, 'it's someone she knows. Suicide. Moonface wonders if it's any kind of answer.'

What, was Moonface beginning to get moral?

'The traditional banks, however—'

It was Dubois, in full professorial mode.

'Damnation,' said Eggy, 'here we go.'

'The traditional banks, they're obliged to play less fast and loose with our money. We lend them money. They, in fact, borrow from us. Most people don't get it.'

Moonface stood before us, hands on hips. I looked up at her without looking into her eyes, lest I behold more vacuity than I wished to see.

'Oh, it's so sad,' she said, 'really sad.'

I supposed it was. I supposed she had me convinced. She walked away, Dubois being rather ho-hum in respect to her pronouncement.

'Anyway,' said Eggy, 'thank God for Churchill.'

'Algiers was the opening bell,' I said.

'Vietnam was unnecessary,' Eggy countered.

And then, what was essential and truly of the moment, impossible not to have them—there in each their person, Miss Meow and girlfriend—filed past our table, each abreast of the other, the coats they wore blazing. Fire engine red. It seemed they had added to their repertoire, no miaowing this time around. Instead, the senior partner uttered: 'Yummo.'

The other chorused, 'Mmmm.'

They went giggling inside the café where Moonface greeted them as long lost friends. From the looks of it, it had something to do with solidarity among women, three male gasbags lording it over the terrasse.

'Yes,' said Eggy, 'I don't think I told you this, but I told Moonface I made a mistake. She should always have been my Number One, not Number Two, reserve position. Hoo hoo.'

Dubois guffawed. He had melancholies of his own, just that he was too much the gentleman to bring them to the table. Eggy's head began to droop in the general direction of his chest. The wine intake. And that he had spent all morning reading a military history of Quebec. And it was eternal, the wine, the maples, the old women and their pooches, even the boom-boom cars with their infernal music. A red-skirted girl with saucy ankles, cell phone at her ear, smoked a cigarette and strode across the landscape, militant. It seemed Dubois's heart might break.

The Ruling Classes

So Moonface was sad. And, as she used to do, she swung her legs up on my couch, began pulling at the tresses of her hair. She had already asked if she might phone Sheridan; I reminded her I did not have a phone. Of course. She had forgotten. She missed her apartment but did not think her apartment missed her. She felt she was just camping out, however, at Sheridan's place. If she still had not returned the books I lent her, it was because she was afraid; it would mean commitment, not to me but to a fork in the road, a decision pending. She asked: 'Did you ever know a suicide?'

She directed her gaze into space.

'Yes,' I answered, 'she threw herself out a window.'

'Oh, that's awful.'

'Whiskey?' I put it to the girl.

'No.'

'The ruling classes rule. That's the thing of it, all there is to say on it.'

'Avuncular, Randall.'

'So how's it going otherwise?' I asked.

'We're going to Ecuador, you know.'

'I know.'

'Pretty exciting. And we're getting things sorted out.'

I supposed it was the sex thing that was getting sorted out, and that she meant me to know as much. She had never seemed so sexless. Or else, I had absolutely no interest just then in her charms, only that she was a friend and was confused.

'I know you're not happy with me,' she offered.

'Why should I be unhappy with you?'

'Come on. You're not. You think I'm doing everything wrong.'

'Are you?'

'You tell me.'

'I think it's great you're going to Ecuador. You need it. About time you see how the rest of the world lives. Sheridan? Well, he seems solid enough.'

I lied, but even so, she let my less than emphatic recommendation pass unchallenged. Sheridan did not have a clue and yet, he might learn.

'I just want to paint my nails, flirt, get drunk, boff my brains out. What do you think?'

'Really?'

'I could just lie here and fall asleep.'

'Why don't you?'

'I can't.'

'I'm going to pour myself a whiskey,' I said.

She rose from the couch and stood there. A grin manifested on her face, one which indicated she was not exactly sure what it was she would do next. She might as easily perform a striptease as put her John Henry on a Declaration of Independence. As sign someone's death warrant. As kneel down and pet a stray dog.

'Maybe I'll see if my bed will have me,' she said.

'Pleasant dreams,' I said, avuncular, once again.

Sortes Virgilianae

There would come a day, and Current President would pass from the scene; and all the world step back from reviling him, free of this burden. Was this not the vaunted perspective the wise had always cherished? Daydream? Moonface high-stepping in a swirling, carnal red gown, her shoulders thrown back, countenance proud—daydream, too? Truth, beauty, justice—just more daydreams? On TV, the sound muted, the running back spun off the force of the tackle. Breaking loose, he danced in for the score. Cheerleaders in orange. Helmets bright. As I lay on my couch, I opened the *Aeneid* and read in Book Nine how the Trojans in primordial Italy succumbed to the lust for glory.

Earlier, in the Blue Danube, I sat with Eggy, fruit cup and coffee his lunch. The old man regarded me with shrewd eyes; and it was somewhat disconcerting. Now and then, when he was not hamming it up, and though the looming crack-up of America was not, perhaps, paramount in his thoughts, he nonetheless grew sombre, if not meditative. He said: 'How are you getting on with your work?'

My work? It did not seem a proper association—my person and work. Eggy continued: 'Yes but, and well, what do I know, but I think Moonface makes love without enthusiasm.'

'Are you asking me to corroborate your statement?'

'I don't know. How would I know?'

'How would I? I've not slept with her.'

'I don't say you have or that you should.'

A portion of peach, by way of a spoon, was embarked on its perilous journey to Eggy's maw. And either the operations of the universe unfolded according to a set of laws or they did not, and there was no guaranteeing when and if the spoon would deliver its load.

'Well,' said Eggy, 'you're the writer. You're supposed to know these things.'

'Know what things?'

'How it is with Moonface. Effing hell.'

What, was Zeus-like Eggy calling a poet to his duty? And what might that duty be?

Perhaps Cassandra was mad, as in less than well-adjusted as per the specifications of the ologists, more Medea than a bride compromised by the goof she married. She was chewing gum, her cheeks those of a placid squirrel. There were two ways of seeing how it was with Moonface, and each, almost but not quite, contradicted the other. She was either adrift, or she was doing as well as could be expected. I rose, and as I did so, I instructed Eggy to behave.

'Oh, I will, alright,' he replied.

Loneliness rushed back at his person, one that was a tiny frame, the waist set high.

'Oh,' he called out, his finger raised, 'I'll have to win the lottery. Or else I can't take Haitian Nurse out for her birthday.'

'Well then, good luck,' I said.

'Hoo hoo.'

So much for Eggy, Moonface, Cassandra. I unmuted the TV. Heard out the silk and gravel voices of the play by play; as drums were pounded; as the very sky itself seemed part and parcel of an echo chamber, shadow consuming more and more of the field on which athletes assembled in opposing formations. On the snap of the ball, these formations lunged forward, fragmented, scattered, formed new groupings, piled on; and then a ball was whistled dead, terminating the action. I held Virgil's book in my hand; it was a journeyman's translation of the Latin, one rendered at a time when Sonny and Cher sang *I Got You, Babe* and Johnny Unitas knew post-season heartbreak. It was not mere affectation to say that, just as the field of honour was divided as I have described by light and shadow, so was I divided between love and hate of the spectacle. That there was joy in the game. That there was a money-machine in it. The great lie was that it was America at its finest. The great truth lay in the fact of America's genius for hoopla—the trumpets, drums, chantings of thousands upon thousands in an enormous stadium, an immense beating heart of want, so many hopeful faces already betrayed. But never mind. The despotic head coaches, their prowess on display, incurred my distrust. Virgilian warriors in shoulder pads and cleats mugged for the cameras. It was one's stab at glory; it was one's culpability in the brightest of voids. If life was meaningless, or if I had been wrong all this time about *X*, *Y* and *Z* and all stations in between, perhaps my enemies the ologists were more right: the gene pool's ability to withstand infections was what signified, nothing else. So much for an unknown bit of Mozart music that had just turned up. So much for the humongous bailout of the banks on the part of the Feds. So much for another pound of flesh gouged from the idea of a republic. Crisis? Why not have it said that a section of reef had only shuddered and fish exploded in watery space and then returned to calm? There was no more meaning, let alone sense, in it than that. Even so, with an unabashedly heavy heart, I could lament the life and death of a nobody, some butcher, baker, candlestick maker of imperial Rome, and wonder if the meaninglessness of that existence added to or, two thousand years later, subtracted from my own. Here was ancient graffiti: *You are Venus, babe. So and So sucks So and So's cock all through the harvest.* It was twenty years at least since I last read Virgil's epic. *Sississboomboombah.* I set the book down like one might a mortally wounded animal. Someone knocked. It was not a good time for Marjerie Prentiss to present herself at my door.

A dully booming voice put it to me: 'Is Phillip here?'

'No.'

'Well, can I come in?'

'You won't find him in any of my closets. He's not under the kitchen sink.'

She gave me a look. Faded red button-down sweater. Denims. Flip flops. And she saw that I had been watching a football game. She saw the book on the low-lying coffee table. Perhaps she noted I was in an agitated state of mind.

'I wouldn't take you for a sports fan,' she said.

'Maybe he's at Eleanor's,' I suggested.

'Maybe.'

It was evident that she was reevaluating me by way of my furniture. A few chairs. Couch. Shelves. TV and ghetto blaster. A writing desk that I now only used as a place to stack books and various papers. A few prints on the wall of sentimental value, one of which was of a prince of old astride a prancing tiger. The football game was a dancing on graves punctuated by timeouts for ads. Quaintness, so I had read somewhere, was but viciousness turned on its head. Marjerie Prentiss was abused as a girl, so I had been made to understand. If I had sympathy for what the girl had undergone, I had none for the woman she had become, even if, so far as I could determine, she had committed no crimes against person or state. There was always someone somewhere who rubbed one the wrong way; perhaps, for me, she was that being. She sampled love like certain gourmets sample cuisines—empirically. She had the heart, mind, body and soul of the executioner, and it was all legal, all sanctioned, to be expected. She seemed so much more disciplined than I, but to what end? She might never figure in any scenario such as might push for collective darkness; she might as easily pursue her obsessions on the quiet as head a movement; but she was, nonetheless, geist, cipher, paradigm, gateway, permission, full steam ahead for all that was twisted and inane. Perhaps we all of us were that. She had been abused but she had been somehow pampered, her allure the petulance of a beauty pageant contestant. One had courage in the face of certain dangers and none for others; and in regards to Marjerie Prentiss I was a coward and she knew it. Those watery dead eyes. I initiated a shoo-ing gesture with my right hand. I grinned mightily so as to apply a veneer of good nature to a pretext.

'Look,' I said, 'I'm expecting an epiphany at any moment.'

'Oh, one of those,' a voice boomed, and she bought it and went for the door.

Picture Father Rome lolling on the banks of the Tiber, calculating odds for the next thousand years—

§

Book VII—The Rain in Spain

Bash

No tree was properly a tree unless hanging from a stout bough were riffraff and runaway slaves, enemy spies, treasonous liberals, sacrificial virgins. Lyre birds aping the moans of the dying. But where were we? Ah, Marjerie Prentiss. She was pretty much as I anticipated, the spitting image of a socialite cum cultural renegade; barefoot, she wore a long, slinky dress. Plunging neckline. Fake tiara. Ironically self-referential. One might compare the forces her mind and body could bring to bear on her surroundings to those of an event horizon. Otherwise, country rock emanated from a machine; I supposed the croonster was crowned by a white stetson, his looks seemingly waxed onto his frame. As I write these words, as I commit to a sheet of paper, to some bit of space-time fabric, as it were, Moonface waitresses here in the Blue Danube. She was absent from the party. She is slipping away from us, her future departure for Ecuador already eliciting the crocodile coos of Traymoreans. Now she majestically imposes on a street cleaner (operator of a machine that vacuums fallen leaves) who has blundered into the café. *Monsieur?* And even as, with half a mind I watch her, my mind's other half elsewhere, it strikes me how she in her other-worldliness, and in her misguided grasp of reality (she has the air of a woman who considers the results of human history thus far a travesty, and so has better ideas), stands in my mentations at the border of dream and waking state, and has, despite her want of confidence, the power to consecrate souls. It is the way she flashes her nails. It is the way she unconsciously grabs at her inner thighs. Her sexuality, seemingly at a far remove from the humdrum realities of serving customers in a café, is, even so, as inseparable from the air we breathe as the scent of flowers after a summer's shower. In any case, I not only attended the party, I dreamed of it, afterwards. Who is to say I will not just now confuse the one for the other, dream for the miserable waking reality that was lived? Well, it went something like this: Marjerie had invited people who were strangers to me. Some women, for instance, whose smiles were too desperate. A Francophone poet, one Merrill Maynard, let me know he was obsessed with physics at their most bizarre. I cannot say I understood a word he put to me, but I liked him all the same. Eleanor sulked. And that she sulked was not expected. She had arranged herself rather fetchingly on the mattress, a quilt of many colours covering it. On one of the overstuffed pillows scattered around the room Dubois perched, a little at a loss. Eggy sat primly on a chair, his grin uneasy. Moonface was invited by way of a card slipped in her mailbox. She chose to ignore it. She did not like the issuer of the invitation, even if she could not tell me exactly why. Now Ralph and Phillip looked for all the world like Errol Flynns in the role of Robin Hood, now like scantily clad bum boys of a Neronian court. Eleanor waved me off as I endeavoured to get to the bottom of her mood. Which should have been, I supposed, Dubois's business, only he seemed abstracted. Perhaps Eleanor and Dubois had had a quarrel. Well, let us say one drink led to the next. I knew early on it was going to be an evening of dangerous drinking, as when one's soul chafes at unpleasant company but that the body has no defining limit, and the drink simply disappears in one's gut. Marjerie Prentiss, for a while pleased with herself, pretended that all she had desired was a casual get-together; but she was, as it were, working the floor, laying claim to the status of the Traymorean one had most to reckon with. Perhaps friction had developed between herself and Eleanor in this regard. Ralph chatted up one of the female strangers. His passion was restoring old houses. Phillip stood in a corner, moodily drinking. Truth to tell, he did not stand so much as pace in ever diminishing circles, and I worried he might worry a hole in the floor and vanish. Now and then he caught Eleanor's eye. 'Hoo hoo,' said Eggy. But no one noticed. Zeus-like Eggy in some godless realm. And when Eleanor rose and made good her escape, she pompadoured as ever, I thought it significant. Phillip followed her, Dubois startled to see it. Meanwhile I was deep in conversation with the poet. He attempted to explain to me the possibility of other universes by way of the physics that would allow for such. It was something to hold onto, this conversation, a ruse with which to fend off the boredom that I figured was coming for me. Dead watery eyes glittered at the back of my head. 'But the economy,' I heard myself saying. Merrill Maynard thought me an idiot. Did I not know? Black holes had four dimensions, one of time and three of space, whatever that meant. A woman introduced herself to us. Oh, she did not pay much attention to politics. Her garden and her dog were her handful, she divorced, her only child off with his father in California. The movie business. The poet, physically short of stature, nattily attired, bit his tongue: he was irked. How nice that this woman had a garden and a dog and was divorced. What was this, over and against the near certainty that the universe would simply swallow itself in some far distant prospect of time? So much for beating one's head against the wall in pursuit of the perfect poem. 'Oh,' I said, 'not going to happen.' Well, what was not going to happen? Perfect poem? Self-cannibalizing universe? The latter, I said. And I was not to be asked how I knew, just that it was an opinion I had read. The woman, losing interest in us, drifted over to Dubois who had, by now, slid his pillow-perch next to Eggy. Eggy poured on the charm. And so it went—country music, physics, loneliness. The drink, of course. Somehow we were all of us preoccupied enough that Marjerie Prentiss slipped away, unnoticed. Perhaps in the corner of my eye I saw her leave. The poet thought Yeats overrated. I assured him he was mistaken. The falcon cannot hear the falconer, and all that. Merrill Maynard promised he would reconsider, his bugbear Victor Hugo. Send a man out to the store for cigarettes, and a depiction of said action would come to 50 pages in a Hugo tome. I shrugged; I had the opposite problem; sometimes I could not see what was in front of my nose. It was as if my mind, in its stubborn insistence that there was some other more vital reality, had no use for reality, only that words failed the ineffable. Merrill Maynard gave me a look. Eggy was reciting dirty ditties, his finger raised. Maynard gave him a look. 'The man has a fabulous memory,' I explained, indicating Eggy, 'but look at what filth has come to rest in it. Now when a star collapses, doesn't it fall through to its neutrons, and then collapse further, some inconceivable density achieved, and then—what? Nothingness? I'd say Eggy has reached the neutron stage.' Maynard smiled somewhat nervously, unsure the analogy was appropriate. I looked around. In fact, the party was a rank failure. The woman whom Eggy would charm evidently figured him as uncouth and a loon, Dubois too much the know-it-all. Two other women who had set up shop, huddling together on the mattress, discussing subjects unknown to us, rose and made their excuses to depart. They mistook me for the host; I passed them on to Ralph who now looked every bit the man of the house-renovation world. He managed to detain them a while with his best I-am-not-a-sexist-but-I-am-master-of-my-universe smile. In other words, he was a decent fellow. Yes, there were serious absences, gaping holes in the immediate social fabric of a gathering. Eleanor, Phillip, Marjerie. I could only assume they had gravitated to Eleanor's kitchen, a fine room for socializing. Yes, I was curious. And yet I had the feeling that, were I to join them, I would be getting in the way of something that was none of my business. Perhaps Marjerie, realizing that the bash was a bust, so to speak, had thrown in the towel and they were having a high old time of it there in Eleanor's salon, Maynard the poet and I at an impasse. He was understandably importuned. So now I sit here in the Blue Danube, writing an impression of it all down. Here is Moonface to ask me what really happened. She rolls her eyes up and to the side. It is something she does, and it is, at times, in an appealing way, characteristic of her nature. 'All hell broke loose,' I answer, and then return to my reverie, giving Moonface no more reason to hang about. Dubois saw me leave the Prentiss living room, the look on his face that of a man who was amused by something or another, but who was wondering what this other fellow, namely me, was getting up to? The gesture I provided him expressed the fact that I had no idea. I could see Ralph was troubled; even so, he would trust to the fact that, in due course, all would be revealed and explained. He was collecting glasses for the washing up, the room emptied now of all persons save for Dubois, Eggy, Maynard and myself about to step into the hall. And Maynard, seeing that I was about to exit, decided it was as good a time as any to take himself off. I suggested we meet in the near future at the Blue Danube. 'Actually, the café is named Le Grec,' I said, 'you go out the door downstairs and turn right. Can't miss it.' I have to say I got the impression Maynard was not much interested. I entered Eleanor's digs. Her knickknacks and plants and overflowing ashtrays. The lived-in look. She was a solitary who loved the company of men. She was a thinker who, nonetheless, did not vex herself overly much with somber reflections. I raised the kitchen. I was very tipsy. It did not render me anymore sober that here, here was Eleanor in the arms of Phillip, who was backed against the kitchen counter by her hips. Marjerie held something in her right hand. My stuporous eyes made out a pair of scissors that she was about to wield as a weapon.

It seemed unnaturally quiet. I supposed that sound had even less chance than light of escaping the gravitational effect of a black hole. It seemed an odd ballet of hooded figures in a deer park, a sky beginning to darken and squall. At first, Phillip was fascinated by Marjerie's arm so evidently poised to deliver a mortal blow. Then he was mildly alarmed, so much so he wrenched Eleanor aside just as I got to Marjerie from behind, yes, in the nick of time. 'Jesus effing Christ,' Eleanor said, unable to trust her eyes. Marjerie, in my grip, did not resist. I locked my free arm around her waist so as to render her immobile. She did not register contact. Woman confronted woman. The amazed and seemingly slow-to-boil Eleanor regarded a sullen Marjerie. Then a grin took hold of Eleanor's countenance, and it was her disbelief, her guilt, her, hey, stuff happens grin. Phillip searched the refrigerator for a beer. There was none to be had, and he mumbled something about Marjerie's fridge. Marjerie surrendered the scissors to me and I let go of my captive. She was temporarily bereft of sense, and yet, Eleanor should consider herself put on notice. 'I could've killed you,' Marjerie dully announced. 'And you,' she said, facing me, 'you're an accomplice.' If there was any truth in the statement, it lay so deep beneath the surface of things that it could not matter. Here was Dubois. Dubois, to be sure, understood drunken and crazy behaviour, only that the atmosphere in the room was supercharged. 'Roll me a ciggie, sport,' Eleanor asked of me, her hand on her belly, she swallowing. And now, so as to complete a tableau, I supposed, here was Ralph put to the wise by Phillip. 'Come on, Marj,' spoke a man resigned to picking up the pieces. Marjerie, as if in a fairy tale, stomped her foot, bare heel striking a faux parquet kitchen floor. Then they filed out, three lost pilgrims without benefit of the world's understanding. In shuffled Eggy with his cane. 'What's going on? Effing hell.' Dubois took a chair and sat. It was no time for me to be sticking around. Let Eggy and Dubois sort things out. In my digs, the TV switched on, I watched a history of old Warner Brothers films. I learned why Bette Davis was what she was, that her complaints vis-à-vis the studio system notwithstanding, in no other venue could she have articulated her vision. Ditto for Crawford and Stanwyck. Bogart, in the filming of *Casablanca,* wondered why a man in his right mind would give up Ingrid. My eyes got heavy, even as they rested on the latter starlet's marvel of a face. I suppose that, in my dream, I relived the evening's happenings, only in a more confused and lurid light, the details of which I had thought to recount and then thought better of it. 'Well,' I say to Moonface back at my table again, wanting her due, 'things did get nasty.' 'Oh dear. Eleanor and Phillip? But I don't feel sorry for Marjerie. I think, you know, she plays with fire. Anyway, I'm happy. Happy, happy, happy.' 'I'm happy you're happy,' I answer, and it seems a foolish response.

Negative Externalities

Consecrated souls, indeed. *The rain in Spain. Hang the bastards. Hoo hoo.* No movie should depict us, Eggy and me and Eleanor and Dubois and Moonface. Poem or song should boycott us. Comedians should just throw in the towel and novelists run for the hills. Or betrayal shall finish what betrayal began. Still, Cassandra's eyes are bemused witnesses to human antics. The old woman and her *schatzi* of a dachshund on our noble boulevard? God's judgment on a failed experiment, the hairline cracks of Dubois's wine-red cheeks not the worst of it. Words, true today, are tomorrow's betrayals. And then, at some moment, time and space as we have known it, shall simply cease.

§

Part Four

Grandeur

Book I—Pavilions of Gold

Eggy *In Extremis*

Cranach might have painted her, pranked her out nude in pearls. Moonface as Venus. The same unbearably pale skin. The same thin lips. Just that she was not as insipid-looking or as cold to the contemporary eye. Even so, the dear girl never looked so ethereal, the alarm in her gentle eyes genuine enough. She stood behind the cashbox at the counter, prepared to engage the phone. Old Eggy, his chin on his chest, lips turning blue, seemed in a dream-state; if so, it did not appear to be an unpleasant dream-state, his expression somewhat pensive but not unduly troubled. Dubois placed a hand on Eggy's forehead, then stroked the sallow cheek of an inverted triangle of a face. Perhaps he figured he was saying goodbye, the way he called Eggy's name, yes, as softly as a south wind in the trees. He looked on the old man as a father might a beloved son.

'I think,' I said, 'we'd better have that ambulance.'

And Robert Dubois signalled Moonface to go ahead, and she punched the numbers that declared an emergency was in progress. Wherever Eggy was, he was deep in that place, and I figured as well that this was it: the old bugger was finally wearied of us. Dubois had the air of a man born to manage a crisis, blue eyes glittering with intelligence.

'How long?' he asked.

'They're on the way,' answered Moonface, hopefully.

She was in her working garb: coarse white shirt, black denims. Her hair, sandy-coloured, without highlights, was wound tight at the back of her head; it seemed, for her, a new look. Her eyes, black in the light of the purple tear drops—lamps suspended from the ceiling—were actually a rich, golden brown. Eggy continued to dream, Dubois quite serene. Elias popped out of the galley to see what was up, a silly grin his worry. I wondered if Eleanor might show and come across yet another corpse, remonstrating with Death as one might with a cat who drops a bird or a mouse at one's feet.

We recognized the siren for what it was: the clarion call of consequence. Soon enough, three youthful medics tramped through the door, two men and a woman in uniform. They brought gear into Le Grec aka the Blue Danube. Immediately, they removed Eggy from his chair and set him on his back on the floor. The woman attempted to communicate with her charge.

'*Anglais*,' Dubois advised, '*anglais*.'

This was how things were in Montreal, our faded Jezebel of a town.

Even so, Eggy would have understood the woman's French.

'Sir,' she said, turning Eggy's head so that his eyes, still closed, would look straight up, 'what's your name?'

Moonface brought food to Miss Meow and her companion. Eggy may as well have been a floor show. Miss Meow miaowed. At his table, the Whistler whistled and stomped his feet. Oh, he had seen death before, so those feet of his seemed to indicate, feet that were, allegedly, those of a fighter pilot who had flown for the Israeli air force.

'He'll live,' the Whistler whistled somewhat sardonically between clenched teeth.

Other regulars were missing out on the spectacle—Blind Musician, for instance. Gentleman Jim had not been seen in a long while. Antonio the Italian-Albanian waiter was off-shift, he who would kiss Eggy's pate for luck now and then, much to Eggy's disgust. Cassandra, wife to Elias, was presumably at home or at French lessons. Gregory, too, was home, perhaps attempting, as Eggy often put it, to incur fatherhood.

The ancient homunculus stirred, roused now, wires attached to him. A machine spit data like ticker tape. Moonface rolled her eyes up and to the side, a characteristic gesture of hers. Dubois and I went to smoke cigarettes outside on the terrasse, and in the autumnal dark we puffed and observed silence. I had wanted to talk to him about bank failures and the credit freeze, he a man of business, semi-retired. His faith in the system was nearly blown. I understood he would accompany Eggy in the ambulance; clearly, it was going to come to that. I would go and let Eleanor know.

'You wait,' Dubois finally said, 'in a few minutes he'll be giving the nurses a hard time. He's not going to like staying in hospital overnight.'

'I hope some social worker doesn't get a hold of him, and he gets stashed in a nursing home.'

'Not a nice thought,' Dubois the arch-materialist countered.

An old woman, her dachshund on a leash, stared through the window, shaking her head at the scene. Foolish men. The sidewalk was slathered with cold, fallen leaves. The absurd dog whined.

'Come on, *schatzi*,' the old woman said, innocent in Babylon.

People went in and out of the venues across the street—the liquor store, the video store, Drunkin' Donuts. Life was good. Dubois and I went back inside. The medics, still hunkered over Eggy, discouraged him from raising his head.

'Your blood pressure dropped,' said the female medic, her tone severe, temper bad.

'How much do you drink?' she thought to ask.

Eggy lied shamelessly, his voice frail and riddled with guilt.

'And your name?' she asked.

'Effing hell, I told you.'

It was old Eggy's old, thundering voice. Dubois guffawed.

'You passed out. Do you know that?' the woman hectored her rebellious charge.

'I'm not exactly a simpleton.'

She rose to her feet and shrugged. *What a horrid old man*. Dubois gave her a look that suggested she should lighten up. He said something in French to the two male medics who then grinned. In the end, they put the old Eggy carcass on a stretcher and wheeled him out to the ambulance, Dubois at Eggy's side. And in the process Eggy gave me a look, and it was a look that said *I know you, but you know, I haven't really seen you before. Effing hell. Oh well. The rain in Spain. Hoo hoo.* It was not quite Eggy with his customary death-is-just-over-the-horizon-for-me eyes; it was Eggy in discovery, and yet, it was understood the epiphany would pass. Eggy and his entourage now out the door, the café returning to normality, my eyes were all over Moonface. She did not appear to mind. She had been heroic on the phone, supplying relevant details, responding to the 911 operator's questions. The episode, all told, had lasted roughly half an hour.

Eleanor Restless

Those who touted the felicities of progress as their greatest happiness were idiots, so I had long since concluded. They were not unlike pushers pedalling highs. I was Randall Q Calhoun, All-American boulevardier. All-around layabout. Passive observer of an on-going farce. Mr and Mrs Civic Smile, of course, had no reason to take me seriously. Why should they? They were busy being civical. Traymoreans dealt with me as they would the weather: day to day, but that I was somehow inevitable. How inevitable had Current President been, eight years of his regime written in stone, try as one might to forget them? Previous tenants of the Traymore Rooms—the so-called pseudo-Traymoreans Marcel and Lucille Lamont and Osgoode—were now mythical, as shadowy in their Tartaruses as Tantalus, origin of a curse that could not be broken. Marcel Lamont may have drunk himself to death, consuming himself, so to speak; Lucille may have killed him, leaving her husband with that lethal case of gin before she buggered off. Osgoode, no doubt, was even now floating from cult to cult, pedophile and Holy Roller. The man was all methodical gusto, American-born. Was there something in his way of pursuing aims that was distinct from how his Finnish or Venezuelan counterparts pursued objectives? On what might an ologist chew?

So there had been nothing more to say or make of Eggy's swoon. Besides, Moonface was caught up now with walk-in trade and phone customers. I took my leave of the café that, on some nights, was more an asylum than the taverna Gregory and Elias wished it to be. Eggy was going to survive the night just as he had before, when his heart acted up. He would live to consume more wine; he would thunder at us. Zeus-like Eggy. He would explain to Moonface why she was his complementary function all the while she rolled her eyes, Dubois guffawing.

I returned to my digs, climbing the Traymore stairs. Mrs Petrova's radiator pumped heat. There was a rather large spider on the wall, perhaps drifted indoors for the winter season. I unlocked my door, entered the apartment, switched on a light. On my couch, I opened a book at random and read these words: *the proper disposition of materials.* It was, after all, a book of ancient literary criticism. Once more, I knew why I had failed literature. Eleanor. Oh dear. I had yet to catch her up to speed with things Eggy; that he was in hospital for the duration; that Dubois was there, hanging about. I got up from the couch, poured a whiskey, drank it, and made for the good woman's door.

En route, I stood at the window at the end of the hall, seeing nothing, really, and everything. *Was I properly disposed*? Lit windows. Flickering TV screens. A cat in the back lane. A raccoon was absolutely comfortable with its existence. By day, the maples blazed in their yellows and oranges and russets. There was a great poem in it; I would never write the thing. In any case, as it turned out, Eleanor had already heard the news. This woman of gilded curls, wide gypsy skirt and pompadours, got a call from Dubois, he talking to her from the medical centre in Verdun, Montreal comprised of various municipalities.

'So,' said Eleanor to me, 'is the old fart on his last legs?'

There was a peculiar look in her eyes.

'Oh, I don't think we've gotten rid of him, yet,' I drolled.

Usually, we carried on in her kitchen. She liked to bake and cook; and, as I would watch her go at it, I would roll her a cigarette and she might offer up an amaretto, and we would converse. Gossip. Political views. It even went so far, at times, that we flirted. Just at this moment her intention was stunningly clear; she planted on me a searching kiss. We had been through this before, these forays into unvisited territories that were, even so, heavily touristed.

'Not this time, Calhoun, you're not getting off so easy.'

It would seem that, in me, the customary whimper of protest died away, extinguished, I supposed, by the effrontery on her part, and the timing of it, and who knows what operations of the random? Had Eggy's near-death episode realigned the stars?

'What about Bob,' I said, 'for God's sake, Eleanor.'

Bob Dubois, so Eleanor reasoned, was going to be occupied for a while.

'But this is not good,' I pointed out, beginning to look for refuge in the possibility that she might find the situation faintly comic and so, come to her senses.

'Of course it's bad. That's the point, you boob.'

'Eleanor. Eleanor,' I said, repeating her name, 'we've been through this. Either I get cold feet or you get cold feet, and mostly I get the cold feet.'

'I guarantee you they're going to sizzle.'

By now, she had led me into her bedroom, she cheery and frolicsome. She was a woman who had set her mind, oblivious of hazard.

'Yes,' she said, 'I'm going to get to the bottom of you. Here's what we'll do. We'll howl, a little, at the moon, you and me. Meanwhile, I'm going to lift my skirt. Observe. Like this. I'm going to lubricate, *voila*, with this. Get the picture. You're going to make available your manhood. You're going to rise to the occasion. The rest should fall into place, pardon the pun, ha ha, that is, if you remember how. If not, I can provide pointers. This isn't literature, this is life, poet schmoet. Prentiss down the hall gets to have her two studs and they don't have to take turns. Afterwards, we might feel awful, who can say? God knows, you'll climb up on a cross. I can smell that coming as we speak. Later, I'll get Bob's report on Eggy and I'll kiss him good night, unless I'm asleep, already. I'll feed him fine cuisine for a week, my penance. Maybe he'll take me to the Caribbean. Always wanted to go there. Let's get cracking, before I lose my looks.'

And so, what had been faintly comic was serious now, a matter of moment; she fussing, she enthused.

A Note from Dubois

No doubt, Dubois slipped his note under my door at some ungodly hour of the night. He had tapped it on his keyboard and printed it off.

To: Randall Q Calhoun,

Here is a quick report, given that it is now 0330 hrs.

The doctor at Verdun Hospital is beautiful. But she does not believe Eggy has only a glass of wine a day. It appeared probable she would have him transferred to Montreal General in the morning. He was already looking alright to me by the time I left. He made sure I was to realize that he was all there by recounting his recollection of the events: what happened before he lost consciousness, what went on after he came to again following the arrival of the paramedics, the ride to Verdun H, the beautiful young female doctor . . . all in absolutely clear and exact details. In my own mind, I could do nothing else but to pronounce him fit to venture into the Blue Danube again as soon as he is discharged. At first, in the ward of patients in rather bad shape one way or another, he looked quite out of place. He thundered a little. Moonface would have felt perfectly at home with his comportment. I hung around a while, and then it was quite late. Anyway, it's looking up, in no uncertain terms in my book. I'll see you in the café. Best regards.

Robert Dubois
Conseiller d'affaires sr / Senior Business Consultant

An Apology of Sorts

I did not believe Eleanor meant me harm. Nor did I believe she intended herself any. I figured I had, at one time or another, become familiar with many of the facets that were the many-sided diamond of what transpired between man and woman, enough to know Eleanor was not mean-spirited, just daffy now and then. She would back hope over experience without a blush; she would then land hard and sound for all the world like the voice of realism. There we were in her bed, pilgrims who blundered into some realm, the particulars of which we seemed to know before the fact and yet, the knowing did not mitigate folly. So that she, after a fashion, apologized. It was not so much what she said as what she did not say. She had not, in fact, gotten to the bottom of me. Well, fancy that. Since when did human beings ever get to the bottom of one other, humankind eminently predictable, but that there was always scope for a little surprise?

'No,' she said, 'I should've learned my lesson a long time ago, and maybe, I didn't, that I'd only properly know a man in bed. Well, Calhoun, consider yourself reprieved: you're an effing enigma.'

I refrained from itemizing a thousand reasons and more that might tell her she was wrong. Among all the varieties of sex one might experience, there was sex that maintained the status quo agreeably or otherwise; there was sex that promised much and delivered little; there was sex that, now and then, quickened the spirit. There was sex that one anticipated ruing and wound up not regretting, really, perhaps because, for one reason or another, no one (Dubois, for example?) had been betrayed by it. Eleanor and I simply collided; our bodies obeyed the physical laws. Her body pleased me. Her mind, pursuing her pleasures and her questions, as well, pleased me, too. If I managed to reciprocate in kind, I wondered if she would tell me. She did not.

'So, lover boy,' she said, 'roll me a cig.'

Yes, I would roll her a cig in this, our new world, one made new by foolishness; one made old by new miseries.

'I think you think God made you for other purposes,' she offered. 'But I can't imagine what purposes those might be,' she drolled, 'you poet schmoet you.'

'There's no god who makes us for any purpose,' I said, somewhat miffed, 'just that I do believe something whispers at us every once in a while, and we are either wise or very stupid to listen.'

'Whatever.'

She was not impressed by my attempt at wisdom, and evidently, she did not find herself in a new world so much as she lay in surroundings quite familiar. She was disheveled at my side, the look in her eyes half smug, half quizzical, what with her gilded curls framing the pleasant features of her face.

'You certainly have a splendid bosom,' I said, yes, like a man who has long loved an image by way of book or print, and then, confronted with the real item, understands why he had been in thrall to it.

'Of course,' she said, 'whatever else would my breasts be but splendid. Crikey, Calhoun, it's not like you to trip over the obvious. How would you describe them? Ripe melons?'

'I think you were a lover boy once upon a time,' she continued, 'but I think you've retired from the fray.'

I handed her a cigarette, my thoughts now drifting elsewhere. It had just popped into my head: *next, Moonface.* It was a demented thought; it was not entirely welcome. I saw the girl begowned in my mentations, whirling, waltzing, singing a tune with coquetry and point. *How will I look Dubois in the eye?* I bridled, too, at Eleanor's mention of Marjerie Prentiss with whom two men were obsessed. There was Ralph her beau and intended husband, and Phillip her lover boy. The intricacies of this three-way were what she and Eleanor would talk to death in Eleanor's kitchen. And then, one evening, Marjerie had come across Eleanor and Phillip in an embrace; she flew into a rage and was just this side of murderous. Subsequently, she and her swains retreated to the Townships to cool off, there where Ralph had a house on which he was working. I supposed that if Marjerie and Eleanor had not gotten so chummy, I would not be lying there just then, *in flagrante* with the latter, *as if Marjerie's hold on Eleanor's psyche had made it possible.*

'Look,' I said to a dear friend, 'we've misbehaved. I should have my head examined. But I really don't want Bob to catch us here like this. I'm going back to my digs.'

I kissed the good woman's cheek, a tear forming in her eye. Even so, she said with some heat: 'Well, it's been swell. But you're just going to leave me here beached like a whale?'

'You're home,' I answered, 'how can I be leaving you anywhere? Unless you're a little uneasy in your mind?'

'Uneasy? You bet, I'm uneasy. Alright, so it was my idea. You didn't have to go along with it. You never do.'

Hell's bells.

'I'm going to miss this, whatever this was, but I'm not much of a lover boy. Never really was. Too effing sombre. If I was hauled up to the Pearly Gates and made to account for my deeds, no hope of bluffing my way through, it's what I'd say. "God," I'd say, "take it or leave it."'

The thing of it was I had just lied. I had been something of a lover boy, once upon a time, my experiences mixed. Some had been good, some a horror show, some sublime. I had been a prince, a cad, a saint. The gamut, you know.

'I feel damn silly now,' Eleanor observed.

'Well, don't,' I put it to Eleanor, pique stealing into my voice.

I got off the bed, hitched up my pants, tucked in my shirt.

'Can't I come over and we talk a little?'

'Now you really are being silly. What's to say?'

'I just might come over.'

'If you must, you must, but right now, I'm going.'

SET-PIECES
Canadian Beige

We are motoring down the 401, Toronto-bound. Dubois is at the wheel of the van, a white tuque with red stripes slopped on his vain and handsome head. He is happy. Perhaps there is something of the nomad in him, Eleanor in the seat at his side, fetching and chatty, wearing her tarty boots. She says: 'Why, it's beige, Canadian beige, the dread colour of November. The colour of those cornfields.'

Dubois guffaws. It was to have been presumably quite the party of like-minded souls making the trip. Eggy, Evie Longoria, even Moonface. Joe Smithers, aka Too Tall Poet, thought he might be interested; hence the rental of the van now conveying only four lost souls toward the bitch city, Eleanor having arranged that her cousin should lodge us all for a couple of nights as she had a large house. But Eggy did not think he was up to the trek, just out of hospital. And Evie figured that maybe she ought to stay behind and keep an eye on him, an intention which occasioned in me an uncharitable twinge of envy. Too Tall Poet cancelled predictably enough.

Moonface, however, does occupy a corner of the back seat; I have the other. Her right leg propped beneath her, her hips a force, she plays with her sandy tresses. And I read Champagne Sheridan in her eyes and his jealousy of her affection for other males. It does not bode well for Ecuador, where she and he are going in January. In any case, Eleanor is determined not to let Moonface's moodiness affect group morale.

'Did you see that,' she asks, 'that sign? A Conversation in Jewellery, my arse. A shop full of whispering earrings? Yuppie heaven.'

Dubois guffaws. Bright sun. Cold landscape.

'It's like the icing on a Tim Horton maple doughnut.'

The slightly musical moan belongs to Moonface.

'What is?' asks Eleanor, playing along.

'The fields,' answers the sighing, long-bellied goddess at my side.

But, as it is, I am distracted by the sight of Eleanor's knee. Well, it is a welcome distraction from stubble and the first snow and a dead animal on the highway's shoulder. I worry now that it is a bad idea, this going down to Toronto for a poetry jamboree in which I am slated to participate along with Vietnam-era war resisters, citizens now of a phantasmagorical land. What will I have to say to them after all these years? Nothing, it would seem, as the years have bled away in that which keeps breaking and will break, forever; as anger has a longer shelf life than hope; as I am perversely skeptical of the celebratory.

'It's going to be vile. Let me warn you.'

'Calhoun, for God's sake,' says Eleanor.

'A double-digit line-up of readers? It'll take forever.'

'More reason to drink,' Eleanor reasons, 'speaking of which—'

The good woman rummages in a commodious bag and extracts her amaretto.

'Anyone else?' she says, after she has had her swig.

'No? Roll me a cig, then.'

And so commanded, I roll her one. Then I address myself, like this: 'Here you are, Calhoun, with people for whom you have the warmest feelings. No accounting for it, but there it is. Dubois is doing what he does best: shepherding. Eleanor is Eleanor, which is to say, sexual, and she doesn't care who knows it, and she has no trouble looking Dubois in the eye, and consequently, I have no trouble, either. Moonface drifts as she has always drifted, in her body and in her intellect. The part she has to play in this drama of the moment is not a major one for her; there may not ever be a major part for her, but if there is to be one, it's, as yet, in the future. Look, she yawns. Her thin lips disappear as she yawns. She rolls her eyes up and to the side. You are probably mistaken, but the look she gives you, though she's abstracted, is remarkably like an interested party look. Her eyes settle on you.'

A Reckoning in Eleanor's Kitchen

'So, you filthy beast,' she says.

I shrug. Then I blurt out the worst thing I could possibly say, given the situation: 'Is it any of your business?'

The good woman gives me a quick, a startled and rather hurt look, then returns her attention to the dough she is working with penitential hands.

'No,' she says, her voice unusually small.

But the harm is done, and the truth is, it is not any of her business, and a further truth is that my words might have suggested to her I had had intentions all along, when it came to Moonface; and a yet further truth is that I had no such intentions, at least, not just then; the girl simply came upon me in the wee hours of the morning in that Toronto basement, the Moonface aspirations nothing with which to trifle.

'But you're not going to let it become an ongoing thing,' Eleanor says, her voice confident again.

'No, I'm not going to let it.'

'Good.'

'Because?'

'She's going to Ecuador with Sheridan. It's love.'

'She seems to have moved backed into the Traymore. I guess she's letting Sheridan know what's what. And what's what is that she's tired of his jealousy.'

'Maybe he has reason. I hadn't realized she could be dangerous.'

'He always has to know where she is, and what woman likes that? Do you?'

'No.'

'But she loves Sheridan, I think, and maybe she'll make a man out of him.'

'She has to make a woman of herself, first.'

'Eleanor, now you're being, what, avuncular.'

'I can't believe I'm jealous of that twit of a girl.'

'You don't expect me to keep paying you bedroom visits?'

'No, I don't suppose I do.'

'Well, good. We got that straight.'

'But you might want to.'

'I might want to, but I can't and I shouldn't.'

'What's with the scruples? Since when have any of us ever had scruples? You know, I think it's only Bob who has ever had any, and I know how he gets, sometimes. He can charm a woman's knickers off at a hundred yards.'

'He evidently charmed yours.'

'He certainly did.'

I have always admired Eleanor when she cheerfully admits the obvious, and it is as if the discovery is all hers. The good woman slaps the dough around.

'Just a few days left until reckoning time,' she says.

'What reckoning?'

'The election.'

'Oh that. Yes, well. How about some amaretto for the dread in my gut?'

'Only if you roll me a cig, please.'

A Reckoning in the Blue Danube

'So you finally did it.'

'Did what?'

'You know what you did.'

'You're going to have to spell it out.'

'You boffed Moonface.'

'She boffed me. There's a difference.'

'Some difference.'

'Anyway, it wasn't what it may seem.'

'It never is.'

'We were drunk.'

'I'll say.'

'I was too drunk to perform.'

'Did you get a look at her bosom?'

'Do you need to know?'

'I guess you did. You know, you must take me for a fool. You and Eleanor. *Merde*. No, she hasn't said anything. She's been too good to me, lately. It's been a long time coming, I guess, but I think the time for it came, you and her. I don't know whether I appreciate the fact you haven't said anything, or she, for that matter, or whether I'm really pissed off because when the cat's away, the mice will play. So, what do you say?'

Dubois fixes those blue eyes of his on me, his soup spoon holding steady halfway between the bowl and his mouth. I have no way of knowing whether he is furious or amused or all of the above.

'Nothing, really,' I say, 'you know what Eleanor's like.'

'Yes, I do know what Eleanor's like, but what are you like? Tell me that.'

'Well, I suppose I'm an ass.'

'No you're not. Too easy an answer.'

'I'm not?'

Cassandra approaches the table with the coffee pot.

'What's he like?' Dubois asks her, regarding me.

Her smile ravishes. Her eyes are large and luminous.

'I don't know,' she answers, 'what's he like? Nice. He's, you know, nice.'

'Yes, I think he's nice, too,' Dubois says, stifling a guffaw.

A stifled guffaw on that man's part portends a journey into irony.

'He's nice but he's a sonofabitch,' he laughs.

'Sonofabeetch,' Cassandra mimes.

'God,' says Dubois, 'if Eggy finds out what you've been up to, he'll—'

'He'll what?'

'He'll be beside himself.'

Cassandra, smiling, turns around and leaves.

'The next thing you know you'll be doing her,' says Dubois.

'Don't be silly.'

'I'm not being silly. You're a menace.'

'I've nothing to apologize for. It just happened.'

'You've been fighting her off all this time and you finally gave in?'

'Something like that.'

'Nothing ever just happens.'

'The war in Iraq?'

'Let's not get off the subject.'

'And what's the subject?'

'I just came from seeing Eggy in his rooms. He's had another episode. I'm going to call his doctor. I think it has something to do with his medication. I hope so, because I don't know what else to think, and thinking that thought doesn't feel good.'

'Oh dear.'

Either Dubois was a prince among men or he, too, was fatally flawed, preferring to fixate on Eggy's health while choosing to ignore the little matter of my penance.

Dead Bird

Mornings, and she used to cross the hall and enter Eggy's lair. And it delighted him, and delighted, he thundered, Zeus-like Eggy, that she was his complementary function. That she—pajama'd and berobed, in beaded slippers—would allow him to think he could reach for her, and he would miss and he would mutter, 'Ungrateful wench'. However, now Moonface joins me instead, here at the window at the end of the Traymore hall. There is the duplex, half of which Edward Sanders aka Fast Eddy once owned, that abuts Mrs Petrova's little yard. To the right, on the roof of a garage, head bitten off, breast broken open, is a dead bird. Wind-ruffled feathers are stuck somehow to the rooftop tar. Dead, most lonely bird.

'Cat,' says Moonface, 'a cat got it.'

Orange-leafed maples. That winged carcass. My inert notebooks. Great shouting out of futility. A blast of rock and roll music erupts from somewhere but is immediately extinguished. I have been part and parcel of a generation that wasted itself, however much was invested and saw handsome returns. Corruptions all around.

'Have you called Sheridan?' I ask the girl-woman at my side.

'No,' she answers, rolling her eyes up and to the side, that is to say, away from mine.

The Moonface countenance darkens briefly.

'But I will. I will very soon.'

'What will you say?'

'I don't know,' she says, more brightly now than is necessary.

'I'll say I like being back in my apartment. I'll say it's definitely on for Ecuador.'

'Are you angry with me?'

'Yes, but then, I've always been angry with you, even if I have no reason to be. The other night was all me.'

'Well, there was a lot of you all of a sudden.'

'I don't know where all that lot of me came from.'

'I don't know, either.'

'I was just trying to be pretty Emma. Emma pretty. I'm angry, you know, because I don't really look like Garbo.'

'Why would you want to?'

I know well enough my words are lame, but Moonface does not seem to mind.

'My face is ugly. You say my ears are too small. I'm too bony—'

'Stop it.'

'Well, it's the truth. And I can't stick to anything. Can't finish anything. But I can get boys in my bed and make it seem like it's a church picnic. And then women will tell me it's just, what, a behavioural pattern, all to do with lack of esteem and success, I guess.'

'Ah, the ologists.'

'Oh Randall.'

Erotic burblings. Those pale, slippered feet. And I kiss the cheek of a chameleon-like creature. She will return to Sheridan, or to some other Sheridan, but on renegotiated terms, I suspect. Suddenly, we hear Eggy in his digs thundering at the TV.

'Hang the bastards. Effing hell, they ought to hang. Always.'

Wherever Moonface and I have just been, the world itself, in all its sad and murderous disarray, has taken a hand, by way of Eggy, suggesting destiny or worse—that all love-making is theatre, a theatre of confusing gestures and sorry words.

As Noted

—Emma MacReady (Moonface) Jottings

Got in late, Montreal twinkling in the cold. Like Eleanor said it would, Bob's foot grew heavy on the gas as soon as we crossed the Ontario-Quebec line. 'Like a horse smelling his barn.' Bob only grunted. 'See,' he said, 'there's the sign. Danseuses.' 'Been there, done that,' said Eleanor. Randall's warm hand was inside my shirt, and sometimes he'd squeeze my breast. Like he didn't want to disengage. I didn't mind. Because we both knew it couldn't continue. No one said anything for miles and miles except when, now and then, Eleanor asked Bob how he was doing, if he was getting sleepy or anything like that. Every hour or so, he'd pull off at a service centre for coffee and a pee. No, he was doing fine. He'd get the troops home. It was snug, nestling up against Randall. And then when Bob dropped us all off and he went to take the van back to the rental place, and when, in the hall, Eleanor said to us 'Dahlings, ah bid you adew', she really was quite amused by something, and I think I knew what it was but I certainly wasn't going to ask her. Randall wanted to come in but I told him no, it would be too much. He almost seemed relieved. 'You read well,' I said. 'Did I?' he came back with. 'Awful lot to go through,' he said, 'for so little.' Have to deal with Sheridan, soon. He'll be going out of his tree.

Here's what happened. It was after the reading at the bar restaurant, and we were all of us at Megan's place. She's Eleanor's cousin, the one with the big house. Big, expensive, empty, sterile. But she's a nice woman. Divorced her husband after a long marriage. Got pretty well what she wanted. She's one of those women who doesn't wear make-up, partly because she doesn't have to, she has good features, and partly because she couldn't care less. Her hair was long, white and fine. Her eyes very sad. But anyway, we sat around in her kitchen, talking over the evening, drinking more wine. Randall was kind of downbeat. He didn't know why. He had expected more. 'Sentience is what you expected,' said Eleanor, 'something other than a bunch of depressives.' 'That's putting it a little strong,' said Bob. Megan said she saw those kinds of guys around town all the time. The hang-dog look. Eleanor wasn't having any of it. 'Hell, they're stuck in the Sixties. Still congratulating themselves for that as there doesn't seem to be anything else in their life to congratulate themselves for.' 'Now now,' said Randall, 'better that than the great yuppie sellout.' 'Oh, I don't know,' said Eleanor, 'what's wrong with a few material comforts I want to know?' 'I think it's a lot more than a few material comforts,' Randall answered, 'that yuppies have to answer for.' 'Well, I'm all yuppie,' Megan said, 'and I won't apologize for it.' Me, I kept smiling at Eleanor all through the evening. She doesn't have a high estimation of my powers. Don't know how Randall managed it, he was so drunk. By the time it came his turn to get up and read, it was so late in the evening and people were irritable. He could hardly stand. But he surprised us anyway: wasn't boring. 'Haven't read to so many Americans,' he said, 'since I read my What I Did for Summer Vacation essay to my fourth-grade class.' That got a laugh. We were in the back room of some bar-restaurant. Back at Megan's, and Randall went down into the TV room where he was going to sleep. Bob and Eleanor had a bedroom for themselves, and I another, but I hated it. It smelled of something that was supposed to have happened but never did. A clock chimed two in dark, cavernous space. I said to Randall, 'Guess who?' 'You're hands are cold,' he said. I wonder if he knew I was coming. He was stretched out on the couch with a blanket. I kissed him, and he sighed. His mouth tasted of cigarettes and wine. I didn't mind. 'But I don't know what you think you're going to get out of me,' he said, 'it's late, I'm drunk, I'm old, I'm shot, and I'm just another has-been Yank living off the fumes of some virtue that never was—' I shushed him. 'It doesn't matter,' I said, 'I don't care.' I unbuttoned my blouse. Enough said. Well, neither of us wound up sleeping much, not because of the hot sex, there really wasn't much of that, but because the couch was lumpy and narrow. Maybe at one point, I said, 'Emma pretty.' I hope I didn't, but if I did, I don't care. 'Eggy will be jealous,' Randall said. 'And so will Sheridan,' I said, 'but I'm not telling.' 'Don't,' said Randall, 'he won't understand.' 'What's to understand?' 'You're right, what's to understand?' Yes, but there's this much to understand: Randall got avuncular. He said this couldn't become a thing, that it was a one-off thing, and all that, and we were drunk and tired and maybe not at our best. 'Whatever,' I said. 'You took advantage of me,' he said, 'you minx.' 'Maybe,' I said, 'maybe I did just that.' And maybe I said that I was giving him my body in place of the poem I had yet to write for him. 'In that case,' he said, 'may the muse never darken your doorstep.' In the morning, I got a look from Eleanor. Oh, I felt like a woman. Oh, she was trying to tell me she was on top of things and fine with everything, but I think she was a little taken aback. She and Megan and Bob were putting together a big breakfast. Pancakes and bacon. There was snow in the yard that was deciding whether or not to melt. Randall was embarrassed and sheepish and hung-over, too. 'Well,' said Eleanor, 'I don't think you're in any danger of winning the Nobel Prize.' 'No?' said Megan, 'why not?' Maybe she was interested in Randall, but she might've thought it somewhat untoward for him to be playing around with a girl half his age. I would. We hung about in Megan's place for most of the day. There was a pool table in the basement. Eleanor kept waggling her rear end when it was her turn to shoot. Normally, I'd find this display disgusting, but I could see why she was doing it, especially after she said she hated the thought of getting old. Bob was worried about Eggy, speaking of getting old. I hadn't given the old bugger a single thought. No, I was wondering what I was going to tell Sheridan, how I was going to tell him I was moving back into my apartment, but that we could still go to Ecuador, seeing as the tickets are paid for.

A Bit of Academe

Already in the Odyssey three who are surpassingly guilty detach themselves from the grey crowd of the shades who lead an uncertain life in Hades—Tityus, Tantalus and Sisyphus. All three committed grave assaults on the gods, who in revenge condemned them to eternal torture: the gigantic body of Tityus is unceasingly gnawed by vultures; Tantalus is plunged in a pond the water of which flees from his eager lips, while above him is a tree of which the fruit escapes his hand as he wishes to seize it; Sisyphus unendingly rolls to the top of a hill a rock which always tumbles back down the slope. These souls, in order that their suffering may be more cruelly felt, have in Hades a vitality beyond that of the common run of the dead, who are pale, flimsy, half animate phantoms.

from "After Life In Roman Paganism" by Franz Cumont

'... but it is a truth that the country, caught up in its ruthless ambitions and moral decay, can learn on my dime. I don't know who will lead us through the '90s, but they must be made to speak to this spiritual vacuum at the heart of American society, this tumor of the soul.'—Lee Atwater, campaign manager for Bush 41 and death bed convert to Catholicism.

'... for here there is no place that does not see you. You must change your life.'

from "Archaic Torso of Apollo" by Rainer Maria Rilke

The more things change, and all that—RQC

§

Book II—In Continuation

More Lollapaloozas

Church bells pealed on a Halloween night. Once again, I stood at the window at the end of the Traymore's hall, ghouls to be seen in the back lane. The residence of Edward Sanders aka Fast Eddy, he no longer with us, had been sold and renovated and placed on the market again. It struck me as rapacious, the asking price, the market system a morality, an ordering principle. Young Augustus Caesar could tell himself many things, oh, that he made of the imperium a peaceable business; but for proper delusion he must have a firm grip on the reins of power. Eleanor stepped out her door.

'Roll me a cig, please,' she said, 'pretty please?'

She followed me into my rooms. And she commandeered my couch as I rolled her that cigarette, extending her body across its length, leaning back on the arm rest. She fully intended to be seductive; she was partially succeeding as she exuded body heat.

'I know you won't talk about it.'

'Talk about what?' I asked.

'I'm dying to know. You know, you and Moonface.'

'None of your business.'

'Oh, come on Randall,' she said, a certain unspoken trilling in her plea.

'I mean I know, basically, what happened. But the details, the details, boy, that's where all the lollapalooza is.'

'Eleanor, you're a thousand times more perverse than I.'

'I know. Ain't it grand?'

Eggy, homuncular man, was frocked in a blue blazer and dark trousers. A red poppy. A smoke-grey pocket square. It was a one-point fold, tip showing. Zeus-like Eggy was lost in that blazer, but nattily so. I handed Dubois my birthday gift to him. He felt the bag so as to determine its contents. The bottle was as decent a sherry as I could find on short notice in a nearby liquor outlet. I figured the substance would go well with his red cheeks and their hairline cracks. Evie Longoria was Eggy's symbolic date, she playing the part with some humour.

'Don't rush me,' she mocked-protested, as Eggy would have her get on with it—the signing of the birthday card.

'Bob is a complicated man. Simple words for a simple occasion will simply not do.'

'Effing bloody hell, woman.'

Dubois guffawed. Even so, I could tell the birthday boy was in a mood. Where was Eleanor? Evie Longoria, Alberta cowgirl, looked for all the world like a medium of a kind—a reader of palms and Tarot cards. Her hair was swept away from her pale temples, a knitted beret set on her head. Matching sweater. Voluminous skirt. Finally, she passed the birthday card to Eggy who promptly and painstakingly wrote his encomium and signed the thing. He slid the card to me. I read that Evie thought Bob a great guy. I read that Eggy thought Bob had kept him interested in life. I wrote than an arch-materialist ought to enjoy many happy returns of the day. So spaketh spiritual Calhoun.

There we were in the Blue Danube, Montreal losing badly in its hockey game on the flat screen TV. Moonface kept appearing every five minutes or so to ask how we were doing, her manner sincere, her thin-lipped smile a bit too over-zealous for the occasion. Eggy's chin raised his chest. Evie Longoria looked out the window into the darkness, passersby all at the outset of revelling. It struck me that she was the marrying kind. It also struck me she was in the hunt for a man, Dubois and me under scrutiny. Dubois endeavoured to keep the conversation going, now that it had to do with Evie and her plans. She was, she said, thinking of moving to Prince George, British Columbia. She interested me, no question; like Moonface, she, too, was a gentle creature, but with levels of rage in her I would not care to encounter should they surface. She did not believe that her daughter was doing at all well, slipping in school. Perhaps a smaller, less sophisticated town...

'And you,' said Dubois, 'what about you? Where in Prince George will you see dance and opera and theatre? In the local beer parlour?'

'I know,' she answered, 'it's occurred to me, too.'

Her eyes moistened. She was a woman who loved both the arts and cowboys. I studied her face like I might a map of the cosmos, in its features my own fallibilities. The eyes set wide apart. Prominent nose. Strong cheekbones. The small, even teeth. Long fingers worried a scarf wound loosely around her neck.

'I just get so tired of it,' she said.

Whatever was she tired of? The fully formed tears—they were Rembrandtian pearls. And Dubois took her hand and held it, Eggy slipping deeper into a torpor.

'It's alright. Let it out,' Dubois coaxed, Evie endeavouring to smile.

Just then, though she had all my sympathy, I determined to keep my distance from her. And just then, Eleanor showed, evidently in a mood of bravado. But when she saw what was taking place, she only said: 'My, my, what have we here?'

She struck the wrong note.

'I'm sorry,' said Evie who, perhaps, had nothing for which to be sorry.

I rose to offer Eleanor my chair, as it would seat her next to Dubois; she took it and she kissed her Bob, and let him know he would get his birthday present, later. At any other time but this, Traymoreans would ooh and aah Eleanor's suggestive tone.

'Well, I'm sorry, Randall,' the good woman addressed me, 'for stealing your spot.'

'I'll get another,' I answered equably enough, 'besides, I was just going to step out for a smoke.'

'Hang the bastards,' thundered Eggy, returning to the land of the living.

Traymoreans laughed, as did Evie, somewhat shame-faced.

'What do I have to do to get a drink in this place?' Eleanor demanded to know.

'Moonface,' Dubois called out.

And Moonface appeared, her eyes very sexy.

The Proper Pitch of Grandeur

Moonface knocked on my door in the morning, a look of accomplishment in her happy gaze. She had phoned her Sheridan, a personable young man whom I deemed deluded as to the *Xs* and *Ys* and *Zs* of this world, to the nasty particulars, his parents arty and liberal but otherwise cutthroat when it came to their ambitions. Moonface had dealt with her Champagne Sheridan who, at least, had the sense to want everything and would, most likely, wind up settling for a great deal less.

'And what did he say?' I asked.

'He said he was sorry.'

'Did he mean it?"

'Why wouldn't he mean it?'

'Don't know.'

I supposed, on the basis of our exchange, that Moonface loved the jealous boy.

'Anyway,' she said, 'I just thought I'd tell you. I'm stepping out to have coffee with Evie. We haven't talked in ages. I don't think she's too happy.'

'That's the impression I have.'

'She might go away.'

'So I hear.'

'You don't seem too bothered by this.'

I shrugged. Below us, Mrs Petrova was unlocking her shop for the day's business. Nothing seemed to defeat the old woman whom one never regarded as old, not in the sense that Eggy was ancient, with his 902 years worth of age or thereabouts; not in the sense that my bones ached (rain, perhaps, in the offing); not in the sense that age was the thing of which Eleanor was terrified. How many men would she yet torment before she succumbed to the inevitability of the human condition? Of course, such torments as she had to bestow were pleasant, agreeable, even delicious torments and so, by her way of thinking, why would men complain? We heard, Moonface and I, Marjerie Prentiss and her two swains descend the Traymore stairs. We knew we would hear more from this quarter in the coming days.

'Well then,' I said, 'give Evie my best.'

Moonface gave me a look. It would suit her fancies well that she and her Sheridan carry on in mutual harmony and bliss, and that I settle down with someone, Evie Longoria a prime candidate. The look I gave the girl suggested she think again. Traymorean weaknesses were also strengths: the catch-as-catch-can affair that was Eleanor and Dubois, decrepit Eggy who was, even so, Zeus-like, feckless. Moonface, of course. The indomitable Petrova. And then there was myself: cynical egghead of some vaguely realized but unexportable gifts. Taken in our entirety, we, as such, presented a front of a kind against a thieving world. And what was the world if not a thief horning in on one's ratty spirit? Marjerie Prentiss was of that world, determined to strengthen the beachhead she had already established in our midst. How very Christian of me to reason it out in these terms and yet, the pagan in me had fought the Christian for years, Dubois with his arch-materialism of no especial aid or help. I was beginning to conclude that one cannot be in and of the world with all its beauties and horrors without some internal mainstay, be it art or be it prayer, be it love or even, as it were, hatred; be it profit-motive; be it some sort of counter-balance, in any case, to evolutionary drift. It was perhaps unnerving to think a brief interlude of physical passion had occurred between us and yet, for all that, here we were in separate universes with our separate hopes and separate anxieties, all of the Grand Canyon filling the chasm that separated her ignorance from my irresolute nature.

'Off you go,' I said, like a father to his child.

Perhaps she figured the conversation had not truly ended. That flickering in her eyes of panic giving way to good cheer was her riposte to me. Often enough, I had seen her on the street performing—as Eggy called it—her chicken shuffle, a pout to her countenance: the world, damn it all, never seemed to cooperate. Seeing her like that, one could never, in a million years, regard her as a beauty or a powerful mind. It was a mystery to me—the source of her peculiar charm.

'Off I go,' she replied, somewhat rueful, her thin-lipped smile revealing bright incisors.

'Oh,' she said, just outside my door, and she gestured in the direction of Eggy's digs.

She meant that I should check on him. I nodded. She clattered down the stairs. And I did go and check on Eggy, and he was just fine, thank you very much, and he would deal with me later, so I ought to get out of his hair.

Unfinished Business

One might say I went into seclusion, this after the election's impending result was clear. Ohio called for the Illinois senator, and I left Eggy, Dubois and Eleanor in the Blue Danube to carouse. I could confess to mixed feelings, to some bewilderment; to the barest glimmer of a recognition that my adult life, rooted as it was in the bad old days of the Vietnam War, was going to be complicated with something like authentic hope, and I might have to see America in a new light. I ascended the Traymore stairs; in my digs I turned on the TV. Soon after, the Illinois senator was President Elect, and all that remained to round off the evening were the speeches to come. And even when the Arizona senator, officially conceding, quelled the boos emanating from his crowd of supporters and showed he was a gentleman; even as I told myself that America was still a collective madness, I saw no reason to wax cynical against that sea of tearful and hopeful countenances in Grant Park, the victor's crowd. Perhaps in no other empire but Rome did the contradiction run so deep, that one of an idealistic vein and the political machinery calculated to starve idealism of nurturing gases. Soon Dubois and Eleanor were hauling Eggy up the stairs, and the homuncular old man was singing, singing something like *a quack quack here and a cluck cluck there eee aye eee aye oh.* Dubois guffawed. I assumed Moonface was at her Champagne Sheridan's, as her digs were silent. I might not have minded a visit from her just then, and God only knew to what such a visit could have led.

In the morning, the air unseasonably warm, I occupied a bench in the nearby park. This park had the shape of an arrowhead, of the prow of a ship bearing trees of yellow, tattered leaves to some fabled port of call. But it seemed to me I was sleepwalking even as I sat there, alone with such emotions as I was sure no Traymorean would appreciate, much less comprehend. Sleep, so far as I could determine it, had been dreamless, the night before. There is the bottomless well of self that no light ever penetrates. Even our noble boulevard seemed unusually quiet, the morning's commute spent. I rolled a cigarette and smoked it. Passersby had the manner of feudal subjects. I half-expected her and, soon enough, I was set upon by Sally McCabe, she a beauty queen from my high school days, misbehaving daughter of a VIP. Her voice had long since been a mainstay of my mentations. She spoke: 'So, Randall, here you are. Are you not pleased? Here I am and, in America, a page has been turned. Or don't you know how to handle the pleasure? Aren't you just a little homesick now for the desert we knew, for the grandeur of that emptiness, for the teenage cruelties which attended our every breath? Especially now, now that the people have proven, once again, that they can turn an argument on its head and confound the world. That man as president—what audacity. Oh Randall, don't give me that look. Don't you recall how grimly you lusted for me, how steadfastly; how I was the whiskey, the boffing, the splendid starry nights? Alright, so it was all a horror to you, but where else, where else in the whole wide world is this possible—me and electoral surprises? I mean, really, Randall, here you are in this most staid of phantasmagorias, long in the tooth, condemned to the sidelines, a feckless, inconsequential poet. You miscalculated. Don't you see that now?' I answered: 'Sally, oh Sally, no doubt you have a point. No doubt I have missed your charms, even if I can't say I ever really had the experience of them, save for the singularity of a kiss and a cheap feel. Still, I'm not ungrateful for what little there was. I remain open to your blandishments, just that, well, I'm accustomed to the life here, to the provincial doldrums of this Jezebel town, and I'm not persuaded that history has been turned; that there is plenty of scope for it to turn yet again, and not for a happy outcome. Surely, you recall what you taught me: the infinite promise of your thighs a more compelling infinity than the hazards and happenstance of justice, as welcome as they are, at times.'

She wrinkled her delectable nose.

'Randall, you were always a little stuffy even when heroic, but I'm flattered, nonetheless. Care for a kiss? Randall, Randall, just kidding. Alas, we've gotten wise. I do note, however, that certain women hereabouts have made inroads on you. Lucky you. But don't worry. As it gets said, this, too, will pass.'

I was in Eleanor's kitchen, uncomfortably so, for all that the room was the finest of Traymore rooms, a commodious salon. Perhaps the source of my discomfort lay in the persons of Marjerie Prentiss and her carpenters Ralph and Phillip. Ralph and Eleanor were discussing the election results in tones that registered their approval. Phillip smoked and paced. I gathered he had hit up Eleanor for another loan, he in arrears to the Magog constabulary in the Townships on account of some drunken foolishness of his. Marjerie had not bothered to dress, she in drab, linen nightwear that reached her mid-thighs. It was garb in which a girl might sleep who still lived in the depressive air of the parental home. And perhaps Marjerie figured that no one was paying her sufficient attention. Or perhaps it was her argumentative streak, but she pooh-poohed the President Elect, saying she did not know why everyone thought him the Second Coming of Jesus Christ. Ralph gave her a look, one that said, no, that was not the point.

'Things are looking up,' I offered, uncharacteristically cheery, 'but the fact remains that the Americans are still bombing wedding parties. I mean, how many wedding parties can they blow to kingdom come?'

It was a question made to order for rebuttal.

'As many as they want,' a dull voice boomed.

'Really?' I said, knowing I was about to get dangerous.

Eleanor shifted her weight in her chair, dubious as to the turn the conversation was taking.

'Just bomb them all,' Marjerie recommended, fixing impassive eyes on me.

Phillip lit another cigarette and continued to pace, any politics but a workingman's politics alien.

Ralph frowned. Marjerie's intended had a comical set of ears, as they were large and they stuck out from his head; and they, to my mind, imparted Britishness to him. In fact, one of his parents, I could not remember which, was a Brit.

'What's that going to solve,' he asked, 'this bombing everybody?'

'Yes, well, what's talk going to solve?' Marjerie shot back, the acme of reason.

'Honestly,' said Eleanor, a little distraught, 'I don't know, sometimes, what I see in you, girl. Tell me, Marj, what it was I saw in you?'

Eleanor poured herself a taste of amaretto. She was rarely unsure of her mind, but in this instance, it seemed that conflicting loyalties were taking a toll on it. She asked me to roll her a cig. His gaze passing from woman to woman and back again, Phillip, no doubt, was confused as to which of them was most his heart's desire. Or did it matter, and he would have them both, if he could, in no particular order, and not necessarily separately? Ralph, with the air of a man who was forever picking up the pieces, wondered aloud why Marjerie was always, what, a contrarian, was always wishing for hateful things to happen to people she chose not to like.

'They do hateful things to us,' was Marjerie's simple reply.

Yes, and she had only to arch her back, as it were, which set off her bosom to advantage, nightwear lifting from her thighs so as to remind the man she had ascendancy; she called the shots when it came to lust and considered opinion. Eleanor, no stranger to the arts of seduction though she had not the patience for them, found this little demonstration of prowess on Marjerie's part irksome, Phillip about to leap out of his pants. He had the air of a man who had been overlong in the woods and was not uplifted by the experience. Marjerie's eyes narrowed. I was sensible of her charms, but I was also getting used to them, a development which permitted me to see the woman in a somewhat farcical light; that she really was rather provincial. And, as I was about to reach across the table so as to deliver Eleanor her cigarette, Marjerie intercepted my hand, held it in a show of significance, extracted the cargo, and placed it between her teeth, the only insouciant but empowered entity in the room. And she waited until one of us thought to offer her a light, and Ralph was the first among us to cave, as a gentleman does gentlemanly things. It seemed to me that whatever one thought of the woman's performance, she meant that one should think on it, and if one thought her contemptible, so be it. She squirmed like a coquette, just to put icing on the cake, she getting to be a middle-aged sex kitten, a Lolita who had unfortunate views. As there was no gainsaying her, I rolled another cigarette. And when I finished, I rose from my chair, went around the table to Eleanor's perch, and placed the item with its rightful recipient all the while I stood behind her. I lit it. I grazed her cheek with mine, she somewhat bewildered.

'Must run,' I said.

'Must you, dahling?' Eleanor trilled, now discovering her role in this most minimal of dramas.

'Yes, I must,' I asserted.

'Gentlemen,' I said, in acknowledgment of them.

'Marj,' I said, perhaps over-familiarly, addressing a wench, a woman who had not in her the slightest iota of the capacity for love, 'you are a piece of work.'

Perhaps I paid her tribute. Perhaps I served notice. A few mirthless chuckles in the room.

'Whatever does he mean?' she asked, as I departed.

I heard Ralph reaffirming that President Elect was good for the world. I heard Marjerie snort. Phillip wondered if there was any beer.

I stood a while in the hall, staring out the window at a backyard world. Towering maples. A lilac turned yellow. A dead white bird on the roof of a garage—It was a splendid day, bright and warm and very autumnal. I was not surprised when I heard the padding of Marjerie's large and unlovely feet on the carpet. It would not have been like her to leave loose ends hanging, and having reached me, she resumed an old conversational thread: 'You don't like me much.'

To be sure, I was weary of being told that I did not like her much. I wished I could say I thought her confused, because misinformed. Or that I could sympathize with the fact that, as a girl, she had been abused, passed by her brother from friend to friend. I could not. She was, how could I say it, perverse from the outset, though the ologies might argue that no one is born predispositioned. I could see that, despite the charms of her body, she had other charms as well, and could jest and smile and bat her eyelashes and treat anyone she chose with the warmest regard; but that, in her case, there was always a hook, all roads leading to it.

'I hear you've been having adventures,' she said, with ill-concealed amusement.

'Well, well,' she added.

I turned and looked straight into her. She really was amused, her watery, dead eyes registering the fact that her mental landscape had somehow been altered in interesting ways on account of my shenanigans.

'It's not any of your business,' I said.

'Why is what I do your business?'

'I've not made any of it my business. In fact, I'd say you go out of your way to make it my business, and that's what I don't like. And, if you must know, I don't know that I like that you make it Eleanor's business, but then, it's between the two of you.'

'Right you are.'

There was no mistaking it: she really was amused. And Lucille Lamont, pseudo-Traymorean, was now saying that, yes, it had been murder, and she had done it because she could do it; oh, not because she hated Marcel so much (she had loved him now and then), but because if she had not killed him he would have killed her; that is, his drinking and his problems would have eventually ruined the marriage and she believed she had deserved better. Lucille Lamont was a woman who knew what she knew, and what she did not know could hardly have been relevant to anything that mattered. In any event, she had gotten away with it. Death by misadventure, so the police put it. Was Marjerie Prentiss a witch that she could summon this voice of Lamont and have it plague me? Just as I was beginning to think

I would get the worst of this exchange with Marjerie, Eleanor stuck her head out her door and called down: 'Are you going to have coffee with us or what?'

Well, she was not inviting me.

'I'll be right there,' a dull voice boomed, and then it said, addressing me, 'it's not like I have to sleep with every man I meet, because I don't, and I'm actually quite selective.'

Those words of hers, I assumed, explained everything. She had placed the tip of her forefinger to the corner of her mouth, standing there playful yet myopic and, as ever, tickled. Perhaps one had to surrender all arguments to her if one wished to keep one's spirit intact. I resorted to an extreme measure: 'The rain in Spain,' I said, 'always.'

Long Fingers of Crimson Cloud

And perhaps I was, after a fashion, in love with Moonface, the realization a bullet taken smack between the eyes; she a woman still pretty much a girl. But that it could happen to anyone, yes, this love-state, even to a cynic such as me. And how like a boy: this urge to tell her of this love. *Say, did you know swans mate for life because courting uses up too much energy?* Now Dubois was political; he had organized and campaigned; by way of his business dealings, he had helped to direct flows of cash to needy coffers. He read the memoirs. Brian Mulroney. Paul Martin. Ex-prime ministers. He must have known his René Lévesque chapter and verse, how the man had been born in New Brunswick and was raised in Quebec. He argued Trudeau and Diefenbaker with Eggy. Suggest that the Kennedy brothers had made possible the liberal confidence, if not the swagger, of a Trudeau, and Dubois would more than likely agree. I myself had no desire to impose my sensibility on anyone; it is just that I resented being imposed upon, I a muttering egghead hoping against hope that President Elect, asked to walk on water, would not sink like a stone.

The sun shone in the hazy sky, the celestial entity on a line complementing the axis of our noble boulevard. It would make the hour of day roughly three o'clock. The Blue Danube terrasse was littered with crinkly leaves; I swept some off the table at which I sat. Moonface brought me soup, generic minestrone the offering. And girls in tight denims and boots went by, no particular cares troubling their gazes. Blooms were surviving the odd night of serious chill, but their days were numbered. A pesky wasp. The autumnal light put me in mind of Venice, as when one might look in the direction of Mestre, pollution augmenting the red glow of sunset. In receipt of some windfall, I would whisk Moonface off to a hired palazzo, and we continue our session and argue the merits of Goldoni or Titian, or of the painter—his name always escaped me—who depicted the snake-bit Eurydice in a time out of mind and far beyond the crassly banal. It was my natural milieu, so it seemed to me just then, and it ought to have been Moonface's, as well, her hips too much slimmed down, so I figured, alarmed. She went back inside, not a word exchanged between us, none needed. I had figured, too, that Eggy would take advantage of the warm temperature and avail himself of the terrasse, not many opportunities for that left between now and late April. I half-expected to see the homuncular man at 82, or was it 902? years of age, stumping along with his cane, hardly able to contain himself, what with some new tidbit of gossip concerning a nurse or a bank girl. Perhaps Dubois would show, vain and handsome Dubois with whom I remained on easy terms, despite Eleanor. Some skies could afford the histories that unfolded beneath them. Perhaps this one could, too, this New World sky lacking—and here was the painter's name—its Giorgione and the enigma he depicted and suffused with menace. Was I not thoroughly conversant with the poetry of heartache, the pop tune lyrics of my youth?

Long fingers of crimson cloud, the sun about to expire, and here was Marjerie Prentiss. Yes, here she was, party girl all made up—lip gloss and eye cosmetics—and her triumphal mood was the wind in her sails. She had the air of a woman who, but an hour ago, had overcome a particularly besetting fear. It did not seem she was just passing by, she taking a chair, her voice dully emphatic: 'You see, we don't need to ask your permission.'

I had no idea what she meant. Short skirt. Striped leggings. Modish jacket. And in the corner of my eye, I saw Moonface stiffen inside the café, exchanging polite words with the Whistler. Chameleon creature, daughter of a minister (United Church), Moonface was a girl who was too lady-like to admit that sex was carnal and yet, propose to her a somewhat off-colour joke and her dimples might surprise one, and one might wonder what she knew and when she knew it. And she who, otherwise, insisted on justice for all her customers no matter how irritating their behaviour, was not pleased to see this latest advent of Marjerie Prentiss. Moonface was somehow wise to this woman, but in ways of which she was entirely unaware.

And here were Eleanor and Phillip and Ralph, the threesome arm-in-arm, tipsy already, up to no good, a procession scattering leaves. They might as well have been skipping home from school, their pace, however, ceremonial, Eleanor's shiny, black boots contrasting greatly with the men's sneakers. I knew the look on her face, and now Marjerie's remark was effectively explained, my heart sinking at the knowledge, Phillip flicking a cigarette into the street. Collegial Ralph, his natural instincts those of a prince among men (and yet how blind he was), steered Eleanor onto the terrasse, his eyes large and luminous with what he understood as spiritual love, Phillip now bringing up the rear, seemingly bored. Well, the sky was spectacular, worthy of note, the light near silvery-gold, what with the autumnal trees. The eyes of Moonface were a rich, golden brown, or so I reminded myself. It was as if nature had designed them for this moment, and this moment only, the many atmospheric variables producing the effects to which we were all witnesses, unlikely to combine again in quite this way, that sky aching with transcendence. Sex was, in part, a desire to satisfy curiosity. Even so, Marjerie Prentiss had not, in the preceding minutes, aroused my curiosity; rather I was experiencing an unaccountable urge to defend my person.

'Randall, me boy,' Eleanor breathed, as she bent to kiss the back of my neck.

Marjerie's eyes narrowed. And the gentlemen grunted their greetings, chairs being drawn along the surface of the terrasse, bodies falling into place. The evening commute was at its most intense, a steady stream of buses discharging passengers. Car horns. Trucks. Squealing brakes. Phillip hunched his shoulders and looked around. He had the air of a man who has just had his bliss and would now attend to other appetites. *Ah, who is this girl? Moonface, you say.* It was clear these interlopers intended to hang around.

Eleanor, too, was made up to party, and she looked rather lovely, her gilded curls crushed by a soft felt hat, a fedora of sorts; it was an item I had never seen on her head, and it imparted a celebratory aura to her open expression. There was a vulgar way of putting it: she had been well and truly treated with, no question, and quite recently. And yes, there was nothing bad in the woman, just trouble and foolishness. Meanwhile, for Moonface, there was nothing for it but that she had to step out, menus in hand. She wound up for her peculiar little shuffle, forcing her steps to bring her in our direction.

'Emma,' said Eleanor, good-naturedly, addressing the waitress by her proper name.

'Eleanor,' said Moonface, unsure what to say next, rolling her eyes up and to the side, expecting the worst.

'A beer,' said Phillip, cutting to the chase. He was the one entity in this party who did not believe anything out of the ordinary had taken place within the last hour or the last ten centuries; he may as well check this girl out as drift into some other, perhaps, more entertaining bar.

Eleanor smirked. What a braggart she could be. Moonface, at least, had a script to follow: 'And for you?'

She rose nervously on her tiptoes and settled back down again on her heels, clasping those menus to her bosom as if they were protective layering. Beers all around, though Eleanor would have wine.

'Of course,' said Moonface, she knowing the woman's preference.

I had always supposed it was best that we each follow our natures, that to resist would bring even more grief on our collective heads. It had been a code of conduct for me for quite a long while, but I further supposed that the dictum could not entirely hold all the time. If Eleanor were an eminently sexual being even to the point of regret, she was not one, however, to succumb to the machinations of others, sex or no sex, and she was under a spell.

And all my life I had grappled with the problem of evil, or so it seemed; and the funny thing was, and it was embarrassing, that when confronted with its reality, one gasped like a fish out of water; one was an idiot in a state of panic, words, let alone complex sentences, grossly ineffectual. What was I going to do? Shoot this woman who was Marjerie Prentiss, the author of a humdrum coup? Current President—here was a man, a being, an entity against whom charges could be laid for heinous crimes, though he was as innocent as the day was long; inasmuch as some people had to die and he had decided who was to die, *and so forth and so on*, like any warlord of ancient days. One shrugged, thoroughly conversant with the American Way. Marjerie Prentiss, on the other hand, was a different matter altogether. The ologies aside (and I had no great faith in their determinations as to what booted it for the human condition), I had no doubt that, in this woman, there was no regard whatsoever for the well-being of others, not a trace of it; and if it were not tantamount to evil, it was very close to the diabolical. And yet, to whom was she obviously bringing harm? And on what scale? And the proof? Was not Eleanor pleased with herself? Had not Ralph and Phillip worked out an arrangement between themselves even if, at times, the arrangement broke down, and jealousy and the humiliations of rage gained the upper hand between them? How had Marjerie convinced these people that there was no other reality but herself, no other way of proceeding in this world but that she was its lowest centre of gravity? She could see how upset I was. Yes, and from out of nowhere I heard the near repugnant voice of Vincent Price addressing his dog in a horror movie scene: *You know they're out there, don't you, you poor driven thing.* How driven was I? Marjerie Prentiss was amused. For all that, Moonface was not, and no further instructions forthcoming, she turned and went back inside. I could easily enough surmise that she was angry; it was the flush that had crept up her neck, the long but thin cascade of hair that had escaped its clasp, obscuring her countenance. It was her thin-lipped mouth drawn small, a hissy fit of a mouth suggesting that somewhere in her being there was a frustrated moralist. I doubted she knew why she was angry, though I supposed I should not doubt her capacity to divine intangibles such as spell out the obvious; that Eleanor was a sucker and the gentlemen were hosers, Marjerie Prentiss smug. Should the conversation fail or prove awkward, I for one, would not come to its rescue. Even so, there was rescue of a kind, Eggy hoving to, making the turn to the terrasse, his cane uplifted, his tough, old eyes excited.

'Greetings,' he said, pleased to see a crowd, especially one of familiar faces.

I set him up with a chair.

'Moonface,' he thundered, demanding service.

'Well,' he wondered, 'what's the occasion?'

And I was surprised to see, and perhaps it was too good to be true, that Marjerie looked scuppered of a sudden; this homuncular man—for all that he had been mean to his wives and yet, in his own way, was devoted to Traymoreans—was somehow an antidote to her person. Moonface was happy enough to see him, she bringing beer and wine and glasses on a tray, and setting them down in each their proper place with the fastidiousness of one warding off evil.

'Who's cooking?' Eggy wished to know.

'And why haven't they got in those spinach pies, yet?' he said, incensed.

'They've got the cheese ones,' Moonface suggested.

'Don't want cheese pies. Effing hell. Damn Greeks, Albanians. What's the world coming to?'

But she would go and consult Serge, an Albanian, the worldly wise cook in the galley. Perhaps something could be arranged, and she would, while she was at it, get Eggy his wine.

'Oh yes,' he said, 'please do.'

And when she was on about her self-imposed task, Eggy addressed me, saying: 'You know what she needs? She needs to spend more time on her backside.'

'It seems she has been, lately,' Eleanor drolled, her turn to be amused.

'Well, that's what I'm saying,' Eggy observed with some heat, his finger raised.

Ralph and Phillip grinned. Marjerie was fading away. I almost felt something like pity for her, she upstaged.

Jeu Blanc

Things got more interesting. There we were at table, Eleanor, Marjerie Prentiss and her swains, Eggy and I. Moonface kept clear, the Whistler and now Miss Meow her only customers inside.

'Well, there he is,' gushed Eggy, his arm pointing, the object of his attentions vain and handsome Dubois, his worn and venerable attaché case in hand. Perhaps, within it, was a neatly folded copy of the *Globe and Mail,* business page at the ready. And something like alarm manifested for the briefest of moments in the man's glittering eyes, and then was gone. Marjerie slumped deeper in her chair.

'Honey,' gasped Eleanor, allowing a private endearment a public airing, suddenly sensible of what she had been up to that afternoon.

'Honey what?' asked Dubois, taken aback.

Oh, he knew.

'Gentlemen,' he said to various gentlemen, bringing over a chair from another table. 'And ladies,' he added.

I wondered if he could feel the heat of Marjerie's watery, dead eyes.

'Imitation,' said Eggy, 'is the sincerest form of flattery.'

'And what's this all about?' Dubois wished to know, even if he was not so sure the knowing was worthwhile.

'The Prime Minister,' Eggy thundered, 'well, you know, he's just consulted Bay Street—'

'Now wait a minute,' said Dubois, attempting to play along.

And Moonface brought Eggy the pies that Serge in the galley had managed to prepare, and they were spinach pies, and, as Eggy noted, a little on the burnt side. But he would live with it.

'I think you should,' said Moonface.

'Here it is,' said Dubois, 'her M-tone.'

'M-tone?' asked Eleanor.

'It's something new. Matronly Moonface,' Dubois explained, choosing, perhaps, to remain oblivious to the fact that when the cat had been away, the mice had been playing.

Moonface, rolling her eyes up and to the side, noiselessly tapped her foot.

'Bob?' she said.

'Well, I think I'll have some wine,' he said.

At which point Eleanor rose, and gripped Dubois's shoulder, and it was a gesture that said she had had enough for now, and would see him, later. Dubois, apparently, had no objections. And Marjerie rose likewise, and her rising signalled her lover boys that it was time to go.

'Was it something I said?' Dubois guffawed.

'Yes, Bob,' said Eleanor in a mock display of pique, 'it's always something you've said.'

Ralph engaged Moonface in an earnest discussion regarding the bill, and he went inside with her.

'What's happening,' asked Eggy, 'why's everyone going so soon?'

'We must have the plague,' Dubois suggested, and then, turning to me: 'And you? What's your explanation for this?'

It would take me an hour to provide him one, and he had not the patience, so I figured.

Ralph paid for a round of drinks, and then escorted his party down the street—to the Traymore, I assumed. We were alone now, Dubois, Eggy, and I. A slight chill had settled on the evening, though it was not yet chill enough to drive us inside where Moonface was now engaged in high level talks with Miss Meow. This woman always wore a heavy coat no matter the weather, had one wonky eye, was beefy, and did not much care for the presence of the Whistler. The louder he whistled and stomped the louder she miaowed. The only person missing for full-out cacophony was Blind Musician; a single bray of his could drown an entire performance of *The Flying Dutchman.* In any case, as amusing as these observations might strike me, my mood was strictly sombre. I did not know what Dubois had made of the scene he initially encountered; I did not wish to know. It seemed that good people were quite capable of inflicting pain, of atrocities, as well; it seemed, too, that bad people might pass through life without committing anything remotely resembling a violent act.

'I think,' I said,' that we should hit upon a minimal definition of evil, at least.'

'Say what?' said Dubois.

Eggy's chin had raised his chest.

'Yes, it's time. I propose that that which most minimally defines evil is what robs a human being of his soul.'

'What has that got to do with anything?' asked Dubois, genuinely confused.

'I was just thinking aloud.'

'Well, maybe you could, you know, provide some context.'

More miaowing. More whistling.

'Boys,' said Moonface, come upon us, clear of a cacophony for a few precious moments, 'will there be anything else?'

'Ah, the M-tone,' said Eggy, his chin still on his chest.

'I know. Matronly, matronly,' Moonface sing-songed, her mouth tightly pursed.

Even so, I could tell she was happy, happy that no viper was now turning the heads of her boys; happy that her Champagne Sheridan was telling her how exciting it would be, Ecuador, that is; but that if her boys were imagining naughty thoughts in respect to her own charms, at least she was the object and not that Prentiss woman, most unpleasant and unwelcome person.

How get Eleanor back her soul now that I decided it had been stolen? I mulled it in a hot bath; I mulled it on the couch, Letterman jesting on TV. Eggy and Dubois, contented drunks, had already been a commotion on the Traymore stairs. There was revelry in Marjerie's apartment. I wondered if from Moonface I would receive a visit, questions in her eyes. Otherwise, she was still half *in situ* and half the time at her Champagne Sheridan's, perhaps because he was behaving as she wished it, having curbed his jealousy. I could hit on no stratagem that would return to Eleanor her errant identity, not that it was all that imperilled; but that, yes, Marjerie had made her inroads. I could not believe Eleanor would reach the point where she would desire all Arabs nuked and liberals and blacks strung from trees. But I could easily enough see her desporting herself among quite local and quite jaded Sybarites, Marjerie, to be precise, and her consorts. Was Dubois a born cuckold? If so, I had a hard time seeing it. But then, I was not, by nature, an out and out philanderer, and yet, here it was I had exchanged intimacies with his sweetheart, and with Moonface, too. And say I was right, and there was no guarantee that I was right, but say there was in the Prentiss woman a streak of evil, what was it on a sliding scale in regards to Iraq, the bombing of wedding parties in Afghanistan, Wall Street and its predatory scams? As I had already observed, there was nothing Marjerie was inviting Eleanor to do that was, on the surface, against Eleanor's nature. But then one might argue that that was the thing of it, as when in some movie I had recently seen, one of the more smug characters suggested that the devil's achievement lay in persuading people he did not exist. And was this good, this citing a less than memorable flick over and against, say, Reinhold Niebuhr? What of Aristotle (or was it Socrates, or was it, for that matter, Daffy Duck?) who asserted that no one would do bad who knew the good? Well, the ancients, as wise as they were, were in some matters remarkably naïve such as would give comfort to present day ologists for whom there are no mysteries. I did have a visitor.

And it was Eleanor, oddly but familiarly dishevelled, drifting over from Marjerie's.

'Randall, Randall, Randall,' Eleanor breathed, 'whatever are we going to do with you? You go to Rome. You come back a stuffed shirt. I try to boff it out of you and you get stuffier. Then you damn near commit incest with Moonface. And then I have a little session, you know, with-what's-their-names, and you get this look, this sourpuss, judgmental look, this what-do-you-think-you're-doing-bitch sort of look, and I say, man, who's he to talk? Hell, I ought to haul your arse back there. What do you think they're doing there? Got the mattress in the middle of the floor. The one is behind her, the other on his knees. Get the picture? Effing hell, Randall, don't you hear what I'm trying to say? I can't believe myself. And I was always such a good little girl.'

Letterman winked. Tears now—full throttle, as it were. She was drunk and she smelled of drink. She was on her knees at my side. One thing was going to lead to the next unless I put my foot down. I rose and got to my feet. I grabbed her by both arms and coaxed her up. She was pie-eyed. What would Mrs Petrova think? Orgies and out of control symposiums. Eventually, I got Eleanor to her bed, thought better of undressing her. I would advise Dubois of the situation, but when I knocked on his door, he either did not hear me or he would not answer.

Fifteen Per Cent Per Annum

I agreed to meet with Dubois downtown at Steerburgers at some appointed hour. He was in his business finery, all in black when the hour arrived and we met up. He studied the menu or endeavoured to, as something else was on his mind. We perched on counter stools, the restaurant cavernous, a friendly, middle-aged waitress fielding my English and Dubois's French. Once every other month or so, I wound up here. Occasionally, I ran into Arsdell, one of academe's finest examples of a tenured fraud. 'Eleanor,' said Dubois, eyeing me.

'Who else?'

'What to do with her?'

'Well, what's to do with her? Read her the riot act? Play the heavy? It won't work.'

'I think you're right.'

'Marry her, Bob.'

'Marry her? Why on earth would I do that? I like my life the way it is.'

'It's what she wants.'

'What she wants is beside the point.'

'Is it really?'

'Damn you,' said Dubois, somewhat flustered.

And then, after a pause for reflection: 'And then what? We get married. And then she's expecting fifteen per cent per annum. Utopia. And she likes her little assignations—'

'I don't know that she likes her assignations.'

'What else has she been doing?'

'Screwing around. But maybe she's trying to get your attention.'

'You think so? She's always been like this. Long before you knew her. And even when I pay her plenty of attention. I don't mind so much, so long as she doesn't rub my face in it. I wouldn't mind screwing around, myself, you know. It's just that, well, it hasn't happened. I can't really say why, or rather, I won't.'

The waitress made a great show of taking my friend's order, obviously smitten with the man. Some bantering in French. She giggled. He guffawed. Our coffees served, I loaded mine up with sugar, worried, however, that my advice was less than sound.

'What worries me,' said Dubois, 'is that she'll want me to give Eggy up, and you.'

'I doubt it. As it is, she's practically the heart and soul of the crew.'

'Not since Marjerie moved in.'

'True.'

'That's when the trouble really started.'

I took this as a shot at me.

'It was bad enough with the Lamonts and Osgoode,' I observed.

'It's worse. I don't know what that woman's game is, but she has a way, you know, of getting under your skin. It's like she crawls inside, parasite looking for a host.'

'Nicely put.'

'She's got Eleanor on her hook.'

'It's what I've been thinking.'

'Démoniaque.'

I believe I got Dubois's drift.

'So marry her, Bob. Keep the same arrangements, if you must. Credit the woman for some sense. She knows better than to set you against your will.'

'It's not been my experience of women.'

'I know that when two people have been sleeping together for a long time, and maybe even cohabiting, and they decide to marry, it's often the end of a good arrangement. But in your case, Bob, I don't know, but you've got your apartment, she has hers, you come and go as you please, just that she knows she's your port and you're hers, come the storms.'

'It's what Eggy says. Make a respectable woman of her. The old-fashioned way.'

'He has a point.'

Dubois's hamburger arrived. A friendly, middle-aged waitress imparted a loving look, Dubois so distracted with his troubles that he did not notice. An intense but briefly felt bout of loneliness on my part. Eleanor could very well spirit Dubois away, and then, Moonface off with her Sheridan in Ecuador, I would be left with Eggy and, good God, the Prentiss woman. Perhaps Dubois had partly read my mind: 'You know about the equator, how toilets behave there?'

No, I did not know.

'Well,' said Dubois, taking time now to swallow what was in his mouth, 'you see, depending on exactly where you are, when you flush the toilet, the water either goes straight down or goes around counter-clockwise, not like here.'

It was my turn to say it: 'What has this got to do with anything?'

'We Swear by the Men of Marathon'

Moonface changed her mind, saying: 'I don't think I could bear it. No, really.'

We stood in a queue, the old hockey arena now a Cineplex.

'Haven't we seen enough bad epics?' she said, her voice a slight musical moan.

She had a point. A film about Alexander the Great—well, what sort of cheap thrill was I chasing?

'What do you propose?' I asked, my tone avuncular.

Which is to say I was playing the part of attentive suitor. The chameleon creature at my side, looking pretty for a change, despite her nondescript garb—the denims, the athletic pull-over, its hood framing her tresses and countenance—considered what she might wish to propose, rolling her eyes. It was as if her dimples had each an epiphany: 'A drink, maybe.'

Now Moonface did not often propose that we sit somewhere and drink. On the other hand, she often questioned my aesthetic judgment when it came to movies. She never read the books I wished for her to read as she was lazy; as she could argue she had gotten enough of the canon in university. It was bad reasoning on her part, but what could one say? Now and then I glimpsed something wild in her. I envied her Champagne Sheridan his opportunity to get to the bottom of her, if he did, in fact, get to that fabled bottom. And my guess was as follows: that which was wild in her was also tentative and lacked courage and was foolish, to boot. It landed her in situations she regretted. She was spooked, of course, by her propensity to fits, brain seizures and such. She must always be in control, and perhaps, it was why she did not drink much. Her mouth was drawn tight and small; she looked vaguely oriental, as per Madama Butterfly or Lady Kaeda. It gave pause to any erotic burblings as might be irrupting in me. Even so, just then I had an urge to rent a room in some down-at-heel hotel. We would draw the curtains, break open a bottle; and in the dark, our bodies become, as it were, spiritual, we would talk, and just let it flow—this talk, talking of whatever came to mind. '*Oh, I hated my mother, you know.*' '*Me, I ran over a kitten in the family driveway once, and the fact of it still shames me.*' Better the grungy room than a raucous bar, the music so intense it separates one from one's thoughts. I feared that such a bar was what she wanted after all, that, and a bottomless pail of booze.

A light drizzle fell to the street. Panhandlers were ghostly. Yellow trees were bathed in lamplight that was at once hot and cold. I might kiss the cool and clear complexion of Moonface's cheek. I did not. I figured I might spring for the taxi fare and we would return to our neighbourhood, have an evening with Eggy and Dubois at the Blue Danube; but then I doubted this would much appeal to her who saw enough of them.

'Ah,' I said, 'I know. Remember Gareth Howard, my old journalist friend? You know, we visited his grave once, and you said you didn't like cemeteries... Anyway, we used to drink at a place nearby. The Cloister. Now I don't much like the clientele, smug lawyers and their smug wives or mistresses, but it's a fairly quiet place, and we could have a decent conversation. That is, if that's what you're in the mood for.'

We headed for it, the sidewalk an excuse for leaves to fall, indeed, in this our faded Jezebel of a town, one I loved at times when I was not conscious of the fact it seemed to have little use for me. We might have been lovers, she and I, were it not for the difference in our ages. She had on her Marilyn Monroe eyes, the lashes prominent. That her eyes were laughing, were lazy, and were ripe with questions. She was worried for Evie Longoria, she let me know. It would seem that Evie Longoria was deeply unhappy. Well, who was happy? Happiness, like sex, was overrated. Perhaps justice was overrated, too, for all that there was so little of it about. Marjerie Prentiss was a horrid woman, was she not? Well, Eggy was a horrid old buzzard, but at least he liked poetry and the study of history. Beautiful women, of course.

As I suspected it might (though I had been willing to chance it) The Cloister broke our mood. The usual clientele. One showed off one's income and, failing that, one's sophistication gleaned from travel books and best-selling novels. Or one simply sat there in a much humbler sense, letting the content of bottomless martinis slide down one's throat, not caring in the slightest who knew it. But these older, more disillusioned spectres were dying off, all the comers, pretenders each, replacing them. Mercifully, there were two vacant stools at the end of the bar that would afford us a measure of privacy. The Ojibwa barmaid whom I had not seen in a long while recognized me. She sized us up, me and Moonface, and smiled, and it put Moonface at her ease.

'Well,' I said to the girl-woman at my side, 'what will you drink?'

Ah, a grown-up drink—whiskey. Neat. I would have a glass of red. My but the barmaid was a sight to behold, curiosity and irony and concealed contempt in her eyes; a great deal of intelligence, as it were.

'Do you know her?' Moonface asked.

'No. I would like to have known her. But like I said, I used to drink here with Gar.'

'So,' I continued, 'what's on your mind? The war in Afghanistan? The demise of journalism? Exotic acts of copulation?'

'Oh, you're so clever,' her dimples said.

It seemed a good fit—Moonface at the bar, leaning her elbow now on the marble, and regarding me with bemused, almond shaped orbs.

'There's such a lot on my mind,' she bragged.

The barmaid brought our drinks. Her look might have been regarded as professionally neutral were it not for the barest sliver of mischief in her eyes.

'But where's it all going,' Moonface thought to ask, 'you, me, life, America, the Electee?'

Well, there it was in a nutshell, the question of the hour. The barmaid mock-chanted: 'Round and round she goes, and nobody knows—'

What a fetching smile she had. And when she turned and walked away, I believed that a certain shimmy to her walk was meant for me.

'You bring out the beast in women,' Moonface observed.

'Maybe,' I said, doubting it, as there was every reason to believe Moonface was having fun at my expense.

On the way back, Moonface got out of the taxi at Sheridan's.

'Good night,' she said, in control of things, pursing her lips.

Other than this, she could not quite disguise the fact that she was drunk. Back in my digs, I heard Dubois and Eggy on the stairs. I heard quite clearly Eggy's quaver: 'Sir Eglamore that valiant knight, fa la lanky down dilly, he took up his sword and went forth to fight, fa la lanky down dilly. The rain in Spain. Oh yes. My oxygen level is at 98 per cent, I'll have you know. Well, it's what the nurse said.'

'What next?' Dubois guffawed.

I heard Eleanor open her door. I could not see her but I could see her entreaty, Dubois summoned. That was what was next for him. As for Moonface, she did not yet know what she believed. She wished to know in what I believed. I supplied her my standard if inadequate answer: art and loose women, love if you could get it, and the good esteem of one's peers. Hearing me out, she thought me stuck in a time-warp. I answered that if such were the case, it was a time-warp that had stood the test of time for five thousand years, and probably more. But did I not, she asked, believe in God and community and family and doing right? I did not think God required my belief, as my god was the god of Plotinus. But that was so much an eggheaded concept I kept it strictly to myself. Community? We had community—the Traymore, the Blue Danube. We did not need the sanction of society to make ourselves official in this respect. Family? I could not get far enough away from what family remained to me. But that, no, I would not like to see its destruction. And sex—what about sex? Moonface wished to know. My, but it seemed she had troubles there. Our brief gropings in some Toronto dark could hardly pass muster for the sexual act, but even so, it was not that she and I had had troubles as such; it was all between her and her Champagne Sheridans. So then, what exactly was troubling her? It was her own sexuality, as it turned out. Why, had she exotic fancies? Would not that just turn Eggy's toes, were he to know? But no, no, it was nothing like that. Or that no, she meant she was not into women, but thought she might have a taste for pain. Well, whose pain? Would she be the inflictee or the inflicter? And if she told Sheridan about it, the problem was, he had his own fancies. Such as? None of my business. Anyway, it was not pain as such. Alright then, then what? She did not mean to mislead me in this—she … she … oh damn, she wished now she had not brought it up. Well, you know, confusion was a part of it. I was not going to offer any advice.

See a sex therapist, if it came to that, see some dreaded ologist. If it was all about just feeling something, anything; if it was love she was desperate to feel, and I allowed my answer was lame, give it time. If she did not now love Sheridan, she might, later. If she could never love Sheridan, she would love another. Perhaps she was a cold fish, just that I did not think she was a cold fish, and we were all of us confused, just that, being young, her confusions ate up more oxygen. The look in her eyes suggested I had failed to satisfy her questions but that it was the best she had gotten in a while. By then she was fairly tipsy, the hood down, her countenance flushed, her hair radiant. It had gone back and forth like this—the Q&A, the Ojibwa woman with her chiselled but quite appealing features now and then checking in, as it were, as if to test the truth of what was honest and what was bald-faced lie. I thought I had scored a few points in her eyes. I was not likely to see her again. But now, just now, and what an unlikely hour for it, it would seem Eggy stuck his head out the door so as to assail no Traymorean in particular, but to put someone or another in the picture by his thundering: 'We swear by the men of Marathon.'

Oh dear. My lids heavy on my eyes as I lay on my couch, James Bond smooching with some lethal creature on TV, I attempted to divine Eggy's meaning. And, in fact, I knew it, without equivocation, without a doubt of any kind, and he would, that 902-year-old bugger, address a sad world that thought it remembered what was once true and necessary but had, in actuality, quite forgotten.

The Garden Path

I could have done without the turgid heavy-metal grind emanating from Moonface's apartment, the furor which helped crown the pursuit of mindlessness as a cultural and political boon, however much it had cause to disdain the liberal hypocrisies. No wonder the girl-woman was divided against herself. Perhaps she quarrelled with her Sheridan in the night, and it drove her to come seek her own bed. I stood at the window at the end of the hall. Rain pounded on a dead bird. Leaves fell in their singularities, and each seemed a sentient being. President Elect, or rather, the fact he had been elected in the first place, seemed a less marvellous event that it had been a few days before when people could not believe their eyes and ears, breathing now for the first time in years. What would he do to prove himself serious? And if serious, what would he be permitted to do by those whose main aim in life was keeping the money machine primed? The steps ascending the Traymore stairs were Evie Longoria's. She greeted me while pointing at Eggy's door, her explanation for being on the premises.

'Be careful he doesn't take your head off,' I warned, 'I think he had quite the night, last night.'

'Oh, I'm used to it,' she said, brightly enough.

'And is Emma in?' she asked, referring to Moonface by her proper name.

'I guess,' I said, 'she's got that godawful music blasting away.'

Evie Longoria understood.

'Anyway,' she said, 'I'll be taking His Nibs to Walmart. He said he needed a new shirt and underwear.'

'I hope he's paying you enough to make it worth your while,' I said.

'Oh, he is,' she answered, just a hint of dubiety in her voice.

She had the air of a woman who likes to sound firm and quite decided about things. I liked the looks of her. The light, all rain-gloom, seemed to divide and flow around me, reaching her.

'Well,' she said, waiting to see if I had anything else to say.

I had nothing to say, really, except this: 'Emma will probably try to tell you that I took her out last night and attempted to seduce her. It's only partly true.'

Evie Longoria was unsure as to whether I was jesting.

'And Eggy's oxygen level,' I continued, 'is at 98 per cent.'

'Oh,' she said, 'robust health.'

'We are incurables, we Traymoreans,' I said, 'and some day, maybe, I'll tell you why.'

'Incurables,' she said.

'Yes, incurables.'

'Like in people who had leprosy.'

'Yes, sort of. Like that.'

'It seems rather rum.'

I liked her for her use of the word *rum*.

'But anyway, I'm on my way out,' I said.

Truth to tell, I had nowhere to be. For all that, in the course of a morning, I managed to raise a coffee shop, a cemetery and a sports bar, not necessarily in that order. But among the headstones of a riverside graveyard, the sky squalling rain, I made my hello to Gareth Howard and heard nothing back. I rolled a cigarette and smoked it, cutting a figure of a kind in my solitude there, advised as to the limits of reason, suspicious of abrupt mood swings, leery of emotion and yet, all the world was a stage, even as death was foreground and backdrop. 'What about the election? I asked, and surely Gar must respond, he not one to have let history in the making go unremarked. Tyrants and their eventual demises came and went, but not black American presidents. And Gar's silence did not surprise me; he was, at times, a surly bastard. What did surprise was the wreath on his marker. And because it could not have been Clare Howard's, as she, too, was buried, but buried elsewhere, I could not imagine whose gesture it might have been, Gar a dear but far from endearing man who, it was suspected, had had mistresses, a consequence of his travels. No, Gar had seen too much of America and what it had done in the world to believe, of a sudden, that the elevation of a black man to the presidency was redemption for Iraq. Or so I interpreted the resounding quiet, one punctuated by the splattering of rain on stone and the brooding calls of crows. And if Gar had viewed nature with suspicion, I wondered if now his bones were making peace with it, the effort consuming all his consciousness and his speech. Clare, or so I attempted to convince myself, had been the love of my life, she tall, beautiful, elegant, well-educated, deeply read, and as loyal to her husband as circumstances permitted. To characterize her as noble went against the tide, but there it was, and if an instant of passion, if one could deem it as such, had transpired between us, we quickly retreated from the possibilities, her mistrust of my lack of ambition fatal to one such as me. One might say her attitude to me was one of cheerful condescension, though when she laid my hand on her breast, her state of mind was not one of cheer; rather it was a turbulent state: contending measures of disgust and sorrow. She tolerated the fact I was Gar's drinking buddy, so to speak, and his sounding board, for literary matters had been much on his mind as well as politics, and he was a frustrated novelist. Never had I more wished to make love to a woman as when we stood there, one afternoon, ceremoniously before the dignity of a casket, she genuinely devastated. Perhaps it was not possible to discern the fine line between betrayal and simple loneliness, but despite the sometimes troubled marriage, lack of love had not been an issue for her and Gar. In any case I began to shiver. The idyllic site—riverside patch of grass and stone and birch—now seemed a horror. It was not difficult to tear myself from the spot, though I was roundly defeated in my attempt to commune and hear the dead speak. That I brought my hand to the bill of my baseball cap dripping with rain in a salute was almost farce, and how his bones must have snickered at the spectacle. I bused it back, and downtown, and in a coffeeshop, the music, as usual, overloud, I committed a few words to a notebook; and though I subscribed to the notion that history is a continuity, I would have agreed that one, at times, could be hard put to discern what connected *X* to *Y* and *Y* to *Z* and so forth and so on. Grief, of course. Regret. That I had not managed to commit to a woman was, no doubt, cowardice on my part. We all of us had our sweet spots, that portion of our souls which the world could always find and strike, reminding us of our absolute aloneness. And then, I exchanged the students and the music for a sports bar and drink. A bank of TVs. College football. A pre-game show in which, by way of video cam, it was seen how it was a coach was whipping his charges into a spiritualized, competitive froth; and it was as if, given the history that had just been made, their time was running out, so go out on that field and take no prisoners, show America what real Americans are made of. And they were not the legions but the barbarians of a deep and impenetrable forest, rich in deities and barbecues. Yes, and it was an excuse to reach deep into my shot of whiskey for the consolations of skepticism. Athletes? How about brutes? It was no mystery to me why Jakes, my old history teacher, had blown his brains out. My second whiskey was landing me in waters too rough to properly navigate with my little craft of self. But that I slapped the counter's surface with an imperious hand and called for a third from a weary-eyed barmaid suggested that I was claiming for myself an abiding clarity about things. I could see the merits of all arguments.

The Checkers Speech

Marjerie Prentiss was up to something. Since when had she come by personality? How was she now hapless and vulnerable, a star-crossed lover, a clown for whom the world had much laughter and sympathy, if not love?

'You are a dear girl but—', said Eleanor, playing along with a stage performance.

'And what's this but?' Marjerie interjected, we at table in a fine room, Eleanor's kitchen.

'You're always in my hair.'

If Eleanor was truly exasperated, she was also at pains not to offend. I was offended, Marjerie's skimpy garb but a night shirt, one that proclaimed for the wearer the right to trot all those intimacies such as had accrued to her body over time from place to place without the inconvenience of a critique, without regard for modesty of any kind, be it that of body or spirit. If Eleanor had invited me over for a dollop of amaretto, a substance I did not just then need, having come from a bar, it was clear that what she really wished from me was moral support. Eleanor's objective, so I could plainly enough see, was going to prove a futile quest.

'But I thought you liked me,' a dull voice boomed at its host.

The quality of that boom was like the expansive and yet spirit-numbing sound of a standing clock in an empty room.

'I do like you. Effing hell. But I don't need to know every frickin' reason why you can't just yet marry Ralph because Phillip, you know, has his rights, too, and you can't marry both, but it seems you have, anyway, God love you.'

So Eleanor had her five cents worth.

'You make it sound like I'm greedy.'

'That you are, girl. That you are.'

'And you, well, I know you don't like me, but what do you say?'

I supposed Marjerie Prentiss could not wait to hear what I might have to say. To call her a whore was an insult to whores, but betrayal was another matter; and I did not believe that either Ralph or Phillip had understood what they signed on for, and she was always throwing pixie dust in their eyes. She had a bottomless supply of pixie dust. I shrugged.

'I don't think it matters here what I think,' I lied, taking the coward's way out.

'It might matter,' Marjerie briefly allowed.

'Alright then,' I grimly responded, 'it might.'

Hers was a massive ego; there could never be enough on hand to feed it.

'There's nothing wrong with me,' Marjerie observed.

'No one said there was.'

Now Eleanor was lying.

'Men do what men do. I do what I do.'

'But I don't always need to know about it,' said Eleanor, returning to an earlier insistence of hers.

'Why not?' asked Marjerie, 'everyone loves a sordid tale.'

Was the woman capable of levity? She would claim the high ground of emotional, sexual and spiritual honesty, no matter the shine of the innocence or the richness of the depravity. What I did not say was that she simply liked to talk about herself to the exclusion of all else, sex a ready-to-hand confusion, an infallible source of the self-referential.

'I've nothing to hide or be ashamed about,' said Marjerie Prentiss. 'I'm going to marry Ralph. I like having sex with Phillip. They know it. They understand it. They're happy with it. Well, maybe they're not always comfortable with it all the time, but men, you know, they ought to face up to themselves. Confront their sexuality. If they only knew it, they'd know they prefer to be in bed with me than out in the cold with no one.'

'You really believe that, don't you?' I said.

The look I got suggested I was a simpleton. The look I returned her suggested she was demented.

'I don't know,' said Eleanor, 'it sounds to me like you're talking through your hat.'

The look Eleanor shot my way wished I would say something useful.

'Roll you a ciggie?' I offered.

'Besides, you've had your adventures,' and it was Marjerie addressing us both rather pointedly.

'I beg your pardon,' said Eleanor, a little chuffed, 'I'm an adult, and I don't go around rubbing Bob's face in it.'

'Really?' said Marjerie, on the verge of a triumph.

I heard Nixon challenging Stevenson to an audit.

'Oh dear,' I said, Eleanor and I alone now in her kitchen, Marjerie Prentiss gone off to dress and get about her day's business. She had sailed out of the room, prevailing winds favourable to her.

'Yes,' said Eleanor, 'I know.'

But what did the good woman know? That Marjerie Prentiss was so obviously delusionary? That sex, for her, was a military campaign? Perhaps I was guilty of hyperbole in this, but then ours was a culture much given to overblown speech, our collective existence sheer bravado, our resources over-extended, our reason to live but a jamboree of consuming them, and here it was that I was a creature fully persuaded of the pleasure principle.

'I like to think,' Eleanor said, 'that I know what I'm doing, and even when I'm clueless I know what I'm doing, but lately—'

'The mind is the source of all treachery,' I commented, the pedagogue in me rising.

And this fact of its rising could not be good news for a simple man and a simple woman engaged in a rather simple ritual, one consisting of amiable chit-chat, cigarettes, amaretto, flurries in the forecast.

'No kidding,' Eleanor snapped.

'Besides the sowing and the reaping, what's religion but the attempt to get the mind in hand,' I continued, somewhat perversely, the pedagogue always angling for his moment in the sun.

'Dionysus is what it's all about. Striking the balance. Worship him over much, and you'll slit your own throat. Worship him not enough and he gets peeved and resentful and retaliatory—'

'Don't know about any of that, Mr Calhoun. You're the expert. I just want some peace and quiet.'

Coming from Eleanor, these were stunning words.

'You? It doesn't seem like Eleanor, Eleanor.'

The good woman gave me a look.

'I'm only ologizing, and God knows that ologizing is the enabler of all treacheries in the mind. If only DH Lawrence had been more tough-minded, he might have been on to something—'

'Sod off, Randall.'

The good woman gave me yet another look.

'You don't have to fight her or reason with her or, in any way, attempt to correct her behaviour. Just don't feed what fuels her fires. She'll lose interest and go and bother someone else.'

'You think so?'

'I think so.'

'She's like one of those dogs, all jaws, that can't let go once a grip has been got.'

'Could be,' I said.

'Well then,' I surmised, 'maybe drastic action is required. It's just that should you lay down the law she'll see it as an excuse to circumvent it. She's not one to shy from a challenge.'

'Why is everything so complicated?'

'Lack of good will,' I explained.

'Is that all?'

'It's a miracle anything good happens at all.'

'You cynic.'

'Card carrying.'

She was beginning to get that look in her eyes, the sweep of which would melt everything that was solid in me. It was not that she was something on the order of a wanton slut, far from it, but that for her the body was truth, and if not that, then the essential reality. The mind was a necessary evil.

'Randall,' she purred.

Life was martial arts, and I must somehow turn the force of her momentum to my advantage.

'Yes, Eleanor?'

'Oh,' she said, 'I don't know. I don't know nuttin'. Damndest thing.'

'You know more than you think you know. You just don't like the burden that knowing entails.'

'Effing hell,' she said, that look of hers a little glassy now.

And it was then, though I had always known it, that I knew for a certainty how Dubois was her complementary function; as he, despite the fact he was vain and handsome and considered himself beyond reproach in most matters, especially those of intellect, was born to manage, and to manage not for his own gain to the exclusion of all else, but for the commonweal. Unless pressed very hard to the wall, he could take this woman who had been the apple of his eye in stride whereas I, cravenly selfish, had not the patience. But best I not bring up his name; it would only suggest she was something of an idiot for not having cottoned on to this truth, herself.

'So you see,' I said, apropos of nothing, 'where there is will there are ways. Life just doesn't give up the ghost. On the other hand, I have a hard time relinquishing the suspicion that, in the human mind, evolution is at odds with itself. It's why I get overwrought and drink and pray. The poet's S.O.S.'

Yet another look, one approximating shrewd calculation.

'You're a strange bird,' Eleanor said, 'otherwise I'd fancy you.'

It seemed I was let off the hook.

So I went to the Blue Danube to drink and, as it were, to pray. I prayed to the long-bellied goddess bringing me wine.

'Emma,' I said, calling Moonface by her proper name, 'I'll wager you that most of the culture wars would simply disappear if men and women just stopped talking so much nonsense about sex.'

'Whatever do you mean?' said Moonface, rolling her eyes in anticipation of cheap entertainment.

'Well, women think they know what men are and men think they know what women are, and none of it is the case, in any case—it's just so much bad will and ill-temper and too much indulgence in ologizing—'

'Avuncular, Randall, avuncular.'

'Yes, I suppose.'

A long-bellied goddess had just quelled my effusions. I looked around to take stock of who was who and what was what—Gregory picking at his food, Cassandra discussing food, to be sure, with Serge in the galley. Miss Meow sat alone, her eyes turned in on herself, her conversational patter directed at unseen entities. Blind Musician had not been seen in ages; I assumed he was on yet another cultural tour of the provinces; or else, he had, like Fast Eddy and apparently, Gentleman Jim, departed the neighbourhood. Joe Smithers aka Too Tall Poet was forever passing by and looking in, but it seemed he could not bring himself to enter; perhaps human contact, above and beyond that of faculty and students at the college where his pedagogical gifts were employed, was simply too much for him; but that he had settled for *Drunkin' Doughnuts* over the amenities of the Blue Danube seemed a political statement calculated to twit the hoity-toity regulars here.

'So?' asked Moonface, 'are you finished?'

'I think it's a good idea you're going to Ecuador. Not a bad idea, at all. But I should've taken you to Rome.'

'Yes, you should've,' Moonface agreed.

It had to have been chance, I reasoned to myself, that wrought such fragile propinquity between us. Or else it was the ghost of Virgil loath to allow his shrine-fires to flame-out, Moonface and I the last Virgilians, how inconvenient, when we might have been the vanguard of our respective ages, bringing the blandishments of change to the world and its numberless dilemmas.

Executive Orders

I had every reason to believe I enhanced the cause of Traymorean life. Was not Eleanor the beneficiary of my wisdom? Did I not supply Moonface with riddles on which to chew as she, with rolling eyes, viewed her future?

Dubois must reconsider his shabby materialism in respect to my challenge of it, and only Eggy, and only because he was a consummate drunkard, safely danced, cane and all, beyond my ability to corrupt his *raison d'etre;* besides, he was Zeus-like Eggy and one does not second-guess a master of the universe. For all that, the failure I most assuredly was invited fresh rounds of self-castigation. That I existed on my father's blood money was suspect. I might have sharpened my wits and written for a living, or worked at something, at least, even at the horrors of an academic regime. But no, I idled, and in the idling, besides redemption, I assumed that thought might bloom in my mentations as a natural consequence of the ebb and flow of failure and the learning experience. In other words, the contemplative life required leisure, and I was, perhaps, conceited enough to believe it. I sat there a long while in the Blue Danube. It was wintry outside, not that it snowed but that it was windy-cold and ugly. Now and then I looked up at Moonface as she went by the table to serve a customer, and I may as well have been a child searching the face of his mother for signs of trouble. Had Moonface maternal instincts? Were those babies hanging off her hips as she mulled over Ptolemy Soter? I was briefly married once; I avoided fatherhood. I had not marched in the streets since my teenage years. My faith was all catch-as-catch-can, as much a matter of whim as anything like true conviction. God was convenient; God was inconvenient, depending on which side of the bed one fell out of in the morning. Likewise, justice. I was surrounded by people who believed that, on the strength of self-empowerment, they had mastery of their lives if not of life itself, and I was always just this side of genuflecting to the spectacle, ready to concede it my sloth and over-all inadequacy; just that, deep down, quite far down in my grotty soul, I could not for a moment believe it true. Which then gave me cause to question how great a portion of illusion was crucial to the maintenance of Civic Life and the well-being of Civic Smiles. Did I in my person represent the arts of the diabolical, or was the devil in those other details—those fabled leveraged margins and dinner and *digestifs* at the St James Club? Perhaps these were old and quite hackneyed concerns and, if so, why was I still on about them? It was being written that President Elect and his team were reviewing the executive orders that Current President, over the course of his tenure, had so far issued; one assumed they intended to reverse the thrust of, for example, the torture regime, the surveillance state, the undermining of environmental protections and the like, all in the name of a free market system and liberty. Well then, well and good. I would be the first to acknowledge the *better good* of their virtues over my craven vices; and I would not be the last to worry that it was all so much whistling Dixie; that the apostles of the absurd had had it right all along, Judas Iscariot having been one of those; that, yes, even when in the presence of a Loving God, there was no rhyme or reason, just time and its unfolding; in time the leaves falling; in time Moonface rolling her eyes.

And in my digs, the wine inviting sleep, sleep bringing on Dreamland, the realm was one in which I hailed Moonface with 'Hail Ptolemy Soter!' A crazy wild realm, Moonface dancing on her long toes, Traymoreans cheering their own.

§

Book III—Mixing-Bowls

Caprice and Beguine I

—'Bliss was it in that dawn; to be alive and to be young was very heaven.' Zeus-like Eggy, his recital complete, his finger raised, now thunders: 'Wordsworth, I'll have you know.' Eggy's choice of pocket square is a two-pointer for this evening. Elegant Zeus. Gregory, at another Blue Danube aka Le Grec table, picks at his dinner. Build it and they will come.

Caprice and Beguine II

—He, of course, is a playboy of the western world. Live a thousand years, and one might have a go at just about anything. So Eggy says, waving Moonface over with a tiny claw, 'Here's a story. Thor, you know, the god, he thought to reveal who he was to a lass he'd just ravished. What do you think he said? Well, of course, you don't know, but I'm telling you. He said, "Hi, I'm Thor." She said, hoo hoo, she said, "So am I but I'm satisfied."' Dubois guffaws, he who has an ear for the subtleties of the language. Moonface: sad Queen of the Night with the ghost of a smile.

Moonface Epistle

Dear Moonface, Ptolemy Soter to you! Marjerie Prentiss remains relentless. I begin to think the only thing that will bring her inner peace (and she lose interest in Traymoreans), is a buggering, her *somatophylakes,* her filthy beasts, her bodyguards, at her beck and call. Or do you care to know? You, I suppose, were at a blues bar, playing at depravity. As ever yours,—RQC

§

Book IV—In Continuation

Protective Camouflage

I was in a state, making my way down our noble boulevard. I would chase away the images in my mind of an adolescent Prentiss, she with her 40-ish body being set upon by her brother's pals in the parental home. Some were tickled; some were frightened; all were louts. And she, apart from the fact that she was sullen and unenthusiastic, would scrutinize the faces of her ravishers and file away her gleanings for future considerations. And the sinking feeling in me was that I suspected I would, sooner or later, wind up in her psycho-drama, no less a cretin than the boys taking their pleasure, she pursuing her research. In the way cold bodies in space roam about until larger bodies capture them through gravity, one of us would cease to wander. I shivered. Not only was I weak and craven and possessed of a vivid imagination, I was paranoid enough to believe the woman had transferred her interests from Eleanor to me.

And in the poor man's super mart, I bumped into Eleanor. Literally. The good woman was examining the tomatoes and their winter price. She drolled: 'When Moonface turns her music up, I know she's having sex.'

Really?

'When she turns her music up,' I said, 'she's usually twitting me for being an old fuddy-duddy.'

'Is that it? Is that it, Mr Calhoun?'

I supposed Eleanor was in a mood.

'Well then,' she said, changing the subject, 'is it warm enough for you?'

'No,' I said,' shivering, yet again.

A cold, bright day, was it not?

'Yes,' Eleanor sighed, 'I think not. And these tomatoes will have no taste. I was thinking of making something tomatoey, with capers. Any ideas?'

'No, none at all.'

'So what are you good for? A poke in the sack? A little moral outrage? Honestly, Randall, what's with you men?'

'You women.'

'Ungentlemanly, sir, ungentlemanly.'

At least, there was something like a flash of humour in her grey-green eyes. We returned together to the Traymore, she with her tomatoes and I with my bread. On the way, she put it to me: 'It may interest you to know that, in respect to Marjerie, I'm beginning to have doubts. The alarm bells are going off in my head.'

'Better late than never,' I said, but with some caution, 'and I would think when she tried to stick those scissors in you, that that might've given you pause.'

'She was somewhat justified. I was in a clinch, if you remember, with her lover boy.'

'I mean it's not that she turns your head and you start behaving badly. You were always going to behave badly. But that it's not you doing it, it's her, it's that woman gotten into you.'

'You make it sound so creepy.'

'It is.'

'Well, how do we get rid of her?'

'How do we get rid of her, indeed?'

'How ignore her? Either I leave or she leaves? I can tell you, I'm not going to leave.'

'And I can tell you she's not going to leave.'

'Actually, she might. Ralph keeps talking about a house out there—in the country.'

'A nest?'

'Sort of. Not clear on the details. I think he's been slowly working on one, renovating and stuff. But maybe he might rent something else, at any rate, in which to live while he works on the other place.'

'And he'll have Marjerie move in with him. And there won't be enough room for Phillip. Cunning plan.'

'I think that's the plan.'

'Well then, I suppose you ought to whisper in Marjerie's ear as to what a great thing commitment is. Soul mates in one another's arms. Until death do us part and all that. Enable, Eleanor, enable.'

'Yes, maybe, I'll whisper away.'

And by now, we were coming on Mrs Petrova's shop. She was snoozing in a chair, waiting for customers. And by now, we were climbing the Traymore stairs, Moonface's digs silent. Perhaps all the apartments were deserted. Untimely erotic burblings. What a nuisance. But when Eleanor invited me into her kitchen for an amaretto each, something with which to warm ourselves, we fell to talking politics.

'Don't tell me,' she said, 'that you don't think things are looking up.'

'I've got my fingers crossed.'

'How silly you are. Of course, things are looking up. Even the idea of the man, if nothing else, is a huge improvement on the reality of the man still in office.'

'True,' I said, 'and the feministas will observe that he's still the male gender.'

She gave me a look. And she began to get that look. And when that shambling grin of hers broke out, I made my excuses, and left.

I read a while, recumbent on my couch. Perhaps the weight of these words, the words Lucan's, tugged my eyelids down: *Also the votaries of Cybele, the womanly Galli, tossed their bloodstained tresses and wailed to the world of its ruin.* And perhaps, falling through sleep, I raised a realm of fitful dream in which Moonface, a wild-eyed rebel, exhorted men to overthrow an unspecified oppressor. Then perhaps, the crisis addressed, she was pleasuring *in the thin warmth of the Cordilleran sun.* There in Ecuador. It also seemed that someone was knocking on my door. I climbed back into wakefulness and went and answered the door. Marjerie Prentiss.

She got to the point.

'I gather you and Eleanor have been having words.'

'What's it to you?'

'What it is to me is that Eleanor thinks I'm a bad influence on her. You put the idea in her head.'

'Yes?'

'Well, did you?'

'What Eleanor and I have to talk about isn't any of your business.'

'It is when it concerns me.'

Her eyes were mascara'd. Blue silk shirt. Faded lavender denims. She was beginning to get ideas. Perhaps, I was beginning to get ideas.

'You know, I could twist you around my finger,' she asserted.

'I'm sure you could.'

'I could do it right now.'

'I guess.'

'But I won't.'

'I guess you won't.

'Because I'm expecting Phillip.'

'To the victor the spoils.'

'You're not a nice man.'

'I never claimed to be.'

'Well, this is getting silly.'

'It surely is.'

'And you're sure he's not here?'

'Jesus, woman.'

'Alright then.'

Detail, Details

I was moved to write a dead man a letter. I addressed it to Jack Swain, Palermo, *Poste Restante.* I would risk the ire of a sad, careerist Sicilian mail clerk who would have, by now, disposed of my previous missives by grisly means. I went to complete this mission in a bone-eating cold. However, as I stood in the queue at the postal outlet, awaited congress with a mightily bored representative of a national service, a few things occupied my brain. Eggy, for instance, had broken a rather strange silence that had befallen Traymorean males in the Blue Danube the evening before. He would probably die, he said (only not now, he was having too much fun) before they would ever get to the bottom of JFK's assassination, and it was rather sad, that, not knowing, and he would certainly like to know. For what if one went to one's grave, in error, and for all that one had, on a Parisian stage, observed lesbians at play? The only decent idea a certain American poet managed to bequeath to discourse was the notion that we, as he put it, do not change; we just stand more revealed. Eleanor was still hanging out, as it were, with Prentiss and the lover boys. I understood they had sampled a sex club, Eleanor getting a taste of bondage. Further plans included a Bob Dylan concert.

'Well,' Eggy pointed out last night, 'and before you two lower the boom on me, I'll say it's not a thought original to me, just that we died a little when Oswald or whomever it was plugged Kennedy, likewise with King and the other Kennedy. The rain in Spain.'

And Dubois allowed that it was true, his glittering blue eyes, however, turned inward on his personal sojourn. So I stood there in a postal queue, approximating patience, my thoughts concerned with the aforementioned such as ebbed and flowed and, otherwise, drifted in me. *Yo, Swain. Came across one of your old missives. What can I say? I knew a man once who believed that family history was self-indulgence. What mattered was what Lenin said, that night in April, 1917, when the workers lifted him on the armoured car in the square and he speechified. Or rather, the route out of family that pathology took was always beside the point. Dunno. Perhaps history is that business that can't spiritually afford reflection, at least, not in the heat of the moment. But then, you're right, we're sots, the kind who, in a crowd, stamp their feet in mushy snow and say, "What's this then? Something's got Lenin by the short hairs. Could use a drink." Americans say power doesn't have to corrupt. Really? Since when? Did you know that Rousseau was a bully; that Shakespeare mixed rubbish in his plays; that Paul McCartney is rated a cut above Schubert? What's the world but a mouth in love with the noises it makes? Some day, I'll get over your way, and we'll have a fine time of it, and we'll do us some gelato at the Liberty Bar. All the best, RQC.*

Football. The less said the better. But if I despised my old coach for his leer; for his collusion with knuckleheads in haphazard rites of manliness; for his always pregnant dolt of a wife, I could never come around to seeing how he saw things. Sally McCabe regarded me as an oddity, a bit of comic relief, perhaps, from the endless pageantry of her life: her beauty, her cheerleading, her car sex, and the fact she was a VIP's daughter. She became, over time, part and parcel of my mentations, a conscience, as it were; and if not a conscience so much, then an inquisitor, albeit a lovely one. Much laughter. Many nose-wrinkling smiles. If the history teacher was a drunk and blew his brains out, so what? What was not to like in life? As with Moonface's apparent fits, McCabe would arrive without fanfare, and often, with questions: 'Randall, what was always your problem?'

'You know, now that you mention it, I wonder if I know. Did Seneca die well? Or better than he had lived, at any rate?'

'You see, there you go again. Such an egghead.'

'It's true.'

'You weren't a bad kisser, though there's always room for improvement. I never interfered when the guys used to pound on you, though I could've done, because they thought you different. Don't hold that against me, and you were different. I won't hold it against you that, deep down, you really thought us dumb hicks. Anyway, forewarned is forearmed. You're going to have a problem. Prentiss. She really is clueless. Don't flatter yourself on her account. All she wants from you is that you acknowledge her perfection. You're driving her mad because you won't.'

'Yes but, she's mad to begin with.'

'No matter.'

'Well, thanks for the tip.'

'My pleasure.'

'Anything else? The economy? The endless war? Woodrow Wilson?'

'No. But ease up on Eleanor. She'll sort things out, eventually. Moonface? Now there's a girl I don't quite get. Would I wish her on a hairy beast? Evie Longoria. She's—'

But the visitation was now at an end, even if I was somewhat taken aback by what I took to be a hint of dismay in McCabe's throaty voice. Still, her laughter was not unkind. Generous countenance.

Later that morning, I had Eleanor on my hands.

'No, Eleanor, no.'

'Why, Randall, why not ever for?'

'Haven't you, with all the men you've taken to bed, rung all the changes on sex there are to ring?'

'You credit me with experience I don't necessarily have. Roll me a cig.'

So I rolled the good woman a cigarette.

'And while you're at it,' she said, 'tell me what the meaning of life is, because damn if I know, anymore.'

'So it's gotten that bad?'

'Kind of.'

Eleanor of the gilded curls, unassuming voluptuary; Eleanor of the keen political mind; good woman who used to play the trombone until she decided it was a silly thing to do; Eleanor who had stumbled on even sillier things to do such as explore her sexuality, but only because someone, Prentiss, had parked a theme park of the notion in her head, was distraught.

'You know,' she said, 'I miss it when I was a girl growing up in the country. There was a pond we kids used to splash around in, rich kids, poor kids, middle of the road kids, smart, stupid, assertive, shy. Can you believe I was shy? Can you believe Bob was shy? We had the same childhood pretty much. I think we were wiser then.'

'Maybe.'

'But don't you think so? All those dramas. It was life and death, but then, you know, in an hour it was all over and forgotten about.'

'I suppose I had a long memory.'

'Yes, well, that is your problem, isn't it?'

'You think me vindictive?'

'I don't think you're petty, if that's what you mean.'

'Thank you for that. If there's anything I can't stand, it's pettiness.'

'No, you can't just let things happen. You always have to know why it's happening.'

'Is that a crime?'

'No crime. But when do you live? I guess I'm a shoot first, ask questions later kind of gal.'

'That you are.'

Eleanor gave me a look.

'Not even a teensy-weensy smack on my bottom?'

'Eleanor. Good God.'

'You know, I go over to Marjerie's some time ago, and there they are, she and her lover boys having at each other, and it put me off, I have to tell you. It troubled me, because I thought I should've liked it, but it didn't feel right. And then we go to this club, and I'm put off again, only worse... well, I don't say anything to them, my mistake, maybe, but it's in my head and I can't get it out of my head, and now—'

'I think you're bored, sweetheart. I think maybe you're over-dramatizing. It's just sex, that's all. It's one brand of power drink as opposed to another. It's neither here nor there.'

'It certainly is here and it certainly is there. You think it's nothing to think about? You're the one always going on about ancient mysteries.'

Rudess

Israel would pound Gaza a while, a boxer punching a bag. A round of outrage. Then a few weeks would go by, and the world would forget, as the world always forgets. And when lover has brought lover to the point of discharge, what has the rights of man to do with sensation, the eyes rolled over with their bliss, some god having flooded the soul with an instant of eternity? As for Marjerie Prentiss, there was neither rhyme nor reason why she had set her sights on me. It was not sex she wanted, least of all love; it was just that I was there, a few steps down the hall, her curiosity her morality, and it was indifferent to any pain but her own. I may as well have been nothing more than a quivering item of Jell-O of exotic flavour, and she must sample. No, she was not even a predator so much as she was an entity in motion, a cloud pushed along by the wind. She might mingle with other clouds should any happen to get in her way; she might drift forever, unimpeded in the skies of day and night.

At the Blue Danube, I sat alone, a party of Greeks sampling the moussaka which, every two days, Cassandra prepared afresh, so Gregory explained to those Greeks. I sat and drifted. And when I collected a thought or two, and was about to treat with those thoughts in a notebook, in waltzed the Whistler; or rather, in he sashayed, swinging his arms violently, a man on martial parade. He astonished the Greeks. He was curt and precise with his order. Would have his coffee hot, not lukewarm. If there was no cheesecake, then apple crumb. Three scoops of ice cream. And I wondered, as he commenced his routine—the whistling through clenched teeth, the stomping of his feet—if he understood that the so-called white voter backlash to the candidacy of President Elect had not materialized as predicted, especially not in western Pennsylvania. Had he heard, too, that Jews were not now considered outsiders but as indigenous to Canaan? They had put their bosses and sweatshops behind them on the coast and broke out for the hills. They did so well that they did, in fact, raise up a David and a royal house. Assyrians, in time, spoiled the party, on their heels, Babylonians, Jerusalem gotten to be a swinging door. The man whistled and stomped furiously. Antonio, waiting on him, as much as any man can who wishes to get through a day with minimum fuss and bother, sighed. And I moved on. Inside the Traymore, as I climbed the stairs, I caught a good whiff of pot roast, Mrs Petrova's. Warm, consoling aroma. Consolation would come with peas, potatoes, gravy, perhaps. And apple sauce? At the top of the stairs, a flash of bare ankles. Marjerie Prentiss. She had just left Eleanor's. She looked around and cocked her head, smirking. I made a show of thinking nothing of it. Perhaps Moonface was at the library, researching Ptolemy Soter. She was resuming her scholarship, taking the odd class now, nothing burdensome. It was a full life: her Champagne Sheridan, the Blue Danube aka Le Grec, classes and, of course, the night life. I observed myself settling down to a familiar routine. I rolled a cigarette. I selected a book. Patted the couch; propped a pillow. At random, I opened the Old Testament. Judges 16. *Then went Samson to Gaza, and saw there a harlot, and went in unto her.* I knew it was coming—the next onslaught of Prentiss. And when she arrived and had knocked and I had answered, she smirked some more.

'Phillip isn't here,' I said.

'I know he isn't. He's in the country, doing handiwork.'

'I guess he owes Eleanor some money she lent him.'

'No, he owes me. I paid up his debt.'

It seemed a perfectly useless conversation.

'So, if you know Phillip's not here, are you looking for Ralph? In which case, he's not here, either.'

'Ralph's in the country, too.'

'Handiwork?'

'Working on our house.'

'So when are you moving in?'

'When it's ready. Am I to be admitted or are you leaving me out here to dry?'

'I'm leaving you out there to dry.'

'I don't think so.'

And she made to move past me, and I might have blocked her entry; but then I thought that to do so would have been childish, and we must put away childish things.

'Well then, what's on your mind?' I stupidly asked.

She took my couch as if it were an objective in battle. She would not be moved off it, it was obvious to see, unless I was to resort to violence, in which case I would lose this little skirmish, if not the war. She studied her nails, her night shirt exposing more of her body than seemed warranted.

'I guess it's kind of a Mexican stand-off between us,' she said, that voice of hers a dull boom.

One had to admire her effrontery, even so. I could not recall the particulars of the Samson and Delilah story, but I knew it had not come to a good end.

'I'll have a cigarette,' she insisted.

I complied, rolling her one.

'I know,' she began to reason, 'that not at all men have sex on their brains all the time. But most men want to have sex with me. I don't see why I should think you're any different. But you see, it's not sex I want from you. I just want you to approve of me.'

'Yes, well, there it is. There's the thing. I don't like you. We've had this conversation before, more than once, I think, and we always wind up at the same place. I don't like you. But we live cheek by jowl, so I just want to get along.'

'Fair enough.'

'More than fair, I should think.'

'But you've done Eleanor. You've done Moonface.'

'What's this doing you keep talking about? I don't do anybody. I find "do" is repulsive when employed like that. I'm no paragon of virtue. I'm not the most considerate of men, but I don't do people—'

'People do people all the time.'

'I think not.'

'I mean, if you want sex, I can give you sex.'

'No prelims? No strings? No sweat?'

'You're going moralistic on me.'

'If I have to.'

'So you're not going to like me. Isn't that doing me? Like you made up your mind and you don't even know me?'

'Like I made up my mind and I don't even know you.'

'Well, I guess that's it,' she said.

I refrained from making a show of agreement. America would live through to the bitter end America's circus of dark arts. Prentiss sprang to her feet, and she stood before me, looking into my eyes. I attempted to look into hers, though I was reluctant to know her reasons and what it would cost me to know them. All I could see, in any case, were those watery orbs. And then a great deal of fury possessed her face. Her cheeks set hard, she struck me one, and it was hard enough—that blow she struck—that I lifted my hand to rub away the pain. She caught my wrist and held it a moment.

She was nothing if not deadly serious: 'That,' she said, 'was for any dirty thoughts you might have been thinking.'

Hair Shirt

Failure by one's own lights was bad enough; to fail while in thralldom to someone else's set of lights was worse. Sure, I would iron a shirt. I would attend, as invited, a gala of academe. Arsdell's, one of academe's finest, had alerted me by way of a note in the mail. It read: *Perhaps you might be interested. Art, Literature and the Condition of Women.* Yes, go and mutter imprecations as you go. But who would want to stand around and take questions as to the fate of projects such as one had yet to complete and would never complete? *Ah, Calhoun. Haven't seen you since the days of the woolly mammoth. Since Caesar lost his legions, at any rate. Me, I'm just keeping up appearances. How the hell are you?* First, I would get myself some genuine sustenance. Eggy was nonplussed.

'She hit me,' I said to the homunculus.

'Who hit you?' asked Eggy, there in the Blue Danube. And here was the foul-speaking hag, so I observed, returned to us after a lengthy absence, and yet she was far gone. She stood at the window, shaking her fist at an uncomprehending world. Ratty sneaks. Gaudy leggings. Thick coat with immense buttons. And I wondered if she was thinking just then how, in the blink of an eye, she had gone from girlhood to decrepitude and rage? Eggy reached for his glass of wine with a tiny claw, this sparrow of a man.

'Prentiss,' I answered.

'Oh, her. Why, she always seemed promising. But I guess she figures I'm not her type. Hoo hoo. I asked her to lunch, you know.'

'Yes. Well.'

'Why, you must've done something.'

'What something? I only answered the door.'

'There you go. You answered the door. The rain in Spain. Always.'

What worried Eggy was that he might have to quit drinking.

'Well, if you didn't do something, it must've been something you said,' he thundered.

'Apparently, it's what I'm not doing and not saying.'

'What do you mean?'

'Just that.'

'My wife used to hit me,' said Eggy, somewhat wistfully, 'well, she was bigger than me. You know what they say: a stitch in time saves nine. They should hang the bastards.'

Eggy was drunk.

'What if I get to the gates and I don't recognize Peter? At least I didn't get Alzheimer's. Touch wood. Hoodeehoo.'

It was glacially slow, the rate at which his eyelids fell. Eggy's chin raised his chest. I signalled Antonio to bring me a glass, and I would help myself to Eggy's supply. The hag went silent and still. It occurred to me she might not have any idea where she was. I rather liked her for her conviction, the way she would exhort passersby to go to church or she would ram something up their arses, but she was, even so, hard to take. It seemed Antonio was up on his tippy-toes, bringing me the glass, lest he call the woman's attention to himself.

Terror grabbed me in some part of my being that did not seem connected to my person. It was not terror at the prospect of an afternoon among parodies, so many minds committed to caring, sipping wine and munching cheese. For that sort of crowd, I could manage a kind of sickly contempt. Perhaps the terror was not mine but Eggy's; that he had, somehow, transposed his onto me, saying, 'I'm tired, you carry the load a while.' He might not wake up. The hag departed, leaving in her wake an unquiet, almost palpable substitute for her presence. I doubted that Antonio was a religious man, but he had made the sign of the cross on account of her vehemence. He shook his head, and he did not care who saw him do so. For all that the Albanian in him was uncouth, he was the gentlest of men. I worried for his contradictions. Rippling banks of grey cloud to the south, a cold sun in the west. Pool tournament on TV. Looking vaguely professional, a woman seeking the prize analyzed the table while chalking her stick. Her game was methodical, lacking flair. Eleanor had recently asked of me the meaning of life; I let the question die, assuming she was not serious. Marjerie Prentiss wished for me to like her, no, not like her, but worship her as a force. Art, Literature, and the Condition of Women, if it was at all in its right mind, could not possibly desire my presence. I would do better to sit here in my hair shirt, stupidly atoning for I knew not what, monitoring Eggy, staring out the window—

And somehow I got Eggy home safe, although I do not know who leaned most on whom.

'You know,' said Eggy, 'you seem to be glowing with wisdom.'

'Don't look now,' I answered, 'but I'm three sheets to the wind.'

'Why does everyone refute me?'

'If I say you're glowing,' he thundered, 'then you glow.'

And now that we had negotiated the Traymore stairs, had not climbed Everest so much as raised the moon where sat our domiciles, the homunculus fumbled about for his keys. Eleanor stuck her head out her door; Eleanor saw our condition, each gilded curl of hers a grin.

'*Les* boys,' she purred.

'*Le* wench,' Eggy shot back.

I was not up for such neck-snapping levity. The great thing about Eleanor, I figured, was that though her soul was imperilled, she did not confuse language with knowledge or the presumption of understanding. But then I was drunk, and drunk, I was skeptical of my powers of logic.

'Not now,' I said to the good woman, she getting that look she always gets when feeling mischievous.

One heard Eggy curse some idiots on his TV. Effing hell.

'You look like a whipped dog,' Eleanor said.

'Eggy said I looked wise,' I countered.

'He's in error.'

'What, Eggy mistaken?'

For the briefest of instants, her grey-green eyes sorted through mine for the remote possibility they might encounter wisdom.

'Come on, I'll make you some coffee,' she said, like an old sport.

I followed her into her kitchen, admiring her charms as I did so, as she meant me to. Clearly, there was something on her mind, but that, now, it was apparent to her she had in me no interlocutor. Even so, she persisted: 'A good time was had by all.'

'The concert, you ninny,' she explained, seeing my incomprehension. 'Dylan. I rather liked him though he's not been my cup of tea. And then we went to some rich man's Old Town loft, someone Ralph knows, and some babes hanging around had to have been hookers. I didn't like the looks of it, so I took a taxi home. Like a rolling stone.'

I nodded my approval of her decision.

'So now, I'm here,' she sighed, 'and where's Monsieur? Did you see him, tonight?'

'No, it was just me and Eggy holding down the fort.'

'Wonder where he got to?' said Eleanor, with good nature, but perhaps, fearing the worst.

The coffee machine began to gurgle, my mind a very dim bulb indeed.

'Just how drunk are you, Mr Calhoun? And the meaning of life?'

My, how grim Eleanor now sounded.

'The meaning? It's called being star-crossed.'

'You think so, Calhoun?' said Eleanor, her tone suggesting she had familiarity with the notion.

Then Dubois was upon us, he wearing his martini face. He had been downtown, helping an old colleague from the business world celebrate a 50th wedding anniversary. Dubois blew on his hands, the hairline cracks of his red cheeks all smiles.

'Cold out,' he said, 'and I'm not getting any younger.'

'Who is?' said the apple of his eye, Eleanor.

But she was, even so, pleased to see the man.

In Like Flynn

Late afternoon, and I sat with Dubois in the Blue Danube aka Le Grec. Moonface pranced about, earrings dangling from her earlobes. The thin circular bands seemed to have elevated her spirits; she blushed from her throat up to her cheeks as we complimented a dear girl.

'They suit my long face,' she explained, pretending modesty.

Dubois was recounting a portion of his business life, especially that period when he first became leery of certain developments in the world of finance. Stock traders would get at the portfolios of money managers, this under cover of the banks. But legal, legit and destructive.

'The traders,' said Dubois, 'they weren't all that smart, though people thought they were. "Hang on a minute, got to take this call from my broker." Remember those days? The buyers just had to know when to buy and the sellers when to sell, the smart guys in the room the money managers. But anyway—'

His words were going through me like so many indigestible bits of gristle.

'Still, the traders were smart enough, I guess.'

Now Moonface chatted up two young men who, to judge by their pinched expressions and workaday suits, might have been officers from the bank at the corner.

'Yes,' she said, 'I'm learning Spanish words. Going to South America. Yes, really. Words for please and thank you and where's the toilet. Those kind of words. Enough to get by.'

Her words tailed off in a pall of failure. She giggled. The men were polite. The commute underway, snow in the forecast, the sun exploded in the sky, and then, it was dark. Cold passersby walked briskly. The ebb and flow of humanity, its collective tread almost noiseless.

'The system needs a real good purge,' Dubois observed, he who once had faith in it, 'and this is it. Think of all those martini bars that sprang up like mushrooms, catering solely to stressed-out traders. I wonder what'll become of them?'

His mouth was full of rice and salmon. He topped up my wine. I thought it best to keep my altercation with Prentiss to myself; even so, I had let Eggy in on it. If I were counting on his discretion, I was only showing myself up as a fool.

'Spirituality,' I said, 'is not reality; it's the objection to reality. This explains you and explains me.'

Dubois guffawed. He was not sure, but I might have been jesting.

'You can't maximize profit forever,' he said, 'and we can't afford to have everyone motivated to the point of super-performance, though it's still what they teach in business school.'

I answered: 'People, when confronted with what ought to prove fascinating, especially in the realm of metaphysics, are usually unimpressed.'

Now Dubois knew I was jesting, and the hairline cracks of his cheeks, in their assemblage, laughed. A taxi pulled up, inside it Eggy, this swashbuckler in the back seat.

'Here's trouble,' I said.

'Oh no,' said Dubois, 'he must've been to the Claremont.'

'He was,' affirmed Moonface, 'he called here from there. I'll bring another glass.'

'You'd better,' Dubois replied, 'or there'll be hell to pay.'

With Herculean effort, Eggy hoisted himself to a standing position outside the car, then took his bearings. His pins began lifting like pistons. When his feet got their traction, he moved ahead onto the terrasse and through the door.

'Officer on deck,' I cracked.

'Oh eff off.'

But Eggy was in the greatest of moods; he had wined and dined Haitian Nurse, so he said.

'Such large earrings you're wearing,' he leered, Moonface decanting wine into his glass. He continued: 'You know what they say—' Indefatigable, he said: 'Oh oh, I might say something untoward.'

Moonface blushed the colour of peach, her rich golden brown eyes savvy. And when she left us, Eggy could not help himself: 'You know what nursie once told me. Said women who wear large earrings have—'

This time, Dubois cut him off, saying: 'Don't want to hear it.'

'Why the effing hell not? I mean nursie ought to know what she's talking about. Well, don't you think?'

'Couldn't say,' answered Dubois.

Even so, it would seem that certain vulgarities, after all was said and done, were quite satisfactory for Traymorean males of a certain era, males who had seen it come and go and might not see it come back again, let alone truth, beauty, justice. And Eggy, in the interests of Moonface's future, would have her scale the heights of Machu Picchu and pray at Delphi and write up a monograph on Winston Churchill, to boot, Eggy buried in his winter coat, his scarf long, white and plush. Why, he looked like Errol Flynn, if homuncular.

Jubilee

And the next evening, the Blue Danube packed, Moonface circulating like a host-queen, what with her earrings, Eggy was over-excited: 'Bring the good 'ol Bugle boys. We'll sing another song, sing it with a spirit that will start the world along… Hurrah! Hurrah—!'

His raised finger, marking the beat, was a dangerous weapon. Two nights in a row, and Dubois was dining on rice and salmon. Miss Meow miaowed; the Whistler whistled. Students, paired off, played with their electronic gadgets while waiting on pizzas, smug with their lot. A lonely old woman perhaps inwardly thrilled to the almost festive atmosphere, picked at her dinner one deliberate mouthful at a time. A table of Albanians caroused, and, as their decibels rose, so did Eggy's: 'Hurrah! Hurrah!'

Cassandra, too, bustled about, and was still nursing a secret source of bemusement, working chewing gum, her cheeks dimpling. *A feast is made for laughter, and wine maketh merry: but money answereth all things.* Ecclesiastes 10: 19 And when Eggy began to speak of the auto industry, Dubois held up his hand.

'Whoa there, hold it. How did we get on to this all of a sudden?'

'What do you mean, get on to this? It's what I've been saying. And what is Ontario going to do if the Americans don't bail out Detroit?'

'The Canadians have just got to wait and see.'

'Yes but—'

'You still haven't answered my question.'

'What question?'

'How we got from marching to the sea to the making of cars.'

'Well, if you won't pay attention.'

And if, as Eggy had said, Haitian Nurse was writing a paper on the homeless, I thought it timely.

'Effing hell,' he had said, 'I corrected her mistakes and she got snotty.'

'Points of grammar or her social theory?' Dubois wished to know.

'Oh, eff you.'

And now here was Hiram Wiedemayer, he an acquaintance of mine, and shortly thereafter, here was Evie Longoria. Even Too Tall Poet showed, apologizing for the fact he had been making himself scarce, of late. Evie regarded him with some astonishment. What manner of God had fashioned this manner of creature? Hiram volunteered to cross the street to get wine, he delighted with the fact he chose a good night to stray into our neighbourhood. Dubois said he would go with him, Eggy saying: 'Of course. What are we? Duffers? Hurrah. Hurrah.'

Evie shushed him, sensing he was perhaps getting carried away. Large-boned Evie looked as fragile as ever, as delicate a neurotic as rare china. And here it was I wished to spend a quiet night, Moonface rolling her eyes up and to the side, pleased there were so many friends of the café about, and her life had meaning. And we all got roisterous.

And for all that Eggy managed to annoy me (that Too Tall Poet was a real poet and I was not), it must have been quite the evening: Evie Longoria in my bed, Hiram Wiedemayer on my couch. Fascinated with Blue Danubians, he nonetheless lamented the fact he failed to bring his camera and capture our mugs.

Eggy had said, 'We might've had a picture of Moonface on her backside.'

That Evie wound up in my bed had nothing to do with sex; it had everything to do with wine, and, as it was, it got the best of her. Even so, she said, before her eyes went shut: 'It's terrible of me. I'm so greedy. I'm so lonely.'

I most likely said something as idiotic as this: 'Think nothing of it.'

Hiram and I once more argued Israel-Palestine, but he was all thumbs up for President Elect. And then, a bad hour come around, and I woke, Evie's face a peaceful countenance. It was as if she had prayed and made her peace with God, let the executioner's blade do its worst. In any case, when I next woke, she was gone. Hiram, too, was gone; perhaps they had left together.

I would take my hangover to the library. Let winter-bundled mothers pushing strollers cluck their tongues. Let squirrels bark derision and sparrows wing-rub their bellies in glee. But could science explain the premonitory? Might I chance upon haruspex specifications in *Myra Breckinridge*? I did not get far, Eleanor accosting me at my door.

'What was all that about?' she asked, innocently enough.

She could only be referring to the evening previous.

'First,' she continued, 'Eggy's on the stairs, singing at the top of his lungs. Then Bob throws himself on me, and he hasn't done that in a while. Tells Marj who was over that if she wants in, get in, otherwise get out. Then I hear Eggy's little helpmate became your playmate. And that Hiram fellow—'

'Please,' I said, 'I would love to paint you a picture but the brain's all fuzz. Permit me to pass, unless you know something about the science of premonition.'

She gave me a look, her lip gloss too bright to contemplate.

'I foresee,' she said, 'that with you I'll never get my just desserts.'

'Justice? What justice? There's no justice.'

And as soon as the words were out, I knew I was possibly in error; that a page had been turned, and we were living now in a new history. So it seemed. I pitched myself past the good woman. Down the stairs and beyond. I pulled up at the scene of the evening's crimes where Cassandra, pitying me, gave admission early.

'Ko-fee?' she asked, knowing what was required.

She had been stringing Christmas lights, this goddess of terrible aspect indulging the felicities of the domestic. She was as fresh as a daisy despite what had been, for her, a late night. And I saw in my mentations long-bellied Moonface, sinuous Moonface performing a veil-dance peculiar to her as she circulated among lotus-eaters, some of whom were Albanians. Yes, it must have been quite the evening. There had been, for instance, a strange stringy blonde in a track suit yelling: 'Go, Habs!'

Hiram Wiedemayer: 'Who would've thought it? What a nightmare it's been. We were on the Titanic and now we're on the Good Ship Lollipop where the bonbons play.'

Well, the man was entitled to speak of it, he—along with Eggy and I—an American transplanted.

Evie Longoria: 'I should really call my daughter.'

Some homuncular voice: 'Ah, young talent.'

Dubois: 'Bring on the virgins!'

Go, Habs!

Too Tall Poet: 'John Newlove's the poet to read.'

A chorus of voices: 'Who's he?'

And so forth and so on.

And then, in my digs, and before she passed out, Hiram snoring on the couch, Evie said, her eyes just then enormous: 'If you're going to ravish me, do please be gentle. But you'll find I'm no beauty. I'm so embarrassed.'

And either I spoke it or simply thought it, the words these: 'Something in your voice touches me. Even so, you're in no condition to be ravished.'

And perhaps, as the woman slept, I could hear snow falling, the night now so quiet when all had been boisterous clamour; could hear each flake asking pardon for disturbing another.

Rank and Status

It was time to pay Eggy a visit in his lair. Evie Longoria had complained of its old man's smell.

'Yes, she was here, and we made a pact,' Eggy said. 'I won't go on about her earrings anymore if she doesn't give me the matron treatment.'

Theirs was a relationship that Dubois once described as an old married couple's.

'Well,' I said, 'earrings in the ancient world indicated rank and status. The women who wore them certainly didn't do chores.'

'No,' replied Eggy, 'they were probably on their backsides.'

He raised a finger so as to punctuate his remark, and whatever else he had to say evidently slipped his mind. Zeus-like Eggy.

'I wonder what's on the talk shows,' he finally said, now a lonely urchin.

I shrugged.

'I know,' he said, with a hint of eureka in his rising voice, 'it'll be all New York senator the new Secretary of State to be. She's at last got an ample pot to piss in.'

Yes, she had that, and opinions on the matter were rife, and rumours, and huzzahs and faint praises and excoriating curses.

'Well, we'll see,' I said, my tone awfully lame.

'What do you mean we'll see? Of course, we'll see. She's a warmonger and she'll bugger something. They should hang the bastards. All of them. Back when they had the chance. But the Democrats, you know, they've got spines of tissue paper.'

'What's this, Eggy? Poetry?'

'Don't get cheeky.'

Here he was then, surrounded by his books, family photos, memorabilia. He was a quite ordinary man who was somehow not ordinary, the whys and wherefores of it hard to pin down. I supposed he had been everywhere he had claimed to have been and done what he said he did. Now and then truth-telling infected his patter, and one was led by it to conclude his affairs with women had been rather minimal, his portion of love on the meagre side of a half-empty chalice. And just when I might begin to think I understood the man, I would know I did not and probably could not ever; there was fancy leg work in his old pins, yet, and the occasional and rather alarming irruptions of a twinkle in his tough old eyes. The secret of the secrets he seemed to have was that they would remain his secrets—*for me to know and you to find out*—and, otherwise, eff you. He was not all that pleased to see me, even if he, hating loneliness, had an instinct for the social; even if he had been mean to his wives. He had always, in a certain sense, told me what I needed to know, though the knowing might not have taken the guise of words. A look, a gesture, an intonation of voice, and I should understand that even if history were continuous, each discrete part of it as was a human life was not knowable; yes, it was a one-off deal rendered moot by death. So that we could talk about Kennedy all we wished, but so what? And we could slag the Prime Minister for his glass jaws. Great fun. And rue the miseries of the earth's peasant classes. Oh dear. That they were getting a screwing the likes of which had never been seen before, but that, well, *the rain in Spain. Hoo hoo.* In what did Eggy believe? Of what was he the elitist, the aristocrat? And of what was he just some old bugger on a street corner, churning his way toward a jug and the ministrations of wenches? Truth, beauty, justice? Yes, there was all that in him, in some room of his soul cordoned off with thick silk rope; a room that was mostly given a miss, yes, even by his own footfalls, but that awaited its honour. Of this, I was certain. And how did he do it? How did he pay for the overhead, so to speak, the ogling minions of a phantasmagorical land dwindled down to a trickle?

'I think,' said Eggy, 'that Moonface hasn't given up on academe. She's writing Sheridan's papers now. He isn't much of a student. But he's her lover boy. Effing hell, I was never that. No wench offered to cross my *t's*, except, you know, in the sack. Do you think they'll drop the bomb? Oh dear. What if they did? I mean, it'd be tits up, wouldn't it? Alright then, I've got a thing about black bottoms. What's the harm in that? It's a damn sight better than squeezing some nuclear trigger. Haven't you read *A Thousand Days* yet? And you call yourself a student of history?'

Current President seemed a tad vindictive, what with his eleventh hour granting of sinecures to those who had played ball and would complicate matters for the incoming administration. It was nothing new, but the scope of it was unprecedented. As it was too miserably cold for a constitutional stroll down a noble boulevard; but as I was feeling some impatience with a homunculus, I would hide away in my digs and await the inevitable calamities of social unrest and climactic distemper. Even so, Eggy was startled when I rose to leave, saying I would, no doubt, see him later. His seeming lack of pleasure in my visit had been his coyness. What startled me was Moonface in the hall. She had a burble in her throat; her mouth drawn small and tight was mischievous: 'I give you leave to come see me in my chambers.'

It had been a while. And her rooms were not as they had been before: cozy and tasteful. They reflected now that she was half here, half there; half vagabond and half prodigal. Her laundry lay about for all to see. Plants were neglected. She cleared a love seat of its pile of books and magazines and other debris. Would I like a coffee? Would I roll her a cigarette? She did not often smoke.

'Sheridan was going to take me to the movies,' she said.

It was I who used to take her to the movies.

'You used to take me,' she accused.

'Well, how can I now, what with your hectic schedule?' I answered, defensive.

'True,' she said, rolling her eyes.

The coffee made, she handed me a hot mug and I placed a thin stick of cigarette in her mouth and held a lighter to its end. She inhaled smoke, and parked herself on a floor cushion. She would use an empty orange juice bottle for the cigarette ash. Her hair uncombed, her shoulders slumped, she was just a moping, ungainly girl without a clue as to what to do with herself, the goddess in her off on a fool's errand.

'So,' I said, 'what occasions this?'

'Oh,' she answered, her voice thick with rue, 'I don't know. I'm not happy.'

'Sheridan?'

'Yes, well. He thinks everything's cool. How grand it is we're going to Ecuador. All his friends think he's Mr Grand. I'm just the chick who warms his bed. Do you see?'

I looked down upon her as a father might a daughter. It was not a role I wished to have.

'Well, do you see?'

She got off her cushion, and on her knees, she wriggled toward me, an insipid smile on her drawn mouth. She laid her head on my lap. And then she said she could not bring her father anywhere; he always monopolized the conversation, going on about the oppression of the Flemish language.

'Good God,' I said, 'didn't you raise him right?'

Next up, was Eleanor. It went like that, sometimes, and I might consider myself a reader of Tarot cards with a clientele. An ologist of a sort with a steady practice. But all Eleanor wanted was a cup of sugar, she too lazy to go out and fetch her own. She was wearing a fabric of gaudy colour such as clashed with her clear and innocent countenance, one that belied the fact of her sinful urges. She was still unable to account for Dubois's renewed attentions.

'But I'm not complaining,' she let me know.

At any rate, something sugary was in the offing. I was reading that bit in Lucan where an Etruscan seer, in his attempt to expiate Rome, J Caesar's arrival imminent, analyzed the entrails of a bull and was horrified by the putrescence he saw, and by the diseased and malformed liver. He would sugarcoat the result for his anxious audience, but inwardly, he quaked. *I fear an unspeakable outcome.* I knew Prentiss's knock for what it was—trouble, and I sucked in my breath and answered the door. She said: 'You know what gets me about you people is that you don't do anything. I'm a doer.'

Her voice, a dull boom, nonetheless seethed with rage. I supposed *you people* were none other than Traymoreans.

'Well, Bob's always busy,' I said, 'and Eleanor cooks. Eggy provides counsel, as befits a senior member. But if you mean me in the particular, I guess I have to plead guilty.'

Was I not amiable?

Why Is Anything Anything?

Eggy, but a pea in his pod of a winter coat, answered Dubois's query.

'Why, the doctor tried to set me up with his secretary.'

'Oh well, that's something,' said Dubois, feeling, perhaps, that his question was answered, the state of the old man's health put to rest by this promise of an assignation.

I figured that Eggy's response was part and parcel of yet another apocryphal tale. And he regarded, with a lamenting gaze, the cheese pies before him. And it was as if, by regarding them, some morsel of it all would appear in his mouth, and he circumvent the perils of transference. More often than not, food wound up in his lap. Effing hell. A dead night in the Blue Danube. The Habs on TV, my attention wandered.

Moonface and I on a ballroom floor, the palace a monument to broken dreams. Moonface and I poised beneath the star bursts of a glittering ceiling. I would place my hand on the small of her bare back. A dip in the knees, and on the beat… Would she freeze or trip? Or was she born, after all, for the spectacle of grace? Yes, while about us in the shadows, hooded figures, the indigent and the homeless, played the games of the dispossessed. For it looked like there would be much dispossession to come. There it was: the taunting flicker of a tongue. There it was: that love is a pitiful force, up against the crushing immensity of space.

'So,' Dubois put it to me from out of the blue, 'are you any closer to finishing your book?'

What book? What impertinence was this?

'Oh,' said Eggy, raising a finger, 'he's just a poet, and poets are, why, you know, riffraff.'

'I rest my case,' so I announced.

Serge in the galley had cooked up for Dubois a special burger, served it wreathed in pickle slices. Eggy was miffed, no such honour for him. Gregory joined us at the table, bored and tired. But he was up for a wager on the game's outcome.

'He's the man,' said Gregory, 'he's the man,' this in reference to President Elect.

Perhaps Gregory was expecting a rising tide, and his fortunes improve. Tiny blue Christmas bulbs, so many tear drops, adorned a small evergreen. Outside, it was dark, of course, and dreary, the street quiet, the lamps that lit it baleful. In some unhealthy street-glow a runt of a tree was having a go at life by the liquor outlet. Eggy had taken to wondering whether it would survive. The figure of Artemis in her niche did not move; try as I might to cause it to move. Perhaps I had not consumed sufficient amounts of wine.

'Gentlemen,' I said, addressing the table, 'I fear an elegaic mood has taken hold of me.'

'Oh Christ,' said Eggy, yes, with some disdain.

Dubois guffawed. Gregory looked very afraid.

'And because it has,' I continued, 'I think it the better part of valour that I remove myself, what, from this distinguished company of noble and stalwart souls—'

'Here it comes,' Dubois interrupted.

'So as to answer, in my solitude, whether that which is over, *finis*, deader than a rotted fish, can generate beginning. What was it that Eliot implied? That the beginning is only a thing that comes around again, like one's tax returns? As for Ottawa, hell, it's but stale beer compared to champagne. Antonio, my bill.'

And Antonio, who had been keeping to himself, nothing to do, now had something to do.

'Well, take care of yourself,' said managerial Dubois, as if he cared.

'Rot your socks,' said Eggy.

'Sure, rot your socks,' Gregory repeated, trying out a new expression for size.

I dreamed (after Letterman had had his cheap laughs on his TV show) that Prentiss and her prankering men set upon me.

Prentiss: 'Well then, let's have it—the meaning of life.'

Calhoun: 'Aristotle said it was happiness.'

Prentiss: 'Let's have it from you.'

Calhoun: 'I have no idea.'

Prentiss: 'Don't you?'

Calhoun: 'I could presume.'

Prankering Men: 'Heigh ho, heigh ho, it's off to work we go.'

Calhoun: 'But if Aristotle said these things, that happiness is the meaning of life, that the soul is the perfect expression of a natural body, does it follow that the soul is happiness?'

Prankering Men: 'What's he smoking? Because we've got to get some of that.'

Prentiss: 'I am the meaning of life. I am your happiness. You can lick me. Come on, haven't got all day.'

Prankering Men: 'No m'am. Haven't got all day.'

I supposed the dream was a variety of nightmare. What was a dream? Electrical disturbance in some organ of sense? Reason? The constant support of an intelligible world? How fragile Aristotle thought the world to be. Had he known the half of it? When I woke, it seemed I had been one of the chattering classes all by myself. Heard plumbing. A Traymorean was up and about. *Do you remember when we met? That's the day I knew you were my pet.*

It seemed to me that if Marjerie Prentiss loved her swains, it was a shallow love, at best; she loved herself first and foremost, and the melodrama in which she was its epicentre. There might be ologists who would venture to say that this overweening self-regard on her part was, in actual fact, a species of hate, one that men had foisted on her, and they might have a point. However, in Prentiss's case, if in no other case, and I would stake a wager on it, self-hatred was self-idolatry. I was low on money. And in wet snow and wind and waning light I would go to the bank machine at the corner. I did so, and there was Eleanor, fancy that, withdrawing cash; she doing a sort of shimmy at the machine, a shimmy bespeaking her impatience with technology; how it is convenience creates more time, yes, only that it is time less lived. Nonetheless, transaction completed, she turned, and turning, spotted me.

'Randall,' she said, 'we have to talk.'

Well, I was enqueued.

'Now,' she said, 'bugger this.'

It was going to require a bit of a hike, away from the Traymore and the Blue Danube, as she wished for us some privacy. I balked at this and was overruled. And so, in a boulangerie smelling of warm pastries and country bread, just down from the little park that looked depressive under the pall of sodden snowflakes, Eleanor unloaded: 'I was over there, you know, *there*, at Marjerie's.'

Her cheeks were flushed, grey-green eyes animated. A knitted cap was pulled down on her gilded curls; she was very appealing.

'Well, we were just talking, kicking the can around, Marjerie saying this and that, nothing of any great import. Ralph heard her out, as stoic as ever, Phillip pacing the floor with his cigarette and beer. Then Marjerie started going on about what men find attractive in women, and I thought it so much bollocks, and just then, and I think he jumped in without thinking, Phillip said he liked women he could put his arms around. Maybe he was saying he liked his women large, I don't know. Anyway, and I don't think he'd meant to imply any criticism of her, but Marjerie took it wrong. She gives me this look. Well, I'm not exactly large but I guess I'm larger than her, more, how shall I say it, oh effing hell, I've got more meat on the bones. She gives Phillip this look. Could've been the light in the room playing tricks with her eyes. It was something, at any rate, and Randall, here's the upshot, I could've sworn that if looks could kill, Phillip was a dead man. I got shivers. You know. That feeling I get, sometimes. How did I know Lamont was dead when he was? Fast Eddy, too?'

'I hate that feeling,' she added.

It was then she took my hand and held it a while, her eyes asking me whether or not she was crazy.

'Yes, you're crazy,' I said.

'Look,' I said, 'Marjerie's a prima donna, a Lamia, too, but—'

Eleanor shushed me.

'Actually, you know, I don't want to hear about it. Here, let me pay for this.'

The interview was over. We parted ways at the bank; I still was in need of some cash, and I planned to dine at the Blue Danube, Moonface scheduled to be on shift.

Lucan against Alexander

Most of the time, Moonface patrolled her realm with an eagle eye. If Miss Meow wanted her water topped up, she got water. If the Whistler thought his coffee not hot enough, he was served another, no matter that his thank you patronized her. If Mr and Mrs Civic Smile wished to compliment their meal for its Greekness, Moonface was sure to pass on the commendation to the galley, even if she could not quite refrain from rolling her eyes. Dubois, at table, sharpened the crease that he had already applied to his *Globe and Mail* copy. I opened a book I happened to be reading at random. Here was Lucan fomenting against Alexander the Great and adventurism. Here was Eggy the Great, braving the elements, making his grand entrance into the café, he thundering:

'A glass, damn it, and I don't care who knows it.'

His cane was lethally brandished upright. He was a hulking sparrow of a man in his winter coat, his bolshie cap suggesting that history was just around the corner, mind yourself. A dear girl went to get wine glasses.

'And I suppose,' Eggy continued, addressing me now, 'you've got your usual quota of doom and gloom to report.'

'Three bags full.'

In truth, I did have as much: the economy, Iran, Iraq, Israel-Palestine, *posse comitatus*, smarmy bookstores, and the fact that, fewer worthwhile books being sold, fewer worthwhile books were being read.

'Oh,' said Moonface, returning with glasses, 'here's Evie.'

Moonface waved at Evie Longoria just coming through the door. And she, the collar of her pea coat high, warily approached the take-out counter. She acknowledged the presence of male Traymoreans with a distant smile.

'I was thinking,' she said in Moonface's direction, 'that I might have a pizza for taking out.'

And now she asked Eggy: 'Do you want me to come around, tomorrow?'

'Well, if you're going to give the place the once over, I suppose, but it means I'll have to clear off.'

Eggy was chuffed.

'You can give me a once over,' Dubois said, attempting a joke.

Evie avoided my gaze. Her hair was drawn back tightly from her forehead and temples, her brow revealed as expansive. She had the air of a woman suffering a migraine.

'I don't have to come tomorrow,' she said, now unsure of herself.

'Effing hell, don't come, just sit with us.'

Dubois gestured at the wine. She was tempted.

'Uh oh,' I said to her in my thoughts. 'Have a care.'

She caved.

'That's better,' Eggy observed.

Dubois signalled Moonface to bring yet another glass. *S'il vous plait.* And Evie Longoria got quite drunk, and soon enough, tears were moistening her cheeks. Convivial people at a convivial table did not notice or were kind enough to pretend not to notice. I lost track of which man had done her the worst, though Evie liked men, loved them to pieces, and why did everything always have to get so hellish, anyway? Moonface had no opinion, she overhearing one of these outbursts as she replenished our glasses with more wine. She rolled her eyes up and to the side—characteristic gesture; she had troubles of her own. Well, was Ptolemy Soter one of them, or so I wanted to know, misfiring on a point of levity? I could not deny I was interested in Evie, though something about her caused me to hang back. Were I to respond to her depictions of her relations with men, I would fall through space, and fall forever. Either I was a coward or I was eminently sensible not to respond. She was a movie buff.

'Oh,' she said, '*The Philadelphia Story.* Love that movie.'

'How can you not love Jimmy Stewart?' I said, relaxing my grip on my tongue.

'I know. He's so sweet.'

She was smiling, the tears on her cheeks very nearly naked things. Dubois and Eggy went silent, eavesdropping.

'I know,' Evie repeated.

I wondered if I could believe her. But did it matter or ought it to matter, she a woman who, perhaps, had not failed to love? It was just that she had had bad luck. And once again I noted she was tall, but not that tall, large-boned, her teeth small, even, sharp. She was a devotee of the arts and cowboys—her singular charm. I was beginning to believe she was a great deal more intelligent than she was willing to let on. I was also beginning to believe she was not especially able to defend herself against the machinations of certain people, be they husbands, lovers, or just anyone. So then, why? Despite the meal I had been eating—some spinach concoction, the wine was getting to me. I would, with a verbal backhand, sweep away all the nonsense that lurked in the woman's complaints, and it would be a violent act, and I would regret the act, even if I could not but believe she was inviting it.

'Ladies and gentleman,' I said, rising from my chair.

'What's with you?' Eggy thundered.

'Effing hell, man, sometimes I think you're afraid of a little fun.'

'I've got some work to do,' I lied.

Dubois, knowing it for a lie, guffawed.

'Since when?' he said.

A giggling Moonface was at my door.

'Mithradates,' she said, by way of a salutation, invoking the name of an old enemy of Rome.

She was accompanied, Evie Longoria embarrassed and somewhat pale. The other woman I recognized from the neighbourhood, she quite the looker. They commandeered my couch, these three wise ladies come a great distance.

'To what,' I burbled, 'do I owe the pleasure?'

I switched off the TV which was broadcasting images for BBC of calamity in Mumbai.

'Well,' said Moonface, 'Gregory closed up. Slow night. But Bob and Eggy are still down there, being admitted into the brotherhood. Greeks and Albanians. Eggy's horrified. Gloria here, this is Gloria... Gloria, meet Randall... he's cool... Gloria came in just after you left, but Gregory wasn't going to serve any more food. So here we are.'

'I've got nothing to feed you with.'

'Do you have a phone?' Gloria put it to me.

A measured tone. Plush chestnut-coloured hair. Fatal. The heavily made-up eyes.

'It's okay,' Moonface said. 'We can order out from my place. Anyway, we just popped by to say hello. Now we've said hello.'

'Just a minute,' I said, 'what's the story here?'

'The blues bar,' Moonface explained.

Well, that explained something, at any rate. If Clare Howard, wife to my oldest friend dead in his grave, had borne some resemblance to Sally McCabe the lovely beauty queen of a year in my youth, Gloria was an even more striking resemblance. And yet, I could see at a glance that she was stuck on herself, which Sally had never been though she would have had her excuses. A cold amiability. Or perhaps she was just awkward in the company of a stranger.

'Gloria Jarnette,' she said, holding out her hand for me to shake. Awkward? Her voice was assertive and usually got what it wanted.

I shook the hand. It was neither the hand of the idle rich nor the hand of a peasant.

'She sculpts,' Moonface boasted, 'and she's awfully good.'

'Well then,' I said.

The sculptor gave me a look; apparently, I was free to challenge this news at any time. Evie, meanwhile, looked to be ill, and what could I do to alleviate her discomfort? She had obviously had too much to drink.

'Tea,' she managed to say, with the ghost of a smile.

But I did not have any tea in my stores.

'I have some,' Moonface announced, 'it's herbal. Is that alright?'

And it was alright. Evie indisposed, Moonface gone to her apartment for the tea, I was left to make conversation with the Jarnette woman.

'So,' I said, 'I take it you like blues.'

'I just go to pick up men,' she said, without a trace of irony.

Boffo the Clown in me was beginning to get restive.

'And you?' she asked.

'It seems I'm retired from the fray—'

Moonface, the dear girl, was back with the tea.

'I would've put the water on,' I explained, 'but I was distracted.'

'I'll bet,' Moonface responded, rolling her eyes.

And now, Evie really was ill.

'Going to be sick,' she proclaimed.

Perhaps it was the whiskey that brought Jarnette to my bed. It was certainly wine that did in Evie; she would pass the night in Moonface's digs, the world spinning hideously for her. At a certain evil hour, one heard Dubois and Eggy on the Traymore stairs, Eggy singing: 'Bongo, bongo, bongo, don't want to leave the Congo—'

and Dubois saying: 'That's not nice,' and Eggy saying: 'Yes but, there's a divinity that shapes our ends.'

'Just get those pins moving.'

'The rain in Spain. Hoo hoo.'

I, too, had too much to drink; even so, I asked Jarnette if she had ever experienced a premonition.

'Are you serious?'

'I am.'

She was, just then, beginning to remove her clothes in the dark bedroom. She was shaking out her hair; she seemed very business-like.

'I'm thinking,' she said.

She could not, in fact, recollect having had such an experience. But wait, yes, there was this: she knew a doctor, had been his mistress, actually, and once, at a party he remarked to her of some stranger in the room that he knew would be dead in three days. Well. Bang on. Internalized clues on the doctor's part probably explained the accuracy of the forecast. I supposed it was so. I was warming toward her. It seemed she might be the equal of anything life might throw at her.

'You're an odd character,' she said, and for the briefest of moments, she looked for a reason to like me and found none.

Even so, she alighted on my bed. And a vision of allure rose on her knees, Jarnette attending to herself, her head thrown back. I attempted to kiss her, but she pushed me down, the look she gave me pleased, mischievous, spiteful, utterly innocent. No, it was she who was decidedly the odd character. And in the morning, I watched her dress with the air of man who was not likely to behold such a vision ever again; watched her pull on wool socks and lace up her hiking boots, her fingers sure and expert even if, truth to tell, they were only dealing with footwear and not sculpting deathless items of clay.

'Well,' she said, leaning back now on the couch, looking around at a room to which she was not likely to return.

'Indeed,' I said.

There was nothing to say.

'Goodbye,' she said, in any case, draping a scarf around her neck, her eyes some tawny colour.

I nodded. She made for the door. And I figured that if she stopped to look back at me, it would mean… I had no idea what it might mean. She did look around and immediately regretted doing so.

'Well,' she said once more, the drama of her exit spoiled.

We humans were but shabby creatures. She was angry now; I wished her gone. Later, from Moonface, I learned that Evie, despite her condition, had simply walked home, thinking the air would do her good, she very much distraught and tearful and above all, embarrassed.

'Oh dear,' I commented, Moonface drinking of the tea she had brought over the night before.

'And you?' asked Moonface, her voice a slightly musical moan, a rising question.

'And me,' I answered, 'well, I'm not sure what happened, if anything. I think I was blindsided.'

It was clear that Moonface got my drift.

'Was it pleasant?'

'Let's say it wasn't unpleasant.'

'Cool.'

'Are you jealous?'

'Why should I be jealous?'

'Don't know. Just wondering.'

The dear girl never seemed to think the worst of anyone.

'And Evie?' I asked.

'I don't think she'll remember much about last night.'

'I hope she doesn't. What was up with her?'

'Can't say. We're friends, but I don't know her that well.'

Moonface's tone was matter of fact, and she was beginning to lose interest in our conversation.

'And you,' I said, 'have you ever experienced a moment of premonition?'

'No,' she said, her countenance brightening to the question, 'but I'm having one now.'

'Having what now?'

'That Eggy is going to knock on your door.'

Well, sure enough… And it was Eggy. It was some homunculus in a state: *why, effing hell, why hadn't he been invited to this little shindig?*

And before he could settle down, before he could feast his good morning eyes on Moonface his complementary function, I said to her that I worried Evie was suffering.

'Oh Randall,' said Moonface, 'avuncular.'

'Evie? What's this about Evie?' Zeus-like Eggy demanded to know.

§

Book V—A Ward of the Traymore

Caprice and Beguine III

—It is the anniversary of a fatal bullet, how one such projectile rocked JFK's head back; and Jackie, in her famous suit, crawled across the limousine for the rapidly disappearing promise. Judge as you will the thousand days of roses and fizz and elegant chatelaines. Yes, and once more, expectations rise, like a wave that would grasp at beams of light as it rolls across the stench of a sea. Or, like I saw it, last night, leafless maples parade so starkly, so therely in the winter dusk, the sky blue-black, but glossy as a football helmet. Once again, Cassandra, wife to Elias who would be a philosopher-prince and a restaurateur, has admitted me early. I assail my notebook, pound to the thickness of onion skin the unwanted and unlooked for and long twitted grief for a dead president. Drum rolls. Echoing hooves. Janus-faced tears. No warlord, no monarch, no Caesar, no head of state was ever put to rest with such agonized solemnity. 'It's Sunday. Sunday all day,' Cassandra points out. It is our little joke, the jest of which helps her acclimatize to a phantasmagoria.

Caprice and Beguine IV

—I stand on the Blue Danube terrasse, having a puff. Morning commute. Sparrows shiver in a hedge, plaintively twittering in below zero sunshine. That Eggy has been spewing verse-oddments of Baudelaire. (For example: *Voici le soir charmant...*) That Dubois revealed to me he was once president of the Chamber of Commerce in the good city of Sherbrooke, some 150 km east of Montreal the fair. That Eleanor R has loved and lost. Or rather she has lusted and been burned, her wings carbonized. That Moonface contemplates life beyond Ecuador. One assumes then that she expects to have a future. That Mrs Petrova perhaps slips into madness, but that it is barely noticeable, hardly worth mentioning, the operations of her shop and the Traymore in no jeopardy. It is the look she wears in the morning as she, with verve, arranges the shop window with the gewgaws she sells; that she, at 80 plus years of age, still gets a kick out of life. But that Eggy's tree, the scrawny piece of work by the liquor outlet—it looks pretty pathetic. Evie Longoria? Is she not panicked? I believe she has made herself a to-do list, and has yet to check-off—just below the pick-up-the-dry-cleaning and get onions—the getting of a man. If only she would not ascribe all human behaviour to bipolar disorders; this sort of relentlessness on her part grates on my nerves. Some people genuinely dislike their family members. Watchful starlings high in unleafed, sun bleached maple twigs… That Augustus Caesar, the more deeply he was in hock to his private deities, or what we call vulgar superstitions, the more he troubled himself to run the empire on a rational basis. History is the gaudy display of ironies.

—*Crépuscule*: from *crepusculum*: from *creperus*, meaning doubtful. To wit: *crepusculum* the doubtful hour. Eggy has done this to me, planting in my mentations the French word for twilight. Must pinch Eggy's intravenous feed to his most highly regarded claret.

—Was it W.C. Fields who observed he did not drink anymore, just that he did not drink any less, either? I can just barely recall the sissboom, pop, crackle, thud, squeal and squeak, splat and pffft, and kerfuffle of Spike Milligan and his musical cohorts, but no estimable quotes. *All I ask is the chance to prove that money can't make me happy.* I suppose a pennywhistle could be perceived as a Dadaist ploy, but clearly, enhanced interrogation techniques are torture. No civilization is impervious to its own stupidities, but you know, those Yanks, they always were and always are a cut above, the dears. Not only that, they have been torturing the wrong people, people unlikely to appreciate win at any cost managerial principles, and so are unlikely to forgive their tormentors. Perhaps Evie Longoria wonders why I have it in for screeching electric guitars, but the interrogators have made no mistake about it: they understand that such guitars jelly brains, blasting the paradisal groove 24/7 into torture cells. I will run away with Cassandra; we will begin anew on a desert island where, swacked on coconut juice, I will noodle on the clavichord. She can handle the lyrics, prancing about like Dorothy Lamour in a grass skirt. We will inaugurate a new Bronze Age. Current President is beyond describing, yes? Eight years of him, and still, words not only fail, they curl up in fetal positions and die. He has all the arrogance of an A-Team member for the shabby aspirants to the D-Team. Well yes, his distrust of the ologies, his anti-academic prejudice I share, so I confess. Why encourage poltroons? Because he knows—it is the silver spoon with which he was born—that, at bottom, most people seek power and leverage and disguise the unattractive appetites as noble intent. Those who turn power down are not quite right in the head. It is possible that, at the core of this man, there is evil, as we are all of us capable of exercising evil; but it is so much more likely that, in this man, there is no core and so, there are no forces vying for his conscience, if, in fact, he is in possession of the item. The man follows a script, but who has written it? If Quixote wore a curd-pot for a helmet, the Presidential bucket comes complete with night-vision goggles. If all I had wanted in life was good living –babes and booze and a beachside shack—I might have been tempted by crime. As it was, I got noble and silly, living off blood money, my father entirely legal and legit, and a moral obscenity, to boot: those chemicals he mixed in the name of science. 'The workers,' Evie Longoria has said, with unsuspected spleen, 'why have sympathy for the workers? They were hand in glove with the bankers, wanting what they couldn't afford. They're just going to bail out capitalism, anyway, and run the loop again. I say, let it crash. Revolution. Hoo boy.' Eggy thought her a woman who cannot handle drink. Dubois got his mental cue cards ready, just in case he must come up with a devil's apology. Alberta cowgirl, indeed. Well, I think he was seeing in the woman possibilities of a creature comfort sort. I, being somewhat worldly, and not unfamiliar with the nuts and bolts of emotional transactions, knew those possibilities could not come at par. But why tell him and spoil his fun? This world that is our daily omnibus has gotten so empty, insipid and lethal I am almost prepared to grant a ponce on the order of Rousseau his point: oh for noble savages and loping dogs.

—Green-sweatered Sally McCabe. Her pom-pom antics. They were meant to light fires in the fans in the bleachers, in absurd athletes torn between the solitary satisfactions of shooting rabbits in the desert and the demands of a corporate body which was a football team coached by a pervert. McCabe's crew of girls was more a Greek chorus than a glee club of short skirts, as we never won; as we never knew a change of lead except for that one time when fluke, not hope, trumped reality. Her nose wrinkled with mirth, McCabe's did and so, she registered I was that fluke; how I caught the football and ran with the thing; how I tripped into the end zone as if looking to undo ironclad laws. Tumbleweeds drifted across Polson Field, and I was mostly cold. 'I guess,' Sally McCabe must have said to herself in some unguarded moment of her mind (perhaps in the girls' room, or in the parking lot smoking a cigarette, or in the back seat of Coop's car, suffering kisses) 'that Calhoun boy has introduced a new variable into the equation. Will wonders never cease.' And now when I watch a game of football, it in no way resembles the game I knew; the athletes warriors, not absurdists just passing time, drunk and not minding getting knocked about; winning or losing beside the point. Meanwhile, like children in a school cafeteria, Dubois and Evie Longoria are playing bumpsies, knocking shoulders here in the Blue Danube. Some desultory talk of Ottawa and a prorogued parliament. Just a few words, nothing more. 'Well, you know,' says Eggy, hoo hooing at Moonface, 'you are always in my mind.' 'Always,' agrees the long-bellied goddess topping up our glasses. 'My belly button was showing,' she lets us know. 'Oh let's see it,' says Eggy. And Moonface beams. Has that been erotic burbling in her voice? 'And for you an extra splash,' she says to me, 'because you're you and there is no other.' My, whence this zest? She rolls her eyes up and to the side. One wonders if Evie Longoria is not thinking to herself: 'So, this is the way we're going to play it, tonight, fast and loose.' She taps a newspaper folded to the crossword section and says, 'Okay, somebody, let's have it—a word for penultimate.' 'Yes but,' Eggy thunders, 'there is no one word.' 'How can you be so sure?' Evie wants to know. 'I don't know, I just know.' 'Randall?' I am asked. 'Beats me.' 'Well, you're no fun,' I am told. Dubois shrugs. 'Last but one,' Moonface advises, passing by. The Blue Danube is expecting a large dinner party that has not yet arrived. *It just might fit, if I'm allowed. I mean, who's keeping score?* Evie taps the eraser end of a pencil against her small, even and sharp teeth. I am not so sure now that she is mad, but she is giving off, as it were, signals, she not the sort of woman who, like Eleanor, would just barge ahead and storm the castle, forget the intricacies of a plan. I had written Dubois a longish note, one I slipped under his door. It explained why there was no book, why I had yet to write it; *because I will not write programmatically.* Dubois's return of note was a single word. He wrote *guffaw*. He is on a roll of sorts, Eleanor in the country for a cousin's funeral, his blue eyes glittering with intelligence and fun.

—Cold. Verily, an inhospitable climate. Had Paul been born a Canuck, there would have been no church, not in winter, at least. Epistles of Paul the Apostle to the Winnipeggers? That pagan Prentiss is heard in the hall, saying, 'He'll get his. I'll sit on his face, yet.' Of late, Moonface has been ravishing. Whom does she ravish? She still looks to vote with her feet: Champagne Sheridan and Ecuador. Perhaps he has the sense to realize he is weak; he will have to hobnob with the right crowd to get anywhere, only which one? Eleanor once exercised that option, hanging about a nightclub that copycatted Studio 54, she a fetching wench but perhaps too much the country girl. Drugs drove her from the scene as she could not handle them. Amaretto will do nicely, thank you muchly. *Couldn't act my way out of a paper bag, anyway. Don't know what I was thinking. No, really, I'm fine. I just don't fit in anywhere. Sexpot den mothers won't do, these days. Yada yada. You'd better go. I think I'm gonna cry.* And yet, whether or not the good woman cares to notice, sexpot den mothers are everywhere, writing books, spouting comedy, curling Ovid's toes. For a return to sanity has been much anticipated. Complete sentences shall minister unto foreign policy. The Yanks will prevail in Afghanistan with better grammar. Cicero will get his head handed him.

—The chill terrorist, young Octavianus, Augustus Caesar to be. One-third of a triumvirate, Mark Antony and Lepidus the other partners. The *Lex Titia* formalized the arrangement, giving the men legal sanction, dissolving the republic. Perhaps the proscriptions were not as bloody as rumoured, but they had the desired effect: no in-house opposition. Now Octavianus had only various generals to defeat, and in the end, Mark Antony. Who was an amiable sort. And it takes two to tango. And he could hold his own in a game of poker, but everyone underestimated young Octavianus. Everyone always does. Now a looker, heavily sweatered (and what the cold has done to her cheeks and flashing eyes ought not to be legal) waves Antonio over to her Blue Danube table. 'Now there's an eyeful,' says Zeus-like Eggy, his finger raised, keen-eyed still at 902 years of age. But his heart belongs to Moonface. 'I'm going to opera her,' he informs me. 'Well, don't tell Sheridan,' I advise. 'Oh no. Hoo hoo.' Yes, and the connotations of a noun put to the uses of a verb, one taking a direct object, are rich in possibilities. 'Tell that woman

I'll buy her a drink,' Eggy thunders. Antonio, passing by, shushes him with a wink and mock-simpering lips. 'Oh, eff off.' The looker perhaps wonders what she has done to deserve this. Eggy, in any case, is on to other business. 'We'll be gathering here, tonight, to watch the election results.' What, we have priorities? 'I'll Handel her,' Eggy puns, grinning like a cherub. I suppose he means he will oratorio Moonface, part of the build-up to Christmas.

—So, like the crew we are, we wind up in Eleanor's kitchen. Eleanor's kitchen is a not unfamiliar haunt; but everything is at sixes and nines, Eleanor not her usual expansive self though she is in her pompadours, Dubois subdued. Marjerie Prentiss shows. She has the air of a woman scouting new recruits in an exhausted field. And it is not long before she and Dubois are arguing federal politics; for each it is a lame attempt to amuse. And for a woman as much given to sex as she is, everything is political, and what is politics are no more welfare and coddling of immigrants. I cannot state it with any more specificity than that. She is, in fact, Ayn Rand incarnate, so it strikes me just now. She is the cobra, Dubois the mongoose who has some sentimental regard for the social contract, whatever that is, on a snowy night in this our faded Jezebel of a town. Dull voice booms that liberals never get it. She coquettes Dubois with her breasts and the force of her hips, the sulky way she smokes her cigarette, dead, watery eyes fielding all her interlocutor's talking points as so much routine. His blue eyes glitter with intelligence; he is Huck Finn looking for his getaway raft. Eleanor is irked because Eleanor is old-school: territorial. Eggy, Zeus-like Eggy, is out of his depth because mired in the mediocrities of mortals. He will commit opera with Moonface. 'No kidding,' snaps Eleanor who, in any case, fails to see that Moonface is operable, men so easily besotted with what are but trifles. 'Bloody hell, what bee got in your bonnet?' asks Eggy, with reason. He is ignored. Prentiss trots out Reagan, Dubois Iran. I trot out Cicero, but no one pays me any mind, as well they should as my sense of the absurd fails to cast any light on the absurdity of the situation; just that Boffo the clown in me, well, he wonders if I might not Benito that woman, as in Mussolini, but that, good golly, such a crude response, and with such unreliable hormones, too.

§

Book VI—Buffoonery and Cowardice

Druids, Templars and the Medici

In the next district over were the ritzier girls, money the bloom on their pretty and sheltered countenances. I went for a passport photo, the shop a portrait gallery of fetching brides of a sub-continent. The proprietor was as hyper as he was dapper, his two minute service more like ten, his mind elsewhere. I, too, thought it a bit strange that in me a somnolent urge might be close to waking, and I would jump my Traymorean orbit for Rome or, why not Istanbul, or Yerevan on the river Razdan? Downtown, at a cut-rate discount, I bought books from yet another dealer bowing out of the fray, a book each on Druids, Templars and the Medici. Desultory talk of Ottawa politics. And then, back in the neighbourhood, I stopped by the Blue Danube, Cassandra run off her feet, Dubois on site. Miss Meow miaowed. She, according to Dubois, had been reviewing her day, her table companion a suppliant to a host of woes, the complaining incessant.

'And when her reel ran out,' observed Dubois, 'there was the replay button.'

He was pleased with his quip. Which was when Eggy showed, the homunculus looking like a movie star.

'Well,' he said, 'I was at the Claremont, drinking Pernod. Always.'

It explained everything. It explained credit-default and barometric pressure. It explained why love was love and gold was gold. Why Helen, Spartan minx, did not mind so much that men fought over her favours, but did they have to fight so clumsily and messily, with an eye always on sacking the city? Wasteful. And it explained why, in his heart of hearts, a man might live for love, and it was the only grandeur life might afford a tough old carcass of quite ordinary lineage. It explained why anything was anything. And what is more, Eggy explained he would finagle Moonface into some outing or another, the opera, maybe, and he might smack her bottom, figuratively speaking, of course.

'Rots of ruck,' Dubois guffawed.

And where was Eggy's wine, no glass set before him?

'Cassandra,' Eggy called out, hopefully.

But Cassandra was serving up pizzas and pitas and moussakas.

Dubois told a flowerpot man that all good things would come in due course.

'To conviviality,' I said, clinking glasses.

'Hear, hear,' said Dubois, in his best imitation of a light moment in parliament.

Perhaps we spoke too soon. One could not say a shadow darkened our table: too cheesily dramatic, too much the stalest of stale clichés. But then, it did seem that the temperature suddenly dropped.

'Hullo,' a dull voice boomed.

Three figures now towered over us: Marjerie Prentiss and those who consorted with her—Ralph and Phillip. Dead, watery eyes assessed Traymorean males for entertainment value.

'Hello,' answered Eggy, and I thought he answered without properly taking stock of a situation now arising.

And, well, he was irked by the fact that some tension in the air was suddenly constraining him and he did not know why; he had no quarrel with these people.

'*Bon jour*,' said Dubois, his tone neutral.

I said nothing. Ralph studied our faces, yes, with the air of a man for whom the notion of brotherhood was a birthright. Phillip shambled even as he simply stood there, both arrogant and insecure and not a little bored. They might have, perhaps, shaken our hands but that the presence of Marjerie somehow rendered the proposition ludicrous. Was the sex they had fun? A broad, tree-lined avenue to life's great mysteries?

'Eleanor,' said Marjerie, 'is on the way.'

'Oh,' said Eggy, relieved to hear it, 'why, it's been a while since she's graced us.'

Marjerie gave him a look, and it was, in fact, her most fetching look, one emanating from narrowed, bemused eyes; just that, who was Eleanor to dispense grace, she only a foot soldier in a game of takes-no-prisoners in which Marjerie was Napoleonic? Perhaps I was mistaken, but there it was, and whatever it was it had to do with Marjerie having, at last, stolen a march on us. The equivalent of a circus harlot become head of state just made it official: a breach had been effected in Traymorean society, and through it Eleanor fell to Marjerie like an apple from a high branch of a tree. If it were striking Dubois in this way, he was keeping mum, his attention drifting now to the TV, hockey game about to start.

'Well, *bon appetit*,' he said, as matter-of-factly as that.

His tone suggested he could do nothing about nothing; such company as Eleanor chose to dine with was her business. She knew where she could find him; indeed, he was only a hop and a skip away from a sane arrangement among equals. Phillip went and took a table, one now up for grabs. Miss Meow miaowed, sensing turbulence. Cassandra on her way to the galley gave Marjerie a brief looking-over. Marjerie continued to hold her position, she a woman who had had her triumph, and yet was still short-changed. What was it about her that frightened us so, if fright it was and not a spell robbing us of speech? It was Eleanor who relieved us of a deepening quandary, she arriving like a fresh wind; her gilded curls resplendent; her cheeks bright; her tarty boots imparting swagger and high spirits with each clicking of heels on Blue Danube tiles.

'Hey boys,' she said.

I supposed Dubois gave her what he hoped was an amused glance. Eggy, however Zeus-like he was, could not be sure he knew what was afoot.

'Hello, Eleanor,' he said, giving the good woman the benefit of his doubt.

I shrugged.

If Eleanor would tell me in confidence she found certain aspects of her friendship with Marjerie and her swains troubling, why then was she, in the next moment, as it were, the belle of their party-times? It was, of course, her rightful place; she was born to conduct her life as the belle of some party. Had Traymoreans failed her in this? How had Marjerie Prentiss copped her soul? I went out on the terrasse for a puff. I soon had company.

'I can't believe I'm saying this, but I think I've got the hots for Phillip,' Eleanor told me, lighting up a tailor-made.

It was cold, she shifting her weight from foot to foot, summoning warmth.

'He's really nice, really a gentleman deep down,' she said, appealing to me for a blessing of a kind. 'He's had a hard life. Sure, he has a temper and drinks too much and womanizes, and well, you know, he certainly has the hots for Marjerie, and I tell him he can't keep going on like that. Ralph's his friend, a loyal pal, and it would be a shame if they came to blows over that woman. I mean, she can really be quite charming and attentive and all the rest of it, but I don't know that she deserves the attention she gets. Oh hell, I don't even know if I know what I'm saying. Say something, Randall. You always do.'

But no, the truth was I did not always say something, and just now, I did not know what to say. So I said: 'It seems to me they've got their hooks in you.'

Perhaps I had just seen panic in her countenance, but I could have been mistaken; I frequently was.

'Yes, well,' Eleanor replied, out on a limb of her own devising.

'The almighty hooks,' said Eleanor.

Marjerie was checking us out from within the café. As was Dubois with the odd sidelong glance. Eggy was a tiny sparrow of a man tiny in his chair, he, in any case, impervious to any treachery that mortals lesser than he might foment.

'Look,' I said, 'if you want to boff Phillip, then boff him. Just don't pretend it's anything other than lust. And anyway, it's too much mixed up with whatever it is Marjerie's got going in her brain. Your having the hots, so to speak, is going to bite you on your arse.'

'What's it got to do with Marjerie?'

'You know it's got everything to do with her. She doesn't care who's doing what to whom so long as she gets to pull the strings. I have to confess I've never seen anything like it. To describe her as manipulative seems too tame. It's not about what she wants from you or me or anyone else; she just wants to run the show, any show, even a flea circus.'

'I just worry I might lose Bob,' she said, her voice uncharacteristically smallish.

'I wonder if you haven't, already.'

I had intended, just then, to be angry with her; I was, in fact, quite angry, but the words came out of my mouth with an element of whimsy to their import.

'I'm cold,' I said, stating a categorical fact.

She had already flicked the remnant of her cigarette into the street. We were each in that state of drunkenness when thought was still lucid, the blood running royal. I had a lot of affection for the good woman; I was not, even then, unmoved by her obvious charms. Even so.

'For God's sake, Eleanor, sometimes I think you're a few bricks short of a load.'

And my head spun with druids and Caesars; it was the wine. With terrorists. With moguls of finance devoted to ritual sex practices. It was the wine. And my head spun with Eleanors and Moonfaces and Gloria Jarnettes somber in their birthday suits, they lamenting the last of their glory days, the poetry of their lusts and the cheek of their satirical outlooks on the world. For yes, when some guru said to them there was no mind-body separation, and that Wall Street was as much a part of God's mind as a bump on a log in the forest, they told him to drop dead. It was the wine. And my head spun with Evie Longoria who was a hundred times lonelier than Too Tall Poet, for instance; who was himself, ten times lonelier than the proselytizing hag who was lonely enough. It was the wine. American crimes spawned by American reach—the wine. That is, it was impossible to list them all, just that, in their entirety they were a kind of pulsation, a throb. When I left the Blue Danube, they were deep in commaderie—Marjerie Prentiss and her faction, Eggy and Dubois. Perhaps the imminent removal of my person permitted it, as if my person had been a spoiler to their fun. Moonface in the Traymore hall appeared to be troubled, or was it only theatre? The look in her eye—it was the look she had when, not so long ago, I came across her and some rat-like boy having at it. I shrugged; she retreated to her digs. And, as I fumbled with my key, up came a slippered Mrs Petrova on the Traymore stairs with a pot of soup in her hands. For whom? Her mythical son no one had seen, though Eggy, thundering, always claimed he had had the privilege? Mrs Petrova had the look of a girl caught out in an act of minor naughtiness, her hair in curlers, scarf wound around her head, two bright patches of rouge each for her cheeks. I did not wish to know to what extent she was secretly demented; I bade her a good night, and through my door, I raised my couch on which I collapsed. Lucan had ascribed to druids in their groves weird doings. In the middle of the night, my heart racing, I woke from an unfriendly dream.

Subsidence

The Blue Danube was a Benedictine atmosphere of Christmas lights and labour; Cassandra brought me a coffee and her dimples, those dimples cheer-inducing. I wondered if Dubois had something to live for now that Ottawa was in an uproar, the game that was afoot as worthy of the romance of skullduggery as any in Washington. Eggy? Politics to him was but an excuse to see that certain bastards should hang, as he always put it; otherwise, Moonface was his complementary function. Eleanor had the hots for Phillip Dundarave, or so she believed, she sensing, perhaps, that he was her life's last great fling. There was no reason to gainsay her in this, just that Phillip Dundarave was not a loving man, a hoser pure and simple. Bits of a dream turned up in my mentations now like so many bottom creatures forced to the surface of a lake. Marjerie Prentiss, it seemed, had entered my digs. She herself was like a woman just roused from a dream, one that had been pleasant enough, her eyes sleepy, mouth a lazy grin. She made of her right hand a piece, thumb cocked. *What's your hurry? Why resist? You know I'll shoot.* She was enjoying herself as she advanced, I back-pedalling. I attempted to study her conscious mind and drew a blank. I would divine her secret urges and got that lazy grin and her dead, watery eyes, instead. I turned us around somehow so that I was now backing out my door. Her contempt for me was rather superfluous, almost a distraction from her intention, which was to expose me to the world as a clown of no consequence. I was out the door, she still convinced I could not escape her. I was running down the Traymore stairs, buffoon and coward. Mirthless chuckles. And on the street, Evie Longoria was passing by, she gone mad, her arms folded across her chest. She was saying over and over that death was not defeat and defeat was not death; and, try as I might, I could not believe her. Though I snapped my fingers, jumped up and down, and in a hundred ways made a fool of myself, I could not rescue her from the spell that had consumed her. She was a more terrifying sight to behold than Marjerie Prentiss now shown up as an amateur, even with the gun. Moonface appeared from nowhere, clearly upset, but she had no more luck than I in dealing with Evie. I should have disarmed Prentiss; should have coaxed Evie into a kinder light; should have consoled Moonface. A very mediocre poet once told me, this the one thing he had been right about, that there were in life no should-haves. Cassandra was now making noises, something like concern in her large and luminous eyes.

'Soup now?' she asked.

The dream seemed to settle through my body like subsidence.

'Sure,' I said, 'thank you. You're spoiling me rotten, you know.'

She touched my arm, only too happy to plead she was innocent of the charge.

Eleanor was frantic at the café window, looking in. She had not even bothered throwing on a jacket. Red button up sweater. Gypsy skirt. As eager as she apparently was to see me, once inside, she approached the table with something of the air of a woman shielding herself from infectious disease. She waved off Cassandra and took a chair.

'Bob and I had a fight,' she said, too cheerfully.

'He said why don't we take that trip he was always promising me? I said I wasn't keen, anymore. Maybe next year, but not now. He wanted to know why I wasn't keen, anymore. Like, what gives?'

'Well,' I put it to the good woman, 'what gives?'

'Phillip.'

She fished a cigarette from the pack she had in the palm of her hand and placed it between her lips. They were exaggeratedly pursed. She was all braggadocio and lip gloss; she was just this side of tears.

'Virgil,' I said, giving way to the rising pedagogue in me, 'wrote that love's a curse and the one who's smitten is to be pitied.'

'Do you think I care what Virgil wrote who knows how many centuries ago?'

'Phillip,' I countered, 'will hose you for a night. It'll probably be glorious. In the morning he'll hit you up for a loan. In the afternoon he might bring his laundry. In the evening he might introduce you to some chick he just picked up in the street. Worse, he might reacquaint you with Marjerie Prentiss while he holds her hand and swears to her his eternal devotion. I mean, just how badly do you want to have your face rubbed in it?'

'I know.'

'You know?'

'I'm not a complete retard.'

Now she twirled the cigarette between her thumb and forefinger, dying to smoke the thing.

'So I take it you don't mind being hosed, being squeezed for money, being a laundress, being a cuckold, and being downright humiliated?'

'You can bet your booties I mind, but it's beside the point.'

'So what did you tell Bob, if I may ask?'

'You may. I told him pretty much what I told you.'

'Hell's bells, Eleanor.'

'Hell's bells me all you like, but I'm resolved.'

'Resolved?'

'To depart my senses. To be a silly goose. Phillip can do with me what he wants. I'll beg for more.'

'Knowing him, he'll be too swacked to be of much efficacy.'

'I'll take my chances.'

'Right. So it's already been arranged: a night of coition and a melding of souls.'

'No need to get snide. But yes. Tonight.'

'Good God.'

'God's got nothing to do with it. Bob said I needn't come cry on his shoulder.'

'Good old Bob.'

Eleanor gave me a look. Then, the cigarette back in her mouth, her hands flat on the table, she leaned back and drew a deep breath.

'I guess that's that,' she said, not exactly meeting my eyes.

She rose. Such a handsome figure of a woman she was as she rose, as she stepped behind me; as she bent and bestowed on my person a kiss. It was a kiss that would challenge me to stop her if I could; and, of course, it was understood I could not, being but a passive observer of folly, and being all too susceptible to her charms, besides. She exited. And it was Cassandra's turn to look seven parts curious and three parts troubled. Even so, she was the last woman on earth who could rightfully claim unfamiliarity with the woes such as love brought one. I assumed she had long since forgiven her husband his past indiscretions. Something flashed in her eyes to suggest she had not.

It had not even the dignity of a farce. Tragedy was too remote a consideration with which to describe certain events about to unfold; though tragedy, so to speak, just might have sneaked in the backdoors of various workaday lives. I was sitting in the Blue Danube, Eggy and Dubois my companions of an evening. Moonface humoured the Whistler. If something was troubling her, and something had been, she had left it at home, and she was bright of countenance and solicitous of our needs. She was now headed for us.

'Gentlemen,' she said, rolling her eyes, sexual and sexless, chameleon-like creature.

'My dear,' said Eggy, summoning mischief from his foggybottom depths.

'Is everything all right?'

Traymorean males were unaccountably at a loss for words. Eggy had been on about how Europeans had never eaten so well as when they first raised the Holy Land and encountered pomegranates.

'Tell Serge,' said Dubois, pleased with his dinner, 'that he's outdone himself, tonight.'

'Oh I will,' Moonface cooed.

My eyes filled with her slim hips and modest bosom. There was between us ancient history, one as recent as Toronto, one as ancient as Orpheus mooning over his lost Eurydice, the cock-up in that little matter his fault.

'About those crusades,' I said, 'especially the first wave—'

Dubois arched his eyebrows; Moonface scooted off.

'Especially the first wave,' I repeated, 'that, having survived the vicissitudes of transit, and they were arduous—climate, lack of food, among others; having repulsed the Saracen arrows and so forth and so on; having raised Jerusalem, at last; having breached the walls, they set about slaughtering like there was no tomorrow. It was their reward. They were as happy as pigs in the proverbial you know what. And thereafter, after we got serious about nation-states to which the Templars were, perhaps, the prelude, the first multi-national corporation, came the monotony of a history of class defending its privileges. What say you, you my intellectual betters?'

It seemed that Eggy was worried for my psyche. Dubois guffawed. Even so, a tiny sparrow of a man, homunculus, smiled his superior smile, that one that put to me a single unassailable observation: if I expected better from humankind I was barking up the wrong tree. Zeus-like Eggy. Whereas Dubois, in respect to the drama in Ottawa, was concerned that clowns had been set loose among the levers of power; and even if Current Prime Minister had to go, as the man was a spiteful spirit dressed up in velvet parliamentary accessories, and had overplayed his hand; the opposition was, perhaps, on the brink of overplaying theirs. In other words, second thoughts had occurred to Dubois in this matter as he dined on his hamburger steak. Hamburger steak was not on the Blue Danube menu, but Dubois was a favoured customer…

'Effing hell,' said Eggy, the other favoured patron, 'there hasn't been this much fun since Billy gave us the meaning of is.'

Eggy had just referred to President the 42nd and his penchant for exploratory sex and protean verbs.

'He certainly had been is-ning,' I pointed out.

'Is-ning,' said Dubois, not entirely impressed.

Is-ning, for Eggy, was a bridge too far. Even so, President Elect was raising hopes that the normal operations of intellect would soon return to the White House. And just then, all is-ning aside, and I was vaguely preoccupied with Moonface and her troubles and her charms; just then, as I looked out the window, I saw Eleanor charging by; and if she was not deeply troubled, her body language could have fooled me.

Whores, Pimps and Whatnot

So Eleanor had just passed by the café, clearly in trouble. I debated whether I should remain with my comrades, eat, drink and be merry, or go and give the good woman a good measure of succour. I could not imagine what had happened; on the other hand, I could imagine all too easily that Phillip Dundarave was at the root of it. The Whistler now unleashed his whistles and stompings.

'Waitress,' he called, his voice reedy, 'could I please have a cup of coffee with two ten per cent creams?'

One saw something like a sigh briefly shadow Moonface's countenance.

'So, do you think they'll drop the bomb?' Eggy whimpered at me.

Dubois had the air of a man for whom levity might just have engineered a new lease on life.

Eleanor, having come back around to the café, in search, no doubt, of succour, signalled at the window. It spawned confusion. And when she pointed at me, her grin the measure of her abasement, Dubois was not only startled, he was sad and disgusted.

'What's she want?' Eggy innocently wondered.

Embarrassed for us all, I said I would go as summoned.

'I'll get back to you,' I said to Dubois.

'Don't bother,' he answered.

I wondered if Moonface guessed what was up, her fingers briefly brushing Dubois's shoulder.

'Damn it all,' thundered Eggy, 'what's the mystery?'

Zeus-like Eggy did not like being the one in the dark. Moonface sighed and the Whistler whistled. The hairline cracks of Dubois's cheeks threatened to consume his once equable temper.

It had better be good, or so I was telling myself, as I went out the Blue Danube and down to the Traymore. It was probably going to be worse, I surmised; for as I climbed the stairs I could hear Phillip pleading: 'Come on, Ellie.'

The trouble was, the man's pleading was more on the order of parody; but in any case, to call Eleanor Ellie was almost a first. Not even Traymoreans resorted to this endearment, at least, not often.

'Go screw yourself,' I could hear Eleanor suggest from her kitchen, her tone awfully partisan.

Had I ever witnessed her truly angered? Even so, there they were: Phillip with a sniggering Gloria Jarnette in the hall. He was pawing her with his carpenter's hands. From Marjerie Prentiss's open apartment a dull voice boomed: 'Oh, just leave Ellie alone.'

Marjerie Prentiss was drunk. Phillip, clearly, did not think me much of a challenge. Gloria Jarnette, in mock-annoyance, pulled Phillip's hand off her breast.

'She's all yours,' Phillip grinned at me, genuflecting at Eleanor's door.

The thought crossed my mind I should pound him one and clear his face of its insipid leer. But why should I stoop to such silliness? Because, and the answer stupefied me, it would occasion retaliatory pain. Surprisingly, however, I had no attitude toward Jarnette one way or another; she was decidedly a free agent. I gave a Phillip a look as I entered Eleanor's digs; he was mock-alarmed. So yes, Eleanor had been laughing, crying, seething, and otherwise, giving vent. She was seated at her kitchen table, noticeably perfumed. She had poured herself an amaretto.

'Ellie?' I said, with a questioning tone.

'Don't start,' she snapped, 'I'm not Ellie to you.'

'So that's how it is,' I said, as gently as I was able.

'Effing right. That's how it is.'

And, as it turned out, and as it had been arranged, close to the appointed hour, she went out on the street. Walking down our noble boulevard in the opposite direction from the Blue Danube, feeling somewhat like a whore, she flagged a taxi. It took her down on St Jacques, motels and strip bars the prevalent venues. She rented a room, then called Phillip's cell phone, one he had borrowed from Ralph. She waited on her demon lover. And he showed, but with Gloria Jarnette.

'I couldn't even get angry,' Eleanor said, her voice husky, her shoulders shaking slightly.

'I mean,' she continued, 'I was so flabbergasted. What was I thinking? I didn't even wait for him to explain himself. I could've clawed that woman's face, she so effing pleased with herself. Thank God, I hadn't stripped. Can you imagine? I just grabbed my purse and ran out.'

'How did he come by having Gloria at his side?' I wanted to know, just a little curious.

'You know who she is?'

'Yes.'

'I'm so mortified.'

'I'll bet you are.'

'I mean, it's all just sex to him. And here's he been telling me how much he loves his daughter and wants to do right by her. That I would ever believe it.'

'Maybe he does love her, but even so—'

'Oh even so yourself. He's an effing loser.'

She smacked her forehead with the heel of her palm.

'*Caramba*!' she said, almost comically, 'idiot.'

'Stop it.'

'I mean, one night, just one effing night and—'

'And then what?'

'I wasn't asking for marriage—'

'Neither was he, from the looks of it.'

Eleanor gave me a look, her head cocked.

'I've cooked my goose with Bob.'

'He'll come around. He loves you.'

'Don't be telling me lies.'

'No, really. He does. Well, after his own fashion.'

'And what fashion might be that be?'

There was not going to be any telling the woman anything.

'I've used up my three strikes. I'm out.'

Marjerie Prentiss materialized, barefoot, sullen, stuporous.

'Well, what do you want?' asked Eleanor, and she was livid.

Our neighbour stood there, saying nothing, intent on studying our faces; just that her mental operations were, perhaps, compromised by drink. Perhaps Phillip came to fetch her, as now he was on site; and he placed his hands on Marjerie's shoulders. She shook them off.

'I think you should both go,' I found myself saying.

It seemed Phillip thought it a not bad idea.

'Come on, Marj, the party's elsewhere.'

One heard Gloria Jarnette's tinkling laugh; one assumed she was engaged with Ralph or with a tinpot dictator or Prince Charles.

A slow grin broke out on Marjerie's face; it was one of the more deadly grins I had seen in a while.

'Oh, you're a cunning woman,' a dull voice boomed.

I rose to my feet. The atmosphere was heating up.

Crépuscule

One might in old age consider that one had arrived at the end of the road, anticipating that one had finally cleared the mystery up, and here was what one had been all this time. And yet, here also was laughing Death, and the core of one's being was no more than sparkling sunlight on the sea, and there had never been any knowing in anything like a final sense. In other words, when Moonface put it to me, saying she did not know what to believe, I would simply provide stock replies. Art, literature, love—these endeavours would always do in a pinch.

Evening, and I was angling for virtue. Sobriety. Wisdom. Compassion. All for naught. I was reading words, and they did not register. How was one going to mount an understanding of things if the words would not register? *The news of the disasters that had befallen the Holy Land was brought to the Pope, Urban III, who was then in Verona…* One stared into the televised eyes of Current President, seeking his reasons. One might forgive an utter fool, but him? An homunculus named Eggy, 900 and some years of age, was still interested. If it was contemplation of Moonface's backside that kept his brain fluid enough so that he might pass his attentions to political memoirs and accounts of Genghis Khan, all the while he vitiated against talk shows, so much the better. *Crépuscule*, so he had told me, and I could not remember when, was his all-time favourite word in any language, the word French for twilight. Had he gotten it from a poem? And twilight in what sense? A Montreal summer, resplendent maples so many erotic burblings? The long shadow of the Austro-Hungarian empire? I lay on my couch, eyes growing heavy. *When Josias, the Archbishop of Tyre, arrived in Palermo from Tyre in the summer of 1187, sent by the barons of Outremer*... Why, was not Eggy born around that time? Sally McCabe thought it possible, just then manifesting her beauty and her gentle irreverence.

'You've still got it good,' she said, this pom-pom girl and object of desire. VIP's daughter. Teen-aged queen. Immortal.

'Here you are,' she continued, 'with your Eggy, with your Moonface, both of them so, well, what, so eternally smitten with life, you old cynic. And now Jarnette, too. When it rains it pours.'

Sally McCabe wrinkled her delicious nose.

'Yes, what of it?' I answered.

'They're what the show's all about.'

'Really? Would you, say, pass the time with Eggy?'

'With that old bean?'

'That dry old bean.'

'Well, I might, if he amused me enough. I've had stranger tumbles.'

'I suppose you have.'

'Of course. Don't you recall our tumble?'

'Sort of.'

'Sort of? Is that all?'

'The memory only torments me.'

'You poor dear.'

'No, really.'

'Alright then. Be a stick in the mud.'

'I don't mean to be a stick in the mud, just that—'

'Look, I know you better than you know yourself. We should be cutting a grand figure by now, you and I, after all we've been through.'

'What are you suggesting?'

'I'm young still. Well, I'm eternal, open to adventure. A little whiskey, moonlight, commodious car, desert wind—none of that ever hurt.'

'Yes but, Mr Jakes blew his brains out back then.'

'It's what you get from teaching history to louts.'

'Is that all you have to say for that poor man?'

That Sally McCabe chose to yawn at that moment was all she had to say for my life's first suicide.

'You're such an egghead. But I'll give you this—it's what I always liked about you. With a little training, shaping… Well, you kind of got away from me. It was like you got religion or something only it was just that you went to Canada.'

'Yes, there was that.'

'Too late now.'

'Too late.'

'But we can still have these chats off and on.'

'We can.'

'Good. I was worried, you know.'

'Worried. Why?'

'That you were going to think you'd out-grown me.'

'Oh no. Nothing of the kind.'

'Well then, bye.'

Voices not in my head but in the hall brought me out of my swoon. Phillip Dundarave wheedled. Marjerie Prentiss's dull voice boomed. She was hurt and confused. Trampings down the stairs. Then Eggy thundered and Evie Longoria said that, alright, she would come around again in a day or two to take Eggy to a hardware store so as to get the spent fluorescent replaced; but Eggy supposed he could live without it, only that Evie reminded him he would complain of it at their next meeting. She sounded tired. More tramping down the stairs. Awake now, and I reached for a magazine Dubois had left on the table beside me. CEO of the year had weathered a storm, one precipitated by the fact his food plant put polluted meat into stores and people died, eating it. Ah, one must needs have redemption, a wringing of hands.

It was now a point of contention between Eggy and Dubois, that word *crépuscule*. Eggy was saying, his finger raised, and we were in the Blue Danube, carrying on: 'Effing hell, *crépuscule*. You know, *du soir*.'

But none of us knew, though I had a suspicion.

'You're kidding,' said Dubois.

'Eff you,' Eggy thundered, and he continued, Dubois cringing as he did so: '*Voici le soir charmant, ami du criminel; il vient comme un complice, à pas de loup; le ciel—*'

'Stop,' said Dubois, in obvious pain, Eggy's French a tribulation to his ears.

'What a guy,' he added, proud, perhaps, of his cultured friend.

'I don't know,' said Eggy, 'a lover told it me. That's how I got it.'

'Lover? What lover?' Dubois guffawed, looking to get a rise.

'Alright,' said Eggy, 'have it your way, but she said it to me, and that's all I can remember.'

'Likely story,' said Dubois.

'Why, it is the story, and that's that. Bloody effing hell.'

And man is tired of writing and woman of making love. Baudelaire: *crépuscule du matin.*

And they were all that had stayed in my mind of the verse, other than that of men in barracks, in their bunks, restive with unhealthy dreams. We were gathered, Eggy, Dubois and I, for the occasion of Current Prime Minister's address to the nation. So, he would ask to have parliament suspended, after all. Or he would have all the first-born rounded up and put to the sword. Moonface had a stately air, perhaps in light of the speech to come. *Behold the sweet evening, friend of the criminal*—At a table of their own, in a world far distant, Marjerie Prentiss and swain were having a lover's quarrel, only that one knew they would kiss and make up, soon enough. Phillip Dundarave, like Dean or Brando, had the air of a man gobsmacked by the incapacity of the female to understand, and yet, he was too smitten to deliberately alienate the affections. Marjerie's face was stained with tears, and she was blinking and frightened. What an act, so I put it to myself. And a vapid fool was blundering into the trap, the more so because he was so pleased to put things right.

A Dream or Not

Had I dreamed the following: that the Current Prime Minister, addressing the nation, had wrapped himself in the flag; while Current Leader of the Opposition, in his field holler, wrapped himself in the sackcloth of duty and humility? Were all Traymoreans regarding the TV with sex-inflamed eyes, making no more sense of the images on the screen than if they had been cats? And Quebec was, as ever, the whipping post of a phantasmagorical land, Blue Danubians of the moment, willy-nilly, seditious. The winter dark outside was debilitating to the spirit, the wine so much liquid light of the sun, Moonface pleased to pour.

'Gentlemen,' she said.

She dimpled from ear to ear. Elias, husband to Cassandra, partner to Gregory, overseeing things, regarded us with astonishment. What manner of creatures were we, and he a Greek? Marjerie Prentiss and Phillip Dundarave rose to leave, having attained rapprochement, her face soft, more so than I had ever seen it. Phillip, stepping up to the cash so as to settle the bill, grunted in our direction. He assumed he was very much in control, and perhaps, for the time being, he was. Nothing could have been more transparently obvious: Marjerie was due for a hosing, she pretending her Traymorean neighbours here at table did not exist.

'*Sois sage, ô ma douleur, et tiens-tois plus tranquille*,' said Eggy, almost with a sigh.

It was as if he had been to every Paris of which the world could boast, and knew each intimately, cognizant of all their mysteries.

It was Dubois's turn for a display of astonishment, even as he cringed at Eggy's mangling of French vowels, however soft-spoken the delivery was.

'Now that's Baudelaire,' he observed, his voice as husky as a lover's.

Eggy beamed.

'Don't ask,' he said, 'but it came from somewhere, but which woman, oh, I don't effing know. The rain in Spain.'

Not all hooded figures were necessarily malevolent; some stole what kisses they could amidst the rubbish piles of alley ways or in the shadows of Roman ilexes. One did not know about Eggy; either he had come to his sweet melancholies late in life, and he was something like 902 years of age, or he had more of a track record than he was willing to let on, always obfuscating the details. I found two notes slipped under my door. Evie Longoria. The one invited me to lunch on the morrow. The other, with abject apologies, rescinded the offer. Perhaps I should have thought more of the gesture but I did not. She entered a vision before my eyes, she appealing enough, a ton of unhappiness in her. She passed through and was gone.

Eleanor Addicted

The season's first true snowfall had been, as ever, like a dream in its silence. And now, one crunched along, each step one took, even on a city street, as solitary as any taken on remote tundra. Christmas ornaments festooned with electric bulbs were affixed to lamp posts. Stars, bells, candy canes. A woman, waiting for a bus, sang to herself, her lips bright red, eyes anxious. I thought her harmless, if barking mad. My heart went out to her, yes, for some inexplicable reason, though there was something mean in her anxiety that repulsed. How much of the drama of our lives is contained in these wordless exchanges of an instant? The shovels were out. Dogs snuffled, poking their snouts where snow had banked up. It was not unusual that I would run into Eleanor at the poor man's super mart; and there she was, peering through reading glasses, inspecting the fine print of a tinned food item.

'It's the gift that never stops giving,' I said.

'And to what do you refer?' she asked, not at all surprised to hear my voice.

'Eggy. His lecherous turn of mind.'

'Oh that.'

She was in a mood.

'Corruption, American style.'

'Yes, there's that, too.'

Middle-aged stock boy, sallow-faced, disenchanted man who would die lonely and bitter and beyond the reach of miracles, was pricing the goods on the shelves. What, he might have wondered, was this an outreach clinic, this aisle of bean and tomato tins and bags of pasta, men and women discussing the mental health of old sots and a nation-state?

'I think I'm addicted,' Eleanor announced, going for the haricots, after all.

'Oh,' I said, intensely skeptical, 'to what?'

'To sex.'

This assertion caught me off my guard. Stock boy sniffed.

'Nonsense,' I thought to say, 'what silly rag have you been reading?'

'It was something I read. Men get all the reportage while women suffer their compulsions in silence.'

Body heat poured through her winter coat. A look of utter helplessness swept her face.

'Want to drive yourself nuts,' I suggested, 'then subject your every whim to some ological inquisition. Want to conduct your life in a strait jacket, it's easily enough done.'

It would have been my pleasure to help her through this latest crisis, but life is not always amenable to convenience. There were complications. We were obstructing traffic, as well. The poetry of whim was my *raison d'etre*.

Eleanor's kitchen. Amaretto. Conversation in lieu of boffing, of relieving delinquent urges. I was getting off easy, though I was, perhaps, if not the cause, then the excuse for the look on her face; how it confessed her embarrassment, as the good woman had gotten glassy-eyed as she trapped me against her kitchen counter.

'See?' she said, her husky tone one that might get her stoned in a biblical time.

In me, Boffo the clown muttered. An entity, one Randall Q Calhoun, was not doing him much good. They were tired and old refrains, me pleading Dubois, Eleanor her need.

'So roll us a cig,' she said, and she was weary.

I complied, shredding tobacco with some energy. An insistent breeze threatened the still hopeful flame in her grey-green eyes.

'I don't know what to say,' I said, pitting my plea against what had been hers.

'So don't say anything,' she snapped.

'You're not addicted,' I offered.

'I'm lonely. Can you get your pointy head around that?'

'Eleanor.'

'I mean, I'm getting shut down on all fronts. Bob. He's so intermittent. You, you're all the time mooning me with your eyes but when it comes time to put the pedal to the metal, oh no, you've got scruples. Phillip? What a prince, ready, willing and able, can make a girl feel she's of no more account than a box of cereal. What gives? Since when did men decide to behave? And since when did they decide to behave even worse? And what's with this Jarnette woman, anyway? Don't tell me you gave her a ride? I mean, effing hell, she's a, she may as well be some effing grave robber. A vampire. I know her type. And you think Marj is bad news. I mean, why should I feel so effing apologetic? And why should you prefer Moonface to me? I know you do. She has no more sex appeal than a turnip.

What's she got that I haven't got? She hasn't got tits, for one thing. Come on, fella, out with it. I mean, what are the rules, anymore?'

Eleanor very nearly wailed. I handed her a cigarette.

'And don't change the subject,' she said, smiling grimly.

My turn for some effusion, I said: 'You're right. And when you're right, you're right. I love all of you. I let you all down in a million ways. No, there's nothing lovelier, more a sight for sore eyes, than a warm, willing, comely wench with mischievous eyes. What else do you want me to say? You're a very good friend, alright? Only it would be a lot less trouble taking Marj to bed. For her, it's research. If she could but test her political convictions to the extent she tests the soundness of her sexual notions, she just might have a mind, after all. Well, I'm as curious as the next man, but she would cost me my self-respect.'

'Really?' a dull voice boomed.

'Eleanor,' I said, without missing a beat, 'I wish you'd lock your door once in a while.'

Barefoot Prentiss in a night shirt now stood behind Eleanor, throwing her arms around the good woman, all the while she regarded me with what was for her a companionable grin. Eleanor blushed, all her command of a situation in tatters. I had not blushed in years; even so, I counted myself as having been exposed.

There were committees for everything, from garbage collection to counting the dead. And yet, no committee was going to prevent Marjerie Prentiss from following me to my digs. She padded behind me in a parody of a tribeswoman, whose only lord and master had declared her an outcast, effectively sentencing her to death. She was tearing at her hair; she was wringing her hands, having a grand old time of it. It was in my thoughts that it was not until they were conquered and confined to the margins of existence that druids took up writing; not because they lacked the art but because they would protect what they knew. Could I not see the Gazans, for instance, in this light? I was angry, angry with Eleanor, angrier still with my pursuer, for she had caught me out in a vulnerable moment. I did not believe that the revelation of a soul in its entirety was a good thing, no matter what romantic comedies and the Eleusinian mysteries and a father confessor might suggest to the contrary; but an overly-cloistered soul was equally injurious to well-being. A soul had to breathe. I was mid-point in my living room when, like a cornered animal, I turned, Prentiss much amused. She might as well have said: *And you thought, what with all the magnificent volumes in your library, it would take me many lifetimes to read them, and here, I've snapped my fingers and I've read you in an instant.* Yes, and I had not the faintest idea of what I might say. But, as when in a movie, the delirious are besieged with fragmented and haphazard memories and voices, so it was with me; and here was a smiling Sally McCabe, a friendly warning in her eyes. Here was the only woman I married, she who tossed herself from a high balcony, her expression both gentle and impassive as she fell. Here were lovers whose names, let alone their faces, I had forgotten. Here was Jack Swain in full thrall to his self-mockery, so great his disdain of North American hypocrisies. Here were the Howards and the Klopstocks, every one of them dead. And so forth and so on. They had only me to rely on for a memory of their existences. Prentiss minced forward, her hands grabbing at the hem of her night shirt, drawing it tight across her hips. She was grotesque. With all the grandeur of truth on her side, as if truth were the sole divine presence to which her mind would grant a hearing, she was mocking the notion of sex itself; she was saying that, in fact, there was no such thing as this sort of congress, not in any elevated human sense; that what was about to ensue amounted to nothing more than some other function of the body; that our souls were no more than dead leaves such as we trample beneath our feet. Pagan lust? Secular lust? No, what she had going was more than a clinical outlay of hormones. She looked straight into mine with her hateful eyes. It occurred to me she had never been taken for all she might have been abused and coerced in her past. It was the source of her insufferable certainty. *Come on, silly man, take me, and see where it gets you.*

'Marry Ralph,' I said, my tone of voice that of a man quoting from a book in which he does not much believe.

She tarried. She fingered my wrist. She wet my lips with her tongue, her eyes fixing mine all the while.

'For God's sake, Marj,' Eleanor said, 'leave something of the man to himself.'

The good woman had my gratitude, she who had just come to my rescue. Prentiss shrugged, blinked, turned, and minced out the way she came. Eleanor grinned, much entertained.

For years I lived like a rat in various rat-holes, underwritten by a trust-fund, courtesy of my father who was not rich-rich but wealthy enough. I did not, in principle, object to riches save when the well-heeled behaved badly, money their moral ascendancy and fraudulent prestige. Such people are better seen and not heard. For all that, I would not have minded having the gold of Croesus at my command (so that I might spirit myself elsewhere) as I entered the Blue Danube, and it seemed oppressive and ludicrous as a refuge, the winter night a pall. To be sure, the trees that lined our noble boulevard sparkled prettily, encased in ice. Bright cheeks. Muted sound. Crunched snow. Even so, one might consider whisking Moonface away to Rome or Venice, to the pockets of lovely quiet each of those cities contained, and we hold hands on a stone bench, and recite bad Renaissance poetry with neo-platonic agendas. I could even present Dubois sitting there at his table with his folded *Glove and Mail*, that mind-teaser, with a company to manage, one of those wonder-working companies that eradicate disease or purge the land of toxins or elevate the poor; that somehow vouchsafe truth, beauty and justice for the as yet unborn generations whom, as we knew, would honour them; as they had to, for we had not. Dubois, for the most part, retained his faith in the system, though now and then, his air was that of a man who knew all along the system was no more than a farce with executive sanction, and it got people killed. How tragic for one who believed there was no problem that did not have its solution, if only the will be there, and the appropriate knowledge, and the votes. Where a poet might see a blinded and fated Oedipus, he saw the disgrace of inefficacious method. Moonface had a new pair of boots.

'Ask to see her boots,' Dubois said, as I took a chair like a man just relieved of guard duty.

And Moonface giggled like a schoolgirl, but she was not going to show off her boots, and I would not have been interested unless, of course, she was going to treat us to a full-blown floor show. Perhaps it was what Dubois had in mind, the rotter.

'Eggy,' he said, 'will not grace us with his company, tonight. He's terrified of the ice.'

There was no wine on the table. I could still taste the empirically-minded tongue of Marjerie Prentiss. My run-in with her, and the fact that Eleanor witnessed it, had tickled Eleanor's funny bone, and I supposed it a spiritual advance of a kind; that perhaps she was on the way to uncoupling herself from Marjerie's machinations.

'You looked so silly standing there, like a man afraid to disturb a sleeping puppy,' she had laughed.

I had given her a look and she laughed some more, her own recent humiliations, for the moment, forgotten. Paleolithic men, squatting around a fire, discussing the next day's hunt, seemed the height of sanity. And while Eleanor laughed, there had been a trooping on the stairs—Ralph and Phillip. One heard them calling out to Marjerie to get dressed; they would take her to dinner. Chinatown. It was not much of a Chinatown in this our faded Jezebel of a city, but even so, Eleanor now mock-wailing over her plight. What was she expected to do, subsist on berries and bugs? Well then, throw on a coat; the train was due to leave the station. Oh, a fine, fine woman she was, but when was she going to learn? One could see her in the backseat with Phillip, saying something like: *give me your body, man, it's effing cold,* she keeping it light while, in the front seat, Marjerie would display how adept she was in the role of the traffic-conscious wife. Phillip was hers to give, and he did not seem to mind being passed around—this arrogant and shambling carpenter who would inherit neither heaven nor earth.

'So,' I said to Dubois, opening up a conversational front, 'we've got a new Liberal head.'

'Apparently so,' he replied, pretending that it was not a shocker; that the past few days had not, in fact, been a reaping of whirlwinds.

'We'll see,' he continued, 'we'll see.'

Dubois drew a knife through his *filet mignon.* The only other customer in the café was chatting up Moonface, the man clearly lonely and yet, in his tone one heard that Moonface lacked certain credentials (a fully pronounced bosom, perhaps); only that, it being the kind of night it was, one had to go with the cards one was dealt. I could have pounded him for his shabbiness; Moonface seemed oblivious. *Emma pretty. Pretty Emma.*

'She's really beside herself,' Dubois said, 'with those boots.'

It was true that one did not often associate the dear girl with conspicuous consumption.

'Have you seen Evie?' Dubois asked.

It seemed rather suspicious that he would ask.

'No,' I answered, 'not lately.'

Dubois regarded me with some suspicion of his own. One heard a party of men and women in high-spirits pass by the café.

'Oh look—' Moonface began to say.

My warning eyes caught hers. Yes, it was Marjerie and her swains, and Eleanor. I would have wished to spare Dubois the sight.

Seven Leaguers

I was restless and wanted to go, and even Dubois pleaded he had a meeting early the next morning. Still, neither of us made a move, the café cozy, winter outside. Save for Serge as reliable as ever in the galley, and Moonface, we were alone in the place.

'You still haven't shown him your boots,' Dubois said to our waitress.

'They come over my knees,' she exulted, now a sex kitten, once a Plain Jane.

'Seven leaguers,' I said.

'Seven what?' Dubois wanted to know.

'Boots,' I said, 'that give the wearer magical properties. Covering vast distances in a single bound. The ordinary rules of time and space not applying.'

'They're fur-lined,' Moonface said, vainly attempting to bring the boots in question back down to earth.

'I'll bet you look good in them naked,' Dubois drolled.

Moonface, blushing deeply, had taken on the hue of the centre of a rose.

Every once in a while, vain and handsome Dubois got vulgar.

The phone rang and Moonface went to answer it, her hips swaying somewhat. This seemed a new development. We were going to miss her when she was down in Ecuador, vainly and frantically trying to find herself. She and her seven leaguers ... could transport me to ancient capitols ... Yesterday, the universe was infinite and today, it is considered finite, though perhaps it might be granted an extension on the morrow—

A Modernist Painting

We were gathered in the Blue Danube, Eggy, Dubois and I, hockey on TV. I could see that Dubois was on high alert. For a tiny claw with a mind of its own was making for a glass of wine and managed to tip it, as it was right at the edge of the table. And just as it was about to fall through space, I reached out and snagged it by its stem, righting the glass as I did so. There was no reason why a certain recollection should occur to me just then, but one did, of a football I caught once in the midst of chaos way back when. Dubois said to his flowerpot half: 'I don't think you'll be drinking any wine just now.'

A terrible silence. Now Eggy's chin had raised his chest, but at an odd angle, breathing laboured. If man has a soul, and if Eggy had one, it was in a state of consternation, roused from some torpor, not much liking the whisperings of demons and angels. Not only that, but Eggy was composing a modernist painting, what with that inverted triangle of a face askew. Dubois gave me a look, the back of his hand flush with Eggy's brow. We would not just yet call for an ambulance. Meanwhile Miss Meow and her companion miaowed. The Whistler whistled, his face within kissing distance of a book on which he was intent. Gregory and some Albanian friends were about to uncork a bottle. I looked up at the TV, and the Habs were already down by a goal. Snow fell. Serge, who from the galley, had noticed something was amiss, was now at the table, wiping his hands with his apron. Dubois motioned to Moonface to come over.

'Get a wet cloth,' he said.

Moonface went white, her countenance hardening. For they were still great friends, she and Eggy, though she did not much visit the old man like she had before when they would gossip and he would pinch her bum, to no avail.

'It will draw the blood to his head,' Dubois explained, Moonface having brought the cloth.

The phone rang. Gregory inwardly scowled. Bad for business, this scene unfolding. Or else he was merely frightened at the prospect of death, even one not his own.

'I don't know,' I said, Eggy looking awfully frail, 'maybe we ought to call that ambulance.'

Serge nodded that it was a good idea but, the phone engaged, Moonface was now handling an order; in any case, Dubois thought we should wait.

'You there?' he inquired of a tiny sparrow of man.

'Can you feel this? If you don't like how it feels, just say so.'

A fluttering of eyes. Dubois removed the cloth from Eggy's forehead, and he was deliberating if this was it—Eggy's last hour. We were all of us as if wrapped in a winding sheet of bad winter light, silly Greek pop music and the TV. And while Mark Antony was playing at house and empire with Cleopatra, Augustus Caesar-to-be seized on this as an affront to Rome's dignity. Actium. A battle to the death which, in the end, was nothing more than a skirmish, only that it changed the known world. History was like that: immense energies summoned and then the absurd. Eggy come back around, Dubois put it to him: 'Can you eat some ice cream?'

Eggy, eyes fluttering, thought he could; and when Serge brought a bowl of *crème à la glace*, Eggy pronouncing it *krem à la glass*, he dug into it with sparrow-like gusto.

'How's things?' Gregory asked him.

'Georgie Porgie, puddin'and pie, kissed the girls and made them cry—'

Gregory had no idea.

I was perhaps asleep by the time Dubois got Eggy up the stairs. Now and then, in the course of the night, some restive wintry breeze rattled the ice-slicked lilac tree in Mrs Petrova's yard, making of it castanets. Augustus Caesar had not the bother of the press: donning seal skins, he haunted his private underground grotto, putting to the shade of Romulus questions that had no answers, pretending to Apollo above ground—there on the Palatine—that he had not been a terrorist in his youth. For the empire was now a viable proposition, if men only kept their heads screwed on right. He had been circumspect enough, had he not, to permit the illusion of a free people, checks and balances and all the rest of it; and the senate could lord it over North Africa where the grain was, excepting Egypt which was his special concern? Give Moonface another ten years and she would be beautiful in a distinguished sort of way, her rich, brown golden eyes a bit wiser, cheekbones more refined, voice a note deeper, posture less defensive. But of course she already had a wonderful telephone manner, the fact of which, when she remarked on it, caused Dubois to guffaw and Eggy to hoot and I to roll my eyes and she to blush when she caught our drift. To say that God was dead had long since failed to carry import. Not all excess led to wisdom. Some wisdoms grew wiser or at least held their ground; others shrank, chipped away by a relentless barrage of the inane.

Legal Tender

Eleanor entered my digs, larger than life in a short skirt and heels. Dark leggings. She was bemused by the sight of me attempting to sew a button on a pair of trousers.

'What? No more group grope?'

These were the first words out of my mouth. A kind of bark broke from her throat; I took it as laughter.

'Whatever are you thinking?' she asked.

'We were playing *Scrabble*,' she explained, 'and Ralph won because, unlike the rest of us, he wasn't stoned.'

She parked beside me on the couch, and squirmed a little.

'I thought you didn't care for drugs.'

'A bit of weed now and then I don't mind.'

'Well, to what do I owe the pleasure?'

'Must there be a reason? You not pleased to see me? Don't you think I look, how do you always say, fetching?'

'Not sure.'

'Oh?'

'Well, I haven't managed to prick myself. That's something, at any rate.'

I snipped off the end of a thread with the scissors and then put spool and needle and scissors back in the shoebox where I kept such items. Eleanor went on a brief tirade.

'You're such a liar, Randall.'

'How so?'

'You'd love to get into this.'

She patted her hip.

'I never said I wouldn't love it.'

'Honestly, I don't know how men without women survive.'

'You'd be surprised.'

'You're in a mood, aren't you?'

'I wasn't, but now I am.'

The radio was tuned to opera. Eleanor hated it.

'Opera,' I said, 'is only Italian country and western. Think of it that way.'

'Country and western, my arse.'

'Only it's Handel,' I said, and I may as well have been talking to myself.

'Tell you what. Some day I'll treat you to one.'

'You promise?'

'Sure. Why not. It would give you a reason to dress up.'

She shifted slightly so as to be able to scratch the bottom of her thigh. I no longer knew her, it seemed; no longer understood what about her was innocent and what was something on the order of a tired agenda. We heard Evie Longoria in the hall. We heard Eggy answer his door: 'Go out? Go out where? It's effing cold. Orange juice? Eff orange juice.'

'Your blood sugar, my good man.'

And so forth and so on.

'You're right,' I said to Eleanor, 'I'm in a mood.'

And though she looked fetching even if she was just flirting, I was not eager to play along.

'Please go,' I said.

Perhaps I had just then hurt her. Perhaps I was entitled. But then, one was never entitled.

I put on a thick coat and went out in the bitter cold. On a street corner, I stood and had a puff, a complete and utter loon. In the sky above, a crow chased off two river gulls. Another crow, on a ledge, called to a crow high in a sparkling tree, the rays of the sun catching the ice just so. I was almost rapt with the spectacle. A finger poked my shoulder. Evie Longoria's eyes perhaps wondered if I was mad. Would the fact of my madness make her feel less lonely?

'Eggy's in a state,' she said.

'We're all in a state, I think. The reasons are legion. Where shall we begin?'

She took my response as gentle and inviting. A car, stuck in the snow, spun its tires, the world, otherwise, a colossal solitude. I could offer to get some wine, and we sit in the Blue Danube and drink. Perhaps she read my thoughts better than I might have credited her; but she must go and collect her daughter; they had a movie date. Soon they would fly to Mexico to spend Christmas with family in a timeshare. She expected to have a great time, only she could not get her weight under control. She would have to wear a swim suit. It was what one did.

'There's nothing wrong with your weight that I can see,' I said, the last gallant man on earth.

'I'll bet you say that to all the girls,' she said, striking a false note.

I did not know what to say so that she might recover a true one. She did not have a light spirit.

There was something in her that could crush light itself. Oh dear. Some lout, sporting large earrings, shoved his way past us, expelling foul verbiage at a furious rate. *Awaken in my heart the wrath of an offended soul…*

'Well,' said Evie, 'got to go.'

For the first time, I saw something like scorn in her eyes, scorn of man who could not make up his mind.

'Well, have a good going,' I said, as silly as could be.

'Yes,' she answered, 'a good going.'

In the Blue Danube I wanted soup and garlic bread. Antonio the waiter had three thousand years of skepticism going for him; even so, for me, he would bring a banquet. He kissed his fingertips.

And I went for a whiz and when I returned, Marjerie Prentiss was at table. She wore an old coat. A tuque narrowed her face, her eyes comically myopic.

'You think I'm a monster,' her voice dully thrilled.

She spoke like a woman who had every intention of humouring me.

'Now that you mention it,' I said, but only in the security of my mentations.

'No,' I lied.

Antonio had set the bowl of soup on the table. I offered the woman a glass of wine from my bottle.

'Why not?' she shrugged.

Johnny on the spot, Antonio brought her a glass, then walked away from a valued customer who was obviously in trouble. I poured and I toasted: 'To you. You've certainly brought interesting times to the Traymore.'

'Have I really?'

'I would say so. For a woman who isn't upscale society or celebritous, you do carry on.'

'I don't know what you mean. Besides, my mother was well-connected. Until she married my father who'd been in the merchant navy. He didn't like society. He read a lot of books. He encouraged me to think for myself. It's my brother I hate. I could kill him.'

'Because?'

'It's not a pretty story.'

'I think I've heard something of it—from Eleanor.'

'So do you think you have my number?'

'Does anyone know anyone?'

'I know my guys.'

'Yes, I suppose you know.'

'Anyway, so who do I remind you of?'

'Messalina, maybe. Ever hear of her? Wife to a Caesar. Challenged a whore to a bout of sexual endurance.'

'That's how you see me?' she replied, bemused.

'I don't know. Maybe the shoe fits. Maybe you've yet to find yourself. Anyway, it's your life. I'll tell you what I don't like. You've got your hooks in Eleanor for whatever game it is you're playing.'

Dead, watery eyes looked so unspeakably innocent.

'What game am I playing?'

'Well, there you got me, because I can't say as I understand it. For some reason, you've got some kind of hold on her, and it's like you need a witness, someone to watch you walk your tightrope.'

'Interesting.'

'Yes, but let's not get too interesting. Know what I mean?'

'No.'

'Sure you do.'

'Tightrope. What tightrope would that be?'

'We all walk one. You seem to require extra degrees of difficulty. Naturally, you'd like the world to notice.'

'You really are a nasty piece of work.'

'I never claimed I was nice.'

'You're always saying that.'

'Well, I'm saying it now.'

'This is insane.'

'I'm sane, but it's not clear that you are.'

'Lately, I've been thinking that sanity is overrated.'

'I always assumed you were intelligent. Are you? What does your father think of your politics?'

'He doesn't.'

'He doesn't like them?'

'Yes, he doesn't like them. But he's not terribly enamoured of liberals, either.'

'Who is?'

'Well, you're one.'

'You like thinking you can screw the worker in the name of realism. Nuking Arabs. Orgies in the palace. Proust on the half shell—'

'You're a little vague.'

'Just wondering how literary your literary turn of mind is.'

'The worker's such a dinosaur. I'm the economy, anyway.'

'What, you charge for your services?'

'I'd laugh, but you're not all that witty.'

'More wine?'

Marjerie Prentiss, as we used to say in the Sixties, split. She departed the café, resolved to be Marjerie Prentiss until her final breath. I could not change her even had I a magic wand. I was a little disappointed when she suggested yet again that I just wanted to sleep with her, as most men did. I replied that most women like to think of themselves as attractive, nothing wrong in that. But I did not believe most women wanted advances upon their persons 24/7. Nor did I believe that men, once past a certain age when they were apparently dominated by their hormones, so the ologists would have it, necessarily wished to be advancing all the time. Marjerie countered that Eleanor, not she, was the sexpot. I said I supposed it was true, but that she liked sex for its own sake; it was not for her a three-ring circus. I myself was a somewhat complicated creature. Prentiss tittered. Oh well. One tosses one's enemies a morsel once in a while. She said she would contribute to the cost of the wine—in legal tender. Of course, she would not, so I put it to her. She was, perhaps, in good spirits when she left. Antonio approached the table, wiping his brow. It was to suggest I had had a close escape. I did not attempt to alter his opinion.

Admission of Helplessness

Moonface relieved Antonio, and the place filled up. Elderly women of a church social, the nicest women one could imagine. It struck me then, Moonface's father United Church, that these were people she understood better than Darwin had his iguanas. At another table, two men wearing baseball caps talked the gold standard. The Americans would devaluate their dollar, the hoarding of gold to come.

'And then,' said the loudest of the two, 'you won't be able to buy diddlysquat.'

Besides being a child of Yankee positivism, I was also a child of the Sixties, apocalyptic thinking second nature. These men, much junior to me, thought doomsday a parlour pastime or a computer game. They would have a rude awakening. The last person I expected to see was Eleanor.

'Eleanor,' I said, a bit disconcerted.

'Your tone, Mr Calhoun –it's not exactly welcoming.'

She attracted stares as she seated herself, slipping her jacket off. She could care less for the good opinion of respectable old biddies. Two men wearing baseball caps were not oblivious to her charms. Still, they were more interested in gold, Eleanor's gilded curls notwithstanding, her blouse providing revelation. She was frightened.

'Never felt anything like it,' she observed to me, 'like I'm a puppet on a string. Or should I say strings? And Bob, well, we talk and he listens. He listens like the gentleman he is. And then he excuses himself, sometimes with a kiss. Early morning business to attend to and all that. What's he trying to prove? That he's so effing superior? That he would never get himself into such a sticky mess? I think of going away. But I'd only be coming back to the same situation. I thought she—well, you know of whom I speak—I thought she and Ralph were working on a house and she'd move away. It's like waiting for the troops to come out of Iraq, waiting for her to get to her endgame. Alright, I made a fool of myself with Phillip. But we never really did it, you know. Just some petting, you know. Like you and me. Thing is, I liked it. You can put your hand up my skirt any time you like, but you won't, not unless I plow you a road, give you a map and security clearance. And then Marjerie keeps talking about herself. Endlessly. And the more she talks the more I feel paralyzed, sex the only true privacy. It doesn't make any sense, but there it is. Roll me a cig, will you?'

'Obviously,' I said, not pleasantly drunk but drunk enough, 'the solution is, it's staring you in your pretty face, don't talk to her. Effing hell.'

'I can't not talk to her. Then she brings Phillip over. And she knows I can't resist him. I turn into some silly twit of a girl, like our waitress here.'

'I don't know what to say.'

'You've been saying that a lot, lately. You going to roll me that cig? Shall we get more wine?'

'I've had enough.'

'No you haven't. There's never any having had enough.'

I could not console her. On the way back to the Traymore, it was not so much she cried, but that her eyes went glassy for reasons other than lust: grief expressed without tears. She had no idea what had come over her; she was separated from the core of her being. Or else she had arrived at that mythical place and did not like what she saw. When one goes mad, I said, one strips one's world down to a besetting terror or two, the other terrors in their multiples being what gave one the appearance that one had been sane. She gave me a look. I had persuaded her to foreswear the wine; we would watch a movie and indulge a splash of amaretto each. Alright then, it was quite possible the movie would bore her, as she did not much like art movies, but even so, it just might distract her from her troubles, let the chips fall where they may. The TV was tuned to football. I explained that, no, I no longer had a great love of the game; but that it was still a source of jargon I would never employ; *three and out*, for instance, or *negative yards* or *play-option*. I would file these suggestive but essentially meaningless epithets in my inner archives along with *Pantocrator* or *Unam Sanctum*. She gave me a look. Was I always going to toy with her mind? So I put my arm around her, we on the couch. I rocked her a bit as she intently studied her folded hands. She choked something down, a spasm, perhaps, betraying her inner turbulence. I had always admired her selfishness, just that it was so often inconvenient. She had not a mean bone in her body, but even the gentlest of people may do damage, a play mistimed, frustration gathering force, then discharged blindly. She searched for a kiss I was not sure I had to give. I recalled Eggy proclaiming he could spend an eternity with Moonface, well, if the circumstances had been different; and I supposed he meant it, greedy, querulous, sometimes nasty Zeus-like Eggy the true romantic among us. As if it were an entity that possessed a corporeal body, I watched the eternal slip away from us, Eleanor and me on that bordello-green sofa or couch or divan, language inadequate and lost to chaos. I could have slipped my hand under her skirt as she had recently invited me to. I was on the verge of doing so when it occurred to me that, perhaps, I owed her an apology.

'I'm sorry,' I said, 'that I was mean to you earlier.'

'Really? I don't remember... oh, that, when you told me to go. Maybe I deserved it.'

She was confused.

'I guess,' she said, 'I've made my bed. Best I lie in it.'

I had nothing to say to this.

'Well,' I said, that single word of mine cheap at the price. 'Well,' I repeated, and regretted the lameness of it.

I set my hand on her thigh; immediately, she covered it with her hand.

'No.'

'I don't want to watch your lousy movie,' she added. 'But I don't mean to be critical. I just want to be alone. Believe me, I haven't said that in a while.'

She grinned now, and was appealing. A tear had finally formed. Perhaps it was all she had wanted, some material expression of a grief she was not even sure she understood or why it was there to understand in the first place.

'Nice of you to have had the thought,' she said.

'Of course,' I said, angry with myself.

She left me the amaretto.

Desire Does Not Sleep; It Slumbers

That it would be an ordinary day was fine by me. I would stay in as, footing on the pavement, what with rain slicking the ice, would, no doubt, prove treacherous. I would write or read. Would harass Zeus-like Eggy, putting questions to him as pertained to druids or Justinian or Charlemagne. *Effing hell, man, how do I know?* Mid-morning, and I heard: *alley alley in for free,* the voice a slightly musical moan. Moonface at the door. She rolled her eyes up and to the side. Was I not a lucky man to have her at my door? However, she was juggling schedules. Her Champagne Sheridan. Her studies. Her working hours. Add to these considerations was the fact of the trip to Ecuador. Lift off soon.

'I'm happy,' she said, long-bellied goddess settling on the couch like a bird.

'Oh,' she said, 'my boots. So sorry.'

She was not wearing her seven-leaguers, just old rubbers.

'It's alright,' I said.

So she was happy and she was busy. Dropped by to let me know she would sublet her apartment. Now I was warned. I was mad with desire for her. The girl who would be moving in was also in classical studies; she had better grades than Moonface as the girl was more serious.

'She really applies herself,' Moonface explained.

I was to be nice to this girl. Eggy was to keep his hands to himself. She was kind of cute, the girl, and otherwise, pretty cool. Moonface then bussed my cheek and touched it with a cold hand. She was out the door. Love hurts. I supposed I could listen to Moonface forever in bemused patience, biting my tongue on account of her naivety, her horizons so endearingly narrow, that is, if she thought truth, beauty, love and justice would prevail. Yes, and America might go communist. As was Caracalla's scowl, so was Current President's smirk carved in marble. But these digressions were taking me far from Moonface, from her incisors, her modest bosom; from the way she blushed upwards from her strong throat, emotions quickly registered, as she was a chameleon-like creature.

A chill rain fell on ice. I stayed in. Now and then I stuck my head out the door, as when Evie Longoria, pounding on Eggy's door, could not raise the old bugger. She was dropping by to let him know she would be away.

'Locked?' I asked.

'Locked,' she said.

I went downstairs to Mrs Petrova's shop for the key. I managed to get my landlady to understand I must check on her oldest lodger. In her eyes was a girl's awe at the prospect of death, though she must have seen death before. Eggy, dwarfed by his armchair, had only been sleeping. *Effing hell, can't a man sleep in peace?* Her mission discharged, Evie Longoria now sat primly on the edge of my couch. Her feet were close together, her skirt long and black, boots shiny and expensive. And how exactly did I occupy myself? Well, I read a little, wrote a little. Published? Oh, there had been an item many years back. I flailed about a lot, waving my arms like a drowning swimmer. But do you think I could get the world's attention?

'Why,' she asked, with irksome logic, 'because you want attention?'

'No,' I chuffed, 'because the world loves a charade, and I'm happy to oblige.'

It was, perhaps, for the woman, another occasion to suspect I was bonkers. Nothing flattered the senses more than knowing someone else was in even worse shape. Her reading was restricted to Booker Prize lollapaloozas. Was she edified? Whether she was or not, it was how she got her eyes to close at nights. Still, she had an appealing side to her nature, this Alberta cowgirl with a yen for the arts. The red jewel-like hair clasp just behind her left temple was a nice touch. Her brow was almost massive but not overbearing. It bespoke great intelligence, though it seemed she was at odds with this gift. I could have been mistaken; I often was. In any case, the warm feelings I had had for Moonface were, by now, dissipated. Conversation at a standstill, Evie Longoria remarked on the weather.

'It's disgusting outside,' I said.

'Yes, it is,' she replied, like a woman consumed by stark realism.

Then she sighed. Christmas, and she would be in Mexico, and perhaps, sometime in the new year, she would relocate to British Columbia.

'Don't you like me just a little?' she asked, her voice quite weak. 'Oh,' she said, rattled now, 'I don't know where that came from. But you seem so perfunctory, almost like you disapprove.'

She was deciding whether to laugh or cry. We had known one another for a thousand years; we had only just met, stunned by something like a family resemblance.

'I'm just an old dog long in the tooth,' I answered.

'I ride an old paint and I lead an old Dan,' she half-sung, through her tears.

She brushed them away with the back of her hands. And she swore; and it was about as black and as private a curse as I had heard in a while.

'Bipolar dysfunction,' she said.

She was looking for a note we both could sing.

To sleep with her would be like sleeping with a white flame and yet, was it fire or ice that would apply the heat? It would be a lovely flame, no doubt, of choiring angels long since used to the fact they went unheeded, no god in the slightest bit interested. It seemed she had flamed like this for so long that, though outwardly she was well-constructed and apparently real, touch her and she would fluff apart, tissue gone to ashes. She knew me for a coward. Her men had been crazy men, crazy enough not to have noticed, until too late, her spiteful fragility. Failed golf pro. Failed novelist. Where was that cowboy, anyway, bad habits and all, whose imperious hands-on treatment of her just might keep her intact? It was very likely that, after this meeting, I would see little of her.

If I shut my heart to Evie Longoria, I had not intended cruelty. Or did someone else, inhabiting my thoughts, steer me toward rebuffing her? It was an overly ghoulish thought, but then Marjerie Prentiss lived just down the hall. I helped Evie with her heavy coat, she frantic to leave as I bit my tongue. At the instant of her departure, I would flail my arms about and talk at the ceiling. Why was the worst kind of pain that which one endeavoured so hard not to inflict? Eggy would not care to know, and so why bother him with it? Eleanor would have scant sympathy, as she thought most women clueless and the authors of their own tribulations. *You can't keep rearranging the furniture in the doll house—sooner or later you have to live in it.* Yes, it was the sort of thing she would say. I recalled Dubois's recent seeming interest in Evie. Had he stepped up to the line and then declined to cross it? The sentences of a book on druids danced off the page helter-skelter; reading was futile. I closed my eyes. Here was Sally McCabe, looking troubled, but charmingly so.

'She had you going there, didn't she?'

'Why, was it you who came between us?'

'No. Would I do such a thing? But yes, what's happened to you? Once upon a time you would've said, "Come on, girl, let's see what pleasures we can prove." You weren't born like that, but I instructed you well. I see you're drinking whiskey, eating pistachios. Kind of puts me in mind of faded aristocrats or bitter pedagogues. Remember Mr Jakes? Our history teacher who blew his brains out? Now why do you suppose he did that? I can never get it out of my mind. I never bought the explanation he was out and out nuts.'

'I think he took a look around him and realized it was hopeless. But that would be the romantic view of it. They said his marriage was bad and he had debts.'

'They always say that.'

'I know.'

'Poor man.'

'I wonder if his shade is heartened to hear you say it?'

'You know, I'm not eager to find out.'

'Why not? You were always more than just a pom-pom girl.'

'A compliment? Late, but I'll take it.'

'My pleasure.'

'The girls now—they might look sexier, but it's all show, I think. We actually boffed you guys, though maybe we were insane to do so.'

'I don't recall you boffing me.'

'You were a special case. Handle with care. This one has scruples.'

'Are you kidding? Scruples? It was more like I didn't rate your favours back in high school.'

'Sure, you rated them. But you thought us all drunken sheep fuckers, which we were.'

An Additional Piece of Time Accorded

Dubois was having lunch in the Blue Danube. Where I had gone, quite out of sorts. Despite my being out of sorts, Dubois expatiated: 'These days,' said Dubois, 'because of medical breakthroughs, a man has an additional piece of time accorded him, enough that he might set the record straight so that the wrong people don't claim him for the wrong reasons as their patron saint. And what about you?'

'I had no idea.'

'Well, why not?' Dubois put it to me.

'You've thought a lot about things,' he added, 'and you just might publish those notebooks yet.'

I was flabbergasted. Vain and handsome Dubois was serious. He was lunching on a plain burger slathered with pepper and mustard, having slurped up his soup. And then his cell phone went off, and it was Eggy on the other end, inquiring as to conditions outside the Traymore. Could he negotiate the sidewalks? A hockey game was slated for that evening.

'We'll get you here,' Dubois assured him, 'be ready to go at 1830 hours.'

I still had not done an honest day's work, whatever that might have been.

'You plan on showing?' I was asked.

'Sure,' I said, and continued: 'Goethe was claimed by communists, Christians, pagans and everyone in between. But then, don't mind me. Just an idle observation.'

'Piaf thought Montreal Mickey Mouse. But when Lévillée played piano for her, she was disabused. He was going to go to Paris whether he wanted to or not.'

Dubois was a patriot. But what was he on about? And such words as we had exchanged up to this point were sufficient for an afternoon's Apollonian discourse. I went home, having promised I would come back around in the evening. There was a note tacked to the outside of my door; it accused one Randall Q Calhoun of unnatural acts. It was signed *E* and *MP*. High spirits, perhaps. Man proposed; woman disposed. A tittering behind Eleanor's closed door. I inserted my key in my lock, having ripped the note from its tack, crumpling it in my hand. A door, not mine, opened, and here were two blithe spirits in the hall, female Katzenjammers. Eleanor in ceremonial dress. Marjerie Prentiss in a night shirt. Her shinbone was nicked where, presumably, she had recently shaved. Blood coagulated.

'We're going to give Eggy his thrill,' said Eleanor, her voice curiously strange, off-centre.

Gilded curls flashed with unnatural sparks.

'But his heart,' I said stupidly, no other words forthcoming.

'He'll die happy,' a dull voice observed.

'But he wants to watch the hockey game this evening,' I explained, somewhat panicked.

'Mortal man has seen enough hockey,' that same dull voice pointed out.

What drug was in their systems, Eleanor glassy-eyed, in the embrace of a punk Dionysus? They were like a comedy duo, the taller Eleanor in her heels nudged against her shorter and more plain counterpart who was, nonetheless, perhaps a great deal more lethal.

'Shoo,' I yelled, now waving my arms, hoping to scatter a couple of carrion birds.

'Aw,' said Eleanor, grinning, 'we're only kidding.'

'But we had you there,' a dull voice noted.

'We wouldn't hurt Eggy Schmeggy. Wouldn't touch a hair of his sainted head. God knows how long we've put up with him. A little more won't be much skin of our nose. The way he's knocking it back, it won't be long now.'

Marjerie seconded Eleanor's assertion.

'Eat, drink and be merry,' she boomed.

'Did you know that in Manhattan,' she went on to say, 'nobody gets drunk anymore. Nobody smokes. One imagines they go home and have virtual sex. Where are the literary lions?'

Was Marjerie Prentiss a closet critic? The ancients warned that godhead revealed was always a moment hazardous to mortals. I had been stuck with the role of mortal in this tableau. It did not seem I could claim, as mortals would come to claim, that I actually got more out of life than the gods, seeing as pleasure, because ephemeral to transient mortals, was more intensely had by them. As if to remind me for the *nth* time of what I had been missing, Eleanor waggled a pompadoured foot. Not that she any longer cared. Marjerie simply stood there, barefoot dormitory wallflower.

'Yes, well, see ya, Ran-dull,' said Eleanor listless now, but in possession of enough vigour that she might sport with the last syllable of my pronomen.

'Bye,' said Marjerie, waving limply, her expression all disdain.

What were men but children unworthy of sport, especially the sport of those truly evolved? There was a stench of death in the hall, even if, in reality, all one might smell was Mrs Petrova's cabbage. Orpheus got to be a cynic. Perhaps now one might understand why. I shrugged. Three adults in the hall of the Traymore Rooms were faintly aware of each their absurdity.

'Have to pee,' Marjerie said, folding her hands on her crotch, on the verge of an ugly bout of laughter.

She minced into Eleanor's apartment. Eyes locked—Eleanor's and mine, all space between us gone neutral. In fact, her eyes were less glassy now; but I could see nothing in them; nothing of sadness; nothing of anger; no hint, even, of curiosity. I was there and not there. I was a fact some rational mind had to register, as it was what rational minds did—locate, identify as threat or non-threat, *guarda e passa*.

'Eleanor,' I said.

Mention of her name perhaps dislodged her, for a moment, from her trance. She muttered something, and stepped into her digs.

For an instant, for a duration of time not much more than the flitting of sub-atomic particles through human air, I figured I was back among the sane in the Blue Danube, the atmosphere nearly festive with Greeks and Albanians temperately drinking wine. The hockey game was on, and the match would prove to be a parade to the penalty box for the Habs, the referee having it in for them.

'*Merde*,' said Dubois, who was more apt to render profanities in English.

Then Eggy, his tough old eyes angling mischief at me, mock-crooned: 'The vicar is a bugger and the curate is another so they bugger one another immobile—'

Dubois guffawed.

'Well,' Eggy hoo hooed, 'it's true.'

But that the economy was in dire straits; that Dubois agreed it was, so hang on, the ride would get rougher yet. Gregory approached the table.

'How's it going, guys?'

'You don't want to know,' said Eggy, his finger raised.

'Tell Serge,' Dubois said, 'that he's done it again.'

'Good steak?' said Gregory.

'Excellent,' Dubois countered.

Antonio, with a wink, unfolded a serviette and made of it a bib; he tucked it in Eggy's many-splendoured shirt.

'Yes, well,' Zeus-like Eggy responded, 'teach Moonface to do that and it would be something.'

Traymorean hoots resounded through the café, Greeks and Albanians startled.

'And I'd smack her backside,' Eggy added, for good measure.

'Moonface,' said Antonio dreamily, wondering, perhaps, how a girl had come by that name.

Gregory returned to his boon companions. I went out for a puff. And outside, on the terrasse, as I puffed, I listened to the music of ice crackling under footfalls, thought it almost beautiful, street lamps lurid. I would write a novel about Frederick of Hohenstaufen who drowned a man in a barrel of wine just to see if the man's soul would fly out, the emperor a man after Dubois's own heart. But of course, if a soul were to have been witnessed leaving a body behind, there would have to have been a natural explanation for the phenomena, no truth but in nature.

'Moonface is the enigma,' I heard Eggy chorusing as I reentered the café. 'Why she's the real enigma, not why the universe keeps expanding when, according to the logic of gravitational pull, it shouldn't. I'd drill her one.'

'Eggy,' said Dubois rather off-handedly, 'you're getting rambunctious these days. You've been getting pretty wild, if I may say so.'

'You may. The vicar is a bugger and the curate is another—'

I was getting drunk, beautifully drunk. Ice crackled. Moonface in my mentations beamed. But I was rudely interrupted.

'Think they'll drop the bomb?' Eggy said, peering up at me, 'I mean, oh I don't know, but will they?'

'Relax,' said Dubois, 'they might, but not yet. So eat your pies. Serge went through a lot of trouble cooking those up for you.'

'There once was a cook named Serge who as he cooked gratified an urge… effing hell, doesn't scan, just flying by the seat of my pants.'

'It doesn't, properly speaking, rhyme,' Dubois noted.

'Oh eff you. You're worse than Randall, always correcting me.'

'With you it's one thing, then it's another. You keep changing the subject. When did we last have a proper conversation, let alone a debate?'

'Oh, I don't know. A few minutes ago?'

Eggy was on a roll: 'The vicar is a bugger and the curate is another—'

'Will you stop that?'

Perhaps Dubois was irritated; perhaps he was truly enjoying himself. But I was back in the Traymore hall in my mentations, men and women there sizing one another up, no mistaking what was wanted.

Foggybottom

That she was civilized about it surprised me. But then I was inebriated, and the machinations of insider-traders might have struck me just then as polite transfers of wealth. How she did it never ceased to amaze me: that, for a woman who was not conventionally a looker, she managed to transmit such heady allure. Once more she had minced her way into my digs, her air conjectural. What might she find? What manner of beast? Otherwise, like adversaries, we stood in the middle of my living room.

'The boys are away,' she explained, 'I'm lonely. Is that too hard to grasp? We're adults, you and I. We don't, you know, have to do it.'

I was, in any case, too far gone to do it, having just come from the Blue Danube. And she was, at least, wearing something other than that nightshirt, item of wear as might qualify her for residence in Bedlam. Comfortable smock and slacks. Her hair was freshly washed. There was nothing about her that did not seem wholesome and companionable. She was making it seem like we were strangers on a train, and it was going to be a long haul, why not make the best of it? *North by Northwest?*

'I was going to watch Letterman,' I protested.

'Why? You think he's funny?'

'I don't watch him for the humour, which is a pretty cheap sort of humour, anyway.'

'Then why?'

She was making an effort to seem interested.

'If America has a collective brain, even if it can't compete with China in mathematics, he's its cerebrum, or he's the canary in the cage, if you get my drift.'

'I don't.'

I shrugged.

'He gives voice to what sticks in the craws of Yanks.'

'Like what?'

'Like Current President. Or death. Or taxes. Smelly cabbies. Overbearing women.'

'He's a pig,' a dull voice boomed, 'that Letterman.'

She pressed her hip against mine. Infinite suggestion. So yes, what was the harm, life a rum business in which man and woman (while elsewhere on the earth, people starved or otherwise led wretched existences) might ingeniously conceive short-lived escapist behaviours? When I woke in the middle of the night, head throbbing, Marjerie Prentiss was gone. Perhaps I snored and drove her crazy. Perhaps I only imagined her presence in the first place. I trudged to the toilet, cursing my stupidity, even so. No doubt she was crowing to half the world, her computer the only light-source in a dark room, that she had cracked the Calhoun code. Love, of course, was not dead; but saying so was a way to make a point. Had we actually boffed, Marjerie and I? Until one of us began giggling? *Three and out. Negative yards.* Ah, here is what happened: we sat on my couch, Marjerie Prentiss and I, heard out Kissinger the realist on TV, he rattling on about this and that and the balance of powers. Marjerie approved; I was disgusted. Charlie Rose moderated, this man who knew less about more than any other being on earth.

Love was dead and yet love lived, was this and that; was here and there, inside and outside the soul. St Francis of Assisi was not as pacific as all that; he approved of the Crusades and death to the Saracen. Moonface, so I knew well enough, would have failed me and I her had we become an item. Pretty Emma, Emma pretty had squatter's rights in her psyche, one sometimes compromised by the pills she ate for her fits, that robbed her of her personality, or so she complained. Hence her chameleon-like nature. Her hair was elegantly wound at the back, her lashes long as I took a seat in the Blue Danube in the afternoon. The tight-fitting top she wore revealed the pale swelling of her bosom, so much so she seemed the living portrait of a quattrocento love object. The radio blared its over-amplified, courtly come hithers. Gregory once again drank with his boon companions, if in broad daylight. They monopolized Moonface when she was not dealing with the phone or with customers. Tiny Christmas bulbs festooned Blue Danube window glass. Moonface wished to be normal; I had pushed her to reach for more than she could reasonably grasp. In this I was a scoundrel. And yet, was she not extraordinary? Not for reasons due to her looks, perhaps, or her intelligence. But that, in her brain chemistry, there was something like a divine fire. And, as the poets once understood, it was not the sage but the fool who best knew the thoughts of God. She wished me not to leave too soon. When she had a moment, when she was not front and centre in the censuring gaze of Gregory (who would, understandably, run a tight ship), she said to me: 'I've been to see my neurologist. He told me the kind of epilepsy I have is potentially fatal. I'll have to be careful in Ecuador. But if I keep taking these pills all the time—'

'I know,' I said, cutting her off, 'you're being managed rather than doctored.'

'I know,' she agreed, her moan slightly musical.

'You know those scenes in old westerns when a scout puts his ear to the ground to listen for the approach of men on horses? You'll have to listen to your body like that. You'll have to wing it. I wish I could say something helpful.'

'Yes, I know,' she said, rolling her eyes up and to the side, the phone ringing, interview concluded.

§

Book VII—*Spolia Opima*

In a Peace Concluded by Love

It was to me a surprise. Perhaps Eggy had something to do with it, he a mischievous gnome at table with Eleanor and Dubois, those two lovebirds convivially shoulder to shoulder. Sunday afternoon in the Blue Danube aka Le Grec.

'Randall,' said Dubois, as I approached, 'pull up a chair.'

'Yes, do.'

The silky purr was Eleanor. They were well along in their consumption of wine, representing, perhaps, the pagan end of things. And on cue, here was Antonio to kiss Eggy's pate.

'I love you, Eggy,' simpered Antonio.

'Oh eff off.'

Eggy was most disgruntled. Cassandra dropped menus on the table; I supposed a feast was in the offing.

'Will you eat with us?' asked Dubois.

It was a natural enough question, but it seemed so oddly put. And Eleanor looked most fetching. The low-cut high-collar blouse. The glossy lips. Throwing on her coat, she joined me on the terrasse for a puff.

'Oh, I can see the wheels are turning,' she said, 'Randall's stripping gears in his head. I knocked on Bob's door, shoved him into bed and basically raped him. Anything wrong with that? Sure, he put up a fight. He was a bit worried about his heart. Then he wondered if I meant it. How could I not mean it? It's work, exciting a man, especially one of his age.'

Moonface *Obbligato*

We woke, Moonface and me, still wearing what clothes we had on us when we went to bed. That we were garbed, still, testified to our innocence, though some might contend that to be naked in paradise is the only true badge of innocence. Even so, I cannot say I did not touch the dear girl and that she did not touch me. I cannot claim we refrained from conversing on matters of God and life's meaning, her thinking on it all pretty conventional, in any case. The usual stuff about a first cause. The usual wall beyond which human comprehension obtains no traction. No matter. There are moments (even moments that, when strung together, comprise a lifetime in a single night) that require no genius. Her eyes, richly golden brown, may have been gods, for all I knew, and more than enough intellect for me to handle. She had, or so she put it to me, felt in between beds; that her own was not quite her own any longer, given that she was mostly sleeping in her Sheridan's bed, plus the fact she would soon sublet her apartment. She also put it to me that she was a little frightened as well as excited in respect to what the immediate future might bring her. Perhaps I could now, now that it was morning, recall my hand on the small of her back, as if—even as we had lain there face to face in the dark, a high wind whistling outside—we were promenading on a dance floor. And yet, something like sleep shivered inside me and took me with it and away from her. I figured my snoring would drive her away; it did not. In the morning then, and she went to her own digs which were next to mine, but that she would return when I had the coffee made. She did so, and we were with one another on a much more prosaic basis, drinking coffee, shelling walnuts, my one concession to the holidays. I suggested to Moonface that she might drop in on Eggy, and she replied she had it in mind. The pedagogue in me began to speak of abduction as perhaps the ultimate cause of an effect we deem human history. As I spoke on the matter, it triggered a memory of the dream I had had in the night; that Eggy was Zeus and Champagne Sheridan a puppyish Dionysus; but that I was only a mortal hero whose attitude towards women, if playful, was fairly superficial, pirating and football everything. And she did go and visit Eggy only to retreat from him and back to me, she blushing from her bosom upwards; that the octogenarian had finally succeeded in pinching her bum. It had been a hard pinch, and the old chuffer was now gloating. Hoo hoo. We listened to music while she got back her equipoise. The viol.

Sainte-Columbe. I might go weeks and not listen to a single note of anything, excepting the overly hopeful pap one heard on the Blue Danube radio and on TV. Then, orgiastically, I would indulge and lose myself in what can only be described as exquisite sensations; or, indeed, I would rediscover some part of me that had gone missing. I might see parrots flitting between the umbrella pines of a Roman park. I might recollect some old amorous adventure. I might come up against my mortality.

'You know,' I said to Moonface as she sat on the edge of my couch, cracking open a nut, 'your life is going to take a turn, and this will prove to have been the last of it, our being able to pass the time like this.'

'I know,' she answered, her thin lips drawing tight against her incisors.

The dear girl had come dangerously close to acknowledging that, between us, there was anything at all. She blushed anew. Were we not cowards to the extent that I, even if greatly her senior, had not truly ravished her while she, with all the arrogance and indifference of the young, had discounted my mentations as not rating much merit, being old hat? So much for Virgil. So much for the human cycle of gain and loss. So much for the corrupt and debased regime of Current President. She might, push come to shove, admit she was more afraid of her sexuality (and certainly, she feared her fits) than she was of thunder and lightning and old biddies of the church, but I supposed I could build a case that what she most feared was her intellect and its affinity with poetry; that she had gifts which she might end up wasting.

'Reality trumped the gods,' I said, 'and we got poetry as a consolation prize, whether or no anyone cares to notice. Science in all its glory keeps rubbing salt in those old wounds, no matter how many physicists quote Dante. Poetry's about the only thing we have to keep the house honest. That and love, even if it amounts to nothing more than a transience, a touch on the lips, and we're briefly warmed, and then it's gone and we're cold. And then there's logic. But that's another can of worms and maybe I should just shut up.'

Moonface gave me a look, she perhaps distressed. Damn it all. Damn the pedagogue. And Moonface said she had better be going. Busy day, including a doctor's appointment. Yet another considered opinion on her epilepsy.

'Randall,' she said somewhat brightly in her best imitation of a worldly-wise woman, 'you do go on. But I'm glad you do. No one else in my life does.'

I went to the closet for her coat, I a silly man. She pulled on her seven leaguers, the magical boots. She put on her coat, jamming her hands into its pockets. A grin dimpled her face.

'A kiss,' she said, 'you filthy beast.'

A kiss, then—this at the door. She clambered down the Traymore stairs. In the corner of my eye, an unwanted presence. Marjerie Prentiss in a night shirt.

'Expose Thyself to What Wretches Feel—'

I stood at the window in the Traymore hall. Snow madly swirling off rooftops and sparrows at Mrs Petrova's feeder were the spectacles of the moment. I was angry with myself, dipping into such mentations that were convinced most endeavours were futile. I had persisted in seeing in Emma MacReady aka Moonface what was not there—a young woman of special gifts. A typical liberal failing. I was silly with wanting to believe. Or perhaps it was even worse; that I wished her to recognize something in me that was her way through the inanities, and of course, she could not see it, seeing only a man past his prime, one who had failed all standard indicators of success. Now bare feet padded my way on a carpet. Can a bipedal creature, shark-like, smell blood? Now dead watery eyes said it all: Arabs were getting knocked about in Gaza. Marjerie Prentiss knew what was right and proper and who was civilized. That the weak got in the way of the strong. Her shoulders were hunched, the night shirt a faded blue. She rubbed the back of an ankle with a foot, her arms enclasping her chest. Her freckles almost danced. That is the way it was with her. No woman I had ever known could so simultaneously attract and repel.

'Eleanor says you know everything,' her dull voice boomed.

'Eleanor is too kind,' I said, 'and anyway, I'm sure you've heard it: the more you know the less you know.'

'No, I hadn't heard it. And if I had I would've said it was a dumb thing to say.'

Her eyes, for all they were watery, were burning through mine down to some core, and then beyond as we fell through space.

'Care to escort me to my bed and play the groundskeeper?'

'No.'

Her grin declared I was in a state of untruth. But I was not just then telling an untruth.

'Maybe another time,' I said.

'Why not now? It's winter. The world's cruel.'

Her dull boom of a voice was falsely magnanimous.

'Eleanor says you're sweet.'

'Hoo hoo. High level talks?'

It was Eggy peering out his door.

'Can I join in?' he asked, 'or shall I just get drunk?'

'No,' I said, sharply, 'you may not join in, but, by all means, attend to your intake.'

'Effing hell.'

Then Eleanor. She of the gypsy skirt and pompadours. She who liked a circus. Dear old Eleanor.

Dear old Eleanor took one look at the scene, at what was her pleasure to behold, and she tossed her gilded curls and laughed. It seemed to me Marjerie Prentiss looked a little chuffed at this, Eleanor's laughter, perhaps, dismissive.

'Expose thyself to what wretches feel,' I quoted at Prentiss, now that there seemed an opening for the words.

'King Lear,' thundered Eggy, his finger raised, even if he had no effing idea what in effing hell was going on.

Here was Dubois come up the stairs, his face radiant from the cold wind, his tuque very much the mark of a man of active life, as if he had just climbed Mt Everest and liked it.

'You've all got mail,' he noted, 'checking my mailbox, I noticed.'

'Well,' he continued, 'everybody seems to be having a good time.'

'A great old time,' said Marjerie, dull voice booming with menace.

And Dubois, removing his gloves, looked at her with his glittering blue eyes like a connoisseur might, and he arrived at no particular conclusion. Either this particular woman was someone he could take in his stride at any hour of the day, or he was putting up a show. But either way ...

'Monsieur,' said Eleanor, crooking her finger at him.

Dubois grunted. The woman in the night shirt stole away like a ghost put to rout.

Eggy beamed, for no rhyme or reason.

'How's the sidewalks?' he put it to Dubois.

'Passable,' Dubois answered.
Weather was everything.

Ringing in the New Year

It would have to have been richly comic, what transpired in the Traymore Rooms on New Year's Eve. Or else the comedy was in Eggy's depiction of the event, Dubois correcting the old sod's errant grasp of details.

'You're always reminding me of my ignorance.'

'No. But let's be clear on the basics,' said arch-materialist Dubois.

'Roll me one of your ciggies,' Eleanor commanded me.

'Effing hell,' thundered a homunculus.

The heart of Traymorean society was *in situ* at the Blue Danube on the first day of the new year: Eggy, Dubois, Eleanor, and myself. Moonface was there as well in her capacity as a long-bellied waitress. Gregory was there, *cappytan* of the ship. Elias and Cassandra. Antonio was nursing his hangover.

'Oh, let me kiss you,' he breathed on Eggy's pate.

'Effing hell, eff off.'

Moonface uncorked a fresh bottle of wine, her nails red again, the pop of the sprung cork ever so soft. Dubois: 'That was the most delicate pop I've ever heard.'

Eleanor: 'Behave.'

Eggy beamed. Dubois guffawed. I had missed the theatrics that featured nudity, coarse language, violence in the Traymore.

'You know, she was starkers,' said Eggy.

'Starkers,' said Dubois, unfamiliar with the import of the word.

'Yes. In the all-together, you know.'

'Well, Randall,' Eggy continued, 'you couldn't know because you weren't there. Because you went down the street to the Irish bar to drink with Moonface and Sheridan.'

'Only because Gregory closed early last night,' I pleaded.

'That's right, Gregory-Smegory, why did you close so early?' Eggy thundered.

Gregory smiled an apologetic and somewhat harassed smile, Cassandra tending to the ferns, Elias going about in circles, beyond the help of rhyme or reason.

‘That’s right,’ Eggy went on, ‘he closed early. So Bob and I go back to the Traymore. Eleanor was going to have us over—’

‘But I fell asleep,’ said Eleanor, ‘can you imagine that, me falling asleep on New Year’s Eve?’

‘So there she was, Marjerie, that is, there she was starkers except for that, what do you call it, that pink thing—’

‘Boa,’ said Eleanor, supplying a word.

‘Yes. There she was wearing nothing but that boa, packing a sidearm, walking up and down the hall. She was, hoo hoo, you know—’

‘She was kissing it—’

‘Yes, kissing it. Hoo hoo.’

‘She was kissing the gun?’ I asked.

‘Yes,’ replied Eggy, ‘she was, you know, intimate with it.’

‘So these are the unassailable facts,’ I said, a bit dubious.

‘Of course,’ thundered Eggy.

‘I have to say it’s what I saw,’ Dubois said, in support of a tiny sparrow of a man.

‘Well,’ I said, ‘then what?’

Miss Meow and her companion were miaowing. The Whistler whistled and stomped. I had warned Eggy and Dubois not to go on about the recent business in Gaza because the sight of the man gloating might put me over the edge. It was bitter cold out. We, convened indoors, would make up, that afternoon, for what had been lacking the entire year previous: libations raised to the spectre of hope. For now was the year and now was the month Current President went his merry way to his legacy and President Elect would take office.

‘Well, now I’m not sure. What happened, Bob?’ Eggy asked.

Dubois cleared his throat, his red cheeks florid, their hairline cracks emblematic of a man who, despite his recent travail, was vastly entertained.

‘It seems,’ he said, ‘that as I stood there, trying to get to the bottom of her intention or intentions, whatever they may have been, you hustled yourself into your apartment. Eleanor, like she said, was sleeping—’

‘It was a nice dream I was having,’ Eleanor confirmed.

‘And then I went into my apartment, debating whether or not to call the police. Or maybe I could bluff it out with her and get a hold of the gun. Then Ralph and Phillip showed up. And I thought, good, she’s their charge. That was going to be the end of it. She started to go back into her place.

They couldn't see she had a gun as her back was turned to them. So I had words with Ralph. "She's got a gun. Do something about her." Ralph's face went white. Phillip just laughed. What a guy that guy is.'

'And that's when you came to wake me up and tell me,' Eleanor now kicked in, 'that she had an effing gun. So I got all the sleep out of my eyes and called the police. You can't screw around with that. I didn't want to see another corpse in the Traymore. One was enough. Then I thought, well, I should lock the door. Then we wondered, Bob and I, whom she meant to shoot. And then Bob said he thought Ralph could handle it. And I said I wasn't so sure, and Phillip might be so drunk he just might cause something to get out of hand.'

Dubois resumed the narrative: 'So I went over there, which was kind of stupid. I was pretty nervous.'

Dubois guffawed.

'Our hero,' Eggy beamed.

'Hang on til I get back,' Eleanor said, throwing on a coat to go out for a puff.

'Me, too,' I said.

'Here, I'm getting to the nitty-gritty, and you're going to have a smoke break—'

Dubois was incredulous.

'Effing hell. Where's Moonface? Effing wench,' Eggy thundered.

We her only customers, Moonface had been in the restroom.

'Settle down,' said Dubois, mildly rebuking a god.

'Good god,' I said to Eleanor once we were outside.

'Don't we know,' she answered, cupping the flame of my lighter with her hands, and inclining her head to it, 'first the Lamonts, then Osgoode, now this.'

I had nearly forgotten them, those previous tenants of the Traymore whose antics had incurred a police presence.

'I just don't get her, I really don't,' said Eleanor in respect to Prentiss.

'Nor I,' I agreed.

'I'll tell you what I think,' said Eleanor, and crisply at that, 'she didn't want to shoot anybody. She wanted to scare someone, and I think she wanted to scare Bob. Because I followed him in, you know. Because, oh I don't know, I couldn't just let Bob... well... anyway, that's what I did, I followed him in, and there was Ralph trying to talk her into giving him the gun. Phillip just stood there, swigging from a beer, smoking a cigarette. But he was watching her very closely. As soon as Bob shows up, the look she gave him. If looks could kill and all that. I mean, she pointed that thing right at him. For a minute there, I thought Bob was going to faint. I nearly did. "What in effing hell are you doing," I yelled at her. She ignored me. Bob motioned me to shut up. Then Bob said the police had been called and they were coming. That's when Marjerie gave Bob the gears about being French and thinking himself so clever when really, he was just full of himself, a know-it-all. Come on, let's go back inside. I'm frozen through.'

So back in we went, Eleanor and me. Evidently, Dubois and Eggy had now gotten Moonface up to speed.

'You're kidding,' she was saying, rolling her eyes up and to the side, yes, in that way she has.

How far away she had gotten from Traymorean life. Good for her, I supposed. Even so, I was not so sure.

'Anyway,' said Eleanor, 'I got Randall up to the point where we were in Marjerie's and she was aiming the gun at you.'

'She wasn't going to shoot me,' Dubois avowed, and then was interrupted once more, as Moonface went to settle a customer's bill, her hips swaying slightly.

Dubois waited, and Eleanor studied his face. Perhaps it was a face she loved, though the universe was so vast nothing in it was certain.

'But she was pointing the gun at you,' Moonface burbled, returned now.

'Yes she was, as a matter of fact,' said Dubois, 'so I tried to talk to her. I said I didn't know what she had going on inside her head, but that she couldn't be serious—'

'And she said she was,' Eleanor interjected, matter of fact.

'Hoo hoo,' said Eggy, 'I'm sorry I missed that.'

'No you're not,' Dubois replied, 'and I'm sorry I didn't miss it.'

Moonface, to top up our glasses, poured. She and I exchanged glances.

'So, what happened?' I asked.

'So I said, well, I didn't know what to say. So I said the first thing that came into my head. I said, "What's being French got to do with it?" And she said the French beat their wives. "Really," I said, "my father didn't. If anything, my mother beat him up. But they loved each other." I guess she didn't believe me. Then she just sort of started shaking and she lowered her arm, and Ralph stepped up and grabbed it, and anyway, the gun wasn't loaded. That's when I felt like slapping her one.'

'I could've slapped her,' Eleanor observed.

'And then the police came,' Dubois continued, 'and then all the questions. And then, well, did we have to charge her? They thought I should. It's a very serious matter, playing around with a firearm. I said I didn't want to press any charges. They could do what they had to do. So they took her to the station, I guess, and Ralph and Phillip went along. And that's all we know.'

'Rot your socks,' I said, raising my glass.

'The rain in Spain. Always,' said Eggy, tuckered out.

A Letter

Montreal, Qc., Canada
The First Night of the New Year

To: Evie Longoria
To be hand-delivered to her at the Blue Danube when circumstances allow
Subject: Elucubrations

Dear Evie, and holder (apparently) of the secret key to the secret door to you know where, my heart,

It's cold outside, today, very cold, and you are in Mexico. Therefore, as it is, today, in Montreal, weather to which we are regularly subjected, we, meaning I, finally get around to the shared project of us staying in touch, and to this end, here I am (in my West Wing, so to speak) writing you a letter so that you will not be able to totally forget us, despite your best efforts.

We don't quite know what the fall-out will be, but a major event has taken place in this our distinguished residential establishment with which you were familiar in your capacity as Eggy's house-cleaner and chauffeur (indeed, Eggy misses you though he refuses to admit it, his Haitian nurse and all other such women having long since abandoned him, and yes, Eggy is still among the living); but that Marjerie Prentiss, pseudo-Traymorean—perhaps you don't recall her—went, how shall I put it, bananas, was walking around the residential hall in a state of undress, excepting the boa, that is, and the gun, and well, it's pretty complicated to explain. I have come to believe she was sleep-walking in a way and meant no one any harm. Eggy said she was wearing her BMB, which is to say, her boff me boa, but she had no takers. Calhoun—remember him?—has no opinion. Eleanor thinks I was the intended victim. Enough said.

Our preferred hangout is still the same place, and we, we residents of the Traymore Rooms, still prefer to call it The Blue Danube, though the effing Greeks and Albanians would run the place into the ground as Le Grec. Our table, which you were often eager to join, even when we were busy discussing state matters, now has a name, courtesy of moi, which for sure you will find most appropriate: Animal Table. Mostly, it remains attended by one Arthur Eglinton, Eggy to you (this Yank you know as an exile from a sorry place) one Calhoun, Randall Q (another Yank immigrated to Canada to get away from the Evil Empire and a bucking poet about to come into his own after a writing career of some 40+ years), and a French-Canadian (Canadian nevertheless who thinks we need Jean Chrétien to return to the helm in these uncertain times as he was, like me, Shawinigan-born). We entertain visitors sometimes, particularly when we think that such a visitor might have a contribution to offer, like a good intellect, or plenty of good quality wine. Not too many have made the grade to membership so far; sorry you do not come often enough for us to come to some favourable assessment, but had you, we would have fast-tracked you straight to the chairwoman's chair. In the summer, of course, the said Animal Table moves to the terrasse when the sun is out, and then back inside when the rain hits. A very favourable arrangement. Calhoun calls it our grandeur. If you want clarification on this matter, you will have to take it up with him. It's too bad you're in Mexico. By the way, Eggy is in love again. He might have given you to think you were the only one, but sorry to say, you were not. It is believed that he might be trying to hit on a new black nurse or the beautiful doctor he met when at Verdun Emergency. Can't blame him; she was beautiful. And Moonface aka Emma MacReady, your friend and ours, is very soon leaving for South America with her beau on, they say, an academic expedition. There is some question in Eggy's mind as to the pose she'll strike on the beaches. We are afraid that Moonface will never be the same again when and if she returns, given what might catch her over there.

We hope that your health is fine; surely it must be.

The others of the Traymorean menagerie are doing fine. Mrs Petrova, as per Calhoun, is an immortal.

We hope that, if this letter reaches you despite the unpredictability of the snail mail, you will write to us of your exotic (I almost said erotic) experiences in Mexico.

Have a great 2009.

Friendly regards.

Robert Dubois
Traymore Rooms
Montreal, Qc., Canada

§

Part Five

Moonface Returns

Book I—The Page Turned

Chicago School of Physics

Who can know what is around the next corner? Edward Sanders, aka Fast Eddy, happened to turn a corner and went smack against a sparrow in flight. It was the rudest of surprises, and then he died. Marjerie Prentiss stays elsewhere, for the time being, either with her mother or with Ralph, her intended, in the Townships. It was necessary that she go. Dubois considered she had not been in her right mind. Right mind or not, the police pointed out she had had no license for the firearm she waved about, starkers in the Traymore hall. The inevitable ologists perhaps have had their way with the woman. Robert Dubois, impossibly vain and handsome in his 66th year is, even so, less vain and less handsome of late, the result perhaps of what he calls cluster headaches. He had suffered from them mightily prior to the time I arrived on the scene, and now they have returned, the pain so intense he lies on his bathroom floor dry-heaving for hours on end. Eleanor R, the long time apple of his eye, she simply leaves him to it, unable to bear the spectacle of his discomfort. Arthur Eglinton on the other hand, Eggy to Traymoreans, in his 82nd or 83rd year—I have lost track—is hale and hearty, so to speak. He has had his little episodes and his little strokes and still, all bundled up, stutter-stepping with his cane, afterburners switched on, he makes his trek from the Traymore to the Blue Danube almost daily, and drinks his wine and holds forth. His memory of verses is not, as it turns out, as limitless as it has seemed: he repeats himself, but no matter. Good verses can stand the repeating. A new president sits in the White House; and though, one's expectations rise and fall like a yo-yo on a string, at least the man is not as despised as was the previous occupant. We are a few days shy of Valentine's Day. The air reeks of rotting snow. For the time being, it looks like Phillip Dundarave will hold down Prentiss's apartment, he one of her stalwart swains who very nearly wrecked Eleanor's relations with Dubois. My name is Randall Q Calhoun. A student sublets Moonface's digs while she is away in Ecuador.

Runaway Train

Life moved too fast for the critical conscience. By the time one worked out the nature of one's relations to A; by the time one established whether or not one could live in some uneasy peace with an obscenity, the world had already put B in one's path, and one flailed one's arms about. The futility of it all. In any case, I joined Dubois in the Blue Danube. Glowering afternoon. Dirty snow on the streets.

'Well,' I said, 'what's the word on your headaches?'

'Catastrophe,' he answered, leaning on the French pronunciation of the word.

He had had to cancel his breakfast engagement with an ex-prime minister, a childhood friend of his, also a Shawiniganite. They would try again but Dubois was not holding his breath. He compared his pains to the birthing pains of women in labour. I suggested he ought not make too much of a point of that; women might resent the comparison. Antonio, the Albanian-Italian waiter set a grilled cheese sandwich on the table. Antonio's dream was to play for a great soccer team. AC Roma, for example. Antonio awaited our customary badinage, but as none was forthcoming, he drifted into the galley where Gregory the owner was cooking. It seemed that he, along with his partner Elias, had made a go of things with the place. How a possible recession would affect business remained to be seen. Cassandra, wife to Elias, was also in the galley. She had the body of a fertility goddess. She was tired, and she was biting her tongue. I said I had a bad feeling about things. Dubois arched his brows. He knew what was coming: politics.

'Israel is tacking hard right,' I said, 'and you know what that means.'

'Yes,' said Dubois, 'so what does it mean?'

His tone indicated he did not much care. And I knew better than to insist. As for Moonface—classical scholar, waitress, would-be sexpot and now, world traveller—no one had heard from her. She had, however, airmailed our way a snapshot of herself *c/o* Le Grec aka the Blue Danube. It showed her posing on the scree of some Ecuadorian mountain. There was no way of telling from the somewhat diffident smile whether she was in good spirits or bad. It would seem the dear girl continued feckless, even in an exotic landscape. Eggy was sure she would ditch her Champagne Sheridan there, and return to us, her true companions, wiser for the experience.

Yes, and now that Moonface had been absent from us for some weeks, it could be determined, however imperfectly, to what extent she was central to the lives of Traymorean males. There were fewer erotic burblings, perhaps, to do with her sandy hair and prominent incisors and modest bosom and child-bearing hips; but she had, even so, pride of place in our hearts. By virtue of her presence, if nothing else, she was always putting us in mind of our less than noble pasts. She was sharpening our views of what the future might portend, for in wishing her well, we would speculate as to what obstacles might complicate her happiness. Eggy pretended not to take her absence amiss. No, he would note that the café did not seem as well run as when she waitressed, patient and polite with her customers even as she parried our raillery. And he would go on about the poor review a performance of Verdi's *MacBeth* had recently received; and then, with one of his rabbit leaps of logic, he would speak of Haitian Nurse—a charming young woman of his acquaintance—and how, ambitious, she was intent on rising in the world of medicine; and how, in her busy schedule, she managed to fit in visitations from the man (alas, not Eggy) whose sole purpose in life was to attend to her sexual needs. Cozy arrangement, so Eggy reflected. Eggy had had his wives and mistresses, but one might conjecture that the course of love and lust in his life had not run as smoothly as he might have liked. Well, Dubois was suffering. All the world could see it was so, he holding his head as if it were the most fragile of flowers, attempting to entice the pain to go elsewhere. The trademark hairline cracks of his cheeks which had, however inexplicably, given him a somewhat distinguished air, seemed to be widening into chasms.

By reputation the finest of all the Traymore rooms, Eleanor's kitchen had become a home away from home for me. It was her salon; it was, at times, a trysting-site. She was crocheting when I entered, having left Dubois in the café, he wondering if he might just curl up in a fetal position on its floor.

'Lampshade,' said Eleanor, she of the gilded curls and revealing blouses and flambouyant skirts and pompadours.

'But it's not human skin,' she drolled morbidly.

What PBS documentary had she been watching?

'I'm relieved to hear it,' I said.

'Bob's having another attack of those headaches,' I continued.

'Oh that. Well, he'll be lost to us for a while,' she sighed.

'Is Dundarave now a full-timer among us?' I asked.

'No idea,' Eleanor said, with exaggerated innocence.

She and Dundarave had been almost an item.

'In fact,' she went on to say, 'I think he's found himself a woman.'

'Not Jarnette?'

I saw in my mentations a smiling and confident looker of rich chestnut tresses with whom I had had a brief episode.

'She's moved on to other pastures, I should think. Phillip's going to bring his new flame around for me to check out.'

Eleanor's tone seemed utterly neutral. And I rolled myself a cigarette and I was suffered to roll Eleanor one, as well. I turned down her offer of an amaretto.

'Well, I'm having one,' she announced.

And she lay her crocheting on the table and went to the cupboard for her supply of the amber; and she dispensed some into a brandy snifter.

'Are you sure?' I was asked.

I was sure. Perhaps it was an hallucination: sunlight salon of hardwood flooring and high, mullioned windows. Tall and leafy plants. Grand piano. Some Noel Coward-like figure in a white smoking jacket having at Debussy. The beautiful Sally McCabe playing peek-a-boo from behind a Chinese folding screen, large birds and arbutus painted on it. She was an on again, off again visitation in my thoughts. We had been at Polson High together so long, long ago, down there in an America the most peaceful rustics of which were lethal.

'So what do you think of Suzie Q?' I inquired of Eleanor, shaking off the vision.

The student subletting Moonface's apartment went by the name of Susan, cognomen unknown.

'I think she was warned off us by Moonface. She's minding her own beeswax, and anyway, she's rather plain and broad in the beam—'

'Yes, but she's bright, or she looks that way. Moonface said she was one of the more dedicated students in her classic's class.'

'Well, maybe you two will have something to talk about one of these days. Who was it? Virgil? The poet, you know, you were always going on about?'

'The very same.'

'Virgil Shmirgil. Anyway, I'd say we've had enough excitement in the old Traymore to last us a while. And I'll be very surprised if Moonface hangs around when she gets back. You guys aren't getting any younger, and she's waking up to the fact she's got a life to live. I mean, Eggy grabbing at her tush non-stop—is that a life?'

Unable to settle down to any work in my digs, I retreated to the Blue Danube, a Traymorean watering-hole. I did however add to the hopeless incoherence of my notebooks that little salon-interlude, the hallucination that waylaid me in Eleanor's kitchen. I had not actually heard the music. Debussy's *Canope*? Eggy and Dubois were hammering out the terms of a wager, Dubois looking freer in his countenance.

'Let's get this straight,' he said, 'by this time next year, if Canada shows a GDP rate of growth at 3.5 per cent or better, you'll pay me 50 bucks?'

'That's the general idea,' Eggy said.

He was wearing a dark sports jacket of thick tweed, a royal-purple one-point kerchief peeking out of the pocket. Natty, Zeus-like Eggy. It was Dubois who had been showing his age, of late.

'And I suppose Moonface is on her backside somewhere on white sand, looking up at the stars. *I will lift up mine eyes unto the hills—*'

'Sacrilege, Eggy,' I observed, 'the way you intend it.'

'Well, why not? Effing hell. *From whence cometh my help—*'

It occurred to me that, earlier, Eleanor had not made the slightest attempt to flirt with me. This was new. And Eggy was old, 902 years of sin and meanness and angelic cheer.

'You'll renege as you always do,' said Dubois.

'I beg your pardon.'

Eggy was chuffed. Now Antonio stroked Eggy's pate.

'We love you,' said the waiter.

'Oh eff off.'

'Well,' I said, 'the new Current President, you know, the Unflappable One, the one in whom millions of wretches have invested hope, he's at the controls of a runaway train.'

'Who asked you?' Dubois put it to me.

'Oh, I think he's right,' Eggy said, his finger raised.

'That's all I need,' Dubois noted, 'two more pundits righter than rain.'

Had I misjudged Marjerie Prentiss? Was she such a loathsome creature as she seemed? Was she not just looking for love in the way any weed seeks the light of the sun? Could she, over time, learn to be less repellant? How failed was my failure? That I had not written *Hamlet*, let alone "Easter, 1916". That I would lie on my bordello-green couch and my bones mock my sentience. That morning, Mrs Petrova, as she always did, arranged her gewgaws for display in her shop window, she in curlers, a bloom on her cheeks, and great age. It did not look like she knew the meaning of failure.

'Yes,' said Dubois, 'two more effing opinionators.'

I left my two colleagues arguing Wolfe and Montcalm and the Plains of Abraham. They would be on about it until the last star flamed out in the galaxy. It was their immortality. Then again, Eggy, about to get bested in the exercise of logic, would abruptly shift gears, and waving his arms, indicate that a certain coterie of bastards ought to hang. Hoo hoo. But Dubois, of late, seemed to have lost interest in the evils of the American empire: torture, greed, hubris, whatnot beyond measure. In any case, as I went up the Traymore stairs, Susan the new lodger was coming down them. I greeted a pair of wary eyes of indeterminate colour. Eleanor was wrong: this Susan was not as plain as all that, her bulky winter coat giving her the appearance of being broad in the beam. I made way for her descent. She might have thanked me; she did not. And yet, as she reached the bottom of the stairs, she turned, and looking up at me, said: 'You're Randall, aren't you?'

'That I am.'

'Oh.'

She pushed through the door into the small foyer and then, presumably, gained the street. Her voice was not unpleasant. As I was about to unlock my door, Eleanor popped her head out hers and motioned me her way.

'I've got company,' she whispered, 'help me.'

A strange woman was at table in Eleanor's kitchen. Phillip Dundarave, beer and cigarette in hand, was pacing the floor like a caged bear. Women found him attractive. He had the air of a man in whom rage and shyness were always vying for the upper hand. Wanda Schneider was a stunner to look at, and yet, she left me cold. It was a mystery to me why some women, however advantaged with physical charms, simply did not move me, when even women who some might consider homely could turn my knees to jelly. Moonface was no beauty in the accepted notion of the word, and yet she had captured every iota of my being.

'Wanda, this is Randall,' Eleanor said, and she seemed unaccountably stiff in tone.

'Hello,' I said, and the woman and I exchanged nods.

I thought her a tennis player, perhaps. Tanned, athletic-looking. Sharp, clean features.

Sally McCabe Presents Moonface

I had need of music, whiskey, a smoke. I gave Eleanor a look which she knew well, and she did not press me to stay; Wanda Schneider itemizing her interests in life: real estate and hiking. She had met Phillip some years ago in the Townships, employing him to do carpentry work on her cottage. They had a fling, and now, it seemed they had resumed relations. For the well-heeled, sex often seems an entitlement.

'Take care,' I said to Phillip's air of menace, as I initiated my exit.

He was bored with the conversation.

'Pleased to have met you,' I added, addressing his new bedmate, Wanda Schneider regarding me with speculative eyes.

In my digs, I collapsed on my couch and closed my eyes, foregoing the music and the whiskey. Before long, a familiar voice was gently teasing me, and it belonged to green-sweatered Sally McCabe, cheerleader, beauty, daughter of a VIP.

'Randall, you poor boy, at sixes and sevens, it seems. Who will feed your fantasias now, Moonface in Ecuador, Prentiss not in her right mind, Eleanor observing the straight and narrow? Wasn't there someone else, as well? What was her name? Evie Longoria? Who went to Mexico over the holidays and hasn't been heard from since? No, I don't know what's happened to her, if anything. As for Wanda Schneider, new talent, the new Wonder Girl, she's another—like Prentiss—another phenom incapable of love. She does it for the prestige, and what's prestigious is, but of course, herself. That she would latch on to Dundarave makes sense, if you think about it. He comes from a good family. Had a decent education. He just got weary of the conventions of his class, hence the James Dean schtick he's never outgrown. Or he's like the man in *Mildred Pierce*, the Beragon guy, who claimed he lost his awe of women at an early age and is not sentimental about them. Dundarave probably sees that the way in which Schneider is a head case can't be undone and so, the easy sex, no ological muss, Schneider much too busy polishing her image to notice he really doesn't think much of her. Is this a fair estimation of things as they currently stack up? Well, you've always got me, kid. The war in Iraq seems to be winding down. The new president is getting the feel of things. You'd think something like sanity is gradually seeping back into the collective psyche, but you and I know better, don't we? In any case, it's not me you want. And to show you I've always had your best interests in mind and that my heart's in the right place, I give you Moonface. Here she is, your long-bellied goddess up on her tippy-toes, wending her way towards you. She's been having a good time down there, no question. Even so, sometimes, she's afraid and not sure why. It might have something to do with her Champagne Sheridan who loves her, yes, but it's, how to say it, an uninspired kind of love. She needs you just now. Your tenderness. Your irascibility. The way you get on your pedagogical horse and will be avuncular with her. The way you have even, at times, touched her, for all that you're old enough to be her father. She's calling to you. "Q," she's saying, her voice slightly musical, her eyes rolling, her red nails flashing, "I think I'm in trouble. Everything's cool, but, I don't know, it should be better. Nothing but blank pages in my new diary.'

Dundarave Settles In

Sunny afternoon, snow receding from the streets, and Eggy's call that it would be an early spring looked to be correct. The Schneider woman knocked on my door, and before I knew it, she was presenting me the glories of her body in my bed. She had the air of a woman in a rush to make last-minute purchases, lest some scheme of hers go in want of attention to details. I have no idea why she figured I could add lustre to her polished self-absorption, but there it was; and it was not a crime, what transpired, but that the world was basically absurd.

'This will not happen again,' she informed me, her tone clinical, she putting on her clothes.

'I don't expect it will,' I answered, just a touch chuffed.

It seemed I was checking a certain quadrant of the sky for the imminent storm that had already come to pass, blown over, and now was all pleasant breezes in a landscape of ruin.

No doubt, she and Phillip Dundarave were perfect for one another, each a predator who sheared rather than butchered. And yet, I was beginning to think that, in comparison, Marjerie Prentiss, the poor dear, was just one of those women who went through life misunderstood. There was no mistaking Schneider, intimacy not high on her list of priorities, let alone a debate over American foreign policy and the philosophical overview of Ayn Rand, that whore with a heart of rhinestone at whom Socrates, open to all comers, would have looked askance. Now standing at the window at the end of the Traymore Hall, Schneider gone, I saw a crow steal some item of food from where a squirrel had evidently stashed it, the squirrel chasing the bird out of the back lane tree. A section of pizza crust dangled from that crow beak. The Eggy and Dubois apartments were quiet. Eleanor opened her door and regarded me with a withering look. Now and then, even for her, man crazy as she was, men were disgusting creatures and not to be trusted. I was sorry to be, in this instance, the source of the male gender's bad reputation. I shrugged. Downstairs, at street level, the door banged open. I heard Dundarave's voice and the sound of boxes slid along the floor. He was giving instructions to someone. He was propping open the foyer door as I stood at the top of the stairs and called down: 'Need any help?'

'I already got it,' Dundarave answered, not batting an eye.

I recognized a couple of hosers from Drunkin' Donuts, the doughnut franchise nearby.

I worried that Dundarave had caught sight of Schneider as she left the Traymore; if he had, it did not seem to bother him.

'You know,' Dundarave grunted, lifting a box from the floor, 'I'm not really moving in. Just looking after the place. For Marj.'

What, was she returning?

Eggy had a gift for social intercourse. And when I gave him the news in the Blue Danube that Dundarave looked to be staying on, he was nonplussed.

'Well,' he said, somewhat archly, 'another toper. The more the merrier.'

He was sweetly oblivious to the implications. That Prentiss had gone about the Traymore brandishing a gun was as much something to be remarked upon as was his conviction that Moonface had been born to live her life on her backside. That Prentiss was the centrepiece of a threesome, Dundarave one of her bookends, was simply one phenomenon among others, as in the way crows were black as opposed to red, and that the previous vice-president ought to be impeached if not hung upside down à la Mussolini. To what extent Eggy had shed his West Virginia upbringing I could not say. Eggy would point out his politics had always been left of centre, and he was a Quebecker though his French was atrocious. I did not see any point in relating to this homunculus the recent Calhoun-Schneider episode. He was sure to respond with something crass. He would cast through his mind for the most polite way of rendering a vulgarity, and then inquire: 'Well, did she give your knob a good rub?'

Korea had been his war; for Eggy, it had been the beginning of things going wrong. In fact, he and I, American expatriates both, had a curious way of regarding Americans. They were to us exotic life forms. I saw them as if I were a ghost looking at Romans through a palace window on the Palatine or catching street scenes in the Suburra. Tacitus and I. F. Stone could have been an instance of transmigration of souls, so far as I was concerned, for all that the former had been circumspect in the reign of the paranoid Domitian and the latter could breathe so much more freely in respect to Nixon's administration. Even so, it was not good to push the Rome-Washington analogy too far.

'Well,' asked Eggy, 'do you think Moonface will come back to us?'

'Why wouldn't she?'

'Effing hell. I don't know. Seems to me she was happy to be quit of us or she would've been back, by now.'

'Yes, I doubt we're that big a deal in her life.'

'You boffed her, didn't you?'

Eggy was peering up at me with mischievous eyes.

'What makes you say that?'

'Bob told me.'

'Bob doesn't know anything. He doesn't know what happened.'

'Well, he was there, wasn't he, when the bunch of you went down to Toronto?'

'So what? We all got drunk on the night of the poetry reading and Moonface couldn't sleep, afterwards, and she came to me and we just sort of, how can I say it, hung out.'

'Hung out? Is that what you call it, these days?'

Cassandra was waitressing, she wife to Elias, one of the owners. She appeared at our table to check on us.

'Homesick?' I ventured to ask her, noting the look in her large eyes.

'A lot,' she answered, vaguely quantifying homesickness.

'I really miss it, you know,' she added, 'family, climate, life-style.'

She walked away.

'She's certainly getting more comfortable with the language,' Eggy noted, his finger raised in the air, 'hoo hoo.'

His all-time favourite movie was *My Fair Lady*. All women, according to his lights, were diamonds in the rough who wanted education. Sometimes I wondered if the ancient chauvinist had not the interests of women more sincerely at heart than the progressives of my generation.

Busman's Holiday

I boarded a bus at the downtown terminal and was driven east through the cornlands and into the hills. Twittering cell phones. Conversational hum. That sissing sound of hideous music being relayed by wires from portable CD players to human ears. Light snow squalls added to the thin crust of snow on the fields. Birches, spruce. Powerful-looking crows. In a town at the top end of a long finger of lake extending into Vermont, I rented a hotel room. The room was stark but not entirely shabby, the exterior of the hotel pink. My original intention had been to stay at a nearby monastery and exist in silence and purge some demons; perhaps I was carrying around one too many. Even so, I figured I would only have felt foolish in such surroundings, and besides, I considered I did not have in me an iota of spiritual talent. A man could come to no less devastating conclusions about himself in a lounge over a drink as in a penitential cell. So I drank and watched TV. Now and then I braved the lakefront and the cold wind; walked and regarded the Catholic steeples of the town with a wary eye. Now and then I smiled at the hotel staff so as to reassure them I was not entirely mad. It seemed a plan. In my dreams I had tempestuous sex with Sally McCabe, and she seemed grateful. *Calhoun, there's more in your quiver than has met the eye.* And then she and I would attend some Roman dinner party of a dying breed of pagan luminaries. Late 4th century. And someone would quote Virgil and someone else would tut-tut, and swallowing the grapes he had ingested, quote instead from the scatological novel of Petronius. And yet another debauchee would ruefully note that the glory days had killed Rome, but that they had been glorious days, nonetheless. McCabe and I, holding hands like two teenagers on the verge of falling in love, would find the world—even as it was on the precipice of calamity—a beautiful spectacle. I hardly noticed that while it was McCabe who had always been plotting my return to the American desert, I had somehow turned the tables on her, bringing her to Rome for more than just a tourist's experience. After two days, I had enough of this self-imposed solitude and time away from Traymoreans, and I took the bus back to the city. And on the return drive I realized that I had hardly given Gareth Howard, my oldest friend, dead now, a thought. He had a shack in the area near the American border where we used to drink and carry on like a couple of prophets so terribly sure that things were fatally amiss and could not be set straight. I saw the lovely Clare Howard in my mentations who had had to put up with Gar's travels and his rage. He had been a foreign correspondent. She, I believe, did not deny him his truths but would have preferred a life and a marriage less obsessed with politics and his wandering. Old, old water now under an old, old bridge. And perhaps even more to the point: one's thoughts, however laden with regret and something like sorrow, matter so very little. Crows pecked at roadkill by the side of the highway. What I had seen of Quebec so far, when it was not drearily suburbanized, was a haunting place. The Old World that had come here was still in evidence; it was the New World that looked so provisional as one crossed over the Champlain Bridge and saw the downtown office towers seemingly frosted in the frigid air; as one thought hockey and beer and Jesuits. Vendors of grilled sausages and hot mulled wine might add a little extra colour to wintry Ste Catherine's.

I paid my first call on Eleanor, she of the gilded curls and reliable welcome. But I found her pensive, she crocheting in her kitchen, her small black and white TV tuned to a melodrama, the sound muted.

'What's up?' I asked blithely.

TV ghosts with consummate cleavage confronted ghosts who looked virile but seemed suspiciously effeminate.

'Things,' Eleanor answered.

'Things,' I echoed.

'You know,' Eleanor went on, somewhat agonized, 'no Bob. He's been locked in his apartment for two days. I don't know if His Nibs is alive or dead. And Marjerie called. And then Ralph, who's still her intended, wouldn't you know. And I had a visit from Phillip, and that was strange. When it rains it pours.'

'So how's Marjerie?' I asked, unsure if I truly wished to know.

Eleanor set down her little project. She stuck her chest out and sighed.

'I suppose,' she said, 'you'll be wanting a little of the amber. It'll cost you a ciggie.'

But she made no move to procure the precious liquid.

'Well,' she said, 'can you believe it? The wench has been having coke parties out there in the boonies. Ralph has had enough of her antics. Phillip flipped his lid when he heard of it. Called her a useless cunt. Cocaine had cost him his wife and a stint in rehab. I guess you didn't know.'

'No, I had no idea.'

'Yes, and then Marjerie tells me she laid it on a bit thick when she was telling me tales of how her brother used to fool with her. There wasn't any, oh what's the word, penetration. As if I didn't know the word. He'd bring his pals around, and, as a way of returning the favours they'd done him, he'd get her to perform some little show. But you know, *entre nous*, I think she got to like it. Anyhow, Ralph has had enough. Had it up to here. But I told you that. Don't get me wrong—I like the woman, but she can be such a cow, at times. And Phillip came over, and guess what he asked me? Asked me if I wanted to see him naked. I mean, he's a grown man. What gives? And no, I didn't want to see Mr Drop Dead Gorgeous naked. But yes, I did, I'm sorry to say. He has the body of a god. And he got stripped off and then this silly grin got a hold of his face, and he was all shy and sheepish, and then he said he was very tired and heartsick. Can you imagine it—that man using the word heartsick? So, could we just lie down together and not do anything, just lie there? So we did, and we didn't do anything. And I don't think I slept a wink, but he slept. Slept like a man who was at long last at peace. Just that, when I tried to sneak out of bed, his arm wouldn't let me go. That was last night, as a matter of fact. And then this morning, he starts up again about Marjerie, that she hadn't got the brains God gave a goose. That if she continued messing around with coke he would never ever want to see her again, and I think he meant it. I know you don't think much of him, but he has some honour in him, a kind of honour, if you can call it that. He said he never intended to sleep with me because of Bob. Sure, he'd flirt. He didn't think that was against the rules. Come to think of it, Randall, it was you who caved, dear boy. I'll bet you're missing Moonface.'

'Well, if you're not going to offer me some of the amber, I think I'll—'

Eleanor shimmied to the cupboard.

'Here,' she said, 'is this what you had in mind?'

I had my drink with Eleanor, our conversation drifting into generalities. To do with the new presidency and the state of capitalism. She was surprised, and yet not so very surprised, that things had turned out as they had. She once worked for a powerful man of business (she had been his mistress, as well, and it was an agreeable arrangement); and though the gentleman had not missed opportunities to turn a buck to profit, he had been somewhat uneasy in respect to where the financial world had seemed to be heading.

'I don't know,' I said, 'but from the outside looking in, it looks like a world of unconscionable greed and not much else.'

'I was on the inside for a while,' Eleanor said, 'and it's not exactly that. Business is a game some people like to play. For my boss, money was just a way of keeping score. But yes, there was a darker side, and I met plenty of men, and women, too, who gave me the shivers. They just didn't care. Not one jot. Then I met Bob. It wasn't that he was some rebel who was going to change how things were done, but he wasn't blind, either, to the realities. Anyway, we clicked, and that's the story of my life. Some life, say what? You'd better go. I can feel a crying jag coming on.'

'Oh dear.'

I pecked her cheek and left. And I went out the Traymore and across the street—to the video store. I rented the movie *W*, a biographical treatment of Previous President. On the Traymore stairs I met Suzy Q, a knapsack slung around her shoulders. She was headed for the library. I said I intended to watch a movie later on, and I told her what it was about.

'I despise that man,' she said, cheerfully enough.

'Well, if you're at loose ends, come over and we'll watch it together.'

Her eyes narrowed.

'It's an innocent invitation,' I said, a trifle irked.

'Really?' she answered.

And she wondered if there was such an item in the panoply of man-woman relations.

'Suit yourself,' I shrugged, 'but if you hear me throwing large objects around in my apartment, you'll know it got to me.'

She went by with a show of bravado, I some ludicrous impediment to her plans. In any case, I figured I might let Eleanor know of my plans. The movie might take her mind off her unhappiness. If she figured that eight years of 'W' had been enough, what were two more hours? In other words, to mark some time, she just might come over, her Bob still incommunicado.

Conquest and Empire

Left of centre critics had panned the flick. I could see why. Its shallow portraitures, for starters. The premises underpinning the quest of the American Dream pretty much unassailed. Suzie Q saw in the once upon a time president only a callow male whose overweening boyishness was repugnant to her; she could not in the slightest see why women were attracted to the man. Eleanor, I figured, saw a deeper picture, but if so, she kept silent on it, noting only that the movie version of the First Lady made her out more intelligent than she seemed in actual fact. I saw that Suzie Q was not quite the dowdy creature Eleanor had described her as being; she was simply a shorter version of Eleanor's body-type, if a tad more thick in the hips. Eyes set wide apart. Open countenance. It did not embarrass her to let one know she was a serious-minded young woman of definite opinions on the progressive side of issues. So then, whence her interest in the classics? Looking for chinks in the armor of those ancient world-dominating males? I saw hooded figures, deer park conclaves of intriguers and assassins, all zealots. I figured, dread in me, that certain chickens had not, as yet, completely come home to roost. Or that the rose petals a once-upon-a- time president had so assiduously strewn about the world's exotic parts were not yet emptied of their fragrance: unquantifiable miseries, violent deaths.

How did Marjerie Prentiss come by the weapon with which she half-frightened Dubois out of his arch-materialist notions of causation? When I treated with the episode in my notebooks, it had not occurred to me to inquire of anyone who might know. For all that, Dubois was sequestering himself in his rooms, and on the evening following, I found Eggy all by himself in the Blue Danube, his back against the wall.

'Have you heard from Moonface?' he asked, happy to have company.

'Well, Bob hasn't,' he went on to say, 'and I haven't. If you ask me her Champagne Sheridan, her Merry-Sherry lad, is censoring her mail. Why else wouldn't we have heard from her? Or else he's got her on her backside 24/7.'

'Perhaps,' I said, 'she isn't interested in us. Perhaps she's too busy with whatever her duties are down there, and I don't mean servicing her beau. If you recall, she was to be part of a crew. Her prospective father-in-law is making a documentary about South American music.'

'Effing hell,' said Eggy, 'a movie. I think it better she was on her backside.'

What could one do with such a homuncular lecher?

'Well,' I drolled, 'it would seem that in the annals of the film world, making movies and being on one's backside are not mutually exclusive enterprises.'

'Randall,' said Eggy, 'are you threatening me with wit? The rain in Spain—'

Save for Elias and Antonio, we were alone in the café. No Miss Meow, in tuque and heavy coat, could be seen to glint myopically at a world gone mad. No Blind Musician. No Whistler. No Gentleman Jim. Especially no Moonface.

'The military strategists,' I said, 'are saying that were it not for the politicians, counter-insurgencies would have carried the day for the Yanks and Vietnam not rankle. We are seeing the end of *laissez faire* capitalism. The god-particle is close to being isolated. You live in interesting times, Eggy.'

'Well, you live in them, too,' retorted Eggy, his finger raised.

He was not one to be caught alone with a hand in the cookie jar.

'But I keep telling you,' he continued, 'the bastards ought to hang. *Because my eyes have seen thy salvation, which thou hast prepared before the face of all peoples*... Now why do I remember those words? *Nunc dimittis*, you know. I haven't practiced religion in centuries. Hoo hoo.'

'I don't suppose you have,' I idly remarked.

Now coming through the door were Dundarave, two smiling women on his arms: Schneider and Jarnette. Antonio rued their coming. He would like to have settled down to watching soccer on the TV. And well, the women did not seem at all surprised to see me, given they had both graced my bed in recent times. Though in the case of Gloria Jarnette, I was not much more than a by-stander; and in the case of Schneider I was but a whistle-stop while she hobnobbed for her leverage.

'Hoo hoo, what have we here?' Eggy wondered, sniffing out the prospect of festivities.

'Good people, have a chair,' Eggy crowed, and then he observed: 'One of us will have to spring for a bottle. Randall, what is the state of your wallet?'

I supposed it was respectable enough. And Eggy beamed at the women. And he did not think he had been properly introduced to either one. Phillip did the honours.

'Hang the expense,' Eggy thundered, rounding on me, 'effing hell, I'll square it with you, later.'

I rolled my eyes, indicating that I had in him complete trust, even if it made me a stooge. But, as it turned out, we were a gala affair; the wine flowed. Eggy held forth like a well-oiled machine, the women in fine form. Dundarave was at pains to be on good behaviour; he was not just a bumpkin from the Townships out of place amidst city sophisticates. He had no idea where Prentiss had gotten hold of the gun. Gun? What gun? The questions belonged to Schneider having a moment of alarm, she fetching in a white shawl.

'She was starkers,' Eggy crowed, relishing a certain recollection of the Prentiss woman, 'except for the boa.'

He was speaking of the night when Prentiss staged her floor show in the hall of the Traymore, she caressing the gun, the arrival of the cops the dénouement to the action. Eleanor, taking no chances, had called them.

'Maybe her father collected pistolas,' I said, addressing my words in the general direction of Dundarave, who shrugged.

It seemed to me he knew what the story was, but that it was not my business to know. I looked at the man with new interest, given that Eleanor had informed me there was something of honour in the man. I wondered what his intentions were in respect to the good woman, if any, but I kept such wondering to myself. Schneider was planning to attend the winter games in Vancouver in a year's time. Eggy allowed he had once visited Innsbruck; had even had relations there with a starlet of renown. This tickled Dundarave's funny bone, and he grinned. Jarnette thought she might tease the homunculus: 'Oh sure. And she was Sophia Loren, I guess.'

'Why, how did you know? Of course, it was her.'

All that was missing was Dubois at table, letting loose a guffaw.

'Men and maids at time of year,' I said, quoting all I could remember of Anacreon.

Dead Flowers

Evie Longoria, back from Mexico, came looking for Eggy. Sun and surf had done her good, though the fact that it was going to prove to be the last Christmas for her dying father had been much on her mind. Just the thought of her father produced a tear in her eyes. She still intended to move to B.C. where she expected to find a healthier life than what our faded Jezebel of a town could offer, Evie convinced that Montreal was making her daughter neurotic. In any case, Evie did not stay long in my digs. She seemed to indicate I was no longer on her list of possible claimants to her affections. Fine by me. I promised I would let Eggy know she had come calling. She succumbed to a full-blown crying jag.

Moonface *in absentia,* a help wanted sign in the window, Cassandra and Antonio covered the shifts. Sometimes, when it got busy, Gregory lent a clumsy hand, bewildered by the likes of Miss Meow and the Whistler. It was one thing when they were part of the background noise of a café, and it was quite another to have to actually communicate with these miscreants, the Whistler more agitated, of late, with his whistlings and stompings and need of immediate service. Cassandra was on the floor when I entered the café, her only customer.

'Where is everyone?' I asked, making a mock-show of concern.

Her cheeks dimpling with a smile, Cassandra shrugged.

'Ko-fee?' she said.

The fact of New President meant that a page had been turned and the sun would once again favour the Shining City on the hill. It was from this very same city that my old friend Jack Swain fled, only to die in Palermo. But now it was to be a hopeful time, a problem-solving time, a time to set things straight and put the country, if not the world, on a more even keel and introduce sanity to its dealings. As Dubois the arch-materialist would have it, one could overdo pessimism, for all that his cluster headaches were causing him such havoc; yes, just when Eleanor was still vulnerable to the machinations of Prentiss or the allure of Dundarave. It was difficult to put one's foot down when one was dry-heaving into a toilet. If my expatriation of many years once spoke for my politics, it was now possible that my politics no longer were even remotely applicable to the geist of the moment. Now and then Cassandra allowed me to flirt with her. It seemed a consolation of sorts.

The wind was too stiff and coldly unpleasant for a walk. I returned to the Traymore, and in my digs I opened Tacitus at random and read: *Messalina believed that Decimus Valerius Asiaticus, twice consul, had been Poppaea Sabina's lover. Messalina also coveted the park which Asiaticus was beautifying with exceptional lavishness. So she directed Publius Suillus Rufus to prosecute both of them.* The implication was clear: what Messalina wanted she got. I was already sliding into sleep and a subsequent dream. In which I could hear but could not see Eleanor baking in her kitchen. And then Suzie Q showed up. It was immediately apparent that she was one of those women who did not ravish at first glance, but who grew on one over time. She had piled her hair on top of her head, revealing her ears and a fine neck. She had in her hand a bouquet of dead flowers which, shyly, she thrust at me. She said she would not discriminate against men because they were too old, suggesting that sex was sex, no matter what. Highly principled. Eleanor coughed a warning. But Suzie Q was stubborn, her wide-set eyes gone sultry, her countenance honest and determined. I woke, groggy and a bit shame-faced.

The Mystery of Zeus

A famous comic was often saying that God was a silly god and had done the world incalculable harm. The pity of it was that I, an unbeliever, wanted to shout from the rooftops that a godless world would prove infinitely worse; but that to do so might get me arrested; it would assuredly rate me the scorn of a generation or two, not to mention the generations yet unborn. I was convinced of the reality of Venus, who had prevailed against the insurgency of Psyche or the inner life, Venus's realm of the senses both lovely and brutish. What did in Psyche was an overdose of self-absorption, not to mention the narcissism and literary pretensions of my peers. Sometimes it seemed to me that Venus's vengeance had been as harsh as any Dionysus exacted from humankind, the goddess ensnaring her subjects by way of greed and empty lust and hateful politics. I myself could confess to a soft spot for Psyche, and sometimes I wondered if there was not in Moonface just a splinter of that goddess. And sometimes it seemed to me that Eleanor, however much she inveighed against the calamities of the recent past and mind-destroying unction such as trumped everything with bread and circuses and bloodbaths, was quite at home with Venus's work even so, the bawdy wench confident of the supremacy of the flesh over the ephemeralities of a less carnal love. I myself had long understood I was divided in my loyalties. Some might say that the Sixties in which I came of age promised an accommodation between body and soul, a way out of life-negating dualism. It seemed to me the accommodation was rather short-lived; or that it only enjoyed a partial success, one predicated, perhaps, on parodies of the notion of body and soul. I had slept with women who were always on a mission. I had slept, too, with women for whom the sex had been almost an accident and not entirely unwelcome, and it was as if we had slaked our thirst at some oasis before pressing on with the grim realities of life. The mystery of Zeus was that he was both the guarantor of justice and the source of caprice. Ah, Zeus-like Eggy. Chip off the old block, so to speak. Nonetheless I went to him for a palaver on various matters, the pedagogue in me getting the upper hand over Boffo the Clown. Eggy, dwarfed by his armchair, baby blue fuzzy slippers on his feet (courtesy of Longoria?), bade me get to the point. He was old and time was precious.

'Yes, well,' I said to Eggy, 'I think I'm coming down with a case of God again.'

'Is that all?' the homunculus answered.

'Just thank Christ you're not in the Sudan,' he continued, 'and anyway, I was blissfully contemplating Moonface on her backside when you blew in.'

'My apologies.'

'None needed. But you know, why, I can see her contemplating God on her backside. Why the effing hell not?'

'Champagne Sheridan might have something to say about that.'

'What's he got to say? He isn't the brightest penny—'

'Perhaps. But I think it's more to the point that when Moonface is on her backside contemplating God, what she's really doing is contemplating the fact He can't be contemplated, as He does not move and can't be moved.'

'Convoluted, Randall. Kitchen-sink Plato. But I'll grant you this: I for one don't think it laughable that you should wish to have a serious thought or two at this stage of your life and then wash it all down with some wine. This is, after all, the true gift of pleasure: that we don't take ourselves too seriously.'

'The ways in which you're incurable continually amaze me.'

'Do you think they'll drop the bomb?'

Speech! Speech!

Mrs Petrova was passing from her shop to her suite as I entered the Traymore. She grunted, regarding me as a mad man. She, in her 80s, still had a weakness for the operas of Puccini, but she was otherwise a sensible woman, and she expected of men an honest day's work. Still, she could not object that I had ever been remiss with the rent. I proceeded to my digs; and, as I unlocked my door, I was waylaid by Eleanor, who was glassy-eyed and perfumed.

'I intend to watch the speech,' I said, attempting to forestall any ideas she might be having.

'Oh,' she purred, 'can I watch, too?'

I supposed she could. She arrayed her splendour on my couch; and I supposed the least a gentleman could do was to offer a good woman a whiskey, and she accepted.

'A kiss?' she burbled.

I thought not. There was already a respectable amount of wine in me, and that was the way I wished to keep it—respectable. I filled a glass with water and switched on the TV. She had heard from Prentiss, that evening. Apparently, Prentiss was most charming on the phone, even apologetic.

'No kidding,' I said.

I smelled trouble.

'And how's Bob?' Eleanor asked.

'Seemed fine to me,' I answered, and then it hit me: perhaps she was a bit put out that Dubois had elected to spend an evening in the café with Eggy rather than pass a spate of time free of headaches with her.

In the middle of the President's State of the Union address Eleanor fell asleep, gently snoring. I viewed it all through the eyes of Tacitus: whose enemy was one's future ally? I was pretty much of that world when Eleanor woke, embarrassed.

'Oh god,' she said, 'did I snore?'

'Well,' I said, 'you missed quite the speech.'

'Was it so stellar?' she asked.

She rose to a sitting position and began to rub her eyes. It was the first time I had ever seen her rub her eyes, their colour a grey-green admixture, her shoulders sloped. She seemed most vulnerable.

'Another whiskey?' I offered.

'Oh no, that would destroy me.'

She was on her pompadoured feet now. She tousled my hair where I sat in my chair.

'Randall,' she said, 'Randall, Randall. Whatever are we going to do with you?'

'I don't know that there's anything to be done,' I countered, 'just that I just witnessed a sane and civilized man assume he was addressing a nation of grown-ups. I mean, I don't know that it testifies to a page of history having turned for the better, but still, even so—'

'Randall,' said the good woman.

She buried my face against her comely and full-figured body, yes, like the loving wench she was.

'Randall, Randall, is that all you live for now, politics? I think you need Moonface. I would never have thought it a good idea, but I think you need her.'

'I need her,' I drolled, 'like I need yet another hole in the head.'

She half-lurched, half-slinked out of my apartment. She always had to let me know what I was missing. And when I finally went to bed, it seemed Eleanor's perfume had become inseparable from the molecular structure of my face. And I dreamed a bad dream. New President, sans security, availing himself of an ATM machine on some street, took a bullet, and a few seconds later, the headlines at a newsstand screamed the fact of his death; and I was witness to my own rage.

A Bit of Academe

Remember how long thou hast already put off these things, and how often a certain day and hour as it were, having been set unto thee by the gods, thou hast neglected it. It is high time for thee to understand the true nature both of the world, whereof thou art a part; and of that Lord and Governor of the world, from whom, as a channel from the spring thou thyself didst flow: and that there is but a certain limit of time appointed unto thee, which if thou shalt not make use of to calm and allay the many distempers of thy soul, it will pass away and thou with it, and never after return.

From the Second Book of the Meditations of Marcus Aurelius

§

Book II—Delicate Pops

Demon Love I

—There is no Moonface to serve us wine. Missing: those delicate pops of corks extracted. Those flashing nails. Those eyes of hers that seem somehow born of another, more rich sensibility than the aplomb of present-day dead enders—or so she might like to have us believe. That Moonface smile, baring strong incisors, ironically naïve. It is not that she is a sex goddess—she is far from that, but then she is a chameleon-like creature. Moonface: backwater waitress. She has read Virgil in the Latin despite her birth in the outback of Ontar-I-O. (Did she not spirit a copy of Catullus to Ecuador?) Unfailingly polite and incalculably rude, she is, in any event, hopelessly a girl of her times. Her bad taste in music does not preclude an evening at the opera, she shimmeringly begowned. Trouble is, I fear I make more of her charms than they warrant. This quite ordinary daughter of a United Church minister who may or may not find herself lost, one day, to the dreary suburbs, has comprehended one notion, at least: that there is life and poetry beyond the clutches of logic and the strictures of conformity as well as the inanities of alternative culture. I am to investigate DVD machines for Eggy as his, the one Moonface lent him and that her Champagne Sheridan hooked up, has packed it in. Too much hot sex. Lesbian liaisons. Eggy the empiricist.

—A new photo of Moonface arrives from Ecuador. In the Blue Danube Antonio the waiter, as if in receipt of a holy relic, hands it to me. There she is, standing in a brick plaza, much greenery about, colourful shops the backdrop. *She has gotten free of the phantasmagorical mediocrities.* Well, perhaps.

But hers is very nearly a come-get-me-boys-if-you-dare pose. Denims. Black tank top. Arms bare. Her face is quite red—from the mountain sun, most likely. Her smile (or is it a leer?) is just this side of unattractive, coyly raunchy. Her eyes are different, her head turned somewhat from the camera so that she looks out at one sideways. Ah yes, a new Moonface. One that has not been seen before by these eyes. For good? For ill? Eggy, no doubt, looking upon the photo, will have much to contemplate. Flashing nails. Hint of midriff. Antonio: 'Maybe she drunk.' The photo, roughly a 3 X 5 affair, raises more questions than it answers. Is she happy? Is she getting properly boffed? I cannot believe she can be missing us.

—We quarrelled, Dubois and I, last night. There in the Blue Danube, where else? Dubois reported that he believed Americans to be benevolent. 'Benevolent?' I answered, and went on to say: 'That would imply a certain amount of disinterested virtue, and the Americans no longer do disinterest or virtue.' Dubois seemed stunned. Meanwhile, all that mattered to Eggy was Moonface and the fact that, upon examination of the newly-arrived photo, she did not look preggers. Perhaps Dubois was peering through a dark tunnel for signs of an oncoming gale in the form of a migraine. 'New President,' I said, 'will have to perform the work of both Hadrian and Diocletian. The former scaled back the empire and put a more humane face on the imperial fist, Jerusalem excepted. The latter took the economy in hand which was in a parlous state, and he imposed reforms, albeit in draconian fashion.' Dubois continued to sit there, bewildered. 'And in any case,' I said, flirting with frivolity, with signature cynicism, 'the solutions only brought on new and more onerous cans of worms.' 'You're a piece of work,' Dubois let me know, wondering if it would be worthwhile to spring for another bottle. Yet, there being no Moonface about, there was no one to audit our debate and so, what was the point? And I thought that in his glittering blue eyes old age was beginning to get him over a barrel. Even so, I wound up agreeing, it seems, to some wager or another: that, in 2012, we would reconvene—Dubois, Eggy and I—at Animal Table, and know that the world was more or less intact, I having indicated that I lacked confidence in this regard. And then, it was on to Duplessis, a sort of Huey Long figure; how that Quebec premier played the church and its cardinals like a violin; and if Eggy had resided in the province for fifty years and did not yet understand this, he did not understand Quebec. On this point,

Dubois enjoyed all the ascendancy, and neither Eggy nor I would dream of gainsaying the man. 'Oh,' said Eggy, 'to be a sailor, and sail the wide, wide sea.' (He sang this refrain, later, as he attempted to coax his drunken pins up the Traymore stairs.) 'Oh to be a sailor, my arse,' said Dubois, 'you're forever changing the subject.' 'Oh, eff you.' But now, did Moonface, the dear girl, have delicate paps? What was that look of hers in the photo? Well, I was drunk. Dubois, equally drunk, considered there was no such thing as a broken system; all was evolution; systems merely evolve. History, I believed, proved him wrong. But what was history?

—Will I cave again, Eleanor up to her old tricks? We sit at her kitchen table, she in a mood. 'Who cares, Randall? I mean, listen to yourself. And if you're not going to stick some effing something up my twat, then get the effing hell out of my kitchen.'

—I wake with the crows, and in the day's first light, I stand at the window at the end of the Traymore hall. Leafless trees. Snow heaps. Brick dwellings. The crows, screeing across the sky, alight on this or that tall maple. There is a certain apocalyptic quality to their communications and yet, it is only nature testifying to the fact that life goes on and one is alive. The Traymore is silent. Ah, but that is Dubois's clattering keyboard. Has he been checking his stock portfolio? Squirrels nimble out of a squirrel's nest. Prentiss whispers at me the softness of her thighs, her smile a tryst-offering, her dead, watery eyes gateways to a mirage. Well, perhaps one ought to enjoy it, the old hourglass of time not as rich as once it was with either chance delights or random treacheries.

Demon Love II

—When I last saw Dundarave and Suzie Q together on the Traymore stairs, suspicions formed. Aggressively neutral looks advised me I should mind my own beeswax. Trust Dundarave to spot the promise in an unpromising package—the humourless and methodical Suzie Q. Am I jealous? I would go and complain to Eleanor of life's essential unfairness, but then it would only incite laughter on her part, and besides, it would exacerbate a jealousy of her own. Though she insists that relations between her and Phillip are strictly Platonic, it remains obvious that she regrets this state of things.

Speaking of Plato, I have reached that part in his *Symposium* when wily Socrates, pleading ignorance and lack of speaking polish, nonetheless turns all the previous arguments honouring love on their heads. And so, love is not a god but a spirit, a demon, if you will; and, as such, it consecrates humankind to a longing for immortality by way of the procreative and the creative. Even the finches in their *couleurs nuptiale* know as much.

—I took Suzie Q to the movies. Going to the movies was an activity sacred to Moonface and me. Suzie Q, I am certain, only agreed to the proposal so as to spite my moral drift. I was convinced of this when something like a hot branding iron came to rest on my thigh, and it was her hand. The sweeping new epic on the screen, all melodrama, was gathering momentum, and one was growing accustomed to the actors drawling away in Australian. 'What are you doing?' I hissed. Heard, and the voice, irritatingly reasonable, stifled bemusement: 'Always wanted to touch a man in the dark.' Well, for the love of God. Yes, was she feral in her mind? I dislodged the hand. And the movie eventually fell apart into bits and pieces of such platitudes as would ennoble the human heart and only cheapen sentiment. Back on the street, and I said to the amorist: 'You know, despite the advances in man-woman relationships, I think I preferred it when women were demure and still got what they wanted.' Heard: 'What could you possibly know about getting?' Indeed. Even so, I did not consider that the girl meant me injury; it was just that her notions of love and lust were theoretical: her hand had had all the rationale of an experiment. I sprung for a taxi and it was a silent ride through the city. Drab snow in lurid street lights. The phantasmagorically smug in the windows of tony bistros. One was weary of winter. 'So what did you think of the flick?' I ventured to ask. 'It was kind of silly.' 'You're probably right.' 'Why only probably?' Well, she had a point. Our respective *Xs* and *Ys* and *Zs* were meeting in neutral space, looking one another over, and concluding there was not much to be gained from the one set gainsaying the other. That Suzie Q was most likely a better scholar than Moonface, a sounder intellect; that she might even make someone in life a more steadfast partner (as she was fundamentally a serious person) was evident; but apart from her study of the classics, she had not an iota of the poetic in her; or there was none that could be reached and wakened. Even so, I thought I might as well add to the iniquities I had committed against the memory of Moonface and stand the girl beside me to a drink. This she refused. 'You're not so hard to handle,' she added to her disinclination to swill. Oh yes? Since when? But I was bored now by the game, bored with the girl and her false claims to a knowing air. I lacked the patience, or so I said to myself with the air of a man headed elsewhere. I paid off the yawning cabbie and bid the girl good night, hoping that for her it had not been entirely a waste. Eggy was alone in the Blue Danube. Which is to say, Dubois was in his rooms, under the gun, pain run amok in his head. 'Rogue gene,' said Eggy, 'and it's about time someone came to keep me company.' The homunculus had already worked his way through most of the wine but there was enough in it for a glass, and Antonio, winking, set one on the table. 'So,' said Eggy. 'Oh well,' I answered, 'I took Suzie Q to the movies.' Eggy was nonplussed. Or rather he raised his finger and declaimed : 'Her lips suck forth my soul—' I tried to imagine Eggy alone in life, no one at hand to badger with rabbit-like leaps of logic.

From Dubois

To: Randall Q Calhoun:

The widely recognized best investment management performer in the world tries hard never to make predictions.

Best regards.

Robert Dubois
Conseiller d'affaires sr / Senior Business Consultant

§

Book III—A Dying World

Back in the Saddle

She was back, and everyone was to know it. Barefoot and perky, despite the dead, watery eyes, she knocked on my door.

'Hullo.'

One might have said that, her business completed, she scampered away. What now for Ralph her intended, and Dundarave her pick me up? What now for Eleanor? And me? Dubois, when he heard the news, only grunted. The cluster headaches had taken him to a new level of consciousness, different priorities. To rich holding patterns, as when he lay on the floor in agony. But we were in the Blue Danube, he, Eggy and I.

'Well,' I said, 'the Prodigal Daughter has returned.'

'What, Moonface?' asked Eggy, something like hope lighting up flinty eyes.

Dubois guffawed, and then, addressing me: 'You see, you see of what his thoughts are made?'

'It's Prentiss of whom I speak,' I said.

'Oh, her,' said Eggy, 'well, she's not so bad. Never gave me any trouble. Hoo hoo.'

We sat there at table, at Animal Table, to be precise, three defanged lions gorgeous to behold. And so far as I was concerned, a mortal enemy was among us once again in much the same way that certain agents of President #43 were still yanking strings in Washington and ponying up in the new casino. Prentiss had restyled her hair; brown bangs careened down to her made-up eyes. Cleopatra had employed a variety of hairstyles with which to proclaim her power and efficacy in the rough and tumble Roman world.

'Well,' said Eggy, 'I guess you think trouble's coming.'

'You're nothing but trouble,' Dubois declared of Eggy, albeit with affection, 'and you know, this time around, speaking of Prentiss, of course, I don't much care.'

'Oh, you don't?' asked Eggy, somewhat incredulous.

'Getting through a night without pain—that's what I care about.'

Dubois helped himself to more wine. The late winter dark had settled on our noble boulevard, and one did not know, anymore, about the Habs. Either they would win the Stanley Cup or they would stink up every arena on the continent.

It was a misty evening in Montreal when I checked myself into the Blue Danube, Eggy saying: 'You just missed Bob. Why, soon as he ordered his dinner, he had one of his attacks. Had to go. Effing hell.'

'Oh dear.'

'Don't oh dear me and don't oh dear him. It's what it is, nothing more, nothing less. Maybe it's something in the ambiance. Too many Albanians. The rain in Spain. Always.'

Homuncular eyes brightened with mirth.

'You're getting cheeky in your old age,' I noted.

'Why, I suppose I am. So effing what? But you may as well hear the news. Prentiss and Dundarave had a row. Over that woman who was coming around. What was her name? Schneider, I think. She could've come around to me, but I guess she didn't see fit to do so. Eleanor, the loon, she tried using her charms—well, on Bob. She thought she might distract him from the pain. Of course, it wouldn't work. Any idiot could've told her that. Bob went out of his tree. You might better go see her. Poor woman. She tries, you know. I fell in the elevator going up to see nursie. Hit my head. Might've bled to death but for the meds I was on. Well, that's what nursie said. Anyway, I'll live. Well, you can see that.'

Lunch with Dundarave

Perhaps Dundarave got the idea from Prentiss who got it from Eleanor: a certain Traymorean mode of communications. For when I woke the next morning, I found a note shoved under my door. The unusually flowery scrawl was Dundarave's. It recommended that he and I have lunch. No hint in the words of *or else* as one might expect from a man who had no patience with the subtleties. A warm front had parked in the area. March did not show the town to its best advantage, the streets filthy with accumulated debris that receding snow revealed. One felt rather than observed that the sparrows were thinking it high time to breed. Was there more to Dundarave than met the eye? One could see in him a top-flight Roman general in conversation with Caesar, gossiping about poets and courtesans, military operations on hold for the moment. Did not the better sort of bathhouses include libraries on their premises? A practical people, those Romans.

Dundarave had already claimed a table at the Blue Danube when I showed. Eggy and Dubois were also there, Dubois with his *Globe and Mail*, that mind-teaser. I signalled that something was up and I would not be sitting with them. Eggy turned his face from me, disgusted. What was so effing important he could not be a part of it? Dubois arched his brows and swallowed a guffaw. Antonio, meanwhile, seemed to be showing a girl how to use the café's billing apparatus, some touch-screen gizmo. So then, a new waitress was on the scene. Her name was Mercedes, as it turned out, at first glance, a beauty. I hoped Elias would keep his hands to himself. Cassandra looked to be keeping a sharp eye on things. Then Dundarave said (he had the air of a cowboy who, having departed the outback for a town's innocent pleasures, was now disillusioned): 'I'm going nuts.'

It seemed an astonishing statement. And yet, in exactly what way was he going nuts? I would like to have asked, and did not, fearing how the question might seem to the man once I put it to him.

'I'm already there,' I drolled.

The look I got from Dundarave suggested he was not amused.

He was difficult to sum up in a sentence or two. That he was stereotypically a man's man; that he had a deadly effect on women. That he presented himself to the world as a simple carpenter, one who did not pretend to fathom the motives of his superiors, but that they would surely exploit him if they could. He was more intelligent than he let on, and he enjoyed the ruse. Perhaps he had read a book or three. He was intimate with fast living and country solitude, the Townships his fallback position when the city got to be too much. Drugs had ruined his marriage; he had a daughter he seemed to dearly love. But why would he confess to me the state of his wherewithal? I was on my guard.

'And I might as well tell you, Ellie put me up to this.'

By Ellie, he meant Eleanor, she who had been something of a confidante to him.

'She thought,' Dundarave went on to say, 'that I might find your perspective useful.'

'She did, did she?'

Well, if it did not turn out well, this little exchange of views, I would have Eleanor to blame.

'So,' I asked, in the most casual and inoffensive tone I could muster, 'what gives?'

'You know what gives. Marjerie.'

'To be sure,' I said, 'to be sure.'

By now our orders, by way of a nervous Mercedes, had been brought to the table. A simple burger for my interlocutor. Lentil soup for me. I would like to have paid more attention to the fact of the new waitress, but now was not the time. So, to the matter at hand: Dundarave and his apparent torment. What does one tell a man who is about to divulge that he has lost his wits on account of a woman who toys with him at her leisure and then twits him with his own helplessness? I was certain words like these were coming, even as, perhaps, he wondered how he would frame his sentences. It had not occurred to me that he might have reason to fear me a little; that Eleanor would have talked me up to him in such a way as to suggest I was wise and could read his thoughts. Then again it was equally possible he was not in the slightest bit intimidated.

'So,' I said, 'you're in love with Marjerie but she's going to marry Ralph.'

Once more Dundarave had occasion to take exception to something in my tone.

'No, it's not like that. I don't love the silly bitch. Pardon my French. But she's the best sex I've ever had, and I've got to have it.'

'And there's a price to be paid,' I suggested.

'You got that right.'

It seemed he was cramming half the burger in his mouth.

'What about Jarnette? That Schneider woman? Eleanor, for that matter?'

'I was never going to do anything with Ellie. I respect her.'

'Oh you do.'

'Yes, I do,' he affirmed, reaching for a serviette.

There was always something in the man of menace.

'Are you willing to pay the price that comes with doing business with Prentiss?'

'I like the way you put that,' Dundarave said, grinning for the first time in the proceedings.

'Look,' I said, 'my opinion in respect to Marjerie isn't favourable, if you must know. I don't understand what she thinks she's up to. But she certainly needs to have a show to run. The show's more important to her than the well-being of the cast. Give her a good cause and she might actually do some good. Just that she'd get bored with it. She likes to be bad. Wants to be bad. Ralph? He's her insurance. Good man who, one of these days, is going to walk. Get my drift?'

'Got it.'

'Anyway, you don't need my advice,' I said with an involuntary surge of authority.

'Well,' said Dundarave, the burger devoured, 'I do know what I'm going to do. I'm just going to keep on doing what I'm doing until I really really can't stand it, anymore.'

The look he gave me suggested I ought to feel free to second-guess his decision. I shrugged. And he would boff Marjerie and she Ralph, and they would have their three-way; and then Marjerie would, perhaps, seek to extend dominion where she could; it was just her way of having fun.

Dundarave picked up the tab and left, but not before I heard him suggest to Mercedes that she would do fine in her new job. Was it a line or was he sincere? I joined Animal Table.

'Good God,' I said to all and sundry there—to a Dubois tested by migraines, to an Eggy contemplating a snooze.

I supposed my tone of voice was overly dramatic, but I wished my companions to know I had had words with something like the devil.

'Yes, what was that all about?' Eggy wanted to know. 'As if we didn't know.'

'Prentiss,' I said, 'getting your brains boffed out but not sure you're liking it.'

'What's not to like?' Eggy asked, forgetful, perhaps, of his now ancient travails in the boffing department, he wise after the fact.

'Oh, he likes it, but he doesn't like the price tag, which is Prentiss and her whims,' I said.

'There's always that,' Eggy agreed, demonstrating that he, too, had an ounce of sense in him.

His chin began its precipitous drop to his chest.

'Going, going—gone,' Dubois guffawed.

And it seemed to me he did not rate Dundarave as worthy of further discussion, Mercedes appearing like a dream, coffee pot in hand. And when I got back to the Traymore and was about to climb the stairs, the Schneider woman manifested at the top of them, and she was distraught.

'I want to talk to you,' she said, and there was no mistaking her tone.

Oh dear God. She was the sort of woman who signed up for classes at the golf academy. Perhaps she had already put in some time at life-studies, drawing nudes.

'Must we?' I countered.

'We must.'

How could one argue with an expensive pair of boots and perfect hair? Well, someone had, from the looks of it. There was loud music now in the Prentiss apartment. A thudding bass. One could safely assume there was boffing in the works. I trudged up the stairs and unlocked my door, taking it for granted Schneider would follow me in. I would hear the woman out, but nothing more than that; and she started in on me once we were in the living room: 'I don't like games.'

'Really? I don't like games, either. But what I really don't like is pettiness.'

'Pettiness?' she said, somewhat taken aback. She continued: 'I'd say it was petty of you to tell Phillip to dump me.'

'I did no such thing.'

'But you did.'

'I'm afraid not.'

'Then what's going on—?'

'You've been downsized. Or else you're just a tourist on the premises. I don't know how else to put it.'

'I went to bed with you—'

'I rest my case.'

Unspoken

Wisdom? What was the thing? The avoidance of pain as came of excess, so the ancients had it? Yet they, too, had their Bacchic frenzies as mitigated against convention and stuffiness. I considered that of wisdom I had precious little; all was, in any case, evolutionary drift. But what had been haunting me of late were certain memories, ones to which no events in particular, let alone faces, were attached. Some amorphous but palpable sensation would take hold of me and stop me in my tracks. And finally I realized these incidents had to do with the first time I sensed that the world was a construct of infinite sadness; as when, for example, I was twelve and tossing a football back and forth with a friend; and the world was fine; and I loved the autumnal smell of fallen leaves and the feel of the leather object in my hands; and the running and the leaping, and so forth and so on; and then I was suddenly on the verge of tears for no rhyme or reason. Perhaps it was as simple as understanding that it was a transient hour, and the beauty of it all was perishable. I described this early epiphany of mine to Dubois and Eggy, and asked them: 'Well, how about you two?'

It seemed strange to sit in the Blue Danube at an evening hour and it was not yet dark outside. Inside, we were the only customers, the Habs on TV. Eggy wished to withdraw his wager as to whether the Habs would take the Stanley Cup, Dubois saying: 'See? I knew it would come to this and you'd change your mind.'

'Oh eff off. If you insist, I'll be a gentleman about it.'

Then Dubois put it to me: 'So what's this business you're on about? Epiphany?'

'Never mind,' I answered, a bit peeved.

'Well, you know,' said Eggy, '"Ozymandias"'

'That's not quite what I had in mind—'

'Ozzy-what?' Dubois guffawed, 'and there you go again. You don't listen.'

'I do too listen,' thundered Eggy, 'I always listen.'

'Yes, he listens,' I sighed, 'but sometimes it's not clear to what he listens.'

'You can say that again,' Dubois agreed.

'Oh, we love you,' said Antonio the waiter to a homunculus.

'Eff off.'

'Dundarave isn't particular where he puts it, is he?' so Dubois put it to us out of the blue.

'A man's man,' said Eggy, very nearly giggling.

Dubois gave me a look, one that asked why he did not just stomp on the old bugger then and there and have done with it.

'"My name is Ozymandias, King of Kings: Look on my works, ye mighty, and despair."'

Eggy had orated, finger raised; but then Dubois interrupted:

'Ozzy-what?'

And then the Habs scored one, tying the game. And not too long after, they scored another.

Antipathy

I do not know who was more strange, Dundarave suggesting that what I needed were more shelves for my books and TV, and he was the man to do it, he being a simple carpenter; or Prentiss garbed in some tunic and black tights at his side, lollipop in her mouth. All she was missing were bells and a jester's cap. Perhaps the clown in me experienced antipathy to the spectacle of a rival, she unnaturally nubile, as jiggly as a teenager. And then, because my door was open, in walked Evie Longoria, her face drawn, eyes anxious. Prentiss registered the fact of her with a grin, one that said: *well, would you look at this? What have we here?* One always had the sense with Evie that she was about to sit for a job interview. I could not recall if Evie and Marjerie had had the pleasure of each other's company; I did not offer introductions. Dundarave, as ever, sized Evie up with his quiet eyes; and perhaps he found qualities about her person to admire.

'Sure,' said Dundarave, 'no problem. I've got the wood. I just need to measure the TV. Hell, a few screws and *voila!*'

The man was enjoying himself.

'Yes,' said Prentiss, 'you live like you're just passing through. Hang up your coat, Calhoun, stay a while.'

Who was she to command? Then Evie spoke and said she would come back around as I was busy, and I told her to wait.

'Look,' I said to Dundarave, 'why are you doing this? I can slap together my own shelves if and when I think I need them.'

'It gives me something to do,' the man replied, giving Prentiss a significant look. He continued: 'Anyway, it's been decided. And they won't have been slapped together. It'll look decent.'

Prentiss's eyes, fixed as they were on me, seemed far away, and they were full of plans.

'The man's got company,' her swain observed, and then to me he said: 'I'll be back.'

It seemed a threat.

Dundarave and Prentiss now out the door, I invited Evie to have a seat on the couch. It was an offensive item of bordello green furniture getting shabby. But I would have no one, especially Prentiss, doing over the décor. And Evie sat there, knees pressed tight together underneath her ankle-length skirt. A tear had formed in her eye. She dabbed at it. She uttered an expletive.

'There I go again,' she said, 'what is it about you that always causes me to cry?'

'I don't know,' I suggested, 'but I have to say I find it disconcerting.'

'Me,' she said, 'I would find that woman disconcerting.'

'You mean Prentiss?'

'I guess. If that's who she is.'

'She is a trial.'

'Are all women a trial for you?'

'What gives you that idea?'

'The way you distance yourself.'

I shrugged.

'Can I get you something?' I asked.

'Actually, no,' she answered, beginning to brighten a little, 'I came around to see Eggy about our schedule, but he's either asleep or he isn't in. So I thought I would just say hello. Hello. And I thought to tell you that I can't make up my mind whether to stay in Montreal or go out to B.C. and live in the boonies with my daughter. I hate my indecision. How's Bob?'

'He's been having headaches,' I answered, wondering if my tone was not verging on cruelty.

Evie Longoria was one of those women whom one would never wish to hurt, and yet somehow, it seemed she was forever drawing cruelty to her person.

'Well,' she said, rising to her feet, 'we all have our crosses to bear.'

There was something in her tone that wished to injure me, her smile a half-finished thing, her eyes rueful. She began to approach my door so as to see herself out, looking back at me as she did so. I resented the inadequacy she aroused in me. There was something like hatred now in her gaze. She backed out the door, and I could almost hear on her lips *effendi.*

So I crossed the hall to Eleanor's, and she was not having my complaints, as I was a mature and responsible adult, and should know how to manage my affairs.

'You probably led her on all this time,' she said, in regards to Longoria. 'You men are silly enough, but women, well, I have to say they're sillier, most times.'

This last pronouncement seemed to exhaust the possibilities of conversation. I sipped my amaretto. And the look she gave me was one I would have placed as being somewhere between fancying a tumble in the sack and wonderment as to why God made such creatures as myself.

'Well,' I ventured to ask, 'how are things with you?'

Things might have been less than satisfactory for Eleanor, her kitchen in disarray, the counter a horror of heaps of unwashed dishes and food left out and what not. If the woman was not the most fastidious of housekeepers, she was no slob, either and so, one could only surmise she had her reasons for her inattentiveness to the room's condition.

'I don't know,' she said, 'but I have this sense of foreboding, like something bad is going to happen. Maybe Bob has a brain tumour. Maybe somebody will shoot the prez. Maybe the next flu bug will wipe us all out. You could fall in love with a woman and she whisk you away.'

'Why, would that go hard on your feelings?'

'Don't flatter yourself, dearie. It's the woman I'd pity.'

'Alright then, what's really eating you?"

Eleanor gave me another look. None of my beeswax.

'In any case,' I said, 'Prentiss seems to have a new lease on life. If there's a woman who gets even more of a kick out of reducing men to mincemeat than she does, I haven't met her.'

'Can you believe it,' Eleanor countered, 'she tells me she's lonely. She's getting older and this frightens her to death. Her looks, you see. And she still can't settle down with Ralph. The idea gives her the willies. And then Ralph calls me up, practically in tears, at wit's end. He knows Marjerie and Phillip are boffing one another senseless like there's no tomorrow, and then the wench she's just going to show at his place and announce that it's time to play house, like there's nothing going on, and even if there is, it's nothing he should worry about. Good God, Randall, when do people ever get wise to themselves? She sort of overdoes it, you know. That's really her problem. Otherwise she's not such a bad girl. And then me, well, I'm not much better. Still carrying a torch for Phillip. The effing arsehole. But you'll be pleased to know, my good man, that I'm behaving. I'm a lady. Can only take so much humiliation. There are limits. Even for this old girl.'

And here, the good woman, she of the gilded curls and pompadours, patted her heart as if she were having a case of the vapours.

Her New Routine

The world might have been dying, capitals in trauma, outbacks seething, but Marjerie Prentiss's new variety routine trumped it all. She had, that morning, wound herself and Dundarave in a sheet each, yes, in imitation of Roman dress; and there were garlands, too, purchased, presumably, from a florist. And then, so outfitted, she and her swain had pranced up and down the Traymore hall, intoning *carpe diem* all the while. It brought a smile to Eleanor who stuck her head out. It flustered Eggy who did not mind hoopla, but this seemed *de trop*. God only knew what Mrs Petrova thought of it, if she was even aware of what truly went on in her asylum. Mid-afternoon, and Eggy in the Blue Danube said: 'Why, it puts me in mind of the amateur theatrics the good folk of my hometown used to stage.'

'When?' asked Dubois, 'back when you were feeling up the wenches and popping grapes in your mouth, oh round about Nero's time?'

'No comment.'

'Phillip,' I said, 'is building me shelves.'

'How nice of him,' said Dubois.

'At no charge, apparently.'

'Oh, there'll be a cost,' Dubois observed, 'only in what currency?'

'Well, from what you tell me,' Eggy mused, 'the woman is into some risqué behaviour.'

'You wish,' said Dubois, 'but there's your answer, Randall. Him. Just send the old bugger to her and he'll pay your debt.'

'Are you trying to kill me off?' Eggy beamed.

'It's crossed my mind,' Dubois drolled.

Behind Enemy Lines

It was irregular, to say the least, Prentiss and Dundarave already in *situ,* the latter nursing a beer. At a glance, one could see that his eyes were bloodshot, though his demeanor was cordial.

'Calhoun,' he said, with a sloppy grin.

Prentiss nodded, her mind busy. Red button-up sweater. The Cleopatra bangs. In fact, the Blue Danube seemed rather crowded; Gregory, Cassandra, and Elias were entertaining a young couple whom I guessed were just over from Greece, and were either family or friends; and who were looking over the place they had obviously heard about. Antonio stood at their table with a coffee pot. I grabbed a table of my own. The bright sun showed up the smudges in the window glass. Now and then the wind screeched.

'Come on,' said Dundarave, 'don't be stand-offish. We've got room.'

He waved me over, reveller in charge of revelment. He gave Prentiss a look, one that said there was no telling about people; that life could be so much simpler if its constituents had a notion of how to relax. And with some show that it was, after all, a bit of bother, I exchanged my table for theirs.

'I'll have those shelves for you soon,' Dundarave announced, as I took a chair.

And from his tone I had reason to believe that, in regards to those shelves, he had lost interest.

Antonio walked over, his eyes disguising their own intelligence.

'Ko-fee?' he asked me.

'Hell, have a beer,' Dundarave suggested.

'I'll pass,' I said.

'I'll have some more coffee,' Prentiss's dull voice boomed.

'Sure,' said Antonio, 'no problem.'

He topped up the woman's cup and then left us, imparting to me a look of infinite pity.

'We were discussing fellatio,' Prentiss said, dead watery eyes burning holes in mine.

She was the sort of woman, so Eleanor said, who would always display her charms to best advantage, despite the hand-me-down clothes she liked to wear. Somehow that sweater, buttoned primly to her throat, sheathed endless delight.

'Priming the pump, as it were,' Dundarave chimed in, 'a lost art.'

The man was pleased with his witticism. In any other circumstance, I might have thought myself among like-minded friends; in this instance, I was appalled. I allowed Cassandra to distract me. Her countenance seemed so sweet, as there she was, tickled to death with her company. It was the most animated I had seen her eyes in a while. Elias wore a goofy smile, he the last man in the world to think of bringing anyone harm. Gregory had the look of a saint who would play down his own substantial contribution to some successful venture. Antonio had one foot in the old world and one in the new.

'Look,' said Dundarave, indicating me, 'I think he's a little nervous.'

'Why should he be?' Prentiss wondered.

'Yes,' she continued, 'he's been around. Haven't you?'

If it were possible for dead watery eyes to sparkle, they had just done so. It seemed that what there was of air in the place would suffocate me.

'Sex keeps you young,' she said.

'Look at me,' said Dundarave, 'I'm a regular teen.'

'You do have a knack,' I said to Prentiss, 'of making light of wickedness.'

'Who? Me wicked?'

'Well, aren't you? And proud of it?'

'Hang on there, boy,' said Dundarave, 'let's not get carried away.'

Even so, I would have wagered he was eagerly anticipating trouble.

'Well, what if I am,' Prentiss cheerfully countered, 'you like it. He likes it. Everyone likes it. I'm in tune with the times. I'm all for death squads. Get those loons before they get us. You have a problem with that?'

Evidently, she had watched some documentary, or she had, somehow, read my thoughts.

'Five minutes with me,' the woman crowed, 'and I'll have you sucking my big toe.'

'I'm afraid I've never been moved enough to perform that act,' I attempted to droll.

'You haven't lived.'

'Sure, get a life,' Dundarave suggested, and it was clear he was now beginning to get bored, no trouble in the offing.

'We should all get a life,' Dundarave repeated, a back country *philosophe.*

There were no gods, but humankind was explained by them, willy-nilly.

That evening, Eggy was in seventh heaven; all because the owner of one of his watering-holes had instructed him to keep clear of his sisters and his aged mother. Eggy was an hombre to reckon with, indeed. Dubois was recalling the glory days of Shawinigan hockey and some goalie, in particular, who played his best when three sheets to the wind. Dubois guffawed.

Eggy then fished from the inner pocket of his herringbone jacket a post-card. It was from Moonface, mailed to him from Argentina. Where she was drinking the wine, though she preferred the Chilean vintage. *I'm as brown as a little nut,* she observed. Next up, Lake Titiaca, birth-place of a sun-god. Hello to Dubois and Calhoun.

'She seems to be having quite the time,' I said, handing the postcard back to Eggy.

'Well, why not?' Eggy mused.

He waved Mercedes the new waitress over. I noted how exceedingly pleasant her voice was. And she stood there like the best of sports, waiting for Eggy to make up his mind.

'Effing hell,' he said, 'oh, I'll have that *filet de sole* thing.'

And she went to consult with Serge in the galley who, in turn, popped out, and wiping his hands on his apron, said: '*Mes amis.*'

Dubois and Serge carried on in French, Serge, as ever, the unsung hero of the place who quietly managed the kitchen. Dubois would have rib entrecôte. I made mention of American death squads answerable to hardly anyone. I suggested that Prentiss and Dundarave were running amok. This got Eggy's interest.

'How so?' he asked, hopefully.

'They were in here this morning discussing fellatio.'

Eggy shrugged.

'I'll bet you don't even know what fellatio is,' Dubois said to Eggy, abruptly changing the topic.

'I'll bet I do,' Eggy answered, somewhat aggrieved.

'I'm sorry,' I said, 'that I brought this up.'

There was hockey on the TV, and the Habs would lose to the lowly Islanders.

Falling Out

It was not as if change did not occur, so I learned one afternoon in the Blue Danube. Eggy's chin began to rise from his chest, and his eyes still pasty with sleep, he said: 'Effing hell. Evie and I quarrelled.'

'Oh?'

'Yes but, she said I was MCP, male chauvinist pig, and she said you were arrogant and that Bob was gutless. Well, I don't know.'

Eggy shrugged. It was something new with him, this shrugging, as it saved him the effort of making words. I forbore to tell the homunculus that it was likely Dubois and I had been names on her list of prospective suitors and we were now crossed out. I long suspected that she and Dubois had spent a night together in the not too distant past, but as to how things went, no one was going to know, Dubois, as ever, stingy with those sorts of details.

'I don't think she's coming back,' Eggy surmised.

'You know, I get that feeling, too,' I said, though I had reasons other than those of Eggy for thinking it.

'Yes but, I enjoyed her company. She wasn't a bad sort.'

'No, she wasn't.'

'But she was always talking about her troubles.'

'Yes, she was.'

'Oh well.'

'When is Moonface back?'

'How the hell do I know?'

Eggy was in a mood. He had lost in Evie Longoria an interlocutor as well as a driver and a cleaner. Somehow he was at this moment less of a lady's man than he might have been. And she was, when she was not going on about her troubles, capable of good humour and of holding her own at Animal Table. One saw her small even teeth and broad forehead, how her skin, drawn so very tight against her bones, signalled her intensity.

'And if Moonface,' I said, trying to cheer Eggy up, 'is moving around like she seems to be doing, well, she can't be spending that much time on her backside.'

'Don't patronize me.'

A shot across the bow from Zeus-like Eggy.

'She's going to marry her Champagne Sheridan,' Eggy supposed, somewhat dismally, 'and she's going to do her post-graduate thing and she's going to have babies, and she's well on her way, and you know, I don't know whether to applaud or be appalled.'

'I don't know, either.'

'Why don't you know either? You're good at seeing the future and what a person ought to do.'

'For God's sake, old man, far from it. Moonface is an enigma, and I suspect she'll always be that as she's an enigma to herself.'

'An enigma wrapped in an enigma—isn't that how it goes?'

'Something like that.'

'I would like to have had her on her backside—'

'Evidently.'

'Don't get cheeky, young man. She's my complementary function. Took me a while to discover that, but I discovered it.'

'Yes, you did.'

'We love you,' said Antonio, approaching the table, holding his arms out to Eggy.

'Oh eff off. Back to Albania with you. Where you belong.'

Antonio kissed the old sod's pate.

Confirmation of Evie Longoria's intentions came to light two days later after her apparent quarrel with Eggy. Evie had slipped her note into my mailbox, and when I went to check my mail in the Traymore foyer, I heard Mrs Petrova's new and richly chiming clock chiming the hours of human fragility. There was strange traffic going up and down the stairs, but the footfalls were eventually explained by the fact that Prentiss's digs were the object of their visitations. Dubois once again had sequestered himself after a few migraine-free days. Eleanor was out of town; nothing unusual in this. Nor was Suzie Q in the vicinity. Eggy, no doubt, was taken up by a new DVD machine and hot lez sex. Perhaps this was what had set Evie off, though she was no puritan. Even so, on discovery of the note, I took it to my rooms and read that men, myself in particular, had copped out of the game or had lost interest and did not know what they were missing. Even her penmanship was intense: small lettering, even lines on unruled paper. Well, she was half-right, I supposed, but as I did not blame my grotty life on the likes of her, I did not see why she should blame me for her troubles. I balled up the paper and disposed of it. And just when I was beginning to visualize Prentiss as an entity for whom one might reach and only ever embrace empty air, all self bottomless and she especially so, the woman, utterly solid and immanent, knocked on my door.

'Hullo.'

Cleopatra bangs. Bemused eyes.

'I won't keep you long,' she went on to say, 'just that we're due for spring rites, don't you think? I understand you're conversant with such things? We may throw a party soon. Be advised.'

§

Book IV—Short of Copy

Demon Love III

—On a dank Sunday morning, I enter the Blue Danube early, Cassandra dusting off the Artemis figure in the wall-niche, Cassandra chewing gum, her dimples squirrelling. She gives me a look, the tenderness of which seems to have no rhyme or reason. It disconcerts. Last night in this very place, and it was quite busy, Antonio and Mercedes both run off their feet, Gregory playing the *maître d'*, Serge manfully manning the galley, Dubois worried about Eggy's recent behaviour. The homunculus was spending more time than ever in various watering-holes. Eggy: 'Yes but, it isn't as if I've been between anyone's legs, if that's what you mean.' Dubois: 'Well, if you were between someone's legs, it would explain the puzzled look on your face.' I go out for a puff. Those are spring, as opposed to winter, clouds above. Unfamiliar birdcalls. A squad car accelerates by. No siren, lights flashing. Leafless, sentinel trees line either side of our noble boulevard. Dog walkers. Pooping dogs. It is the time of year for *le grand ménage.* House-cleaning. The ministrations of wax, bleach, ammonia. I suppose Cassandra will set her potted ferns on the terrasse sometime soon, along with the ornamental birds. Was Mercedes cut from the same cloth as Echo? Eggy wondered it, last night, and Dubois answered in the negative. No, Mercedes is not quite the dynamo as was Echo, though she is, in her own way, attractive. So Dubois reasoned it, Eggy supposing that that rational French mind had a point. And then Dubois and I stepped out on the terrasse for a cigarette, Dubois lauding Gregory, who was not, it seemed, afraid of work, and would make a go of the place. 'He knows,' Dubois observed, 'the little things to do, and they add up.' 'Well, he's beginning to know,' I corrected, 'as business is teaching him business.' Dubois in the business world had been one of those men who would trouble-shoot failing companies and bring them back to health. But where were Miss Meow and the Whistler? Blind Musician, for that matter? Too Tall Poet? Had Dubois an answer for these absences? Moonface seemed reduced to the stand-by status of a rumour. She has become in Eggy's mind little more than a minx getting her sentimental education in Argentina, irrelevant now to the great affairs of state as are life in the café. We had our cigarettes, Dubois and I, and we returned to Animal Table, where we found Eggy aghast. His *filet de sole* thing had, horrors, come with Greek potatoes.

Yet More Crying Jags

It was for Eleanor to know and me to find out. Wherever she had been, of late, she was not telling. Another fly-by-night fling in Toronto the Good plus shopping spree? A sunset tryst in Panama City? Eleanor, she of the gilded curls and pompadours, would only top up my amaretto and give me the look of one who had made an effort but had not entirely obtained her heart's desire in matters of love and pleasure.

'You know,' she said, 'took a little trip. The usual. Nothing exciting happened.'

Liar, liar, house on fire—She continued: 'Anyhew, I come back, and what do you know, my kitchen's spic and span. Bob's doing. What's he angling for? And—', and here she lowered her lashes and regarded me fearfully: 'well, what I want to know from you is this ... has ... oh, never mind—'

'Has what?'

'That Longoria woman. Is she still hanging around?'

'She was. But she was hanging around Eggy. You know perfectly well he paid her a stipend for driving him here and there and to do a little house cleaning.'

'Why would anyone wish to hang around Eggy, all gristle and bone and ill temper? Do you expect me to believe that?'

'I don't understand why you won't believe it. The latest joke going the rounds is that he took to wearing a crash helmet when that hulk of a nurse would show up and sponge him down once in a while—'

'Roll me a cig,' she said, ignoring my attempt at levity. I said: 'Bob's planning a trip for us. Quebec City. Last hurrah.'

'Oh is he? I've not heard of it. Is Evie going, too?'

'Boys only, I think.'

'You going?'

'Yes.'

'Want to fool around?'

'Eleanor.'

But her thoughts were already elsewhere, as soon as she had put her proposal to me.

'Prentiss is up to something,' she observed.

'What now?'

'Just a party.'

'With her, it's never just a party.'

'Maybe, maybe not.'

'So how do you know about this party?'

'She told me. Spring rites.'

'Are Traymoreans going to be copulating en masse?'

Eleanor gave me a look. It was a look that suggested I might have hit on the truth of a thing.

'You're kidding,' I said.

'Maybe, maybe not.'

'Well, count me out.'

'So I may as well tell you,' she said, pursuing yet another line of thought, 'I was visiting with Ralph at his country place. No, nothing happened, like I said. I was just his shoulder to cry on. All to do with Marjerie, of course. He loves her dearly, but she won't grow up. Loves Phillip, too. You know, best buddies. But Phillip won't grow up, either. Said he was tired of the sex thing. Said that even if I, *moi*, yours truly, as attractive as you know me to be, tried to seduce him, it would only leave him cold. Well, I took it as a challenge. So I guess I'm lying when I said nothing happened. But nothing did. I tried and I made a fool of myself for trying. Nothing new. It's your old Eleanor true to form. Got my hands in his pants and he just froze. There's a first time for everything.'

Silence. I handed her the cigarette I had taken my time in rolling.

'Why are men always brushing me off?' she sighed.

She then tizzed me: 'Tis a heavy burden to bear.'

'You win some, you lose some, I guess.'

'Come off it, Calhoun. By the way, have you ever had Longoria in your bed?'

'It's for me to know and you to find out.'

'So you have.'

'Not really.'

'Criminey, Randall, with you, it's ... I don't know. I guess they just bring their knitting along and you lie there, holding the yarn.'

'Yes, I suppose I'm really a beast, at that.'

'I hear there's another new waitress in Dodge.'

'That there is.'

'Are you going to make a play?'

'Eleanor, for God's sake.'

'Why not?'

'I don't chase women.'

'How then do you explain your exploits?'

'Happenstance. The stars align a certain way.'

'I swear to God, Randall, you're either the slickest of the slick or you're just the goofy clown you claim to be.'

'Oh, I'm the clown, alright. No question.'

Suzie Q assailed me in the hall as I was about to enter my digs, having just escaped Eleanor. The good woman's voice had gotten husky, her eyes glassy, her heart too noble for my comfort. Suzie Q put her finger to her lips, shushing me. Ah, she was just then incognito. In a sweatshirt. Running togs. Thick socks. She approached me and followed me into my living room.

'What's the big mystery?' I asked, as she seemed more proprietary of my quarters than I would have liked. At least, rather than occupying the whole of it, she only took up the edge of my couch, leaning forward, yes, like an athlete in a locker room miserable with defeat.

'Are you going?' she asked, and she seemed to be addressing the floor.

I waited for clarification. Where would I be going? The Yukon? To hell in a handbasket? She had had her locks trimmed, the curls spilling over her ears, if not the chic-est of hair-stylings, fetching, at any rate.

'The party,' she said.

'I haven't been invited to any party.'

It looked like she might cry.

'I meant to go away for spring break,' she began to explain.

'Oh,' I said, still waiting, 'where?'

'To the country. For a little skiing.'

'That's nice.'

'But obviously,' she said, 'I haven't gone anywhere.'

No, indeed. Of what was she the counterpart to Randall Q Calhoun, this Suzie Q, this clearly intelligent girl who was somewhat haughty, quick to take offense? My fumbling but serious youth not yet given to cynicism? As when a flashing ankle and sparkling eyes and a John Donne sonnet could still answer all that was half-hearted in life and shame it?

'Anyway,' she said, rising from the couch, her tone abstracted.

'Look, if there's something bothering you—'

'You'll think I'm silly.'

'I just might.'

'It's Phillip.'

'Is that all?'

'And her, too.'

'But of course.'

Her eyes registered her panic. Hers was essentially an honest face.

'Why do you say that?'

'I live here, don't I? I've seen how they work.'

Suzie Q blushed. For an instant, and only for instant, she seemed grateful to hear those words. Ah, sweet femininity, yes, in a girl who apparently loathed the appearance of it.

'But I like it,' she said, 'and then again, I don't.'

'You'll have to be a titch more particular.'

'Fucking them.'

It was a harsh word to come tumbling from her mouth, that f-word.

'Oh well, there you go. Are you sure you know who's fucking whom?'

The look she gave me now was that of a snarling, half-crazed dog.

'I mean,' I said, 'what do you want me to say about it?'

'Marjerie's right. You're not a very nice man.'

'When she's right, she's right.'

'They make me feel dirty.'

'I'm told that's half the pleasure.'

Now that was fury, that fury I saw in her eyes.

Virgin Snow with Oatmeal

Wine was conspicuously absent from Animal Table; but Mercedes was there gingerly attending to Eggy and Dubois. She knew she was now massively outnumbered as I arrived, the look in her eyes the equivalent of running up the proverbial white flag. Eggy had no idea what a frightening homunculus he was.

'Well, what's your excuse?' he thundered at me as I took a chair.

I had just been in audience with Eleanor. I had just been given the treatment by Suzie Q, that one which redounded to the fact that all amity, let alone the ebb and flow of critique between male and female, is life and death and give no quarter urgency until the next round of exchange. In any case, it was none of Eggy's business what I had been up to. None at all. Bugger him.

'I'll have a coffee,' I said, without looking into Mercedes' eyes, fearful of what I might see in them.

'Yes but, what's your excuse?' Eggy still wished to know.

And why was the world so indifferent to his wishes? Had it not yet been ascertained that he was a hanging judge; that Moonface was his complementary function for all that she was more than likely on her backside on a tropical beach, and in the embrace of a pretender?

'None,' I answered.

'Says you.'

'Now boys,' Dubois tut-tutted.

'New President,' I said, 'can't decide whether he's the leader of the free world or a satirist.'

'We've covered this ground, already,' Dubois observed, 'and what matters is if they're going to play a game of hockey, tonight, or just go through the motions.'

Dubois referred to his beloved Habs, those low-lifes who were currently self-destructing. The look in his glittering blue eyes suggested he had seen it coming all along, his belief in the good sense of the American people still rather shaky but not yet shattered. I would spare that belief of his the fatal body blow it deserved.

'Yes but,' Eggy interjected, winding up to thunder, raising his finger, 'there was a mutiny and the coach was blindsided.'

'Could be,' Dubois mused.

And it could have been that Eggy had not the game of hockey in his squirrelly mind.

It was evening in the Blue Danube, Animal Table reconvened. Antonio did the honours on the floor. Miss Meow was reading a newspaper. *La Presse. Quotidien montréalais.* I was just in from a puff outside on the terrasse, and in the course of that puff, two goals had been scored, none of them by the Habs. Dubois gave me a look. He squelched a guffaw.

'*Merde*,' he said.

Eggy's chin had raised his chest, and so he missed the disaster unfolding on the ice.

I had passed the afternoon on my couch, Eleanor at my side. Now and then she sobbed for no discernible rhyme or reason. She had not the slightest bit of interest in March Madness or college basketball, all that American hoopla. Now and then she placed my hand on her knee. Now and then I gave her a consoling squeeze.

'God, they're ugly,' she intermittently observed of mid-western tall and gangly physiques, the hair close-cropped, the faces Teutonic and humourless.

Replicas of the Stars and Stripes were stitched to every jersey, without exception.

She understood Florida, so she would claim, but Minnesota or Oklahoma? She had lost the sartorial Dundarave to the machinations of Prentiss. She had lost Dubois to Dubois. At least she could say she had not lost me, as she had not really had me, so to speak. After a while, she sighed and summoned up a sloppy kiss for my person, and then drolled: 'Don't know what you see in any of this, but I'm going.'

'My youth,' I said.

'My arse,' she said.

She shimmied out in her pompadours, thoroughly disgusted. And my eyes must have closed, and I must have dreamed something; and when I next woke I was terrified—for no rhyme or reason. I hoped Animal Table was in session. And it was, and there was comfort in this.

'Well, what's the score?'

Eggy had come to, his homuncular peepers blinking.

Dubois guffawed.

'It's a catastrophe,' Dubois offered, by way of catching Eggy up to speed.

'Oh well,' Eggy shrugged.

He looked around the café for an attractive woman to ogle, and there was none. Miss Meow did not rate.

'Oh damn,' he said, 'it's the Albanian.'

'Eggeee,' Antonio sing-songed, passing by, 'we love you.'

'But he's half-Italian,' I corrected.

'Little good it does him,' Eggy snorted.

His peepers fluttered. It looked like he might swoon.

'Are you alright?' Dubois queried.

'Of course, I'm alright. I was just between someone's legs, that's all.'

'I hope it was worth it,' Dubois said.

'Always,' Eggy responded, if a little grimly.

Along with the wine, melancholy had by now settled in my gut. In my mentations, the dead sounded off. Old friends. The Howards, the Klopstocks. Jack Swain. My first and only wife. Fast Eddy, too. There was the absent Moonface, Eggy's complementary function. A game of hockey on TV was exceedingly unimportant. It might snow, overnight, and the next morning the ground seem virgin. On the terrasse, as I stood there and puffed, geese flew overhead in loose formation, there in the darkening sky; and to their calls, I exulted. For no rhyme or reason. A child holding on to his father's hand had noticed them, too, pointing upwards. One of life's little, unscripted moments that might or might not attach to memory in someone's dodgy old age.

'Well,' said Eggy, 'what's the score now?'

'You don't want to know,' Dubois answered.

'Oh, that bad,' Eggy responded.

It was time to order a meal before the wine destroyed us.

Crows called from one end of the sky to the other, contrarians to a feather. It snowed, as was forecast. I made coffee. And then, as was sometimes my wont, I took a cup of it to the window at the end of the Traymore hall, birds, squirrels, cats and dog my metaphysics. Heavy, weary steps on the stairs. And why, it was Dundarave not so sartorial, returning from a late night of it. His grin was briefly sheepish, his bleary eyes carved from stone. He raised a hand in greeting, one that simultaneously warded off questions. Even so, I smelled the blues bar on him, and possibly Jarnette. Perhaps she had allowed the man to do some of the heavy lifting as pertained to her pleasuring. One assumed that Prentiss would have something to say in regards to her swain's lateness and prowess, too proud to admit to jealousy, but just petty enough to engineer a catty observation or two. Dundarave unlocked a door and was gone. Plumbing. Dubois had just gone for a whiz. In my digs again, I put on Faure's *Requiem*. The music suited my mood. Fallen leaves, sweatered girls, football—was all that the boy I once was? All those amorphous longings. The sweet sissboombahs of an imperishable civic order. At precisely which moment did I cease to believe women in loafers and men in hush puppies? Famished, I prepared a pot of oatmeal. As I buttered and sugared a bowl of the gruel, I was treated, so to speak, to another blast from the past: my parents' loveless kitchen that I always knew would not break my spirit but that would attune me to the hypocrisies of love and the ephemeralities of lust.

A Woman in White

Someone knocked. And it was Marjerie Prentiss all in white, but barefoot. High-collared, somewhat faded blouse, the buttons mother of pearl. Capris.

'Oh,' she said, 'you're in.'

Dead watery eyes mocked. Her eyes were a mounted challenge. And yet, given that her bangs very nearly reached those eyes, she bore an uncanny resemblance to Moe of Three Stooges provenance.

'Needing sugar again?' I drolled.

'No,' she said, 'just cruising. Phillip was out catting all night, and now he's crashed.'

'I'll bet.'

'You always keep me standing here.'

'I'm busy reading.'

'Reading?'

One almost heard the *nyuk-nyuks* of a Moe in her dully booming voice.

'A verse written by a Roman who's having trouble getting it up.'

'Ah, a tragic lament.'

'No, some jesting at his own expense for the amusement of his god.'

'I've never heard of such a thing.'

'There's more to the ancients than we credit them for.'

'Are you going to invite me in or not?'

I shrugged. I watched as she occupied the couch. There was a pile of books on the coffee table. Plato. The British-French wars. American imperialism. Marjerie Prentiss gave each a cursory thumbing-through, and none seemed to gain her interest. I put it to her: 'So, did you ever watch someone die?'

And she, caught a little off-guard, had not.

'Did you ever have a deeply metaphysical conversation with a child?'

'Have you?'

'No, but I continue to believe it's possible.'

'And you,' she asked, 'did you ever achieve mystic union whilst having sex?'

What, was she making promises? The lilac tree in Mrs Petrova's yard was sprouting shoots. The sparrows were burbling. Time for glee and the old maypole.

'I don't know,' I answered, a touch evasive.

'Will you roll me one of your cigarettes?'

'I suppose I could.'

'Well then, why don't you?'

And she sat there and smoked the cig, her touring eyes on reconnaissance, she giving me her Cleopatra profile, what with those bangs she sported. It seemed the conversation had nowhere to go, and I had no intention of winding up in bed. If she had had any idea of what she wished to get from her visit, she either decided there was nothing to get or it was clear to her that I was in no mood to cooperate. She shrugged.

'Hey, it's been a hoot,' she said.

'Likewise.'

She might have stepped out of a beatnik poem, its heroine. She might have been some novel's slutty housewife, one bored beyond any language's capacity to measure. Even so, as she fascinated herself, she was incapable of the bored state. Or so I supposed. She was, of course, working her magic; and I had an image in mind of a bewildered Priapus, a silly and twisted grin on his mug. I attempted to telepathically convey to her that she was near wearing out her welcome; that I had things to do. She got the hint.

'Ta-ta,' she said, as she rose from the couch, and on the heels of her feet, was comically sinuous.

'Keep in touch,' she added, as she went out the door.

Now here was Dubois poking his head in. He gave me a look, one to which he was entitled, seeing as he had just witnessed Prentiss absconding with my integrity.

'Busy, busy,' he clucked.

'What do you want?'

'Are you fucking her?'

'Don't be silly.'

'Alright then. Look, are we on for Quebec City or not? In other words, are you up for Eggy and high maintenance? Is this thing a go?'

'Sure. I already said so.'

'I just want to be clear on it, that's all. I'll do some checking around for rental cars. For now, I won't bother you with such things. When the time comes, I'll let you know what's what.'

'Look, I can help—'

'No, that's fine. Really. See you later at the café.'

Moonface Debriefed

Mid-afternoon, a cold bite to the air, and the Blue Danube was quiet, Cassandra wiping the sides of the soup tureen. Eggy snoozed. His slumped inverted triangle of a face was transparent: that he was guilty, guilty in respect to all his sins, only that his lips slyly demurred. Dubois studied some mind-teaser of a newspaper. An article, no doubt, on derivatives. Now derivatives was one those words that had gotten to be one of those words; I visualized it flying around bat-like (irregardless of the fact that it was March) at the onset of dusk, the sky a darkening blue. I slid into place at Animal Table, which brought Eggy to wakefulness. He raised a finger and was about to thunder or perhaps orate verse, but then thought better of it.

'Effing hell,' he said.

Cassandra, leaving the soup tureen, moved to one of her potted ferns. She was singing to herself the lyrics of some pop tune on the radio, the TV programmed to a soccer match. Dubois looked on, he a paternal figure, his charges in each their proper niche.

'How are you?' he asked me, archly civil.

'Fine,' I answered..

Eggy's cheese pies untouched, the bottle half-full or half-empty, depending on one's theology, I was in the mood for a vigorous discussion of *X*, *Y* and *Z*; my fellow conspirators were not. No, it was a sleepy cantina in a sleepy border town, never mind that drug wars raged all about; that the dogs on the street were rabid.

'New President,' I said, attempting some gambit or another, 'is already up for a lynching. That didn't take long.'

No comment. No takers.

'T-shirts are going the rounds in Israel, ones that read *1 SHOT 2 KILLS.* Any guesses?'

Eggy shrugged in the vernacular. Nope. Dubois waited for the kicker.

'Arab women who are preggers are targets of opportunity.'

'Hang the bastards,' Eggy thundered.

Dubois simply looked out the window. Perhaps he wished I would keep to writing poetry or something.

'Any news of Moonface?' I asked.

This drew a blank, an elongated geometrical construct, one that stretched from hell to eternity, along which three pilgrims, each an unhorsed knight—Eggy, Dubois and I—continued to heed the rumoured grail of love, but that it was a slog.

'I was thinking,' Dubois said, 'of Moonface. I was thinking of her as an old woman, getting debriefed. What I mean to say is I see her seated at some table, all her old lovers seated with her, and everyone's comparing notes as to what they've been and where they've been and so forth. There's a song to this effect sung by Renée Claude. Maybe you could end your book on this note.'

Dubois guffawed, pleased with his pun.

'What book?' I asked.

'The one you're supposed to be writing but evidently are not.'

'Yes, well—'

'Oh, are you writing a book?' asked Eggy, the soul of mischief.

'No. So don't worry your pretty little head about it.'

'Eff off.'

'I can't quite remember the lyrics,' said Dubois, 'but I wrote them down somewhere. I'll pass them on to you.'

'That would be nice,' I answered, endeavouring a polite response.

Once in a while, Dubois got so awfully earnest. He was vain and impossibly handsome, and he truly meant well. Eggy, on the other hand, was a rotter through and through.

Equinoctial Ceremonies

Yet again, I missed out on the action, as when a pistol-packing Prentiss not so long ago, wearing only a pink boa, traipsed about in the Traymore hall. This time around, or so I was told, the action began with me, even if I had been dead to the world, Eleanor and Prentiss regarding me on the couch. Some mirthful debate as to whether I should be wakened, Eleanor all for letting sleeping dogs lie. So now it was the morning after, and the summing up was underway, there in Eleanor's kitchen, commodious room, Dubois and Eggy in attendance. Eleanor, banging a spoon against a pot, had roused me, exhorting me to come and get it. Hotcakes, sausages. Eggy chuckled, bits of sausage falling to his bib with which he was outfitted, his open maw—target zero—still pristine. Even so, he was in possession of some intelligence that, sooner or later, was going to impinge on me. I steeled myself.

'Yes,' said Dubois, slabs of hotcake neatly skewered on his fork, 'you should've seen it. And when Eggy saw it, he fainted.'

'I did not.'

'But you did. At first I thought you were having one of your episodes, the way your blood pressure goes and falls off a cliff. I figured you had no idea what you were seeing, but then it dawned on you—'

'What do you mean I had no idea? Think I was born yesterday?'

'A few centuries ago, maybe—'

'Eff off.'

Even so, and though he was getting the worst of this exchange, Eggy beamed.

'What, for God's sake,' I put it to those stalwarts, 'are you on about?'

'Why, hanky-panky,' said Eggy, his finger raised, 'sport in the hen house.'

Dubois guffawed.

'A little *divertissement* you might say,' Eleanor drolled, her lipstick bright, her curls gilded, her voice shimmering with mystery.

I began rolling a couple of cigarettes.

'Yes but,' Eggy said, 'Suzie Q—'

I shook my head, evincing the air of a man who knew he was being toyed with.

'Yes, she gave it her all,' Eleanor attempted to explain, 'but in the end—'

'Gave what all and to whom?' I interrupted.

'She was polishing His Nibs's knob,' said Eleanor, like a woman who had seen everything and would write the primer.

'Did I hear right?' I asked.

'You did.'

Well then, Prentiss must have had her latest revels, good time had by all, only I slept through the festivities.

'You missed the party,' Eleanor crowed, relieving me of one of the cigarettes and promptly lighting it, 'not that anything happened that you haven't seen before, I'm sure.'

'Dundarave done up as a Roman—' Dubois said.

'In a sheet,' Eggy hooted.

'Dyed red,' said Eleanor.

'They were taking turns,' Dubois duly noted.

I gave Eleanor a look as if to say, *what, you too?*

She answered, and it seemed she blushed: 'No, dear. Not me.'

'Oh God,' I said, 'I don't want to know.'

'*Au contraire*,' Eleanor rebuffed, 'sure you do. The effing minx invited. We watched. How they roped Suzie Q into it, there you've got me.'

I threw up my arms and shrugged.

'Why,' asked Eggy, child-like, 'do you think it was very bad? Will they drop the bomb?'

I ignored the homunculus.

'Well, I guess I wouldn't have put it past her,' I sighed, and then continued: 'So, you all enjoyed yourselves? Slave girls tooting on flutes? Dundarave festooned with floral wreaths? Were you served deadly mushrooms? I wouldn't put that past her, either. But I guess you weren't as here you all are.'

What began as an innocent query on my part got dismissive; and, after a spate of silence, Eleanor answered: 'Oh, I don't know—'

'And Eggy,' said Dubois, keen to retain in memory what comic highlights of the scene had been on offer, 'when he came to, he lit out of there as fast as his pins could carry him.'

Eggy beamed.

'Anyway, that's enough,' said Eleanor, suddenly prim.

'No it's not,' Eggy thundered, 'more details, please. Why, as Bob says, I didn't see it all.'

'There isn't much more to tell,' said Eleanor, her demeanor softening, 'we were invited to watch. We watched. And then Marjerie, the minx, she finished him off with a vicious little yank, if you ask me, and then she said it was over, spring officially sprung, and the world would unfold as it should, let the chips fall where they may. And then, Bob, you got your jaw back in place because it had dropped all the way to the floor, and me, if I were to be honest, no, it didn't do anything for me.'

'Yes but, Suzie Q—' Eggy protested.

'Too true,' Eleanor broke in, 'there was that. You see, Randall, obviously she thought she was up for it, and then she wasn't, and she got upset, especially after Phillip called her a silly cunt and she bolted. Then Marj and I, going after her, got into it in the hall—'

'Yes, I think I might've heard that in a dream,' I said.

'And now,' said Eleanor, 'now all's quiet in the Traymore realm, except for us. But I didn't really sleep right.'

'Why, I slept like a babe,' Eggy let us know.

'I have to say,' said Dubois, 'that I did, too.'

'Shouldn't someone see how she's doing,' I asked, 'Suzie Q, I mean?'

'Tried that already, but she wasn't in,' Eleanor responded.

'Good grief.'

'Do you disapprove?' Eggy put it to me.

'Yes, of course. Not to the sex but to the gamesmanship. Suzie Q's just a kid, for God's sake.'

'Not really,' Eleanor begged to differ.

'Even so,' I insisted, 'you can't just produce some stiffus prickus and say, "Here, go to work on it."'

'I take your point,' Eleanor said, her tone a bit odd, so I figured, 'but I don't think it was like that. They didn't hold a gun to her head. She wanted to do it.'

'Maybe she thought she did,' I countered, 'but she and I, we had a chat recently, and I can tell you she's not all clear about what she's doing with those two. Well, I think they're using her for their little games. And I don't understand why you became a party to—'

'Whoa. What's this? Calhoun the Christian? Since when? Adults play games. Sometimes somebody gets hurt. You can't have an omelet and all that—'

'Eleanor,' I said, 'no. I think not. And you'd better see to her. And I don't mean to come down as a righteous prude and get on your case, but the girl's just a girl, however clever and sophisticated she thinks she is, and sex is one thing, but psychodrama's another, and if they want to diddle one another on their own, fine, but to get you to watch—'

I could not, it seemed, complete my thought, but was I coming off a moral man?

'I knew it,' said Dubois, 'underneath all that cynicism a moral structure.'

'I beg your pardon,' I answered, 'hardly. I'm still very much the cynic. But between those two—Prentiss and Dundarave—they might just have ruined her, and it's a waste.'

'Yep,' observed Eleanor, 'you're still a cynic, alright.'

It was nagging me in the Blue Danube, later, Cassandra, as usual, admitting me early: how I could not just come out and say to Traymoreans that they had conducted themselves poorly. It was going to be a chore, committing to my notebook the gist of what had transpired in Eleanor's kitchen. Why not just write yet again, for the *nth* time, evolutionary drift, and have done with it? Oh, Suzie Q would stew and nurse her wounds and get over it, and then go look for some meek creature male or female that she could manage, and attend to her needs by her own lights, to hell with party favours. Or she might turn hermit or sign up for a focus group and vote Republican. Well now, here was the cynic, right on time. Sometimes Cassandra just stood there, gazing out the window; and then something in her countenance seemed to reach back in her head for a thought that had gone missing and she could not quite find it. And then her feet and her hands recovered their capacity to move, and she would swing her fine head, and her long hair swish about. And then she might come and top up my coffee, I some minute part of a very large equation in her calculations. For Suzie Q, what was done was done. One assumed she would move away on the return of Moonface, and she would forget all about Traymoreans. America's debt just might bring the world down. No doubt, I would get my Prentiss visit in the next day or two, and she regard with me those dead, watery, and sexually smug eyes. I knew that in Dundarave there would be, upon waking, just the barest whisper of remorse in him; not because he could give a toss for Suzie Q's tender feelings, but because it had been demonstrated once more he was not quite his own man, and it would rankle. And then Cassandra announced to me that trouble had arrived; and indeed it had—in the person of an excited homunculus, Eggy rapping on the glass door with his cane.

Eggy on a Mission

'I knew I'd find you here,' Eggy crowed as he settled in for a hit and run.

He waved off Cassandra.

'I have appointments elsewhere,' he thundered, and then to me: 'Got to see nursie. But you know, why, I just saw Suzie Q, and I spoke to her.'

'Really?' I said, alarmed.

'Of course really,' Eggy thundered, 'think I saw a ghost? Why, I told her right there in the hall, I told her I was sorry for last night. But then, I couldn't be that sorry, she should understand, as I hadn't seen everything, well, not much. Because I fainted. Well, according to Bob who thinks I'm on my last legs.'

'And what did she say?'

'Oh hell, nothing. No, she didn't say anything. And I thought, uh oh, she's not liking this very much, and she's going to whack me one, you know, and she looked at me, and then, guess what? Why, she laughed. And then, what's more, effing hell, and she just might become my complementary function if she keeps it up, she bussed my cheek. See? Right there.'

And Eggy, Zeus-like Eggy, he who would have a universe believe he was a harmless old fuddy-duddy, his finger raised, attempted to indicate the general area where it could be understood his cheek and the buss occupied mutual space.

'And that was that,' Eggy concluded, 'I'm short of copy.'

The homunculus shrugged.

'Hoo hoo,' he said, as an after-thought.

§

Book V—False Carnations

Demon Love IV

—Eggy and Dubois at Animal Table are on a roll, the life of the mind glorified. *Duck Soup* meets Aristotle. Outside, dark rain and the shiny boulevard. Dubois: 'The female sparrow will mute the song of her mate should he try to attract some other female with his song.' Eggy (impertinent): 'Yes but, Jews are aliens from outer space. Read your Ezekiel.' Dubois: 'And to think that this man in his 7th decade was going for a doctorate. No wonder they eased you off the reservation.' Eggy: 'Well, you know, I decided to take up drinking.' Calhoun: 'Perhaps Lot's wife posited humanity's first existential question.' Eggy (doubtful): 'Why, is that in Ezekiel?' As busy as Mercedes is, even so, she makes time for the uncorking of Animal Table's second bottle, her smile up close, eyes distant, hips a force. It is very near like an unveiling, this corking rite. Did that figurine of Artemis just move, bending her bow? Eggy: 'They should've dropped the puck by now.' Calhoun: 'There's never a hockey game when you need one.' Eggy (to Mercedes): 'Well, you could pour, you know.' Calhoun (to Mercedes): 'Don't let this runt push you around.' She blushes, this waitress with blue brassiere. Miss Meow at her table not only miaows, she Mao's, her massive shoulders slumped. She has been companionless, these past few days. They seem American, that crew at their table, Vermonters, probably, come to Sin City for a lark. One hears: 'Men look at women and women look at women.' One hears: 'What's perverse and what's normal are normal.' Perhaps one of the members of the crew is a celebrated novelist. Eggy: 'Why, because x equals minus b plus over minus… oh, I don't know, complete the effing square yourself.' Dubois (to Calhoun): 'What's got into him?' Eggy (thundering): 'Coleridge. That's what got into me. *Where Alph, the sacred river ran. Through caverns measureless to man*… But, in any case, Moonface is a scatterbrain.' Calhoun: 'She will have changed when we see her next. She might not know she's changed, but she will have—' Eggy: 'Ah yes, Champagne Sheridan's got her knocked up. Babies and the burbs.' Dubois: 'Not if she's careful.' Eggy (finger raised): 'Has any wench ever been careful?' And Dubois would go for a puff and I would join him, and we leave Eggy perplexed as to quadratic solutions and whether Coleridge wrote the poem or whether the opium wrote him. Calhoun (to Dubois on the terrasse): "I think we're in for an epiphany.' Dubois (guffawing): 'Did you bring an umbrella?'

—To Eleanor's for a sliver of the liquid amber. And what is serious? 'Serious,' Eleanor in her kitchen answers, 'is when your desire aches and can't find its complement.' Since when is the good woman a mystic? The grey-green eyes. Gilded curls. Bright lipstick. Her mind will freely range from subjects as various as the Federal Reserve to Jacob Burckhardt to which high heels might she look good in. And I know and she knows, and even Dubois knows; and all the world knows it: she will marry her Bob, her knight; as he has, for the most part, protected her, try as she might to give his security the slip. With Gambetti the millionaire. With sartorial Dundarave. Even with me. An understanding shall trump desire. (And she will get all his money of which, I suspect, he has more than meets the eye.) But no matter, for the good woman is not avaricious. Even so, she bids me bugger off; she has a date with a mall. And I go and stand at the window at the end of the Traymore hall. The stippling lilac. The deteriorating snow. The elegant river gulls. Sparrows splashing in the dirty ground pools. And Suzie Q is in from classes. And Prentiss is out with a 'you'll never pin me down' look on her face. And no, it does not seem I will have that pleasure.

—Prentiss is of good cheer, dead, watery eyes as frisky as squirrels bouncing off March trees. She stands at my door, a nondescript frock on her. 'You missed the revels,' her dull voice booms. 'So I've been told,' I answer. A bare toe rubs against a bare ankle. Even her Cleopatra bangs calculate the odds of… well, who can say what they calculate? 'Phillip certainly had a good time,' she observes. 'I can imagine.' 'You really don't like me.' And so forth and so on in respect to a conversation that has infinite legs—

A Conversation about the Meaning of Life

A note from Eleanor, slipped under my door at some unknown hour of the night, summoned me for an audience in her kitchen at eleven or so in the morning. I complied. She was not alone; as I walked through her door I heard Prentiss, and this was not auspicious.

'Randall,' said Eleanor, cheerily enough, 'set yourself down.'

'Hullo,' a dull voice boomed.

Prentiss was evidently amused. I declined an offer of freshly baked carrot muffin.

'So what does it all mean?' Eleanor put it to me, her tone suggesting she was prepared to be relentless on this score.

'Diddlysquat,' I said, without thinking.

I might have said: 'Prentiss, your bangs are ludicrous.'

'Come on, Randall,' Eleanor, 'we're serious. What the effing hell does it all mean?'

Once more without thinking: 'You live, you die, you're forgotten.'

'Oh really,' said Eleanor, miffed.

I blessed Marjerie Prentiss with a significant look.

On a cloud-soddened afternoon, I sat in the Blue Danube, noodling in my notebook. I was surprised to see Eleanor coming through the door, energetic in her pompadours.

'That was a poor performance, this morning,' she immediately informed me, 'right poor.'

'I didn't think the question was serious,' I answered.

'You really don't like Prentiss.'

'Not much.'

'Do you think you can tell me why?'

'Eleanor, darling, we've been through this, haven't we? And I don't think her friendship has done you much good.'

'That's my call, not yours.'

'Fair enough. But don't draw me into things between you two, alright?'

Eleanor gave me a look. Man proposed; woman disposed. But then, yes, as she had not a mean bone in her body, it was not in her—for all her stubbornness and the way she would insist on carrying her wishes through to a conclusion—to force the issue.

'I have a funny feeling about her,' Eleanor now said, changing tack.

'Like she's going to finally succeed in shooting one of us?'

'Maybe. But no, it's something else.'

She fished for a cigarette from the packet of smokes she held in her palm; and she placed it between her lips. Where it dangled as her eyes became a pair of reflecting pools, pondering the unknown.

'Hold the fort,' she said, 'I'll be back.'

And she stepped out to the terrasse for her puff; and she had the air of a woman who had much on her mind; and she shivered a little. And when she had had her puff and was settled again at the table, letting Cassandra know she was only passing through, no need to fuss, she said: 'Yes, I have a funny feeling. No doubt about it. But damn if I know what it is.'

Then: 'It's turned cooler again,' she observed.

Well, she had not come wearing a jacket, the sweater that flattered her fairly light. And my noodling was now quite disrupted; I had lost forever some vaguely-realized train of thought, my ability to focus, even on futility, not what it once was. So it seemed. Even so, I was overcome by a wave of sympathy for the woman across from me whose biscuits I had eaten; whose liquid amber I had had generous portions of; whose kisses I had even had the pleasure of receiving, mostly in a spirit of play; nothing outright sexual. She was, after all, not only appealing but a trouper; and she could have accomplished much in life. Ambition aside, and all things being equal, she had a knack for general contentment, though her love affairs or debacles now and then upset her equilibrium. To be sure, Dubois peeved her on occasion on account of his perceived indifference to the troubles she incurred. He was not, in fact, indifferent; just that, in the main, he trusted her, and she knew it.

'Well,' she said, 'I'll know next time not to make carrot muffins.'

'Indeed. Anything but that.'

'Come on,' she said, impishness in her eyes, 'wouldn't you like a roll in the sack with Prentiss? I'll bet she could give you quite a time.'

'Are you pimping? Trying to set my teeth on edge? I can't say she's a bad person. She's just not a good person.'

'You're sure about that?'
'Pretty much.'
'Have you ever slept with a bad woman?'
'Not knowingly.'
'Can one ever know?'
I shrugged.

Critique

What children had I sired? What foundation had I endowed? What book written so as to change the course of history? What revolutionary thinking? My plea would have been that I had endeavoured not to hurt anyone; but my, what weak pleading it was; as, of course, one hurt somebody by virtue of breathing and occupying space. If I had made myself very nearly a hermit, anchorite, recluse, even so, I was bibulous in public, and there had been sex, however haphazard. So yes, as a drinker and smoker politically unaffiliated, if I was sure to annoy the life-style puritans and the political-correctness crowd, I did live simply, much more simply than those who had ambitions and high overheads. Even Dubois, for all he had spent his life in the business world, did not live extravagantly despite the junkets of his younger years—golfing trips to South Carolina on company jets. And when he first joined Royal Trust, they were still doing data-entry with keypunch cards. Could I imagine how noisy it was? Eggy had spent his money on his wives, and on wining and dining prospective mistresses; and I supposed that was what Moonface had always been for him—a pleasure his old age precluded from sex; and he could play the Grand Man of Democratic Tendencies. One had to take Eggy seriously when he avowed he had always held to left of centre views. Eleanor, a shopper, was the spendthrift Traymorean among us, but there it was—that she was a Traymorean indicated a fairly humble circumstance, but one freely chosen; and she, too, was more or less left of centre, even if the NDP had weaselled rightwards. Moonface, apart from the odd time she would swank herself up in an opera gown, was all denim and sneakers, and she liked it that way, even as she liked flashing her nails. We were not, strictly speaking *hoi polloi*, but we were not Park Avenue posh, either. And if Marjerie Prentiss had ambitions, scheming to get rich did not seem to be one of them. Punishing men in bed was her apparent vice; and so long as there was a ready supply of men who craved the punishment, I did not believe her appetites would cost the world, for all they compromised Traymorean tranquillity. Mrs Petrova herself was a fixture on our noble boulevard; and I would have wagered she was well off, indeed, old-style shopkeeper; she was a touchstone. She was the neighbourhood. The sparrows were copulating; the squirrels were squirrellier. Spring again.

I made for the Blue Danube, which would be open for business; and when I got there Dubois was already installed at table.

'Did you ever sleep with a bad woman?' I asked him out of the blue.

Glittering blue eyes searched my face.

'Never,' Dubois guffawed, 'is there such an animal?'

'It seems a statistical probability.'

'And yet, bad and men seem to go together a lot,' Dubois offered.

'Yes, they do.'

'Cassandra,' Dubois called out, 'are you a bad woman?'

'Very bad,' she grinned, 'the worst.'

'Well, in that case,' Dubois said, 'I won't turn my back on you.'

His cheeks were red with mirth; her dimples deepened. The place was appallingly empty and yet, here was trouble about to arrive in the person of Arthur Eglinton, otherwise known as Eggy to people in the know.

'I might be imagining things,' Dubois said, nodding at the window, 'but I think he's steamed.'

And vain and handsome Dubois was not referring to Eggy's churning pins and the piston-like action of his cane, Eggy's countenance noticeably dark. Ever the gallant, Dubois rose and went to help the homunculus through the door.

'That woman's at it again,' the old man thundered.

'And who's going to spring for wine?' he thought to ask.

He fairly ripped his scarf from his neck; then he collapsed into his chair and caught his breath. He peered around, as if unsure where he was.

'What's up?' I inquired.

'Eff you.'

'Is that any way to talk to your friends?' Dubois put it to Eggy.

'What friends? Haven't got any friends. The world's gone to hell. And women ought to be put back in their place. In the kitchen, I tell you,' Eggy thundered some more.

Dubois guffawed: 'What's brought this on?'

'Yes, but she rubbed my nose in it. Alright, so she was starkers. She was knocking on all the doors, making quite a racket. Alright, so I answered the door, and she, well she must've just been there, but she was down the hall. Anyway, she turns around and walks right up to me as pretty as you please in her birthday suit, and she grabs my head, yes, like this, and she shoves my face in her titties. "Here," she said, "hoo hoo on this". I mean, besides being naked, she looked peculiar.'

Well, it had to have been Prentiss.

A Stony Silence

As I was in no mood for drinking, I withdrew from my august company, leaving Eggy to lament the fact that Dubois considered Eggy's depiction of his episode with Prentiss overstated. With any luck, Prentiss might have settled down. Even so, as I went up the Traymore stairs, Suzie Q, knapsack strapped on, unseen of late, was descending them. The look in her eyes suggested she had blundered into a lunatic asylum, but was stuck there for the duration: presumably she witnessed the Prentiss-engineered commotion. She passed me by in what I could only describe as a stony silence. Indeed, what a hash the older generations had made of things. It was, no doubt, what she was thinking. I heard one of Mrs Petrova's clocks. Heard Eleanor's plumbing. Nothing from the Prentiss apartment. In my digs, I powered up the ghetto-blaster. Piano, accordion and oud. I was too agitated for a lie-down and a stew; and if I was tempted to write Moonface a letter, what was the point? I did not know where to send it, and it would only, in any case, compromise her sojourn away from Traymorean and Blue Danubian realities. *Dear Moonface, How are you making out? You are missed. —RQC*

I waited for the knock I knew was coming. My eyes fluttered through a documentary on TV. Heard on the stairs: *ploo sah change ploo say lay meem shose*… Eggy. Heard Dubois complain of the catastrophic effect of Eggy's French on his ears, and would he please get a move on. *Eff you.* And I fluttered through the BBC news. Fluttered at the onset of Letterman, and he was still slagging Previous President who had once incurred the Queen Mother's displeasure. A man's manners were his worth. It was a plaintive rapping laid on my door. It was rapping that said: *for your ears only.* Though all the world, and especially the Traymore, most likely had ears to the ground. I did not know what to expect. Nudity, coarse language, mature themes? She was wearing some tubular, sack-cloth dress. She stood there rubbing an ankle with a bare toe. Her cheeks were wet. I would have regarded such tears as would have emanated from dead, watery eyes as suspect. She pushed me aside and entered my domain. She looked around in the semi-dark of my living room, the only light the light of the TV. She was always putting out sexual energy, but not this go-round. And it did not take long, the woes Prentiss had to relate. She did not, she supposed, love Dundarave all that much. And yes, they had had a row; and it sounded to me like the man may have been reasserting his manhood by withdrawing his favours; and then again, I could have been mistaken. To be sure, Ralph was a good man, and she would most likely marry him; only that he would expect of her a certain wifeliness, and it would chafe. She would probably spend half her time wandering the countryside where they would reside, she in search of distraction. She knew I detested her politics and her views on Arabs. Too bad. The Palestinians were no better than dumb brutes with whom the Israelis were saddled, just as the Americans got as their burden the tribes they conquered and dispossessed; and the liberals were always coddling losers, and she would have none of that. Otherwise, she was a feminist. It went with the territory she trod; and if men could not hold up their own end when it came to sexual role-playing, well, she was not going to coddle them, either. Her cheeks seemed to be drying, and I had the distinct feeling that she was enjoying herself, perched there on the edge of my couch. And what a horrid little man it was, and she meant Eggy. And Dubois was such a know-it-all. And in that department, I was an even worse offender; and she could not, for the life of her, see what I contributed to anything, mooching, as I apparently did, off Eleanor's generosity; and there was a good if somewhat frustrated woman. And I supposed that Prentiss had assumed, vis a vis Eleanor, that she could teach her a thing or two; and I knew that Eleanor, in respect to Prentiss, and for all that Eleanor flaunted her body and tossed her thoughts about as so many bean bags, would never presume to teach back in kind. It was an almost moral position she took.

'So what are you doing here if I'm so useless?' I thought to ask.

'You have an honest face,' she laughed, her voice a dull boom, like that of thunder dying away.

I could not decide, what with her Cleopatra bangs, whether she was some hybrid Pocahontas figure caught between two futilities—those of paradise and those of hell, Captain John Smith her gullible mark; or whether she was as twisted as I was inclined to suspect.

'It's late,' I attempted to observe.

'What of it?'

Her voice was growing huskier. This set off alarms. And then I overshot my mark:

'Actually, if I were Ralph, I wouldn't have you. And if I were Dundarave, well, I don't know—'

'Is that what you think? Oh, I'm wounded. Been put in my place.'

I had no satisfying rejoinder, so I regarded the woman on my couch in silence.

The door at street level slammed; and I was just now learning that Suzie Q could whistle, if tunelessly. And Prentiss had the air of a woman who had taken a man's measure and was sure of her conclusion, and that was an end on it. Why then should I continue to debate?

'I really am tired,' I said, 'so if you've gotten it out of your system, whatever it was that was bothering you, I'd appreciate it if you left.'

'And Eleanor said you're a gentleman.'

'Hardly. And I only hold forth when I'm drunk or among friends or both. And the world makes less sense than it did an hour ago, and tomorrow, it'll make even less sense. I don't know about you, but that's what I have to look forward to. In the know-it-all department, I think you can hold your own. But not now. I'm going to bed. You know where the door is.'

I had not intended to have the last word on *X*, *Y* and *Z*, but apparently, I had had it. And she rose and lifted her arms above her head and yawned, a gesture which caused her bosom to shift under the dress she wore, and her eyes caught mine and they laughed. I had not had the last word, after all. And she quit the field.

True Colours

I learned from Dubois that Eggy was eating his strawberries in the Claremont, a watering-hole in the next district over. He was slated, too, for an evening out, not with us, but with some mystery girl who was young and married. Eggy would escort this prize to the opera, Eggy having got it in his head that he was a rascal, a homewrecker.

'Well,' I said to vain and handsome Dubois there in the Blue Danube, Antonio working the floor, 'speaking of rascals, a certain far right talk show host has really outdone himself. And here's the unfortunate quote: that if the British Prime Minister continues to slobber all over New President at the G-20 meeting, British Prime Minister stands to risk anal poisoning. Delicately put, wouldn't you say?'

Dubois winced.

'Yes,' I continued, 'and one wonders what kind of effect New President is going to have on the course of world history, as it's beginning to look like there will be such an effect, something more than the mere countermanding of the effect of Previous President. Well, I wonder, even if you might not.'

'Oh, I think about it, too,' said Dubois, collegially, 'and I think he's paying attention to the fundamentals, which is good.'

And just then, Joe Smithers aka Too Tall Poet made an entrance. He had the air of a man who had been parachuted into enemy territory against his will, his mission suspect, poorly thought out by his superiors.

'I had a hankering for pizza,' he announced to us, grinning, 'imagine that.'

One had to remind oneself that Too Tall Poet went about his business with his head in the clouds; that it was almost literally true; and that for him a pizza pie might have constituted an exotic object.

'So pull up a chair,' Dubois invited the man, 'don't be a stranger.'

Too Tall Poet consented; and Antonio brought over a menu. It might have been radioactive, this menu, so gingerly did Too Tall Poet handle the thing.

'I don't want to hate life's winners,' I said to Dubois the arch-materialist, 'just in case I happen to become one. Not likely though. Am I such a snob? Help me on this. Tell me that greed and ego are everyone's immutable lot and—'

Dubois guffawed. Too Tall Poet tittered, uneasily.

'There are winners,' I said, 'that succeed in making Prentiss appear spiritual.'

Dubois guffawed some more, Too Tall Poet blinking his eyes, Prentiss an unknown to him.

'You know,' the poet said, 'I only thought I was hungry. Gentlemen, it was good to talk with you. I should do this more often.'

He giggled. *Life's winners, my arse*—Too Tall Poet ducked as he went out the door, one of nature's rare fauna. Dubois returned to his soup. I looked out the window a while.

Demon Love V

—Eggy has had his grand night out, one consisting of preliminary drinks at the Claremont; then with his Lithuanian hottie in tow, *Cosi fan tutte* at the Monument-National—old-style theatre as Eggy depicts it; then nightcaps back at the Claremont until 2 a.m. And Eggy even had time enough to discuss the politics of Lebanon with a cabbie or two. Eggy our homuncular Stendhal. Well, good for him. Meanwhile beheadings, mass shootings, serial kidnappings—all this comprises a goodly portion of American news, not to mention banking fraud and unemployment figures. I am, as snow sleets down bewilderingly, in one of my theological snits; and it is when I am farthest from God, if there is a God; and I do not insist that there be a God, as I would not dream of imposing on secular humanists in their cheap suits; just that *oh those bones, oh those bones, oh those skeleton bones, oh mercy, how they scare* brand of reasoning does not reason all that much, in the end. Yes but, it is National Poetry Week somewhere, celebrities passing themselves off as rhymesters and making poetry tolerable for an hour.

—I put it to Eleanor: 'The drunk understands that much of his fate is in the hands of imbeciles and he is master of nothing, dominant nowhere but in his fantasies. His intelligence counts for nothing. He evades, defuses, avoids. He may despise militant joggers, but he otherwise steps aside when they would schlep by, eyes shining with mastery of situational ethics. For it is time to reinvent society and put it on a viable economic footing. Dumdeedumptum time. We are all in this together, so the lie goes. Since when? What's a drunk to do? Humankind may be one of evolution's products, but human instincts have dulled quite a lot. So where are you all dressed up to go?' 'None of your business. But I do have an engagement. I'd let you cop a feel, but I'm in a hurry. Now if you were to wash those dishes for me, I might could see my way to rewarding you handsomely, later.' 'Ah, there she is—the Eleanor I used to know and love.' 'Don't get smart. Don't stop drinking. Kisses. Must run.'

§

Book VI—Theological Freelancing

Avuncular Once More

Prentiss and Dundarave had upset Suzie Q's equilibrium by way of a sex game, enough so that Suzie Q saw fit to move out. She was going to have to move out, in any case, Moonface's return imminent and yet, I was almost sorry to see her go. Despite her confusions, there was something in her of authentic rebellion and a regard for truth for its own sake and yet, Prentiss and Dundarave had, more than likely, appealed to her vanity and she fell for it. It was my thinking on the matter. I wished she had not been so pouty with me when she knocked on my door, dangling a set of keys before me: 'Emma's. I don't know what to do with them, so I'll leave them with you. Well, goodbye.'

'Best of luck,' I said, accepting the keys.

She was stooped from the weight of her knapsack; and it was a bursting suitcase she was about to heft down the stairs.

'Do you want some help with that?' I asked, with some sincerity.

'I can manage.'

'Was there something you wanted to say to me?'

'Not really.'

'Alright then.'

I raised my hand in a salute, and she went to resume her struggles elsewhere. It was now, what, my third or fourth spring in the Traymore. It pleased me to think I had lost track.

I fought the impulse to unlock Moonface's apartment, enter and occupy her cozy and well-used love seat. A vague impression of her digs came to mind, and it had been a while since I was last in it: the prints, the plants, the books on the floor, items of clothing strewn about, unwashed coffee mugs. In other words, Moonface was not particularly tidy. And I would sit in that love seat, a proper gentleman, and ponder things. Ponder the poet Virgil in the darkness. And yes, how did Christ get to be Christ? And when the last of the Medicis lay dying, death having trumped pride, what was the last Medici thought? I could see Moonface up on her toes, splendidly naked, perhaps; or begowned and somewhat sombre; but smiling, in any case, confident that she was, after all, a girl wonder, and a bridge to a future that would set things right. It was snowing when I left the Blue Danube aka Le Grec, Eggy and Dubois given over to a spate of affectionate bickering, Antonio the waiter appealing to some Italian-Albanian heaven each time Eggy thundered with truth on his side; and the air smelled like October. It seemed I was clapping eyes on the Traymore for the first time, noting the smell of the foyer's radiator heat; appreciating the fact that the lit stairs were not as gloomy as some I had known, the wainscoting a nice touch. I gained the carpeting at the top of the stairs that Mrs Petrova, by way of Herculean labour once a week, managed to keep presentable. I had no intention, after all, of stepping into Moonface's domain; it smacked too much of a violation; though I might have had good cause; as Suzie Q could have inadvertently left the gas on or water running or some such thing. I inserted my key in its lock, and then I noted I was being watched. And yes, there was Prentiss at her door in one of her long cotton shirts, her bare toe rubbing a bare ankle. She regarded me with a look I could only describe as emanating from a distant place; and it did cross my mind that the woman was insane. I was, for a brief instant, alarmed. I had not been witness to the infamous episode when she had an apparent breakdown, prancing about starkers in the hall, ornamented with a pink boa, packing a gun; but I reminded myself that she was capable of anything. Even so, it was clear she had no intention of speaking, of communicating with me in any time-honoured mode. Space and time did fall away; and perhaps, in her eyes I did not exist, or I was but an object, some pebble of interesting colour and shape and yet, not in the end collectible. It was a strange, near violent juxtaposition: those dead, watery eyes consecrated to sorrow, the infinitely malicious smile. One could only hope that the world that occasioned her contemplation was worth the scrutiny. *Aphrodite, her left knee bent*... Indeed, her pose was that of an ingénue, casual and mocking, however weighty her thoughts.

Philosophy, religion, folk wisdom, magic rite, and even science—it was all there compacted in her gaze that extended from one point of a centreless universe to another, and who knew what cosmic wind was at its back? And just then, she placed a hand on her belly and held it there. I signalled with a nod that I recognized her existence, and this gesture seemed to break the spell; and she was momentarily startled. *You?* I escaped into my apartment, not disturbed so much as thoughtful. I had had a conversation the language of which was no language my intellect could grasp and yet, my body knew, and the knowing would kick in at some point down the line. I could look forward to an evening of documentary-viewing, something to do with a phenomenon known as black money, world-wide high level bribery, in other words; and there was BBC news, and there was Letterman, if I managed to stay awake. *Have you got any money? I don't have any money. Where's all the money gone? Walmart has all the money.* Sally McCabe manifested; she had the air of a woman revisiting old haunts.

'You're such a putz, Calhoun,' she let me know, her nose prettily wrinkled, her smile a genial force.

'That I am.'

'People are not moral as such,' she mused, 'but they tend to adhere to the rules as they are understood, and the thing about rules is that one may bend them once in a while, and this is an understood, if not expected, prominent feature of the Great Plan. Otherwise, one takes one's pleasures when and where one is able. I have. You certainly have. Biarritz. Been there? Basque pelota. Ever heard of it? It's said it's a game that goes back to the ancient Greeks. But what do I care about such things? I'm just a pom-pom girl, teen slut with personable patter, and if I've been Isis in your eyes, I suspect I was an Apache princess in another life. Prentiss? Yes, she's an interesting case, isn't she? Now and then I come across her type in my travels. It might be overly generous on your part to consider her a strangely spiritual creature, however twisted. She's bent right out of her tree. If she honours obscure deities, 5 will get you 10 she doesn't even know their names. Well, I see you're about to observe your evening services and I'm in the way. Ta-ta.'

And she was gone before I could inquire as to what state of mind one might expect of Moonface on her return. And what I feared the most was that, on her next Blue Danube shift, the dear girl would blink her eyes a few times, and presto! and she had never spent three months in Ecuador, with sidetrips to Argentina, Chile, Peru. Or perhaps, worse still, she would have no further use for Traymoreans and Blue Danubians, and she would drift into Ottawa and we would never see her again. In fact, the latter eventually was to be expected most; and I figured I had already girded myself for the prospect. *Moonface? Just some girl who used to hang about. Waitressed at our local. Bit of a scatterbrain. Had pretensions to poetry and being a sexpot. Well, she was rather nice.* The Letterman show a rerun, there was no reason to ward off the increasing weight on my eyelids. Perhaps, Americans were, after all, entitled to their belief that they were an exceptional people. What did I know of the place, anymore? One heard it had gone rightwing-crazy-berserk, violent. One heard that it had regained its senses. One heard tripe about *the better angels of one's nature.* One did not know what to believe, if anything. One despaired as it was conceivable that one's mentations had gone up every blind alley and met with every dead-end; had explored every nook and cranny except any that mattered. The point of life was to know that one would live and die and be forgotten, the recognition of the fact one's decency.

Some Excitement

A thin slip of snow lay on Mrs Petrova's backyard grass. A cardinal flashed red in the dun-coloured crown of a maple; and I supposed it or some other bird, passing through, was the issuer of a purling song. Sparrows, perching in the tulip tree, looked fat and spoiled. Then I came away from the window at the end of the Traymore hall, hearing the telltale sound of Traymoreans greeting each their day, and the sound was plumbing. Once, at about this time, a slippered Moonface in pajamas would frisk into Eggy's lair, and they would gossip and he would endeavour to pinch the dear girl's bum. Mid-morning, and the foppish countenance of a grand duke (late 17th century) regarded me from the pages of a book. He was history incarnate, as he was a mediocrity. But he was one who had had the wealth and the power, the impetus and ability to harm. If he punished cruelty to animals, he beheaded sodomites. He put to death wooers illicitly serenading the objects of their affections. Taxed the peasants at extortionate rates. Forbade science but was fascinated by scientific instruments and gadgets. And I went to the poor man's super mart to replenish my stores, and then, back again, I came upon a squad car, its light flashing, parked in irregular fashion in front of Mrs Petrova's shop. Well, it would seem that someone had attempted to rob the neighbourhood's darling, but that someone else had come on the scene and spooked the thief. I approached the door, thinking to see if my landlady was alright; ill-humoured patrolman waved me away like I was pestilential. And that was the last that was heard of it; but that, a couple of hours later, peering through the window, I beheld Mrs Petrova seated, newspaper on her lap, black-framed reading glasses set on her nose; and she was at peace with the world and its treacheries, and I wondered just how pious she was, if at all. A blustery wind blew debris about, the squalling sky, however, a spring sky. It was this world of the boulevard and the elements with which Mrs Petrova, caterer to the local yen for watches and wedding bands and the like, was at peace. I then ducked into the Blue Danube, riding a wave of appreciation for appearances and all the vanities, jolly Antonio winking. Eggy was on site, eyes closed, chin on his chest. I took another table so as not to wake him.

Had my soup. Scribbled a little in my notebook, Prentiss's behaviour of the evening before drifting back into consciousness. What if she had been in some perilous state of mind, and I had offered her nothing but my indifference? One was cognizant of the possibility that tragedy was more often the consequence of missed signals than of malicious intent or overriding fate. I would distract myself with the prospect of Moonface back on shift, but it was a cheap ruse; and it was rendered all the more cheap by the entrance of Prentiss and Dundarave, quarrelsome and drunk, perhaps. They paid me no notice but they woke Eggy. Without raising his head, he peered, so much as his eyes were able, in all directions. A claw, quite on its own, independent of the Eggy brain, reached for the glass of wine it knew was there. Eggy's head levitated, as it were, into position so as to receive the libation; and he drank; and he smacked his lips; and he said: 'Effing hell.'

Dundarave, rather rudely, informed Prentiss that she was the proverbial whore of Babylon; and one wondered just how well supplied he was with literary allusions. A dull voice boomed with something I could not make out, Prentiss slouched, hands jammed in the pockets of a windbreaker.

'Well, you are,' said Dundarave, a note of resignation creeping into his tone.

'So what? You knew what you were getting when you got me,' Prentiss observed.

Was not honesty the best policy?

'Oh that's how it is,' Dundarave shot back with mock-irony.

'Is there any service in this place?' Prentiss wondered, looking around, her eyes perhaps registering the fact of me and Eggy, but not at all interested.

Antonio sighed, and he approached the table, a man on the way to a dreaded appointment.

'What you want?' he put it to them, with a monumental lack of waiterly polish and finesse.

'What we want,' said Dundarave testily, 'is something to eat.'

'We got things to eat,' Antonio asserted.

'Just bring us a couple of burgers,' said Prentiss, highly irritated.

'Burgers. No problem,' Antonio answered, happy enough to begin walking away, 'but how you like?'

'Just whatever,' said Prentiss, her words clarifying nothing, 'just bring them.'

Antonio shrugged. One heard: 'Effing hell.'

It was Eggy advising all concerned that, back among the living, he was an hombre with whom to reckon.

We would not have been surprised—Eggy, Antonio and I—had the couple exchanged verbal remonstrance for a cuff or two; but nothing of the sort happened; and not much changed in the world in the duration. Perdition beckoned from Afghanistan. The radio deejay cavilled against cigarette smoke, her tone *de rigueur*, proof that there was such a beast as progress in human affairs; and she may as well have been Moses parting the Red Sea, the evil Egyptians now just an evil memory. Next up, the bankers. And life was good. But then between the honeymooners—sartorial Dundarave and his happy hour seductress, she a veteran, apparently, of many campaigns—argument stalled, like an airplane of erring pitch. I could see, gathering force in Prentiss's eyes, what was becoming the familiar look of one who was fatally abstracted; and it was as if she were regarding shapes as nebulous as swirling fogs as opposed to starkly delineated objects or the lesser beings of her immediate realm. Perhaps she felt overrun by various homunculi—the Eggys, the Calhouns, the Antonios, as well as Elias in the kitchen, and had need of refuge in her architecturally complicated mind. Eggy supposed that though it had snowed, it was but a last hurrah for snow and soon, spring would be busting out all over. And why, as decency demanded it, we should see that those bastards hang by their chinny chinchins—Previous President and his hardboiled sidekick the Previous Veep. It was one thing to have been, boffo-like and buffoonishly, right of centre; it was quite another the sanctioning of torture, so much so, it had become an item of cult ceremony in a hallowed union of states as was America. Prentiss, whose feet shod in half boots had been square to the floor, now slung one leotarded leg over the other and wriggled a little, getting restless, perhaps. Given the sexual traumas of her late adolescence, one could not blame her for her enduring anger; just that she had made of it all a pearl that could not uncommit, and no solvent made of love could undo its lustre. And Dundarave, wearing something like a military field jacket, town and country man, let a cigarette that he would smoke outside dangle from his lips; and he had the air of a man waiting for a storm to blow over. Antonio somewhat stiffly brought this duo their hamburgers which they proceeded to eat in calculated silence, Dundarave devouring his, Prentiss methodically licking her fingers and blinking. And where they had been oblivious to their surroundings and did not care who knew it, they were now self-conscious, even abashed, customers wandering in for take-out and striding away. All the world knew Prentiss and Dundarave; was savvy to their less than expeditious love of one another. All the world could surmise the nature of their rather ho hum perversions. Eggy, exercised by the recent summit of the heads of the leading economies, said: 'Yes but, New President, well, that's what you call him, charmed them out of their socks as did wifey with her bare arms. Will they drop the bomb?'

He sheepishly extended a claw in the direction of his wine glass. Prentiss coughed. It was a species of sexual irruption, that cough. It was pique as well, the recent election results not to her liking.

Hanging Suits

Dubois settled his briefcase on the floor; slung his jacket on the back of his chair; removed his navy-blue tuque, primping his rather sombre *bonhomie* and vanity all the while.

'Gentlemen,' he said, 'good evening.'

'Eff you,' Eggy responded, breathing wine fumes through ancient nostrils.

'So here you are,' I said, 'our Grease Eminence.'

Dubois guffawed. Ensconced now, he turned to signal Antonio that his attentions were required; but he had his hands full with Miss Meow who was now hissing like a cat in high dudgeon, on general principles. When this woman was displeased with the world, with the errors of its ways, with its increasingly lowered standards, she could also be heard to mutter under her breath dire vocabularies of wrath and ill will at us enablers of sin and corruption.

'Well,' said Dubois, 'don't fall off your chairs when I tell you this, but I'm going to get married and I need a witness for the marriage application.'

Dubois gave me a significant look.

'Eleanor, I suppose,' Eggy mused, not in the least impressed.

'Yes, that would be the case,' said Dubois, somewhat dryly.

'Yes but, you know,' Eggy went on to say, more emotively, 'you bed a woman for years, then you marry her, and effing hell, it all falls apart. Is this what you want?'

'The falling apart,' Dubois countered, 'is all you know, and it colours your prejudice—'

'Rot your socks,' Eggy thundered, his finger raised. 'But if that's what you want, and Eleanor's a fine woman, if a little opinionated, then well and good.'

'Thank you,' Dubois said, 'but look who's opinionated. You're one to talk.'

'No comment.'

A little stunned, I thought to congratulate Dubois, and added that it had probably been a long time coming. I kept to myself the suspicion that marriage would spell the end of Eleanor's playfulness in respect to me. But it was not as if I always jumped when she barked.

'Thank you,' said Dubois, like the chairman of the board that he could be, 'I'll take that as a yes, that you'll go with me to city hall.'

'Sure,' I agreed, 'I'll witness.'

I was not as drunk as I might have been; and the light outside seemed too brilliant for the hour; and I was aghast, desiring the dark pall of winter and the purity of snow over the all too subtle blandishments of early spring. Antonio, freed up—Miss Meow waddling with stooped shoulders out the door, the world beyond saving—approached Animal Table. Dubois figured that he would start off with soup, then the steak, but that the salad was to be wrapped up as he would eat it at home.

'No problem,' said our Universal Waiter.

'Well,' said Eggy, 'Moonface tomorrow. Well, it's what they say, I don't know. Think she misses us?'

'I doubt it,' I said.

'Are you kidding?' Dubois answered, 'she'll take one look at you and she'll hop the next plane back.'

'No comment.'

Monstrous and desolate winds were blowing about within Eggy's tough old carcass. Perhaps we should have—Eggy and I—made more of a fuss about Dubois's impending betrothal to his longtime lover, but the man did not seem to mind, he concerned for the fate of his beloved Habs. Would they make the playoffs? They were running out of chances. Hockey? I would like to have had conversing: the guerrilla tactics of 17th century Florentines, the Department of Justice and torture memos, death-bed conversions; but no, we were going to speculate as to whether Montreal would cobble together a sufficient defense and win a game.

'So you're going to do it,' Eggy said to Dubois.

'Yes, I think so.'

Dubois might have been contemplating a merger, a buy-out, a bankruptcy claim with that analytical tone of his.

Prentiss's door was open, as was Eleanor's. I passed through the latter door, a man headed for trouble. I made my way along the outback of Eleanor's living room until I raised the good woman's kitchen. She and Prentiss, each with an arm slung around the other's shoulder, were glassy-eyed, cigarettes and amaretto on the table. Dundarave paced a circle on the floor, beer in hand. I supposed he had no deep thoughts in respect to marriage one way or the other. It was the luck of the draw, just like life.

'Well, look at what the cat drug in,' Eleanor crowed, and her voice verged on ugly.

'Stag night,' a dull voice boomed.

'Nobody here but us staggettes,' Eleanor giggled.

'Speak for yourself,' Dundarave warned, his grin a shambling affair.

Prentiss regarded me as an entity of indeterminate mass and shape and valences.

'I heard the news,' I offered.

'I'll bet you have,' Eleanor cooed, Prentiss clapping a hand to Eleanor's bosom.

'We're losing her,' a dull voice indicated.

'Going, going, gone,' Eleanor agreed.

She removed Prentiss's hand from her splendid bosom.

'No more hanky-panky,' she added, looking my way, 'not that you were ever much good for it.'

And my, but her voice was thick.

'Yes, it's a coy fellow, it is,' Prentiss observed, and not without malice.

I looked around and was benevolent, happy enough to be judged.

It had never been a credo as such; just an unswerving conviction that every human soul was isolate and very much alone. In light of it, I reviewed Eleanor's kitchen as I lay on my couch. All that horseplay between the women. *What flabby thighs, my dear. Yes, but they could squeeze the neck off a wild turkey. Now why would you want to go and do that? Because I was raised that way: to the manner born.* Giggles. Dundarave good-naturedly tolerant. Had he ever hosed Eleanor? Got his bid in? Desported with the wench? If so, it was not recorded; and Eleanor had always denied it, telling me he had twitted her with Gloria Jarnette that night he and Eleanor were to rendezvous at a motel, he showing up with Jarnette on his arm.

Another Sort of Nuptial

Good Friday morning, and in the Blue Danube, I without a religious bone in my body, thought to write Moonface a welcoming missive; had even considered that she might show, chicken-shuffling through the door as an entourage of one, come to reclaim her ancient privileges.

Dear Moonface, stay away. But if you must come, let it be according to these theatrics: of splashing fountains and terraces of bay and myrtle; cypress grove, faun statuettes. You'll wear a silver gown, and diamonds and pearls and rubies. Pages in black velvet shall attend you. And so forth and so on. Effigies of the great poets shall surround you. Bells shall ring. White horses. Gold spurs. And so forth and so on. Eggy shall scrape the pavement with his brow. Dubois shall read out a proclamation. I shall simply stand silent, a dignified creature, my eyes applauding your delicate bosom which some mediocre poet, and we shall shoot him in due course, will compare to pigeon eggs. Effing hell, hang the bastard.

And then the fuss and bother and pomp of it all over and done, we shall talk, you and I, of pertinent matters. And you shall determine, on this basis, that much has changed and nothing has. 'Oooooh, Bob and Eleanor are getting married. How exciting.' But Prentiss is Prentiss still, and alas, Eggy has thrown you over for a Lithuanian. Can you forgive him? How much did you drink and when did you know it? Did you come across the ghost of Pissaro? What an effer, that guy was.—RQC

Second Mind

Gregory, captain of the good ship Le Grec, known to Traymoreans as the Blue Danube, was back from Disneyland, complaining of airplanes and in-flight headaches due, perhaps, to the change of air pressure brought about by landing. He pointed to the middle of his forehead and looked agonized. Moreover, he did not know when to expect Moonface back from Ecuador or whether she would return to work for him.

'Maybe you should take the train next time,' I suggested.

'Train,' said Gregory, considering it.

Dubois had other things on his mind besides trains and airplanes.

'I don't know,' said Dubois, 'if I'm doing the right thing, getting married to her.'

The man held his head between his hands; and then he blinked, and glittering blues eyes endeavoured to focus. He continued: 'After we left here, the other night, Eggy and I, I went to see Eleanor, and she was drunk, carrying on with that Prentiss woman. Dundarave was flat on his back on the kitchen floor, tracing patterns on the ceiling. He was probably stoned. "Here's my conquering hero," she said, "the pitter of my patter, the butter on my biscuit, the cream in my coffee." I wasn't very amused.'

'Oh, she's just playing with you a little,' I said.

'I hope you're right. But I mean, one minute she's saying, "Oh Bob, we're going to be happy", and then the next, and I'm some schmuck who was good for a night's diversion and nothing more. Thanks for the memories.'

'And Prentiss? She had nothing to say? She's always good for a laugh.'

'No,' Dubois answered, 'she had nothing to contribute, except that she winked. Gave me the look.'

'Yes, the treatment,' I said.

The café was busy, Antonio hard at it. Mostly students, it seemed, their gazes set on getting rich.

'Then what?' I thought to ask, 'did you chase everyone out? Did you take Eleanor in hand and set her straight?'

Dubois guffawed. Who was he to tell Eleanor how to live? Since when had he bossed her about?

'No,' said Dubois, 'I just went back to my place, stared at my computer. I haven't seen anybody, today, just you, though His Nibs said he was going to meet me here right about now. He's probably forgotten, and he's down at the Claremont, courting the Lithuanian. I don't know how he does it or why the girls let him. It can't be his money because he's cheap.'

I nodded my agreement. Zeus-like Eggy was most certainly cheap. And the Apostle Paul, he had had the wit to say that if the Christ had not risen, there was no point in the preaching.

Bitter Chalice

Easter Sunday was raw, what with the wind and the grim associations the holiday always occasioned in me. I had spent a bad night of it, waking around four, continuing sleepless, until first light, in that horrible zone that was all blackness and death. Then I must have drifted off. When I next woke it was due to the fact that Eleanor had come to me on a mission.

'You still in bed?' she said, 'I hate this day. Always have.'

She extended her wrist for me to smell.

'Get a whiff of this,' she commanded.

I complied.

'*Chance eau Fraiche*,' she let me know.

'You look terrible, by the way,' she noted.

'TMW,' I explained, 'too much wine. So it's Easter and we're still here. I was wondering, earlier, if the world had disappeared. Maybe it did. Maybe you're a mirage.'

'I'm effing real, sweetheart, and I'd climb in there with you to prove it, but I don't want to muss my hair. I'm going to do something different, today. I'm going to church. Bob can't believe it.'

I could not say why, but for some reason or another, Eleanor's announcement did not strike me as lunatic.

'Well,' I said, which was all I had to say.

'Also,' she said (she was, by now, gorgeously perched on the edge of the bed), 'Prentiss is treating us all to supper at the café. She already made arrangements with, who is it, Gregory, I guess. It was to be a surprise.'

'Seems extravagant.'

'Some bonus cheque she got for her work. And I thought times were bad. But anyway, everyone will be there, and so will you.'

'Will I?'

'Yes you will, and you'll like it.'

'It's not going to be easy.'

'You'll be among friends, so don't waffle on us.'

'So why the perfume?'

'Self-defense. I just felt like being naughty and pagan.'

'And you're going to church?'

'Why not? I don't see any contradiction.'

'No, I suppose you wouldn't. But if you'll excuse me, my bladder's about to burst and—'

'Of course, dear.'

Gregory, his smile anxious, had slid some tables together so as to accommodate our party, Mercedes uncorking wine. Prentiss, I had to admit, was holding up her end: as engagingly as she was able, she teased Eggy on his love life, and he was flustered. Eleanor, in high spirits, piled on: 'Come on, Eggy,' she implored, 'who is it this time? Who's the object of your suit? Who's your complementary function?'

'No comment.'

I wondered if Dubois had, in a bit of pillow talk, betrayed Eggy to Eleanor on this matter of complementary functions. Dubois did, in fact, look wary. Even so, sartorial Dundarave was willing to play along, saying to no one in particular: 'You don't stop looking, do you?' he said, his tone suggesting that when you stopped looking you were dead.

'I will confess, with cheerfulness, love is a thing so likes me, that let her lay, on me all day, I'll kiss the hand that strikes me.'

It was Eggy at his finest, his finger raised, his tough old eyes focused on his tormentors; Dundarave taken aback, Prentiss goofily grinning. Of course, they probably had not yet had the pleasure of Eggy when he was both in his cups and in his verses. Dubois's smile was nearly a smirk, and he drolled: 'Don't get him started. He can go on like this all night.'

'Oh, eff you,' said Eggy, beaming.

Prentiss did not often wear as much make-up as she was wearing now, and that, and the black silk blouse buttoned to her neck, gave her the air of a rather severe, business-like courtesan, one of high intelligence. Perhaps it was the secret of her erotic appeal: that underlying the casual anything goes demeanor of a fortyish teen, was a much more formidable entity, one coherent and organized, loaded for bear. (But then, perhaps the wine had already gone to my head.) Miss Meow was lonely at her table, doubly so as it was a holiday; and I felt something for her; though it might have been a bit much, inviting her over. The Whistler, on the other hand, was perfectly content at his table to whistle and stomp and demand refills of water, Mercedes his victim. I had been under the impression that we were in for a feast of lamb; but that, to be sure, the galley was not equipped for such an undertaking. Instead, Prentiss had sprung for a couple of large Greek-style pizzas which, when one thought about it; and in light of the fact that it was Easter; and in light of Passover; in light of the Eucharistic and the phenomenon of agape in a secular, technocratic age, did seem appropriate, though I would not relish the ensuing heartburn. And it seemed to me that my eyes were dulling; and I set dull eyes on Prentiss's countenance; and it was a plain face, that face of hers; and once again I was mystified. Did bone structure signify character? The sprinkling of freckles? The overbearing mildness of those dead, watery, and seemingly unassuming eyes? The street was, for the most part, quiet, the air too raw for anything like Easter parades and flowery extravaganzas. And life was a blind thing of arbitrarily assigned meaning; and even if one struggled and managed to get somewhere, one actually got nowhere, and got death. I could not say what Prentiss was up to, if anything; but that she was presiding over a Traymorean *mise en scène*; and it should have been Eleanor's prerogative to preside, if it was anyone's. As if we Traymoreans, in our modest relations, had been Prentiss's idea, not our own; and the more I pursued this line of thinking the less I had any stomach for the convivial. I would eat so much and drink so much as was polite, and then plead my excuses. Eleanor kicked my shins with a pompadoured foot and said: 'You're awfully quiet, Randall.'

'I don't know,' I answered, 'Easter. Never been my favourite time of year.'

'I'll bet you don't like Valentine's either,' a dull voice put it to me.

'He's missing Moonface,' Eggy thundered.

And to my horror, I blushed. Prentiss was beatific. Eleanor simpered. It was undeniable that there were in me erotic burblings occasioned by Prentiss, and I was not sure I liked myself for them. I was stupid, dull, feckless. Dubois, too, was awfully quiet, and it seemed significant. Eggy was snoozing now, and Dundarave looked envious. And then the conversation, such as it was, took a rather strange turn, a dull voice giving mention to pills and bourbon and suicide. Then Dundarave spoke: 'I guess there are worse ways to go.'

'Morbid, Marj, morbid,' Eleanor noted, with the tone of a woman about to put her foot down.

Prentiss responded, and coming from her, her words were most peculiar: 'Christ was suicidal, don't you think?'

At which point, Eggy raised his head: 'Yes but—'

Eggy could not complete the thought for one reason or another.

'How so?' asked Dubois, rallying to a challenge.

'He knew the Romans would get Him,' Prentiss explained.

'That's different,' said Eleanor, 'from swallowing pills and pouring booze down your throat.'

'Really? How's it different?' Prentiss asked, blinking and looking for all the world like an innocent among jaded academics or worse, ologists.

'I'm going out for a smoke,' Dundarave announced, 'all this is too heavy for my liking.'

'I might just join you,' Eleanor chimed in, 'indeed, I will.'

And there was some fussing about for a cigarette on Eleanor's part; and then the scraping of chairs and the putting on of jackets; and then Eleanor and Dundarave, who had once been nearly lovers, went out on the terrasse, suddenly discovering, perhaps, that they did have something in common.

'Well,' said Prentiss, 'I guess I'm not going to get an answer. How about you, Randall, got anything to say on the subject?'

'What? Suicide? The Christ?'

'In your Easter bonnet with all the frills upon it—'

It was Eggy briefly crooning. Mercedes arrived with two giant pizza pies, which she gingerly set before us.

'Is everything all right?' she said. 'Fine. Super. Thank you.'

Gregory stood there and looked upon us, he the proud proprietor, just that his smile was anxious. Eleanor and Dundarave came in from having their puff.

'That was fast,' Dubois guffawed.

And he took a serviette and made of it a bib for himself.

'Are we done with the heavy lifting yet?' Eleanor put it to the table, with something like exaggerated cheerfulness.

Conviviality had flown the coop. Dundarave gave Mercedes the once over.

Perhaps it was the wine, but Prentiss began to get ugly, going on about Islamofascists and the like; and Dubois decided to push back. The facts, *mamselle.* Eleanor knew better than to employ reason, and she decided she had something to watch on TV; and she was the first to break ranks. She offered to leave some money on the table but Prentiss would not have it. With a ta-ta, Eleanor took her leave, and Prentiss and Dundarave left soon after, intending to hit the bar down the street. It was dark outside, our faded Jezebel of a town passing by in vehicular and pedestrian units; and one could not say that there was anything like a noble atmosphere on the noble boulevard; it was all just the getting from A to B, nothing less, nothing more. Even so, I was receiving from nowhere I could identify such pulses of sorrow and dread as threatened to tear me apart. Could be it had to do with some childhood experience of Easter resurfacing. Could be it was the fact of the last eight years, America at sea. A second straight night of TMW—too much wine? Eggy, for his part, found that the evening had not been much fun; it could have used Moonface to lighten things up; but then, and who knew, but she was probably on her backside somewhere and thoroughly indifferent to our lot; in which case, the Lithuanian might have done, just that she was married. Dubois, now that we were Animal Table again and not some botched Last Supper, Mercedes now mopping the washroom floor—Dubois thought Prentiss an odd duck.

'What do you mean, odd duck?' Eggy said, 'effing hell, man, of course she is. You've seen how she gets, sometimes.'

'I mean what's all that with Christ and suicide?' Dubois wanted to know.

'I don't effing know,' Eggy said.

'Beats me,' I ventured to say, and I really had no idea, about to launch into a description of how the woman always had an unsettling effect on me; just that Eggy was in no shape for complexities and Dubois's mood had grown dour. Even so, I continued: 'And what's this about Eleanor going to church? Since when?'

Dubois grunted and said: 'Since when she's always done so, off and on when it suits her. She calls it R, R and R—rest, relaxation and reset.'

'In my day we took the sermon seriously,' Eggy thundered, his finger raised.

'I'll bet you did,' Dubois observed, he anti-clerical.

'No comment.'

Dubois was Eggy's dear friend, but Dubois sometimes had a startling lack of sympathy with certain aspects of Eggy's long life. Gregory said he would be happy to sit with us and drink wine all evening, but as business had died down, and as it was Easter, he would like to close.

'Got to find your Easter egg and keep wifey happy,' Eggy crowed.

Gregory looked bewildered.

'I don't care for pizza anyway,' Eggy said, his barely touched, 'and I don't see why you keep that Albanian hanging around.'

§

Book VII—With a Song and a Prayer

Demon Love VI

—Eggy has had another fall. According to Dubois with whom I spoke last evening, no bones were broken, but a shoulder was seriously bruised.

—It must have been a curse, to have had a beautiful soul in a convention-riddled society, and yet beautiful souls are a dime a dozen now. But enough. Moonface is back. There she was in the Blue Danube, chug-a-lugging beers with Antonio, the hour close to supper hour. And for an instant, she was stunning to behold, her tan setting off her eyes to great advantage. And she was, it must be said, in shock. 'Nothing's changed,' she said. Ah, she had a hold of the rag-end of philosophy. The whiteness of the top she wore also enhanced her features, making of her shoulders something noble. I pretended to wisdom, to knowing all there is to know about culture shock and how to overcome it. She touted Bolivia—its poverty and beauty. All she came across in Argentina were blondes. But of course. She had seen things one does not see in this our phantasmagorical land, violent contrasts—the richness of the rich and the poorness of the poor, for instance. And how time was a very different entity from the time we observe here in the urban north. I was agonized. For she was different and she was the same dear girl, but she was remote, in the sense that some parts of her soul had been isolated from Traymorean and Blue Danubian existence, and this reality would remain so for the rest of her life no matter how deep or shallow the isolating. She had taken the wine tour in Chile. 'Oh,' she informed some vintner there, 'I work in a restaurant in Montreal, and our customers drink your wine all the time.' Seems the vintner was most keen to know how well his wine was regarded. In any case, I could not sit with her long, her presence too overwhelming; and besides, Antonio was eager to know all about the Ecuadorian beaches, which Moonface assured him were very good, indeed, better than anywhere. Trust Antonio to get down to what truly matters. I returned to my digs without having eaten. With a scattered mind I read: *Cosimo would acquire an object because it appealed to his curiosity, like those life-sized portraits of double-headed sheep and calves, rare birds, quadrupeds and monstrous fruit with which he filled the rooms of the Ambrogiana; or because it excited religious emotions, like those swooning Madonnas, weeping Magdalens and martyrdoms by Sassoferrato and Carlo Dolci...* It seemed, for an instant, that I was reading about myself. And it had seemed that, in a Quito bus station, Moonface's Champagne Sheridan had very nearly flipped his wig, people staring at them incessantly. 'We were so tall,' Moonface observed, 'taller than everyone.' She was sure it explained everything.

—Some people have love in their bones, or in their natures, at the very least. Others acquire it like one begins to accept the taste of a suspect dish. Or by dint of effort, grace or luck, one suddenly has love on one's hands and finds this state of affairs preferable to the proverbial two birds in the bush. Still other unfortunates go through life and never love and are never loved. Lack of opportunity? Lack of talent? Absence of humanity? But let us not get carried away with any notions of humanity lest we think too kindly of ourselves on the whole. The thing of it is I have Moonface's apartment keys; sooner or later she will come for them; and it shall be revealed, how she intends to live for the nonce. Either, she will have opted for cohabitation with her Champagne Sheridan (in which case she will surrender her apartment and Mrs Petrova will display the For Rent sign in her shop window), or the girl will enlist in the ranks of independent agents and accept conjugal visits, but not from me. It is just past the lunch hour in the Blue Danube. Cassandra, of course has heard the news, but she does not yet know when Moonface will be back on shift. Cassandra seems less homesick than she has been in recent months. *One gets used to things.* Otherwise, no, I have not much to report. The Spanish justice system may take Previous President to court. Why, because they are not devoid of humanity? Bumped into Wiedemayer, by chance. He had been suffering from what he called conjunctivitis, a flu in his eyes (the old pink eye), and he a photographer and dedicated to the arts. Had I read Robert Louis Stevenson's *Lay Morals*? No, I had not, I answered, but I was fairly certain that Mr Stevenson had not gotten his proper due as a prose artist, his reputation resting too much on his more popular but lesser works. The way of the world. Dread in the pit of my stomach now. For Emma MacReady aka Moonface, now that her eyes have been refreshed by her sojourn, will see me for the ridiculous creature I am. True, one has to be a little on the absurd side to love, but there is absurdity and then there is absurdity. Even so, she has long since forgiven Eggy his silliness perhaps because his silliness was always sincere. Moonface has never accorded Dubois anything but respect. What did he do to rate the honour? I suspect he intimidated her somewhat with his billfold and courtly manner, the odd time he treated her to a martini downtown. I go out and I hail Elias, the man sweeping the terrasse, preparing for the season. It is getting warm enough for sitting out. I walk a little, noting the balcony doors that are flung open to admit the freshening air, air such as will drive the fusty winter blahs into oblivion, radios cranked up. The music's amorphous, enervating energy. It was not Chuck Berry. It excused maximizing profit.

—Yesterday, it was seen that Moonface was back at it. I had seen it for a fact, as I was returning from some peregrination or another, and I happened to peer into the window of the Blue Danube, she one of those pop-up figures of a children's book, one complete with a theatre set purporting to represent a café. Her shoulders slumped, this chameleon-like creature occupied a point in time and space where the crossroads had vanished and she was no longer what she recently was: young woman about the world, open to sensations. Then again, Dubois may come to her rescue, it being his intention to organize an event. Yes, short of going there oneself, what better way to learn of a distant and exotic place than to hear from one who has been there. Emma MacReady aka Moonface shall deliver a seminar, Animal Table to convene at precisely six of the clock on the evening of such and such a date in April, for the express purpose of hearing the dear girl out; and one must listen, and that would mean Eggy, her derring-do more to the moment than that he had once been to Quito, effing hell; and the presence of Moonface's beau, the redoubtable Champagne Sheridan shall be deemed perfectly acceptable; and Dubois shall supply the wine. It promises to be an evening.

—So shall we hear of shagging a gaucho on the pampas, of headhunting in the Amazon? The origins of the Peruvian flute are… fill in the blank. Calhoun, you are bad, and bad, you may darken the brow of Moonface the educator. No, you read of Gian Gastone, the last of the Medici rulers who lorded it over Tuscany; how he, a stinking drunk keeping to a stinky bed, surrounded by his bum boys and wenches, nonetheless repealed the more onerous tax burdens, circumvented the church to some extent, liberalized the laws and lightened up the general atmosphere of tight-arsed Florence; whereas his pious dunderhead of a father had brought about one catastrophe after another. There is, in this, a cautionary tale, history, as ever, paradox. Eggy, I suppose, is in his bed, convalescing from his fall. Dubois has glitter in his glittering blue eyes: boffo idea—to give Moonface the Animal Table floor and free rein, if only for an hour. There is a knock. Why, from the sounds of it, it has to be Prentiss. Shall I answer? Shall I activate protective camouflage? *Nobody here but us grotty, pimple-faced scholars. In which case, you don't want to know… For yes, we sweat, get clammy-handed. We forget how to breathe when a woman would proclaim herself as Venus, one seeking martyrs. And it is Prentiss, wouldn't you know?* And what a sight she is, from the pumps on her feet to the cloche headgear, the hat angled smartly over those ludicrous bangs. 'Hullo.' 'What, are we doing a scene from the *Great Gatsby?*' 'That's close. Not bad. I'm in mourning.' Her voice is a sonic boom. Evidently, she spots the question in my eyes and she clarifies: 'For high old times and robber barons.' 'I think, my dear, you're out of synch.' 'I suppose I am. But so are you. So's everybody. And when everybody's out of synch, anything goes. Want to go?' 'Go where?' 'You know, silly.' 'I think not.' 'Yes, well—' 'Sorry.' 'Don't bother. I'll go and bother Ellie. She'll get a kick out of this.' 'I think she will.' 'Toodle-loo.' And the woman is louche all the way to Eleanor's door, and she just goes right through, without announcing herself. In fact, what has happened is that I have just been reminded that one woman's objectification is another woman's shenanigans.

—Of the pending marriage of Eleanor to Dubois, no word. Eleanor just says, 'You know Bob. He'll get around to it when he gets around to it. Not that he's a procrastinator, he isn't. He's just circumspect. In the meantime, I'll just keep on keeping on, being *moi*, and randy now and then. You know how it is.' Well, I suppose I do, and if I do not, perhaps I ought to. But in any case, because the good woman rarely receives in her living room, the space purely a formality to be incurred on the way to her kitchen, it strikes me I have little of it by way of a topographical survey in my mentations and consequently, barely a mention of it in my notebooks. 'I guess,' I say to Eleanor in her kitchen, she smoking the ciggie I rolled for her, 'maybe Bob's distracted, what with Moonface back, what with Eggy having had another tumble. And don't you think Prentiss has been even more weird than usual, of late, doing her flapper impersonation? I think so. Well, it's the time of year when I begin to get these little bursts of Rome in my head—smells, tastes, sights, sounds. But no matter. It can't possibly mean a thing to you. It's a kind of affliction such as used to revisit tropical travellers by way of residual fevers after their travels were done. I suppose now one just pops a pill. You know, I can sit here and look at you and muse upon what we could get up to, and I'm sure there's a pill for that, too, a shut-down pill. Yes, and when it comes to the pleasures, we Traymoreans are, on the whole, amateurs. We haven't the perks of celebrity. Just an idle thought. Oh the odd thing or two frightens me, but what terrifies me most is emptiness. Are we empty creatures?' 'Avuncular, Randall. How do I know and why would I care? As for Prentiss, yes, I'll grant you she's been a bit dolly lately. She brings out the mother in me. The wench wants mothering though, to be sure. She's off the coke, by the way, so she told me. She was never really into it in the first place. A few house parties out in the boonies. Something with which to get a rise out of Ralph, only it got Phillip ballistic. Only I have to tell you, Randall me boy, Calhoun good sir, that thought of the wench brings me distinct unease, not because of what she can do to me, she can't do anything to me or you, for that matter, she's basically harmless, but—oh, I don't know. Lost my train of thought. Maybe this is it: you see how old Eggy is but you don't see his death. Know what I mean, jellybean? He could go another twenty years. Heaven help us. You and Moonface? I guess you're still carrying a torch for that witless floozy. Even so, she's at the beginning of the next leg of her journey. And it might be all downhill from here. Don't give me that look. I know, I know—journey—another yuppie word. Don't I know it? Now kiss me and bugger off.'

—It is my intention to meander over to the café at about seven and take a little wine, Animal Table in session, hockey playoffs on the TV. Who knows, Moonface might be working. And I do meander over, and I have a puff first before going inside; and I catch the hue of the evening sky. The trees that line the street are definitely up to something, branch tips knobbly. Commuters disembark from buses. And one separates the people that fill one's eyes into categories: those who make a show of occupying their space and those who do not. Perhaps it has bearing on the future. And I go in as I have on so many evenings, thinking nothing of it, thinking nothing of myself; and I expect to offer and to receive breezy greetings as I settle in. Dubois grins, but it is a grin born of a crisis sort of grin; and he is holding Eggy's arm in a peculiar way; and why, yes, he seems to be feeling for a pulse, Eggy's lips and chin more green than blue. How frail, how bewildered, how chuffed Eggy is. How very tired. My questions for Dubois are unspoken, but he gets my drift. Has he called for an ambulance? And if not, should he not? It is looking bad. Is Dubois gambling here, cutting it extra fine? No, we will wait a bit and see where things go, and anyway, what with the hockey game, what with Moonface on the premises, and Eggy will not wish to go to the hospital just now. Indeed, Moonface is working a shift, a frightened grin drawing her lips tight against her incisors, dark eyes clouded. Miss Meow smirks. Lovers each inspect hand-held electronic thingamajigs. Gregory, having his dinner, is clearly resigned to the prospect of Eggy dying in his restaurant. And it seems the old man has urinated; and with apologies, Dubois asks Gregory if there is a mop. Gregory gets the mop and he swipes at the floor. Well, I would break the silence. 'Has he eaten, today? We should get something in him. Some juice, maybe. Anything.' Dubois inquires of the old man: 'Hey, you still with us? Want some juice? A tumble in the sack?' Eggy's head tilted at a certain angle, and that troubled countenance of his—why, it resembles too much the crucified Christ in paintings I have seen. And even the two-pointer stuffed in his pocket seems wilted. 'How about some coffee then?' Dubois persists, but gently, and with the air of a man for whom a recurrent crisis has become routine. A weak Eggy response suggests he might spring for that. And Dubois signals Moonface, indicating that she should bring some coffee, which she does, setting the cup before the homunculus with an optimistic flourish. Somehow he manages to drink, Dubois supervising the effort. Perhaps Eggy has just seen the shades in Elysium and considers the storied place overly hyped. 'How about some sugar?" I suggest. Eggy shrugs. Hey, it is a sign of life. I grab a sugar packet, tear it open, dispense the sweet granules. Eggy looks on, amused. But now he quaffs. Now his countenance clears. Mischief regains his eyes. The hockey game underway, well, is there a score yet? Will they drop the bomb? And Moonface, why, she does not seem much changed. She may as well have not gone away, for all the difference it has made.

Eggy, that's a depressing thought. Effing hell, how should he know? And the dear girl goes and attends to Miss Meow, whom she considers sweet, though I do not see how she can. Still, life goes on, *n'est-ce pas*? Moonface returns to Animal Table. How are things? And if sweetness is wanted, Eggy would have some cheesecake, and, of course, it is not a proper dinner but it is a meal. 'Ummm,' says his waitress. A few moments later, and here is the sweetness: thick slab of cheesecake, monster strawberry on top; and Eggy looks upon it with the air of a man welcoming an old friend. Now Dubois needs a puff, and out he goes, and in the dusky light of evening he puffs and chills; and perhaps he ponders the transitory nature of life; its beauties and its perils. Eggy is methodical, wrecking that slab of cake. He is on about something now, and yes, certain bastards ought to hang; and it does not appear that Moonface, however high up she got on those Bolivian mountains, suffered any untoward effects. No seizures of the kind she may have expected to have. *I mean, boffing at 10,000 feet… hoo hoo… maybe she's cured.* By now, Eggy has fairly demolished what was on his plate, his fork pushing the strawberry around until he can get a purchase on it; and yet, a spell is broken. Even the bloom that was on her tan has worn off, and Moonface is, what, a rather ordinary young woman of predictable plans and wherewithal. Silly me. Silly us. Ridiculous Traymorean males who, by dint of their collective breathing (Eggy's episode notwithstanding), would maintain this chameleon-like creature as well as the dreams with which she would trouble herself. 'Well, young lady?' Dubois puts it to her, having had his smoke, reseating himself. Moonface shrugs. The night sky is upon us. Miss Meow has miaowed. Couples have dined and carried on (and loners, too), all oblivious to the little drama that was being played out at Animal Table, the crisis so much water under the bridge. Perhaps we will get to Quebec City in May, Eggy, Dubois and I. Of a sudden I recall that Dundarave never got around to those shelves he would build for me, but who effing cares?… *Then, if some patriot stern and honour-laden stands forth, the shouting ends, the people stop to hear; his words bring back the public peace…* Virgilian words. To do with Poseidon calming the winds Aeolus let loose on the sea, imperilling Aeneas and his ships and his crews.

Demon Love VII

—*But did it really happen?* Yes, and one minute I am in dreamland, and the next, and Eleanor is smothering me with hot, tearful kisses; and it is not to initiate sex so much as it is to quell the fright she has just received. Naturally enough, I am irritated. 'Oh Randall,' she wails, her bosom a blast furnace, her eyes two yawning gaps in her head repulsing light. Why do I not remember to lock my door at nights? At three in the morning or thereabouts, I had drifted off, the movie I was watching nothing but drugs and ludicrous sex and martial arts cops; and it was devoid, in the absolute sense, of anything remotely registering an aesthetic. And yet, would it have gone any better for me had I watched Bergman's *The Seventh Seal,* and with Death, discussed cinema? As a stricken Eleanor regarded me with an admixture of impatience and despair, Sally McCabe—but just for an instant—flickered in my mentations, she with her semaphoring pom-poms. She would alert me, but to what? 'For God's sake, Eleanor.' 'Calhoun—' It is to say that, in pronouncing my name, she managed to reduce it to the monosyllabic; but that she must inform me of the medics and cops on the way, or they would be soon enough, Bob on the phone. *Cops? Medics? What gives?* 'Phillip's dead,' she whispered, 'but maybe Marj isn't.' And to the incomprehension she must have seen in my eyes, she said: 'Oh Randall.' I rose to a sitting position, and she had the full run of an embrace with me; and then she allowed me to extricate myself from the couch. Now I am in the Blue Danube, attempting normalcy, Cassandra upbeat, preparing for the day to come. Otherwise, the rain comes down pissily and without conviction. Music pours from the radio like raw sewage, the effect it produces in me yet more disgust with the capitalist game; but that I am no communist and I have not a clue as to what to suggest as an alternative to a rigged game. (I have no head, as Billy Bly would tell me, for this sort of thing.) And for some reason, and there is no rhyme or reason for it, I am put in mind of a woman with whom I once had an affair back in my twenties; how she liked to crunch on frozen peas for a treat, and I had thought it peculiar. She crunched, however, with so much gusto that it was endearing, her teeth strong, grin lascivious. *Frozen peas, indeed.* I only got a glimpse of the lovers Prentiss and Dundarave as, just then, cops and medics came trooping up the stairs like some counter-insurgency, Dubois having let them in. Prentiss was wearing one of her long nightshirts, and it was hiked up on her thighs so that one could see the rounding curve of a buttock cheek. She was on her side and turned to her swain, he on his back and staring up at the ceiling. It is all I can say of it, numbness everything for the moment; but that Eleanor kept repeating: 'I knew it. I just knew it.' Well, she must have known something somehow some way as yes, seven in the morning is not an hour when one might venture out to pay a courtesy call. In any case, coming on the lovers like that so still on their love-mattress, she had added to the string of corpses it had been her lot to discover. I left her and Dubois to the cops; and I suppose that Prentiss lives, Dundarave very much dead. And I wonder if there is anything to the fact that—back in the early days of her tenure in the Traymore—I used to address the woman in my mind as Ms Prentiss, and have long since dropped the courtesy title. *Well, whatever. Hoo hoo.* As Eggy might say. Speaking of whom, he had been nowhere in sight during all the commotion, and I worried for him. And I still have Moonface's keys.

—Dubois pokes his head in the Blue Danube door, wondering if he is allowed, as it is not yet opening hour. I wave him in. And he settles to the table, folding his hands on the table top, his eyes almost those of a *bon vivant*. 'What a morning,' he guffaws. 'Well,' he continues, more soberly now, 'to fill you in, from what I understand, Ralph is on his way into the city. Eleanor phoned him. Marjerie is in the hospital. I guess Phillip's in the morgue, and Eggy slept through it all, so I was able to establish. He should be coming around pretty soon. Mrs Petrova got into a state, what with all the traffic. Eleanor will be off to the hospital when the cops finish with her. They've really been grilling her. What did she know and when she did know it sort of thing. As if she was supposed to keep it all from happening and was remiss in her duty. There's always something out there to make somebody expendable and I guess Dundarave was elected, because Marjerie couldn't choose which of the two men she was going to spend her life with. I don't know if that's a theory or not, but it's what I'm thinking. What we used to call the hand of God, only I stopped believing in that hand before I even got to university. I suppose you have your own ideas.' 'Not really,' I answer. Dubois shrugs. And I note that his jowels are getting loose. And I begin composing a letter in my head—to Jack Swain, old friend of mine from the early days. *Dear Jack, it's been a while. But keep an eye out for a departed soul soon to join you in your realm, a certain Mr Phillip Dundarave. He was not really a good man and he was not really so terribly bad. I didn't like the way he played with the feelings of my good friend Eleanor. Anyway, he's likely to be a little disorientated, this martyr to Venus and town and country Pan. Be a dear and give the man a leg up until he gets acclimatized. Gotta run. All the best.—RQC.*

—And now Eggy is upon us with all the pomp and circumstance of a homunculus, being Eggy; Animal Table has its quorum. 'Well, does the wench live?' he wants to know. 'So far as we know,' Dubois replies, bending to his soup. 'That doesn't seem a very enthusiastic answer,' Eggy notes, and then: 'Oh, Cassandra. Spinach pie, please.' It seems a miracle that Eggy leaves it at that; usually, his ordering of a meal is an excuse for theatre. 'Yes but,' he says, 'so what happened? Very simply, just tell me what happened.' 'That's what we've been discussing,' Dubois answers, his tone neutral, 'and we don't rightly know. Suicide? Murder-suicide? Maybe. Randall thinks it was an overdose.' 'Oh, one of those,' says Eggy, the word overdose almost foreign to him, though he has been knocking back the wine for centuries. 'And how are you feeling?' Dubois inquires of him, rather pointedly. 'Well, I'm not going to drop dead yet,' the homunculus thunders. He regards me, his finger raised: 'And you're coming, aren't you, well, you know, to Mamselle MacReady's little talk?' 'Of course,' I answer, 'like you, I wouldn't miss it for the world.' 'Now don't get cheeky. I don't think she was a bad woman, that Prentiss gal. Seems to me the woman liked being on her backside. Is that a crime? I don't know, just suggesting.'

—I entered the Traymore, and climbed the stairs. Went straight to Eleanor's in what seemed the unnatural silence of the place. Her door unlocked, I stepped inside and made note of some furnishings in her living room: the chesterfield, the complementary armchair; the rocker; the drop-leaf secretary with its maple veneer; the steamer trunk masquerading as a coffee table. And I was about to note the various potted plants and lamps and knickknacks, and the overall effect of these items in their aggregate when Eleanor emerged from her bedroom. 'Calhoun,' she drolled, 'are you stalking me?'

Perhaps we both knew exactly why I was there. I had nothing but questions with which to counter the well-I-never-look in her placid eyes. *Phillips' dead, remember? Alright, you remember. In fact, you half-expected something like this would happen. But now that it's happened, how has it affected us? What has his dying done to the Traymorean universe and its inhabitants? Could be Marjerie Prentiss has gotten her little triumph at last, unleashing her peculiar brand of cause and effect on people less evolved than she. Could be I've credited her with more powers than she actually possesses. Could be you're the true beating heart of the Traymorean enterprise, after all, and it's been in me all this time to watch your back, as the vernacular has it? Perhaps I'm yet again front and centre with my own absurdity.* Surely, Eleanor R could read my mind, but she had no such mind-reading talent. She simply stood there in a formless, floor length nightgown, her gilded curls oddly still, she downright dowdy and not at her best. 'Well,' she, at length, offered, 'now that you're here, you may as well roll me a cig. I'll break out the amber.'

And we repaired to her kitchen, the most commodious of all the Traymore Rooms. Or so I would always believe. It was commodious not in the sense of size but in what it permitted by way of free-ranging discussion. And she began to discuss. She confessed she had fallen into a funk (only a funk?), hence the early hour at which she had taken to her bed with a book in the hopes that a history of the emperor Constantine might induce sleep. It almost worked. Then she said: 'Did I say funk? More like a waking dream. Awful things, waking dreams. Kind of like jetlag, only a thousand times worse.' And I saw in her, perhaps for the first time (though I must always have seen it, just not with such clarity) how happiness coincided in her with the operations of disappointment. It is to say the good woman had the gift of happiness, but that, somehow, things had never worked out for her as she might have wished. She said, fixing those intelligent eyes of hers on me: 'I've certainly jacked Bob around, haven't I?'

And how was Bob? He had, for the moment, slipped the Traymorean orbit. His sister rang him, come into town from the state of Texas where she resided, and she was troubled and had need of a shoulder on which to cry. Eggy? Perhaps he had finally dropped dead, but Eleanor had had enough of stumbling across corpses, and if I wanted to investigate things Eggy, well, it was alright by her, but I would be doing so on my own. *Prentiss and Dundarave. Silly people. They'd looked almost noble, lying there*—Torture memos, the economy, here and there some international crisis, the uneasy presidency of New President—all of it would come more readily to our minds than an explanation for an instance of apparent ritual suicide on our doorstep, even if Prentiss breathed yet. 'I'll tell you what,' Eleanor said, 'just before you walked in like a burglar on the prowl, I was thinking how I used to lay awake at night listening to the peepers in the country when I was a girl. It was all the world there was, and all the world one needed. I don't know what changed and when it changed, but change it certainly did. Then I came to the city, I guess, hotshot me ready to grab a cyclone by the tail. And then things changed for everyone, not just for yours truly.'

Eleanor spoke these words and sucked on her cigarette. It was going to be one of those rare evenings in which, no matter how much amaretto she knocked back, her eyes were not going to get glassy; her voice was not going to drop seductively. On the other hand, it might be one of those evenings when I might say something stupid, as in, *maybe you ought to write some of these things down,* and she respond: *avuncular, Randall.* No, she made scarce mention of Phillip Dundarave except to say that, in her opinion, he was more country than town, and that was the tragedy of his life, as if, what, he were a star-crossed crooner of sad songs on the order of a Hank Williams; and that Ralph, well, now Ralph had even more on his plate, for Eleanor figured that Prentiss's condition of mind was probably as bad as it had ever been. 'Yes, she said, 'I've even had words with the woman's mother, and the mother informed me that Marjerie's sedated, otherwise she'd be distraught. Ain't that rich—*distrawt*? The loon. And you? How's all this sitting with you?' And I answered that I had not the words; that I felt numb to some extent, the numbness a convenience. Or else it had now passed forever, the feeling that if I could put my foot down and signal that enough was enough, I could initiate change. I said to dear Eleanor, 'Not that I'm the type, you know, to throw in with a cause, but the Traymore has been something of a cause, only I think Moonface is drifting away from us.' 'What did you expect?' was Eleanor's tart reply. It was in the nature of a rebuke, that reply, Eleanor, however, not unkind. 'You think me a silly man,' I said, 'but you don't know the half of it. Live long enough, and I thought I'd be able to see the shape of things on the way. If anything, it's even murkier. For sure, it's staring me right in the face: doom, revolution, regrouping, renaissance. But all I can see is my little life and little mortality. I'll hear Eggy hoo hoing on the stairs. Won't be hearing Moonface's chicken shuffle much longer, I guess. Maybe you'll want me to kiss you, maybe not.' 'Hell's bells, Calhoun, roll me another cig. And that'll be it for me. I just want to keep it simple from here on in. I think I can sleep. And if Mr Dubois wants to pop in, well, fine and dandy, but he won't find me waiting up for him at all hours.' And that was that. We smoked and we drained each our snifters. Now she was getting that look in her eyes, but she was only pulling my leg. *And now I sit here in the Blue Danube, presenting my review of things to my notebooks, Cassandra and Elias laughing in the galley. Good to hear. I anticipate that, for them, the day will bring them plenty of customers, church-goers especially who will be hankering for pizza.*

Silent Eggy

We gathered, as arranged, in the Blue Danube on a rainy evening. Dubois called Animal Table to order. He read a poem on the origins of the Peruvian flute, the subject matter of the poem and the rendering macabre. And then he enjoined Miss MacReady to *take it away.* Eggy, for the most part, managed to behave. He had been under standing orders not to speak. No interjections. No rabbit leaps of logic, especially between the hours of six and seven when Moonface was to have the floor. But perhaps her experiences were still unassimilated; she spoke and not much came of it; just that water behaved no differently in toilet bowls on the equator than it did in the toilet bowls of the True North. And when she stated that, in certain Argentinian restaurants, she may as well have been in Europe, she seemed to have exhausted her repertoire. So she produced photographs of exotic landscapes. She was partial to Bolivia. 'It was like Mars,' declared her Champagne Sheridan. Yes but, even on Mars, Venus would seem to have had her innings; and it was perhaps grossly frivolous, those photos Sheridan had snapped of Moonface (ones in which she struck certain poses as could only be described as girlie shots) popping up amidst the views of misty Machu Picchu. They were kept, however, from Eggy's eyes lest they trigger a heart attack. Still, at one point in the proceedings, the old man's maw parted and his gut erupted; an up-gushing of wine poured like lava down his chest. Editorial comment? He seemed incredulous that he was capable of such mischief. On the TV the Habs looked to be going down for the third straight playoff game, their chances for capturing the Stanley Cup dimming by the minute. I could not say that Moonface was embarrassed by the pictures that featured her tush and other parts of her anatomy, meant for a strictly limited audience, to be sure; but she was not selling tickets, either. But was Eggy alright? Moonface ministered unto him with a handful of serviettes and some alacrity. With what eyes did she behold the homunculus? With dutiful eyes? With eyes unintimidated by reality? Eyes in which disgust was repressed? Eggy assured her that he was, hoo hoo, alright, thank you very much. Dubois and Sheridan were, at this time, out on the terrasse smoking the last of Sheridan's South American cigarettes, a cloudburst spent. So much for the seminar. Yes, well. And was not experience wasted on the young? If the Moonface eyes had been open, had they seen? With what registrations were they now turned inward?

What conclusions would she draw at some future date? Or would her travels have been no more, in the end, than the chucking of a pebble in a lake? Still, time, distance and experience had done their work; she was not quite the same Moonface we once adored; Eggy's left eye drooping more than ever; Champagne Sheridan playing the young man who had found approval in the eyes of his intellectual betters (and it was not at all clear that he was entitled). Moonface reverted to answering the telephone when Antonio had his hands full with customers. Miss Meow now delighted in pronouncing menu as *may-noo*. She thought it a wonderful joke, even if the Antonio did not seem to get it. What did it mean when one admitted to oneself the transitory nature of things? That one had gotten full of oneself on account of one's perspicacity? I had had enough to drink. I had failed to educate Moonface in anything worthwhile. And yet, when she and I stepped out to the terrasse for a puff—she was taking up cigarettes in earnest—and I told her I was proud of the fact she had undertaken her travels, I got by way of an answer something more than 'Avuncular, Randall, avuncular.' There was fright in her eyes, but there was also desire, a determination to meet life, whatever the terms; whatever the extent of her confusions. For all that this resolve might run its course by the weekend, it was heartening to see. Indeed, she was downright shy and not at all smug. One could almost take seriously the prospect of her as a lover; the fact that it was not in the cards and had not ever been really in the cards of no matter for the moment. *Were the Moonface eyes post-apocalyptic, she the proof that even a humankind stripped down to the quest for food and the pornographic and the endless ologies, nonetheless still has legs?* As I stood there in the street with Moonface, she getting a bit restive now, as if expecting something to happen that was never going to happen, McCabe arched her brows at what was now forming in my thoughts: Eggy's latest episode and how there would be others until he finally ran out of them. McCabe spoke: 'No, he's good for another 900 years or 20. And what's with this Moonface? Do you think she actually has a clue as to what's at stake? Well, you've had your fun with her, but enough's enough. How convenient for you that Dubois, in the aftermath of one of his cluster headaches, will have a stroke of genius. He'll persuade Eggy to alter his will, to leave what loot he has to dispose of to Moonface so that she can become the old wise woman of that song Dubois translated for the benefit of all you dull, English-speaking Calvinists. I can see it, can't you? Shall I paint you the picture? Hospital room, for starters. And maybe Eggy is or is not in his final hour, but he's the centre of attention, in any case, and enjoying it to the hilt; Haitian Nurse attending him, Dubois there, even a somewhat skeptical Eleanor. There's Moonface, to be sure, seated on the bed, looking really rather fetching for once in a skirt. She does have charms, you know, that a change in the attitude of her soul would bring out more. Eggy all the while is trying to be serious; it's his last shot at the grand gesture. It's hopeless. Still, the scene is rich with comic possibilities. That he wants his IV spiked. That he wants to see a few bastards hang, but, oh yes, right, the matter at hand is Moonface and how she's going to live her life. It has long been a staple of conversation at Animal Table. And there she is, the girl, so close to him, and he hasn't far to reach, but he's not quite up to it, though his voice is still capable of thundering: "Look, girl, you've got to get serious. And I'm offering you the means and the wherewithal. Study your classics. Open up a jazz cabaret. Travel. Whatever you choose. Just don't blow it all on your Champagne Sheridan. Nice enough lad but a bit weak." Randall, Randall, really. As Moonface will have it, avuncular.' That was it then, McCabe having had her say. She departed my mentations. I gave Moonface a look she could not possibly interpret as it would entail her to have knowledge of the future. Then I draped an avuncular arm along her shoulder, she flinching a little. False move, false note, but that, sometimes, one has to risk it and suffer the consequences. I directed her attention to the doings in the café. 'What a crew,' I said. She agreed, yes, with a sigh that suggested her overlong familiarity with the place and its denizens. Dubois was carrying on with Champagne Sheridan; no doubt, they were discussing Camus or corporate business models. Eggy was fast asleep, his profile suggesting he had attained something like a measured peace. I let my arm fall away from the woman at my side. Was there a poet in her? I figured she truly was embarrassed by the photographs I had seen earlier. Perhaps she should have been, I did not know. 'Let's go inside,' she said. 'Yes,' she said, 'I want to see if Eggy is alright.'

Ballade pour mes vieux jours
—by Luc Plamondon and André Gagnon, freely translated by Robert Dubois as:

A Ballad for my old days

For my old days, I wish
That all the men I loved
Come sit by my side
In an ancient tea-salon
And that we talk all together
Of what we have been

For my old days, I wish
That all the men I loved
Come walk by my side
In a garden full of pansies
For us to pick together
As flowers of times gone
As flowers of eternity

For my old days
My loves
I wish you
All around
All of you around, all around
All around me

For my old days, I wish
That all the men I loved
Come lie by my side
On the bridge of an English boat
And that we sink all together
Far out on the Aegean Sea
On a beautiful end-of-summer morning.

Eggy's Coda

Eggy was not so immortal, after all. He got away from us following a brief but heartfelt funk in which he stated to a new girl on the scene that he *didn't give a tinker's cuss, anymore.* It is unknown to us whether he on his hospital bed recognized in this girl fresh talent; whether the prospect of it had afforded him one last sliver of delight in a world in which so much delight is bogus. In any case, the terrasse at Le Grec aka the Blue Danube was not the same without the homunculus and his cane and his bell and his thunder. And yet, or so it struck Dubois and me, one afternoon in recent memory, Eggy might not have wandered that far away, even so. There was, directly across the street from the terrasse, and in front of the liquor outlet, a small scrawny thing of a tree that had, now and then, been the object of Eggy's speculation and his sympathy. Would this runt make it? Would it come to enjoy life as a full-fledged boulevard nobility, majestically branched and leafed? The thing, of a sudden, did seem to be doing rather well. It looked to be filling out. It might actually sport splendid autumn colours come September. As it tremulated in a breeze, did it not seem to be waving at us? Or had we just been imperiously dismissed? But for everything gained, sometimes there is loss, and I believe Eggy, or some part of him, at least; that part of him that did care when he was not thundering his indifference, would have been pained to see Moonface beginning to signal that she intended to live life on the cheap in a spiritual sense, she and her Champagne Sheridan. Their relationship might have legs and they stick to one another; it might fall apart by winter; but the thing was she could not seem to stick to anything else: certainly not the Latin studies, and probably not ever the writing of poetry. There was perpetual apology in her rich golden eyes for the fact she had only ever been pretending accomplishment so as to buy herself some regard. She hardly ever spoke of Eggy now. If he had been a trial to her when he lived, he was no good to her dead now, was he? Traymoreans still looked out for one another, but with Eggy gone, one might observe less wind in their sails, so to speak, less reason to give mediocrity the slip. Dubois, I think, missed Eggy more than anyone. They had entertained one another royally for a long time. They had helped one another through a great many rough patches with a minimum of fuss, never mind that Eggy was forever fussing and thundering his disenchantment with idiots. Was he in his person the last of a kind? It is a question, among others, I often put to myself. Was Moonface, in her own right, a warning of a sort, someone whose frustrated existence says that something has died out of the world perhaps never to return? Were we all of us that? Perhaps that is why Dubois and I continued to make a point of meeting on the Blue Danube terrasse so as to clink whiskey glasses and either say bunk to all that nonsense of a diminution of standards or to wear sentience of the finer things as a badge of honour. Perhaps Eggy had worn it, for all the good it did him. "Don't look now," said Dubois to me on the day we were parked on the Blue Danube terrasse, the tree opposite us very much on our minds, looking awfully familiar, as it were, my companion on the verge of a guffaw and something else—some upsurge in him of an unclassified emotion, "but I think I hear the effer. Wants his wine. Doesn't care who knows it. Get those child-bearing hips moving. Hang the bastards. Will they drop the bomb?" No, Dubois was not the type to wax sentimental (though he might go on about his Shawinigan youth now and then), but that he had just come close to shedding a tear seemed to have shocked him and his countenance shatter by way of the hairline cracks of his cheeks. I looked away. Best to let the man have his moment and be done with it. It is what Eggy would have recommended, though he might have wondered why we were in no hurry to go deeper in our cups. Why, were we so cheap we could not toast his memory with another round of libations? Well, will they, in fact, drop the bomb, he would like to know? And now—*what's this?* The old woman and her schatzi right on schedule, the wiener of a dog giving that tree across the way a good sniffing over—Something familiar registering in that dog's tiny brain—As for the old woman, it did seem there was one less old man about with whom she might come the harpy, forever reminding him how shy of the mark he had always been, even as Zeus—

§

About the Author

Norm Sibum has been writing and publishing poetry for over thirty years. Born in Oberammergau in 1947, he grew up in Germany, Alaska, Utah, and Washington before moving to Vancouver in 1968. He has published several volumes of poetry in Canada and England of which *Girls and Handsome Dogs* won the A.M. Klein Prize in 2002. *Sub Divo* (Biblioasis) is his latest collection of poems. *The Traymore Rooms* is his first novel.